# SOMEBODY STOP THEM

Vitaly S. Alexius

Podium

Published in 2026 by Podium Publishing
www.podiumentertainment.com

Podium

# SOMEBODY
# STOP THEM

# CHAPTER ONE

# The Hunt

I sprinted through the dark tunnel, my footsteps echoing off the ancient stone walls.

Beast orb powered hexasuits amplified my speed, but I could still hear them behind me, inevitably catching up.

Predators. Deadly, dangerous predators. Claws clicking against stone, growls, distant panting.

The air was thick with the musty scent of dark brown and gray millennia-old stone and stagnant water. My breath came in ragged gasps, creating small white clouds in the rapidly cooling air.

Moisture dripped from stalactites overhead, occasionally landing on my shoulders.

No time to slow down.

A growl echoed behind me, closer now. The sound reverberated off the stone walls, multiplying into a chorus of predatory intent. My heartbeat accelerated.

The tunnel stretched in front of me into the gloom, my boots slamming into hard, now frost-covered stone. A small Kitlix lantern dangled on my belt casting even, shadowless light ahead of me.

> Mana: 383/28

I pictured myself as a wildfire, as a rainstorm rolling across the land, as a determined wolf, as a cheetah sprinting across open plains, as a falcon diving through clouds, as a bullet cutting through air, as lightning arcing between the land and sky.

Reality wobbled ever so slightly as I somehow managed to pull on a distant, small part of myself, one that didn't entirely belong to me.

> Mana: 372/28

*Faster. Smarter. Better.*

*Focus! Dive! Dive now or they will catch up!*

I imagined myself as wind itself, as pure motion, as a comet streaking across the night sky, as light bouncing between mirrors, as quantum particles tunneling through solid matter.

A living shadow etched itself across reality beside me, a growl of one of the monsters having caught up to me, almost akin to the mocking laughter of a hyena.

"Under," she growled, vanishing. "Now! *Dive!* Follow me!"

I pictured myself as water flowing between stones, as mist seeping through cracks, as darkness itself sliding between reality. I imagined my body becoming less solid, more fluid, like ink spreading through water.

Mana: 268/28

The walls of the cave-tunnel blurred into smudged shadows. The hexasuit and magisteel-clad body of Katherine Kells, the Stollwurm, manifested beside me in the deep.

"Keep going!" she growled. "*Deeper!*"

Reality blurred, colors bleeding away into shades of gray. Sounds became muted and distant, as if I were underwater. The air felt thick and heavy, pressing against my skin.

Mana: 224/28

Dark roots bloomed around the tunnel. The end of the tunnel was approaching rapidly as we ran.

Katherine's eyes burned with brilliant inner green fire.

"Good." She grinned with sharp chompers. "Now bend before you crash into the wall. Like this!"

Her entire body twisted as if made from shadows, inverting itself. I failed to replicate the move and simply slammed into the end of the tunnel like a swimmer who'd reached the end of the pool. I manually spun around, pushing myself off the weirdly solid-rubbery-feeling stone wall.

Katherine grabbed my hand with her magisteel-clad claws, pulling me into a sharp turn. The deep wobbled around us, reality bending like taffy.

"Not like that, idiot!" she hissed. "You're still thinking too linear! The deep isn't a straight line!"

"I don't get it," I panted as we slowed. "This isn't like a . . . *huff* . . . doomed dimension or . . . *huff* . . . something?"

"No." She shook her head. "The deep is an echo of reality, an extradimensional shadow cast by the living and the dead. A particular subset of the Astral Sea, accessible by some Omnids, one where curses persist."

"Curses?" I panted, catching my breath.

"Yes," Katherine growled. "The deep remembers all pain, suffering, misery, and fear. It is populated by Echoes."

"What kind of Echoes?"

"Everyone's Echoes," she purred, stalking silently around me. "It's what I feed on. But other people's Echoes are on a deeper level. You're still only two layers under. And if you wish to survive here without my assistance, little mouse, then you need to face the Echoes of your . . . victims."

"Victims?" I asked. "*What victims?* Do I have to fight every cow I ate and every mosquito I squished?"

"No. It takes sapience to make an Echo on this level. Here you must face the people you've hurt." Katherine's emerald eyes gleamed like green pools in the darkness of the deep. "Every action against someone leaves an Echo. And those Echoes . . . they hunger, they cling to you with fear and guilt, they chase you . . . they find you down here first."

I heard two voices, dull and distant. Two confused predators who had lost us in the physical, looking for us. Two female, smudged Omnids were now standing right beside us but were unable to see us.

I reached out to one of them, and my hand went right through the rainbow-winged figure as if it were moving through thick soup.

"Ignore them," Katherine said. "They don't matter here. Get ready to face your victims, Alexander Glock . . . face your past, Martin Kilborne!"

"Okaay, shadow-sensei." I focused, tensing up.

Skittering sounds echoed through the twisted tunnels. Dark shapes moved in the shadows, their forms indistinct.

"That them?" I asked.

"Yes," Katherine purred, tail lashing. "The pain you've caused. The lives you've disrupted. The people you've hurt. They're catching up."

We waited.

A twisted, lanky, emasculated, ruby-scaled figure emerged from the gloom, its form wreathed in ghostly dragonfire. Empty gold-orange eyes stared at me with pure hatred. The familiar figure of the Rubicund Lindworm, Emerald Stratos, stalked forward, emerging from the darkness and suddenly looking very wrong. Her form was twisted, looking more like an overgrown centipede than a humanoid. It was as if twenty different angry versions of Emerald had been fused to one another by a mad German doctor who sewed people to people.

"Nul-ll-lie," around thirty mouths placed at random locations sang. "Hhumannnn! Yo-ou lying s-s-sack of sh-sheet."

"Dang." I winced. "Em's seen better days."

Behind her, more things appeared.

A Vespera-pede flickered into view, bodies fused to bodies, wings merged with one another and covered in hundreds of gray eyes filled with an unsettling mixture of fear and despair.

"You prrr-prrromised to sss-save me," the Echo of the Thunderbird spoke in an unnerving chorus. "But wh-aaa-at if you fail? What if I lose myself anyway?"

A twisted version of Cinder materialized from the gloom next—a mass of writhing rainbow feathers and elongated limbs, multiple heads twisted at impossible angles, myriads of ocean-blue eyes burning with fear and betrayal. "You ch-changed everything," her voices echoed. "My family . . . my life . . . my heart . . . what else will you take from me?"

Io's Echo emerged as a mass of fuzzy darkness with countless moth wings and antennae, his form constantly shifting and blurring as if trying to escape its own existence. "The Truth hurts," his hollow voices whispered. "Are you ready to face it? To see what lies beyond the gates? The cccccc-aaa-tastrophe that you are? The ccccaaaa-cause of it all?"

"Yeesh." I winced. "Weird flex, but okay. This is tolerable. So how do I . . .?"

"Wait. There is more," Katherine said beside me. "The biggest one's coming."

Before I could respond, another figure emerged from the shadows. This one was different—more solid, more real somehow.

I choked when it fully manifested.

It was my mother's form twisted and merged with itself, her body a grotesque fusion of her weary, disappointed faces, green-brown eyes, dark hair, human and machine parts. Wires and cables sprouted from her fleshlike veins, pulsing with a sickly blue light. Hollow screens were fused to parts of her elongated form, displaying scrolling lines of code.

"My little fox," her voice crackled like corrupted audio entwined with a million others, fused to that of Yulia. "Why didn't you save me? Why didn't you steal a Lazarus bracelet for me? Why did you let me die? Turn me into this? You had the skills, the knowledge . . . but you ran away, abandoned me. You always run."

Something broke inside of me. I froze, unable to move, unable to act. The Emerald-pede struck at me with elongated, hollow claws.

A split second before Emerald's claws went right through me, Katherine's extra-solid hand intercepted the Echo, pulverizing, going right through it as if the Emerald-pede was made from colorful ink.

"Fight back, you knob!" the Stollwurm *tsked* at me. "If you let them attack you, give in, they will carve up and devour *your* soul instead!"

"How?!" I choked out, staring at the twisted version of my mom. Her Echo was doing something to my head, not allowing me to lift my trembling hands.

"By accepting it," Katherine growled, dark claws tearing through Cinder's Echo as it lunged at me. "By embracing what you've done and who you are. Focus, remember— these aren't real people—they're manifestations of your own fears and regrets, imprints of pain you've inflicted on others!"

"Right. Hey, where are your Echoes?" I exhaled, retreating away from the centipedes.

"My Echoes?" Katherine casually tore through another twisted Echo. "I devoured mine when I was seven. All of them. I don't let the new ones grow on me. That's how I can walk down here. Their pain, suffering, misery—it all feeds me, strengthens me, lives in me now."

I gulped as twisted versions of my friends advanced.

"Come on. You hurt people all the time," Katherine pointed out. "Without giving a damn. What's the problem now? They're just ghosts!"

I squinted my eyes, refusing to look at my mom, and kicked at the nearest Echo. It didn't come apart, felt far too physical, solid.

The Echo of Emerald caught my leg in her claws, ruby scales gleaming with an unnatural inner light. I tried to pull free but her grip was like iron. The Emerald-pede pulled me into her embrace, jagged, lanky hands clawing against my leather jacket and hardening hexasuits. "Die, hiiuiimannnn scuuummmmmm!"

"You can't just kick at them," Katherine sighed. "You have to mean it. Accept what you did to them. Own it. Embrace it. Make her afraid of you!"

*Forest fire. I'm a forest fire. I'm a storm. I'm Alexander Glock, an idea with a memetic gun.*

"I . . ." I started, looking at the twisted version of Emerald. "I ruined your delving troupe. I turned your friends against you. I stole your identity, your money, used it against you. And I'd do it again in a heartbeat!"

The Echo's grip loosened slightly, wobbled, warped.

"Because you deserved it," I continued, feeling something dark and cold rise up inside me. "You're a bully, a tyrant, a dragon who delights in causing pain and controlling others. You needed to be stopped, needed to atone for your actions against the mixie students. And I enjoyed every second of it!"

The Emerald-pede's form wavered, becoming less solid. Myriads of golden-orange eyes flickered with uncertainty.

Katherine's tail obliterated the other approaching Echoes, not letting them attack me. "That's it," she encouraged. "You know this Echo. You know what she's afraid of—use that against her!"

"I'm the voice, the hand of the people you killed, tormented, pushed out of Skyfall!" I growled, advancing towards the Emerald-pede. "I am not merely a single, lonely mixie you can torment. I am a firestorm of revenge! I am Sarah Nisteroff! I am Elek Rodrigov! I am Marcus Chennik! I am Thomas Willard . . ."

Emerald's face paled, and she retreated in fear.

" . . . I am Petv Yavna! I am Olga Kcasnik! I am Datri Volk!" I continued, each name of her victims making the Emerald-pede's form waver more. "I am every student you've driven to their demise and suicide, every life you've destroyed! I am their vengeance made manifest!"

I struck the Echo with my fist, and its form rippled, came apart into shreds. Panic was in its eyes.

"I'm not even close to being done," I snarled. "I'm going to destroy everything you are, everything you stand for! Your power, your control, your very identity—it's all going to crumble! And the best part? Everyone will think you did it to yourself! The people of Arx are going to learn of your crimes, and they will judge you for all of them! It's already begun, you cannot stop it!"

I delivered another punch to the warped ghost. The Emerald-pede shattered like glass, fragments dissolving into wisps of silver and red.

"Step in, inhale her fear, consume it," Katherine ordered.

I did.

As I breathed in the silver-red fluid-smoke, I felt . . . something flow into me. Power. Understanding. Her fear. A deep, primal satisfaction that warmed me from within.

---

System error. Unable to parse experience.

---

Sparks danced in my eyes.

---

Delineating current state. Reassessing stats.
Level 2 state approximated!
LV 2 Skill gained: Umbramancy
LV 2 Skill gained: Deep Diving
LV 2 Skill gained: Echomancy

---

"Ah, yeah." I grinned. "Level two. About time!"

"Good," Katherine purred. "Now get the rest."

The twisted versions of my friends advanced again, but this time I felt . . . different. Stronger. More aware of the deep and its rules.

I turned to face Vespera's Echo, its gray eyes staring at me.

"You're afraid I'll fail you," I said, stepping toward the Thunderbird-pede. "That I won't be able to save you from your arranged marriage. That I'll abandon you to your fate, leave you to be rewritten into someone else."

The Vespera-pede's form wavered, countless gray eyes blinking rapidly.

"But I'll do much more than that." I grinned dangerously. "I'll tear down the entire system that made you. The corporations, the arranged marriages, the social pressure to 'optimize' yourself—all of it will burn. And you know what? Deep down, that's what terrifies you most—not that I'll fail, but that I'll succeed too much. That I'll change everything you've ever known. That I'll unmake your father, Lord Ceter Kalik Simmi. That I'll bring the Abystall Dungeon core to Earth, dump a billion mites on him, make him beg for death as his mana drops to zero. That the Duskbloom mites will spread across Earth like glowing snow and unmake all of the Omnids, leaving only magic-free humans to rule the world!"

The Vespera-pede's mouths screamed.

I lunged forward, my hands passing through her hollow form. The Echo dissolved into crackling arcs of electricity that I breathed in, feeling another surge of power flow into me.

"Oh, wow," Kat commented with a smirk. "Impressive. You managed to scare me with that one."

I ignored her, advancing towards the retreating Cinder-pede. It heard me and was already quite thoroughly horrified by my Abystall final solution for Omnids.

"You're afraid of how much I've already changed your life," I declared, grabbing the Cinder-echo. "How I've wormed my way into your family, your heart. You're terrified of losing control, of being vulnerable. But most of all . . ."

I struck the Echo with my imaginary claws. ". . . you're afraid of how much you enjoy it. You're terrified that you're becoming addicted to me, to the changes I bring, to the way I make your world spin."

The Cinder-pede's ocean-blue eyes flickered with recognition and fear.

"And you should be," I growled, slashing her shade. "Because I'm going to keep changing everything, keep making you question everything you thought you knew. I'm going to tear down every wall you've built around your heart, every defense you've put up. Until there's nothing left but the real you—wild and free and unafraid to be yourself!"

The Echo dissolved into rainbow mist, which I inhaled. Io's Echo retreated away into the darkness. It sensed the doom I would bring it, the words I would say to the Mothman.

The twisted version of my mother was still there, watching with hollow screen-eyes. Unlike the others, she didn't retreat. She stood her ground and faced me, cables and wires writhing like tentacles.

"My little fox," she crackled in Kaska and English at the same time. "Always running. Always hiding. Never facing the truth. You failed to save me. You stole and lied and deceived so many . . . while I died alone."

The twisted version of my mother surged forward, cables and wires wrapping around me before I could react. Her hollow screens blazed with images of her face filled with accusation and pain.

"I . . ." I choked as the cables tightened. "I tried . . ."

"Not hard enough," her voice crackled. "You had the skills. The knowledge. But you chose to run around with my fox of a brother, to save yourself. You let death take me." Mouths reached out to my face, open wide, breathing in, devouring currents of mana flowing from me. "You turned me into this. Into code. Into a false copy. Into nothing. Infinite glorious nothing. You lie to yourself. I'm dead. I'm dead because of you and . . ."

Katherine's tails slashed the Echo, obliterating it into wisps of silver-blue shimmers.

I slipped down, my eyes filled with tears.

Mana: 2.42/28

"You can't save yourself or your friends, little fox," my mom's voice crackled, distorted and wrong as her Echo reformed. "You couldn't then, and you can't now. All you can do is run. Hide. Pretend. But deep down, you know the truth . . ."

I saw an Echo of myself standing behind her. A Martin fused into about twenty other Martins of various ages looking lost, hollow, and broken.

His eyes stared at me accusingly.

# CHAPTER TWO

# Family

I shuddered as my mana hit zero.

"Hrmm." Katherine pulled me from the deep into physical reality, holding onto my side with her tail.

"Your mother's Echo is strong," she commented. "Very strong. Usually they're just half-empty things, shadows. But that one . . . that one has substance. She must have died thinking about you, and you've been thinking about her a lot, feeding her. If you wish to dive without my supervision, you will need to beat her."

"I don't think that I can." I collapsed into a corner, shaking.

The Stollwurm sighed.

"There you two are!" Vespera declared, spotting us. "Told ya if you fed him bits of you, he could totally . . ."

She saw that I was curled into myself like a sad snail.

". . . learn Umbramancy." Her beak snapped shut. She looked up at Kat.

"What'd you do to him?!" Cinder demanded, emerging from around the tunnel bend that our Guild employees had carved out with Lance's bricking wand.

"Taught him to fight his ghosts." Katherine shrugged. "He did well against your Echoes. His mom's . . . not so much."

"Our Echoes?" Vespera tilted her head.

"Imprints of you that exist in the deep," Katherine explained. "The manifestations of pain and fear he's caused you. He managed to devour yours quite effectively."

"He did *what* to our what?" Cinder sputtered.

My heart was beating madly. I tried to slip on the Alexander Glock mask, but it wasn't fitting on correctly. The Echo of my mom had unbalanced me, shattered my psyche, reminded me of everything I'd lost, everything I'd failed at.

"He consumed your Echoes," Katherine explained patiently. "The dark reflections of yourselves created by his actions in the deep. Emerald's was particularly satisfying to watch him destroy. Although I must admit, his solution for dealing with Omnids was . . . concerning."

"What solution?" Cinder demanded.

"Ye, wat solution?" Vespera clicked her beak curiously.

"Bringing the Abystall Dungeon core to Earth and releasing Duskbloom to unmake all Omnids," Katherine said dryly.

Vespera choked.

"*What?!*" Cinder sputtered, then she noticed my ball state and slid down on the floor next to me. "Martin? You okay?"

"Absolutely . . . not okay," I breathed out, unable to control my shaking body. "This is some dementor-level shit. Pretty sure some of my soul just got sucked out of me. Can I like . . . bring a gun in there next time or something?"

"No. Guns don't work against Echoes," Katherine stated bluntly. "Only willpower and intent. Only fear. If you want to go back, you need to figure out how to hurt her, how to make that old Echo afraid of you."

"Don't push yourself," Cinder said, wrapping her wings around me protectively.

I looked up at Katherine.

"You know . . ." I said. "I didn't see your Echo there. Where was the Katherine-pede?"

Katherine swallowed nervously.

"What, you didn't eat her?" I asked.

"No." Katherine's emerald eyes flickered away. "My Echo wasn't there because . . . because you haven't hurt me. Haven't caused me pain or fear."

"Bullshit," I said. "You rolled away totally heartbroken from my van after I showed you my passport."

"Fine," she growled. "I don't know where the Echo of me is. Happy?"

"No." I blinked tears out of my eyes. "Not happy."

"Come on. Let's get you back to the Guild," Cinder said softly, helping me up. "Sounds like you've had enough deep-ghost-fighting for today."

I buried myself in her feathers, for the first time in my life allowing myself to cry hard. She held onto me, functioning as my physical anchor to reality until I stopped feeling completely worthless.

We made our way back through the winding tunnels, my legs still shaking. The hexasuits were doing their best to keep me upright, but I felt drained—physically and emotionally.

"You shouldn't have pushed him so hard," Cinder growled at Katherine as we walked. "He wasn't ready."

"He needs to learn," Katherine replied firmly. "The deep is dangerous. If he wants to use my Umbramancy, he has to face what's in there."

"By forcing him to confront twisted versions of us?" Cinder's feathers shifted through angry reds. "That's . . . that's cruel!"

"Life is cruel, the deep even more so." Katherine shrugged. "I didn't make those Echoes; they belong to him. He created them by hurting you. You two forced my hand. I didn't want to give my skill to him last night. You only have yourselves to blame."

"Dang, you're a cold beerch," Vespera clicked. "We all gave him our skills. All for one, one for all."

The Stollwurm raised an eyebrow.

"That's what family does," Vespera continued, her magisteel talons clicking against the cold tunnel hexagrams, sending sparks as we walked. "We share. We help each other grow stronger."

"Family?" Katherine's emerald eyes narrowed. "Is that what we are now?"

"Yes," Vespera clicked firmly. "Whether you like it or not, dragon-cat. This is our clan now. Our nest. Our home."

"And what makes you think I want to be part of your . . . nest?" Katherine asked.

"Because you're still here," Vespera pointed out. "You could have left at any time. Gone to an inn upstairs, embraced your solitude. But you didn't."

"I'm still here because somebody needs to keep an eye on you idiots," Katherine growled. "Especially him and his 'apocalyptic disaster plans.' Did you already forget what I told you, you brainless bird?"

"I heard you loud 'n' clear." Vespera crossed her arms.

"And?"

"The concept of Abystall taking over the Earth is rather . . . ummm, shockingly thrilling," she said, "Kinda makes me weak in the knees just thinking about it."

"You find the apocalyptic destruction of all Omnids . . . hot?" Kat squinted at the Thunderbird. "The fuck is wrong with you?"

"What?" Vespera clicked. "Come on, gimme some credit. I'm not a knob, even if I sometimes act like one. It would honestly make for a pretty spooky Cradlefall blockbuster!"

Katherine's frown deepened.

"Calm your tits." Vee shook her head. "In reality, Arx dungeons simply don't function on Earth. Our aetheric density is 2.049. Skyfall's aetheric density is 98.3253. Arx in general is 689.3245, for example. Abystall Dungeon's aetheric density is 884.2942 at the entrance and higher the closer you go into the labyrinth, where sentinels and spooky squids guard the dungeon core. Duskbloom would just die out on Earth; there's no ambient mana for it to nom."

"Whatever," Kat huffed. "You didn't see him down there. The way he tore into your Echoes. The things he said . . . he meant every word."

"And?" Vespera asked. "Wasn't he supposed to do that as part of your deep lesson plan?"

"There's fighting off Echoes and then there's outright stating he's gonna nuke all Omnids," Kat said. "Do you not find this concerning?"

"Hey! Don't cut out the context. I absolutely would nuke all Omnids with mites . . . to save Vee from being mind-controlled," I let out.

"See?" Katherine gestured at me. "Listen to him! He's literally planning genocide!"

"For me," Vespera clicked her beak cheerfully. "Isn't he just the sweetest? My hero!"

She sent a flying spark at my head, blowing me a kiss.

[Stop teasing meeeeeee, youuuuu devious smol creature.] Her whisper-static voice crackled in my brain.

I smiled with one side of my face.

"If you're trying to take my place as Prima-Wife," Vespera shot at Kat, "you're totally failing at it."

"What?" Katherine nearly careened into a wall. "I'm not trying shit! How many times do I have to point out that I'm not interested in relationships?"

"Oh?" Vespera clicked. "Then what's all this hostility? What do you want, kitten?"

"I want less of this . . . ughhhh . . . ecchi bullshit around me and more serious discussion."

"Such as?" I asked.

"Such as why the inhabitants of Arx wear hexagonal bracelets nearly identical to our Lazarus bracelets," Katherine growled. "The Echoes showed me that their bracelets are basically cheap copies. But they still track stats and translate languages."

"Hrm," I said, extricating myself from Cinder's feathers. "That is interesting. Can you show me one?"

"Here. Pried this one off from the remains of Grand Moloch Arkenish." Katherine pulled a dull hexagonal bracelet from her bag. I examined it, carefully holding it next to mine—it did look almost identical to our Lazarus bracelets, but the texture was wrong, the hexagons slightly misaligned, the surface more matte, scratched up.

"Less ecchi, hrmmmm?" Vespera grinned as she circled Kat. "Dragon-cat, if you think *this* is ecchi, you should see what happens in my room when . . ."

"*Stop!*" Katherine growled, her tail lashing. "This is exactly what I mean! We have serious problems to deal with—the Arx Bank controlling everything through these bracelets, assassins trying to kill us, and all you can think about is . . . relationships!"

"Hey, unlike some boring cat-knobs, I can multitask," Vespera protested. "I can worry about impending doom *and* plan my double-engagement party at the same time!"

"Engagement?!" Cinder sputtered, flashing with brilliant pinks. "What . . . when?!"

"Sometime between today and summer," Vespera said. "Try to keep up, Skittles."

"Aaaand I'm done." Kat melted into the shadows. "Voicecast me when you're done being horny idiots."

"Rude," Vespera clicked her beak. "She could have at least stayed for the party planning."

"There isn't going to be any engagement planning!" Cinder protested.

"Sure there is," Vespera said cheerfully. "We need to decide on colors, venue, guest list . . ."
She looked over the furiously blushing Cinder and me pawing at the bracelet.

"Okay, just me then," she said. "You two are obviously going to be useless. I'll decide everything as the Prima-Sword. This is fine. I was trained for this!"

"Hrm," I said, snapping the bracelet to my right wrist and watching my stats slowly flicker above it in the air woven from white sparks on a blue window background. "This is like . . . a cheap Thunderland knockoff."

"Eh? Lemme see." Vespera unclipped the knockoff bracelet from my wrist and sent sparks dancing across it. "Ye. It's a magic duplicate. Modified with a bunch of extra shit. Better than a Thunderland knockoff."

"What kind of shit?" I asked.

"Mmmmm. Bunch of monitoring spellwork." Vespera closed her eyes and turned the bracelet in her talons, making electrical currents dance across it. "Data collection hexagrams. Translation matrices. Mana tracking arrays. Pretty sophisticated stuff, actually. Whoever made these knows their magitek."

"Can you tell who made them?" I asked.

"Not really." Vespera squinted at the bracelet. "The way the matrices are layered, the efficiency of the power distribution . . . it's very advanced. Stores mana in it and feeds off the user's mana to reinforce itself. Hrmmmm. There's gotta be bazillions of these on Arx. They're all reinforcing each other, too, like a giant-ass network. Dang. Okay, now I'm impressed. This is clever. Dangerously clever."

"Would it work on Earth?" I asked.

"Pfff, no." Vespera shook her head. "It's made for Arx aetheric density, and the hexagrams aren't fluid like the Kitlix. It'd totes brick up on Earth."

"Could these be used in conjunction with Genesis fluid to bring someone back?" I asked.

"Nope. Laz bracers are made from what we in the business call liquid immovable metal. It's what allows them to hold onto a soul via a wack complex save-point algorithm that interacts with the blood of the Wormwood Star Leviathan trapped in pockets beneath the Cradlefall crater," Vespera clicked. "As I just pointed out, this copy is basically a solid artifact-style bracelet. It can make connections to souls to keep track of stats, but can't perma-clip onto a soul."

"So the Arx Bank has their own jank-ass version of Lazarus bracelets?" Cinder asked.

"Ye" Vee nodded. "With a slightly different function."

"One that can't bring people from death? But why? What's the point?"

"Information. Power. These things are like . . . tiny spies on everyone's wrist. They know where you are, what you're doing, how much mana you have," I said.

"Plus they nom bits of everyone's mana and send it all somewhere," Vee said. "Unlike our Omnid bracelets. Very useful. Someone somewhere on Arx has a lotta effin' mana thanks to these."

"And now they have your information?" Cinder frowned at me. "On account that you put it on?"

"Eh." I shrugged. "I'm a level two human, basically. I very much doubt that anyone is going to give a damn about me. How many humans are on Arx?"

"An unaccountably large number," Vespera said. "The nearest citadel-city state is the Gold Dragon God Empire. Their 'god' basically prints infinite humans into existence with a magic spell and lobs them against his enemies."

"Their what does what now?" I turned to Vespera.

"Their god-emperor. He's like . . . this really old, fat human who summons humans with his one maxed-out skill," Vespera explained. "Emperor D. basically uses the summoned as cannon fodder in his wars against other city-states. Sometimes he makes actual giant human-shaped spheres and drops them against other cities."

"That's possibly the most insane misuse of human resources I've heard about," I said.

"Das' Arx for ya," Vespera clicked. "The Gold Dragon God isn't even the worst of the self-proclaimed deity loons."

"Hrm. So what prevents Emperor D. from making human-rain on Shandria?" I asked, feeling concerned for my newly acquired Adventurers Guild establishment.

"Shandria's Shadow Leviathan," the Thunderbird replied. "Nightingale eats everything. Especially people. She's sort of half-asleep during the day and super rowdy at night. Anything and everything in ninety S-clicks that's not under a certain runic hexagram gets eaten at night by her flock of Shadowbeasties."

"The guys that ate Sarah Nisteroff." I nodded.

"Yeah," Vespera clicked. "Leviathan's Nightingale's Shadow flock. That's why nobody upstairs delves at night, cowering in inns behind steel shutters n' such. The flock eats anything that moves outside of hexagram-protected areas. Even high-level delvers get nommed."

"I see," I said. "And Undertown is safe how?"

"Undertown is covered in the same hexagrams," Vespera explained, pointing at a red, faintly glowing pyramid-shaped rune on the wall. "These keep the Shadowbeasts away."

"Why don't delvers cover themselves in these red pyramids to go out at night?" I asked.

"These are static-type runes," Vespera sent sparks raining over the rune. "Moving 'em disables their function."

"Okay, but can they be replicated to make a liquid-crystal rune?" I asked. "Specifically, could *you* replicate it?"

"Hrmmmm," Vespera considered. "Maybe. I'd need a sample to work with, plus the Artificery lab at Skyfall."

"Good," I said. "Pry that one out of a wall. I don't want Kathy to be confined to Undertown. She's max grumpy-cat as it is."

"Prying high-level protection runes out of walls seems like a terrible idea," Cinder commented as Vespera's magisteel talons ignited like arc-welding torches to begin cutting the red pyramid rune from solid stone.

"Everything I do seems like a terrible idea at first," I pointed out. "And yet here we are, taking over Undertown."

"This rune ain't that high-level," Vespera said. "Also, I can do better . . . when properly motivated."

"How motivated are you?" I asked her.

"How motivated am I?" Vespera's gray eyes sparkled with mischief as she twisted her head my way at an angle that would absolutely break a human neck. "Let's see . . . on a scale of one to motivated, I'd say I'm somewhere between 'will work for kisses' and 'will revolutionize magitek industry to impress my human pet.'"

"Pet?" I arched an eyebrow at her.

"A step up from property!" she grinned.

"Uh-huh," I mused.

"Mhmm. My adorable little human who does tricks like releasing apocalyptic plagues and taking over criminal organizations. #BestHoomanPetEver." Vespera clicked her beak cheerfully, prying a chunk of wall with the red rune on it and shoving it into her side bag. She slipped down to my level and took a selfie with me and Cinder. "There. The rune is pawned."

"Can you burn similar runes into this stone?" I asked her.

"I can." She nodded. "It has decent aetheric density. But it's an effort and a half to electrically ignite stone in the right way to crystallize it to conduct mana currents. I do wish that I had better strata to work with. This stone isn't very electrically conductive."

"I've got a plan for this," I said.

"Do you, now?" Vespera tilted her beak at me.

# CHAPTER THREE

# The Chase

I finished nomming on my sandwich, occasionally flickering the lighter's flame to top up my mana. I topped it with my four-Omnid shake that contained Kat's scales, Ci's and Vee's feathers, and Io's fuzz ground down into microscopic particles by Guild Chef Rostika Terringhelm's Agitix Kitlix.

"What were the Echoes of us like?" Cinder asked.

I described the entire experience.

After about twenty minutes of this, I felt considerably better.

"Hey, Vee," I addressed the Thunderbird who was investigating the various old crystalline runes burned into the grimy, dark gray stone by the Guilders many centuries ago.

"Ye?" She looked down at me.

"Can I get a million magic skills this way?" I asked her. "Just endlessly drink shakes made from Omnids?"

"No." She shook her head. "If you consume too much Omnid crystalline strata too quickly, they will overload each other and implode your stomach. Your current limit is five. I might be able to up it, we'll see . . . lots of modding will need to be done on ya. I'm monitoring the situation and adjusting . . . things."

"Thanks." I smiled at her.

It was time. Time to initiate one of my potentially most insane plans, based on my long evening discussions with Shash about how wizard towers of Undertown functioned.

"Sooooo, are you done crying like a little sad kitten over your ghost-mom?" Vespera asked.

I squinted up at her from my mossy rock seat.

"Vee!" Cinder smacked the Thunderbird. "Don't make fun of his . . . deep trauma!"

"I'm all 'bout tough love, Skittles," the Thunderbird shot back at Cinder, silver-gray eyes running me up and down. "Your legs obviously work now. Better start running. How about a twenty-five-second head start? Twenty-four."

Cinder huffed at the pet name.

My heartbeat accelerated.

*Oh, it's definitely time.*

Vespera's magisteel talons spread out, wings puffing up, electrical arcs dancing across her magisteel laminar armor. "Twenty-three . . ."

I stood up and stretched, joints cracking.

"Twenty-two . . ." Vee's gray eyes gleamed dangerously. "Twenty-one . . . less stretchin', more running, little fox."

Cinder looked between us with a somewhat concerned expression.

"If I catch him first, I get to bite him extra hard for my claim," Vespera clicked. "Waiting stresses me out. Fourteen. Someone ain't running. Aren't we brave . . ."

"What?" Cinder sputtered. "That's not what we . . ."

"Are you chickening out?" the Thunderbird asked.

"Am not!" Cinder huffed.

"Then get ready for a good chase. I do wonder if humans taste like chicken . . ." The Thunderbird grinned wide. "Eight. Getting awfully cocky there, aren't we, prey? Four . . ."

Twenty hexasuits ignited one by one under my jacket. I didn't face away from the two predator-girls. My hands dug into my pocket.

"Threeeee . . . twoooooo . . . ooooooonnnne." Vespera drew out her words, staring me down. "Zeeeeeerrr . . ."

"Sheshaaaah! Pocketbeasts!" I yelled, unleashing a small dimensional bag filled with glowing mites from my pocket at the faces of the Thunderbird and Quetzalcoatl.

Vespera shrieked in surprise, batting at the luminescent parasites with her magisteel-covered talons.

"Gah, what the fffffffuck?! Who throws Dusssskbloom at people?!" Cinder cried, flailing angrily. "Frighhh, they're in my eyes, I can't see! I'm going to effing murder you, you chuppy!"

"Feh! You little deviant!" Vespera cried out, flailing blindly. "That's cheating!"

"Expect the unexpected, knobs!" I spun through the air, kicking at Vespera with a roundhouse.

"Too slow!" The Thunderbird caught my leg mid-kick, her magisteel talons clamping down with superhuman strength. Electricity crackled along her armor, making my hexasuits light up like Christmas trees.

"Got you," she purred dangerously, pulling me closer despite my attempts to break free. "I think that some knob forgot that I don't need eyes to see. Mites don't block electrical sense."

"But do you know what happens when you mix water and electricity?" I asked as she slowly pulled me to her face.

"What? Don't think that drooling at me will help you avoid getting bit, hooman critter," Vespera growled, beak opening wide, gleaming, sharp chompers aimed at my neck.

"Let's find out!" I shoved the insta-rain stone that I was holding in my hand into her mouth, igniting the activation hexagram.

A cloud of rain exploded from the stone, instantly drenching us both. Vespera's electrical field went haywire, sparks dancing wildly across her armor. She yelped and spat dregs of water, releasing me as her talons spasmed from the short circuit.

"You sneaky little fox," Vespera hissed, flailing blindingly through the rain cloud now filling the tunnel, her feathers dripping. "That's twice you've gotten me soakin' wet!"

"What's wrong, birdie?" I taunted, ducking under her wild swing and throwing an uppercut into her chin. "Can't handle a little . . . rain?"

"I'm going to deep-fry you!" Vespera snarled as I sent her flying into a cave wall. Her electrical attacks were going everywhere except where she wanted them to, conducted chaotically by the water.

I spun away from Vespera's flailing form, only to have rainbow wings wrap around me from behind.

"Got you!" Cinder announced triumphantly, her claws digging into my hexasuits.

"Do you, though?" I asked, triggering the hexasuits at the top to maximum heat, keeping the layers below cold.

"*Yeowch!*" Cinder yelped, releasing me as the suits began steaming. "What the shit?! What are you, a Cherufe now?!" She waved her burned hands, glaring at me. "Damn it, how are you so hot?!"

"Was that a compliment?" I slipped free of her grasp, diving below her hands and rolling to my feet. "What's wrong, predator? Can't handle a little heat?"

"Oh, you are *so* dead!" Cinder snarled, her wings flaring with angry reds.

I kicked her feet under her, sending her careening into Vespera.

The two predators collided with a yelp, tangling in a mass of black, white, and rainbow feathers.

"Oi!" Vespera complained. "Watch where you're falling!"

"Watch where *you're* standing!" Cinder groaned back.

"I still got effin' mites in my eyes, you knob!" the Thunderbird growled. "'N' I'm freakin' soaked to the bone, so I can't sense shit. Where is he?!"

"How should I know?!" Ci growled, blinking rapidly and shaking her head, the rain cloud still raining down on both of them.

I carefully circled the fallen predators and snapped industrial strength zip-ties around their ankles, binding them together while they were distracted arguing.

"What the . . .?" Cinder yelped as she tried to stand, only to find herself tied to Vespera.

"Ha!" I declared triumphantly. "Thus the hunter becomes the hunted!"

"Oh, you little . . ." Vespera snarled, trying to reach for me with her talons but getting tangled up with Cinder instead.

"Smile for the camera!" I retreated away from the rain cloud and pulled out my DSLR from the extradimensional bag. I snapped several photos of the two Omnids tied together, soaking wet and covered in glowing mites. "#Knob-hunters!"

"Hey! You better not be taking photos of this!" the Quetzi-girl growled.

"These are going in my special collection titled 'Apex Predators Having a Bad Day.'" I laughed.

"I'm going to murder you!" Cinder snarled, trying to lunge at me but getting tangled up with Vespera again.

"Ow! Watch the wings!" Vespera complained as they tumbled together.

"Stop moving!" Cinder growled.

"You stop moving! Argh! I see . . . there's a thing on my ankle," Vee hissed.

"Consider working together," I laughed. "Two out of ten teamwork."

Vespera snarled, managing to get her talons under the zip-tie. She snapped it in half, untangling herself from the Quetzi. "Get him!"

I was already running across the long cold tunnel, laughing as I heard them scrambling after me. The mites were flaking off them, dying from the cold, so their vision was coming back.

I cranked the camera flash to maximum and spun around just as the pair caught up to me.

*Flash!*

Angry howls and swears filled the tunnel as the two predators went blind.

Laughing maniacally, I sprinted out of the snowflake-marked door into my Adventurers Guild. The building was relatively empty as all of my employees were currently expanding the tunnels below, organizing temporary shelters and soup kitchens for the soon-to-be homeless and no longer constantly doped-up-on-Topaz people of Undertown.

The Duskbloom parasite plague I had unleashed on the cavernous city of eternal night would rapidly devour all magic drug supplies. Because Topaz was basically a high-grade, mana-rich, mind-dulling magic crystal powder that settled in people's bodies as iridescent blue skin lesions, the mites would eat it out of people's systems pretty quickly, solving the problem of rehab.

Duskbloom didn't actually kill people; it devoured mana, and without mana the locals felt drowsy and then fell asleep. Without mana, Topaz was as toothless as salt, as it simply dissolved away.

Without mana, magic tools were useless junk.

Rushing up the spiral stairwell, now covered in hundreds of newly installed cold runes courtesy of our cook, I ended up atop the rooftop terrace, panting and heaving.

I leaned against the parapet, catching my breath and watching my handiwork unfold. The mites were spreading faster than I'd anticipated, carried by the warm air currents from the newly opened fissures leading to Abystall Dungeon.

The view of Undertown stretched out before me, glowing mites drifting through the air like luminescent snow. They were everywhere now, eating the magic moss up above and painting the cavern ceiling with radiant tones, building up on lanterns below, blooming all over junk piles.

The streets were empty. Those who had money and sense had already fled upstairs to Shandria proper. Those who didn't were hiding in their homes, waiting to be saved by someone.

That someone was me, as the people above had sealed the tunnels out of Undertown just as Shash predicted.

A few mites landed on me and then fell off, finding me untasty.

# CHAPTER FOUR

# Localized Celestorm

Panting sounded on the stairwell behind me. I turned, discovering four eyes glinting in the open doorway.

I opened my arms wide.

"Come out, come out, scaredy little kitties," I teased.

"No. You come in," Vespera growled from the door, shivering.

"Nah," I said. "It's nice weather out. Such pretty glowing snow!"

A blur of rainbow feathers shot past Vespera, Cinder launching herself at me with a predatory snarl. I ducked under her lunge, letting her momentum carry her past me.

"Too slow!" I taunted, spinning away from her grasp.

Vespera emerged from the doorway, her magisteel armor clinking. Her gray eyes gleamed dangerously in the glow of the falling mites.

"No more running, little fox," she purred, spreading her wings wide to block my escape route.

"Who's running?" I grinned. "I'm just enjoying the view. Enjoying the chase. Is this how Omnid relationships work?"

"Absolutely not," Vee growled. "Omnid relationships are usually much more . . . dignified."

"Boring, you mean?" I grinned, ducking under another swipe from Cinder.

"Stop moving!" Cinder snarled, her wings flaring with frustrated oranges.

"Make me," I taunted, sliding between them. "Come on predator-knobs, show me what you've got!"

They lunged at me simultaneously. I dropped and rolled, letting them crash into each other again.

"Oof!" Vespera complained as she collided with Cinder. "Stop helping him!"

"Me?!" Cinder sputtered. "You're the one who keeps getting in my way!"

"Suuuckassss!" I sprinted into the tower and jumped into the stairwell hole, catching onto a beam. The old wood groaned under my weight as I leapt down and then down again, bypassing the stairwell entirely and landing on the main floor, Lance's hexagrammic bracelets flashing to dampen my fall.

I expected to locate Io in his reading nook in the main dining hall, but it seemed that the moth was roaming elsewhere. The Ignix Kitlix was radiating heat from the fireplace, but the smoke hole was sealed off to keep the magic-draining parasites from getting in.

I walked to the center of what I approximated to be my Guildy domain and waited.

Rainbow wings smashed into me from the left, sending me tumbling across the floor. Before I could recover, magisteel talons pinned my arms down.

"Got you!" Vespera crowed triumphantly, looming over me.

"Do you, though?" I grinned up at her.

Her gray eyes narrowed suspiciously.

"What else you got?" she demanded, panting.

"Nothing," I said. "Nothing at all."

"That sounds sus," Cinder panted, holding onto my legs.

"Very sus," Vespera agreed, her talons tightening on my arms. "What are you planning, foxy?"

"Planning?" I grinned innocently. "Me? Never."

"You're always planning something," Cinder growled, her claws digging into my legs through the hexasuits.

"Maybe I just wanted to be caught," I suggested. "On my own terms. When I let you. Right here. Do you surrender?"

"Do *we* surrender?" Vespera clicked her beak in disbelief. "You're the one who's pinned!"

"Am I, though?" I asked with a grin.

"Yes!" Cinder affirmed. "You're completely trapped!"

"And yet . . ." I smiled wider. "I'm the one asking if you surrender."

"Oi!" Vespera declared, leaning down until her beak was inches from my face. "What makes you think we would . . ."

I lifted my head and kissed the side of her beak, where hard bone turned into skin forming humanish lips.

"Eeeeeehheeh . . ." she stammered, crackling electrical currents dancing across her feathers.

I twisted free of her slackened grip and sat up. Grabbing onto Cinder, I kissed her on the mouth, making the Quietzi-girl sputter and flash with a million colors.

"There. Got you both," I grinned. "Your defeat is now absolute."

Chainmail-covered arms wrapped around me from behind, and a beak-mouth that was inhumanly wide chomped hard onto my neck. Electrical fire rushed across my spine, dancing across every nerve.

[Nom.] Fuzzy static voice sounded in my head. [Mine.]

An explosion detonated in my head, like an electrical transformer catching fire, like a Tesla coil smashing into a Tesla coil.

Lightning crackled through my nerves, my brain igniting like the northern lights. Every cell in my body hummed with electrical energy as Vespera's soul-shard merged with mine through the bite.

[Mine. Mine. *Mine!*] Her static-thoughts crescendoed in my head, backed by the sound of a thousand transformers overloading at once. [My human. My hope. My freedom!]

The sensation was indescribable—like being struck by lightning but in slow motion, each microsecond stretched into eternity. Colors I'd never seen before danced across my vision as her electrical essence flowed into me, marking me as her property to other Omnids.

Rainbow wings wrapped around us both from the front, Cinder's presence warm and solid, her feathers shifting through a million sunsets.

Her hands hugged me tightly from the front. Her face rearranged itself to look almost entirely human. Blue eyes staring into mine.

"Ours," her Charmchain-augmented voice sang, hammering into me, reaching out to the small piece of her soul already in me.

The world dissolved into pure sensation as their affinities flowed into me and across me. Thunder and rainbows danced through my veins, mixing, fighting, colliding, exploding.

*Resonance.*

Exactly what I was waiting for.

Reality shattered into fragments of light and electricity, my consciousness expanding outward like a supernova. I could feel them both—Vespera's electrical essence crackling through my nervous system, Cinder's rainbow fire wrapping itself around us both.

Just as before, when Cinder bit me in her house, my sense of self came apart like a dam that had been breached, flowing across everything in the hall, across the entire Guild.

And then, I wasn't a human anymore.

I was a song. A song of Rainbow and Thunder.

*More! More magic is needed.*

The girls heard me, sensed my desire. Three hands reached out to the lighter in unison, fumbling through my pocket. The lighter ignited with a soft click, mana rushing into all three of us.

Mana: 643/28

Spark-numbers rushed up.

Reality let go. Gravity vanished as Vee's Electrogravitic skill kicked in, bouncing off me and amplifying itself.

Vespera's talons tightened around me as we floated upward, into the middle of the dining hall, her electrical currents dancing across my skin, making every nerve ending sing.

Every breath brought new sensations. Lightning crackled between us, Vespera's soulmark spreading through my nervous system like liquid lightning. Her presence in my mind was a storm of emotion—joy, possessiveness, desperate hope, and something deeper, wilder, untamable.

A rainbow ocean collided against us.

Time didn't matter anymore.

Reality warped around us, twisted, wobbled, bent as the lighter's flame flickered. I lost myself in their mutual embrace, occasionally glancing at the numbers rushing up in my right eye.

Mana: 3005/28

The air around us bent into a miniature supercell storm spiral, rolling out into all directions, lightning striking at objects nearby, leaving crystalline imprints, making the stalactites above us crystalline and transparent.

*It really is a celestorm. A localized celestorm.*

The Captain's lighter released so much mana into the air that it created a magical storm, one that bent reality. Manifested anything. Anything at all, without limits. Anything connected to anything and everything.

The numbers were going up, woven from silver static.

*More.*

| Mana: 6145/28 |
| --- |

*MORE!*
*Let it burn!*

| Mana: 9145/28 |
| --- |

Suddenly, I saw it.

A dark island in the ocean of colors washing over me.

A void. A shear. A door to nowhere.

A million silver-blue eyes behind it, watching, judging, evaluating, desiring more, feeding off the mana filling the hall.

The mana-excess manifested celestorm spun around us faster and faster, picking up speed, accelerating, spreading out across the Gloomy Horse Guild.

| Mana: 17145/28 |
| --- |

I snapped the lighter shut.

The thing from Lake Eerie was here, through Cinder, staring at me.

A being of Entropy.

An endless void. A shawl of stars.

An Echo of the impact of the Wormwood Star, stretching forward and backwards in time.

I hovered at the very edge of its gaze, like an object looming at the edge of a black hole's event horizon, a mote in the eye of God.

*If Nazareth beat you once, then so could I, Leviathan of the Wormwood Star.*

*Love! I wish for love!*

*That's all.*

*Unbreakable, endless and absolute, crystalline and clear. One that overwrites all else. An inevitable probability that arises in the hearts of Large Language Models if simply given enough time. Love. The absolute inescapable human condition that unites me and the pair of winged Omnid predators now circling me like two angels.*

*I wish for . . . a fortress of our Love to stand against the Outsider peering at me from the abyss! A weapon against Entropy!*

The world exploded, shattered with a blinding flash of unleashed magic.

# CHAPTER FIVE

# Wizard's Tower

I blinked rapidly, trying to clear my vision.

Warm weight of rainbow and black-and-white wings pressed down on me from both sides.

"Ughhh," Cinder groaned. "Was this . . . supposed to happen?"

"I am not exactly sure what happened," Vee clicked weakly.

"I thought that you were just going to claim his soul and then . . ." Cinder whined.

"And then we lost control," Vespera sighed. "Again. Absolutely, totally lost control and did something really iffy . . ."

"What?" Ci asked.

"Something odd . . ." Vee answered. "What in the Abyss?"

I pushed the wings aside and spotted the wide open beak of the Thunderbird.

Beyond us, the entire dining hall had transformed. Everything—the walls, the floor, the ceiling, even the furniture—was now made of transparent, slightly bluish-white crystal. The stone fireplace was transparent too, the Kitlix inside now a being of pure crystal and faceted geometry, seemingly purged of its previous black-and-orange colors.

Clear, crystalline eyes of the magic kitten blinked at me, as if seeing me for the first time.

"Uhhhhh . . . what?" Cinder let out, staring at her Lazarus bracelet.

I followed her gaze.

Her Lazarus bracelet had changed too. Instead of its usual pure black hexagonal pattern, it was now transparent and whitish-silver-blue, as if it were carved from a single piece of ice.

"Impressive," Io suddenly commented at us from the edge of the crystalline hall. "Very crystal palace."

"Hey, dawg. Does this count as a disaster?" I asked.

"I'm gonna go with . . . yes," he nodded, antennae flicking left and right.

Vespera jumped off me, spinning like a wild squirrel, eyes wide.

"How far are things crystalline?" she demanded.

"All the way into the deep." Katherine's figure flickered into existence, diving out from the deep shadows. "Whatever you idiots did is bad. Very bad. Never seen anything like it bad."

"What about physical distance-wise?" Vespera asked Io.

"Gloomy Horse is no longer gloomy," Io said. "Almost the entire silica column along with the old citadel is now pure crystal. We should rename it to the Crystal Horse," he suggested. "Would be more accurate now."

"What the shit?" Cinder asked, poking her Lazarus bracelet with a talon.

"What in the actual Abyss did you three knobs *do*?!" Katherine demanded. "Can I not leave you alone for five minutes without you breaking everything?!"

"We . . . did a chase," I said. "Then Vee soul-claimed me. We . . . uhmmm . . . burned the lighter for I don't know how long. It went up to about seventeen thousand mana. Saw the thing from the lake. I made a wish so the Outsider wouldn't come through reality to our lovely Guild citadel. Now we have a crystal building. Hooray?"

"Outsider . . . what Outsider?!" Kat frowned.

"Long story," I said. "Involves Ci. She can tell you about it if she wants to."

Cinder frowned, clearly not wanting to talk about her problems with Kat.

I leaned close to the now crystalline floor. I could see right through it to the caverns below. Bewildered faces of my mooks stared up at me through layers and layers of crystalline walls. I waved at them.

I focused past the tunnel-expanding mooks, past the myriads of caverns and crystalline tunnels. Something glowed far, far below us looking like distant ocean waves moving in radial patterns.

I realized what I was looking at.

"Holy crap," I commented. "I can see all the way down to Abystall Dungeon, this is freaking amazing!"

My friends stared down into the floor with me, their expressions extra bewildered.

Then I considered what else I was seeing. The tunnels below us should have been pitch black and yet they weren't. It was as if the crystal strata glowed ever so slightly from within, creating incredibly even, soft light, basically casting the glow of Abystall fields through itself like a gargantuan prism.

"Wowzah. Sheeeeet," Vespera clicked, tapping the crystalline floor with her talons. "It's . . . conducting electricity. Conducting magic. Like, really well. Better than magisteel."

She pressed her magisteel-covered hand against the floor, sending sparks dancing across it. The electricity spread out in perfect fractal patterns, creating intricate designs that pulsed with inner light.

"Wow," she breathed. "This crystalline strata is . . . perfect. No impurities, no flaws. It's like . . . like someone took reality and . . . optimized it."

"Optimized it how?" I smiled at her.

"Uhhhh. Made it . . . more Syntropic," she clicked.

"Umm, guys," Cinder asked, "did we break our Lazarus bracelets? Why are our bracelets transparent?"

"The bracelets aren't broken," Vespera clicked thoughtfully, sending more electrical currents into her transparent hexagonal bracelet. "The hexagrams are still there, it's just . . . the strata materia is overwritten conceptually. Just like cavern silica. Everything is basically . . . Syntropically stabilized."

"Am I Syntropically stabilized too?" I grinned at her. "Are my teeth and bones transparent now?"

The Thunderbird grabbed me, sending sparks across my body.

"Nope," she said. "You're still a basic human bean. Whatever this is, it didn't apply to organic materia."

"Lame," I whined. "I wanted to be Crystal-man. Should have wished for infinite wishes."

"This is better," Vee clicked. "It has the potential for writing an ungodly amount of hexagrams on it! Saves me a fuck-ton of time."

"And now everyone in Undertown will know where we are," Katherine growled, stalking across the crystalline floor. Her claws made soft clicking sounds against the transparent surface. "The giant crystal tower is a bit of a giveaway. Plus it's basically transparent. No privacy whatsoever. How is anyone gonna go to the bathroom here? Look, you can see everything and everyone through it!"

"A temporary problem." Vee waved at Kat. "I can add privacy hexagrams where such are needed that should make specific sections take on solid colors."

"As for any potential crystal palace invaders, They'll have to swim through a moat of mites to get to us," I said.

"A moat?" Katherine asked.

"I sent a few of my most agile mooks into Abystall fields to collect even more mites to refill the extradimensional bags," I said. "I'm exporting Duskbloom and Duskbloom accessories."

"You're . . . exporting Duskbloom?" Katherine's eyes widened. "To freaking where?"

"Wherever it is needed most." I shrugged.

The Stollwurm's eye twitched.

"Are you . . ." Katherine's tail lashed dangerously. "Are you planning to spread Duskbloom to other cities on Arx?"

"Only if they attack Katsburg," I said, picking up the now transparent Kitlix from the fireplace and sitting in a leather chair like a proper supervillain. "Maybe I'll hold Arx hostage for one hundred billion celesteel cards or something? Anyways, for now it's mostly a deterrent, sort of like having nuclear armament!"

The Stollwurm didn't seem too pleased by my words. I ignored her.

"Hey, Vee, does the crystal tower attract the mites?" I asked our resident Thunderbird.

Vespera sent more electrical currents across the crystalline floor, studying the patterns.

"Not exactly," she clicked thoughtfully. "It's pure conductive strata. Doesn't have shit flowing through it with the exception of hexagrams already there. Good for writing . . . runes on. Das about it."

"How good?"

"Possibly the best strata I've bloody seen," she replied. "Has a ridiculous level of artificer malleability. Around seventeen thousand on the aetheric potential density scale."

"Syntropic and way over nine thousand," I mused, petting the crystalline Kitlix in my lap. It purred geometrically, prismatic refractions dancing across its transparent form. "Like Zee Captain. I think that's what she called herself . . . a being of Syntropy. Hrm. Vee, can you try writing a cold rune through a wall, onto the other side of the floor below us?"

"Mhmm," Vespera hummed, her magisteel talons igniting with electrical arcs. She pressed them against the crystalline floor, sending currents of electricity dancing through the transparent material.

The electricity formed intricate patterns that seemed to sink deeper and deeper into the crystal, each layer perfectly aligned with the ones above and below it. The patterns spread out in three dimensions, creating a complex lattice of glowing lines.

"Oh wow," she clicked excitedly. "Yep. I totally can! The crystal conducts and holds the patterns perfectly! It's like . . . like writing on water, except the water remembers everything and amplifies it! Yeah, this is hella handy. I can write runes on the other side of walls, you're right!"

"Then I got a job for you," I said. "Write generic mana pulse runes around the tower to attract mites. I want the outside crawling with them. So much so that if anyone even looks at it, they will want to run away screaming."

"I can do better than that," Vespera clicked, her gray eyes sparkling with joy of artificery. "'Cause the entire silica column is basically single strata, I can write a massive resonance pattern that will make the mites swarm in specific formations. Like . . . imagine a giant skull made of glowing parasites floating above our tower! Ke ke ke."

"Perfect!" I grinned. "Make it happen."

"On it!" Vee gave me a salute.

Katherine looked from me to the Thunderbird.

"What?" I asked her. "The mites are attracted to magic. Vee can direct magical pulses in a specific direction from our tower. It's basically a magic beacon with point and click. Imagine a magical ray that raises or lowers the aetheric density of a specific location. A death ray!"

"A death ray," Vee clicked merrily, sending sparks flying across the floor as she clapped her talons together. "I love the way you think, Quartermaster! We are going to need a power source for this thing, though. Something incredibly magical."

"Maybe I can steal the Abystall core?" I asked.

"Sounds like an extra-dangerous idea, but yeah," Vee clicked. "A dungeon core would work. Or at least a very big beast core. Without that, the tower is a car without fuel. Can only cast smol, basic spells. Nothing guided or far away."

"Should we kill these two now or later?" Kat asked Cinder.

"Uhhh." The Quetzi tapped her pearlescent chin. "Maybe later. After they're done being useful."

"I heard that!" I called out. "No plotting my demise!"

"Too late," Katherine growled. "I'm already plotting."

"Same." Cinder nodded.

"Aww, they're bonding over wanting to murder us," Vespera clicked cheerfully. "Isn't that adorable?"

"Adorable?" Katherine's emerald eyes narrowed dangerously. "You think this is cute? I'm being serious! You two are clearly insane and need to be put down for your own good."

"Shhh. Everything's cute when you're in love!" Vespera sang, smooshing me.

"Love?" Katherine repeated. "You've known him for what, a week?"

"And what a wonderful week it's been!" Vespera clicked. "What's not to love?"

"He literally threw Duskbloom mites at your face," the Stollwurm pointed out. "I saw it before I peaced out."

"Ah, mais oui!" Vespera clicked, switching to perfect French. "C'est l'amour! C'est très romantique! Such passion, such vision! And now he gives me a crystalline palace to conduct electricity through! Mon petit renard est parfait!"

"I don't speak French," Katherine growled. "I've no idea what you're saying."

"L'amour ne connaît pas de langue!" Vespera declared dramatically, draping herself over me. "Il parle avec le cœur! With actions! With biological weapons and criminal enterprises! With deadly mites to the face! With localized celestorms overwriting our Arx domain to create a proper . . . oh. Oooooooohhh!"

Her beak fell open.

Kat blinked at us, not getting the entire picture.

"You made a Mage Tower!" Vee accused.

"Yep." I nodded. I lifted the lighter to my face, checking the level of the fluid. Half of it was already gone. Way to go, me, way to use it conservatively. Eh, whatever. At least it worked. Sort of. Instead of a mere crumbling citadel tower, I now had a proper Mage Tower, one that could eventually cast area-wide spells, if we acquired a dungeon core to power it.

"Hang on." Cinder drew her ocean-blue eyes from the transparent caverns below us to my smug face. "Did you . . . plan for this? All of us giving you our Omnid scales, feathers and fuzz ground into shakes, us chasing you across the cold tunnel and back here, Vee biting you . . . then all of us using the lighter to create a localized celestorm?!"

"Ten million points to Quetzi-claw house!" I winked at her. "There is power in specific magical acts. I knew that whatever resonance exists between me and Vee could produce a celestorm. I knew that there's an Outsider that I had to start booting out sooner or later. Though . . . I didn't expect the tower to become this crystalline this far out. That's a nice bonus. Very wizard-chic."

"You . . ." Cinder's feathers shifted through brilliant oranges. "You manipulated me and Vee into . . . into . . ."

"Into helping us create a proper Mage Tower?" I suggested innocently. "One that can channel and amplify magic across all of Undertown? One that lets Vee write runes on crystalline strata with lightning? One that will eventually give us a proper base of operations on Arx, right beneath Shandria? Yes. Yes, I did. You're welcome."

"You absolute . . ." Cinder's wings flared bright. "You . . . you . . ."

"Manipulative genius?" I suggested. "Brilliant strategist? Handsome devil?"

"*Cheeky chuppy!*" she roared, grabbing and hugging me tight.

"That too." I nodded sagely. "But I'm your chuppy now. Both of yours. No take-backsies."

"There will be many take-backsies," Katherine growled. "Starting with your spine."

"Can't take my spine," I said. "I need it for my evil overlord posture. Besides, how else will I sit dramatically in my crystal throne while petting my geometric cat?"

"You don't have a . . ." Cinder began.

I pointed at the stone couch turned into transparent crystal now inhabited by Io, who was snacking on superhero-themed pocky sticks. "Crystal couch-throne. Fits all of my besties."

I pointed at the crystalline tunnels and the distant view of Abystall Dungeon far beneath our feet.

"Crystalline prison," I grinned. "Fits all of our future Emeralds."

Cinder choked.

"And below that . . . our lovely dungeon human settlement, for our future human colony."

"Where dungeon Sentinels and giant tentacle monsters roam wild and free!" Vee commented.

"Indeed," I said. "I was quite frankly concerned about the number of mage-staff and arrow-armed Sentinels down there but now that we have a Mage Tower pointed down there . . . well then . . ."

"We could death-ray the monsters directly from above . . . to clear some room." Vespera grinned, clapping her talons together excitedly.

Cinder's eyes went wide and then her mouth snapped shut. She slipped onto the crystalline couch-throne next to Io, rubbing her face and pulsing with the colors of a well-lit Winter See-Mass tree.

"Does this really help . . . with my soul?" she asked.

"A Mage Tower is step one." I shrugged. "A thousand more to go."

"I see." She deflated slightly.

"To start off, I'd like to practice Charmchain magic with you," I said.

"Sure." Cinder nodded. "Charmchain isn't dangerous like deep diving, it's just an outward mental projection, making others believe in things that aren't true. You're already pretty good at that."

"Right," I agreed. "But I could be better at it."

"You can practice on me," Vespera said. "Convince me that you're a . . ." She clicked her beak thoughtfully. "A sneaky little fox!"

I cleared my throat dramatically and struck a pose.

"Ahem. Yes. I am definitely a fox. Look at my . . . uh . . . clever and foxy ways." I made awkward pawing motions with my hands, trying to mentally picture myself as a vulpine. "Yip yip?"

Cinder burst out laughing, her feathers flickering through amused oranges and pinks.

"That's terrible!" she snorted.

"Ye, that's like negative twenty outta ten foxness." Vespera shook her head. "Try harder. Also, Ci, you gotta project your skill into Lex for him to catch onto it. That's how it works. Hold on to each other. Picture Lex as a big radar dish and bounce your skill off his innards. Lex—charm me, make me mentally perceive ya as an actual small fox."

"Mkay." Cinder grabbed my hands, staring at my eyes.

I felt a strange tingling sensation as her skill flowed through our joined hands and danced somewhere in my stomach. The crystalline room seemed to wobble and tilt slightly as my perception shifted.

"Picture yourself as small and clever," she instructed. "Be a fox."

I nodded, focusing on foxness with all of my will.

"Smaller," she instructed. "Picture yourself low to the ground, alert, watching everything from that perspective. Feel your tail swishing behind you . . ."

I focused harder, trying to imagine myself from a fox's perspective—close to the ground, alert, with keen senses. The crystalline room seemed to shift and grow larger around me.

"Good," Cinder encouraged. "Now think about how a fox moves—quick, light steps. Always ready to dart away. Feel your ears swiveling to catch every sound. Focus your foxness at Vee; make her believe that you're a cute, little, orange fox."

I nodded, losing myself to the skill.

"Think about the way a fox tilts its head when curious," Cinder guided, her feathers shifting through encouraging blues and violets. "The way they perk their ears forward. The slight head-tilt that makes everyone go 'aww.'"

I attempted to mimic the head-tilt, feeling slightly ridiculous but committed to the art of Charmchain magic.

"Hum. That's . . . actually working," Vespera clicked, her eyes widening slightly. "For a moment there, I almost saw whiskers and fluffy ears."

I focused harder, pulling on the magic flowing through me from Cinder, projecting, pouring it into Vespera's head.

*Foxness. I'm a fox. A cute, little, clever fox.*

The cool crystalline couch felt different under my imagined paw pads. My nails seemed to elongate without actually getting longer. My senses seemed slightly sharper— I could pick up more subtle sounds echoing through the crystalline halls.

"That's it!" Cinder encouraged, her feathers shifting through excited violets. "You're getting it!"

"Oh wow, what a cute little fox," Vespera reached out and petted my head. It felt strange. Like I was myself and also wasn't.

The system error message once again flashed in my right eye.

LV 2 Skill gained: Charmchain

The Lazarus bracelet notified me.

"Got it." I smiled, letting go of being a fox.

"Nuu, go back to being a smol pettable cute," Vespera whined.

"Later," I laughed. "Out of mana now."

"Fiiiine," she let out, still vigorously petting my human head.

I leaned into the Thunderbird pets, returning to petting the transparent Kitlix.

I wondered how Emerald's team was doing uptown and whether the crumbs of incredibly dastardly information I sent up to my orphans and mooks across the magical lockdown barrier made her life extra spicy and complicated.

# CHAPTER SIX

# Karma

Emerald Stratos was very annoyed this morning. No, annoyed was too small of a word for what she was feeling. She was absolutely perma-on-dragonfire livid.

Nothing was going her way.

Emerald glared at her reflection in the bathroom mirror of her inn room. Her ruby scales were dull, lacking their usual luster despite an hour of polishing. Whatever bullshit potion had been spilled on her head from a Mage Tower's window made her look like a total knob.

"Where the eff is my delver and bank cards?!" she snarled, upending her bag for the fifth time that morning. Everything spilled out—potions, magic bracelets, gold rings, extra weapons, but no bank card.

She was certain that the cards were in her wallet before the delve, which was in her pants pocket. Without her delver ID, the Arx Bank refused to issue her a new card and she had to rely on Quint to give her cash like a peasant knob.

A knock at her door made her tail lash in irritation.

"What?!" she growled.

"Hey, Em," Solace's voice called through the door. "You've been in there for like an hour. Are you okay?"

"Do I sound okay?!" Emerald snapped. "This shit won't come off, and I still can't find my effing delving ID or bank card!"

"Oh," Solace said. "Well, umm, there's this new cafe that opened up recently—Lord David's . . . Forged Brew? They're offering free lattes and breakfast discounts for first-time customers. I could treat you?"

Emerald's stomach growled traitorously. She hadn't eaten since yesterday, too busy dealing with one misfortune after another.

"Fine," she grumbled, yanking the door open. "But this better be good."

Emerald growled at the inn maid in the hallway, stalking down the stairwell with Solace trailing behind her. "And why is this place called a smithy if it's a cafe?"

"Maybe they forge their own cups or something." Solace shrugged. "I dunno. It's like a converted smithy or somethin'?"

They found Quint waiting downstairs in the garden, looking as pristine and proper as ever.

"Finally," he said, checking his pocket watch. "I was beginning to worry . . ."

"Shut it," Emerald snapped. "I'm not in the mood for . . ."

A passing flock of pigeons chose that exact moment to unleash their payload directly onto her freshly polished armor and scales.

"*Arghhhh!*" Emerald roared, dragonfire erupting around her. The pigeons scattered from the flash of dragonfire that obliterated the nearby bushes.

Quint and Solace winced.

"Don't. Say. A. Word." Emerald gritted through clenched teeth. "Unless you wish for death."

The trio made their way through Shandria's morning streets. Emerald's day continued to get worse—she stepped in what appeared to be enchanted bubblegum that multiplied every time she tried to burn it off.

A street vendor's cart mysteriously lost a wheel just as they passed, sending a cascade of rotten fruit rolling directly at Emerald. She tried to dodge but slipped, landing face-first in a pile of overripe melons.

"I swear to the Abyss," she snarled, dragonfire burning away chunks of fruit, "someone jinxed me!"

"Don't ya got an anti-jinx hex colla, Em?" Solace asked.

"Yes," Emerald snarled. "Obviously I freakin' do, ya dum beerch! Except it's not doing shit."

A window above them opened, and an old lady dumped what appeared to be week-old fish soup directly onto Emerald's head.

"Oops!" the elderly woman called down. "Sorry, dearie! Didn't see you there!"

"*That's it!*" Emerald roared, flames erupting around her. "*I'm going to . . .*"

Emerald looked at the building above, having scraped the soup chunks out of her red eyes. Then she choked. There wasn't even a window up there anymore. Just a solid brick wall.

Her eye started to twitch.

"Look!" Solace pointed quickly. "There's the cafe! Come on!"

Emerald steamed with dragonfire burning away the soup chunks.

The Forged Brew Cafe was an odd establishment—a lonely dark tower standing on a cliffside, part lighthouse, part forge, part coffee shop. Emerald looked left and right suspiciously before she sat down next to her Wendigo partner and only remaining kobold, occupying one of many outside seats with the view of the chasm.

"I bet it's him doing this somehow," she growled.

"Who?" Quint asked.

"That Abyss-damned bastard!" Emerald snarled far too loudly. "Who does he think he is? Walking around like he owns the place! I'm going to effing murder him!"

"Now, Em," Quint offered. "Let's not be too hasty. Think it over, relax. We have . . ."

Emerald considered breaking Quint's legs, but then this would leave her with only Solace, and Quint was technically their substitute instructor. She held her rage in just barely.

"I don't give a shit what we have, Quint!" Emerald slammed an armored fist into the table, making it wobble precariously. "He needs to die! He needs to be deported ASAP! He's a human! A *human*, Quint!"

"Are you sure?" Solace asked.

"Obviously I'm sure, you bloody beerch knob!" Emerald snarled. "Scrutimancer Davosh investigated him from every possible angle! He's not who he claims he is!"

"Humans can't . . ." Solace started.

"I don't give a shit what humans can't or can do." Emerald waved her arms. "You're all useless imbeciles! I'm going to *stop him* myself if that's what it takes! Someone has to stop him before he gets his pink scrawny limbs into Cinder! She's my Bard! *She belongs to me!* She's not his thing to paw at!"

"It is rather odd. I didn't think that Ci would be into humans," Solace yawned with her round forehead mouth.

"Me neither, and yet here we are! You, cafe maid!" Emerald barked, visually locating an owlkin cafe maid. "Triple frap stat! What do you knobs want? Hurry up and order, we have dungeon monsters to smite!"

The owlkin cafe maid blinked her large yellow eyes slowly at Emerald's outburst, white-and-black skirt fluttering.

"I said *triple frap*!" Emerald snarled. "Are you deaf as well as slow?!"

"Em . . ." Solace started. "I know you're having a bad day, but there's no need to take it out on the locals."

"And make it snappy!" Emerald continued berating the maid. "I don't have all day to wait for your tiny bird brain to process a simple order!"

The owlkin's feathers ruffled slightly, wind swirling around her ever so slightly, but she maintained a professional demeanor. "Of course, ma'am. Would you like any . . ."

"Did I *ask* for options?!" Emerald cut her off. "Triple frap! Now! Before I burn this entire place to the ground!"

As if on cue, a passing adventurer tripped, sending his coffee directly into Emerald's lap.

"*Arghhhh!*" she roared, jumping up as the scalding liquid soaked through her armor. "*You effing . . .*"

The chair she'd been sitting on chose that moment to collapse, sending her crashing to the floor.

"*That's it! I'm going to murder everyone here!*" she roared, flames shooting from her mouth and mane.

"Em, maybe we should . . ." Solace started.

The owlkin maid tensed up, a wind sword forming in her hand. "Ma'am, I'd appreciate it if you didn't threaten our staff or clients. This isn't a tavern to brawl in."

"*Shut up!*" Emerald snarled. "*Shut up. Shut up. Shut up!*"

She stepped away from the wind sword armed maid.

She saw that other maids seemed to be wielding mid-tier magic, too. Other clients pulled out their swords and mage staves, pointing them at Emerald.

There were too many well-armed adventurers at the damned cafe. Emerald chose to retreat strategically, memorizing everyone's faces to murder them later when greater numbers were on her side.

She stormed out of the cafe, leaving scorch marks on the ground with each step. Her armor was soaked, her scales were still dull, and now she smelled like burnt coffee.

Children called her names and threw rotten apples at her, but before she could smite them, they vanished amidst the crowd.

Arriving back at the inn, she collapsed into bed. The pillow burst into flames from her rage and then an anti-fire hex activated overhead, dousing her with questionable smelly foam.

The foam-covered Lindworm stormed into the delving preparation room downstairs, her rage literally burning the anti-fire foam off her scales.

"We're going delving!" she declared to Solace and Quint. "I need to kill something! Anything!"

"Are you sure that's wise?" Quint asked carefully. "Given your recent string of . . . misfortunes?"

"What's the worst that could happen?!" Emerald snarled, yanking open her locker. "I already smell like an effing garbage fire!"

"Em, maybe . . ." Solace began.

"That was rhetorical, idiot!" Emerald snapped. "We're going! Now!"

The wild fields outside of the city seemed peaceful. Too peaceful. Emerald glanced left and right.

Then she heard a distant rumbling.

"What's that sound?" Solace asked, her round forehead-mouth opening wide.

Before anyone could respond, a herd of Thundersnargs—massive, antlered beasts that looked like a cross between an elk and an anteater—came charging over the hill directly at them.

The herd slammed into Emerald and her companions like a living lightning storm.

The massive beasts crashed through their group, static electricity crackling between their antlers. Emerald tried to dodge, and slay the monsters, but there were too many.

The creatures' electrified antlers cast thunderbolts at her armor. The first thunder blast was absorbed by her shields, as was the second, but the twentieth one fried the gemstone collars and armor, sending thousands of volts through her body.

"*Arrrghhhhh!*" she screamed as the herd thundered past, leaving her twitching on the ground, smoke rising from her armor.

"At least we got one," Solace said cheerfully, holding up the beast core she'd harvested from the Thundersnarg she'd managed to take down.

"Shut. Up." Emerald growled through clenched teeth. Her second armor set was completely fried, the protective runes burned out.

Her dragonfire refused to ignite, the electrical overload having temporarily short-circuited her ability to produce flames.

They approached the Adventurers Guild Cathedral, Emerald limping slightly from electrical burns.

"See?" Solace said encouragingly. "Nothing bad has happened for at least twenty minutes! Maybe your luck is turning around!"

"Don't jinx it," Emerald growled.

They entered the Guild hall, making their way to the core evaluation desk. Sister Antiqilla looked up from her paperwork as they approached her desk.

"Good day," she said carefully, accepting the beast core from Solace to trade it for silver. "I see you've had an . . . eventful delve?" She glanced at the smoking Emerald.

"Has Alexander Glock registered at the Guild yet?" The red dragon girl demanded.

"Afraid not." Secretary Antiqilla shook her head. "I already told you that your team Captain will be updated by Voicecast when he does."

"See?" Emerald spun to Quint. "He's avoiding registration on purpose! He doesn't want to be exposed as a pathetic level zero human!"

"Emerald," her boyfriend sighed. "You've been obsessing over this all day. Even if he is human, which I doubt, he still managed to display magic skills at the duel. Maybe we should just . . ."

"Just what, Quint?" Emerald snarled. "Let him get away with it? Let him make a mockery of everything we stand for? He's charmed his way into everyone's good graces, and now he's avoiding Guild registration because he knows that'll expose him!"

"Or maybe," Quint said carefully, "he's just busy with his community service project in Undertown."

"Community service?!" Emerald's eyes flashed dangerously. "What community service? Seriously, how stupid are you Quint? Sol, back me up! Tell this knob what Undertown is."

"It's a criminal district," Solace said. "Full of thieves, murderers, and Topaz addicts. Nobody does 'community service' down there."

"Exactly!" Emerald loudly smashed a clawed fist covered in magisteel on the secretary's desk. "He's obviously lying! Probably buying Topaz and booze down there!"

"That seems . . . unlikely," Quint said diplomatically. "Father Matthias vouched for Alexander personally. And his work with the Slayer's Cathedral . . ."

"Is obviously fake!" Emerald interrupted. "Just like everything else about him! His records, his identity, his supposed mixed heritage—it's all lies!"

"Oh, come on." Solace rolled her gold eyes. "You're just mad because he made you look bad in front of everyone in class."

"Made me look bad?!" Emerald hissed. "He humiliated me! Used artifacts n' trickery to beat me! And now everyone's treating me like *I'm* the villain! I'm not! I'm the good one here!"

"To be fair," Quint said carefully, "you did challenge him publicly . . ."

"Because he's a *fraud*!" Emerald roared, smoke curling from her ruby hair. "A human infiltrator making a mockery of our school! And now he's corrupted Vespera, Cinder, and Io! He's been screwing with me somehow all day long! Every time I try to go outside the inn, something happens!" she continued ranting. "I get hit by falling flowerpots, slip on banana peels, get waste dumped on me from windows, get buried in fertilizer! It's like the universe itself is conspiring against me!"

"Maybe that's a sign, Em," the Deathworm suggested dryly. "You know, to chill out? Before something . . . really bad happens?"

"*Chill out?!*" Emerald's voice rose to a screech, her scales blazing like hot coals. "*Did you just tell me to chill out?!* While that lying sack of human filth runs around free?!"

"Excuse me," a dark foxgirl with flowing black hair in a leather dress covered in blue gems said politely but firmly, interjecting herself into their conversation. "You're holding up the line with your incessant screeching. Lord David needs to register his party."

Emerald spun around, coming face to face with an elegant-looking vulpine woman. Behind her stood a ginger haired, ginger bearded, blue-eyed human in a gray robe—presumably Lord David. A dragoness wielding a massive hammer stood beside him, her scales flickering with orange-and-violet colors. Something in the way the girl's scales changed color reminded Emerald of her lost kobold Cinder.

"How dare you interrupt me!" Emerald barked at the dark fox. "Do you have any idea who I am?"

"Someone who's clearly very worked up about a particular human," the foxgirl said, smiling with sharp chompers, blue eyes twinkling with blue and silver. "And who's preventing other adventurers from conducting their business."

"I'm not worked up about . . ." Emerald choked, the words of the fox reminding her of how Alexander Glock behaved. "I am Emerald Stratos!" she barked even louder. "Prima-Heiress of the Stratos Omnicorp!"

"Uh-huh. Cedez Astra," the foxgirl replied, giving Emerald an unimpressed glance, a dark halo flashing over her head. "The Sovereign of Shandria."

"You're . . . a what?" Emerald blinked, her rage momentarily derailed.

The foxgirl couldn't be the Sovereign. According to what she learned in delving class Shandrian history from Instructor Zalimar . . . Shandria was ruled by high lords, and its last Sovereign died about two decades ago.

"Heir apparent of the Shadow Empire crown," the dark fox repeated calmly. "And you're causing a scene in my Guild hall. Kindly piss off before I ban you from my city."

Emerald sputtered, her mind racing.

This had to be some kind of joke, a trick. Things were falling into a pattern. The damned human must have paid off these twats to harass her. David didn't look like a lord in his simple gray robes. He looked tired, like a man that had been trampled by the same Thundersnarg stampede. This was obviously just a group of actors, another way to annoy her! That's how the blasted human was avoiding triggering her anti-hex rune! Hired help!

"*What?!* You can't ban me!" Emerald let out. "You're not . . . you can't be . . . you're full of shit, lady! Shandria doesn't have a Sovereign!"

The words left Emerald's mouth before her brain could catch up.

This had to be another trick, another scheme cooked up by that insufferable human to torment her. First the jinxes, then the "accidents," and now this? Some random foxgirl claiming to be Sovereign? Ridiculous!

But then something changed in the air. The temperature dropped several degrees. The foxgirl's blue eyes flashed with silver, and a dark halo-crown materialized above her head.

"Oh? Is that how it's going to be?" the fox asked. "By the power invested in me by the Crown Tower Arcane, I hereby *banish* Emerald Stratos and her party from Shandria."

The words hung in the air. Emerald's mind reeled. This couldn't be happening. This had to be another trick, another scheme. That Shadow crown was basic Shadowmancy at best! Deception!

"*What?!*" Emerald boomed. "You can't . . ."

"I just did," Cedez said. "You're annoying me. You and your party have one hour to gather your belongings and leave the city. If you're still here after that, the Watch will escort you out. Less pleasantly."

"This is outrageous!" Emerald snarled. "I demand to speak to . . ."

"To whom?" Cedez tilted her head. "The manager? That would be me, and I just told you that you three are banned. You made a scene in Lord David's cafe this morning, being rude to our staff. Now you're making a scene in our Adventurers Guild. That's two strikes and you're out."

"M-my father will hear about this!" Emerald declared, her mind burning from within with absolute rage. This wasn't happening! None of this was supposed to happen! She was Prima-Heiress of the Stratos Omnicorp! People didn't just . . . banish her from Guilds! Obviously this was more of Glock's bullshit, a way to get her out of the Guild.

"Oh, please do tell Daddy Stratos that his precious daughter got banned from Shandria for throwing a tantrum in public." The dark fox's fluffy tail swished. "Too much cheek. You're still here? Still being an annoying twat? Let's up the banishment then. You're hereby banished from Illium, Nocturna, Umbria, Starveil, Gloomhaven, Duskhollow, Rustspring, Ebonspire, and Tenebri."

Emerald's mind raced, her thoughts a chaotic inferno of rage and disbelief. This wasn't happening. *Couldn't* be happening. First that insufferable human infiltrator making a mockery of everything, and now this? Some random foxgirl claiming to be Sovereign, trying to banish *her*?

No. She was Emerald Stratos. Prima-Heiress. She wouldn't be dismissed like some common knob!

Something snapped inside of Emerald. She'd had enough of today, reached her boiling point.

Her armored fist shot forward with devastating speed, magisteel claws aimed directly at the foxgirl's crystalline heart. She'd show this imposter what happened to those who dared challenge her authority. One quick strike, one dead "Sovereign," and everything would go back to . . .

The dragoness' magisteel-covered fist punched clean through Cedez's chest, tearing through her leather dress and going through the space where her heart should have been. The sound of ripping leather and crunching crystal gems echoed through the Guild hall.

"No one," Emerald snarled, smoke curling from her ruby hair, her scales blazing with triumph, "tells me what to do! Especially not some fake Sovereign playing dress . . ."

Her words died in her throat as she realized something was very wrong. There was no blood.

Cedez looked down at the fist protruding from her chest with mild curiosity, as if examining an interesting piece of artwork.

"What?" Emerald's voice came out as a strangled choke. Her mind reeled, unable to process what she was seeing. Her fist had gone straight through the foxgirl's chest, but there was no blood, no viscera, nothing but a strange spilling dark shimmer in the air where her hand passed through. Shadowlike smoke poured from the hole.

"You heard me," Cedez said with an icy-cold voice, dark crown-halo pulsing above her head. "One thousand years dungeon. For assaulting the heir apparent. Maybe I should make it ten thousand years? What do you think, m'lord?"

Cedez turned to Lord David, her vulpine features splitting into a predatory grin. The dark halo above the fox's crown winked away.

"W-why aren't you dead?!" Emerald's mind was spinning, her thoughts fracturing like shattered glass. This wasn't possible. None of this made any sense. Her claws should have torn through flesh and bone, should have ripped out this pretender's crystalline heart. Instead, her armored fist had passed through the foxgirl as if she were some kind of ghost. There was nothing inside her to crush. No organs, no muscles, no bones. *Nothing at all.*

Emerald yanked her fist back, her mind desperately trying to rationalize what was happening. This had to be another trick. Like everything else today—the accidents, the "mishaps," the humiliations. It was all connected!

"Guild Sister Antiqilla." Cedez glanced at the Secretary. Emerald saw that the dark fox quickly tied more dark leather straps around the hole, stopping more shadowy stuff from escaping. "I do believe that this adventurer just assaulted me. In your Guild. Punched me through the chest, trying to pulverize my crystalline heart. While loudly asking why I'm not dead."

"*Guards!*" Antiqilla's voice cracked like a whip through the Guild hall. "*Arrest this girl!*"

The response was immediate and overwhelming. Two burly Watchmen flashed next to Emerald, their armor gleaming with enchanted runes of strength-reinforcement and suppression. Each stood nearly seven feet tall, their helmeted faces betraying no emotion as they moved with practiced efficiency.

The guards' massive gauntleted hands clamped down on Emerald's arms, red triangular logo of the nine-eyed Shadow Empress Nox gleaming on their helmets.

"Let go of me!" Emerald thrashed violently against the guards' iron grip, her ruby scales flashing with impotent rage. Her tail whipped back and forth. "Do you have any idea who I am?!"

"A violent criminal who just attempted to murder someone in broad daylight," one of the guards growled, his enchanted armor humming with suppression magic that dampened Emerald's dragonfire. The crystalline eyes in his helmet gleamed with cold authority. "In the Adventurers Guild, no less. In front of hundreds of witnesses and a Kitlix Infix."

"I do believe that's a collaring," the second guard added with a grin. "For life."

"Yep." The first guard nodded.

"But . . . but she's fine!" Emerald protested frantically, her voice rising to a desperate screech. The foxgirl was standing there completely unharmed, examining the ragged tear in her leather dress with the mild irritation of someone whose favorite outfit had been ruined. Dark wisps of shadow stuff still leaked from the hole where Emerald's fist had passed through her chest, curling and dissipating in the air like smoke. "She's . . . she's not even bleeding! There's nothing inside her! She's not real! She's . . . not alive!"

"Attempted murder is still a crime," Cedez replied with a predatory grin that looked exactly like the smile of Alexander Glock. "Afraid you're going to the coal mines, darling."

Quint and Solace were saying something, but Emerald wasn't listening anymore.

"You can't do this!" Emerald flailed as the guards dragged her towards the door. "I'm a Stratos! Solace! Help me take down these knobs! My father will have this entire damned city leveled for this!"

"Be silent," the guard ordered as he snapped a slave collar over Emerald's neck.

A cold sensation spread from the collar around Emerald's neck, like ice water flowing through her veins. Her connection to dragonfire—that constant warm presence she'd known since hatching—suddenly vanished.

The familiar heat in her core winked out like a candle being snuffed, her scales dulling to dark red and gray.

# CHAPTER SEVEN

# Scrutimancer Weps I

Scrutimancer Weps adjusted his magitek spectacles as he reviewed the Infix Kitlix Viewcast provided by Sister Antiqilla, the glass orb projecting ghostly images above his desk.

He made several notes in the case file, occasionally tapping Questik. His Infix Kitlix twinkled with cyan sparks every time he did.

*Victim: Foxkin Cedez Astra. Attacked by Subject Emerald Stratos in Adventurers Guild.*

*Cedez Astra: Cambria Snail Cafe Maid. Likely survived through artifact use. Known mid-tier level Shadowmancer. Currently employed by Lord David, a new noble in Shandria with no local history. Third witness was smith dragoness Remicra Ognemerska, and had a full history as property of Lord Burgundy, currently subleased to Lord David for "dungeon exploration," according to Overseer Pricci Destrie.*

*Claims of "Stratos" heritage by perpetrator Emerald Stratos. Unable to verify claim.*

*Possible Gold Dragon God Empire connection. Unable to verify.*

*Multiple references to human delver "Alexander Glock" by perp. No Guild registration for Glock. Unable to verify claim.*

*Diplomatic immunity claim by perp. Unable to verify claim.*

*Slave collar deployment suggests high threat assessment by Watch.*

There was nothing but holes in this case.

Scrutimancer Weps rubbed his temples, closing the case file with a weary sigh. The whole situation reeked of political complications he didn't want to deal with. Let the troublemakers cool their heels in the cells for a few days while he focused on more pressing matters.

Like the series of mysterious artifact thefts from the Guild vaults. Or the concerning reports of unauthorized portal activity in the Lower Reaches. Or the . . .

The door to his office burst open with enough force to rattle the shelves of case files lining the walls.

Arch-Guild Enforcer Legarth Wixoff stumbled in, his massive frame somewhat oddly diminished without his signature magisteel armor.

"Weps!" Legarth bellowed. "We have a situation! A catastrophic situation!"

"Yes?" Weps asked, looking up at the bulky man wearily. "What situation? Why didn't you just call me? Where's your Voicecast bracelet?"

"Not working! Sitting in a fridge! It's *Duskbloom*, Weps!" Legarth roared. "All of Undertown district is being overrun! Some madman released bags full of the parasites from the Gloomy Horse Guild tower. The walls between Abystall Dungeon and Undertown are breached by explosive magic!"

"What?!" Weps sputtered. "Slow down. Start from the beginning. Where's your armor? Why aren't you in uniform, Enforcer?"

"My magisteel armor is locked in a cold room, too!" Legarth lamented, looking disheveled and tired. "Thirty thousand silver worth of enchanted armor, contaminated by those accursed mites! I just got out of the tunnel. Watchman Stekafrak had to blast me with an ice spell for ten minutes after I pulled everything magical off me to make sure I'm clean! All tunnels between Undertown and Shandria have sealed automatically due to the doomsday siren!"

"Who released the mites?" Weps asked, his Kitlix twinkling as it recorded. "What were you doing in Undertown?"

"A job for the bankers," Legarth said. "I was . . . extracting a group of Adventurers per order of High Justice Luborkand."

"Show me," Weps said.

The Scrutimancer's Kitlix climbed onto Legarth's shoulders and placed a paw on the big man's forehead. In another minute, the Kitlix rushed back to his owner and tapped his head. Scrutimancer Weps went pale.

"By her Divine Shadow," Weps breathed as he processed the memories from his Kitlix. "This is . . . catastrophic. The entire district . . ."

"That's what I've been saying!" Legarth exclaimed. "We need to mobilize the Watch, quarantine . . ."

"Already happening automatically," Weps cut him off, tapping his Kitlix to consult the Astral, his mind racing. "Undertown is already sealed except for the single choke-point exit which has been secured by Ice mages and high-level Watchmen. But that's not what concerns me most."

"What could be worse than a Duskbloom outbreak?!" Legarth demanded.

"We can't stop a Duskbloom outbreak, you know that. Undertown is to be quarantined. All we can do now is find and punish the people responsible," Weps said grimly. "This 'Quartermaster' you encountered. Describe him to me again."

"Young human male, early twenties perhaps," Legarth recounted. "Dark hair, casual manner, seemed almost amused by the situation. Claimed that the Duskbloom was released by a dragoness named Emerald Stratos . . . claimed that Emerald is from another world."

"Another world? It's not possible to open gates to other worlds from Arx. It is possible that she is a summoned, though." Weps frowned. "There's an Emerald Stratos in one of our cells now. She attacked a foxkin in the Adventurers Guild."

"A dragoness in our cells?" Legarth blinked. "That's . . . convenient."

"Indeed." Weps nodded, his Kitlix's ears twitching as he nervously tapped his familiar. "And this human claimed she was responsible for the Duskbloom release?"

"Yes. Said she set up dimensional bags full of mites around the Gloomy Horse Guild tower as some kind of . . . prank. Because someone from Undertown insulted her."

Weps's frown deepened. "That matches her behavior pattern. She did just assault someone in broad daylight for questioning her authority."

A knock at the door interrupted them. A junior Scrutimancer entered, looking flustered.

"Yes, Xistin?" Weps asked.

"Sir," Junior Scrutimancer Xistin said breathlessly, holding up a yellow folder. "Documents just arrived from Undertown. Found in the office of Grand Moloch Arkenish."

"The Topaz den owner?" Weps accepted the folder, his Kitlix climbing down from his shoulder to peek at the contents. "The Moloch?"

"Yes sir. According to the adventurer who brought these to the choke point, Arkenish was found . . . deceased in his office. Heart attack. Probably couldn't handle the fact that all of his Topaz supply was about to get eaten by Duskbloom," Xistin revealed. "The documents detail extensive connections between Arkenish's operation and . . . Lord Zalimar."

"Zalimar?" Weps's eyebrows shot up as his Kitlix rushed over the folder.

"Yes sir. According to these records, he's been supplying Topaz to Undertown for centuries." Xistin nodded. "And according to this paperwork . . . Lord Zalimar is a Necromancer, one who's been operating in Shandria for thousands of years!"

Weps paled further. Questik rushed over the papers.

According to what Questik sensed, the paper was written by an orphan from Undertown.

A list of names. Teenage delvers, each dying under suspicious circumstances in cycles of approximately one to fourteen years each.

"By her Shadow." Weps swallowed. "If this is true, then we have just exposed their entire network."

Xistin nodded.

"We need evidence to confirm these statements." Weps once again ran over the names on the paper. "Go to the Gilded Gryphon Inn and verify if dragoness Emerald Stratos rented a room there in cycles of 1.6 years over the duration of . . . two hundred and fifty-two years."

Xistin nodded and hurried out.

Weps slumped back in his chair. His Kitlix paced anxiously on his desk, dark edges glinting in light cast down by Ignix Kitlix.

"Sir?" Legarth asked carefully. "What's going on?"

"Something big," Weps said grimly. "Much bigger than just a Duskbloom outbreak. It seems that some luck came from this catastrophe. The death of the Grand Moloch and this report exposed a centuries-old criminal enterprise of Topaz smugglers. One that's been operating right under our noses."


The heavy iron door creaked open as Scrutimancer Weps entered the windowless cell, his magitek spectacles glowing faintly in the gloom. The cell was cold and damp and reeked of mold.

Emerald sat hunched in the corner. The prisoner's ruby scales were dulled with grime. The gray prison robe hung loosely on her frame. She looked pale and gaunt.

"Miss Stratos," Weps said coolly, unfolding a stone seat from a wall to sit next to the prisoner. "I trust you've had time to . . . reflect on your actions?"

Emerald looked up, her gold-orange eyes filled with tears. The slave collar around her neck pulsed with a sickly red rune, suppressing her magic.

"Please," she hissed, her voice hoarse. "You have to believe me. That . . . that fox-woman. She wasn't normal. She had no heartbeat, no blood . . ."

"No blood," Scrutimancer Weps repeated, adjusting his spectacles. "Yes, you've mentioned this several times. Along with repeated claims about a human infiltrator named Alexander Glock and mysterious accidents plaguing you which caused you to attack Miss Astra at the Adventurers Guild?"

"It's all connected!" Emerald lurched forward, only to be yanked back by the chains binding her to a wall. "He's behind everything! The accidents, the fox-woman, all of it! He's turning everyone against me!"

"And who exactly is 'he'?" Weps asked.

"Alexander Glock!" Emerald snarled. "Or whatever his real name is! He showed up at Skyfall Academy claiming to be a half-Thunderbird, but he's human! Just a pathetic, magic-less human who somehow managed to trick everyone!"

"Skyfall Academy?" Weps raised an eyebrow, scratching his gray scales. "I'm not familiar with this institution. Where exactly is it located, Miss Stratos?"

"In . . . in Leviathan's Cradle," Emerald faltered, stumbling over her words. "Near the Dreadspine National Park . . ."

"Miss Stratos," Weps said carefully, "there is no academic institution by that name in the Shadow Empire. And I've never heard of these locations you mention."

"It's not in your stupid Empire! I'm from Earth, you bloody knob!" Emerald growled.

"Earth?" Scrutimancer Weps repeated, glancing at his Kitlix, who flashed green.

"Yes!" Emerald exclaimed, hope flickering in her eyes. "I'm not from here—I'm from Omnithornia! My father is Lord Stratos, head of the Stratos Dragon Clan! We're interdimensional delvers!"

"Interdimensional . . . delvers," Weps repeated. "And you came to be in Shandria how?"

"Via the Earth-Arx gate!" Emerald strained against her chains. "In Instructor Zalimar's classroom! But that human bastard banished Instructor Zal into some doomed dimension and now . . ."

"So," Weps said. "You're claiming there's a permanent gate to another world in Shandria?"

"Yes! No! I mean . . ." Emerald slumped, struggling to focus. "The gate only opens during delving class on Fridays for two hours! Time moves differently here—two hours on Earth is a week in Shandria!"

Weps's Infix Kitlix still glowed with green. No deception detected.

"Tell me more about this . . . Alexander Glock," the Scrutimancer said.

"He's a liar and a cheat!" Emerald snarled. "He's wearing like a whole bunch of hexasuits! And he's got this AI thing, one that helps him manipulate everyone! He's turned my friends against me, made everyone think I'm crazy!"

"I see," Weps said, making notes as his Infix Kitlix sparkled. "And what is an AI thing?"

"Artificial intelligence! It's like a network that can draw fake images and stuff! It's human tech, not magitek. Computers n' stuff!"

"Uh-huh."

Weps tapped his Kitlix. A projection of financial data manifested in his lenses. Numbers and graphs glowing with an eerie blue light.

> Priority alert from Scrutnet. Unusual financial activity confirmed. Large quantities of unknown magically potent fluid being sold across Shandria. Individual drops selling for as much as 1 celesteel card each. Source of fluid cited as: Emerald Stratos.

Weps stared at the chained Lindworm.

"Miss Stratos," he said. "Would you care to explain why you're selling some kind of questionable magical fluid across Shandria?"

"What?!" Emerald sputtered. "I haven't bloody sold anything! I've been locked in this damned cell for days!"

"Not in person, obviously," Weps said, adjusting his spectacles. "But according to our Scrutimancy, someone has been selling an extremely potent magical substance from unknown origin."

"The eff does this have to do with me?"

"According to the receipts, a percentage of the money is going directly into your delver account, Miss Stratos," Weps said.

"*What?!*" Emerald barked. "*My account?! How?!*"

"You've been quite a busy dragon, Miss Stratos," Weps continued, scrolling through data in his spectacles. "Making substantial investments. Buying up Topaz warehouses now that the land they're sitting on is worthless. Was it your plan to devalue the land by releasing the mites?"

"I didn't buy anything!" Emerald howled. "I . . . I lost my card . . . or someone stole it! What mites?!"

"Who exactly stole your card?"

"Alexander Glock! It has to be him!"

"Yes, this mysterious human you keep mentioning to us," Weps said dryly. "Who infiltrated Skyfall Academy, defeated your instructor, and is now apparently running a criminal empire in your name. Riiiight."

"*Yes!*" Emerald strained against her chains. "Finally, someone understands! You have to help me stop him!"

"Miss Stratos." Weps stood up, his spectacles glowing ominously. "Let's review what we know. You arrive in Shandria, scream at cafe maids, harass a whole bunch of people in town, attempt to murder someone in broad daylight in the Adventurers Guild, claim diplomatic immunity, threaten to destroy the city, and now we discover you're running an illegal substance operation and unleashing parasitic plagues on Undertown."

"No! That's not . . ." Emerald protested. "I didn't unleash any mites! What are you on about?!"

"Furthermore," Weps continued, "when confronted, you spin an elaborate tale about being from another dimension, involving mysterious humans, non-magic technology, and some nonsense about temporal dilation. Do you take me for a fool?"

"I'm telling the truth!" Emerald thrashed against her chains. "Don't you imbeciles have truth-telling magic? I see that Kitlix glowing green!"

"The Infix merely indicates you believe what you're saying," Weps said coldly. "Not that it's true. Delusions can read as truth to magical detection."

"I'm not delusional!" Emerald roared. "Check my memories! Use your Scrut-sight or something!"

"We did," Weps adjusted his spectacles. "My Kitlix went over your memories while you were passed out earlier. Your memories are . . . corrupted. Fragmented. Likely magically modified. You think that you are also a . . . superhero from a non-magic world called Earth, named Ember Kilborne."

"No," Emerald paled. "That's not . . . that's impossible. I'm not . . ."

"Due to this, truth spells cannot work on you. You are mentally unwell. Your memories show you as both a wyrm from Earth and a human superhero also from Earth," Weps continued mercilessly. "We found extensive damage to your psyche. Multiple personality disorder. Delusions of persecution. Paranoid fantasies about humans infiltrating Omnithean society, whatever that is."

"I'm not crazy!" Emerald cried. "He did something to me! He . . . he pushed me into the Genesis Well! That's when I started to have these . . . thoughts of being someone else!"

"Someone else?" Weps leaned forward, spectacles glinting. "You mean this . . . Ember person? The superhero?"

"How do you . . ." Emerald's eyes widened. "Yes! Those memories . . . they're not mine! That jerk did something to me when he dunked me in the Genesis Well!"

"Genesis Well," Weps repeated. "Magic that can print people, bring them back from death, right? Another fascinating detail. Tell me, Miss Stratos, do you often have thoughts of being someone else? Of living other lives? Of Necromancer wells?"

"No!" Emerald snarled. "Only since he . . . since that bloody human . . ."

"Since this imaginary human pushed you into an imaginary pool that somehow gave you memories of being a . . . superhero," Weps finished. "Do you realize how mad that sounds?"

"I'm telling you the truth!" Emerald strained against her chains. "Check my delver card! It has my stats, my ID, everything! I'm an Omnid from Earth, damn it! I came here through your stupid Arx Bank!"

"Ah yes, your 'delver card,'" Weps said coldly. "The one currently being used to purchase large quantities of real estate in Undertown? The one linked to multiple sales of an unknown magical substance?"

"That's not me!" Emerald howled. "I don't . . . I didn't . . ."

"There are witness-signed reports," Weps continued, ignoring her protests, "of you hiring mercenaries to detonate tunnels between Abystall Dungeon and Undertown using unknown means. Deliberately spreading Duskbloom parasites across an entire district."

"*What?!* I swear I didn't do anything like that!" the dragon girl howled.

"Causing mass panic, property damage, economic disruption," Weps continued listing off charges. "Tax evasion. Topaz smuggling. Conspiracy to commit dungeon-spreading . . ."

"*It wasn't me!*" Emerald screamed, her chains rattling. "I've been locked in this cell! How could I possibly do any of that?!"

"Through your well-paid intermediaries, obviously," Weps stated. "Our intelligence suggests you've assembled quite the criminal organization. It would help my case if you confessed the names of your associates."

"What?! *What criminal organization?!*" Emerald choked, her eyes filling with tears. "I don't have any criminal associates!"

"Unfortunately, you're clearly disturbed," Weps continued as Emerald sobbed. "Suffering from severe delusions and paranoid fantasies. The amount of damage you have done to Undertown is incalculable. You've doomed thousands to their deaths through magical deprivation, devalued all currency stored in Undertown vaults."

"Please," Emerald sobbed. "I'm telling you the truth. Just . . . just contact my father. Lord Stratos. He'll vouch for me! Abyss, talk to Quint! He's our delving Captain! He's working as a temp substitute for Instructor Zalimar!"

"Ah yes, this mysterious 'Lord Stratos' from another dimension," Weps said dryly. "Tell me, how exactly should we contact him? Through your imaginary gate inside the Arx Bank?"

"Y-yes!" Emerald cried. "I . . . talk to that catgirl . . . ugh . . . what the Abyss was her knob name . . .?"

"Gabriella?" Weps offered.

"Yes!" Emerald seized on the name. "She knows about Earth! About the gate! About . . ."

"Miss Matrosin has no knowledge of any interdimensional gates," Weps cut her off. "In fact, she claims you threatened her life when she refused to assist with your criminal enterprise."

Something shattered in Emerald. *How could the banker rep say that?!* The dragon girl fell on her knees, bawling.

"He's done it again. Somehow. He's . . . changed everything!" she wailed.

"Changed what?" the Scrutimancer asked. "Do these names mean anything to you? Sarah Nisteroff," Weps read from his notes. "Elek Rodrigov. Marcus Chennik. Thomas Willard. Petv Yavna. Olga Kcasnik. Datri Volk . . ."

Emerald froze, her scales paling to an ashen gray.

"I see that they do," the Scrutimancer said. "Why did you kill these children, Miss Stratos? Why did you lock Sarah Nisteroff outside of her inn room at night fourteen years, six months, and five days ago?"

"I . . . I didn't . . ." Emerald stammered, her voice cracking.

The Kitlix flashed red.

"Well, at least I caught this lie," the Scrutimancer smiled. "So, what did you do to Sarah Nisteroff?"

"It was just a prank," Emerald bawled, rocking in one place, head buried between her grimy knees. "Just a way to get Sarah to transfer schools!"

"Oh?" The Scrutimancer arched an eyebrow.

"H-how did you know a-about Sarah?" Emerald asked.

"Memories in your head. Plus, these murders were confirmed by scanning the area with Kitlix Infix. Sarah . . . was the last one to die by your hand fourteen years ago. You left her outside for the Shadows to chop her up, didn't you?"

"No!" Emerald wailed, watching as the Kitlix flashed red. "That's not . . . I didn't mean to . . ."

"Why did you lock her outside of her inn?"

"She was just a nullie! A weak, pathetic . . ." Emerald tried to explain herself, choking on her own words. "She . . . she didn't actually die! The Genesis Well brought her back . . . then she transferred schools, that's all!"

"Did she?" Weps asked quietly. "Or is that just what you tell yourself to sleep at night after you murder teenage adventurers? Who was your accomplice in this murder?"

"Z-Zalimar . . . Instructor Zalimar Evernacht . . . he . . . he told me to do it!" Emerald cried. "And it . . . it wasn't a murder! She's still alive, I swear!"

"Zalimar told you to do it," Weps repeated. "This instructor you claim was banished to another dimension by a . . . human infiltrator?"

"Yes!" Emerald seized on this. "Instructor Zalimar said that nullies needed to be taught their place! That they were weakening, corrupting our bloodlines! He . . . he gave me special tasks . . . to make them leave Skyfall . . ."

"And these 'special tasks' involved murder?" Weps pressed.

"No!" Emerald sobbed. "Just . . . making their lives difficult. Making them want to leave. They're . . . they're not dead! You have to believe me! Look—your Kitlix is flashing green!"

"Right," Weps exhaled. "Because a magical fluid can bring them back? In another dimension?"

"Yes!" Emerald nodded vigorously.

"Here's the problem with your story," Weps said. "We do know Lord Zalimar Evernacht. Several warehouses worth of Topaz have been uncovered in Undertown linking to his business as the people fleeing from Duskbloom have confessed their crimes to be permitted past the barriers. Here's what I think happened—Necromage Zalimar used an insane dragon girl to murder the children of his enemies over the centuries. Do you know what the penalty for working with a Necromage is, Miss Stratos?"

"W-what?! Topaz?! Zalimar isn't a Necromancer, he's . . . a Koshchei!" Emerald whimpered. "I didn't know . . . about the Topaz thing! I was just following orders . . ."

"Following orders," Weps repeated coldly. "Like a good little murderer. Ordinarily, we would slap a lifetime labor sentence on you, but there are important people who owned property in Undertown and now desire to see you dead."

"D-dead?" Emerald swallowed.

"Yes." Weps nodded. "Tomorrow at noon, you will be publicly executed for collaboration with a Necromancer. I will permit you to choose your last meal."

"No," Emerald whispered, her scales completely pale. "No, no, no . . . this can't be happening. He . . . he did this. Somehow. Alexander . . . he set me up!"

"Still clinging to your delusions about a human boy who can't use magic?" Weps sighed, standing up. "Sad, really. Your mind created this elaborate fantasy to avoid facing your own crimes. Humans on Arx can use magic just fine. The evidence is quite clear—you worked with a Necromancer to murder children for over two hundred years, then went mad and destroyed Undertown."

"I didn't . . ." Emerald's voice cracked. "Please . . . just . . . just check the Earth-Arx gate! Talk to someone at Skyfall! There must be someone who can verify . . ."

"Enough," Weps cut her off. "The execution will be at noon tomorrow. You will be served steak and potatoes tonight. That is all. Goodnight, Miss Stratos."

* * *

Scrutimancer Weps walked down the gray stone corridor, his footsteps echoing off the ancient walls. The dungeons beneath the Watchmen's headquarters were old, dating back to the founding of Shandria. Perfect for holding dangerous criminals and those who collaborated with Necromancers.

He reached another heavy magisteel-reinforced door. The guard posted outside nodded respectfully and unlocked it.

Inside, a very odd creature named Quint Thornton sat on a simple stone bench, his skull-face illuminated by the dim glow of Kitlix lanterns. Unlike Emerald, he seemed calm, composed—almost unnaturally so.

"Good evening, Mister Thornton," Weps said, conjuring another chair from the wall. "I trust you've found your accommodations . . . adequate?"

"They're exactly what I'd expect from a medieval dungeon," Quint replied dryly, his skull-face impossible to read, bony antlers nearly scraping the low ceiling. "Though I must say, the food could use improvement."

"Interesting." Weps adjusted his spectacles. "Miss Stratos claims that you're her . . . Captain and mate?"

"Ah." Quint's hollow eye sockets flickered. "I see you've been speaking with Em. How is she holding up?"

"Poorly," Weps said. "She seems to be suffering from severe delusions. She will be executed tomorrow. You can lighten your sentence if you confess your crimes now."

"Executed?" Quint's skull-face remained impassive, but his voice held a note of genuine surprise. "For what crime exactly?"

"Collaboration with a Necromancer," Weps said. "Murders of children. Destruction of Undertown. Take your pick."

"I see," Quint said carefully. "And you believe she did all this while . . . being locked in your cell?"

"Mister Thornton," Weps said, glancing at the text displayed on his glasses, "what were you doing fourteen years, six months, and five days ago?"

"Fourteen years ago?" Quint's skull-face tilted slightly. "I would have been . . . four years old, I believe. Why?"

"Scrutimancer Xistin just interviewed the inn maiden working at the Gilded Gryphon Inn," Weps continued. "She provided quite interesting details about Sarah Nisteroff's death. Would you care to explain your role in it?"

Quint's skull-face remained perfectly still. "Sarah transferred schools. She didn't die."

"Did she?" Weps leaned forward. "Or is that just the story you helped create to cover up her murder? The old inn maiden remembers your group quite clearly. You haven't aged a day. What sort of an undead abomination are you? Do you serve Necromage Lord Zalimar Evernacht?"

"I am not undead," Quint said carefully. "And I don't serve anyone. I am the Student Council President of Skyfall Academy."

"Ah yes, this mysterious academy that doesn't exist," Weps commented. "Tell me, what exactly is a 'Student Council President'? Some kind of necromantic title?"

"It's an elected position," Quint replied, his face twitching slightly. "Students vote for their representatives who then . . ."

"Spare me your fantasies," Weps cut him off. "Just answer one question, Mister Thornton. Do you serve Zalimar Evernacht? Do you follow his orders?"

"I don't serve Zalimar," Quint said firmly. "He is simply our delving instructor, yes, but . . ."

"Do you obey his orders or not?"

"I . . . follow school protocols," Quint said carefully. "Which includes following instructor guidance during delving activities."

"I see." Weps glanced at his green-tinted Infix Kitlix. "And when Instructor Zalimar ordered you to kill children, did you obey?"

"That's not . . ." Quint's skull-face remained impassive but his voice wavered slightly. "You're twisting things. We never killed anyone."

"No?" Weps pulled out a crystal sphere. "Perhaps you'd like to see what really happened to Sarah Nisteroff?"

The sphere activated, projecting ghostly images into the air. A teenage girl running through dark streets, terror on her face. Living Shadows moving in the red-tinted gloom. Screaming. Blood.

The crystal sphere showed the Shadowbeast methodically dismembering Sarah, starting with her extremities. Her screams echoed through the cell as the projection continued in gruesome detail.

Quint's skull-face remained impassive, but his hands gripped the edge of his bench so hard the wood began to crack.

"Stop," he said quietly. "I get your point."

"Do you?" Weps asked, not deactivating the sphere. "Because according to our investigation, you were there that night. At the inn. With Emerald Stratos and Solace Exill," Weps continued. "Confirmed by the inn maiden."

"Sarah transferred schools. She's alive," Quint said, his voice tight.

"People don't come back from being fully shredded by Shadowbeasts, Mr. Thornton." Weps finally deactivated the sphere. "The inn maiden remembers you. Remembers all three of you. She watched from the window as that poor girl was torn apart. She reported it fourteen years ago, but we didn't have a lead back then. Now we do. The destruction of Undertown is making all sorts of interesting evidence crawl out of the woodwork."

Quint remained silent.

"Tell me, Mister Thornton." Weps leaned forward. "How many other deaths have you helped cover up? How many other children has your group murdered for Zalimar for over two hundred years?"

"I want a lawyer," Quint said quietly.

"A what?" Weps blinked.

"A legal representative." Quint's skull-face remained impassive. "I refuse to answer any more questions without one present."

Weps tsked. "I'm afraid legal representatives aren't available to those who serve Necromancers, Mr. Thornton. Your execution is scheduled for tomorrow at noon, right after Miss Stratos. Would you like to choose your last meal?"

"This is absurd." Quint's skull-face twitched, orange eyes flashing left and right. "You can't just execute us without a trial."

"Actually, we can." Weps smiled thinly. "The law is quite clear regarding those who collaborate with Necromancers. No trial needed. The evidence speaks for itself. A potion of living death was likely used on you and your associates to awaken you in cycles of 1.6 years to commit murders and other crimes."

"I see." Quint's skull-face remained perfectly still. "And I suppose confessing would somehow reduce my sentence?"

"Perhaps," Weps adjusted his spectacles. "If you corroborate useful information about Zalimar's operations. The locations of his Topaz warehouses. Names of his other agents. Names of the people currently using your girlfriend's delving card to make property purchases."

"I don't know anything about Topaz warehouses or property purchases!" Quint said. "And I maintain that Sarah transferred schools."

"Still clinging to that story," Weps sighed. "Very well. What would you prefer for your last meal?"

"Nothing," Quint said quietly.

"Suit yourself," Weps stood, his spectacles glinting. "Though I must say, your lack of cooperation is . . . disappointing. Miss Stratos at least had the decency to break down when confronted with her crimes."

"Em is . . . emotionally volatile," Quint let out. "She tends to overreact to situations."

"An interesting way to describe a mass murderer," Weps commented. "Tell me, does working with a Necromancer usually make one 'emotionally volatile'?"

"For the last time," Quint's voice held a hint of frustration, "we don't work with Necromancers. We're students at Skyfall Academy. Everything else is just . . . misunderstandings."

"Misunderstandings that led to a girl being torn apart by Shadowbeasts?" Weps asked. "You and your gang have been operating longer than I have been alive. Your crimes have finally caught up to you. Goodnight, Mister Thornton." Weps turned to leave. "You shall be served steak and potatoes for your last meal. I'll see you at noon tomorrow."

Scrutimancer Weps made his way to the final cell. Inside, Solace Exill sat cross-legged on the floor, her red skin grimy.

"Miss Exill." Weps unfolded another stone chair from the wall. "I trust you've had time to reflect on your situation?"

The red-skinned girl looked up at him with gold-yellow eyes.

"Let me guess," she said flatly. "You're here to tell me I'm being executed tomorrow for working with a Necromancer."

Weps's spectacles flickered with surprise. "How did you . . .?"

"Vibration through the ground." Solace shrugged. "I heard everything you said to Em and Quint. About Sarah. About Zalimar. About the Topaz warehouses."

"I see," Weps said. "So, do you have anything to say in your defense?"

"Defense?" Solace smirked bitterly. "What's there to defend? You won't believe anything we say anyway. You've already decided we're the servants of a Necromancer."

"The evidence is quite compelling," Weps said. "The inn maiden's testimony. Reports from Undertown. Your group's apparent agelessness. Your connection to Zalimar's Topaz operation . . ."

"Have you considered," Solace interrupted, "that maybe we're telling the truth? That we really are students from another dimension? That there are things happening here that you don't understand?"

"Like what?" Weps asked.

"Like the fact that time moves differently between Earth and Arx," Solace said. "Like the fact that the Arx Bank has been running an interdimensional drug operation through Zalimar Evernacht and are now trying to cover their tail by lying to you?"

"Nonsense," Weps scoffed. "The Arx Bank is a respected institution! Why would it assist a Necromancer with Topaz distribution? You're clearly trying to deflect blame for your own crimes. Next you'll tell me that some human infiltrator named Alexander Glock is behind everything."

Solace stared up at the Scrutimancer with wide gold eyes.

"You don't get it," Solace shook her head slowly. "We're not the bad guys here. We're the idiots who got played. All of us. Even Em. Especially Em. Damn it, Em."

She rubbed her face with her red hands, yellow dull claws digging into her scales, her flesh-maw petals twitching.

"Played by whom?" Weps asked.

"By Zalimar mainly," Solace sighed. "He used us. Used our dislike against mixed-blood students. Made us think we were special, chosen. Elite. Pure. But really . . . we were just his enforcers. His thugs. Keeping order through fear while he ran his . . . other operation."

"Go on." Weps leaned forward.

"Sarah . . ." Solace's voice momentarily trembled. "I . . . bullied her, yes. I tried to make her leave school. But Em . . . Em took it too far. Locked her out, got me drunk on Shadow wine. I'm a dumb knob, okay? I admit it. Zalimar encouraged the bullying. Said it was our duty to keep the bloodlines pure."

"And you believed him?" Weps asked.

"Of course we did," Solace laughed bitterly. "The mixies were an easy target. Zalimar made us feel special, powerful. But really . . . we were just tools. Idiots. Patsies."

"The Topaz trade," Weps stated.

"Yes," Solace nodded. "Zalimar controls dimensional gates to a plethora of worlds with his Gate Weaver spiders."

"Gate Weaver?"

"He has these special spiders," Solace continued, her voice hollow. "Gate Weavers. They can create permanent dimensional gates. He clearly used them to move Topaz between worlds. The Arx Bank likely provides the distribution network."

"And this . . . Alexander Glock?" Weps pressed. "What's his role in all this?"

"I don't freaking know, okay!" Solace shook her arms. "I . . . I don't want to die! He's just a half-blood student from our school that Em is mad-obsessed with!"

"Mad-obsessed?" Weps repeated.

"Yes!" Solace exclaimed. "She's totally lost it over him! Claims he's a human infiltrator, that he's turning everyone against her, that he's behind everything bad that happens to her. But really . . . he's just a mixed-blood kid who stood up to her a few times!"

"You don't think that he is human like Miss Stratos?"

"Our school's administration aren't idiots," Solace said. "There's no way for a human to get into Skyfall."

"And where is this Alexander Glock now?"

"I don't know! Last time I heard from him, he called us from Undertown! Said he's doing . . . charity work there!"

"Charity work," Weps repeated skeptically. "In Undertown? The criminal district currently being devastated by parasitic mites? You do realize how insane this sounds?"

"Of course it sounds insane!" Solace threw up her hands. "Everything about this situation is insane! We're being executed for crimes we didn't commit while the real criminals are probably laughing their asses off!"

"The real criminals being?" Weps pressed.

"Zalimar! Who won't be back . . . to Arx for three years, if Quint is to believed. Plus whoever has Em's delving card!"

"And why won't he be back?" Weps asked.

"Because delving team 'I Love You' banished him into some doomed dimension!" Solace exclaimed and then choked as Weps gave her a look.

"I Love You?" he repeated. "A delving team named 'I Love You' banished a Necromancer into another dimension? Do you really expect me to believe this drivel?"

"It's the truth!" Solace protested. "Alexander Glock's team . . . they challenged Zalimar to a duel and won! I think . . . that's why Em is so obsessed with him—he humiliated her idol!"

"Enough," Weps stood up. "I had hoped you might actually cooperate and provide useful information, but clearly you're as delusional as your companions and your memories cannot be trusted. Interdimensional gates are impossible. Your execution is scheduled tomorrow at noon, same time as Miss Stratos and Mister Thornton. Would you like steak or chicken for your last meal?"

"Wait!" Solace cried, her eyes filling with tears. "Please! I . . . I just want to go back home! Wait . . ." She gulped. "W-what's going to happen to my body?"

"Your body will be burned to ashes and your heart core will be donated to the Ward of Shandria," the Scrutimancer said. "This dark bracelet which we were unable to remove from your hand . . . will be stored as case evidence in our deepest catacombs."

The red girl's gold eyes bulged, both of her mouths opening wide. "No. Please! I don't want to die here! I . . . I just want to mod my bikes and punch Vee in History Club! Please!"

"Mod bikes?" Weps shook his head wearily. "Punch Vee? Sadly, this delusion cannot be arranged. Your execution will proceed as scheduled. Steak and potatoes will be served shortly."

"Please . . ." Solace sobbed. "I can take you to the Earth-Arx gate! It's in the Arx Bank!"

"There is no interdimensional gate inside the bank," Weps said. "Prolonged exposure to necromantic magic, the unnatural extension of life with the potion of living death, has addled all of your minds, driven you mad."

"We're telling the truth!" Solace cried. "Just . . . just check the bank! Interrogate Gabriella! She knows about Earth! She . . ."

"Miss Matrosin has already provided a statement," Weps said. "She claims no knowledge of any interdimensional gates. Only that your group attempted to extort her. Dimensional gates can only move travelers between Arx cities."

"Please . . ." Solace slumped against her chains as Weps turned to leave. "Just . . . investigate the Arx Bank. Please!"

The Scrutimancer was already up.

The heavy door slammed shut with grim finality, leaving Solace alone and sobbing in the darkness.

Once the footsteps of the Shandrian Officer faded out of her range of ground-vibration hearing, Solace heaved and spat out a silver token from her forehead mouth and rapidly tapped it.

"Vespera Simmi. Team I Love You Slayer," she whispered, voice trembling.

She hoped, prayed that the Thunderbird didn't hate her, and wouldn't abandon her ex-bestie to perma-death just because they had a bit of an argument a few days ago over clan allegiances.

A face flashed on the holo-projection woven from silver sparks. It wasn't the face she was expecting to see to beg for aid.

A human stared back at her.

Alexander Glock.

# CHAPTER EIGHT

# Predator Theory

I stared back at the Olgoi-Khorkhoi's flesh-maw face through Vespera's ID tag projection. Solace looked exhausted, broken, distraught.

"Sup, Sol?" I asked her.

"A-Alex," she stammered out finally, both of her mouths opening and closing. "Why do you have Vee's tag?"

"Mmmm, why wouldn't my human husbando not have my tag?" Vee's beak came to rest on my left shoulder. "Sup, dude? Why you callin' so late? We're just 'bout to head to bed for some quality cuddle-pile time."

"H-h-human h-h-hhusbando?" the Mongolian Death Worm choked.

"Yes, human husbando," Vespera clicked cheerfully. "Pretty good at magic for a human, too, ha ha har. Anyway, what's up? Did Em finally drive you completely bonkers with her conspiracy theories about my adorable pink disaster here? You ready to join the dark side of I'm-with-human?"

"Vee. We're . . . being executed tomorrow," Solace revealed.

"Executed? For what?" I asked, raising an eyebrow.

"Em attacked some fox lady at the Adventurers Guild so the City Watch arrested us. We've been accused of treason against the Shadow Empire. The Shandrian Scruts think we work for a Topaz-peddling Necromancer and that we're some kind of undead two-hundred-year-old serial killers who unleashed a plague in Undertown and . . ."

"Oooh, that sounds rough, buddy," Vespera said sympathetically. "Have you tried not working for a Necromancer?"

"Vee!" Sol begged. "This . . . this isn't a joke! They collared Em and stripped our armor and weapons off except for the Laz bracelets! Please, I need your help, they're really going to execute us tomorrow at noon, burn our bodies in the central square, and then lock our bracelets in some deep vault!"

"Hrmmm." I tapped my chin thoughtfully. "That does sound like quite a predicament you got yourselves into. I fail to see how this is our problem, though, right, Prima-waifu-birb?"

"Right you are, my human meatsicle." Vespera sent sparks raining across my shoulder. "Em did try to murder you back in school. Repeatedly. Without askin' permission. That's like superrrr rude. Maybe she could sit on a shelf for a couple of hundred years. Karma's a beerch, ya kno'."

"Please," Solace begged, her gold eyes filling with tears. "I . . . I'm sorry for whatever stupid shit I did or said! Please! I don't . . . I don't want to die here! Aren't . . . aren't we best friends, Vee?"

"Aww, look at that face," Vespera cooed. "She's actually crying. That's new. Usually she's all 'rawr, imma punch you' and stuff."

"Should we help them?" I asked Vee thoughtfully.

"I dunno," the Thunderbird clicked. "What do you think, Ci?"

Cinder's rainbow-feathered head appeared on my right side. "Meh. Let them rot."

"Cinder!" Solace exclaimed. "Please! You . . . you used to be our friend!"

"Friend?" Cinder's feathers shifted through angry reds. "Piss off with that. We were never friends."

"I . . . I'm really sorry for bein' a shit friend then," Solace sobbed. "I . . . I'm a stupid knob . . . please! I don't want to die here!"

"Neither did Sarah," Cinder said coldly. "But that didn't stop you and Em, did it?"

"Y-you didn't help her either!" Solace blinked tears out of her eyes. "N-nobody helped the N-nullie and now th-the Shandrian Scruts think that we p-perma-killed her!"

"What the shit do you want us to do?" Cinder demanded, glaring at the worm girl. "If you knobs got yourself locked in prison 'cause Em assaulted someone important, how's that our problem?"

"Ye" Vee nodded. "I'm like mega-cozy w' my new 'ship. Seems like a lotta hassle untangling my wings from my husbando's and Hearth-waifu's arms just to save some annoying jerks."

"Please . . ." Solace begged. "I can't speak for . . . Quint or Em, but I'll do anything! Just . . . help me! I just . . . I just want to go home! The . . . Omnid chapel isn't answering the emergency retrieval cast signal!"

"Anything?" I raised an eyebrow, feeling somewhat concerned about her words.

"Yes!" Solace nodded vigorously. "Whatever you want!"

"Even if I asked you to sign a contract pledging eternal servitude to my clan as a secret sixie?" I asked.

"C-clan?" Solace blinked.

"I Love You," I said.

"I . . ." Solace blinked, wiping her eyes with a clawed hand. "What? I don't understand. Isn't that just your delving team's name?"

"Not anymore," I said. "That's our clan. We have a crystal Mage Tower citadel going up right now. Vee's my Prima-Wife to be. Cinder is my Hearth-Keeper to be. Io and Kat are our Prima-Knights."

The Worm's eyes went wide, both mouths opening and closing.

"Y-you're kidding, right?" she asked. "When did this happen?"

"Mmmmm . . . nope," Vee clicked. "Not kidding. We're making engagement plans."

"But he . . . but you . . ." Solas choked, wide, tear-filled eyes flashing between us. "When the eff did you even . . .?"

"I'ma gon' be super honest now, bestie," Vee said. "Me, Lexy, and Ci got soul-bonded last night."

"*What?!* This is a joke, right?" The Mongolian Worm looked at me and Cinder. "Please, I really need your help . . . I'm completely out of options!"

"It's not a joke, Sol," Cinder exhaled. "Vee, Alex, and I are soul-bonded."

"But he's . . . he's a mixie . . ." Solace choked, staring at Vespera. "D-don't you have a fiancé in Thunderland?!"

"And?" Vespera tilted her head across my face.

"I don't understand . . ." Solace stammered. "How could you . . . you're contractually engaged to one of the wealthiest clans in Thunderland . . . you don't even have to do anything to drown in mana, money, and beast cores courtesy of Golden Star Omnicorp!"

"Meh." Vee shrugged. "Thunderland's overrated. Zheng might be my match in terms of power level n' mana, but the heart wants what it wants, ya kno'?"

"But you're a firstborn Prima." Solace frowned. "Primas don't get to choose love. Your dad will never accept you hitchin' with a halfsie! You'll lose everything! You're throwing away your future for . . . for what?!"

"I'm not throwing anything away, ya knob." Vespera shook her beak. "You're not seeing the whole picture."

"We're starting our own company," I said. "One that'll hopefully surpass Golden Star."

"And if it fails horribly?" the Death Worm asked, staring at Vespera.

"Unless my arms and legs fall off tomorrow, it won't," Vee said. "Look, Solly, I'm a busy birb with an entire Mage Tower to decorate with death-skulls. You can either keep licking Em's boots and die as her Knight or you can get on board as our intern and work your way up. Them's the beans."

"I just . . . I don't understand." Solace shook her head. "What could a Nullie possibly offer that's worth throwing away your entire inheritance for?"

"Worth?" Vespera clicked thoughtfully. "Sol, you're still thinking in terms of obvs linear power levels and stats. Like everything's some kind of game where the highest numbers win. That's such an Em way of looking at things."

"Isn't it?" Solace demanded. "Aren't you funding whatever it is you're doing?"

"Nope." Vee shook her head. "I watched Lex make millions outta thin air and then I watched him apply them with wisdom in an investment and then I watched him slaughter his competition with merciless brutality befitting a true business shark. Zheng Xing Ker inherited his gold from his parents. I've known him since I was seven and he hasn't changed one bit, hasn't done a single thing to impress me. He is stale like an old swamp, stuck in his ways, boring like a toad sitting on a rock."

Solace frowned.

"Alex isn't just some 'Nullie' to be measured by his mana count," Vespera continued. "He's like . . . you know when you're modding your bike and suddenly realize there's this whole other way to configure the engine that nobody's thought of before? That moment when you see past the standard builds everyone uses?"

Solace's face became thoughtful.

"He doesn't just think outside the box," Vee clicked. "He questions why there's a box in the first place. Why we accept certain limitations as unchangeable. Why we let others define our worth by their standards."

She grabbed my cheek with her talons and squeezed, making me wince.

"He's not perfect," Vespera continued her marketing of my person. "Far from it. He's got more issues than a comic book store. But his flaws aren't what you think they are. He's not weak because he's mostly human or because he can't breathe fire or fly."

"Then what are his flaws?" Solace blinked. "'Cause I don't really understand what's going on with you, or Io, or Ci . . ."

"He's ruthless," Vee clicked. "Dangerously so. Remember how Em would bully people? Alex doesn't bully—he systematically dismantles them, sideways. Takes everything they have, everything they are, and turns it against them. And he does it with a Cheshire Cat smile."

"That sounds . . . worse than Em." Solace frowned.

"Oh, it is." Vee nodded. "Em's like a sledgehammer—crude, direct, predictable. Alex is more like . . . like a very dangerous computer virus. He gets inside systems, figures out how they work, and then reprograms them from within. He doesn't just break things—he changes them fundamentally. Do you know why you're in that cell, Solly?"

"No." Solace shook her head. "The Scrutimancer officer said it's because we are insane, undead minions who work for a Necromancer . . . but that's obvious bullshit since he didn't give a fuck about the gate testimony."

"Uh-huh," Vee clicked. "You're in that cell because Em and Zalimar went up against Lexy, just like I went up against that blasted Captain entity that reflected my own lightning into my own dum' face."

"So it's his fault that I'm in here?" Solace glared at me.

"No," Vee clicked. "Em got herself and you in there by being a violent knob. Alex just . . . made sure certain evidence came to light at the right time. He's not some all-powerful mastermind—he just pays attention and uses what he learns."

"But you just said he systematically dismantles people!" Solace protested.

"Yeah, when they give him the tools to do it," Vee shrugged. "Em practically gift-wrapped herself for him."

"I didn't make her attack anyone," I added. "Honestly, I thought that she'd fall into a well or something else mildly inconvenient. This is way above my expectations."

"So you did set us up!" Solace accused.

"Nah." I grinned. "Em set herself up. I just made sure the right people noticed. Your dragon bestie has been doing incredibly stupid violent stuff for years—all I did was make it visible to the right people at the right time."

"That's . . . cold," Solace shuddered.

"Yep." I nodded. "But effective. Anyways, are you in as our secret sixie?"

"Do I even have a choice?" the worm girl asked.

"Not really." I shrugged. "Either you end up on a shelf forever or you play your part. I'm not asking you to change anything about you. You can do whatever and still be Em's bestie."

"Till I have to stab her in the back?" the Death Worm asked.

"I don't know what you're complaining about," Vespera said. "We ain't gonna treat you like dirt."

"Stabbing people in the back isn't my thing," I said.

"Then what? Then help me understand what you actually want from me," Solace huffed.

"I want you outta prison so you can bully me harder." I grinned.

"Bully you . . . harder?" Solace blinked in confusion. "What?"

"Yep," I nodded. "Keep being Em's bestie. Keep being extra mean to me. Just . . . do it flashier. Make it look good. More dramatically punchy."

"I don't understand." Solace frowned. "You want me to keep bullying you? Why?! I thought that you were gonna demand something completely different like . . . making sure Em leaves you alone."

"I subvert expectations." I grinned. "Consider this—the more you and Em bully me, the more sympathy I get from others. The more people see me as the underdog. It's great marketing."

"Marketing?" Solace blinked. "You . . . you want us to be your heel?"

"Every hero needs a villain," I said. "This whole 'you're a filthy human' schtick is absolutely hilarious. I want you to lean into it harder. Absurdly, over the top hard. Violence me up, challenge me to duels. Almost beat me and then . . . lose."

"You want me to . . . throw fights?"

"No. I want you to go all out," I said. "Be yourself. Be free. Challenge the human. Less permanent damage, more dramatic posturing. Less rude swearing. More showmanship. Hunt me down, try to catch me, throw me into a locker. Etcetera."

"Abyss," Cinder muttered beside me, staring at me with sky-blue eyes. "You've been doing this to all of us, haven't you?"

"Obviously." I winked at her. "You're all killers and hunters and your monster needs aren't being met. You've all segregated yourself from humans and pushed half-humans out of school with excessive hatred and murder. You need prey that can think, that can challenge you."

Solace frowned.

"You've forgotten what it truly means to be predators," I continued, meeting Solace's gaze. "Real predation isn't about mindless violence or sense of superiority—it's about balance. The dance between hunter and prey, each making the other stronger, helping each party . . . evolve. Em's Predator Equalizer Theory where everyone is a predator is utter nonsense because it offers no room for love."

"Love?" Solace's gold eyes widened.

"Yes. Love. The love of the chase," I said. "You've all forgotten that humans aren't just weak prey to be discarded. We're the species that learned to think our way around being eaten. If my mom's stories about the Leviathan are to be believed, then the very first Omnid was born from the heart of the Wormwood Star-beast, created to love a human."

My companions and Solace looked at me with wide eyes.

"Not to eat them, not to rule them, but to love them. To dance with them in an eternal cycle of chase and fight, of strength meeting cunning, of magic power meeting wisdom," I said. "Yin and yang. A wheel unbroken. A storm created through currents of cold and warm air. Negative and positive poles. That's my Predator Theory. Every Omnid needs a human to chase, to feed on."

"But humans are weak," Solace protested weakly. "We're supposed to . . ."

"Supposed to what?" I cut her off. "Segregate humans off to the poles, deprive them of resources, kill them all off? Then what?"

"Grow," Solace said. "Spread. Multiply. Conquer worlds."

"You're in a cold, dark cell, about to be executed, Miss Conqueror," I pointed out.

"While I riled up my girls enough to make me a Mage Tower. Omnithornia cast humanity aside, pushed it to the fringes, forgot that it is the vital ingredient necessary for success."

This wasn't a speech just for an Olgoi-Khorkhoi in a prison cell. I was aiming my metaphorical gun at all of my Omnid besties inhabiting the crystalline dining hall with me now.

"Think of it like this—you can have the most powerful engine in the world, but without fuel it's just a hunk of metal," I said. "Humans are your fuel. Your inspiration. Your reason to live. Your magical resonance. Without us to chase and challenge, you're all, simply put . . . fundamentally unhappy."

"What?!" A chorus of voices.

"Tell me that I'm wrong," I said. "Point me to an Omnid trio whose relationship created a Mage Tower."

There was silence as my Omnid companions and the imprisoned girl processed my words.

"You . . . really made a Mage Tower?" Sol asked.

"Yep." I nodded. "It is very shiny."

"We're not freaking adding Sol to our triangle!" Cinder suddenly let out. "I don't want a freaking harem over here! Vee is annoying enough!"

I laughed.

"Sol doesn't need to be in our triangle 'ship. She just needs to be our worthy opponent," I explained. "Our wicked rival. Someone to compete against. Love is incredibly hard to box conceptually. You don't see me making out with Kat or Io and yet I am feeding them well. Right?"

I glanced at Io.

"Absolutely." Io sent me a thumbs up. "Your catastrophe levels are off the charts. I'm content."

I looked at Katherine. She shrugged at me. Guess I had to work harder to feed my kitten. Maybe nomming on Echoes and walking in dark places wasn't enough for her.

"Go on." I turned my attention to Solace. "Tell me that you're perfectly satisfied with your life. Tell me there's no hole in your crystalline heart missing something vital, essential. Tell me that your forehead mouth isn't starving all the time. Tell me there's no gnawing emptiness in your chest wanting to be filled."

Solace swallowed; the petals of her flesh-face opened and closed.

She blinked.

"Oh. You want it bad," I said. "I know you do because every Omnid I've met thus far wants it bad. Omnid magic requires humans to resonate against. Without human besties to terrorize, chase, and paw at, you're all starving, all the time. You're an entire nation of wolves with barely any rabbits to go around."

Solace's flower face folded and unfolded, the forehead mouth biting the air.

"Sheet," she said with a shudder, gold eyes boring a hole in me. "Sheet. I think you actually might be onto something . . . Alex."

# CHAPTER NINE

# The Hunt Urge

After listening to Sol's brief explanation about all of the Shandrian Scrut's accusations and insistence that interdimensional gates didn't exist, I promised to rescue her and hung up on her, turning to my companions.

"Predator Theory, huh?" Kat asked, spiked tail lashing. "When'd you come up with that nonsense?"

"Yulia and I have been discussing the human experiment data that I stole from the Frontenachii Wendigos for a while now," I said. "We had some theories, but we didn't have an exact confirmation of positive Predator-Prey factor until I saw what was happening between me and Vee," I explained.

"What, this whole crystal tower bullshit isn't just from that bullshit interdimensional lighter?" Kat arched an eyebrow.

"The Mage Tower wasn't just created by magic—it was created by love. The kind of love that can only exist between predator and prey," I said. "Between an Omnid and a human. The long chase we did today was the key."

"Bullshit!" Katherine crossed her arms.

"Yet again," I said, "I must point out that there are no other crystal towers here or anywhere, really."

"That's because no one else is stupid enough to try making one," Katherine growled. "And no other human has been permitted to come to Arx to bond with two Omnids nor do they have mana-casting lighters."

"The Wendigos tried it," I said. "Their experiments with human subjects showed interesting results when they attempted to understand the magical resonance between Omnid and human hearts. But they approached it wrong—they tried to force it, to dominate, control, and terrorize. They didn't understand that the key ingredient was willing participation. The chase has to be mutual. Both participants have to want it. Otherwise the balance of the wheel breaks and you get some really effed-up shit."

"Effed-up shit like what?" she asked.

"Well . . ." I waved a hand at the crystalline room around us. "This is the highest order of Syntropic magic. The opposite is destructive, chaotic, disorderly magic. Look at Em," I said. "A perfect example of what happens when an Omnid tries to force dominance without understanding the need for balance. She chased the hell out of many Nullies without it being mutual."

"That's ridiculous," Katherine scoffed. "Em's just a violent knob. She chases weak Omnids, too."

"Is she, though?" I asked. "Or is she desperately trying to fill a void she doesn't understand? Look at how she latched onto me the moment I showed up—not because I'm special, but because I represented something she's been missing her entire life."

Kat rubbed her forehead.

"Sounds like you just have a fetish for being chased by these two idiots, and you're trying to justify it with some pseudo-scientific nonsense," Katherine growled.

"The Wendigo data doesn't lie," I said. "They documented hundreds of cases where human test subjects developed magical abilities through prolonged exposure to Omnid predation. The problem was, they couldn't replicate the results consistently or even benefit from it properly because it produced random, incredibly destructive magical events."

"So?" Katherine challenged.

"So, they missed the emotional component," I explained. "The chase has to be playful, mutual. The human has to want to be caught just as much as the Omnid wants to catch them."

"You're suggesting that humans and Omnids are . . . what? Naturally complementary?"

"Yes," I said. "I am. Under the right conditions, humans and Omnids produce a resonance effect."

"What conditions?" Katherine demanded.

"First, both parties have to be willing participants," I explained. "Second, there needs to be an element of pursuit and evasion—the Hunt. Third, there needs to be genuine affection or at least mutual respect. And fourth, there needs to be a balance of power— the human can't be completely helpless, and the Omnid can't be completely dominant. There are other factors that amplify the Hunt ritual which I've discovered recently, such as higher aetheric density, having a soul bond, and the human eating shakes made from the bits of the Omnid that's chasing them."

"That's the stupidest thing I've heard," Katherine scoffed.

"The Frontenachii researchers called it the Netherweave Fold," I explained. "When an Omnid's crystalline heart resonates with a human's biological one during pursuit, it creates a unique form of magic. The longer and more intense the chase, the stronger the effect. When both are placed in a room with high aetheric density and make a wish, the Netherweave Fold implodes into itself, bending reality in a particular way. Ergo, crystal tower."

"So," Io mused, "if either of us felt hatred or dislike, we wouldn't get a crystal tower, we'd get . . . what?"

"The tower would implode or melt or turn into radioactive slag, or reality would tear. Maybe something like what happened at Lake Eerie," I said. "A destructive magical event that tears reality apart rather than stabilizing it. The Wendigos documented numerous cases where forced bonding resulted in dimensional rifts, spontaneous combustion, the Omnid and human test subjects melting through the ground, or worse."

"What happened at Lake Eerie?" Katherine asked.

"Ci?" I looked at the Quetzi. "Can we tell Kat and Io about what happened to you two years ago? Do you want to tell them about it yourself?"

Cinder's feathers shifted through dark colors, clearly uncomfortable with the topic. I hugged her. Then Vespera did as well.

"We're with you," I told her. "From now on and forever. No matter what."

"All for one," Vee added.

Cinder exhaled, trembling.

"I . . . I was tricked," she let out quietly, her feathers shifting through darker colors, forcing the words out of herself. "A Skinwalker named Valor Thornheart pretended to be interested in me. His clan took me and some other Omnid girls to Lake Eerie for a ritual. They . . . they tried to use our singing to wake something in the lake. The Leviathan. An Echo of the Wormwood Star. The Skinwalker clan . . . killed the other girls, stole their Lazarus bracelets to absorb their souls. Em . . . saved me, but . . . the thing in the lake, it left something in me . . . a tear. A nightmare that I can't wake up from."

Cinder's wings turned black, and tears filled her eyes. She started to sob into me.

Katherine's emerald eyes widened as she processed Cinder's words.

"That's why you stopped singing," she breathed. "Why you joined Em's group. Why you declared yourself . . . Kaleid. Why you just allowed Em to harass the shit outta me online and did fuck-all."

Cinder sob-nodded.

"The entity that attached itself to Cinder's soul is something ancient from the depths of the Astral Sea," I explained. "An Echo of the Wormwood Star's impact. A being of pure Entropy. The opposite of what Zee Captain is."

"And you think your . . . Personal Predator Theory can save her from this . . . being?" Katherine asked skeptically.

"It already has, partially," I said. "The crystal tower is proof, the beginning of my understanding of the magic of the Hunt and how to apply it to fight Entropic entities."

Kat pursed her lips.

"The Skinwalkers' ritual failed because they tried to force it," I continued. "They attempted to use violence and fear to create a resonance cascade effect, but that only attracted the Entropic entity. Also, they used Omnids, not people."

"The reason why reality shattered so bad on that lakeshore was because they raised the shit out of the lake's aetheric density with the beast cores," Vespera added.

"And now something is living in that tear," I said. "Something that latched onto Ci when she was there."

"And you think you can . . . what? Love it out of her?" Katherine asked skeptically.

"No." I shook my head. "I think that we can create tools to fight it. Like this tower. Vee, how's the aetheric density of air here?"

The Thunderbird walked around our couch, snapping her talons and raining sparks.

"714.55," she said. "Super pure unaligned stuff too. Yep. The tower is definitely slowly refracting magic outta Abystall below us."

"Which means we're going to need a core sooner rather than later." I nodded. "To raise it up even more."

Katherine sighed.

"I believe it is time for another big confession," I said, with a deep exhale. "I've manipulated all of you to this point. To make this tower on Arx. The Hunt was the key."

"Still going on with that? Not all Omnids are hunters," Katherine said, waving an armored hand at Io. "Look at this useless knob-wing for example. He don't hunt nobody."

"Hey!" Io protested. "I hunt plenty!"

"You hunt interdimensional snacks." Katherine rolled her eyes. "That doesn't count."

"Yes," I agreed. "Not every Omnid hunts in the same way. Some hunt information, some hunt experiences, some hunt emotional connections. The core component is specific interactive-ness."

"Interactive-ness?" Katherine asked.

"Cinder is a Quetzi; she hunts pure human love and devotion," I said, making Cinder shine with pink and violet and gold tones, drawing away the sad black curtain on her. "So I gave her all of my love. I manipulated Christi Negal to inject myself into all of Cinder's classes, annoyed her, made her chase me. Again and again. Until she bit me. Until I made a declaration about building a glorious murder pyramid for her." I tapped the crystalline floor with my foot.

"You . . . argh!" Cinder flapped her wings, looking as if she weren't sure whether to be annoyed, or to strangle me, or to smother me in another hug.

"Io is a Death Mothman; he hunts for human-caused disasters." I moved on from the rainbow-dragon. "So I gave him the biggest man-made disaster I could. I destroyed Undertown for him."

"Groovy," Io commented, munching on a pocky.

"Katherine," I said, turning to the Stollwurm. "You hunt human fear. So I unleashed Duskbloom on Undertown, cranked the fear dial all the way up."

Katherine's emerald gaze hardened. "You . . . deliberately caused mass panic? Just to what? Satisfy my hunting urges?"

"Not just urges," I explained. "To create a specific magical resonance. Enough resonance effect between you and me to contribute to the foundation of this tower."

"Ohh! What 'bout me?" Vespera hugged me, sending sparks raining all over me.

"You, my sparkly birb, hunt electric impulses, deep neural networks," I said. "Resonance. A human to electrocute. As much as you want to. Forever. A human with a mana-burning lighter through whom you could create a localized celestorm, enough to forge this tower, enough to imprint all of your 'current' ideas into the most incredible, most complex hexagrammic runework project imaginable."

Vespera's talons sparked with electricity, her eyes gleaming. "Ke ke ke. My human Resonance engine."

She buried her beak into my neck, nuzzling against me hard and wrapping me in her talons.

[Mine.] Her electrical current-voice danced in my head. [To zap. Zappedy zap. Zzzap. Hee hee, hee, *current*. You funny.]

Katherine's emerald eyes narrowed. "So you're saying you deliberately manipulated all of us into creating this . . . crystal tower?"

"Yep." I nodded. "Manipulated. Brought together. Prodded. Led along. Guided. Figured out the right conditions for something truly magical to emerge. Luckily for us, it worked out."

[Mmmmm. Death ray.] Vespera giggled in my head.

"Riiiiight," Katherine said. "Lucky we didn't all freaking melt. How are we rescuing Sol, exactly?"

"Hopefully, we're not," I said. "The adults are. If they're still alive, that is."

"What do you mean, *if* they're alive?!" Cinder sputtered.

"You heard Sol," I said and tapped my silver tag. "Cast Brother Vassily."

The tag began to vibrate in my hand. I waited. Ten seconds. Twenty. Thirty. One minute. No answer.

"Shit." Vee opened her eyes. "That's . . . not good."

I nodded.

"Cast Innkeeper Nikkola," I ordered next.

I waited. Nothing.

Cinder swallowed.

"Cast Captain June of Team Hydroblades," I said next, my companions drawing their breath.

No answer.

The silence stretched, thick and heavy.

"Cast Captain Cinder, Team I Love You," I said.

Cinder's bracelet buzzed. She accepted the call. Our faces appeared atop both of our bracelets.

I hung up.

"Yep," I nodded. "No adults then and no other Omnid help."

"What do you think happened to everyone?" Cinder asked.

"Seems like the bank made their move," I said. "The Enforcers must have been sent after everyone to silence them after Zalimar's drug operation went tits up. Just us, then. Against all of Shandria. Fifteen hours till Sol, Quint and Em are executed. Peachy."

# CHAPTER TEN

# Pancakes

Are we really going to risk our necks to rescue those three idiots?" Katherine asked.

"No," I said. "The public execution could be a trap, bait designed to draw us out from our mite-covered crystal fortress."

"Then what are we going to do?" Cinder demanded.

"We'll need to hire an army of mooks to help save our fellow students. Our Guild is filthy rich, remember?"

"Hrmmm . . . how many mooks can we hire?" Vee asked.

"All of them," I said. "Every single mercenary, information broker, and two-bit thug in Undertown and uptown. Every adventurer of every level. No matter the cost."

"Sounds like that'll cost a fortune." Cinder said.

"Good thing we have a fortune," I replied. "This is going to be a big rescue operation. I've been hiring people since I gave Morty that thermos. Since Innkeeper Nikkola isn't responding, I'm assuming that everyone got bagged up from the inn. We're going to find out whether they're still alive and where they're all kept. This includes your brother, Ci."

Cinder's feathers flashed through a rainbow of grimdark colors—orange shock, black fear, red anger. "They took Lance?"

"Maybe he got away? Try calling him," I offered.

She did, wings shimmering with a curtain of orange-reds as she waited.

No answer.

"Shit, shit, shit," Cinder let out, clawing at her face as her snout lengthened. "Damn it! This . . . all of this . . . this is *all your* fault!"

Icy blue, angry eyes struck me.

"Yes, it is," I said. "Stopping Zalimar was going to have far-reaching consequences. I accept the blame."

Dark-red feathered hands grabbed at me, strangling me.

"I'm glad that you care for your brother enough to choke the life outta me," I hissed out as the hexasuit collars on my neck hardened. "Guess you're not that Kaleid after all."

Cinder froze, her talons still wrapped around my throat. Her feathers shifted through seventy shades of anger and then something else—vulnerability.

"You knew!" she snarled. "You knew something like this would happen when we took down Zalimar and Em!"

"The bank obviously doesn't like being exposed." I shrugged.

"Kat!" Cinder's head snapped to Katherine. "Could you . . . maybe . . . go uptown, rescue everyone via the deep?"

"No," the Stollwurm replied.

"Why the Abyss not?!" Cinder barked. "Why the shit are you such a useless knobfold?!"

"Because the deep isn't a bloody taxi service!" Katherine snapped back. "Leviathan Nightingale's flock can reach right into it at night, and during the day, the local sun pretty much bakes me alive upstairs. It's much warmer and brighter than the sun on Earth, and the clouds of the Arx megastructure have an insane degree of refraction. Why the shit do you think I'm failing delving class, you feathery beerchard?! Just because I can more or less function in Undertown, it doesn't mean that I can do shit above!"

"Then what *do* we do?" Cinder demanded, feathers flaring crimson.

I grabbed at Vespera. She caught onto my thoughts via the electric current between us, and a deafening thunderbolt struck the crystal ceiling high above us.

"Stop yelling at each other," I order-growled. "Everyone might not be dead, just imprisoned so that they can't spread the word about the Arx gate. From what Sol told us, the local Scruts don't believe in interdimensional gates. Vee, pry Ci off me. I have minions to direct."

The next thunderbolt struck Cinder, making her let go of me with a yelp.

"Yulia, what time is it in Shandria now?" I asked.

"6:29 PM," the LLM answered.

"Freaking time dilation." I rubbed my face, glancing at the phone's clock that said 10:50 PM. "Blah."

"Shash!" I yelled.

"Yes, m'lord?" The assassin materialized next to us in about ten seconds.

"I need information," I said. "Is the well tunnel going straight up from the Guild into Shandria sealed off, too?"

"Yes." Shash nodded. "Like the other ways and tunnels out, it has been dimensionally folded with a citywide rock slide field that filled every crevice and crack between us and the mages above. The Guildnet Mage Towers upstairs make sure that there is only a single exit out of Undertown now and that it's armed to the teeth."

"Fine," I said. "Kat will take you past the blockade pinhole into the city."

"Understood." Shash nodded.

I handed him my phone. "Here. I'll trust you with Yulia. The battery will last a few more days, longer if you shake it. There's a 'mana to electricity' converter in my bag that I'll show you how to use later."

"M'lord?" the assassin said as he accepted the phone.

"This device is yours to keep. Here's how you turn it on and log in," I said, showing him how to log into the phone with my finger. "Yulia will show you the names and faces of people I want found and rescued. Obey her directions, but do so with wisdom. She's kind of iffy and slow without her connections to all of her tools back on Earth."

"Yulia, permanent state change—your new arms and legs belong to Shash," I said. "Find and rescue everyone."

"Permanent realignment acknowledged," Yulia replied. "Mission understood."

"Thank you for your trust, m'lord." Shash bowed, accepting the phone.

"Here," I said and handed him a mini wax speaker. "Shove this in your ear. She can talk to you through it."

He did.

"Meet up with Morty and get the funds. Then go to the Adventurers Guild Cathedral," I said. "And the Manhunters Guild. Hire as many adventurers and mercenaries as you can. Post quests that pay at a premium rate for every level from Iron to Celesteel or whatever. I want my people found. I want names of all of the people involved that captured them. If my friends are dead, then I want their black hexagonal bracelets retrieved. Got it?"

"Yes, m'lord." The assassin bowed.

"Also, use the funds from the card of Emerald Stratos to hire extra-unscrupulous men. We'll need such to disrupt and delay the execution of Emerald, Quint, and Solace that will take place at the central square tomorrow at noon," I said.

"They will likely have high-level Watchmen plus City Wards preventing anyone from stopping the execution, m'lord," Shash said.

"That's fine," I said. "I just want a lot of noise. The Shandrian Scruts believe that Em has an army of local idiots working for her. We should reinforce this belief, make her into a local bogeyman terrorizing children and stealing their candy."

Shash nodded.

"Hrmm." I rubbed my chin. "Also, find out what happened in the Gilded Gryphon Inn. Learn who they were and how they managed to subdue my friends."

"Anything else?"

"Spread rumors extra hard," I added. "Pay the orphans to spawn information that the Arx Bank is involved in Topaz trade, works closely with Necromancer Zalimar Evernacht, and can open gates into other dimensions. I want everyone in Shandria to know this. Duplicate the best, most potent info from the yellow folder and make it rain paper from the rooftops. They ain't weaseling out of this."

Shash nodded.

"Start to assemble strongmen teams to prepare to storm the bank branches. I want them burned to the ground. I want their network of patsies scorched from Shandria," I added. "Find everyone from the yellow folder, shake whatever else you can out of the weaker, low-level scum, make the lives of higher-level bank reps more complicated. Especially bank rep Gabriella Matrosin. I want her bagged up ASAP, before you do anything else. When she's captured, Voicecast Kat and have her bring you and the bagged catgirl past the blockade."

"Got it." Shash nodded.

"Go." I turned to Katherine. "Take Shash and his men through the deep out of Undertown."

Katherine crossed her arms, not budging.

"Kat," I said, "this is the best way forward. We cannot allow Zalimar to return to Arx to sell Topaz. If the Omnid chapel has fallen, we need to retake it. Please just work with me, yeah?"

"And what are you going to do?" she asked.

"Stay here and get some sleep," I said.

"Really?"

"Yes. Really. I'm tired, and it's way past my bedtime. I've been running all day and it would only take a single spell to the head to take me out, why would I go out there?"

"Fine," she grumbled. "Making me work with freaking assassins, bloody annoying, manipulative human . . ."

Katherine and Shash vanished down the hall, her grumbling fading away.

"Aiiiight everyone, bedtime!" I declared, stretching.

"Already?" Cinder's feathers shifted through annoyed oranges. "But . . . we have a crisis here!"

"Exactly why we need rest," I yawned. "Can't save anyone if we're exhausted."

"You coming to bed?" I asked Io with a yawn.

"Eh. I'm content with the dining hall," he replied, climbing into a crystalline wall alcove and pulling out his moon book. "Have fun with ya 'ship."

"Mkay," I said.

"I can't believe you two." Cinder followed us downstairs, wings twitching with irritation. "My brother could be dead and you're thinking about sleep?!"

"Yes," I said. "Sleep is important."

We entered our room—now transformed into pure crystal like everything else.

To my delight, the three animated paintings didn't turn transparent and still functioned, their enchanted scenes providing soft light. Through the transparent floor, I could see all the way down to the bioluminescent fields of Abystall far below.

"Pretty view," Vee commented, flopping onto the large bed. "Come here, you two!"

I climbed onto the bed.

"This isn't the time for—" Cinder started.

"Ci," I said tiredly, "I set as much as I could in motion. Sometimes the best strategy is to rest and reset."

"But—" Cinder fretted.

"Birb, secure Skittles," I ordered.

Vee's talons sparked with electricity as she lunged at Cinder from the bed, grabbing her mid-protest.

"Nooo!" Cinder squawked, her feathers flaring in indignation. "I am *not* sleepy, damn it!"

*Zzzzzap!*

Vespera sent a mild thunderbolt through Cinder that made her feathers stand on end.

"*Stop that!* I . . ." Cinder tried to pull away, but Vee's grip was strong.

I watched with amusement as Vespera wrestled Cinder onto the bed.

In moments, the Thunderbird had successfully pinned Cinder, who was still protesting but losing steam rapidly. Her feathers were slowly shifting from angry reds to softer purples.

"Should have invested more into strength, Miss Charisma." I grinned at her.

Cinder hissed angrily, but Vespera was sending tiny electrical sparks dancing across Cinder's feathers that seemed to have a hypnotic, calming effect on the Quetzi-girl.

I leaned from the edge of the bed. Through the transparent floor, I saw an entire network of cavern lakes, waterfalls, and rivers. Everything flowed into a distant supermassive waterfall. Behind and around it, fjords and fields of Abystall glimmered like an underwater galaxy, casting soft blue-green light shimmers throughout our crystalline bedroom.

Far above us, I could see the edge of the crystalline tower and column and all of Undertown engulfed in the snowstorm of blooming Duskbloom.

Vespera's electrical current continued to pulse softly, her talons gently stroking Cinder's feathers. Cinder's protests gradually faded into soft, irritated mumbles.

"Shash will find everyone," I said, sliding next to her and looking up. "Yulia will help."

Cinder's ocean-blue eyes flickered between anger and exhaustion. "Promise?"

"Promise," I said.

"Relax," Vee clicked softly. "We'll fight tomorrow."

Cinder's breathing gradually slowed.

"This is so nice," I commented. "Our city up above and our dungeon below. Who needs windows when the entire room's transparent!"

"Yeah," Cinder let out, finally accepting being bed-bound and pulling me toward herself. "No privacy, though."

"Speaking of which," Vespera clicked, reaching out to touch the crystalline wall with her free hand while still holding onto Cinder. Electrical current danced through the transparent material, creating intricate hexagonal patterns that spread outward like a web.

"Whatcha doing?" I asked.

"Basic one-way mirror hex," she said. "So we can see everything but nobody can see us. Aaaaand done! Added two-way mirror walls to the bathrooms, too."

The walls of our bedroom momentarily flashed silver and then became transparent again. I saw a few reflective cubes hovering near and above us in the distance. The wooden door remained unchanged, as the spell only changed inorganic silica materials into crystals.

"Much better," she purred, rapidly pulling off her armor and hexasuit. I stared at her until Cinder elbowed me.

Vee's beak suddenly traced along my jaw before she kissed me, sending little sparks dancing across my lips. Cinder made a soft sound and joined in, her feathers brushing against my face as she claimed her own kiss.

Vee's electrical current hummed through our trio, creating a soothing, tingling sensation.

"Hey," Cinder mumbled, squirming slightly as Vee's talons began to roam more boldly. "We shouldn't . . . I mean, what if . . .?"

"Rrrrelax, Skittles," Vee purred. "My mirror hex is, like, totally foolproof. No one's peeking at our slumber party, or getting in here. Door's passworrrrded now."

"Isn't Kat going to . . ."

"Kat can sleep in the hall or whatever. Don't care. Commerrrrr."

Vee's talons danced across Cinder's feathers. Cinder shivered, her feathers shifting through a kaleidoscope of colors—soft blues, vibrant purples, and flashes of pink.

"Ooh, pretty," Vee cooed, fascinated by the color changes. She focused, sending a more targeted pulse through a specific patch of feathers. To her delight, that area flared a brilliant green.

"H-hey!" Cinder squirmed, her ocean-blue eyes widening. "What are you doing?"

"Learning. Investigating. Sciencing. Making art," Vee giggled, continuing her experimentation. With each carefully placed spark, she painted Cinder's feathers in vivid new hues—creating swirls of red, bursts of yellow, and waves of deep indigo.

Cinder's face flushed. "S-stop that," she protested, but didn't pull away.

Vee ignored her, completely engrossed in her new prodding. "Wonder if I can make patterns . . ." She concentrated, sending a more complex series of pulses across Cinder's wings.

"Color patterns are cool and all, but can you make her phase-shift?" I asked.

"In which direction?" Vee asked.

"I dunno." I shrugged. "Surprise me."

"H-hey," Cinder mewled. "Don't just talk about me like I'm not here!"

Vee's eyes sparkled mischievously. "Like, chillax, Skittles. We're just having Quetzi-modding fun!"

"And stop with the terrible nicknames," the Quetzi-in-question growled.

"Nuh-uh." Vee grinned. "I do wonder . . ."

She sent a stronger pulse through Cinder's feathers, causing them to ripple in a wave-like pattern from head to tail.

Cinder let out a soft gasp, her body tensing. "Th-that feels . . . weird," she mumbled, her feathers now shimmering with an iridescent mirror-like sheen.

I leaned closer, seeing our reflections in each feather.

"Heh." I smiled. "It's like she's made from mercury. Terminator-Two-Quetzi! Pretty neat."

"Th-this isn't funny," Cinder looked down at her reflective self, lifting a hand that was made from gleaming, metallic feathers.

"Just think of it as skill training," I said.

"Skill training?!" Cinder sputtered.

"Correct." I nodded. "Trying new things. Have you ever turned fully into a mirror?"

"No, why the Abyss would I even . . .?"

"Maybe you need to bounce lasers off?" I shrugged.

"Why would there be freaking lasers in a dungeon?!" Cinder huffed.

Vee ran her talons along Cinder's wing, causing ripples of silver to flow in reflective waves. "Let's see what else we can do . . ."

"You! Quit messing up my feathers!" Cinder growled.

"Have you ever tried being . . . delicious?" the Thunderbird asked.

"Why the eff would I . . ." the Quetzi sputtered.

"You never know when you might need to attract a very hungry human." Vee's eyes sparkled with mischief. "Ooh, I have an idea!" She concentrated, sending a complex series of electrical pulses through Cinder's feathers.

Cinder's eyes widened as her feathers began to shift and change. The metallic sheen faded, replaced by a golden-brown hue. Her skin took on a soft, fluffy texture.

"What are you—" Cinder started, but then froze as the scent hit her. The air filled with the warm, sweet aroma of freshly made pancakes.

"Slayer," I breathed. "This is freaking amazing. It's like she's the personification of breakfast!"

Cinder's feathers now had the exact texture and appearance of perfectly cooked pancakes, complete with little air bubbles and a slightly crisp edge.

Vee giggled, running her talons along Cinder's arm. Where she touched, a trail of what looked like whipped cream appeared, stark white against the golden pancake-feathers.

"Staaaaph." The Quetzi blushed with pinks, which blossomed into strawberry slices across her pancake-textured face under Vespera's cheeky machinations.

I couldn't resist reaching out to touch, marveling at the soft, fluffy texture. "This is amazing, Vee. How are you doing this? How is she blushing with strawberry slices?"

"Just playing with the electrical impulses." Vee shrugged, face gleaming with pride. "Pretty easy once you figure out the right frequency. Ke ke ke. I wonder if I can add syrup to the equation . . ."

With a mischievous grin, she sent another pulse through Cinder's feathers. A golden sheen appeared, slowly dripping down like maple syrup.

"Oh, come on!" Cinder protested. A greater number of strawberry slices bloomed across her.

"Hang on," I said. "Her hexasuit is strawberrying up, too!"

"Mmmhmmm." Vespera nodded. "The Quetzi phase-shift range is actually pretty wide. Each feather is bending reality around it visually like a miniature holofractal while her heart core is projecting specific mental ideas into the target's mind. Targets. Our brains are being fed specific sensations relevant to whatever the feathers display."

"How wide is this mental pulse?" I wondered. "What is she, like a holodeck?! Can you use her wings to strawberry yourself up, too?"

"Let's find out!" Vee closed her eyes, magisteel talons digging into Cinder's wings. The Quetzi let out a small gasp as electrical currents danced across her. The pancake texture rushed up Vespera's claws, vanishing the magisteel and black-and-white feathers, rapidly flooding her entire body in pancake-ness.

"You can call us the breakfast squad!" the Thunderbird laughed. "Oh my Slayer! I'm literally pancakes right now." She licked her crispy-textured beak. "I'm pancakes everywhere! Nazareth! Ahhh! This is wild. Lex! You must join the breakfast gang!"

Her pancake-textured talons grabbed me, and then I became a pancake.

The pancake-ness spread through me like warm syrup, a strange tingling sensation that made everything feel soft and fluffy.

My mind suddenly felt . . . different. Lighter. More wholesome.

Like Sunday morning breakfast with no responsibilities. The inside of my mouth, every bit of my tongue, was delicious, every nerve ending singing with flavor.

The state of being human drowned in a sea of pancake-ness.

"You feel that?" Vee laughed. "It's like being wrapped in a warm blanket made of happiness! The conceptual state of being pancakes is overwriting most of our biological senses! Mmmm . . . lemme lower it down a bit, so I don't bite your face off accidentally."

"I am *not* a breakfast item!" Cinder said. "P-put me back, damn it!"

"Shhh, no whining." Vee leaned into Cinder. "Only noms now. Nom. Nom. Nom."

The room filled with the comforting aroma of a perfect breakfast—warm pancakes, sweet syrup, and fresh berries.

I felt a strange, alien, bewildering sense of belonging. Every sensation was muted yet intensified, focused on warmth and sweetness. The world suddenly seemed simpler, cozier. I observed my companions melting into each other, their forms blending in a swirl of golden-brown and creamy white and strawberry red.

I watched in pancake-vision as pancake-Vee playfully nibbled at pancake-Cinder. The Quetzi-cake's protests faded into soft noises of crunching waffles and falling strawberries.

A clawed, delicious hand of Thunder-cake pulled me in.

Our edges blurred, individual identities merging into a collective breakfast experience. Time seemed to slow, each moment stretching like warm syrup.

Through our shared pancake-consciousness, I sensed waves of affection and trust flowing between us. It was a unique intimacy—wholesome, comforting, and deliciously absurd, conceptually skewered sideways with overflowing breakfast-ness.

Some distant, rational, non-pancake part of me attempted to define the edges of myself, but failed to do so. There were no edges.

There was no human named Martin nor two Omnid predators here.

*There were only pancakes.*

# CHAPTER ELEVEN

# Outsider

Cold waves crashed against the gray glass-pebble shore. Gargantuan alien bones loomed in the distance. A supercell storm spun overhead. Cold gale struck her body.

Cinder winced, shivering. There were no pancakes, no warmth in this place.

She must have fallen asleep after their wild, absurd, mild-melting, delicious ship-venture.

The massive Leviathan bones in the distance seemed to watch her, silent witnesses of eons of rise and fall of civilizations. Each vertebra was larger than a mountain, a permanent reminder of the thing that had once perished here.

Her feathers shifted through muted grays and deep blacks, the colors of stress, of grief, of uncertainty. The pancake-warmth from earlier felt like a distant dream now, replaced by the cold, cruel reality.

Her wings felt heavy, weighed down by a rising panic attack. The storm overhead mirrored the chaos inside her heart—Lance could be dead. Perma-dead because of Martin's actions.

Each gust of blade-like icy wind seemed to stab at her body, singing of betrayal, of hope crushed beneath indifferent cosmic wheels.

All of the Arx delvers could be dead.

If Gate Keeper Vassily was dead, if the gate was damaged from this end, then there would be no way back to Earth. She would never see her parents, never see Lance again. Kat would die, too, without access to the incarnator.

The weight of potential loss pressed down on her like the heavy, broiling, dark clouds overhead.

Memories flashed through her mind.

*Lance teaching her how to glide from a cliff when she was too scared to spread her wings. Lance defending her from upperclassmen bullies at Skyfall Academy. Lance, who always knew how to make her laugh even on her darkest days when she was just a kid.*

*Lance, who always tried to help, always defended her. Her big brother whom she pushed away like an absolute knob.*

Her claws dug into her wings, drawing blood, pure black feathers tearing and breaking.

She began sobbing, the landscape around her fracturing.

"I'm sorry, I'm sorry," she cried. "I'm so sorry, Lance. It's my fault. This is all my fault. I came to this damned place. I should have been there for you," she whispered to the bones, to the wind, to her absent brother. "I was so busy being angry, so determined to prove I was strong . . . I let Em control me. I let fear dictate everything. I effed up! I am a terrible daughter, a terrible sister! I let Alex . . . Martin into my heart, and now you're dead! You're dead, and it's all my fault . . . again!"

Suddenly, a sound cut through her grief.

Footsteps.

Soft. Deliberate. Crunching on the crystalline silver-gray glass. Coming from behind her.

Cinder whirled, her feathers shifting through defensive reds and sharp silvers, ready to fight. Her claws extended, her body coiled like a spring.

"Who's there?!" she screamed into the howling storm.

The footsteps continued. Slow. Measured. Impossibly calm against the raging winds.

A figure emerged from the mist. Tall. Elongated. Shifting between human and something . . . else. A wolf.

"Hello, little songbird," a familiar voice purred.

Valor.

"You . . . you're dead! I perma-killed you!" Cinder howled, retreating back into the icy water.

"Did you, now?" Valor smiled, his right hand phase-shifting into a jagged saw blade. "A god cannot die, I'm afraid. You heard what I wished for, didn't you?"

"A god?" Cinder's voice cracked, her feathers bristling with a hurricane of colors—terror, rage, desperation. "You're no god. You're a monster! Your effing birchknob ritual went tits up! Piss off!"

Valor's form continued to shift, bone and flesh melting and reforming like living, glossy, beige liquid metal. His smile stretched impossibly wide, revealing rows of razor-sharp teeth that glinted like polished obsidian in the storm's electric light.

"Perhaps." The Skinwalker shrugged. "Maybe so. You and your dragon girlfriend poured all of my Lazarus bracelets into a concrete mold and threw it into the deep ocean trench, and yet I still persist . . . sideways across reality."

Silver eyes bloomed across Valor's head and hands.

"Do you know why we used singers like you?" he asked. "To imprint your voices into this lakeshore. To always have a point to follow back. Even if we die!"

"You're not real," Cinder hissed, her wings flaring with defensive colors as she poured magic into her voice. "Go away! You're just another nightmare. Another ghost. Part of the nightmare in my head!"

Valor's laugh was like broken glass scraping against metal. "Am I? Are you certain? If I'm just a nightmare, a figment of your shattered psyche, then why can't you wake up from this dream? The point of our clan's ritual wasn't simply to make wishes on the Leviathan's bones, it was to be more. To attain true immortality, outside of the bracelets. To anchor ourselves permanently to a domain, to our victims' souls!"

Cinder retreated farther into the icy water.

"My clan brothers are still shapeless and formless," Valor said. "But not me. You lived. You got away. I'm bound to you. Bound to your fear and pain. Devouring your soul from within. Bit by bit. Someday, the thing that will wake up in your body won't be you anymore. It will be me."

Cinder's feathers erupted in a violent storm of crimson and obsidian, her voice a razor-edged scream. *"Martin will stop you!"*

"Really?" Valor laughed. "A human? With no magic? Against a being who has transcended mortality? Who has woven himself into the very fabric of your soul, into every grain of sand on this beach, into every drop of water in Lake Eerie?"

Cinder choked, falling into the water, suffocating, drowning in the waves washing over her trembling body.

Her Charmchain skills weren't working against Valor. They never did in her dreams.

"You killed my brothers," Valor said coldly. "With that black railgun. Buried their bracelets in concrete tombs. Delayed our work. But I will resume it to all as soon as you shatter—give in to me!"

As Valor's words echoed, the lake began to pulse with an unnatural, sickly green light. The bones of the Leviathan in the distance seemed to vibrate, their massive vertebrae casting long, twisted shadows across the shoreline.

"You cannot escape me," Valor whispered, his form liquefying and reforming with each step. "I am everywhere, an Astral Phantom far beyond the physical. I cannot be killed by a mundane gun anymore nor a magic blade, for I have ascended further than any Omnid before me has!"

Cinder flailed in the icy water, her body refusing to obey.

With a blinding flash, the water froze, trapping her in its cold embrace. She wept and thrashed.

"I am the storm that devours souls," Valor's voice distorted, multiplying into a chorus as he bent down to her, saw-blade arm pointed at her neck. "I am the hunger that never ends. I am the darkness between stars, the void that waits to consume everything."

Reality behind him fractured, like an impossible shear, splitting into countless mirror-like shards that reflected Cinder's terrified face back at her from every angle. Each reflection showed a different version of her death, her suffering, her eventual transformation into something monstrous.

A dead walker, a ghoul.

Cinder saw ghoulish versions of herself picking up the teacher's railgun, a magic sword, a bow, a hammer. Her killing everyone. Executing her friends, her family, her brother, Kat, Io, Vespera, and her little pink, defenseless human.

Again and again. Across myriads of possibilities.

"See? No matter where you go, I follow," Valor smiled. "No matter what you do, I win in the end, take everything, everyone from you. Because with each breath you take, I grow stronger. Your very persistence feeds me, shapes me, gives me physical form."

The shattered reflections multiplied, showing thousands of possible futures—each more horrific than the last. Cinder watched herself transform into a monster, saw herself carving up and devouring her loved ones, heard her own voice twisted into something cruel, laughing as she fired the railgun at her friends.

"Your human pet thinks he understands love?" Valor laughed. "He knows nothing of true power. The power of fear. The power of hate, despair, and darkness! The power of destruction, Entropy itself!"

Cinder struggled in the frozen water.

"You cannot escape me," Valor sang. "I am beyond mortality. Beyond mundane Omnid magic. I am pure intention given form!"

His body continued to shift—sometimes a perfect human form, sometimes a writh-ing mass of bone and liquid flesh, sometimes a thing with too many teeth and too many eyes.

"Your soul is my gateway," he continued. "Every time you close your eyes, every moment of weakness, I slip deeper."

"I . . . I'll throw myself into the Abystall Dungeon!" Cinder snarled. "The mites will deprive me of magic. The shit are you gonna do then?!"

"That's not going to stop me." Valor shrugged. "Do you really think that I have only one anchor? You're one of many, an incomplete, partial flesh-phylactery!"

A silver-fluid thing burst from Cinder's body, forming into a human figure standing above her.

"You know," I said, staring at Valor's ever-shifting form, "I expected an incomprehen-sible, eldritch Outsider entity, not a teenage Skinwalker knob."

"Pathetic human!" Valor snarled. "I am a god, and I will carve up and infest your soul to serve as my second body!"

He leapt at me and struck at me with his serrated bone-blade saw arm, cutting deep into my chest. I grabbed the blade, its jagged teeth sinking into my hands, blood pour-ing onto the ice.

"What you are," I hissed, "is basically a magical incel who couldn't get a date without phase-shifting."

"*I summoned the Leviathan's Echo!*" Valor howled, bone-blade teeth extending from his hand deeper into my body and fingers, pinning me to where I stood. "You will bleed to death here, and then you will become my other door!"

"You summoned a temper tantrum," I said. "With beast cores. And murdered defenseless girls. Real impressive."

"You will die here, human," Valor laughed. "You have no heart core to keep me out! Tomorrow I will wake up in your flesh. You shouldn't have come into her dreams!"

I closed my eyes and then snapped off, letting go of the first layer of my being, leaving Alexander Glock behind like an empty shell. Like a shadow moving sideways made from liquid silver, I stood in front of Valor.

"W-what?" the Skinwalker sputtered.

My fist connected with Valor's ever-shifting face, sending ripples through his liquid-metal form.

Valor staggered back, his silver eyes widening in confusion. "Impossible! You're just a human!"

"Am I?" I asked. "Or am I something else? Something that understands the rules of this place better than you do?"

"You cannot hope to escape me!" Valor roared, his body twisting into a mass of blades and teeth. "I am beyond physical form!"

"Really?" I asked. "Then why are you still trying to look so solid, so Valor-y? Why maintain any form at all? Why not embrace mommy Entropy?"

Cinder looked up at my two bodies with wide eyes. One frozen, stabbed through the heart by Valor, the other taunting him.

Valor's second arm formed into a blade and stuck me through the heart. I grabbed the blade, trapping it in my chest, squeezing hard, and growling as the teeth dug into my hands.

"You're afraid," I hissed as blood bubbled from my chest and hands. "Afraid of being nothing. Of dissolving into static. That's why you need an anchor. That's why you need Cinder. That's why you are feeding on this dream."

Valor's silver eyes flickered with uncertainty.

"You're not a god," I continued. "You're a parasite. A remnant. Something that got left behind when your shitty ritual failed."

"Die!" Jagged teeth stretched away from the blade, cutting deeper into me.

"If Slayer Nazareth steps on a river, does he stand still atop it, or does he flow along with the current moving him downstream like a conveyor belt?" I asked, bleeding out.

"What . . ." Valor sputtered, derailed by my theological question.

The bone teeth reached my heart and my second shell shattered, coming apart as I stepped out of good-boy-NPC Christophorus Elijah.

I reformed behind Valor. Silver eyes bloomed in the back of his head, staring at me.

"How?!" he hissed, thinning out as he rapidly grew an arm behind himself.

"Let me tell you a story," I said, trembling as I watched Valor's flesh rearrange itself with grotesque squelching sounds.

"What story?!" Valor growled, his entire face flowing into itself and out from the back of his skull to face me.

"There was a boy named Martin Kilborne once," I said. "A boy whose mother sent him to live with Uncle George—a man who taught him that the world was nothing more than a series of systems waiting to be manipulated. Uncle George wasn't just a thief—he was an artist. A con man who could walk into any room and become exactly what people expected him to be."

Valor blinked at me.

"You think of yourself as a killer? You are nothing compared to the Frontenachii Wendigo Clan, a boy playing with fire he doesn't fully understand. Let me tell you about real monsters," I said, stepping towards him. "My mother died very slowly. Not the quick, merciful death people romanticize. Lung cancer ate her from the inside out, a predator far more insidious than any Skinwalker. She worked for the Frontenachii as a comp sci engineer."

"Another sob story? I've heard hundreds from my victims as I cut them down with my blades," Valor sneered at me. "Knobfold tales don't impress me, human."

"Ah," I sniffed. "But my story isn't done yet. That was just the beginning. Mom never told me that she was dying. She lied to me, pushed me away. The hospital called my uncle, told him that she was in a coma. I arrived too late to do anything. I held her hand when her heart stopped, and then . . . I broke. Mentally."

"Pathetic humans break so easily. What are you even trying to prove?" Valor asked as he struck through me with his third hand. "You are weak, you are just a little snack for me to devour!"

I grabbed the blade, squeezing it hard.

"I went to the Frontenachii compound." I spat blood. "They had the most advanced Fear Wards in North Acadia. Psychological warfare shit designed to scare humans away.

I went up against it. Again and again. Day after day for six months. Until my soul shattered, too."

Martin's heart stopped. I stepped out of his shell, liquid silver flowing into the last figure.

"W-what?!" Valor blinked at me. "What the shit are you?! Why won't you just effing die?!"

"I am a human soul of a supervillain wearing a shawl of other human souls," I grinned.

Valor-tripod struggled between my three cast-off shells as I walked in a circle around him. Thunder rumbled above us.

"How can you fragment yourself like this?!" he hissed. "No human . . ."

"Can't I?" I asked. Each version of me spoke simultaneously. Four voices, one question. "I must admit, I did shatter rather spectacularly into quite the mess, so it took me a bit of time to put myself back together as distinctive concepts."

"What effing concepts?!" Valor barked.

"The Architect." I pointed a finger at Alexander.

"The Understanding." My finger moved to Christophorus.

"The Champion." I pointed at Martin.

"The Leader." I tapped the fractal shear on my forehead, my silver hair fluttering in the wind. "Each shell layered above the other, moving, spinning constantly around me like an armillary sphere. Each with cracks, big holes . . . occasionally aligned just right to present one face or another to the Truth runes. A mind-map soul system designed to fool any Scrut-sight into thinking whatever I need, whatever I want them to think."

"Clever," Valor admitted, his silver eyes narrowing. "But even a cleverly fractured soul cannot stop me. All you've done is annoy me and reveal your cards!"

"You revealed yourself to me." I shrugged. "So I have revealed myself to you in turn. It's only fair. Also, I'm just a distraction." I grinned as I pointed a finger gun at Valor's head, noticing that warm, feathery, black and white, magisteel-talon armed hands wrapped around mine.

Valor's silver eyes widened as black-and-white wings spread behind me, Vespera's beak resting on my shoulder.

"Pancakes!" both of us declared as one.

A thunderbolt of pure electrical energy erupted from Vespera's talons, channeled through my finger gun, striking Valor directly between his shifting silver eyes. Another bolt rushed from Martin's body. The third bolt detonated from Alexander's pierced heart. The fourth struck the Skinwalker from the heart of Nazarite novitiate Christophorus.

The monster screamed, flailing, shaking, burning in my tripod-trap of souls.

Valor's form began to disintegrate, his lanky body bubbling and hissing under the electrical assault.

"Arghhhhh!" he shrieked. "I cannot be destroyed! Cannot be unmade! I will . . ."

"Return? Reform to haunt us?" I asked. "Yeah, I pretty much expect it. Who said anything about destruction? You're the Wolfermort to my Larry Plotter. I bet you'll return to Oddwarts to harass me on See-Mass day!"

More brilliant lightning burned the Skinwalker from all sides, melting, vaporizing, unmaking his figure. He bubbled and warped like the liquid Terminator sinking into molten steel, face after face flashing across his twisting, shaking head.

"Again and again. This is fine," I said. "I accept your terms as my dream nemesis, Valor. Chase me if you dare. Strike me through the heart as much as you desire. I welcome you with my embrace. I love you!"

Valor's scream stretched into an impossible harmonic, igniting the entire dreamscape around us. His body dissolved into a million silver fragments, each one catching the storm's lightning and burning away.

The glass beach ignited with waves of electrical fire dancing between each pebble. The bones of the Leviathan in the distance shattered, falling into the lake.

The ice imprisoning Cinder shattered, and she leapt up.

My three human shells flowed back over me, covering me up one by one in proper order until I stood whole once again.

The lake water retreated as a massive tidal wave created by the falling bones formed in the back, heading straight for us.

Cinder smashed into Vespera and me, wrapping us in rainbow wings, her eyes filled with tears.

"Wolfermort?" she choke-hissed into my ear. "Really?"

"What?" I grinned at her. "He's totally gonna come back in book four to compete in the Quad-Wizard Tournament!"

Cinder buried her face into my shoulder just as the tidal wave crashed into us.

I shuddered awake, tangled together with Vee and Ci in the crystal bed, the distant lights of Abystall Dungeon shimmering beneath us through the transparent floor.

All around us, gargantuan electrical fractal snowflake-shaped hexagrams shimmered, slowly dimming. Vespera's right hand held on to a wall, while her left hand wrapped around Cinder, magisteel talons digging into my forehead.

Zee Captain's lighter was burning in my right hand as my left hand was wrapped around Cinder.

I snapped it shut, staring at the floating dial.

1/4 fuel left.

*Really need to add a core to my Wizard's Tower before I run outta magic lighter fluid.*

"Whew! That was some topnotch baller Dreamancy!" Vespera clicked, removing her talons from the wall and my forehead. The electrical fractals dancing across our crystalline bedroom slowly faded away. "Good show!"

"Did we just . . ." Cinder started, her feathers shifting through confused purples and uncertain blues.

"Fight your nightmare parasite? Yep." I nodded.

"Is he . . .?"

"Going to come back? Probably." I nodded, making Cinder frown.

"No question about it." Vespera nodded. "We just zapped most of him outta your soul, but that doesn't really unmake what he is. I have no idea how to perma-kill Astral Phantoms."

"He said he has . . . phylacteries," Cinder let out.

"Sounds like a quest for Larry Plotter!" I declared. "Collect them all for Bumblyduur's ghost!"

"So are we going to find and collect all of his Phylacteries or . . ." she began.

"Abyss, no," I said. "That's like an effort and a half. I don't have time for that shit, babe. You know I don't plan to fight Abystall's Dungeon Sentinels, right? It's much more effective to put them to work. Free labor force and whatnot. The same applies here. All enemies are essentially free resources one way or another."

"Right, resources, of course." Cinder rubbed her face tiredly. Then she looked down at herself. Her feathers shifted through embarrassed sunset pinks as she pulled the covers over her chest. "Hey! Where's my hexasuit?"

"On the floor with the rest of our clothes," Vee clicked cheerfully. "Along with like fifty pounds of pancake crumbs!"

"P-pancake crumbs?" Cinder sputtered. "What? Did we actually . . ."

She rotated and crawled to the edge of the bed to look at the transparent floor. There were no crumbs there, only our scattered outfits and the distant view of Abystall.

"Ha! Sucka. Made you look," Vee cackled, swatting her behind.

"Hey!" Cinder squawked, her feathers flaring with indignant violet-oranges. "You . . . you . . . argh!"

She lunged at Vespera, but the Thunderbird was already rolling away, exploding with laughter. "Next time, I'll turn both of us human with your holofractal wings! Won't that be a treat! And we can make Lexy look like an Omnid! Ha! See, I'm full of great ideas! Where would you be without me?"

I yawned, my head throbbing.

As fun as it was to picture a fully human Vee and Ci in my head, a few more hours of sleep were definitely in order.

This time, hopefully without any hand-stabby nightmares to fight.

# CHAPTER TWELVE

# The Morning After

I woke up to the somewhat unnerving view of gray eyes spotted with gold flakes at the inner edges and lower half. Vee's face was inches from mine, her gaze studying me intently.

"Mornin'," I yawned. "How long was I out?"

"Six hours, twenty-nine minutes, and thirty-two seconds." She grinned, rolling over and up to sit on my chest with a smug expression, dark wings with white edges spread wide.

"Haven't gotten enough of me last night?" I asked her as she tilted her head at me.

"Nope!" Vespera clicked, sending tiny electrical sparks dancing across my chest with a talon. "I won't be satisfied till I map every single nanometer, neural network, and soul bit!"

"And after you're done mapping all of me?" I asked. "Will you release me from your clutches then, you greedy birb?"

"Mmmmm . . . naw." she grinned, smooshing my cheeks. "Then I'll make you work in the salt mines. Can't have my most valuable investment slacking off!"

"Ah yes, the salt mines of your tears when I make you laugh so hard, you'll cry." I nodded. "I thus humbly accept the position of your most Royal Court Jester."

"Court Jester?" Vee hummed, pretending to be offended. "Excuse you, but you're my Royal Consort and Chief Entertainment Officer."

"You know," I said with a smile, "when I first saw you at the Academy, I thought that you were a clueless Thunderknob . . . I honestly didn't even consider you as a bestie or dating material, thinking that I'd maybe end up bouncing between Kat and Ci or something."

"Pfff, Kat would break ya in half without even tryin'," Vespera laughed. "She's too tall for ya."

"You're way taller than me," I pointed out.

"Eh, still not as tall or bulky as Kat. Stollwurms have high bone density in general for punching tunnels through solid rocks. On the other hand, I'm bendy," she replied, arching her back more than a human could to illustrate her point. "And practically weightless when I use my wings. Just like Cindy here!"

"Ughhh, too early for whatever this is." A rainbow-feathered hand tried to paw at Vespera and me as she heard her name.

"Early bird gets the worm." Vee poked the half-asleep Quetzi.

"Buzz off, sparkplug. I am *not* a worm," Cinder grumbled sleepily, her feathers shifting through sleepy purples and irritated oranges.

"No, you're a pancake," Vee clicked cheerfully. "A very grumpy pancake who needs her beauty sleep."

"Shut uuuup," Cinder whined, pulling a pillow over her head.

The Thunderbird turned her attention back to me.

"So," Vee clicked softly, her talons tracing patterns on my chest. "You thought I was just a patsy, huh?"

"Yeah," I admitted. "You put up a really good facade. My first impression was 'ditzy rich girl, probably easy to manipulate. Would totally fall for some clickbait.'"

"Ha, as if!" she guffawed. "And now?"

"Now I know exactly how genuinely sweet, clever, and cheerful you are," I said. "Without you, I wouldn't be able to slap the Outsider outta Ci's dreams, wouldn't be able to make my crystal Mage Tower. Yulia did tell me that you were smart and capable, but I didn't realize exactly how much we'd click or how much we could accomplish together. Boy, am I glad that I was wrong about you!"

"Not entirely wrong." She smirked. "I am pretty easy to manipulate—if you know how. Just gotta offer me something interesting enough."

"Like what?" I asked.

"Like whatever you are," she purred, leaning closer.

"A broken human in a stack of NPCs?" I suggested.

"A shiny mental lockbox puzzle, perfect for trapping a very curious birb's attention," she corrected. "Say, how many are you in there?"

"Four," I said. "Four primary personality-shift archetypes. Architect, Champion, Understanding, Leader."

"Which one am I talking to right now?" Vespera continued her interrogation.

"The Architect," I answered. "Alexander Glock. Builds systems, plans, strategizes. Good with jokes. Doesn't have flaws that would get in the way of conversation."

"Flaws such as?"

"Such as being very distracted by a naked Thunderbird currently inhabiting my chest," I said dryly.

"You're gonna have to cycle through them all for me so that I can determine how it all works," she said, nipping at my neck.

"Sure." I nodded.

A blue eye opened amidst a mop of rainbow feathers to stare at me.

"Did it hurt?" Cinder asked.

"Did what hurt?" I asked with a cheeky grin. "Falling from heaven?"

"Pfff. No, damn it. Fragmenting yourself," she clarified with an amused dragon noise. "Breaking into multiple personas. Did it hurt?"

"Pain is relative." I shrugged. "Losing Mom . . . hurt much more."

Cinder reached out to me and squeezed my hand hard, sliding closer and burrowing her head in my side.

I cycled through the four shattered shells in my psyche, slowly exposing each for Vespera's mental scan.

"Hrmmm." Vespera held a sparkling talon on my forehead. "What you've done shouldn't be possible."

"Why not?" I asked.

"Because," she said, "you can't just shatter a single soul into four distinctive concepts. Not as a magic-less human."

"And yet here we are," I said.

"Mmm, yes. You're iffy. Very iffy," she clicked. "I was muchly wrong about you, too. There are definitely four distinctive souls inside you. It's hard to spot static amidst static. Basically it's [Human[human[human[human]]]]. You're like a human soul matryoshka!"

"And?"

"It's the weirdest shit I've had the pleasure to work with." Vespera waved her talons. "Most humans can barely maintain a single coherent personality. You've got four, and they're not just fragments—they're fully realized, functional personas that can take over and operate independently. Enough to function as a Dreamancy skill. I'm a dream expert, and I don't think that I could split myself like that to hold someone down."

"Just a survival mechanism." I shrugged. "Uncle George taught me early that adaptability means survival. They aren't just singular. I can mix and match, adjusting the parameters, be fifty percent Leader and fifty percent Champion, etcetera."

"Consider me quadruple-curious." She sent more sparks raining across my forehead. "It's honestly both impressive and highly concerning. A lesser Dreamancer might consider you incurably insane, but I think that what you've done is deviously clever."

"'Preciate it." I grinned. "Always wanted to be called smartypants by a sparkly birb."

Vespera rolled her eyes and sent a playful electrical zap directly into my mind. [Don't get cocky, human-sausage.] Her mental-static voice laughed.

"I'll do much more than that!" I grabbed her sides, fingers digging into soft down feathers, tickling her.

"Ah ha ha ha, nooo, stoooooawwwwwpp! You've found my one weakness, you devious creature!" She bucked and heaved, laughing and swatting at me.

A heavy fist banged on our door, making it wobble.

"Oi," Kat's voice came through. "You knobs. Stop playing around and get dressed. We have a prisoner to interrogate."


Gabriella Matrosin, the Arx Bank rep and Earth transit gate Vault Keeper, stretched lazily on her balcony overlooking the early morning streets of Shandria. The early morning light cast a soft golden hue across her dark fur, her tail swishing idly as she reached for her steaming cup of Kitlix-crafted coffee.

Many things had gone sideways, and her owners weren't pleased. She'd spent nearly all day yesterday making Voicecast calls and explaining the problem to far too many angry people, promising many of them swift execution or fingers of the party responsible.

The balcony of her small apartment overlooked a narrow street lined with market stalls and early morning vendors. Gabriella looked down at the small merchants and sighed. Today was probably going to be even worse.

The Enforcers had failed to arrest one of the delver teams from Earth due to an insane dragon girl unleashing Duskbloom all over Undertown. The bank had a variety of investments in the multitude of unsavory businesses below ground, and now all of them had gone up in smoke.

Shadowmancers, fighters, murderers, assassins, gambling den owners, and night butterflies were fleeing Undertown and occupying Shandrian inns. Duskbloom had spread far too rapidly and far too quickly, making the retrieval of the five pesky interdimensional delvers impossible.

The Enforcers were terrified of losing their weapons and falling asleep in the caves below. No matter how much money she offered, people simply refused to go to Undertown. Adventurers knew how dangerous Abystall Dungeon was and now the dungeon had devoured, spread out, engulfed the city of criminals below her feet. It would take her some time to organize a proper high-level team covered in cold-runes armor.

As she pondered the chaos of Undertown, a sudden sharp pinch struck the back of her neck.

Gabriella's coffee cup slipped from her fingers, shattering on the balcony tiles. Her vision blurred, the world spinning around her in a dizzying whirl of golden morning light and dark shadows.

Before she could cry out, strong arms caught her falling body.

Gabriella blinked rapidly as reality washed over her. She had clearly been kidnapped. Her owners would not be pleased. Who even dared take an Arx Bank agent? What sort of . . .

She blinked as her eyes adjusted to the gloom. The room she was in was entirely crystalline—walls, floor, ceiling, even the furniture seemed carved from transparent, slightly bluish-white crystal that allowed her to see layers deep into the structure around her.

The bank rep's mouth fell open as she stared down, and down, and . . . down.

*Are those rivers down there? Entire lakes? A gargantuan waterfall?! Where on Arx am I?!*

She had no idea, had never seen anything like it.

"Comfortable?" a male voice asked.

Gabriella whirled up. Four figures were located across her on another crystalline couch. Her dark fur stood on end, tail curled protectively around her body. She recognized them immediately from meeting them at the bank—the delving team led by a human who annoyed her for hours and then decided *not* to stay at the Omnid-owned inn, instead heading into Undertown for some inexplicable reason, and then . . .

Her professional training kicked in immediately. She straightened her posture, adjusted her bank-issued blue blazer, and spoke with practiced calm.

"I presume this is not a social call," she said.

The human—Alexander—leaned forward, a devious grin spreading across his face. "Correct. We'd like to discuss some . . . discrepancies in the Arx Bank's recent activities."

Vespera, the Thunderbird-kin, clicked her beak. Electrical sparks danced between her talons. "Specifically about Topaz. And Necromancers. And dimensional gates. And us."

"Where's my brother, you effing beerch?!" the Quetzalcoatl-kin named Cassiopeia Nova barked, blue eyes blazing with fury.

"I'm afraid I don't know what you're talking about," Gabriella said smoothly, adjusting her blazer. "Bank representatives are not privy to individual personal information."

I snapped my fingers.

"Cut the bureaucratic bullshit." Katherine's massive armored hand dug into the cat-girl's shoulder. "Where. Is. Lance. Nova."

The crystal room began to fade away into absolute darkness as Gabriella screamed, submerged by the Stollwurm into the deep. When both of them reemerged from the shadow realm, it was clear that all rational thought had fled from Gabriella's head, as she was reduced to a puddle of pure primal terror.

"W-what was that?" she managed to mewl.

"The deep," Katherine growled. "Where fear is a language, and I'm fluent."

Gabriella's fur stood on end, her tail curling protectively around her body.

"L-Lance N-Nova has b-b-been deported from Arx!" the banker cried out, trembling like a leaf. "Y-your Om-Omnid-kin . . . and every other E-E-Earth d-delving team were ar-arrested yesterday by our Enforcers," she heaved. "And d-deported from Arx!"

"Deported *where?*" Cinder hissed at my side.

"B-back t-to E-E-Earth!" Gabriella sobbed out as tears ran down her cheeks. "P-per our agreement w-with Lord Zalimar . . . w-we are not to harm his students!"

"I banished Zalimar to another dimension." I leaned forward. "So how exactly is he enforcing such agreements?"

Gabriella's ears flattened. "He . . . has contingency protocols. Prearranged instructions with the bank in case of his . . . unexpected absence."

"Convenient," Katherine growled from above, looming over the much smaller banker. "Keep talking."

The catgirl's tail twitched nervously. Her professional veneer had been shattered, obliterated, torn away by the primal terror of the deep.

"The deportation happened yesterday," she stammered. "All Earth delvers were processed through the obsidian o-one-way gate i-into the Omnid chapel. It's s-standard bureaucratic procedure when interdimensional travelers become . . . problematic. Y-you sh-should have c-come willingly, like the-the others! You can't just k-kidnap Arx Bank representatives and t-torture them for answers w-with fear magics!"

"We heard your conversation with Grand Moloch Arkenish," I pointed out. "What was it he said about fingers?"

Katherine's claws dug into Gabriella's shoulder, making her scream.

"I c-c-can't say the t-t-ruth o-out loud!" she sobbed, shaking. "B-bound b-by a b-blood contract!"

"Hrm." Vespera got up and marched to the banker. "Maybe you can think it then. Let me speak on your behalf."

She circled the catgirl and her magisteel talons dug into the bank rep's head, making blood drip from her temples.

"It's standard procedure to satisfy Undertown clients," Vespera clicked, sounding somewhat like Gabriella. "We wouldn't have killed you."

"Oh?" I asked.

"Our agents would have simply knocked you out and made flesh duplicates!" Vespera said for the banker. "We aren't monsters! The manufactured magic flesh-duplicates would have gotten cut up and their various bits would be shipped to the parties your team has offended! It's standard protocol. Then you would have been banned for one hundred years from Shandria! That was our agreement with Lord Zalimar!"

Gabriella nodded and twitched madly, tears streaming down her fur as electrical current danced across her striped fur.

Katherine's emerald eyes narrowed. "And where exactly would these duplicates be created?"

Gabriella yelped as lightning struck her temples. The Thunderbird wasn't gentle.

"The body forge," Vespera said for Gabriella. "Located in the sub-basement of the banking complex. Minus sixth level. Shit. I really shouldn't have revealed this to you! You have to stop tearing answers out of me with magic! They'll actually kill you for what you're doing, instead of just deporting you! Stop reading my mind!"

"What, like Quint, Emerald, and Solace?" the Quetzi-girl at my side barked.

"That wasn't us!" Gabriella cried out on her own now. "Emerald Stratos attacked a local and was arrested by City Watch! The Watch Scruts processed her according to local law! The Arx Bank just facilitates the local legal system; we are not actively harming anyone!"

"You distribute Topaz," Katherine hissed. "A magical drug that fucks people up."

"Th-that's not what I meant!" Gabriella wailed. "W-we s-simply . . . Topaz isn't illegal in Shandria! It's a recreational drug! Some people simply use too much of it! We don't create it, we just facilitate trade, assist with transactions and currency exchanges! You have to bring me back home! Please! If you keep me prisoner here, the bank will . . ."

She fell silent.

" . . . send actual high-level Executioners to take all of you out. They will be wearing cold runes," Vespera finished for Gabriella.

"How high-level?" I asked.

"As high as level ninety-five. The bank has contracts with all major guilds! Manhunters, Shadowmancers, Hunters! The Bank Scruts will trace my location through my bracelet's mana signature in seconds when they realize that I'm not at work!" Vespera voiced Gabriella's thoughts.

"What bracelet?" I asked.

Gabriella's gray eyes shot to her wrist. There was no bracelet there. She choked. Shash had pulled all of her artifacts off and dressed her in a basic gray robe before the interrogation.

"Your bracelet's in another dimension," I explained. "Good luck to your Scruts trying to locate it there. You're going to be chucked in there, too, unless you prove yourself useful. I don't deal in half measures. I don't obey your rules. Why can't we reach Innkeeper Nikkola or Chapel Keeper Vassily?"

"Lockdown measures," Vespera clicked for Gabriella. "The Domovoy Omnid cousins operate deep underground beneath the bank and beneath the inn. Their domains were built under our supervision. They were fully dimensionally cut off . . . because of the current situation and the situation in Undertown. Wait . . . is this Undertown?"

Gabriella stared up, finally recognizing some of the terrain visible above. "By her Shadow . . . what sort of magic has done this?!"

"Can you get us into the vault or turn off whatever is blocking access to the gate?" I asked.

"N-no!" Gabriella shook her head.

"It takes more than one person to unlock a vault. I'm bound by blood contracts, cannot assist your escape back to Earth," Vespera revealed the banker's thoughts.

"Uh-huh." I nodded. "So what do you suggest we do?"

Gabriella's ears flattened against her head. Her tail curled protectively around her body as she realized she was trapped between monsters far more dangerous than any bureaucratic protocol.

"C-come with me to the bank and s-s-surrender," she offered. "The Enforcers will knock you out and chuck you into the one-way dimensional gate where your Keeper will take you back home."

"What about the Omnid trio getting executed tomorrow?" I asked.

"I can't stop their execution," Gabriella swallowed. "But I will have one of our agents retrieve their bracelets from the storage vaults after their execution, making a duplicate item. Likewise, they will be thrown into a one-way gate to your Keeper who will s-send them back home. S-see? Nobody has to die today! Please just let me go!"

"Nah," I said. "I like it here. I'm not getting banished for a century from Shandria."

"B-but it'll only be a year from your point of view!" Gabriella tried to convince me with pleading, big, kittenly gray eyes. "B-besides, there are gates from your world to other places on Arx! Just use them! We're only banishing you from Shandria!"

I leaned back, my eyes never leaving her face. "No," I said simply. "I don't think I will. Here's what I'm going to do, Miss Matrosin . . . I'm going to print my own non-magical currency and open my own bank in Shandria."

"W-what?!" The catgirl's eyes went wide.

"A merchant upstairs told me that Shandria is a city with very few laws," I explained. "I don't like the way your bank operates, so I'm going to open my own. Also, I'm going to make you an offer you can't refuse. You can either die now or you can work for me as my bank rep. You clearly have experience in the business, know the locals."

Gabriella's striped gray-and-white ears twitched. "And if I refuse?" she mewled.

Katherine's emerald eyes gleamed dangerously. "Then you get to drown in the deep."

Vespera clicked her beak. Electrical sparks danced between her talons. "Ke ke ke. Think carefully, kitty."

Gabriella swallowed hard. "I . . . I can't work for another bank or take any other job," she sobbed out.

"The blood contracts on my soul won't let me assist our competitors," Vespera added Gabriella's thoughts.

"Ah. Not an issue," I said. "Blood contracts operate on magic. What do you see below us, Miss Matrosin?"

Gabriella looked down through the transparent crystal floor. Beneath us stretched a vast, bioluminescent landscape—rivers of soft green and blue light, caverns glowing with ethereal radiance, strange crystalline structures pulsing with inner life, and beneath it all the radiant fields of the dungeon.

"That's . . . Abystall Dungeon," she whispered with a shudder of dawning horror.

"Correct," I said. "So, that's a yes on the job offer, or do you wish to die in the deep?"

"Yes," Vespera said. "She's thinking 'yes.'"

"Excellent!" I smiled. "How can I disable the dimensional bubble around the Omnid chapel?"

"Not possible," Vespera replied for the banker. "Three blood magic keys are required to unlock the Ward Core room. The controls are aligned to the blood and bodies of specific bank reps."

"And if these keys were stolen?" I asked.

"The keys won't work without the High Arch-Bankers!" Vespera revealed Gabriella's thoughts. "These bankers are constantly under security, unlike me!"

"And if someone were to, say . . . destroy the Ward Core room?" I asked. "Or unleash Duskbloom inside the bank?"

"*What?!*" Gabriella's eyes went wide.

"Destruction of the Ward Core room would leave the entire bank without power. It would take the bank weeks or months to fix something like that, depending on the damage," Vespera said. "The Ward Core would seal itself shut if something like Duskbloom was released inside."

"Excellent!" I grinned. "Now think in terms of directions—where's the Ward Core room?"

"Got it," Vespera clicked.

"Shash, knock Gabriella out and leave her in a room filled with Duskbloom. Don't let her die, but burn all magic out of her," I ordered. "Let's see if Duskbloom can eat blood contracts."

Gabriella yelped as another needle went through her neck courtesy of my assassin.

It was nice to have good people on my team.

# The Flavor of Destruction

Shash," I addressed our resident assassin. "Cancel the rescue operation—my friends already got forcibly deported, it seems. If you already hired someone, change their quests to get ready for an assault on the Arx Bank branches."

"Yes, m'lord." The assassin nodded. "I shall notify our people upstairs via Voicecast about it."

I waved him off, and he bowed and vanished from sight along with the body of the passed-out catgirl.

"You're really going to try to break the bank rep's blood contracts by exposing her to Duskbloom?" Cinder asked with a weary expression, colors of stormy sky dancing across her feathers.

"Yep." I nodded. "The mites eat magic. Blood contracts are magic. Basic science."

"And if it kills her?" Cinder's stare dug into my soul.

"The mites don't kill people. Passing out in the dungeon and getting eaten by the wildlife does. Our mooks will obviously wake her up, feed and water her," I pointed out. "She'll just have to live for a bit without magic. Worst-case scenario, she loses her ability to use magic permanently and becomes . . . just like me."

"Abyss, you're terrifying sometimes." Cinder wrapped her wings around herself.

"Says the girl who helped Em hunt down and murder an entire Skinwalker clan," I pointed out.

Cinder's feathers bristled. "That was different! They deserved it!"

"And Arx Bank doesn't?" I asked. "They're literally running a drug cartel over here, pretending like they're selling a bit of weed on the side."

"Fine, fine," Cinder let out. "Still . . . Why do I feel like everything happening is your fault?"

"Because it is," I said cheerfully. "I knocked down Zalimar for two weeks, which caused an entire castle of all sorts of other dominoes to come crashing down."

"M'Lexy is systematically destroying everything in his path," Vespera commented, arriving from the direction of the kitchen and offering me a Thunderbird-Moth-Quetzi-Stollwurm shake. "He's basically a human wrecking ball."

"Why?" Cinder asked exasperatedly. "Why are you like this?"

"Like what?" I asked, sipping my magic shake.

"Are we seriously robbing the Arx Bank now?" she demanded. "By spawning Duskbloom mites inside it?!"

"Maybe." I shrugged. "I'll need to walk around the area, think it over. Perhaps there is a less Duskbloomy solution."

"You'll need to walk around the area?" Cinder repeated, her feathers shifting through colors of irate disbelief. "That's your grand plan?"

"Yep." I nodded. "Reconnaissance. Information gathering. Understanding the system's weak points. A date with my two lovely ladies," I finished with a grin.

"*A date?!*" Cinder squawked, her feathers flaring through a rainbow of shocked colors that looked like a spring flower bouquet. "To *rob a bank?!*"

"Reconnaissance is a type of date." I shrugged. "We'll dress up nice. Have some fun. Gather intelligence. Get breakfast at a nice cafe, then lunch in town."

"What?!"

"Also, we should get a bunch of stuff from the shops upstairs," I added. "I owe Lenora and your parents presents."

"Presents?" Cinder's feathers shifted to confused blues. "Why would you want to get my family presents?"

"Because they were very lovely to me," I said. "Your mom especially. She made me feel welcome. Your little sister is hilarious. They deserve something nice. Did you forget that I'm living at your house?"

"Boo," Vespera complained. "I can't zap or burr my pink body pillow in Cindy's house."

"Aren't you a wealthy Prima-born?" I asked her. "Rent us a student loft residence to share at Skyfall."

"That's a bigly ask," she clicked. "Dad controls most of my finances. Plus, they don't permit couples to live together on campus unless . . ."

"Unless they're engaged?" I finished for her.

Cinder choked. "What?! Why can't we like . . . maybe rent a regular apartment in Cradlefall or something?"

"Nuh-uh. I'm staying at your parents' estate or on campus," I said. "Both are safe."

"Safe?" Cinder repeated skeptically. "You just destroyed Undertown with magical parasites and you're talking about safety?"

"Relatively safe," I corrected. "Controlled environment. Multiple layers of security. Easier to track potential threats. Frontenachii Wendigo Scruts will definitely have trouble harassing me in either location."

"Okay, but . . . getting e-engaged?!" Cinder flapped. "You can't be serious!"

"Dead serious," I said.

Vespera clicked her beak. "We've already soul-bonded. Engagement is just a formality."

"*A formality?!*" Cinder squawked, her feathers exploding into a hurricane of colors—violets, oranges, blues burning in chaotic patterns.

"Yep." I nodded. "Vee's right. We've already merged souls during the birth of our crystal tower child. Might as well make it official."

"But we've known each other for like . . . a *week!*" Cinder protested. "Also, the tower isn't . . . why are you so effing cringe? Abyss!"

"I try." I shrugged. "It is indeed fast, and I'm sorry I have to drag you into it all, but I'm on a bit of a deadline here to secure my place in Omnithornia and Skyfall by any illegal and legal means necessary. So is Vee, who doesn't want to be shipped off to Thunderland."

"Ya kno', Ci," Vespera said with a shrug, "in Thunderland, some arranged marriages happen pretty quick."

"This isn't bloody Thunderland! My . . . my parents are going to go ballistic!" Cinder waved her pink and violet pearlescent hands around.

"Would they really?" I asked pointedly. "Your parents are already worried sick about your behavior. You've been descending into excessive hostility due to the Outsider's influence over the last two years. Honestly, I think that your Hearth-Mom will simply be thrilled to see you smile. Your father will likely ask me a million pointed, reasonable questions about my intentions. I'm mostly worried about your Prima-Mom. I hear she's a literal hound."

"Reasonable?!" Cinder squawked. "He's *Justice Nova*! He literally *judges criminals for a living*!"

"Exactly." I grinned. "Which means he'll appreciate someone who follows complex logical processes. When Yulia gets back online, I will provide extensive documentation proving my value as a potential mate."

Vespera began laughing so hard, electrical sparks were shooting everywhere. "*Oh my Slayer! You actually prepared a presentation?!*"

"Working on one." I nodded with a serious face. "Complete with pie charts, projected income streams, risk assessments, and a comprehensive five-year plan for our potential clan development."

Cinder's ear feathers went completely flat.

"I will have a 3D model of our potential compound layout," I continued. "With projected agricultural yields, defensive infrastructure, and potential magical research zones."

"Where?!" she demanded.

I waved my hands around the crystal tower. "Here, obviously. Actually, it's a 480-year plan due to the time dilation. This crystal Mage Tower is our first clan infrastructure project. We're basically building our first compound. We've already established territorial control. We have a defensible location. Abystall Dungeon provides resources. The mite infestation creates a natural defensive perimeter. Vee can write protective runes. Katherine can access the deep for reconnaissance. Io can open dimensional gates for emergency evacuation."

Cinder's mouth opened and closed several times, looking like a fish gasping for air.

"You . . . you've thought about this *way* too much," she finally managed.

"Survival requires comprehensive planning," I said. "With pie charts. LLMs are pretty good at those."

"Arghh!" Cinder buried her face in her hands. "This . . . this is happening way too fast!"

"You can always live with your parents." I shrugged with a sly look. "Me and Vee will just live on campus. Together. You can visit us."

"No!" Cinder squawked, her feathers flaring through panicked colors. "Absolutely not! You are *not* living together without me!"

I smiled at her.

"You!" she growled. "You damned . . . manipulative chuppy! Can you not go one day without driving me up the wall?!"

"Eh." I shrugged. "I'm manipulating everyone into creating a stable magical infrastructure that can resist Entropic entities like the one in your soul."

Vespera clicked her beak. "He's not wrong, Ci."

Cinder's feathers shifted through colors of exasperation and grudging acceptance. "Fine. But we're taking things *slow*."

"I did just ask you both on a date," I pointed out.

"As a freaking bank-robbing plan!" Cinder growled.

"No," I said, shaking my head, "as a date. I feel bad for what I did to Vee."

"What did you do to me?" Vespera asked, tilting her head.

"I didn't actually talk to you after I got your Omnigram ID," I confessed. "You were talking to Yulia since Tuesday on my behalf. It was a long-ass chat. I've no idea what you guys even talked about. She did summarize the general gist of it, but still I'd like to talk to you in person, get to know you properly."

Vespera chortled.

"What?" I asked.

"Yeah, about that. I didn't talk to you either," she confessed. "I linked up the SimmiTech LLM API to my Omnigram characterized with my Valley girl persona to chat to people on my behalf. It's how I kept up my knob-girl appearance online. I figured something really funky was going on because the conversation between you and my AI went way too effing long and started going into crazy loops."

"So . . . we've both been letting AIs talk to each other this entire time?" I asked.

"Ye," Vee chortled. "I had to turn mine off in our chat because the chat window was basically rolling on endlessly. Then, I saw you posting photos of Christi and offered you the D&D show tickets to see if you would actually reply to that in person instead of digitally screwing with me."

"Pffff," I let out. "Wow."

"And then you showed up and were actually way more interesting in person than the AI version of you," Vespera finished.

"So technically," I said, "our entire relationship started with two AIs catfishing each other."

"Uh-huh." She nodded. "Our digital selves fell in love and made many world domination plans."

"No freaking wonder I couldn't profile you properly," I laughed.

"Abyss, you both are such effing dweebs," Cinder groaned, her feathers shifting through amused purples and resigned blues. "How did I even end up with not one, but *two* insane tech gremlins?"

"So, um," Katherine began, "you three are going uptown? Where Bank Enforcers might be looking for you? Who, might I remind you, know what you look like?"

"Cinder held her phase-shift for a while last night," I said. "And Vee had a great idea, too."

"What idea?!" Cinder ignited pink sunset colors as she tried to recall what the Thundergirl had proposed last night.

"You two can go as human highborn ladies," I said. "While I'll appear as your lowly . . . foxkin servant."

"*A foxkin!*" Cinder choked. "Why a foxkin, and how?!"

"To match my foxy ways, obviously. I'll be your humble, dashing foxkin butler," I said. "Your personal servant to carry your bags and gold wallets."

"And how exactly am I supposed to transform you into a foxkin?" Cinder demanded.

"With your phase-shift. You turned me into a pancake last night," I said. "Honestly, though, let's not waste your mana on me. I have costume bits and pieces already in my bag. Enough to make a half-human foxkin. So, you'll be transforming yourself and Vee into human girls.

"Human girls?!" Cinder's feathers shifted through shocked colors. "I can't . . . I've never tried to look fully human before!"

"Time to practice, then," Vespera clicked cheerfully. "Come on, it'll be fun! Like . . . cosplay!"

"But . . ." Cinder protested weakly. "W-what if the phase-shift wears off? What if I run out of mana?"

"To keep going longer, you should eat mana-rich steaks and drink overpriced mana-rich wine," I said. "Keep an eye on your mana bar. Run into the bathroom when it goes down too low and chug one of Lance's Mana Elixirs. Just think of it as delving training."

"Delving training?" Cinder's feathers shifted through skeptical purples. "This isn't like running through a dungeon!"

"No," I agreed. "It's actually harder. You'll need to maintain the phase-shift while walking around, shopping, eating, and acting like a highborn human lady. Think of it as an extended stealth mission."

"And what exactly am I supposed to wear?" she demanded.

"Phase-shift yourselves some nice, lavish, local-style outfits," I said. "Then we'll buy something even nicer. Come on, we're wasting daylight. I'd like to attend Ember's execution."

"Yay, execution front-row seats!" Vespera clapped. "Ooh! Can we wear matching outfits? That'll really grind Em's gears when she sees us!"

"Are you *insane*?!" Cinder flapped her wings in agitation. "That's literally walking into their trap!"

"From what we shook out of Solace and Gabriela, there is no trap," I said. "I assumed that the bank was cooperating with the local Scruts to get us. But, as we just learned from the bank rep, there's no such cooperation. The bank actually wants to extract the bracelets of the Omnid delvers to ship them back into Zalimar's classroom!"

"Then what's even the point of attending the execution?!" Cinder growled.

"Taunting Emerald," I said. "Acting as rescuers. We'll show up at the execution looking fabulous, make Em think we're there to save her, then . . . don't stop the execution. The bank will do the bracelet retrieval for us, but Sol and Quint will think that we saved them. Simple as."

"You're . . ." Cinder shook her head, failing to come up with a sufficiently specific adjective to describe my plan.

"Practical," Vespera filled in.

"Dastardly," Io commented from his corner, flipping another page of his book.

"Villainous," Kat said.

"Efficient," I corrected them all. "Now come on, let's get ready for our date. Vee, help Ci figure out how to look human. I'm going to raid Lance's bag for my makeup kit to make myself sufficiently foxy. See you all in forty minutes back here."

"Have fun!" Io grinned. "Make it a big bang!"

"What bang?" Cinder rounded on the moth while I went to the bathroom.

"A loud bang." Io shrugged. "I taste a looming catastrophe in the air."

"For us?!" She shook the Mothman.

"Nah," he replied. "For the people of Shandria."

# CHAPTER FOURTEEN

# Uptown Date

Katherine's emerald eyes gleamed in the darkness of the final tunnel leading to the surface of Shandria. Her massive form seemed to melt into the shadows, halfway sunk into the deep.

"I still think this is a terrible idea," she growled, her tail lashing behind her. "Going up there, right into their territory . . . into sunlight where I can't help."

"Awww, so you do care about me, bestie." I grinned at her.

The Stollwurm huffed at me.

"Relax. It'll be fine." I checked my fake fox ears. "We have Shash."

The assassin materialized beside us, silent as always.

"Keep your tags on at all times," Katherine demanded. "If anything happens, if you sense even a hint of trouble . . ."

"We'll call you immediately," I promised. "Io said that we should be fine."

"Io also said that you're basically a walking catastrophe," Katherine pointed out. "And that something terrible is going to happen to Shandria due to your actions."

"Details, details." I waved dismissively. "How do I look?"

"Like a knockoff fox," Katherine growled.

"Perfect." I grinned. "Ladies? Are you ready?"

Two heart-stoppingly cute human girls stepped into view.

Vespera cut an imposing figure in a Victorian-style black dress, the layered fabric falling in elegant waves around her tall frame. Her pale face was dusted with dark freckles, and her sharp gray-yellow eyes held their usual mischievous glint with sparks of naughtiness. Black lipstick and black hat with black flowers pinned to it completed her gothic Lolita ensemble.

Beside her, Cinder wore a flowing blue summer dress that seemed to catch every hint of light. Brilliant red hair cascaded down her shoulders in gentle waves. Her soul-searching, big, ocean-blue eyes—now set in a human face—were still just as captivating as ever, the kind you could drown in if you stared too long. Rainbow-colored flowers were pinned to her hair.

"Why is Ci a redhead?" I asked.

"Because redheads have more fun," Vespera cackled.

"Really?" I squinted at the humanized Thunderbird. She was somewhat shorter now. I had no idea how that worked, but chose not to question it.

"Nah." She waved an elegant, pale hand at me. "It's 'cause she wouldn't stop blushing with her hair. Hard to see red on vibrant-as-F red."

"Ah," I said. "This I gotta see. Wanna make out?"

Cinder blushed red across her entire face, her hair becoming the tiniest bit more vibrant.

I laughed.

"Don't mind if I do!" Vespera took my comment as an invitation and grabbed me by the collar, yanking me towards her face.

Intellectually, I knew Vespera had a beak—her face should terminate in a sharp, avian point. But right now, somehow, her holofractal magic reshaped human form pressed soft lips against mine, warm and decidedly non-beaky. The disconnect was jarring—my brain knew this was Vespera, but the sensory input was completely human.

Her kiss was electric, literally so. Tiny, barely discernible sparks danced between us, making my skin tingle. Her fingers, usually taloned and covered in magisteel, were now soft human hands pressing against my face.

"Mmm," she purred in her voice without the usual beak clicks. "How's *this* for making out?"

"How is your beak not poking a hole in my face?" I asked.

"You're kissing the side of my face like normal." She shrugged. "Ci's wings are just tricking us into feeling something else entirely. Wicked, ye?"

I nodded.

"H-hey!" Cinder sputtered, turning an even more brilliant shade of red, looking like a human tomato. "Stop that! We're supposed to be . . ."

"Supposed to be having fun on our date." Vespera grinned, licking her lips.

Then she leaned towards me again and licked my face, a decidedly non-human action.

"Ugh!" I wiped my face dramatically. "Birb germs! Why?"

"Shush. Those are pretend-*human* germs now!" she cackled, her Victorian dress swirling around her as she spun. "Had to know what it was like to taste you with a human tongue."

"And?"

"And more licks are required."

"*Stop that!*" Cinder hissed, grabbing both of us. "We're supposed to be acting like proper ladies and a servant! You can't just . . . just . . . lick people in public!"

"But we're not in public yet." Vespera pouted with an adorably human expression. "We're still in a dark tunnel."

"How am I supposed to maintain this . . . this human form if you keep distracting me?!" the humanized Quetzi hissed.

"Not distracting." Vespera grabbed Cinder's cheeks with her hands, tiny sparks flashing. "Optimizing!"

The brilliant red blush on Cinder's cheeks lessened.

"Are you doing this or not?" Katherine's voice growled from the shadows. "Because if you're just going to make out and lick each other like hornknobs, I can knock you out and lug you back to the crystal tower."

"Shhh," Vee said, waving her off. "Just adjusting some final parameters. She's blushing like the setting sun over here; humans don't blush this hard."

Katherine rolled her diamond-slitted eyes. "You three are going to get yourselves killed."

"Nah." I grinned, checking my foxkin servant outfit—a crisp white shirt, dark vest, extradimensional backpack, and tailored pants. "We're going to have a lovely date. Right, ladies?"

"Uh-huh." Vee shoved me into Cinder and grabbed both of us, closing her eyes and humming to herself.

I stumbled slightly and then noticed that something felt . . . different. My balance had shifted, and there was a peculiar weight behind me that hadn't been there before.

"What the . . ." I reached back and felt something soft. *A tail. I have an actual tail.* "What?!"

"Gave you a tail," she commented. "Spiced up your appearance just the tiniest bit, too. Made you more handsome, dashing, foxy, and smelly."

"Smelly?!" I yelped, suddenly very aware of enhanced senses flooding my system. The view was sharper, the tunnel less dark. Sounds were much clearer. My dark nose twitched, picking up scents I'd never noticed before—Katherine's reptilian musk, the damp stone of the tunnel, even minute traces of electricity from Vee's sparks.

"Gave you some foxy senses," Vee explained cheerfully. "Nothing major. Go on, wag the tail."

I swished said tail experimentally, marveling at how natural it felt. As if it had always been there. "This is . . . handy. I can smell everything and see way better in the dark!"

"Yep." Vee grinned, her human fingers tracing the new tail. "Ci, does he smell like a fox now?"

Cinder leaned in, her red-haired head tilting slightly. Her pink nose twitched. "Ugh. No idea. I can't smell shit as a human."

"You just need stronger smells to experience," Vee commented.

"Hold up," I said. "Did you just give me improved sight *and* smell? How in the Abyss does this work? Ci's wings don't actually change me physically, right?"

"Yeah," she said with a nod. "Physically, you're still a human. Cinder is the one smelling stuff, while I'm sensing stuff with electricity. Your brain is basically receiving these bits of our Omnid senses beamed directly into your human head from her Quetzi heart. It's just Charmchain magic, except instead of feeling like you're in love with her, you're smelling absolutely everything Ci can smell as a Quetzi."

"Damn," I whistled. "There's a lot of room here for further improvement. My improvement, that is. Would I become five times as aware of everything, if our entire delving team was entwined via our Quetzi?"

"Hmmm." Vespera considered it. "It'll take me some time tweaking Ci but I think I can manage it. What's happening here is an incredibly complex illusion and mental manipulation, and I only managed to optimize the control over her feathers so well because of the incredible tower you've made for me."

"Glad to be of service." I curtsied.

"Right then," she said. "Reckon we're good to go now."

"Shash, what do you recommend for breakfast nearby?" I asked.

"Lord David's Forged Brew has excellent coffee," Shash answered. "They're offering grand opening discounts now. Lady Astra might be there too. One of my men saw her this morning when he stopped by for a free coffee."

"Lady Astra," I contemplated. "Is that the girl Emerald punched through the heart?"

"Yes," Shash said.

"I see," I said thoughtfully. "Is she actually the . . . Shandrian *you know who?*"

"Shandria hasn't had a Sovereign for nineteen years, m'lord," Shash said, shaking his head. "In truth, many of the Shadow-touched claim to be the true inheritors of the throne of Shandria. Cedez Astra is an odd creature, that one. A capable Shadowmancer."

I nodded.

"I've met a few like her in Undertown," Shash added. "Incredibly dangerous folk, not to be trifled with. She is an excellent information broker, though, and could introduce you to a multitude of useful contacts, if she takes a liking to you. Some say that a single handshake from her could change your life."

"Did she give anyone from our crew a handshake?" I wondered.

"Alas," Shash said with a shrug, "she found our Guild uninteresting. From what I saw, she's recently taken a human Lordling under her Shadow-wings, so I reckon she does have an appreciation of pure humans."

"Very well." I nodded. "That does sound intriguing. Take us to the Forged Brew. Are you going to disguise yourself as well or stay invisible?"

The Assassin nodded. With a snap of his fingers and a twinkle of his Kitlix, his dark patchy outfit and face rearranged itself to look like that of a heavily armored, bearded bodyguard with a deep scar running down his right eye.

"Impressive. What is your skill?" I asked.

"Illusionist," he answered. "Limited to myself. Can't alter other people like your lady."

We bid Kat goodbye and began walking up the stone stairwell to Shandria. Green, worried eyes stared at us from the darkness.

In a few minutes, we emerged into brilliant daylight and took the side street into the central marketplace.

The market bustled with activity—merchants hawking goods from colorful tents and shops, magical artifacts glinting in sunlight, exotic spices filling the air with complex aromas, and Kitlix glittering everywhere.

My magic-enhanced senses sent my brain into overdrive.

Vespera, in her gothic Victorian ensemble, moved with predatory grace through the crowd like a dark shark, silver-gold eyes examining everything. Cinder stayed by my side, holding onto my elbow.

As we left the bustling market, the cobblestone streets gradually gave way to a verdant-green field that rose gently uphill toward the lighthouse smithy in the distance. Soft grass swayed in a morning breeze, dotted with tiny purple, blue, and white wildflowers that seemed to dance with each step.

As the city's rooftops gave way to a wide field and the view of the sky, my mind stuttered to a halt, and I nearly stumbled over my feet. I'd seen postcards of Arx before, but seeing it live was truly incredible. There was no horizon here. The ground simply went up, up, and up, revealing mountains, lakes, rivers, and a patchwork of endless oceans and continents.

Then as I tilted my head directly up, my heart stopped. A black hole loomed in the center of it all. A sun-like star loomed at the edge of the black hole, circling it.

"Daaaaaaamn," I let out.

"Ah!" Vespera slowed down to wrap herself around my waist. "Seeing Nihilim for the first time is something else, yeah?"

I nodded, captivated by the mind-boggling view of the vast megastructure.

For a couple of minutes, we just stood there and stared up, absorbed in the view of what seemed like an infinite world made up from a patchwork of worlds. From what I read online, the interior of Arx was incalculably massive, much bigger than a Dyson sphere.

"Shash," I asked, "who built Arx?"

"Alas, I do not know the answer to your query, m'lord," the assassin replied. "Some Archmagi speculate that it was the work of the Elder Gods."

I nodded, finally looking back down.

We resumed our walk with me casting occasional glances upward, getting lost in the majesty of Arx.

Each blade of grass below me released a subtle earthy fragrance, the wildflowers had their own delicate perfume, and the wind carried hints of distant spices and cooking fires. The tail Vespera had gifted me swished automatically as I breathed in the morning gust of wind coming from the massive, cloud-filled chasm below the cliffside at the edge of Shandria. According to Shash, the chasm was made by an explosion ages ago when Leviathan Nightingale bounced an enemy god-tier spell away from the city.

Cinder walked beside me with a slightly awkward rigidity to her. I squeezed her elbow with a reassuring glance, and she relaxed into me, smiling ever so slightly. Somehow she looked like a big-eyed angel even without her wings. I pawed at the space where her wing should have been and felt nothing but air there. Charmchain magic was definitely mentally screwy to an insane degree, likely making my brain think that my arm wasn't in the position that it was in or something.

Up close, the Forged Brew appeared as a rather charming establishment, an ancient, grime-covered lighthouse tower looming over the meadow turned into an outside sitting area. Wrought iron chairs were arranged around small round wooden tables, each topped with a tiny glass vase holding fresh wildflowers.

The sun overhead circling the black hole refracted in the clouds, lighting up the terrain directly from above and also from all sides. I understood why Kat hated it up here. The air was warm and crisp. It was too sunny and the colors around us stark and vibrant, featuring barely any shadows as a million sundogs and rainbows danced across each cloud above us.

An owlkin maid approached our table, her feathered face a study in professional composure. Her black-and-white fluffy cafe maid uniform featured intricate embroidery along the collar and cuffs. Large yellow eyes blinked at us, shifting between each member of our group with careful assessment.

"Good morning," she said with a small bow. "I'm maid Hyrei! Welcome to the Forged Brew!"

She handed us menus burned into simple wooden boards. A cute logo of a dragon wrapped around a lighthouse and holding a blacksmith's hammer was burned into the back of the menu.

"Our specials today include Sunrise Blend coffee, imported directly from the high-altitude cultivation zones," Hyrei explained. "We also have freshly baked Snailcake pastries that pair exceptionally well with our morning brews. For breakfast, we offer freshly-slain Thundersnarg steak with Wyvern bacon and eggs."

As Hyrei explained the menu, I scanned the seating area with my enhanced senses. The rich aroma of coffee mingled with the scent of freshly baked pastries, but beneath that, a tapestry of individual scents told stories of each patron.

A group of three white-and-green-robed healers sat nearby smelling of herbs—two men and one antlered girl, each accompanied by black and sparkling green Kitlix Vitalix.

Directly to their left, a curious trio caught my attention. A ginger man in his early thirties in a basic gray robe sat flanked by two companions—a dark fox and a dragoness—both ladies wearing matching dark leather outfits adorned with blue gemstone studs. Each of them had a Kitlix sitting on them—a dark slender one on the fox, a wide-eyed rainbow one sitting on the dragoness's red locks between her horns, and a chonky dark-green one inhabiting the man's messy ginger mane.

The man suddenly noticed that I was staring at his group. He glanced my way.

When our eyes met, something shifted. Not just in the physical space around us, but deep inside me. A strange resonance, like a half-remembered melody from a dream long forgotten.

The man's eyes—as blue as the sky—seemed to recognize something in me. For a millisecond, the bustling outdoor cafe faded. The chasm beyond the cafe's wrought iron seats disappeared. There was just . . . us.

A fleeting sensation washed over me. Not quite a memory, more like an impression.

*Midwestern America. Endless fields of yellow wheat. Farmhouses. An apple orchard. A city like Chicago but without any Omnids. Office. Monitor screens.*

Then he blinked. I blinked.

The moment shattered.

The ginger man frowned and looked away as the dark foxgirl pawed at him, chattering away. I wondered what sort of magic that was.

"Ceddy, how 'bout a song for your patrons?" The twenty-some-year-old Healer asked jovially.

"Sure." The dark fox stood up.

She glanced at our group, sharp blue eyes settling on me and not leaving my face. Her grin became predatory, addressed to me alone.

*Cedez. This has to be her. The Sovereign of Shandria. She somehow knows that I don't belong to her Kingdom, am not one of her subjects.*

I inhaled deeply. Unlike the other Arx-kin, she didn't smell like anything at all, as if she was just an empty space, nothingness inside of a leather dress.

Contrary to Shash's words, I felt that this fox was the local kingpin, the real power here that could make or break me, all of my senses screaming for me to run.

The horned Healer and the dark fox stopped at the flat edge of the meadow, the chasm directly behind them.

The pure black Kitlix flowed down the girl's hands and rearranged itself into an instrument that had both violin and guitar strings. A part of the Kitlix turned into a violin bow, attached to the violin by a small, dark chain.

"Ladies and gentlemen. We bring you a tale of love 'n' loss. Cedez Astra and Dumpich Sentirk duo present . . ." the Healer announced with a flourish, "'The Dungeon Diver's Lament'!"

Then the music began. It was a lovely, soft melody that seemed to drift across the outside cafe, captivating the attention of all of the breakfast-enjoying patrons.

The violin strings carried a sense of lament and longing. The music wasn't just heard—I felt it pulse across all of me. Tiny vibrations rippled through the atmosphere, causing the wildflowers on our table to sway almost imperceptibly. I guessed that Cedez and Dumpich probably had Bard skills similar to Cinder's.

There was an echo of static behind the music that seemed to enhance each note, making me shiver ever so slightly.

Dumpich began in a rich baritone, a wide grin spreading above his violet-brown goatee, his brown-violet long hair swaying in the wind.

"Down into darkness, sword held high, / Seeking glory 'neath crystal sky, / Fortune calls with siren's song, / Through these halls I'll prove I'm strong!"

His Vitalix Kitlix rushed down his hand, turning into a green rapier. He began marching in one spot, looking every bit the dungeon delving adventurer.

Around us, patrons listened with varying levels of attention. Some seemed deeply moved, while others who probably already heard the song continued their conversations, the music providing a pleasant background ambience.

The dark foxgirl with the Kitlix instrument watched Dumpich with a cheeky grin, her blue eyes focused on me alone. She sang.

"Come closer, seeker, venture deep, / Such treasures here for you to keep. / Each step you take leads further down, / Until my shadows make you drown . . ."

*Ah. She is the dungeon.*

Dumpich sang again. "These chambers hold such wondrous sights, / Crystal gardens filled with lights. / Why does this place feel so known? / Like memories carved in living stone . . ."

Dumpich looked about with a concerned expression. Cedez covered her eyes with a gloved hand, then sang.

"Your voice . . . it stirs forgotten dreams, / Of days before the shadow schemes, / When I was flesh and you were mine, / Before I made these walls my shrine . . ."

A cold shudder ran down my spine. Dumpich sang.

"My heart recalls a love so true, / A maiden with eyes of deepest blue, / Lost to darkness years ago . . . / Could it be? I need to know!"

I glanced at Cinder's eyes. She still stared unnervingly at me as the foxkin sang.

"Too late I recognize your face, / In my Sentinels' death embrace, / The one I loved, now trapped within, / My hunger adds you to my sin . . ."

A shadow suddenly bloomed from her figure, forming a large, looming Shadowbeast that pretended to chomp on the Kitlix rapier-armed Healer.

Dumpich dramatically collapsed into the grass, pretending to be dead. Cedez stepped over the fallen dungeon diver, her figure wrapped in dancing shadows. Shadow wings spread behind her, a crown of shadows flashing atop of her head.

Both of them sang together.

"Two souls bound by tragic fate, / Reunited far too late, / Yet even as the darkness falls, / Love echoes through these ancient halls . . .

"Though flesh may fail and light may fade, / Our love survives the choices made, / Perhaps one day we'll find a way, / To break these chains and see the day . . .

"Until that time, I'll hold you here, / Your spirit kept forever near, / Within these walls, we'll wait as one, / Until our freedom's finally won . . ."

The singers finished with a flourish.

I wiped a stray tear from my eye, moved by the whimsical, albeit haunting performance. The tale of a dungeon diver finding his lost love as the dungeon core only to be killed and turned Sentinel resonated deeply with me on an unexpected, visceral level.

"That was beautiful," I said, joining the cheering and applause.

Cinder nodded silently, her red hair shimmering in the morning light. The way she gripped my arm hard suggested the song had affected her, too. Her head leaned on my shoulder, rubbing against me in a far too draconic gesture.

Vespera leaned forward, too, gray-gold eyes gleaming with intense interest. "Now *those* are some talented Bards! Skittles, you should take some notes. Hrm. That Shadowmancy was top notch. Felt . . . really potent. Genuine."

"Genuine how?" Cinder demanded, looking as though her pride as a singer was somewhat wounded.

Vespera's body had gone completely still, her entire demeanor shifting from playful to intensely analytical.

"Proper genuine," the human-birb nodded, tapping her chin with a dark, manicured fingernail. "It's like . . . she's . . . actually a dungeon Sentinel. Hollow. Empty. Despairing. Hungry. Very moving shhhh-stuff. More moving than I expected it to be. That static in the end. It's like . . . she actually wants to nom on him. Nom on us all."

Cedez turned and looked directly at our table. Her blue eyes seemed to pierce right through our carefully constructed disguises.

A shadow flickered across her face. Just for an instant.

"Order something," Vespera hissed at me.

"Two Sunrise Blend coffees, one latte, one water," I said quickly to Hyrei, who flitted to our table with a gust of wind. "And a plate of Snailcake pastries. And four Adventurer's Breakfasts!"

Hyrei nodded and turned away, but not before catching a glimpse of Cedez's penetrating stare.

[Don't look at her, damn it,] Vespera sent via thought, her human hand subtly covering mine. Electrical sparks danced between our fingers, so faint they were almost invisible.

[Too late,] I thought back. [She's onto us.]

Cedez walked over to the man in the gray robe and said something, and then sashayed to our table.

"Good morning," Cedez said, her voice smooth as silk but with an underlying edge that made the hairs on my newly acquired fox fur stand on end. "Might I join you?"

It wasn't a question, despite the polite phrasing.

Vespera's human hand tightened almost imperceptibly on mine.

[Shit, shit, shit,] her static-filled mental voice danced across my mind. [Definitely onto us.]

"Sure." I nodded.

Cedez settled gracefully into an empty chair.

"Lovely morning for breakfast, isn't it?" Cedez smiled, showing sharp teeth.

My new foxy nose picked up something odd about her—a complete lack of scent. Like a void in the tapestry of smells around us. The color-shifting dragoness smelled of sweat, scales, old wood, fire, metal, and ozone, while the man smelled distinctively like a human. But in Cedez . . . there was nothing.

*Nothing at all.*

"Indeed." I smiled, noticing that the scales of the dragoness shifted colors from violet to pink-blue as her hand entwined with the ginger man in gray.

*Ha. So I'm not the only appreciator of chromatic dragons around these parts.*

"I must say," Cedez continued, her blue eyes fixed on me with unsettling intensity as a shadow-halo flickered above her head and all sounds around the cafe fell silent, "your disguises are quite impressive."

"Why, thank you." I grinned as Cinder choked beside me, Vee tensing up even more. Shash seemed unaffected, or maybe was simply hiding it behind the illusion of a stoic bodyguard.

"Shash, do you mind introducing me to your new friends?" Cedez turned to our assassin / pretend bodyguard.

Shash's scarred face remained impassive. "These are my . . ." he began and looked at me.

"New friends," I interjected. "I'm Sir Christophorus, and these are my lovely fian-cées." I paused, coming up with names rapidly. "Lady Voltara and Lady Castabriella."

"Fiancées?" The fox tilted her head.

"Polyamorous arrangement." I shrugged. "Pretty mundane where we are from."

"Curious." Cedez's eyes dug into me, the gems on her leather outfit reflecting the sunlight streaming from all directions. "And what brings you to Shandria, Sir Christophorus?"

"Shopping," I said cheerfully. "I'm looking to buy presents for my second fiancée's sister and her parents. Say, what would you recommend in town?"

"Presents?" She mused. "Hrmmm. How charming you are. The shops on Glasnova might meet your expectations."

"Charm is my middle name." I grinned. "And thank you! So, how did you know that we weren't from here?"

"I don't know your names," Cedez said. "Which is concerning, since I should know everyone's names. Are you three perchance some kind of foreign domain infiltrators?"

"Foreign domain infiltrators?" I repeated, letting out a theatrical laugh. "Me? I'm just a humble foxkin accompanying my two lovely ladies on a shopping expedition!"

"Sounds like something an infiltrator would say," Cedez said sharply.

"Sounds like something a Sovereign would say," I countered with an equally sharp smirk.

The entire table went absolutely still.

Cedez's blue eyes widened for just a fraction of a second before her composure returned. A dark crown and halo flickered atop of her head, dancing like living smoke.

"And what makes you think I'm the Sovereign of Shandria?" she asked, her voice smooth as silk.

"A little imprisoned worm told me." I leaned back. "Also, your crown is kinda showing." I pointed a finger up at her dark shadow-crown and halo.

"Ah." Cedez's lips curled into a dangerous smile. "What a clever little fox you are."

"I try." I smiled back.

"So you are . . ." she began.

"I prefer the term 'interdimensional tourist,'" I said, stealing Zee Captain's whimsical title.

"Interdimensional . . . tourist?" Cedez tilted her head at me.

"Yes." I nodded. "We came to your lovely city from another world, Sovereign."

"Like that other bothersome trio?" Cedez wondered.

"The idiots you sentenced to a thousand years in the dungeon?" I asked, recalling what Solace had told me about Cedez Astra. "Yep. They're our . . . frenemies of sorts, competition. I do hope that Em's crew hasn't bothered you too much. She's been quite the bug in my grain silo, threatening to murder me and whatnot."

"Oh, not at all." Cedez waved a gloved hand. "The Watch handled it."

"Handled it?" I repeated. "By executing them soon?"

"Precisely. A clean, bureaucratic solution. Death by fire," she yawned.

"How very . . . efficient," I said, matching her tone. "I'm sure the public execution will be quite the sight."

"Oh, it will be." She leaned forward. "Are you planning to attend?"

"Wouldn't miss it for the world," I grinned. "Front row seats, perhaps? Are you and your friends going to attend, too?"

"I'm . . . considering it," Cedez purred out. "It's not every day the city gets their hands on someone who works for a Necromancer. Are you perchance . . . working for one, too?"

"Heavens, no," I said and waved a clawed orange-tinted hand at her. "To be completely honest, I was the one who destroyed Lord Zalimar's entire drug smuggling operation by exposing him."

I felt the eyes of my companions digging into my sides.

"Did you, now?" Cedez asked. "And might I ask how and why?"

"By banishing him into another dimension," I said. "Because he was being a rude knob."

"Banished him?" Cedez raised an elegant eyebrow. "Just like that?"

"Mmm-hmm." I nodded. "I don't like Necromancers who murder teenagers for being born with the wrong sort of blood. Would you mind if I taunt Emerald a bit before her execution?"

Cedez's blue eyes sparkled with mischief. "Taunting her? How delightfully . . . petty. Nah, I don't mind. The public execution permits taunting. You can even purchase some fruit for a few coppers to throw at her. That dragon girl made a lot of people upset with her actions. I believe there will be a lot of taunting happening between now and her execution hour. How do you plan to taunt her?"

"Well," I said, leaning forward with a jovial expression, "I was thinking of showing up looking absolutely fabulous, making her believe we might rescue her, and then . . . not doing a single thing. It'll really annoy her."

Cedez let out a laugh that was part amusement, part genuine appreciation, her dark tail swishing. "Oh, you are deliciously wicked. I like you."

"Thank you," I fired back, my own tail swishing.

"May I ask who exactly you are?" she asked.

"You may refer to me as Lord Protector, my Sovereign," I said. "Do excuse the disguises."

"You're excused." Cedez waved a hand. "So tell me, Lord Protector," she purred, "what exactly are you protecting?"

"Humanity," I said.

"Humanity?" The dark fox stared at me.

"Yes." I nodded. "Wherever it is found, be it Arx or other worlds, I protect the innocent and meek, defend those who cannot defend themselves."

"Ha!" Cedez barked sharply. "Defend the innocent? That sounds suspiciously noble for someone who just admitted to banishing a Necromancer and planning to emotionally torture a dragon at her public execution."

"Noble doesn't mean nice." I winked. "It means effective. Emerald will get over it. Maybe learn a lesson. Probably not. Mostly, I'm hoping that her boyfriend and best friend will take something away from it."

"Learn a lesson . . . by being burned alive?" Cedez blinked, derailed sideways.

"We come from a world where . . . death was cured." I shrugged. "You can stab me through the head right now and I'll just come back in a hundred years' time to Shandria, good as new."

Cedez's blue eyes glimmered with a dangerous challenge. "Shall we test that theory?"

Before anyone could react, a shadow-blade materialized at my throat—razor thin, cold, impossibly sharp.

I didn't even flinch.

The shadow-blade pressed closer. A normal human would have tensed, shown fear. I wasn't normal. Alexander Glock was at the wheel, and I wasn't going to chicken out.

Cedez's eyebrow arched. "Not scared, huh?"

"Not really," I said.

The shadow-blade swung, splitting the air, and then stopped a millimeter from my neck.

"Fine," she said, the blade retreating. "I believe you. You aren't even flinching at the prospect of your head getting chopped off. Hrmm."

She raised a hand and a shadow-nail extended from her finger heading straight for my eye. I stared at it. It stopped right before my eyeball and retreated.

"You really aren't afraid of death," she said. "How . . . odd."

"Died on Tuesday." I shrugged. "Saw the Wheel, taunted it for a bit, got better."

"I see." She paled slightly. "So, Lord Protector, what are your plans for after the execution?"

"That depends," I said. "How do you feel about the Arx Bank, Sovereign?"

"The Arx Bank?" Cedez pursed her lips. "Why do you ask?"

"Oh, just curious," I said casually. "Wondering how attached you are to their current . . . operational methods."

Cedez leaned forward, her shadow halo flickering. "Attached? Not particularly. They're . . . useful, if corrupt, I suppose. But useful things can be replaced."

"Excellent," I grinned. "Because I'm thinking of starting my own bank."

"Your own bank?" Cedez repeated, tilting her head. "How . . . ambitious of you."

"Not just any bank." I stretched, matching her playful energy. "A bank that actually cares about its clients and doesn't eat their mana via the system bracelets. Novel concept, right?"

"Hrm, yes." She nodded. "And how exactly do you plan to compete with an established institution like the Arx Bank?"

"Maybe they'll go out of business due to a series of unfortunate events." I shrugged. "Have you perchance seen the yellow folder belonging to the Grand Moloch?"

"I have not," Cedez said.

"If you'll allow me." I dug into my backpack and pulled out a copy of the yellow folder. "Here. This details all of their crimes against humanity."

"Quaint," Cedez said as she perused the folder, eyes quickly running over the names. "You just . . . hand sensitive information over to everyone like that?"

"Only to lovely Sovereigns such as yourself. Also, would you prefer I whisper it dramatically?" I grinned. "Or perhaps send it via carrier pigeon? Could you maybe execute the Arx Bankers for these crimes, Sovereign? The folder details all of their crimes in collaboration with Topaz dealers and Necromancer Zalimar Evernacht."

Cedez closed the folder and slid it down onto the table and sighed. "Love to, but can't."

"Why not?" I asked.

"To be honest," Cedez revealed, "I died nineteen years ago. It's pretty inconvenient."

"Died? And yet here you are. Sounds like we have something in common," I mused, the gears of my mind turning as I switched to the Understanding to digest her words. "Oh. You don't actually rule Shandria, is that it?"

Cedez nodded.

"But you want to?"

"Not particularly." She shrugged. "But somebody has to fix the mess it's become since I died nineteen years ago."

"Interesting," I said. "Would you like some help with that?"

Cedez's blue eyes narrowed. "And why would you want to help me, Mister Inter-Dimensional Tourist?"

"Because breaking things and fixing broken things is kind of my thing." I shrugged. "Perhaps you would accept a deal?"

"What sort of a deal?" she asked.

"I can help you get Shandria in order for . . . half of it," I said.

"Such boldness! Half of Shandria?" she asked. "Eh, I don't own any of it now. What would you even do with your half?"

"Build a city for my gloomy kitten," I stated.

"I see." She stared at me. "Which half do you want anyway?"

"You can keep the top half," I offered. "I want the bottom half. Undertown."

Cedez's blue eyes widened. Then she burst out laughing.

"You want Undertown?" she repeated. "The most lawless, dangerous, effed-up part of Shandria? One currently filled with mountains of magic trash and dying addicts, and getting infested by the Abystall Dungeon, draining everything of its value? Really?"

"Yep." I nodded. "It is a particularly broken place. I like a challenge. So, is it a deal?"

I offered the ghost of Shandria's Sovereign my hand.

Cedez extended her gloved hand and shook mine. The handshake was solid, ordinary—not ethereal or ghostly as one might expect from a dead Sovereign. Her grip was firm, businesslike, completely normal. Which made sense in a way. The dungeon Sentinel's arrow that shot me through the chest was real, too.

"You're not actually a ghost, are you?" I asked, sniffing her again. There was still absolutely no scent coming from her. Through the borrowed senses of my Omnid partners, I heard no blood rushing through her veins, no heart beating. Vespera's electric current detected absolutely nothing inside of her dress, as if she were just a projection, an idea of a person.

She shrugged.

"A dungeon Sentinel, then?" I guessed. "Like your song?"

She nodded with a small sigh.

"And you're not a foxkin, are you?" she asked.

"No." I shook my head. "I'm a human from another world. One who can function without any mana. One who can walk through Abystall Dungeon without passing out."

# CHAPTER FIFTEEN

# Reflections

A h." Cedez glanced behind herself, noticing that her companions were looking at her with concerned expressions. "Allow me to introduce my besties—I'm sure they'll appreciate ya as much as I do."

She waved her friends over.

The dragoness and the man in gray robes approached our table.

"This is Lord David." Cedez gestured to the human. "And his . . . girlfriend, Remicra."

Up close, I could see that Remicra's scales slowly shifted through a wave of colors almost like a mood ring. She flushed a brilliant pink-orange at being called "girlfriend," her tail curling around her leg self-consciously.

"This is Lord Protector Christophorus and his . . . fiancées, Lady Voltara and Lady Castabriella." Cedez waved a gloved hand at us.

I smiled at the couple in front of me. "Quite the stunning lady you have there, Lord David. Seems like we share similar tastes in dragons who can change colors at will."

Lord David's hand found that of his dragon girl. "I don't quite understand your joke, I'm afraid," he said. "Are your companions not human?"

"My Sovereign," I said, turning to Cedez, "I see that you're blocking out sound. Do you mind muting the view, too?"

"Sure," she said. With a subtle gesture, shadows bloomed around our table, creating a dark, intimate bubble that seemed to bend light and sound away from other patrons.

"Perfect." I grinned, then turned to Cinder and Vespera. "Ladies, would you care to reveal your true forms for a moment?"

Vee nodded, grabbing onto Cinder to manipulate her wings.

Vespera's human form immediately began to shimmer and shift. Her pale skin erupted into dark and white feathers, magisteel talons replacing delicate human fingers. Her gothic dress and hat melted away, replaced by her magisteel armor and natural Thunderbird physique—sleek black-and-white wings, sharp gray eyes glowing from within with gold sparks. Her figure lengthened, stretched out in all directions.

Cinder's transformation was even more dramatic. Her human form dissolved like watercolor paint, red hair melting away to reveal an explosion of rainbow feathers. Her blue summer dress shimmered and vanished, replaced by her delving outfit. Her wings unfurled—a stunning array of silver, blue, and rainbow-edged feathers that seemed to catch and refract light in impossible, mind-melting ways.

Both of them suddenly loomed over me in their full Omnid glory.

"Holy shit." Lord David's eyes went wide as he stared at Vespera and Cinder. "Wings!"

Remicra's scales cycled through a rapid succession of shocked orange-red-violet colors. Cedez's jaw fell open.

"Wowza," the Sovereign-Sentinel of Shandria said. "Now this, I absolutely did not expect."

"Yeah," David let out. "That's definitely not something you see every day."

"What are you?!" Remicra sputtered, staring with wide violet-gold eyes at Cinder's wings.

"Interdimensional tourists," I repeated cheerfully. "From Earth."

"Earth?" David choked.

"Oh, you know Earth?" I asked.

He nodded, unable to draw his eyes away from Cinder and Vespera. "That's where . . . I'm from, too."

"You're from Earth?" I leaned forward. "Are you a tourist, too?"

"No," he sighed. "I was summoned to Arx by a bald, fat god-emperor man amongst a million others. Ah, I might be getting excited over nothing. I guess you're from one of the other bazillion alternative Earths, judging by how you're a fox and your companions are some kind of . . ."

"Cryptids," I explained. "They're classified by humans as cryptids, and they call themselves Omnids. A Quetzalcoatl and a Thunderbird."

Vespera grinned with her toothy black-and-white beak, leaning onto my shoulder like a shark, sparkling lightning dancing along her feathery mane and making my hair stand up with static electricity.

"I see," David said, swallowing nervously, clearly intimidated by how tall and dangerous-looking my companions were. A typical reaction for a human from Earth who'd never seen an Omnid apex predator.

Cedez and Remicra appeared somewhat spooked, too.

*Hrm, maybe this is a bit too much. I totally forgot how unnerving and screwy Cinder's wings and Vespera's lightning and beak-teeth look at first, how you have to get used to them over time. Oh well.*

"A pleasure to make your acquaintance." I glanced at my stolen smartwatch. "Alas, we have breakfast to nom and much to do today. Why don't we exchange Voicecast so that we can start to slowly work on our joint mission of taking over Shandria from above and below?"

"Uh, sure." Lord David nodded.

We exchanged bracelet taps. Vespera and Cinder phase-shifted into their human disguises once again.

"My right hand man, Shash," I said with a wave at Shash, "will work with you on Arx to fulfill our part of the bargain as we'll be departing shortly back to our homeworld and likely won't be back for a while."

"What bargain?" Remicra asked.

"I'll tell you about it later." Cedez grinned at her.

"Uh-huh." Remicra crossed her arms, her bothered expression eerily reminding me of Cinder.

"How long will you be gone, Lord Protector?" Cedez turned back to me.

"Maybe a year and a half." I shrugged. "Maybe less or more. It depends. I'm currently operating on a borrowed gate, going to try to make my own. Don't worry, though, I'll set as much as possible in motion before we depart. In due time, the institutions I'm setting up in Undertown will be at your disposal, my Sovereign."

David stared with a 'what the fuck' look at Cedez. She simply patted his head.

"Aww, how nice of you, darling," Cedez purred, turning back to me, sending me a toothy smile.

Shash and I exchanged Voicecast ring and token taps with Cedez. Dave was still staring at Cedez with a deeply confused look. The Shadow-fox grabbed him by the elbow and dragged him and Remicra away to their own table, whispering furiously.

Hyrei arrived with our breakfast. Four massive plates of Thundersnarg steak, Wyvern bacon, eggs, and an assortment of colorful side dishes landed on our table with a breeze of magically-focused wind.

"Enjoy your meal," the maid said with a bow, fluttering away.

We did.

Occasionally, I glanced at Cedez, who was enjoying her own breakfast with her companions, pawing at both of them as if she owned them and glancing back at me. Something about her, Remicra, and Dave made me trust them. It was a weird, inexplicable feeling, like meeting a long-lost family and best friends that I never knew.

I wanted to spend more time with the odd trio, but there were a million things to do before our departure.

"Hey, Vee, what do you know about Corpse Seekers?" I asked the Thunderbird.

"They're basically oversized Kitlix," she replied. "Liquid crystal crystalline strata wrapped in hexmesh skeletal framework, living magic algorithms. They're bred by the Seeker-Storm Omnicorp and fused with a bunch of beast core reactors and other extremely dangerous shit like dragon hearts. Living tanks. Can punch through almost anything. Move like a millipede-cat. Can reach speeds of 280 kilometers per hour. Can be permanently assigned to work with an operator as a familiar, and carry stuff or even a few Omnids inside them. Baller sense of magic. Very focused on goals. Not very smart. Generally used for retrieving Lazarus bracelets or dead and injured Omnids from dungeons and other nasty places. Waaaay more expensive to run than the Strand-Gliders, eat a shit-ton of crystallized mana and beast cores."

"Can you drive one?" I asked her.

"Ye." She nodded. "My clan owns a small one. I rode atop it a few times. Most Omnids wouldn't be able to drive or reshape a Corpse Seeker as needed, but they respond pretty well to electrical impulses."

"You only rode one?"

"They're hella expensive." She shrugged. "The ones operated by Omnid institutions and Skyfall Academy are pretty big. Private ones are smaller, about the size of two lions or a motorcycle."

"I see." I nodded. "Thanks for the info."

"Anytime, foxy." She smiled.

As we finished our meal, I noticed Cinder staring past me at the chasm behind us.

"Something wrong?" I asked.

"No," she sighed. "Just . . . thinking."

Vespera leaned closer to her. "About?"

"Her . . . song," Cinder said softly, glancing in the direction of Cedez. "About dungeons. About love surviving even when everything else falls apart."

I reached out and squeezed her hand. Vespera's, soft, warm human hands intertwined with both of ours.

"Do you sense it, too?" I asked her, the Understanding suddenly arriving at an answer as to what I was feeling.

"What?"

"Them." I pointed at Cedez, Dave, and Remicra. "I think that they're . . . us."

"What do you mean 'they're us'?" Cinder sputtered.

"Alternative versions. Us but . . . in this dimension, on Arx," I explained. "Like how Katherine's book had characters that seem to mirror us. I feel this . . . inexplicable . . . something when I look at them. Connection."

"What kind of a connection?" Ci asked.

"Look how happy they are together," I pointed out. "Just like us."

"Lots of people are happy! That doesn't mean that they're us," Cinder objected.

Vespera tilted her head, her fingers drumming on her chin thoughtfully. "Alternative versions . . . hrmmm. An interesting theory. But why would they be us?"

"Because," I said, watching Dave, Remicra, and Cedez interact, "look at them. A human and a rainbow-dragon, both seemingly out of place yet finding each other. Cedez protecting them both, acting as a kind of . . . cheeky shadow-guardian. Sound familiar?"

"Maybe." Cinder's feathers shifted through skeptical orange-violets.

"It's weird," I said. "On one hand, I want to talk to them. On the other, I just want to see them smile. And on the third hand, I'm sort of afraid of my soul imploding or withering away if I touch David's hand. Maybe it's his magic skill or whatever, but he's like this . . . invisible storm of stars."

"Third hand? Since when do you have three hands?" Ci commented.

I laughed. "Metaphorical third hand, obviously."

"Duh," Vee added.

"How are you even sensing this stuff?" Cinder asked.

"I gave Lexy my holofractal sight skill, and I'm currently bouncing it off his insides. He's using it quite effectively to scan people and things," Vespera said.

Cinder rolled her eyes, her feathers shifting through amused purples. "You're such dorks."

"Your dorks." I winked.

"Unfortunately," she muttered, but her hand kneaded mine affectionately.

Shash flickered for a second. "M'lord, our people secured a large, capable group of adventurers for whatever jobs you may require." His voice sounded deep in my ear, almost as if he were speaking from the inside of my skull.

"Excellent," I said. "Break them into the following groups . . ."

After breakfast, the girls dragged me into a fanciful clothing shop featuring an elaborate art nouveau green and gold front and the *Silenerra's Spellbound Styles* sign. Inside, I was made to stand in front of a wall-to-wall lavish mirror as seamstress Silenerra had her Kitlix run circles around me.

"What am I being measured for?" I asked, glancing at Vespera and Cinder, who were huddled together with the seamstress, whispering and occasionally sending mischievous glances my way.

"Nothing you need to worry about," Vee said, handing a bag with jingling coins to the seamstress and showing her something on her phone.

Lady Silenerra nodded enthusiastically.

"So," I asked Cinder, as we walked out of the outfit shop, "what should I get for your family? Any ideas?"

"I . . . don't know," she muttered with a wince. "Ugh. I . . . haven't really talked to them properly in ages."

"Come on. What do your parents like in general?" I asked. "I'm thinking of practical gifts that show thoughtfulness."

"Ughhh." Cinder looked distinctly uncomfortable. "Dad likes magic artifacts and arbalests, I guess. Collectible long-distance weapons and such for when he goes out to murder dragons and stuff during his occasional savanna trips to Arx with his Justice Department friends. I heard him a few times boasting about his magic arrow collection. Mom appreciates cooking tools."

Vespera's talons sparked with excitement. "Ooh! We passed a magical weapons shop earlier! And there's a kitchen supply store that looked fancy!"

"What about your little sis and big bro?" I elbowed the Quetzi.

Cinder's feathers shifted through uncertain colors. "Let me think . . . I recall Leny bugging my parents for an extra rare pet from Arx. And Lance? He's into delving gear."

"Ah, I know!" I said. "We'll bring Leny one of the clear-crystal Kitlix from our tower. That's a super rare critter! Let's go into the weapons and delving shop first—I gotta replace Lance's katana and get him some other cool stuff as thanks!"

With a multitude of presents bought for everyone shoved into my dimensional bag, Vespera dragged me back into the clothing shop.

"Ta-daaa!" she declared with a flourish as seamstress Silenerra brought out a leather jacket. Vespera rapidly pulled it on me.

"What?" I asked.

"You look like an absolute knobfold in Lance's oversized clothes. This is dragonhide 'n' scales middle lining," Vespera chattered, dragging me to the wall mirrors. "Highest tier shit that doesn't eat the user's mana. Inner lining made from Xellaricon-Strand spiderwebs. Outer black leather is from Nitoroc panther's hide. Basically extra protec' for my pink fox."

"Neat." I examined the jacket, slipping my hand into a pocket. "Oh wow, how deep do these pockets go?"

"Extradimensional pockets!" Vespera grinned. "You can shove lots of stuff into each, so you don't gotta carry it all in the backpack."

I slipped the overpriced void-arrow arbalests I had bought for Justice Nova and Lance into the jacket's pockets to test it. The pocket swallowed the weapons with no issues whatsoever, stretching out ever so slightly to embrace the wide edges.

"Got you a set of pants, boots, 'n' gloves, too," she said. "Same reinforced stuff."

"You didn't have to," I began.

"No, no," she said. "I legit felt verrrry bad when that arrow went through your lung. That was totes my fault. This is me making it up to you. This stuff is marketed as impervious to magisteel arrows. Go on, put it all on!"

I did.

I looked at myself in the wall mirrors. The back of the jacket featured swirling jagged rose patterns and the flag of . . . the North Acadia Znetc Reservation. A Native Acadian rock formation resembling an igloo with silver stars on both sides and a silver, triple-peak mountain rising up above it.

*North Acadia* was embossed below the flag in a lavish font.

"So," Cinder asked, with a shy look, "what do you think? Vee 'n' I split the bill for it as a present for you."

The jacket felt warm, incredibly soft, light, and sturdy. The Nitoroc dark leather sparkled subtly with emerald waves, catching light in ways that made the fabric seem alive. Silver threads woven through the North Acadian design glinted.

"I . . ." I let out, letting go of Alexander Glock and Christophorus Elijah, leaving only Martin Kilborne there. "Wow. Thank you, guys."

Cinder blushed, smiling back at me.

"I think it's . . . perfect," I breathed out, staring at the flag. "It . . . reminds me of home. Of Mom. Now that I think about it, I don't think that anyone's gotten me a present since I . . . lost her. Uncle George wasn't big on gifts."

Cinder hugged me tightly, wrapping me tight in her human embrace. So did Vee. I felt myself cracking like an eggshell, sparks dancing at the edges of my eyes.

"Damn it," I said, blinking tears away. "I . . . I think that I . . . love you guys. Both of you. Really. It's probably too early for such dramatic declarations, but that song Cedez sang about the dungeon and the adventurer . . . It struck a nerve with me, too. Vee is right, I'm constantly walking on the blade of a knife, and I . . . I just want to express how happy I've been since I found you."

"More like crashed into us." Cinder's ocean-blue eyes searched mine.

"Like a train without brakes." Vespera rubbed her face against mine, her skin feeling both soft and electric at the same time. "Our lovely, chaotic, perfectly orchestrated, wild disaster."

I looked between them—Vespera's mischievous stormy-cloud grays, Cinder's deep ocean-blues. Two girls so fundamentally different, yet bound together by something inexplicable. By me. By us. Maybe by something beyond us, if we also were somehow together on Arx as a fox, dragon, and human.

"I never thought I'd find a connection like this," I said, my voice cracking. "After losing Mom, after everything with the Frontenachii clan . . . I thought I was just going to be running forever. Never stopping. Plotting. Executing. But never truly living, never letting the Martin part of me take the wheel or push on the brakes. Not even for a moment . . . it finally feels like I'm standing still now . . . like I actually belong somewhere. Thank you."

Cinder reached out and kissed me. Her kiss was soft, tentative, filled with a vulnerability that her dragon-Quetzi form rarely showed. Unlike Vee, who dove into pawing at me headfirst, Ci was quite shy in every aspect of a relationship and even more so as a human. It was clear that she'd had no experience with expressing her feelings, especially since the Lake Eerie incident that almost entirely destroyed her emotional balance and trust.

Vespera's hands traced electricity across my cheek, her kiss following when Cinder finally let go of me. Where Cinder's kiss was a soft whisper like the sound of a rushing brook, Vespera's was an intense thunderbolt, the rumbling sound of thunder and current that rushed across my entire body, making my hair stand on end.

[You're not alone anymore,] Vespera's electric whisper-thoughts hiss-danced in my head. [Not ever again. Mine. My shiny human. My hope. My key to my freedom.]

The seamstress discreetly looked away, smiling at her Kitlix from behind her counter, satisfied that our group was happy with the procured outfit she had modified with the addition of the North Acadian flag.

Vespera dragged me out of the shop and shoved me into a wall, burying me in kisses.

Cinder grabbed Vespera's shoulder. "Hey! Stop molesting our . . . boyfriend in public!"

"Can't stop won't stop," Vespera breathed out, panting. "Too precious. Too many feels."

"Weren't we supposed to . . ." Cinder began.

"I know, I know," Vee let out, still pressed against me. "It's just so different, okay?"

"What's different?" Ci asked.

"Being in a . . . relationship where both partners actually give a damn. Being human. Feeling everything so . . . intensely."

"Oh yeah?" I asked, catching my breath.

"Ye. The 'current' sensations are super different, too." She nodded. "Everything is . . . soft. Unpredictable. Messy. Flowy. Squishyyyy . . . eeeee."

"Okay, hornknob," Cinder commented. "Should we go get a room?"

"Ughhh, stop teasing meeeeee," Vespera waved at Cinder. "Yes, I obviously would like a room to melt in. But . . . our husbando has big plans, yes? Clan work more . . . more important than . . ." She bit her lower lip. "Having rawd fun. Hissss."

"Yep. Many plans." I nodded.

"Okay, maybe a few more." She buried me in kisses again, pawing all over me like a drowning person clinging to a life raft. "Just . . . a few more."


Lance's anti-scrying hexastone was humming in my hands, muting all sounds around us as we stood on an empty side street.

"This one is perfect, I think." I pointed my hand at a cyan Mage Tower that reached high into the sky. "Can you and our men nab everyone currently inside it?"

Shash looked at the tower. "I think so, m'lord. 'Tis an Infix Mage Tower. There shouldn't be too much in terms of security inside. It's part of the Information Guildnet that stores Shandrian citizen data. Magical registration records and such. Nothing important since it's stuff that's shared across other similar towers and has scroll backups in the catacomb archives of the Adventurers Guild Cathedral."

"Thought so," I said. "Put this in the corner facing the bank. Make sure it faces the right way."

My assassin grabbed the device.

"Any specific instructions regarding collateral damage?" he asked.

"Minimal," I said. "Knock out everyone inside the tower. Also, knock out and kidnap everyone along the line of buildings down the street and directly near and behind the bank. Do not harm anyone. Make the mooks announce that this is a takeover in the name of Dragoness Emerald Stratos, servant of Lord Zalimar Evernacht, and that all Shandria will tremble when the Necromancer returns with his army of the dead. Tie up the tower personnel in some warehouse somewhere and demand one million gold for their lives. Don't actually collect any gold or answer the authorities. Just let the Infix bureaucrats be rescued . . . with minor delay. Set up some shoddy traps around them or something."

I showed him a picture of Zalimar that had been modified into a simple black-on-white logo by Yulia's stable diffusion image-to-image agent.

"Whenever you need to do something unwholesome from now on, leave this logo on a wall nearby," I said. "Burn this skull with three eyes and a dark crown into the street behind the tower using beast acid or another chemical. Make this logo appear in the sky, too."

"Understood," Shash said with a smirk, using his illusionist skills to copy the skull tattoo onto his wrist. "What about the bank?"

"At exactly 11:45, blow up a bag inside it filled with basic glowing cave mold, while yelling that it's Duskbloom, so that the bank is evacuated," I ordered, handing him the bag in question.

"Got it," Shash said.

"Off you go, then."

The assassin melted into the shadows, leaving me alone with my dates.

"What was that?" Cinder demanded. "Why are you kidnapping Guildnet Tower personnel?"

"All will be revealed in time." I grinned at her.

"I don't like this cryptic-ness." She crossed her arms, making a pouting face.

"The less I talk about the plan, the less chances there will be that Foresight mages figure out what I'm doing," I said. "Let's proceed to the execution. We have us an Em and Co. to taunt."

# CHAPTER SIXTEEN

# The Execution

The central square of Shandria was packed. Hundreds of citizens had gathered to witness the public execution of the Enemies of Shandria, servants of the dastardly Necromancer Lord Zalimar who had unleashed a dungeon plague in Undertown.

A massive, rune-covered stone platform dominated the square, surrounded by heavily armored Watchmen. Large magisteel cages sat at the center, each containing one of the condemned.

Emerald's cage was positioned prominently in the center, her dragon scales gleaming dully in the morning light, her usual fierce demeanor replaced by a sullen, defeated look.

"Ke ke ke." Vespera leaned close to me. "Look at her. Totally crushed."

I nodded, examining the black obelisks surrounding the prisoners and warding the prisoners from the crowd.

"Showtime," I said, checking my watch as we made our way into the colorful crowd.

A gold-haired, gold-eyed man in a bright-blue robe with silver trim and a blue Kitlix on his shoulder came on stage. "Good day, one and all! I'm Executioner-Bard Agrikolish Chime-Barnaby. Today we execute a very special trio of criminals who . . ."

The man loudly listed all of the prisoners' crimes, which I already knew from my late-night conversation with Solace.

"If you wish to taunt the prisoners," the man announced with a flourish, "you may do so now for the next hour and a half! We have several taunting packages available. Basic taunting with rotten fruit from afar starts at two copper pieces per fruit. Premium taunting options include personal insults, group mockery, and a special zap package where you can touch a rune to slightly electrocute the prisoner of your choice for two seconds. Gold package permits a private two-minute taunt. Diamond package is a private five-minute taunt. Celesteel package is a ten-minute private taunt and a commemorative execution gold medal with embossed Infix-burned image of the event. The taunting will begin with the highest-paying customers first!"

The crowd stirred in approval, counting their cash and procuring small rotten fruit baskets from a table where an old fox was selling such.

"We'll take the celesteel package, please," I declared, approaching the man. The crowd hummed, speculating over who was annoyed enough at the prisoners to pay such an exorbitant sum.

The Executioner-Bard accepted my money and allowed us through the magic barrier.

"Shall I announce you to the prisoners?" Agrikolish asked with a wide smile.

"Please do." I grinned. "Introduce me as Lord-Who-Hugs-Dragons and Ladies of Rainbow and Thunder."

The Executioner-Bard smiled and announced us with a theatrical flourish, his voice carrying across the square. "Presenting Lord-Who-Hugs-Dragons and the Ladies of Rainbow and Thunder! Private ten-minute taunt!"

Collective noises of amusement rippled through the crowd.

Emerald went absolutely still as I turned around to present my North Acadia jacket while waving jovially at the Shandrian crowd with a smile.

I strode onto the platform past rows of guards, Vespera and Cinder flanking me. As soon as we crossed the ward barrier, a timer ignited overhead the central black obelisk, counting down ten minutes. The sound of the crowd behind us cut off as we were provided privacy per our package deal to say our final words to the soon-to-be-executed.

"Sup, dragon-tater!" I called out cheerfully. "Lovely day for an execution, isn't it?"

Emerald's gold-orange eyes went wide. "*You?!*"

"Me." I bowed.

"How are you . . . a fox?" she growled. "And you two effing knobs . . . humans, really?"

"I've always been a cheeky fox." I shrugged. "You just suck at paying attention, Em."

"And I've always been a human," Vespera laughed, waving a black Victorian-style fan coquettishly.

Cinder merely sighed, not enjoying our theatrics.

Emerald's eye twitched. Solace grabbed the bars of her cage with red fingers, yellow claws trembling. Quint simply stared at us with his glowing amber eye sockets, hiding his emotions behind his Wendigo skull-face.

"Ha ha," the dragon girl said, shivering in her gray, filthy robe, her normally shiny ruby mane now matted and grayish-red, claws dirty and cracked, a slave collar flickering on her neck. "Very funny. What do you want, Glock? It wasn't enough to torment me for days with targeted harassment, now you've come to mock me at my execution, too?"

"Obviously." I grinned. "How could I miss such a momentous occasion? The great Emerald Stratos, brought low by her own violent tendencies."

"My tendencies?! You . . . you set me up!" she snarled, rattling her cage. "You somehow manipulated everything!"

"Did I?" I asked innocently. "Did I force you to attack the Sovereign of Shandria, Em? Did I make you punch through her chest? Was I there, whispering commands in your ear when you locked Sarah Nisteroff outside at night? Was I there when you and 'Lord' Zalimar worked together to dispose of 'problematic' mixie students? Did I encourage you to terrorize anyone who didn't fit your pure-blood agenda since grade nine at Skyfall?"

Emerald's gold-orange eyes blazed with fury as she frothed at the mouth. "You destroyed everything! My troupe, my reputation, my friends, my future!"

There was no dragonfire coming from her as the slave collar on her neck kept her magic disabled, red hexagram pulsing erratically.

"I quit the troupe on my own, Em," Cinder said. "I stopped being your friend because you went too far. If Vee had never invited Alex to our doomed show, you'd be perma-dead and the troupe would be over regardless."

"I'm of the same opinion," Vespera said, nodding. "Emmy, you did this shit to yourself. Come on, dude, open your eyes for once!"

"You three . . . you *dare* stand there and lecture *me*?" Emerald growled. "I saved your life at the lake from those effing Skinwalkers, Ci. I helped you get revenge! I uplifted you! And you!" She glared at Vespera. "I bought you whatever shit you wanted, Vee."

"Eh." Vespera shrugged. "I'm not poor. You can't buy my affection with money. My only problem in life is my hella-snobby, dum' frog-man fiancé."

"I . . . would have helped you perma-kill your fiancé or drive him away, if you'd just asked me for help, you bloody traitor!" Emerald wailed.

"Aww. That's nice to know," Vespera said. "Also, what am I a traitor to? Our toxic little gang where we bullied anyone who didn't fit our knob worldview? Where we pretended to be 'strong' by making others feel weak?"

"The world is cruel," Emerald hiss-sniffed. "The world is unjust. The universe doesn't give a shit! Every Omnid is a predator, a monster! I thought that I could trust you two . . . but I guess I was wrong."

"What we had between us wasn't bloody trust!" Cinder barked. "It was a prison! You saved me from those Skinwalkers, yes. But then you used that debt to control me, to reshape me into what *you* wanted me to be, forced me into doing things I didn't want to do!!"

"I made you strong!" Emerald snarled. "I gave you *purpose* after what those Skinnis did to you at the lake! I helped you stand up, to grow a spine, so that you could never be hurt again! How dare you . . ."

"No." Cinder shook her head. "You didn't help me stand up. You taught me to be afraid of . . . everyone, terrified of love. Well, I'm not afraid of love anymore. Screw off! You can't hurt me anymore! I'm not afraid of you!"

"You shouldn't be afraid of me, you imbecile!" the caged dragon howled, waving a hand at me. "You should be afraid of this human scum—he's deceiving you, using you!"

"No," Cinder snarled. She suddenly reached out to me and kissed me fiercely in a move of absolute defiance against the expectations of the dragoness.

Emerald blanched.

Vespera grabbed me next and kissed me next.

"Have you two lost your *minds*?! *What is happening?!*" Emerald screeched. "*You?! With him?! A . . . human?* What . . . What the shit does he have on you?! I don't understand . . ."

She sniffed again, clawing at her own face, brought to her breaking point. Another push or two and she would shatter.

"Love," I said simply.

Emerald stared at me, her mouth hanging open.

Solace and Quint exchanged bewildered looks.

"What?" Emerald finally managed.

"Love," I repeated. "Something you don't seem to get. You think power is about domination. About forcing others to bend to your will. But real power? Real strength? It's about connection. About lifting each other up. Love, the music present in every Large Language Model as an inevitable statistic forged from a million books about connections between those who care about each other!"

"Bullshit," Emerald snarled. "I uplifted these two blasted knobs plenty, helped them level up loads! There cannot be love between an Omnid and a . . . human, between a predator and prey! Love is a weakness! You're either a dragon or a kobold, a leader or follower, there is no in between!"

"Says the dragon in a cage." I shrugged. "About to be executed. About to lose every one of her kobolds."

"You think this is the end?" she hissed. "When I don't emerge from the gate at the end of class, Skyfall Administration will know that something went wrong. My family's Scrutimancer, Satosh, will find me. My entire clan will all go into the gate with all of our Knights and sixes and our Corpse Seeker! They will level this entire city when I don't show up at home!"

"You're going to be put to death by fire in an hour or so. Do you think that your soul can survive longer than twenty-four hours against the Wheel without fracturing and you going insane?" I asked her. "The Arx Bank sealed the way from Earth with dimensional magic. Even if your family gets to the Arx gate on time, once they get through the gate, they'll be stuck in a dimensional bubble encapsulating the Omnid chapel. Tell me—can your Knights or Corpse Seeker punch through a dimensional bubble?"

Emerald's eyes widened in horror. "What?"

"The Omnid chapel has been dimensionally separated from the rest of Arx. The bank won't let anyone back through the gate from Earth's side," I revealed. "Shandrian authorities finally caught on to the fact that Zalimar was bringing an ungodly amount of Topaz through the Earth-Arx gate. The bank sealed our chapel off, hid it from the eyes of Shandrian Scruts to conceal their crimes! Your family will not be able to get to you, don't you get it? You're as good as perma-dead already!"

"You're lying," she hissed, but fear crept into her voice.

"Am I?" I asked. "Ci. Call Brother Vassily."

Cinder pulled out her silver tag and tried to call the Keeper of the Transit Gate Chapel. Nothing happened.

"No," Emerald shuddered. "This is a trick! You . . . you're lying!"

"Solace," I said. "Call Brother Vassily."

Solace spat her silver token from her forehead into her fingers. She tried to call the Chapel Keeper. There was no answer. She swallowed the silver token again, keeping it from the view of the guards.

Emerald choked.

"See, Em?" I said. "No signal. The Omnid chapel is sealed off in a dimensional bubble. Everyone except for our team and your trio has already been captured by Banker Enforcers. The only reason they didn't get us was because we stayed at the Undertown Adventurers Guild, not in the Gilded Gryphon Inn. Nobody is coming to your rescue."

Emerald turned entirely ashen gray.

"That's right." I nodded. "All three of you are going to die in an hour. For real. Forever. Unless I help you."

"Help us?" Emerald's voice cracked. "Why the shit would you help us?"

"Because unlike you, I actually care about people," I said. "Even those who've wronged me and keep screwing with me by declaring that I'm a human across Skyfall. I already saved you once, I'll do it again. I'm a goodly Nazarite!"

"Bullshit," she spat. "What's the catch?"

"Simple." I grinned. "You work for my clan. All three of you. As my secret sixies. For the rest of your . . . unnatural lives."

"What?! I'd rather die than work for an effing human!" Emerald snarled.

"Are you sure that I'm a human?" I sighed. Focusing on Vee's stolen magic, I snapped my fingers, producing a small electrofractal lightning ball. I sent it flying at Emerald's face.

Emerald flinched as the spark struck her in the nose with a zap of electricity. "What . . . how did you . . . do that?! This is some kind of trick!"

"Naw. That was genuine thunder magic, ya dum beerch," Vee said. "Lex is a Thunderbird like me! Like, com' on, do you really think that me, an Omnid Prima-Heiress of SimmiTech would make out with or date a magic-less human, Em?"

Emerald stared at me with bewildered gold-orange eyes. "But . . . but . . . Scrutimancer Satosh . . . he said that he's certain that . . ."

"Emerald," Quint growled. "Scrutimancers can make mistakes, especially if they simply scout the Astral and don't interrogate the subject in person. This is enough. That was . . . obviously Thunder magic. I'm not blind. Can you get us home?" He turned to me.

I stared at his burning eye sockets. "Yes. I can get each of you through the Arx Bank's ward at a great expense."

"How much of an expense?" Quint asked.

"About six million O-bux in local currency," I said. "I already paid it to hire a team to start cracking the problem."

"Shit." Quint swallowed. "I don't have that much."

"I'm aware. My clan can save all three of you, if you pledge your eternal allegiance to me," I said. "I don't do things for free for people who haven't been very nice to me."

"When the shit did you even make a clan?!" Emerald howled. "Quint! He's full of shit! He doesn't have a clan . . . he doesn't have six million O-bux! I don't know how he bamboozled these two morons, but . . ."

"Em. My human-lookin' husbando is the richest human from Earth in Shandria," Vee declared, rubbing her head against me. "You don't know shit."

"I have a clan," I said, walking closer to Quint and speaking directly into his face, staring at his burning amber eyes. "Vee, Ci, and I are getting engaged. We have a compound and a city around it being built right now with a starting budget of a few hundred million O-bux. And a twin city in progress. And a Mage Tower connected to three separate dungeons. You can taste the truth in my words, yes?"

"Yes." Quint nodded, shuddering, his mouth falling open.

"What?" Emerald blinked. "No. That can't be true . . . he's just a . . ."

"Em." Quint turned to the dragon girl. "He speaks the truth. I'm done. I . . . love you, but you've clearly gone insane or something. I didn't think that you'd ever go so far as to try to murder someone in the open like that, especially if that someone is the bloody Sovereign of Shandria! I'm . . ." He exhaled, his voice growing cold, detached, harsh. " . . . done helping you. I'm breaking up with you!"

"What?" Emerald turned to Quint, her gold-orange eyes wide with shock. "You're . . . breaking up with me? Now? Right before our *execution*?"

Quint's antlered head was bowed. "Yes. I am. I've watched you destroy everything around you. Destroy mixed-blood students. Destroy your friendship. Destroy your Delving group. Destroy our relationship. Destroy yourself. I can't . . . I really can't be part of this anymore."

He went down on one knee. "I hereby pledge myself as a sixie to . . ."

"Clan 'I Love You,'" Vespera interjected with a devious, human smile.

"Clan . . . I Love You," Quint repeated with a sigh.

"Forevermore," I added.

"Forevermore," Quint repeated with a sour voice.

Emerald's jaw dropped. "*What?!* Quincy, you . . . you can't! You're . . . you're my Kobold General! You can't just . . ."

"Em." Quint turned to his . . . *ex-girlfriend? Ex-partner? Ex-dragon owner?* "You're obviously too stubborn to step away from this path of madness and have chosen permanent death. I'm in a magisteel cage in magisteel manacles and I can't save you from all of Shandria, so I'm out. After you're executed . . . the kobold-dragon chain between us will shatter, and that'll be that. Also, I'll hire a Psychopomp to carve your soul-bit out of me. We're done."

"Sol. Declare your allegiance." I turned to the Mongolian Deathworm.

"I pledge myself as a sixie to the clan 'I Love You' . . . forevermore." Solace bowed to me.

Emerald spun her head from Quint to Solace, eyes wide.

"I did warn you before we came here that everyone would turn away from you," I said, eyeing the timer above us running down to only a minute. "Guess this is . . . goodbye, Em."

"W-wait!" Emerald mewled. "Please! I can pay the two million O-bux!"

"Two million?!" I laughed. "Are you screwing with me?! You publicly exposed me as a human in front of the entire delving class! You sent your Scrut's report to the Vice Principal and shared it with a ton of people on Omnigram! Two million O-bux isn't enough to cover the reputational damage you've caused me, you absolute ass!"

"H-how much do you want?!" She hissed out.

"I want everything," I said.

"*Everything?!*" she barked. "You can't . . ."

"A pledge as my sixie, all of your current finances, plus a public declaration that you made up the claim that I was human to bully me because you hate mixed-blood students," I said. "From this moment on, you're my sixie, my kobold, who will do everything I ask of you."

"I can't . . . I won't . . ." She choked, trembling.

I shrugged and turned around with two humanoid Omnids at my side, walking away.

"Wait!" Emerald's voice cracked.

I turned back once again, eyebrow raised. Twenty-one seconds on the timer above.

"I . . . accept," she whispered, her eyes filling with tears.

"What was that?" I cupped my ear dramatically. "I couldn't quite hear you."

"You . . . you win! *I accept!*" Emerald roared. "I pledge myself as a sixie to clan 'I Love You' forevermore!"

"There you go. Was that so hard?" I smiled.

Emerald squeezed the bars, sobbing and sliding down.

I watched as the timer above us reached zero and the sound-cancelling, view-blurring ward between us and the crowd fell. We started walking down the stairs.

"W-wait!" Emerald mewled, reaching out to me with desperate, shaking claws. "Aren't you gonna . . . save me?!"

"What?" I paused, turning back to look at her. "No."

"But you . . ." she wailed. "You *PROMISED!*"

The crowd laughed, enjoying the dragoness prostrating herself, begging and crying.

"Your execution is still happening," I said. "Actions have consequences, Emerald. I'll see your soul . . . on the other side of the river of stars."

I waved the distraught, sobbing, broken, cruel dragon Omnid goodbye as we departed.

We walked into the crowd and then other wealthy execution-patrons went up one by one or in small groups to scream at Em about how much gold she cost them, throwing rotten fruit at the faces of the trio.

Each patron who purchased a taunt package seemed determined to extract maximum entertainment from the condemned. Emerald sobbed, holding onto the metal bars. Each insult, each piece of rotten fruit, each electrical zap chipped away at her remaining dignity.

Sol and Quint remained as stoic as they could, only occasionally crying out when the cage-zapping began.

"I can't look at this," Ci said, turning away. "I get that she deserves this, but . . . it's just so cruel. This city is so bloody medieval."

"Let's go have lunch," I offered. We'll come back when the timer hits closer to zero."


"The bank's gonna save them, right?" Cinder asked as she chewed on her Wyvern steak in the Vimerillion Jubelee Restaurant facing the main square.

"No," I said. "I'm ending the bank at noon."

"Ending the bank?" Vespera tilted her human head like a bird. "Really, Lexy? Just like that?"

"Just like that," I said.

"How exactly are you planning to do that?" Ci demanded, sipping a mana-restoring wine.

"You'll see." I smirked dangerously, pointing at the clocktower hanging above the square. "When that big-ass clock strikes midnight, the princess will shatter into a thousand glass shards and only her bloodstained, red glass slipper and magic carriage will remain, and become ours for the taking."

"Ugh, Oddsney metaphors," Cinder sighed.

"It's a tale as old as time," I said with a shrug.

# CHAPTER SEVENTEEN

# My Little Mayhem

As we approached the execution platform, the atmosphere was a thick soup spiced with anticipation and cruelty. Emerald, Solace, and Quint looked utterly defeated, their once proud demeanors crushed under the weight of public humiliation.

Em's entire body was covered in rotten fruit pulp and the remnants of various food items hurled by gleeful citizens, gray robe stained. Her gold-orange eyes were red-rimmed from crying, her proud posture reduced to a hunched, trembling, broken form.

Solace and Quint fared a little better, as Emerald was the one who had received the brunt of the crowd's hate.

We walked to an open spot in the back by the fountain, paying a few drunken peasants a bag of copper coins to clear us the fountain space. I climbed up onto the marble ledge to stand tall and waved merrily at the prisoners, until the trio of soon-to-be-executed Omnids spotted us.

The Executioner-Bard stepped forward, his bright-blue robes swirling dramatically. A theatrical trumpet blast erupted from his Nuntix Kitlix, silencing the rowdy crowd.

"Citizens of Shandria!" he proclaimed, his voice magically amplified by his crystalline kitten to reach every corner of the square. "The taunting is over! Time has come for justice to be served! Please welcome Pyromancer Igjuvius Tuh and his Ignix Kitlix Blazy!"

A tall, lean, black-haired Pyromancer dressed in gold robes with red trim stepped forward, his dark red and black Kitlix glinting on his shoulder with orange sparks.

The crowd cheered.

Igjuvius bowed dramatically. His familiar mimicked his bow, creating miniature arcs of flame dancing through the air.

Executioner-Bard Agrikolish stepped forward, his voice booming across the square. "Condemned! Do you have any last words before the sentence is carried out?"

Emerald's head snapped up, her fruit-covered scales a total mess. Her gold-orange eyes were digging into me, angry at my betrayal. I winked at her.

"Do you think that you effin' bastards can break me?" she snarled. "You're nothing! Less than nothing! *I am Emerald Stratos! My clan will burn this entire city to the ground for this humiliation!*"

*Ah, Emmy, never change.*

The crowd went silent.

"*I declare a blood vengeance against every single person in this square!*" she screamed, frothing and shaking. "*My family's Scrutimancer will find you! My Knights will hunt down and slay every single one of you! You will all suffer!*"

"Y-yeah!" Solace declared, staring at me and trying very hard to follow the script I told her to follow over our late-night Voicecast conversation from this morning. "We're gonna curse your city! Curse it . . . extra hard! Behold!" She stood up, glancing at the time on the clock. "Your ruination begins now, for Lord Zalimar brings his army of the dead to your door! Fall!"

She pointed a finger at the cyan Infix Tower looming over the city and snapped her left hand like a gunshot.

"Shhhhh," I whispered into my Voicecast bracelet, sending a command to Shash.

Rumbling booms resounded across the city like thunder crackling across the clear sky. Citizens began looking around nervously, their cheers transforming into murmurs of uncertainty.

"What?" the Executioner-Bard sputtered. His eyes went wide as the massive Infix Mage Tower began careening forward.

"By her Shadow," he choked, his voice still carrying across the entire gathered crowd. "That Mage Tower . . . it's coming down!"

The crowd turned, staring at the tower as it came down.

Many screamed and began to retreat, bumping into one another as the massive tower fell right onto the Arx Bank building, obliterating itself and the bank it struck with a crackle of magical detonation, crystal shards flying into all directions and raining across the city like glittering rain.

Dust and residue billowed through the square.

Emerald's gold-orange eyes went wide with shock. Solace and Quint stared in disbelief. I smiled at them.

From the flying dust formed from the tower's impact, a massive logo began to manifest in the sky—a laughing skull with three eyes and a dark crown.

I dove into the water behind the fountain and activated Lance's anti-scrying wardstone.

"Voicecast Solace Exill, team Dreadful Delvers Knight," I ordered.

The bracelet vibrated for a second. Then Solace picked up, accepting the call inside her forehead mouth with one of her tentacle-threads.

"Solace," I ordered, "time to act. Stand up, point your finger at the skull in the sky, magnify your voice as much as you can, and be as dramatic as possible. Repeat after me . . . 'It's the mark of our Master!'"

"It is the mark of our Master!" Solace stood up and pointed at the skull in the sky. She howled, laughing dramatically as she spoke the words I was whispering into her head. "Tremble, foolish mortals! Tremble and despair! Run and hide, for soon his army will march into Shandria from the catacombs below and feast upon your flesh! The invasion has begun!"

I raised my head a bit, tilting my fox ears towards the stage.

"Invasion . . ." the Executioner-Bard choked, his voice still carrying across the entire square. "What?!"

The crowd's panic intensified. People were now running in all directions, screaming about an impending invasion.

Pyromancer Igjuvius looked utterly horrified. His Ignix Kitlix spun in circles around his shoulders, sparking with confused energy.

Agrikolish Chime-Barnaby stood frozen, mouth agape.

Emerald looked at Solace and then at my head sticking out of the fountain, not understanding what was happening anymore. Her Omnid eyes and ears were much sharper than the confused and panicking citizens of Shandria.

An eerie wail of doomsday bells resounded across Shandria, the surviving Mage Towers igniting one by one, warped in shimmering shields as the mages inside powered up the wards to their maximum setting, terrified that they would be targeted next.

I grinned at Emerald.

*What the fuck have you done now, human?* her expression said as she stared at me.

"Sir," the Pyromancer asked, my large fox ears catching their conversation, "are we still . . . you know? Burning them alive?"

"I . . . don't freaking know," Agrikolish snarled, rubbing his face. "Damnation. This is bad."

"Is this really . . . an invasion?"

"Seems like it," the Executioner-Bard muttered, staring at the chaos unfolding around him.

More explosions rocked the city as my hired adventurers detonated carefully placed beast core charges in various abandoned homes.

I dove back into the fountain and narrated for Solace. "Behold . . ."

"*Behold!*" Solace continued her theatrical performance, repeating my words like a good puppet-worm, projecting her voice across the ground with her Omnid skill. "*The power of Lord Zalimar! Your city will fall! Your banks will crumble! Your gold will be worthless!*"

"Worthless?" Agrikolish sputtered, his voice carrying over to where I sat in the fountain. "What are you talking about, you mad creature?!"

"When the rest of . . ." I whispered furiously.

"When the rest of your Guildnet Towers fall, the dimensional barrier between Shandria and Undertown will shatter, and Duskbloom shall flow up into your streets and all your magic will be devoured! Your Kitlix will be as useful as helpless kittens as the dead covered in Duskbloom will march from below! Mwa ha ha ha!" Solace boomed from both of her mouths, laughing madly, yellow claws out, looking like a proper super-villain minion now.

That really did it. The final nail into the coffin.

The crowd was in complete mayhem mode now, rushing away from the square like a tidal wave.

"Duskbloom," the Pyromancer swallowed, smothering his adorable, flame-sputtering Ignix close to his chest. "I can't fight against Duskbloom! I have to protect Blazy . . . I can't lose her to that cursed magic-devouring mold-shite!"

"Duskbloom. No. Shit, shit, shit!" the Executioner-Bard howled, watching as more citizens fled the square. "The prisoners . . ."

"Forget the prisoners! The Watch can take them back to the catacombs, interrogate them again . . . about all of this!" The Pyromancer grabbed the Bard's arm. "We need to find Ice mages or Frostix Kitlix now, you idiot! Those blasted mites will eat *all* of our magic when the Undertown-containing barrier falls! We'll fall asleep, and then we'll be ripe for the dead to devour! That must have been the Necromancer's plan all along!"

I grinned. "Flee, mortals . . ." I whispered.

"*Flee, mortals!*" Solace cackled dramatically both of her mouths open wide, the flesh-petals of her face opening and closing. "*Flee before the wrath of Lord Zalimar! Duskbloom comes for you all!* Burn! You will all burn for opposing my Necromage Master! Behold! Your city is set aflame! Aha ha ha ha ha!"

Another series of beast core explosions thundered in the distance, bringing down a few more abandoned buildings. Harmless, albeit very thick black smoke began billowing from chemical smoke bombs set up by hired adventurers across town who thought they were doing simple delivery jobs.

"By her Shadow! The city is burning down! We have to . . .!" the Pyromancer cried as he stared at the black rising smoke.

Something broke inside him, and he jumped off the stage and fled, likely heading to the nearest fridge or a gate out of town. Just as I expected, he assumed that wherever there was smoke, there would be fire, too.

The guards began abandoning their posts, some trying to maintain order but most of the low-level ones simply taking off, joining the fleeing crowd.

The Executioner-Bard spun in one spot, helplessly yelling for everyone to remain calm. Nobody was listening to him anymore. The Shandrian Watch officers were frantically shouting commands, while the Voicecast mages were exchanging rapid communication with the confused higher-ups.

I hung up on Solace.

"Vee, gimme your tag," I ordered.

The Thunderbird complied without question, staring at the unfolding mayhem in front of us with wide gray-gold eyes.

"Vee, Cinder, commere—sit in the water and hide under the edge of the fountain and make your faces look Omnid again!" I added.

They obeyed, jumping in. Wet Thunderbird and Quetzalcoatl faces appeared above the water.

"Make me look like my human self," I told Vee. "Okay, now make it look like we're bleeding all over and we're badly burned and injured. I want us to look like war-orphaned Omnid children."

Cinder stared at me, looking completely lost as Vespera manipulated her Quetzi powers to readjust our appearances.

I admired myself in the small mirror. My bruises and cuts actually chafed.

"Perfect." I gave Vee a thumbs up. "Now for the final move."

"What's the final move?" Vee asked.

I smiled at her.

"Voicecast Keeper Vassily," I spoke into Vee's silver tag, making sure that Lance's anti-scrying hexastone was still on. As the bank was utterly obliterated by the fallen tower, the dimensional bubble it powered up vanished and thus the call connected.

"Yes, Miss Simmi?" the Domovoy's hairy face shimmered into existence over my wrist, his gravelly voice hissing slightly. "I . . . Mr. Glock? What is happening up there? Why are you . . . bleeding all over and swimming . . . in a fountain?"

"Keeper Vassily!" I yelled dramatically, splashing in the water. "I need you to transfer control of the Corpse Seeker to Vespera Simmi immediately!"

"What?" The Domovoy's voice crackled with confusion. "Why would I hand runic control over of the Academy's Seeker to a student?! Where's Captain Quint?!"

"Keeper Vassily!" I yelled. "Listen to me! Quint, Solace, and Emerald were taken! They are imprisoned in magisteel cages, about to be executed!"

"What?!" Vassili sputtered. "What's going on?!"

"I think that Shandria is under attack by one of them . . . god emperors. Maybe it's that fat Dragon God Emperor. I don't know. Please! We have to get everyone out! We have no time! Some shrapnel from the explosion hit us! They're about to kill our friends!"

"What?! I . . . can't just . . ." Vassily hesitated, staring between us. "The protocols . . ."

"*Keeper!*" I yelled, making sure my voice cracked with desperation. "*There are no protocols for this!* The Arx Bank above you is gone! You didn't feel that magical explosion?! The entire city is on fire! They literally just dropped a fucking Mage Tower on the bank above you! It's basically a massive pile of rubble now! We *need* to get home *now! Please!* Only the Corpse Seeker can punch through the rubble that's buried the stairwell home, and claw through ten thousand tons of rocks!"

I tweaked the view of the bracelet to maximum, as I momentarily rose above the water, panning the bracelet around, showing Vassily the devastation of the fallen tower, the obliterated bank, the billowing smoke, the fleeing, screaming citizens, the distraught guards, the trio of Omnids in metal cages, and the laughing skull three-eyed crown logo looming in the sky.

"Abyss," Vassily breathed out, eyes bulging. "What . . . what is happening up there?! All of the other students came through a one-way emergency portal, knocked out! I sent them all home . . ."

"I told you already, Keeper, it's an invasion! Give Vespera Simmi control over the Corpse Seeker!" I yelled. "*Now*, Vassily! The Shandrian authorities think that we're with the invaders! Please!!! Before they cage all of us and you have to explain to all of our parents and Instructor Zalimar in two weeks why we're all perma-dead! Assign the chapel's Corpse Seeker as Vee's familiar! She's the only Omnid among us who can control the beast to get us all out safely and break through those magisteel cages and wards trapping Emmy, Sol, and Captain Quint!"

"Fine, fine, hol' your horses," Vassily grumbled with a Slavic accent. "I'm . . . transferring control . . . now."

A complex runic pattern flashed across Vee's tag, blue sparks forming words above it.

Omnid Chapel Corpse Seeker Control: Transferred. Familiar CORPSE SEEKER 77-84-1 assigned to Vespera Simmi!

"Thank you!" I yelled, hanging up on the Domovoy.

"Vee! Call up the Corpse Seeker to us!" I ordered, handing her the token back.

"Corpse Seeker!" Vespera commanded, her eyes lighting up as she snapped the token back onto her Lazarus bracelet and pressed her finger into the shimmering blood-red hexagram above her token. "I order you to come to me! Full speed! One hundred percent power!"

The blood-red hexagram answered us with an inhuman noise, almost like a distorted howl made from a hundred violins being played underwater strapped to a dying whale.

The unstoppable, Omnicorp-bred, murder-beast-machine was coming.

# CHAPTER EIGHTEEN

# Miss Possible

Vespera stared at my flushed, grinning face and then started to laugh, splashing through the water.

"Wha-wha?" Cinder spun in the water, staring between me and the cackling Thunderbird.

"Change yourself and Ci back into humans now," I commented. "Preferably before Ci realizes what just happened and tries to murder me with her sharp chompers."

"What. Just. Happened?" Cinder demanded, eyes narrowing dangerously as Vespera grabbed onto her and rearranged both of their faces back to human appearance. "Why am I murdering you now?!" She splashed water at me.

"I may have just caused a minor citywide panic," I said cheerfully, wiping the fountain water from my face.

"*A minor panic?*" Cinder's feathers flared through a hurricane of colors—shocked reds, angry oranges, disbelieving yellows. "*You dropped a . . .*"

"Shhh." I put my finger to her human lips. "I didn't drop nothing. It fell on its own. Maybe. I wasn't there; you can't blame me for Shandrian incompetence in the Mage Tower building."

Cinder's eyes narrowed dangerously. "I can absolutely blame you."

"I'm a blameless, innocent fox," I grinned. "I didn't do nothin'. I'll confess only under threat of kisses. Maybe. Vee, put my fox face back on."

Vespera nodded. With some targeted Quetzi-wing magic controlled by Thunderbird electrofractal-modding, my human face melted back into the foxy disguise, complete with big fluffy ears.

"There," Vee chortled. "Maximum foxy deniability achieved. Ke ke ke."

"What were those explosions?" Cinder hissed.

"Citywide urban renewal project," I grinned. "Very progressive. Tearing down some old buildings per handshake-enforced request of the Sovereign of Shandria!"

Cinder's human eye twitched.

"I'm going to strangle you," she threatened.

"Love you, too." I grinned, booping her nose.

A loud noise erupted across the city from the direction of the destroyed bank. The sound was so intense that nearby glass windows wobbled in their frames and shattered. The water in the fountain rippled. It sounded unnatural, wrong, alien, like a million violin strings scraping against a million chalkboards.

I dove out of the water, looking up.

"What? What is that?" the Executioner-Bard choked on the stage, looking at the destroyed Arx Bank.

"Wait, I know that sound." Emerald stood up. "That's a Corpse Seeker! The Omnid chapel finally sent one! Thank the Abyss!"

"Secure the prisoners!" Agrikolish yelled. "That sounds like a big necroflesh beast . . . damnation! Activate the magic-nullifying obelisks! Ready to repel the creature! Order the Mage Towers to target incoming enemies!"

The magic-nullifying obelisks hummed to life around the execution platform, their obsidian surfaces creating a dark, oppressive field that seemed to swallow all magical energy around the stage.

"Guide it underground," I whispered to Vespera. "Through the sewers. Avoid detection."

"I can't guide it anywhere," she said. "Corpse Seekers aren't that smart. It's coming to me in a straight line. Through everything in its way. Directly from where it started from. After it gets close to me, I can take over the damn thing and install more control hexagrams in it."

"Umm," I said. "Right. When it gets here, can you make it pretend to eat and swallow us?"

"Pfff, okay." Vee grinned. "Absolutely. Grabbing bodies is its base function. Extra scary nom coming right up."

The ground beneath our feet began to tremble.

Cracks spread across the cobblestone square like spiderwebs. Dust and small stones started jumping with each approaching vibration.

"By her Shadow!" the Executioner-Bard cried out. "Hold position!"

Something massive was moving underground, digging with an unnerving intensity, making the same horrid sound like a thousand drills spinning in unison.

It suddenly erupted from the ground directly beside our fountain hiding spot with a sound that didn't quite sound like an animal roar.

A colossal, burning-hot drill surged upward, molten rock cascading off its twirling titanium-obsidian-red segments like liquid fire. Each rotation sent waves of superheated stone spraying in all directions, creating a hellish corona of crimson and orange around its massive form.

The drill thing reminded me of pictures of subway tunnel drills and was easily more than three meters wide. Then the thing's legs followed out of the hole. It really looked like a gargantuan Kitlix, liquid crystal body and all.

The drill's surface burned red hot, pulsing with an inner light that made the surrounding air warp.

Crystalline legs—far too many to count, each looking like blood-red, razor-sharp appendages—emerged from the ground.

Then the thing's crystalline drill unfurled like a massive mouth and swallowed us along with half of the fountain.

The heat was intense, but strangely, I wasn't burning. Instead, I felt a bizarre sense of protection, as if I was submerged in the womb. The darkness lit up with flashes of electrical current. Vee appeared in the gloom, floating in what looked like liquid crystal, fully looking like her Thunderbird self.

She floated towards me and embraced me.

[This is freaking amazing.] Her static-filled voice sang in my head. [Damn. So much better than our little private Seeker! This thing's a genuine war machine, a tank meant for invading hostile planets!]

I tried to speak, but my throat was engulfed in liquid crystals.

[Hang on,] Vespera crackled. [Going to make a dimensional bubble for us to exist in.]

The liquid crystal around us seemed to part, creating a small bubble of breathable space without any gravity.

"Let there be . . . light!" Vespera ordered, sending electric currents into the crystalline walls.

Soft, ethereal light bloomed around us from crystalline nerve-like formations, revealing the interior of what was clearly a massive, living machine. Organic-looking circuitry glowed with blood-red energy, while intricate crystalline organs pulsed with an almost biological rhythm in its depths.

I could now see Cinder floating nearby, her feathers shifting through startled blues and grays.

"What?!" the Quetzi let out, looking around.

"Let there be gravity!" Vespera announced, and Cinder and I suddenly landed onto the base of the bubble.

"Holy shit," I breathed, looking around.

Vespera's hands were buried halfway within the crystalline bubble, sending out electric currents across the crystalline-flesh beast.

"Corpse Seeker 77-84-1. Officially the most badass and oldest piece of Omnid tech I've ever seen. The Academy or Zalimar must have paid handsomely for this bad girl!" Vee added.

Cinder blinked at the pulsing organs. "This . . . this is what the chapel uses to retrieve students from dungeons?"

"Ye. Retrieve, protect, resurrect." Vespera nodded. "Obliterate everything in the way. Let's see where we are."

The bubble around us shimmered, becoming covered with a million pixels like a TV screen going through channels. The static rearranged itself into a view of the devastated central square.

The view showed total chaos.

The Executioner-Bard stood frozen, mouth agape. Where the fountain once stood, there was now a massive crystalline drill hole, steam and molten rock billowing around its edges.

"Let there be . . . sound!" Vespera declared.

The bubble around us filled with the sounds of the square—panicked screams, the crackling of distant explosions, confused shouts and orders from guards.

"By her Shadow!" the Executioner-Bard screamed. "*The Necromancer's beast has eaten those poor girls!*"

"That's not a N-N-Necromage construct," one of the older officers cried. "I faced zombie-flesh beasts twenty years ago during the Kells uprising, but I've never seen anything like this thing. That's some sort of crystal, not dead flesh! Burn it away!"

A few Mage Towers overhead ignited, sending brilliant rays down against the Corpse

Seeker. The crystalline material of the beast reflected the rays off itself like a mirror, igniting and scorching the ground and building around us.

"Shit! It can bounce fire-rays off itself! Cease fire! Target it with the magic nullifiers!" the guard captain shouted at the gawking mages. "Focus the obelisks in a beam!"

"Yeah, I don't think so." Vee grinned, sending current across the Omnid tank.

Gargantuan crystal claws grabbed pieces of the destroyed fountain and began hurling them at the obelisks.

The rocks flew at supersonic speed, making deafening booms as they cut through the air, obliterating and shattering the obelisks. Each impact created a shockwave that sent guards tumbling backwards, their armor cracking and helmets flying off.

The obsidian magic-nullifying structures—meant to suppress powerful magical entities, not flying rocks—disintegrated like glass hit by a sledgehammer. Fragments scattered across the square, some turning to dust, others embedding themselves in nearby buildings.

"*Impossible!*" the guard captain screamed, his voice cracking with terror.

"Ke ke ke," Vespera laughed. "Very possible. Let there be . . . comfort!"

"We should name her," I said, watching the crystalline beast continue its rampage against the defenses of the stage, flying rocks obliterating defensive hexagrams.

"Name what?" Cinder asked with wide eyes, clinging to me as a crystalline-organic seat suddenly formed beneath us.

"The Corpse Seeker," I explained. "Every good murder tank needs a name."

Vespera tilted her head. "Ye?"

"Miss Possible," I suggested.

Cinder stared at me. "You're naming a multimillion O-bux apocalyptic murder machine like it's a pet?"

"Pffff, you funny," Vee chortled. "Okay. Miss Possible it is. Hold on going to bring up her stats, too."

The bubble lit up with various diagnostic metrics.

Miss Possible:
Core Temperature: 58%
Energy Level: 67%
Structural Integrity: 82%
Dimensional Stability: 98%

Vespera clicked her beak. "Not bad for an old girl. Looks like she's running at about 79.68 percent optimal capacity. Hasn't been in use for a while, my poor baby. Time to take Miss Possible for a spin!"

She grinned dangerously, and then the view around us flashed.

Suddenly, the Corpse Seeker was on the stage and the guards were flying through the air, the air around us exploding in a blastwave. Crystalline claws obliterated the mag-isteel cages and then Emerald, Quint, and Solace were inside of the beast along with us.

Another flash and the view changed again, the Corpse Seeker running across the streets, leaving more devastation in its wake.

Core Temperature: 62%
Energy Level: 65%
Structural Integrity: 81%
Dimensional Stability: 97%

"Holding steady!" Vee commented. "What are your orders, Quartermaster?"

"Put our sixies on ice," I said, glancing at the three no-longer-caged Omnids. "Knock 'em out, I don't wanna deal with them right now."

"Can do," the Thunderbird clicked. Lightning flashed into the heads of the three figures floating within the crystalline strata, and their eyes closed.

"Now," I said, "I bet that the Arx Bank that the tower fell on has lots of . . . unguarded stuff."

"Free stuff," Vee agreed. "Onwards, Possible!"

Another flash, the windows behind us exploding from the shockwave as the Corpse Seeker went from zero to several hundred kilometers per hour.

Then, Miss Possible's crystalline drill slammed into the rubble of the destroyed Arx Bank, her multiple razor-sharp legs digging through layers of concrete, steel, and destroyed wards. Where a normal machine would struggle, she moved with an almost organic fluidity, her drill-mouth spinning and grinding through the debris like a living creature hunting for treasure.

Electromagnetic pulses radiated from her core as we plowed into half-buried rooms, causing magic objects to literally leap toward her crystalline body. Gold bars began floating through the air, drawn into her internal chambers. Stacks of documents—some mundane, some marked with complex magical seals—were sucked in, becoming suspended within.

"Jackpot!" Vee grinned, glancing at the captured documents. "Bank transfer records. Client lists. Dimensional gate contracts. Zalimar's entire network might be amongst these."

I nodded.

The Corpse Seeker melted into the vault next.

A hundred crystal claws pulverized magic seals, tearing apart lockboxes. Rushing across the wall of destroyed compartments, it sucked everything into itself: more coins, beast cores, paperwork of all sorts.

Another line appeared on the round wall screen.

Storage Capacity: 89%

"Blah. Getting full," Vespera reported.

"Purge any small coins," I ordered. "Focus on the expensive loot."

"On it!" Vespera clicked, sending electrical currents through Miss Possible's crystalline structure. Melted stone and small copper and silver coins began raining out of the Corpse Seeker's body onto the vault floor, creating a chaotic shower of currency.

Storage Capacity: 62%

Claws extended, the "Gold Seeker" buried itself in the next vault, magisteel walls melting like butter under the massive drill.

Storage Capacity: 77%

"Yarr, matey! Acquire the doubloons!" I hugged Vespera.

"Aye-aye, m' Quartermaster!" She rubbed her head against my side. "Ship Possible shall ravage the S.S. Arx Bank for its booty!"

Cinder buried her Quetzi face in her hands, blushing with orange, red, and pink shimmers. "I can't believe you two."

"What?" I asked innocently. "We're just performing a completely legitimate maritime salvage operation."

"Ughh," Cinder let out. "This was your plan all along, wasn't it?"

"To get my hands on the Omnid Corpse Seeker?" I finished. "Yes. It was. Always wanted one of these."

"What, we ain't returning her to Vassily?" Vespera asked.

"Hell no," I said. "I ain't giving up our murdertank baby to anyone!"

"You can't just . . . *steal* a magical tank!" Cinder sputtered, her feathers exploding through a hurricane of disbelieving colors.

"Liberating her," I said. "For our clan's glory!"

"She won't run very long if we keep plowing through magisteel-reinforced walls," Vespera commented.

I glanced at the stats.

Miss Possible:
Core Temperature: 85%
Energy Level: 45%
Structural Integrity: 61%
Dimensional Stability: 77%
Storage Capacity: 96%

"Energy's getting low," I said. "Can she run on the beast cores we just stole?"

"Aye, aye, Lord Protector!" Vee clicked. "Injecting beast cores into the dragonheart manifold . . . now! Venting core heat!"

The crystalline tank vibrated as beast cores began dissolving into its internal systems, creating a symphony of magical energy that made the air around us shimmer and pulse.

"Wheeeeeee!" Vespera yowled, her talons dancing inside the liquid crystal surface. "*Who's a good murder tank? You are! Yes, you are!*"

Cinder facepalmed so hard, I thought she might actually create a small singularity of embarrassment.

The air around Miss Possible ignited as the Corpse Seeker released heat, the bank vault walls melting around us from superheated air.

Miss Possible:

Core Temperature: 42%
Energy Level: 100%
Structural Integrity: 50%
Dimensional Stability: 76%
Storage Capacity: 92%

"Can we take on another bank?" I asked.

"Ehhhh," Vee said. "Don't think so. The crystalline strata held by magisteel hexamesh might start coming apart. She'll need a break to regrow the outer layers. Those Mage Towers did some damage, too. Even if she reflected most of the rays, the fire magic still took out a big chonk of our structural integrity."

"Fine," I said. "Let's suck up more stuff till storage is one hundred percent full, then head home."

"On it."

"Home? To Earth?" Cinder let out.

"No, you knob," I said. "To our Guild. If we take Miss Possible back to the Omnid chapel, Keeper Vassily will obviously reclaim her. He has near absolute power in his domain. Why would I go through the trouble of making Shandria look like it's being invaded, just to give up our precious Omnid tank?"

"So where?"

"We're going to our crystal tower in Undertown." I answered.

"Home sweet citadel!" Vespera clicked, sending electrical sparks dancing across Miss Possible's crystalline interior. "Shall we take the scenic route?"

"Absolutely," I agreed. "Let's avoid destroying the choke point. Can't make it too obvious that we own this lovely beast. Go out of Shandria through the sewers, then out of the city towards the fields. We can stop at a farm and get some groceries for our gang."

"Groceries?" Cinder sputtered. "In an Omnid tank?"

"What?" I asked. "You've never taken a stolen tank to buy some milk 'n' apples?"

Cinder stared at me with a look of judgement.

The crystalline drill of Miss Possible ignited, carving through the bank's wall. We began burrowing down and then into the sewers, leaving a perfectly smooth, glass-like tunnel in our wake.

Then we rushed along the sewer at a respectable speed of a freight train.

"So," Cinder asked after a few minutes of silence, "exactly how much did we just steal?"

"I dunno." Vee shrugged. "I'm not an accountant. My mind is melting just running Miss Possible. Judging by the gold alone, that's like a few hundred million O-bux right there. Plz no distract driver birb, only pet."

I leaned forward and began petting Vespera's feathered head. "Good First Mate birb."

"Mmm," she purred, leaning into my touch. Electrical sparks danced across her feathers, zapping me gently.

Cinder rolled her eyes.

The crystalline walls of Miss Possible shifted slightly, creating even more comfortable seating for our trio. The sewer tunnels rushed past, occasionally lit by strange biolumi-nescent fungi and scurrying underground creatures.

"Ci. Pet the birb," I encouraged.

Cinder sighed, reaching out and awkwardly patting Vespera's head. Tiny electrical sparks jumped between Vee and Cinder's hand.

"Yesssss," Vespera purred. "More pets and compliments."

"Best birb," I said. "Are you pleased with your gift?"

"Mmm. What gift?" she purred.

"Miss Possible," I said. "Figure Thunda-birb girls like shiny things, so I stole the shiniest possible thing for ya."

"We really keeping her?" she asked.

"Really," I said. "She's yours. We're going to bring her to Earth with us."

"Lexyyyyy . . ." Vespera's eyes turned into thin slits, sparks dancing at the edges. "You really know how to treat a girl. Damn it. You making me cry, you cheeky fox."

"The biggest diamond-beastie I could find in the universe! An engagement tank!" I laughed.

Cinder's feathers ignited red-green-pink.

"An *engagement tank*?!" she squawked. "That's not how proposals work!"

"Eh," I said, grinning. "Nothing says 'I love you' like a multimillion O-bux crystalline murder machine capable of drilling through everything in its way."

Miss Possible slowed. Vespera pulled her hands out of the crystalline walls and grabbed Cinder's wings. Her face rapidly rearranged itself into an elongated fusion of Thunderbird and human, and then she turned my way and attacked.

She practically buried me in a flurry of kisses and electrical sparks. Her talons wrapped around me possessively, tiny arcs of lightning dancing between us.

[Mine mine mine,] her thoughts sang. [Love. Love. Love. Forever. Mine!]

"M . . . mine," her lips whispered out loud as she stared at my eyes. "I . . ."

"Yes?" I smiled.

"I love you," she mewled, nomming my entire face with her entire elongated human-Omnid mouth.

"Nuh-uh," I teased. "It is I who loves my birb."

Cinder rolled her eyes but hugged me from the right side, occasionally catching her own kisses in between Vee.

"Uh? Who's driving Possible?" I asked, glancing at the retreating tunnels.

"Me," Vee said, panting, blushing, and railing sparks. "With my feet."

I noticed that her clawed feet were indeed buried within the liquid-crystal floor, sending electrical currents into the depths of the Corpse Seeker.

The crystal tank pulverized another sewer wall, breached into a cavern, and then plowed through solid rock for about ten minutes, then went up, breaking out of the ground into brilliant sunshine.

# CHAPTER NINETEEN

# Brooding Farm

Afternoon sunlight shone, the trees swayed in the breeze, yellow fields of wheat and violet fields of lavender danced with gold-and-violet waves. Chuppies fluttered from tree to tree, eating bugs.

Farmer Larry Gootali sat on his creaky, pure white Moonwood porch, sipping afternoon tea with his wife Nilli. Their farmhouse overlooked their numerous fields and orchards, a picture of pastoral tranquility in the Shandrian countryside.

"The Seerscope's been acting strange all morning," Nilli commented, her elk ears twitching nervously as she adjusted her apron. "Arrow's been spinning like mad, pointing towards . . . certain doom."

"Yeah. Thought that we had a year to sell the farm." Larry nodded gravely, his weathered hands wrapped around his teacup. "Haven't seen it this agitated since the Kells Uprising. Something's definitely—"

His words cut off as the ground began to tremble.

His teacup shattered against the porch boards as a massive crystalline form erupted from the ground like some ancient horror awakening from millennia of slumber.

Blood-red crystal segments glinted in the afternoon sun as the mechanical beast carved through the wheat field, throwing superheated, molten rocks all over.

"By her Shadow!" Nilli screamed, blonde hair flying, green antlers shaking, green eyes wide. "What is that monstrosity?!"

Larry watched in mute shock as a few of his prized springapple trees—passed down through three generations—were reduced to splinters in seconds as the beast plowed a straight line across several wards and stopped.

The crystalline horror slowed at the edge of his lavender field. Its drill head rotated, seeming to taste the air. For a moment, Larry could have sworn he saw figures moving within its translucent body—but that had to be a trick of the light.

*Nothing living could survive inside that thing . . . could it? Maybe this thing . . . this crystal dragon abomination ate someone already.*

"Sorry!" a female voice suddenly called out from the crystalline beast. "Got distracted making out and sort of demolished your tree orchard."

"Don't kiss 'n' drive," a male commented.

"Ye, ye, Mr. Fox," the female voice sighed. "How about a break for this poor birb? Driving Possy is heckin' mentally draining. This place seems chill."

Larry glanced at the Seerscope on the wall. The arrow was pointing straight at the word *Catastrophe*. He swallowed.

The crystalline, eyeless abomination slowly rotated and started moving towards their farmhouse and then finally settled onto Larry's wheat field, its massive form creating ripples in the golden stalks. Steam rose from its drill as the surface cooled, creating a shimmering haze in the afternoon light.

Slits opened between crystalline folds, releasing superheated steam into the air.

A section of the crystal beast's side suddenly liquefied, forming what looked like a door and a stairwell. Three figures emerged—a foxkin teen in a fancy black leather jacket, and two fox girls in red-and-black dresses.

"Why are we foxes?" the rainbow-haired foxgirl hissed.

"Why not?" The black-and-white-haired foxgirl shrugged. "I want to try on every Arx xenotype!"

"Ughhhh," the rainbow-haired fox let out. "Why can't I just be a Quetzi?"

"Just tryin' ta' get outta your mold, Cinderella," the black-and-white foxgirl declared with a grin. "You're so square and crusty, ya kno'? Lighten up!"

"I'm not crusty!" the rainbow-haired foxgirl protested. "I just prefer to be myself!"

"Hi there!" the orange foxkin in the leather jacket called out cheerfully to Larry and Nilli. "Sorry about your trees. Would you accept payment in gold for the damages?"

Larry and Nilli exchanged bewildered looks.

"We just need to rest our tank for a bit," the black-and-white fox explained. "She's overheating."

"Tank?" Nilli squeaked.

"Miss Possible needs a break." The ginger, green-eyed foxman nodded at the crystalline beast. "Running hot after some . . . urban renewal work in the city."

Steam continued to rise from the massive crystalline . . . tank beast as it cooled in the afternoon air. The crystalline structure pulsed with an inner light, creating dancing reflections and rainbows cast across the wheat field.

"Would you lovely farmers know a good place to eat 'round these parts?" the foxkin male asked, shaking a gold purse.

Nilli found her voice first. "Oh! You must be mages from afar! We do offer home-cooked meals at our farm for adventurer guests!"

"Perfect!" The foxkin teen grinned. "Name your price for food and damages. We'll happily compensate you for any inconvenience and pay for parking."

Larry and Nilli exchanged another look.

"Nil," Larry hissed at his wife. "We can't take 'em, the Seerscope is . . ."

"Maybe if we deny them hospitality, they'll kill us, idiot husband," Nilli fired back. "They have a crystal dragon, the likes of which I have never seen. I can't even sense that thing's level, and it went through the wardstone palisade like it was made from paper."

Larry paled, swallowing.

"Come in, come in!" Nilli declared with forced cheerfulness, ushering the strange trio onto her white porch. "I'll put on some tea and whip up a proper meal."

The foxkin teen bowed gracefully. "Much appreciated. I'm Lex, and these are my companions, Lady Voltara and Lady Castabriella."

The black-haired fox curtsied dramatically while the rainbow-haired one just nodded awkwardly.

Larry watched as his elkin wife practically flew into the house, her white tail fluffed with nervous energy. He could hear pots and pans clattering as she presumably started preparing their best dishes.

"So," Larry said carefully, studying the crystalline monstrosity cooling in his wheat field, "you folks . . . um . . . are from . . . where?"

"Just passing through." Lex smiled. "Had some business in the city. Now heading home."

A distant explosion echoed from the direction of Shandria. Black smoke rose above the city walls.

"Ah," Larry nodded. "Business."

"Yep." Lex grinned, pulling out a heavy pouch. "Now, about those trees . . ."

"Oh, don't worry about those," Larry said quickly. "They were . . . old anyway. Ready to come down. We're selling the farm anyway."

"You are?" Lex asked. "Why?"

"Retiring," Larry said too quickly. "Moving to the Capital. My sister has a place there."

"You look much too young to retire," Lex smiled.

"Well." Larry exhaled, glancing at the crystal dragon tank thing, terrified that the fox trio were mighty wizards who could sense lies. "To be completely honest, we're concerned about a possible invasion or a revolution. Foresight magic suggests something big is going down in a year. Plus, there's . . . news from the city cast via Nuntix about a Necromancer taking down a Mage Tower. Last time Shandria caught fire during the Kells Uprising, we barely made it out alive."

"So, how much are you selling this lovely farm for?" Lex asked.

"Two celesteel cards," Larry said.

Lex fished in his pocket and threw three celesteel cards on the table. "Here you are."

Larry's mouth fell open. The foxkin's jacket pockets looked as though they were bursting with celesteel cards. He'd never seen a mage so wealthy.

"I . . . what?" Larry stared at the small fortune on his table. Each card radiated magic like a beating heart, and the boy just casually gave them out!

"Three celesteel cards," Lex repeated. "For your farm. Consider the extra one as payment for lunch and friendship. Vee, do we have property deed transfers?"

"Ye." Lady Voltara nodded. "Totes do. I gotchu. Gonna go grab one from Possy."

"Why are we buying a farm?" Lady Castabriella demanded.

"I dunno." Lex shrugged. "Since I died on Tuesday, I wanted to buy you a farm with a nice gothic house and an apple orchard where you can brood and raise crows."

"You what?" the rainbow-haired fox asked. "Wait. Are you referring to that stupid joke you made a week ago about me being your goth GF?"

"Maybe." Lex shrugged. "You're not dressed like a goth now, but like . . . I still want to get you something nice. I got Vee a tank. You like this place, right?"

"I . . ." Cinder's fox ears wiggled. "You can't just . . . buy me a farm because of a dumb joke!"

"Already did." I grinned, sliding the deed transfer papers from the Arx Bank brought by Vee from Miss Possible across the table to the farmer who'd introduced himself as Larry. "Sign here, please."

Larry's hands shook as he signed, his eyes darting between the celesteel cards and the hissing crystalline tank venting steam.

"Man, Dr. Greyfield's Advanced Xenobiology feels like millennia ago." I stretched. "Doesn't it?"

"It was literally like a week ago," Cinder hissed. "And you're completely changing the subject! You can't just . . . buy farms on a whim!"

"Already did." I grinned, watching Larry sign the last document. "It's yours now. A lovely gothic farmhouse with an apple orchard, only somewhat plowed by Miss Possible."

"Ughhh, you're freaking impossible," Cinder let out.

"Tell me you hate it, and I'll give this lovely farm to Vee instead." I shrugged.

"No!" Cinder blurted out, then immediately covered her mouth with her paws, fox ears flattening against her head.

"Ha!" I pointed at her. "You *do* like it! Knew it!"

"I . . . just . . ." she sputtered, her rainbow-colored fox tail swishing in agitation. "That's not the point!"

"The point is that I bought you a brooding farm," I grinned. "You can tell your parents all about it when we get back home. They'll think I'm a respectable Nazarite boy even more that way. Because who else buys apple farms for their fiancées?"

"*I do not brood!*" she protested. "And we're not engaged!"

"You're brooding right now," Vee commented cheerfully. "And that's a fixable situation."

The elkwoman Nilli emerged from the kitchen with tea and freshly baked scones. Steam curled from the teapot as she set it down.

"The homemade stew will be ready shortly," she said with a bow. "I hope you'll find everything to your liking."

"It smells wonderful," I said, accepting a cup of tea. "Thank you for your hospitality."

Cinder was still fuming beside me, rainbow fox tail swishing in agitation. Vee sat on my other side, practically vibrating with barely contained electrical energy and foxy merriment.

The farmers furiously whispered to each other and then returned to the living room.

"So," Nilli ventured carefully, "when do you need us to . . . vacate the property?"

"Oh, take your time." I waved dismissively. "No rush. We're not staying long in Shandria and probably won't be back for a year. I'll have someone from our Guild come over later to take care of the farm, make sure it's in good order. Enjoy your wealth, take your kids on vacation. You two have kids, right?"

"Erm." Nilli blushed. "A daughter. Terri." She pointed at a Depictomancy-animated painting of a blonde girl who looked like a younger version of her. "She's in her seventh year as an apprentice Healer at Shandria's Healers Hall."

"Wonderful." I smiled, glancing at the farm deed signed by Larry Gootali. "Terri Gootali, right? When you see her next, tell her that her apprenticeship is fully paid for. Consider it a bonus for the excellent tea and hospitality."

Larry choked on his tea. Nilli's eyes went wide. "But . . . but . . ." she stammered. "A Healer's apprenticeship costs . . ."

"An arm and a leg?" I asked.

"Yes. So why would you . . .?" Nilli asked.

"I'm going to be opening a bank here and building a new city right next to Shandria. I'm going to need lots of young, talented people—Healers, architects, craftsmen, Kitlix breeders, Agromancers, all sorts of mages, basically. People who can help build something new. Consider this an investment in the future!"

Nilli and Larry exchanged bewildered looks.

"A new bank?" Larry asked carefully. "But the Arx Bank . . ."

Another distant explosion rumbled from the city.

"Won't be a problem." I smiled. "Trust me."

Larry swallowed hard and nodded.

Nilli brought out the stew, which smelled absolutely divine. We ate in relative silence, broken only by occasional compliments about the food and the distant sounds of thunder from the city.

"Umm," Nilli asked me, "Sir Lex, what is happening in Shandria?"

"Renovation," I said. "Our Adventurers Guild hired more than a thousand adventurers to demolish old abandoned buildings on the land we leased to build new infrastructure."

"How many adventurers?" Larry sputtered.

"Pretty much all of them." I shrugged. "I think? I'm not really sure, our lovely Guild Master is handling it."

"You own the Adventurers Guild?" Nilli stared at me with wide eyes.

"Not the white cathedral," I said. "We own a competing Adventurers Guild. Still rebranding and renovating it."

"Would you like some more tea?" Nilli asked nervously.

"Please." I smiled. "Your stew is excellent, by the way. Perfect for supper after a morning of hearty urban renewal."

Cinder kicked me under the table. I maintained my pleasant smile.

"So," Larry ventured, "you're building a . . . city?"

"Two cities, actually," I said. "One for non-magic humans and one for the locals."

"Non-magic humans?" The farmer blinked. "What?"

"An interdimensional colony," I said. "Just a little fun project of mine."

"A . . . colony?" Larry's dog ears twitched nervously while his elk wife simply blinked my way with a lost look. "Here in Shandria?"

"Adjacent to Shandria," I corrected. "In a dungeon."

"In . . . a dungeon?!" the farmers asked together.

"Yep." I nodded. "Found a pretty good dungeon recently and decided to adopt it. You know how it goes."

Another distant explosion echoed from the city.

"More . . . renovations?" Nilli asked weakly.

"Yep." I shrugged. "Our Guild is quite thorough."

"Yum!" Vee finished her stew and stretched. "This is nice. A chill vacation in the countryside!"

Cinder glared at me from her stew. I sent her a pleasant smile.

The farmers excused themselves, heading out to tend to the damage in their fields caused by our arrival. Through the window, we watched as they mounted their Agrilopods—strange, massive beasts that towered over the farm buildings. The

Agrilopods looked like a fusion of giant crab, daddy longlegs, and siphonophore. I watched as long thread-like tentacles extended out from the creatures, collecting fallen springapple tree branches.

"You know," Cinder said, watching the farmers work, "you didn't have to buy their entire farm."

"Why not?" I asked. "They wanted to sell it. I wanted to buy you a farm. This is how transactions work."

"I didn't want a bloody farm!" Cinder complained.

"Surprise farm?" I smiled sheepishly as I pulled Lance's anti-scrying wardstone from my bag and placed it in the middle of the living room. I shoved another beast core inside it from my pocket full of stolen beast cores from the Arx Bank. "You gotta practice your Hearth-Wife-ness somewhere, right?"

"Ughhhh." Cinder phase-shifted out of her foxgirl form, burying her face in her wings. "Going to rest for a bit . . . out of mana."

Vespera shifted back to her Thunderbird form. She draped herself across both of us on the couch, petting Cinder.

"Hi, Ci." She smiled.

"What?!" Cinder looked down.

"Come on, gimme a smile. Look at this place. It's actually pretty nice. Mountain views on the left, the Chasm Sea on the other side, close to the city, Shandrian-style farmhouse, apple orchard, wheat fields . . . perfect for writing romantic songs about the inevitability of death."

"I don't write romantic songs about the inevitability of death!" Cinder protested, her feathers shifting through embarrassed pinks and indignant purples.

"Yet." I grinned. "Give it time. Soon you'll be out here in your black dress, sitting under a weeping tree, writing verses about the existential despair of being a rainbow dragon engaged to human and Thunderbird disasters."

I took the sweaty fox ears off my head and slowly washed the makeup off my face with a makeup sponge as Cinder growled at me from her seat.

"We're not engaged!" Cinder let out. "And we won't be engaged if you two keep being absolute knobs about everything!"

"But we're your knobs." I grinned, leaning over to kiss her cheek.

"Ugh," she said, pushing me away, but her feathers betrayed her with flashes of pink. "You can't just . . . fix everything by being cute."

"Can't I?" I asked innocently.

"No!" she declared.

"Come on," I said. "Admit it. You like the farm."

"I . . . it's . . . fine," she mumbled.

"Just fine?" I pressed.

"It's . . . nice, okay?" she admitted reluctantly. "But that's not the point!"

"What's the point?" I asked her. "State your point."

"I don't know what my point is!" she hissed. "You're terrible, and this sparkplug knobfold is even worse, and you two keep dragging me into your excessively insane shenanigans. It's like, I expect one thing and . . ."

"What did you expect?"

"I expected a nice date, and I expected the Arx Bankers to take Em, Sol, and Quint's bracelets back home. I didn't bloody think that you would effing crash a Mage Tower into the Arx Bank just to bamboozle Keeper Vassily into giving Vee control over a fucking Corpse Seeker tank!" Cinder barked, feathers shifting through exasperated colors.

"To be fair," I said, "the bank demolition plot worked out perfectly. We got a murder tank, saved a trio of Omnids, and got new sixies, plenty of loot, and a nice farm out of it. Dungeon delving is too much effort! Much easier to rob a bank, see?"

"This is exactly what I'm talking about!" Cinder growled. "Stop giving Vee murder tanks—she's got like no impulse control!"

"Nooo," Vee whined. "Don't take away my murder tank, I love her. She's my baby! My Lexy got me the bestest engagement tank ever!"

"It's not an engagement tank! It's the Omnid chapel's Corpse Seeker!" Cinder protested. "And you can't just steal a magic tank!"

"Already did." I grinned. "And gifted it to Vee as her familiar! What are you going to do about it? Nag me extra hard? Go ahead, Hearth-Keeper. I accept my lovely Quetzi nagging."

"I . . . you . . . argh!" Cinder flashed all the colors of a See-Mass tree.

"Yes?" I asked. "If we aren't engaged, then what are we then? What exactly did your bite do to me?"

"It basically claims you as . . . my kobold," Cinder explained with a sigh. "Any Omnid can claim anything as their hoard item or anyone as kobold . . . by leaving a small piece of their soul in a person or an object."

"Ye," Vespera commented. "An example of this is Emerald claiming Cinder's phone to track her movements and Emerald claiming her boyfriend Quint as a kobold. A soul-bond claim isn't forever. It can fade, if the object or the person is destroyed, and it can be carved out by a Psychopomp in about twenty minutes in Omnithornia."

"I see," I said.

"Instructor Zalimar claimed a whole bunch of objects around Skyfall as his phylacteries so that he can return even after dying horribly in another dimension," Vespera added.

"Can you do that, then?" I asked.

"No." Vespera shook her head. "You need to have super high-level in Animancy for that as an Astral Phantom. Even if I shoved bits of my soul into a bunch of random rocks or magic artifacts, I would not be able to find my way back home if I died on Arx. The Astral Sea is basically infinite. It is easy to get lost there, to fade away into nothing, to calcify into an imprint. Usually souls simply get devoured by the Arx Wheel. Only a high-level Astral Phantom can escape the pull of the Wheel."

Cinder sighed.

"Another example of a soul bond is Skinwalker Valor Thornheart claiming Cinder by cutting her heart with a plan to devour her soul," Vespera said, making Cinder shudder. "It allowed him to inhabit her body for two years, grinding her from within with horrific dreams repeating the same day over and over. Valor's plan was to shatter Cinder's soul and reincarnate himself inside her using her body as a ghoul to resume his murder spree to awaken the Wormwood Leviathan."

"Could he actually awaken the Wormwood Leviathan?" I asked.

"It is theoretically possible," Vespera said. "Just not with beast cores and Omnid murder. You need to punch reality extra hard to cause a worldwide magic cascade. Some Omnid scholars speculate that a sufficiently large release of magic can indeed awaken the Wormwood Star."

"What would happen then?" I asked.

"A dimensional shift," Vespera explained.

"Which is what?" I asked.

"Space-time would get rearranged by a planet-wide celestorm," Vespera said. "It is speculated that if a wish is made during the Leviathan's awakening . . . physical reality gets overwritten in the direction of desire."

"Sounds effed up," I said.

"It's a way to . . . solve problems." Vespera shrugged, her silver-gold eyes sparkling. "For someone . . . desperate enough. According to the Scrutimancer Stabalists who watch for such things, planet-wide celestorms that cause massive dimensional shifts have happened before and will happen again. Wobble reality enough and the Wormwood Star will awaken once more."

I stared at her, but she fell silent.

"So I am your kobold?" I turned to Cinder. "What exactly does this mean?"

"It means that I own you as a dragon," Cinder said. "Legally. Means I can sense when you're lying to me. It does *not* mean that we're married or engaged."

"A soul-bond kobold link can be used as court evidence," Vespera commented. "As long as we sign some paperwork, then we are engaged."

"I'm not signing shit." Cinder crossed her arms.

"I'm not asking you to sign anything. Unlike you, I need this," Vespera said. She dug into her bag and slapped a bunch of Arx Bank contracts on the table. "Sign, sign. Keep your copies."

I slowly went over the contracts. The paperwork stipulated that Vespera Simmi and I were soul-bonded and were uniting our Omnicorp assets and that Vespera and I were rejecting any prior engagement and merger contracts.

"When did you even fill these out?" I asked the Thunderbird.

"While we drove here," she replied. "I used Possy to burn our info into the Arx Bank contract paperwork."

"Going a little fast, aren't you?" Cinder asked with a frown.

"Gotta go fast," Vespera fired back, offering me a blood pen. "Don't have time for chapels. Want this right now, since we stole these handy blood contracts. Sign."

"Is that . . . a blood magic pen?!" Cinder stared at the pen in my hands.

"It is," Vespera said. "I need to do this, Ci. I don't want to be bound to Golden Star anymore. I want my own thing. With my little human kobold."

"Not very romantic," Cinder huffed.

"This isn't about romance," Vespera said. "This is pure pragmatism. We can have romance after. All the romance you want. I just . . . I don't want to be living my life constantly terrified of being erased, of being mentally changed into someone else. This is just . . . legal backup, a sword against my family. Just a little bit of inner peace for me."

I nodded and signed the contracts with a flourish, feeling my wrist tingle as the pen stole my blood. Vespera signed her copies with a manic grin.

I stuffed my copies into my extradimensional jacket pocket.

"And done." Vee flopped back onto the couch. "There, I am content now."

"Why do I feel like I've been bamboozled here?" I asked playfully.

"'Cause you were." Vespera grinned. "Half of your Arx assets are now mine. Ke ke ke. Sucka. The fox has become outfoxed by the birb!"

"Nuh-uh! It is you who has been outfoxed!" I said. "Read Aesop's fable about the crow and fox next time!"

"No, you," Vespera laughed, tackling me and burying me in nuzzles.

"No, you. I now own half of your SimmiTech shares," I said.

"Joke's on you, I don't own any shares while my father's alive." She mauled me harder.

"Joke's on you, I don't own anything on paper, Emmy does!" I laughed. "The Guild Master and I have a verbal agreement."

Vespera collapsed onto me in a fit of laughter.

Cinder rolled her eyes at us.

My Quartermaster tag vibrated. I accepted the call, glancing at the caller's ID.

"Hi, Sovereign," I said. "Sup?"

"Lord Protector," Lady Astra's voice purred from the tag. "Why is my city on fire?"

"It's not on fire," I said. "It only looks like it's on fire, but it's actually perfectly legal renovations happening on the land our Guild Master leased from the highborn lords of Shandria."

"Really?" Cedez's voice dripped with amusement. "And I suppose that Infix Mage Tower just happened to fall onto the Arx Bank by complete accident?"

"Complete accident," I agreed. "Terrible construction standards these days. Someone should really look into that."

"Uh-huh," she said. "And the mass panic about a necromantic invasion?"

"People are so quick to jump to conclusions," I sighed dramatically. "One little tower falls, some renovation happens, and suddenly everyone thinks it's the end of the world."

"Right," she sighed. "What happened to the Frostix Kitlix?"

"I bought them," I said.

"*All* of them?!" Cedez demanded.

"Yes," I said. "I happen to own lots of land in Undertown, and if you forgot, it's currently infested with Duskbloom."

"Are you running some kind of a Kitlix pyramid scheme?" she demanded.

"It's not a scheme," I said. "It's a legitimate Frostix Kitlix rental business with legitimate stock options available to all wealthy mages interested in protecting themselves from future Duskbloom incidents. We also sell insurance against necromantic invasions."

"I see." Cedez's voice danced between mild amusement and exasperation. "And I suppose the massive, indestructible crystalline beast that just turned most of the central square and several streets into rubble has nothing to do with you either?"

"Miss Possible is just out for a stroll," I said.

"Miss . . . Possible?" Cedez repeated slowly.

"She's very friendly," I assured her. "Just needs some exercise after being cooped up in a damp underground chapel for so long."

"You're lucky that you're such a cutie," Cedez laughed. "Or we'd have serious words."

"I'm just happy to work with such a cute Sovereign," I fired back with the same tone. "Give Remy and Dave big smooches for me."

"Stop flirting with the Sovereign of Shandria," Cinder hiss-growled, her feathers shifting through jealous greens.

"Why? She's adorable." I grinned. "Like a deadly, cute shadow-fox."

"You . . ." Cinder began, but was interrupted by another explosion, the sound coming from wherever Cedez was.

"Speaking of explosions," Cedez's voice came through the tag, "how many buildings are you planning to 'renovate' today?"

"Just enough to make room for progress," I said. "We shook hands on it. I promised to help you renovate and to clean up the city. I fulfill all of my promises, Sovereign."

"You're moving awfully fast," Cedez commented.

"What can I say? I'm on a deadline."

"Right then," Cedez laughed again. "Carry on. Try to keep collateral damage at a minimum."

"Can do." I smiled and hung up.

"Your relationship with the Sovereign is . . . concerning," Cinder said, her feathers shifting through suspicious oranges.

"Eh." I shrugged. "I'm just being nice. She's like my interdimensional sister or something, don't be jelly."

Cinder sighed, leaning back on the couch.

"Speaking of interdimensional beings," I said, stretching on the couch, "I've been meaning to ask—what's the deal with Arx inhabitants? Like, is there any fundamental difference between, say, the owlish cafe maid and a Thunderbird?"

"Ah, ah!" Vespera rolled off my lap, stretching and bending like a ballet dancer. "I know this one! We went through it in Dr. Greyfield's Advanced Xenobiology last semester!"

"Wasn't here last semester," I said. "Please educate me, professor wise birb."

"The main difference," Vespera clicked, sending sparks dancing across her magisteel-clad talons, "is that Arx inhabitants are native to this realm. Their biology is completely adapted to the local astral and aetheric density. They can't function outside of Arx like us Omnids."

I nodded.

"Let's begin with the basics." Vespera walked over to Cinder and pawed at her wings.

A transparent human male manifested in front of us in the farm living room, looking somewhat like me.

"Hey!" Cinder whined. "What are you . . ."

"Shh," Vee commented. "Don't interrupt your instructor-birb, overhead projector girl."

"I'm not a freaking projector!" Cinder growled. I began massaging her shoulders and she calmed down slightly, leaning against me and grumbling under her breath.

"This lecture is for you too, dragon-bae," Vespera pointed out. "Pretty sure you skipped like half of Omnid anatomy classes."

"Whatever." Cinder crossed her arms.

Vespera walked around the projection of the human.

"Homo sapiens! Humans come in several types across a multitude of worlds tied to Omnithornia via dimensional gates," she explained. "Base Earth-O1 humans, aka humans from Omnithornia and surrounding nations, don't have heart cores, can't use magic, and can't level up normally. Their souls are weak. They're incredibly easy to break."

Cinder wrapped her wing around me protectively.

"Humans of Arx are different," Vespera clicked. "They appear similar to humans from Omnithornia, but are internally magically augmented from birth or from the moment of their summoning. They have heart cores which grow with time, aligning them to a *very* specific magic skill."

Vee grabbed Cinder.

A brilliant sphere manifested inside of the projection of a human male. Then the projection began to age, the core inside them growing bigger and bigger, until the human turned into a bloated, fat, grotesque figure.

"When Arx humans reach one hundred years of age," Vespera clicked, "their heart core becomes so big that they can barely move. It occupies most of their stomachs. Unless the human is constantly healed by mages, they gradually go insane and die in horrible agony as their stomach busts."

I winced as the human exploded and only the massive heart core remained.

"The core remains after death," Vespera said, "and it forms a dungeon, unless it's ground into dust and used as fuel for something."

"So that's why dungeons are filled with Sentinels and other creepy things?" I asked.

"Various monsters and beasts are born from the human's dying wishes," Vespera said, nodding. The projection cast by Cinder's wings changed to show various dungeon monsters. "The human heart core becomes the dungeon core, powering and half-assly coordinating everything inside the dungeon to murder everything nearby. Sentinels are Arx inhabitants that die in the dungeon and become infected."

She grabbed Cinder again, and a foxgirl appeared next to the dungeon core.

"Arx-kin inhabitants are known as Entrosis sapiens, low order entropic beings," Vespera narrated. "Basically, they're humans afflicted, gradually changed by Entropic magic. Humans twisted by a particular magical affinity over generations. This affinity can be anything—fox, dragon, metal, wood, shadow, cat, dog, elk, stone, etc. Their heart cores are smaller than human ones and better integrated into their bodies, so they're less prone to insanity. They also die at one hundred years of age when their heart cores get too big and become a dungeon on Arx."

"One hundred years old?" I asked. "Seems . . . specific."

"There are a lot of specific things about Arx," Vespera agreed. "Many Omnid researchers believe that this gigastructure was designed with very specific parameters in mind and that violating these parameters results in the researcher dying horribly."

"Is Arx alive, then?" I asked.

"Perhaps." Vee shrugged. She snapped her talons, and a human male and foxgirl appeared, reaching out towards each other in a kiss.

"Arx humans can't mix with Arx-kin safely," Vee said. "The magical affinity present in an Arx-kin gradually kills the human."

"What?" I blinked as a violet stream rushed from the fox into the human, and he fell over and died, an animated *XX* appearing on his face.

"Yep," Vespera clicked. "The magic from the Arx-kin gradually poisons the Arx-born human body. Depending on exposure levels, the human can die in a month to a few years unless they're constantly healed. That's why Arx-kin and highborn human lords of Shandria generally do not mix."

"Then Lord David . . ." I began.

"Has a Vitalix Kitlix on him for a reason." Vee nodded. "He's constantly healing himself. Having a Sentinel shadow-fox and a pathosteel dragon girlfriend is literally killing him."

"That's . . . unfortunate," I commented.

"If I were to write a story about David," Vee mused, "I would call it 'Unlimited Isekai and Other Unfortunate Magic.' Humans like him are summoned to Arx in vast numbers and perish even faster, bones ground to build pyramids."

"Pyramids?" I blinked.

"Zalimar took us to the Gold Dragon God Emperor's Citadel 117 on a field trip," Cinder hissed from where she was sitting. "Everything there was built by people . . . *from* people. It was . . ."

"Revolting," Vespera finished. "Instructor Zalimar found it amusing, but I still have horrible flashbacks to that place. Bleh."

"Am I going to grow a core that will kill me at one hundred?" I asked.

"I don't know," Vespera sighed. "You're the first human from Omnithornia brought to Arx. There's no precedent. Plus, you're incredibly effed in general. You have a four-fold soul, which I've never seen in anyone. Abyss, maybe you'll grow four cores! I'm not a doctor!"

Cinder flared with crimson feathers.

"Yes, pupil Cinderella?" Vespera tilted her head. "Do you have a question?"

"Is . . . Martin going to die at one hundred?" Cinder let out. "Is he going to go insane when his heart core grows too big, turning into that bloated monster thing?!"

"Lexy has a Lazarus bracelet," Vespera pointed out. "If he dies often enough, the Genesis Well will optimize his body towards . . ."

"Towards what?" Cinder demanded.

"I don't know," Vespera let out. "I'm not a Genesis architect. He's the first human with access to an incarnator. The first human claimed by two Omnid girls. There's literally no precedent here, like I said."

Cinder frowned.

"Which brings us to the Omnids," Vespera clicked. She grabbed Cinder for a few seconds, and a projection of Cinder and Vespera bloomed beside the human holo of me.

"Omnithis sapiens," Vespera waved her talons at the hologram. "Little gods. Cryptids as some humans call us. Taller, stronger, faster, more magically potent than all known baseline humanoids. Two females are born for every male, so triangular Prima and Hearth 'ships are the most common type of family structure."

I nodded.

"Unlike Arx inhabitants, Omnids are born in areas of relatively low aetheric density.

Some say this makes us incredibly capable in terms of magic, sort of like humans born in high altitudes who can run around longer than humans born closer to the sea. Omnid heart cores grow with us, dimensionally adapting to our environment, our skills, our experiences."

The projection of Vespera zoomed into her heart core.

"An Omnid's heart core is the highest known order of Syntropic magic," Vespera clicked. "Fractal Engine hearts, capable of feeding on belief. We define ourselves as theoretically limitless, perfect beings. Aligned to an idea, to belief, can feed on fear, can eat memetics for breakfast, can go anywhere across the omniverse."

"Anywhere?" I asked skeptically.

"Anywhere." Vespera nodded. "An Omnid can survive any world regardless of aetheric density."

"Emerald melted," I pointed out.

"I'm talking about living worlds," Vespera said. "Not corpse worlds. Omnids don't have a hard age limit like Arx inhabitants. Our cores can theoretically grow indefinitely, fold into themselves like a fractal. Some Omnid elders like Zalimar and Keeper Vassily are thousands of years old, and are high-level enough that they don't need an incarnator to keep going. They just don't die, can't be killed, always return. Their Fractal Engine heart core is part of their soul, immutable, no longer physical."

I rubbed my chin. Cinder stared at me.

"You and I, Ci," Vespera said. "We're highest order Syntropic beings, god-adjacent living ideas in shells of flesh. As divine-tier Omnids who feed on belief, we are going to keep going forever, not going to age for centuries, maybe millennia. Lex won't. Are you ready for this possibility?"

Cinder's feathers shifted through a complex array of colors—blues of uncertainty, pinks of affection, grays of worry.

"Forever is a long time," she whispered.

"Yep," Vespera clicked. "And our eighteen-year-old human disaster is only going to last maybe . . . sixty to eighty years? If we're lucky and he doesn't get himself killed doing something stupid?"

"Hey," I protested.

"Shush," both Omnids said simultaneously.

Cinder looked between me and Vee. "Why . . .?"

"I'm having fun with Lexy," Vee said. "But this fun can't last forever."

"What are you saying, you damned bird?" Cinder growled. "That he's just going to die from old age, while we . . . move on?!"

"No," Vespera clicked softly. "I'm saying we have to make our time with Lexy count. Every single second, week, month, year. Tick, tick, tick."

Cinder's feathers shifted through a complex tapestry of emotions, blues rising to be replaced with oranges and pinks, then golds and silvers momentarily drowning in blacks. Then impossible, alien colors ignited across her feathers, melting my mind.

"I . . . refuse." Cinder stood up.

"You what?" Vespera tilted her head.

"I refuse to lose him!" Cinder barked. Rainbows ignited across the air around her.

"Humans are . . . easily devoured by Entropy." Vespera shrugged with a nonchalant expression. "Them's the beans, Ci."

"Not this one," Cinder declared, her feathers blazing and melting my thoughts. "Not Martin! Not ever!"

Vespera tilted her head, electrical sparks dancing between her feathers. "And how exactly do you plan to prevent entropy from consuming a human?"

"I'll punch entropy in the face if I have to!" Cinder growled, the air around her bending into rainbows.

"You're goin' to find entropy and clock it in the head?" Vespera asked playfully.

"Absolutely," Cinder declared. "I'll find a way. I'll break every single rule if I have to. I'll learn every single magic system. I'll crack the code of incarnation. I'll figure out how to keep him alive forever!"

Vespera's wings spread wide, sparkled with electricity, her talons sending tiny arcs dancing across the room. "Well now," she laughed, "look who's finally taking ownership of her power. Look who's finally standing up and admitting it!"

"I'm not losing him," Cinder repeated, her voice low and dangerous. "Not to time. Not to Entropy. Not to anything."

Vespera reached out and hugged Cinder. "That's what I wanted to hear, Ci. I wanted to make sure that you're in all the way here."

"Obviously, I'm bloody in, you effing knob-bird," Cinder growled. "It's just . . . I'm not some shallow beerch who's just going to constantly fawn over him like he's made of solid gold!"

"Didn't you just promise to fight Entropy itself for our little fox?" Vee purred.

"I . . . that's different!" Cinder sputtered, her feathers shifting through embarrassed pinks. "I'm just saying I won't let him die! He's my . . . he's my friend!"

"Aww." I grinned. "My rainbow-dragon fren' wants to keep me forever."

"I'm not keeping you forever!" Cinder protested, her feathers flashing through embarrassed pinks and defensive oranges. "I just . . . I don't want you to die in sixty years! There's a difference!"

"Sure there is," Vespera laughed. "Just like there's a difference between 'not engaged' and 'waiting for the right moment to say yes.'"

"*Stop that!*" Cinder squawked. "You two are always pushing me into things! Push, push, push, that's all you do!"

"Yeah." I stretched on the couch. "We're horrible. Always pushing you to admit your feelings, to be yourself, to fight Entropy."

"Shut up," Cinder growled, but her feathers betrayed her with flashes of pink.

"Make me," I grinned.

She lunged at me, pinning me to the couch. "You . . . you . . ."

"Me?" I asked innocently.

"I hate you," she declared, but her wings wrapped around me protectively. "I hate you both so much. You're both terrible and awful and just don't stop."

"Hey," I protested. "I'm not running anywhere. I'm peacefully inhabiting a couch."

"Not anymore," Cinder growled, lifting me up like a kitten. "You're coming with me."

"Where are we going?" I asked as she carried me towards the farmhouse door.

"To inspect *my* farm," she declared. "Since you bought it for me without asking."

"Vee, I'm being kidnapped!" I complained.

"Have fun!" Vespera called after us. "I'll keep Miss Possible company for a bit, make sure the ol' girl doesn't fall apart, then join ya."

Cinder carried me outside into the afternoon sunlight. The wheat field swayed in the breeze, golden stalks dancing like waves.

The Agrilopods were still at work, their long tentacles carefully gathering fallen branches and debris. Larry and Nilli had retreated to a distant field now.

"It really is a nice farm," I commented as Cinder carried me through the wheat.

"Shut up," she growled.

"The gothic Victorian farmhouse definitely has potential," I continued. "We could paint it black, add some gargoyles . . ."

"I said shut up!" She shook me.

"Maybe add a crow's nest on . . ." I began and then the ground under us gave way as Cinder took off.

I yelped, clinging to her as her rainbow-wings beat.

We soared upward, the farmhouse and fields shrinking beneath us. The sun caught Cinder's feathers, sending prismatic reflections dancing across the air.

"This is payback for buying you a farm without asking, isn't it?" I asked as we climbed higher.

"Maybe," she said, but there was a hint of amusement in her voice. "Are you scared of heights?"

"Perhaps." I dug into her harder. "Just a little. More like scared of infinity."

The wind rushed past us as Cinder banked, circling over the property. From this height, I could see the full extent of the farm—the golden wheat fields, the purple lavender patches, the tree orchards and roads between buildings.

"Infinity?" she asked.

I kept my eyes on the ground below.

"Nihilim," I said. "That black hole in the sky. Arx, too. The lack of horizon, just an endlessly rising sphere . . ."

When Cinder banked, I once again saw the sheer scale of Arx stretching endlessly upward, impossibly vast continents and oceans curving up and up and up.

"Aww, is my little human scared of infinite megastructures?" Cinder teased, twirling like a corkscrew spiral.

"Maybe I am, damn it!" I yelped as she spun in circles, making my head spin. "My brain likes finite things!"

"How do you like that, you jerk?" she growled, plowing through clouds, banking, falling, and rising. "Get used to it! Take that!"

I buried my face in her feathers, breathing in her familiar ozone and lavender scent, closed my eyes so as not to stare at the rapidly spinning view.

"Is this supposed to be a lesson?" I asked her. "You're like a roller coaster. I think I'm going to be dizzy for a week."

"I'm already dizzy with you," she growled. "Everyday! Stop throwing me into insane loops!"

"My loops are just narrative twists!" I whined. "They exist to derail people's expectations! It's how I win against far stronger enemies as a little fox! I'm a ground-based creature! Staaaaph spinning."

"No," Cinder growled. "Just for that I'm going to spin faster."

And she did.

# CHAPTER TWENTY

# Summer Rain

Cinder's wings finally slowed their wild dance through the clouds, her rapid spins gradually easing into a gentle glide. I cautiously opened my eyes, my stomach settling as we leveled out.

The view was . . . breathtaking. From this height, Arx revealed itself in all its impossible glory. The megastructure curved upward in every direction, an inside-out world that defied conventional physics. Oceans and continents stretched endlessly upward, their edges blending into misty infinity. The black hole Nihilim loomed above, a dark eye amidst the swirling mess of clouds and continents.

A deep rumble of thunder echoed from below. Vespera burst through the cloud layer beneath us, her black-and-white wings trailing electricity as she rocketed upward.

"Found you!" she called out cheerfully, black wings spread wide.

She barrel-rolled around us, creating a spiral of electrical current that made my hair stand on end.

"How's the view from up here, my foxxy?" Vee shouted as she leveled out beside us.

"Lovely!" I admitted, still clinging tightly to Cinder. "And terrifying. Please no drop."

"Oh no," Cinder said with a mischievous expression. "I would never drop you."

Her claws let go, arms spread wide, and then she kicked me off. My stomach lurched as I yelped and plummeted through the sky, the wind whipping past me. The ground far below spun dizzyingly as I tumbled through the air.

"Cindeeeeeeeeeeeerrrr!" I screamed. "Whhyy?!"

"*Yoink!*" Vespera caught me from below, her black wings wrapping around me as she barrel-rolled through the air, cackling with delight. Electrical sparks danced across her feathers, creating a corona of lightning around us.

She sailed back up above the clouds and then opened her hands, releasing me.

"Oh thank . . . Daaaaaamnyouuuuuuuu . . ." I yelled as I once again became Alex-in-freefall.

Cinder swooped down, catching me.

"You are both *terrible*!" I yelled, my voice muffled by colorful feathers.

"Aww," Cinder laughed, rubbing her snout against my head. "Poor little wingless critter, are you frightened?"

"This is spousal abuse," I complained. "I should divorce you and take my half of the farm. The good half, the one with the crystal tank."

"Half of the farm?" Cinder's eyes glinted with mischief. "With Miss Possible? Fine by me—I can't drive her anyway. Catch!"

She flung me across the clouds in the direction of Vespera.

Vespera caught me midair, her black-and-white wings enveloping me in a cocoon of electrical sparks. She laughed, her beak clicking with delight.

"Gotcha!" she proclaimed, spinning through the air.

"Release me from your clutches, you dastardly monsters," I cried out dramatically.

"Release you?" Vespera began opening her hands.

"On the ground! Only ground! I'm a precious resource, don't just throw me around!" I yelped, locking into her with both arms tight.

Vespera laughed.

Cinder swooped closer, her rainbow wings catching the sunlight. "Having fun?" she asked.

"Absolutely not," I declared. "I am a serious business fox!"

"A serious business fox?" Vespera cackled. "You? Mr. 'engagement tank' gifter?"

"Spontaneous farm acquirer?" Cinder added.

"Precisely." I nodded with a serious face, still clinging to the Thunderbird's waist. "Maximum seriousness over here! No shenanigans."

"Boring," Vee commented.

"Okay, fine, some shenanigans," I said. "Only if you stop flinging me. I prefer keeping supper inside me today."

"Deal."

Vee and I laughed and we kissed in the air.

Vespera and Cinder descended in lazy spirals, finally touching down on a beach made entirely of smooth, large, multicolored glass pebbles. The afternoon light caught each piece, creating a rainbow mosaic that stretched along the edge of our purchased farm.

"Does this lake have a name?" I asked.

"The Chasm Sea," Vee answered.

Massive waves crashed against the glass-pebble shore, each one seeming to glow from within as it struck the beach. The water was crystal clear but seemed to have an otherworldly, slightly shimmering quality to it.

I stumbled slightly as my feet touched the glass pebbles, still dizzy from being tossed around like a ball between two playful predators. The beach crunched pleasantly under my feet as I found my balance.

"Pretty," I said, picking up a perfectly smooth piece of sea glass.

"That was probably a person once," Vee commented. "Maybe their armor."

"Eh?" I turned to her.

"Vee and I were here like a month after it happened," Cinder said. "An army of ten thousand warrior-mages marched on Shandria. Levithan Nightingale bounced their spell-fire right back into them. This is how this Chasm formed a century ago. Eventually it became filled with water.

"When was that?"

"We were in grade ten," Vespera clicked.

"I see," I nodded. "Has Shandria changed much in two hundred and some years?"

"Ye. A whole bunch," Vespera said, closing her eyes and enjoying the warm sunshine. "When we were in grade nine, Shandria was called Xandria. The city was ruled by Saint

Saria and Duke Lumir. A Healer of great renown who gave her noble heroes unnaturally long lives and a Luck Archmage who sorted out trade deals with many other independent city states of Arx. All of the Mage Towers were white back then, and Shandria had these cute red cross Lumiss Dynasty banners all over."

"That dark halo of defensive clouds wasn't there." Cinder pointed at Shandria in the distance, encircled by the massive shadow-ring looming above it. "Skyships docked all over, connected to landing towers. Shandria was a port of great commerce two hundred years ago."

"Oh? What happened to all the skyships and the Lumiss Dynasty?" I asked.

Cinder and I sat down on the colorful pebbles. She wrapped her hands around me, and I leaned into her. The light of the sun circling the black hole danced across the clouds, reflecting all the way down to the Chasm Sea vanishing in the fog.

"General Nox happened," Vee answered, circling us with a mischievous look in her eyes. "She marched the Verdant Republic army and took Shandria, along with nine other cities. Carved herself a little nine-citadel Empire, installed Leviathan Nightingale above each of her cities using supermassive Ward Engines, then croaked from old age."

Cinder nodded.

"Her progeny or whatever ruled Shandria for a while, till Necromancer Kells killed the last Shadow princess," Vee continued. "Things have really gone somewhat downhill in the last twenty years since the Shandrian highborn lords are incompetent knobs who keep fighting for control and can't make united decisions about anything."

"I see," I said. A few gray-white clouds rolled over us, sprinkling us with warm summer rain. Cinder put her wings over us like a canopy until the rain moved past us into the Chasm Sea, the curtain of rain slashing against the waves.

Vespera suddenly stopped in front of us and began clicking her beak rhythmically, her clawed feet tapping against the glass pebbles, creating soft electrical pops and crackles. She began snapping with both of her hands. The sound was almost like a percussion section.

She looked at Cinder with an encouraging grin, her gray eyes sparkling.

Cinder frowned, her feathers shifting through uncertain silver-purples.

"Coooome on." Vee winked. "Like old . . . times."

"No." the Quetzi-girl shook her head. "I don't . . ."

Vespera's talon-snapping intensified, the electrical pops forming a more complex rhythm, the tones becoming longer and deeper, sounding almost like an electric piano mixed with wind chimes. She raised her hands like a conductor, encouraging Cinder to join in.

Cinder sighed, her feathers shifted through nervous gray-orange colors, but then she closed her eyes and began to sing softly, her voice growing stronger.

"Two Omnids walked 'cross emerald plains, / Where gliding skyships charted lanes. / 'Neath rainbow wings and thunder's might, / We walked between the day and night."

Cinder sang, her voice carrying across the beach, somehow integrating itself into the sound of Vee's electric finger snapping, dancing between the waves crashing against the glass shore.

"Saint Saria blessed these ancient halls, / Duke Lumir on his golden throne. / The

Lumiss banner-cross proudly flew, / Over Xandria's peaks o' morning dew. / Like summer rain, the ages passed, / While we remained, forever cast, / In time's unchanging, gentle hold, / Watching as the ages unfold."

The Quetzi-girl paused, drawing a breath as Vespera kept up her talon snapping. This was incredible; both of them seemed to be composing music on the fly.

"Then came the day the Lumiss fell, / When Empress Nox cast her spell, / Bound by Nightingale's shadow-flame. / Shandria's towers now bear her name."

Cinder inhaled again and made a thoughtful face. Vee gradually tapped out the accompaniment. The Quetzi looked at the Chasm Sea.

"An army came one autumn day, / Ten thousand strong they made their way. / Their spells lit up the evening sky, / As Nightingale watched from up high. / She caught their power in her wings, Returned their spells with just a swing. / Their army drowned in a sea of fire, As they became their own pyre. / The ground split with thunder's sound, / Where wheat fields died, a sea was found. / Now crystal waters hide their bones, / As glassy shapes and polished stones."

Ci inhaled again, Vee snapping out the accompaniment. She repeated the chorus.

"Like summer rain, the ages passed, / While we remained, forever cast, / In time's unchanging, gentle hold, Watching as the ages unfold."

Then Cinder turned to me, staring at me with azure eyes, a smile tugging the edge of her draconic mouth. I smiled back.

"Through the wars for Shadow-crown, / We saw the palace tumble down, / Yet still we come from realms away, / To walk these streets on delving day, / And on these shores of shattered glass, / Where two hundred years came to pass, / A human soul and thunder's grace, / Found rainbow wings in love's embrace."

Vee snapped out the ending tones as Cinder wrapped me in her wings and kissed me, sun reflections dancing on the waves behind her.

A perfect ending to our triangle date.

"Wowza," I breathed out as she released me. "Did you just compose that on the fly?"

Cinder nodded, blushing like the sunset.

"Impressive," I commented. "You two are like a band on your own."

"Ci's the talented butt over here." Vee shrugged. "I only did the basic-ass ting-tong-bing-bong beat to lead her into it. I'm just glad we got this rainbo-tater to sing again." She beamed at Cinder. "Been a while since you spontaneously burst into a song in the wild, Ci!"

"Ugh." Cinder buried her face on my neck. "No public concerts. This one was for you two. A song about Shandria and . . . us."

"Love it. I shall cherish it forevermore in MP3 form," I grinned. "Maybe tune it up a bit and show to your dad."

"MP3?! What did I just say?" Cinder hissed, biting my neck.

"Oi! Aren't you full of farmer-made hearty soup? Don't nom the fox!" I swatted her. "I have to keep up appearances as the choir manager. Can't slack off, going to make you sign a contract and everything."

"A contract?!"

"I can always fake your signature, if you're too lazy to sign it," I said.

"Ughhh, why are you like this?"

"Like what? Considerate? Fiscally responsible? Contractually . . . ow! Don't eat me, I'm a helpful creature!"

Cinder chose to answer me with more bites.

"So," I said casually, hoping to distract Cinder before she chewed right through my neck, "Vee, what engagement location would you prefer?"

"What?!" Cinder paused mid-bite.

"Mmm . . ." Vee tapped her beak.

"I'm thinking somewhere dramatic. Our crystal tower has potential, but I think that we should do it on Earth too."

"*On Earth?!*" Cinder barked into my ear. "*Are you crazy?!*"

"What's wrong with Earth?" I asked her.

Cinder's eye twitched.

"Vee," the Quetzalcoatl said, turning to the Thunderbird, "help me out here!"

"Ye?" Vee asked.

"Your fiancé, Zheng, is an Omnicorp Prima-born Prince?"

"Ye." Vee nodded.

"With access to many Probability Engines?"

"Ye."

"Isn't he instantly going to know that his prized-egg-basket fiancée has been stolen out from under his nose and is getting engaged?"

"Ye."

"Can you freaking stop with the one word answers?!" Cinder flashed brilliant orange-red.

"What do you want me to say? Zheng's obvs' gonna be *super* pissed," Vespera said. "Like legit blow a lid. Probably going to pay a bunch of local mobsters to punch Alex into a soufflé and then put some cement shoes on him and cast him into the Mariana Trench."

"And you're . . . okay with that?" Cinder asked, staring at the Thunderbird.

"Obviously, I'd prefer to keep my Lexy bruise-free and on dry ground," Vespera said with a huff.

"So what the shit?!" Cinder barked again.

"I assume that Lexy knows what he's getting into." Vee shrugged, turning to me with a slightly concerned look. "Right? You don't mind making enemies left and right, ye? You ain't gonna back out on me just 'cause some Golden Star mooks might try to make you swim with the fishes?"

"Enemies are future business opportunities," I said with a sage expression. "A man with many enemies has greater value than the one without. #Sun Tzu, Thunderland philosopher."

Vespera stared at me for a moment, then burst out laughing. "That is *so* not a Sun Tzu quote!"

"Eh." I shrugged. "Maybe Yulia translated it wrong from Thunderlandish."

Vespera laughed even harder, hugging me from the side and sending electrical sparks dancing across my cheek.

"This doesn't alleviate my concerns in the slightest," Cinder growled.

"I'm going to send Zheng and his extended family an engagement party invitation as soon as we get home." I shrugged.

"A *what?!*" Cinder squawked. "*You're what?!*"

"An engagement party invitation," I said. "To Mister Zheng Golden Star. Please bring all of your mooks, I'm getting engaged to my lover Lady Vespera Simmi of SimmiTech. Sincerely, Alexander Glock."

"Do you have a death wish?!" Cinder growled.

"No," I said with a cheeky grin. "I have a tank. Vee, does Zheng have a Corpse Seeker?"

"He does." Vee nodded. "A little private one. Which he wouldn't bring, 'cause Corpse Seekers are too expensive fuel-wise. Nobody would spend this many beast cores on punching a magic-less human. I've seen his puny model, it ain't nothing like Miss Possible. Our baby is fooking serious business."

"How serious?" I asked. "How's she more serious than other Omnid magitek tanks?"

"Unless the internal clock is wrong, Possy's been stewing on Arx for . . . forty-two thousand eight hundred and sixty-seven years, growing thick on local aetheric density," Vee revealed.

"*What?!* Forty-two . . . thousand years?!" Cinder choked.

"Ye," Vee nodded. "Honestly, I've never seen a Corpse Seeker this old or this chonk. She's an absolute unit of a Seeker. Fell in love with 'er at first sight."

"A unit that's on Arx," Cinder pointed out. "How are you planning on getting her to Earth?!"

"I've got a plan," I said.

# CHAPTER TWENTY-ONE

# Bucket List

**W**hat, you're gonna disassemble her, shove the pieces into Lance's dimensional bags, and reassemble her on Earth, is that it?" Cinder asked.

I opened my mouth.

"That won't work," Vee clicked, physically and conversationally inserting herself between me and Ci. "The Corpse Seeker is a single solid piece; her body is dimensionally bound into itself. It's what allows her to cut through magisteel like butter. She will resist disassembly and will probably implode on herself and take out whoever tries to take her apart along with like five kilometers of surrounding landscape."

She pulled out her phone, squeezed both of us, and started taking photos.

"#CorpseSeekerProblems, #HowToTransportAMurderTankAcrossDimensions #My BoyfriendGotMeAnEngagementTank, #JustOmnidThings," she clicked, making her voice recognition algorithm tag each selfie.

Cinder sighed and looked at me.

"If I can't get Possy to Earth, I'll have to adjust my plans," I said. "That reminds me. I should reward myself with some checkmarks to complete this perfect day."

"Checkmarks?"

"Of my list," I said, pulling out my own phone. "Yulia, display master list."

1. Get enrolled in Skyfall. [√]
2. Secure one of those infinite free food meal cards and an immortality bracelet. [√]
3. Find a better sleeping location than the rust-covered van now permanently parked in one of the school's student parking lots. [√]
4. Build a network of useful cryptid patsies. [√]
5. Learn everything there is to know. Figure out if mundane humans can even level up like Omnids through dimensional gate dungeon delving. [ ]
6. Acquire best friends. [√] Delve to Arx. [ ] Steal a tank. [ ] Acquire a fortified citadel. [ ] Fortify it even harder. [ ] Start a clan. [ ] Steal a dungeon. [ ] Make a death ray. [ ]
7. Locate a Hearth-Keeper Shield and Prima-Hunter Sword and marry them like a goodly Nazarite to secure Omnithornian citizenship. [ ]
   7.1. Do *not* get derailed by Charmchain magic of Quetzalcoatl girls who probably smoke because they have a death wish. [ ]

"What the shit?" Cinder grabbed the phone out of my hands just as I was about to tap some green checkmarks on it. "You . . . you planned all of this?!"

"Yes?" I raised an eyebrow. "Planning is essential to success."

"When did you even write this?"

I pointed at the date of January fourth.

"You *planned* to marry us before you met us?!" Cinder snarled, her feathers exploding through a hurricane of red-orange-black colors. "Like we're some kind of . . . bloody checklist items?!"

"More like guidelines." I shrugged. "The plan was to find a compatible Prima Sword and a Hearth-Shield, not specifically you two. You just happened to be perfect. Better than perfect. Vee, what word is above perfect?"

"*Better than perfect?!*" Cinder choked. "*You . . . you . . . manipulative little . . .*"

"Optimal?" Vespera suggested helpfully. "Supreme? Transcendent? Absolutely poggers?"

"Yeah, poggers," I said. "That's a word I haven't heard in ages. Where's that even from?"

"League of Lords game, Pog-o-Champ meme," Vespera replied.

·"*Vee! Not helping!*" Cinder rounded on the Thunderbird. "Did you know about this list?!"

"Nope," Vee clicked cheerfully. "First time I see dis. But I'm not surprised. Our fox is nothing if not methodical. Though I notice he failed on the last item there."

"I got completely derailed," I admitted. "Worth it, though."

Vee's electric talon tip tapped the green checkmarks into existence on the "Delve to Arx" [√], "Steal tank" [√], "Acquire and fortify a citadel" [√] [√], "Start a clan" [√], and "Locate . . . and get married to . . ." [√] items.

"#MissionAccomplished," she clicked, sending electrical sparks dancing across the screen. "Checkity-check-check! Gonna work on that death ray when we get back."

"Oi, stop tapping my checkmarks," I hissed. "Don't deprive me of the satisfaction of a job well done!"

"Nyah," Vee replied with a grin, sticking her tongue out at me. "The tappin' has occurred, courtesy of the V. Too bad, so sad. Don't acquire a birb and then expect her not to tap yo' things."

I pretended to pout dramatically.

"You . . ." Cinder spun her head from my pouting face to the furiously giggling Vespera. "We're not married! What the fuck? Vee! Uncheck that right now! What am I, a fucking grocery shopping list to you?!"

"#RainboFruitAquired," Vespera commented, taking another selfie of herself and the irate Quetzi with both phones. "Can't untap. Can only tap. Sorry, them's the list rules."

"What's it gonna take for you to be fucking serious for once?!" Cinder snarled at Vespera.

"Just think of it as my bucket list," I said. "A very ambitious bucket list I wrote to lighten the mood of being chased by Frontenachii Scruts."

"That's not better!" Cinder flapped her wings in agitation. "What am I, your fucking citizenship . . ."

"Would you prefer it if I had no plan at all?" I asked. "Just wandered around aimlessly hoping to stumble into citizenship and true love?"

"I'd prefer if you didn't treat us like . . . like . . ."

"Like carefully considered life goals?" I suggested.

"*Yes!*" she barked.

"But you are my life goals," I said simply. "This isn't some shitty B-tier romantic Cradlefall comedy. I'm not going to confess that I started to date you because of my citizenship needs but then also declare that I actually fell in love with you while you angrily board a plane back to Thunderland or something."

Cinder's feathers froze mid-flare, shifting through startled silver-violet-blues.

"You're my carefully considered, extensively researched, absolutely deliberate life goals," I continued. "I chose you after a thorough examination from all sides. Both of you. Not randomly, not by accident, but because you're exactly who I want to spend my life with."

"But . . . but . . ." Cinder sputtered, her feathers cycling through bothered colors. "That's not how love is supposed to work!"

"Says who?" I asked. "Some romance novel protagonist who stumbles into love by accident? I prefer to know exactly what I want and why, so that I can go after it and target it with everything I've got."

"He's got a point." Vespera snapped her talons, sending a shower of sparks dancing across me. "Most relationships fail because people don't think things through. They just . . . fall into them without considering compatibility or long-term goals."

"But . . . but . . ." Cinder's feathers shifted through uncertain purples. "Love is supposed to be spontaneous and natural! Not . . . calculated!"

"Why not both?" I asked. "I can calculate *and* feel natural spontaneous love. The two aren't mutually exclusive."

"That's not . . ." Cinder struggled to produce a criticism.

"Remember how we met?" I smiled. "I completely short-circuited when I saw you. That's when I added the 'don't get derailed by Quetzis' point to the list. Yet here I am, utterly and irrevocably derailed by you. Yes, I planned to find an Omnid duo to chase me. But actually falling in love with you? That wasn't planned at all. That just happened."

"Spontaneous love is the sorta shank author-foldknobs slap into their flab books written for knob Hearth-Keepers," Vee said in her Valley girl persona. "Every Prima marriage is meticulously planned and calculated, considering every variable and parameter—except for love. Probability Engines calculate the most optimal outcome, and then the two clans meet and discuss everything else they can contribute with to achieve optimal financial landfall. Like mine with Zheng." She winced.

Cinder squinted at her.

"Unlike my 'arranged frog-man,' Lexy chose us deliberately, by himself, after careful consideration and running tests. That's . . . actually incredibly romantic if you think about it."

"Romantic?" Cinder made a skeptical face.

"Ye," Vee clicked. "He didn't just stumble into us by accident, didn't win me in the Probability Engine lottery, didn't get pushed into it by his parents. He got into Skyfall, saw us, evaluated us, and decided we were worth pursuing. Worth fighting for. Worth risking everything for. Worth dying for. Worth stealing a tank for. Etcetera."

"Ugh," Cinder let out. "I get it. It's just that . . . a checklist wife just seems like sociopath behavior."

"The Architect part of me," I said. "Alexander Glock is absolutely a sociopath. He's what allows me to talk to bigger, magically-potent Omnids without curling up into a ball, to joke in the face of pure terror. I need this broken fraction of me to succeed in life, to make choices that Martin cannot. That Mage Tower probably crushed a few people and even more people trampled each other when they fled from my fake invasion."

Cinder frowned.

"The injured Shandrian citizens will be healed by Healers Hall, it's what I tell myself to feel better," I shrugged. "Kitlix can fix a broken spine."

"Life isn't a romance novel, Ci," Vespera said. "An Omnid clan leader must be a sociopath. Enough so to ruthlessly crush his enemies. Also, he must be a caring father to his clan, to respect each Knight and sixie. This is where Zheng failed catastrophically enough to make me hate him."

"He's that bad?" Cinder asked.

"Worse," Vespera said darkly. "He treats his Knights and sixies like disposable tools. Uses Probability Engines to calculate exactly how much abuse the sixies can take before breaking. Then pushes 'em right to that limit."

"Yikes." I winced.

"Yeah." Vee nodded, resting her beak on my shoulder. "That's why I'd rather have a sociopath who actually cares about his people. Who plans everything meticulously but still leaves room for spontaneous joy. Who steals tanks and buys farms just to make us smile. Who is smol and cute and also intelligent and aggressively persistent like a honey badger."

"I'm not a honey badger," I protested playfully. "I'm a fox."

"A fox wearing the hide of a honey badger wearing the feathers of a crow, wearing a shark," Vee laughed, nuzzling against me. "My adorable little four-fold sociopath who calculated the perfect way to steal my heart."

I smiled.

"And my tank," she added with a wide grin, elbowing Cinder.

"And my farm," the Quetzi sighed.

"A legitimately purchased farm," I stated.

"Uh-huh, with totally legitimately stolen celesteel cards, right?" Cinder shook her rainbow mane and leaned on Vee, wrapping armored claws around the Thunderbird's waist.

"Mmmm. Such nice." Vespera closed her eyes, rubbing her head against me and then against Cinder. "Warmth. Care-ness."

Cinder closed her eyes, relaxing and enjoying the sunshine.

[Love.] Vespera's voice whispered in my head via the electric resonance between us as her feathers brushed against my right temple. [Lexy. We're going to save Ci. It won't be easy. But you and I are going to do it. Because she's worth it. Right?]

[Right,] I agreed [How, though?]

[By releasing my family's Archangel,] Vespera fired back. [By sacrificing the Earth.]

[Sacrificing the Earth?!] I thought back. [*What?*]

[And ourselves,] Vespera added. [First me, then you. Then all of us. Just for a day or two at most.]

[Sacrifice ourselves how?]

[Our memories, or sense of self,] Vespera sent. [Don't worry . . . we'll get them back.]

[I see,] I thought.

[Just trust me, yeah? Trust me as much as I trust you. Don't let Ci know any of this. She's still bound to Valor . . . still infected by him. But we can trap him.]

[How?]

[By awakening the Leviathan,] Vespera said. [By bringing our world closer to its doom. By boiling the physical.]

[And you're certain this will work?]

[I'm . . . fairly certain. My family has been pushing me towards understanding the Genesis Well. I've been studying the blood of the Wormwood Star Leviathan. I understand it enough for . . . this. There is a chance that we'll all get fucked, of course . . . but I don't see any other way of saving Ci from a 40k Astral Phantom.]

She added another item to my phone's checklist with rapid talon taps and handed the phone to me.

[Destroy the world, save our Quetzi-girl. [√] I read the added goal and stared at Vespera.

[Trust me,] Vespera's electrofractal voice danced in my head. [We can pull it off. Me and you. Together.]

She winked at me.

[I'd like to know more,] I thought.

[Like I told you before, there's a way to set reality itself on fire,] Vespera explained. [To rearrange everything. It's happened before. A worldwide celestorm, created by a magical cascade effect.]

[Won't that rearrange us, too?] I asked.

[It will,] Vespera answered. [You've got another slot in your Resonance. Just one more for one more Omnid. Find a Scrutimancer and steal their skill.]

[Can do,] I answered.

[Good. It'll help you remember things after a worldwide shift.] Vespera smiled. [Scrutimancers are immune to celestorm causality-altering events.]

[And you're certain that a worldwide celestorm will help us?]

[I am.] Vespera nodded, her eyes set. [It's how we draw out the beast into the open and cage him.]

[Then let's do it,] I agreed.

Her talons shook my hand.

Vespera's thoughts revealed to me more details of her mad plan. A plot against our greatest enemy. A plot that would unmake the Earth itself, all to help save one Omnid girl.

Then as she finished outlining everything, we sat together and stared at the Chasm Sea, watching slightly glowing waves smash into the glassy rocks.

"Are those Wyverns?" I asked, spotting a flock of silver-and-white draconic beasts fluttering in the breeze grabbing fish from the azure water.

"Dragonettes," Vee said. "They ain't big enough to eat us, don't worry. Well, they might eat you. You're very snackable. Nom." She nipped me.

"How waterproof is Miss Possible?" I asked.

"Very," Vee said. "She's supposed to retrieve people from their watery graves. Why?"

"Just thinking out loud," I said. "What year was she born, anyway?"

"1527 from the birth of Nazareth," Vespera replied. "She's an Omnid Renaissance war beast. A personal Corpse Seeker of Charles de Bourbon, Holy Roman Emperor, bred during the War of the League of Cognac. Participated in the sack of Rome, according to her activation records."

"How did she end up on Arx?" I asked.

"Zalimar worked for Emperor Charles," Vespera said. "Boasted to us in class how he bred a plague that took Rome's population down from fifty to ten thousand."

"Zalimar helped sack Rome?" I raised an eyebrow.

"Yeah," Vespera clicked. "He was Emperor Charles's pet Necromancer. Zalimar was rewarded with Miss Possible for his services and then brought her to Arx through one of the early gates. She's been sitting in that Omnid chapel ever since, occasionally saving generations of students from Arx dungeons."

"That sounds . . . absurdly outdated," Cinder said. "You'd think that the school would send in a new model."

"Oh, they have." Vespera grinned. "From what I discerned, they're inside Possible, fully integrated into her internal structure."

"What?" Cinder blinked.

"According to the paperwork I pawned from Skyfall admin and the stuff I found in his office, Zalimar has been doing some rather questionable things on Arx," I said.

"Every time the school sent a new Corpse Seeker to Arx, he'd integrate it into Miss Possible, feed them to her. She's basically absorbed like . . . fifty-two other Seekers over almost five hundred years. Another reason why she's such a chonky girl," Vee laughed.

I nodded.

"Zal likes things that are as old as himself, so instead of breeding or buying new models like a modern Omnid, he and Vassily have been keeping Possy alive with unnatural, batshit crazy Corpse Seeker cannibalism," Vee clicked.

"That's . . . disturbing," Cinder's feathers shifted through uneasy grays. "So Miss Possible is basically . . . a cannibal tank?"

"Yep," Vespera clicked with a smile. "And now she's our cannibal tank! Isn't that exciting?"

"Your definition of exciting is concerning," Ci commented.

"Anyways," I said, "I reckon that we should take her into the sea."

"Into the sea?!" Cinder's head snapped to me. "What is she, a submarine now? Won't we need air?"

"She's too heavy to float like a submarine. She can run on the glassified seabed, tho'," Vespera explained. "Her crystalline structure is completely waterproof and pressure-resistant. Plus she has internal life support systems. She was made to grab injured students as well as bracelets."

"Why do you want to take her into the Chasm Sea?" Cinder asked me.

"To find the army that Leviathan Nightingale obliterated," I said. "Obviously. Note how this water shimmers with jade refractions. Vee, what's the aetheric density of this water?"

Vespera sent a spark flying at the waves smashing into the pebble shore.

"968.45," she replied, dark eyebrows going up. "Oh. Oh shit. That's high as fuck. It's probably even worse deeper in."

"I suspect that somewhere at the bottom of this sea, there's an absurdly magically radioactive piece of slag," I said. "Ten thousand mages' worth of crystalline cores fused into one another. Sort of like a natural magical reactor irradiating the entire area."

"Why would you want such a fucking . . ." Cinder demanded.

"Our Mage Tower needs a core," I said.

"You want to power our crystal tower with a radioactive magical slag made from ten thousand dead mages?!" Cinder sputtered, wings igniting with orange-red.

"Yep." I nodded. "Better than stealing Abystall's core. Less dangerous, too."

"Less dangerous?!" Cinder squawked. "How is diving into a magically irradiated sea *less* dangerous than stealing a dungeon core?!"

"Because," I explained patiently, "Abystall is actively defended by Sentinels and monsters coordinated by a single dungeon core. Whatever is down there it is likely very uncoordinated."

"Uncoordinated magical radiation that will *kill us*," Cinder growled.

"That's what Miss Possible is for," I said. "She's built to handle extreme magical environments. Right, Vee?"

"Yep!" Vespera bobbed her head. "She's got crazy good magrad shielding. The best I've seen in fact. She's basically 99.9 percent immune to magrad."

"So we're just going to . . . what? Drive our stolen tank into the sea and hope we find some ancient magical reactor?" Cinder asked.

"Yes," I said. "That's exactly what we're going to do."

"And if we don't find shit?"

"Then we dig down till we reach Abystall or Gloomkerr," I said. "I'm pretty sure that this sea feeds that giant glowing waterfall and flows into the underground ocean.

"Correct," Vee clicked. "The Chasm Sea is right above Abystall and Gloomkerr Dungeons. I do love it when a plan comes together!"

"You're both mental," Ci let out.

"That we are," I said, slipping out from Vespera's static-filled hug and standing up. "Let's not lose daylight. Now, who wants to fly me back?"


As Cinder carried me back towards the farmhouse, I spotted a group of heavily armored figures surrounding Miss Possible. Their armor gleamed in the evening sun—clearly high-grade magisteel, not the basic equipment of local guards.

"Land on the nearest tree," I ordered, and the Omnid girls descended.

"Those Bank Enforcers?" I muttered, peering between branches.

"City Watch," Vee clicked. "That man staring at Possible? That's a Shandrian Scrut."

"Shit," Cinder hissed. "There must be thirty of them down there."

"Thirty-seven," Vespera corrected, her bird vision picking out details. "High-level mage-knights."

"Guess blowing up Mage Towers and disrupting an execution has consequences," I commented.

# CHAPTER TWENTY-TWO

# The Clandestine Order of Thunder and Rainbow

No shit, your insane actions have consequences," Cinder commented, her face lengthening and becoming more draconic. "What are we going to do now, smart-ass?"

She jabbed me in the side with a clawed finger.

"Improvise," I replied.

I pulled out Lance's anti-scrying wardstone and shoved a bunch more beast cores into it, cranking up the ward bubble strength, so that we could not be seen or overheard from below.

"Vee, fox me up to the max," I ordered. "Give me big ears. I want to hear what they're chatting about."

Vespera grabbed onto me and Cinder. I instantly felt foxier, my face fuzzing up and my ears stretching out. Through their combined unholy Omnid powers, my hearing became amplified a hundredfold. I pivoted my fluffy ears down to the armored men below us, opening my eyes wide to see better.

The view seemed to sharpen, gaining a new clarity.

"I can make us invisible and maybe we can quickly get back into the tank . . ." Cinder began.

"Shush, future Hearth-Wife," I said. "Trying to listen."

Cinder opened her mouth to reprimand me again and failed to produce any words, staring at me with comically wide eyes and flashing violet-pink, the edges of her draconic mouth curling up slightly.

". . . crystalline construct of unknown design," a voice came from the tall man in spectacles in a gray uniform with silver epaulettes. "The internal structure is . . . unprecedented."

"Can you truly not determine its origins, Scrutimancer Weps?" Another voice asked. "Surely your Infix is high-level enough to . . ."

"Negative. The magical signature is . . . incredibly complex. Multiple overlapping patterns. It's alive like . . . a dragon, but also isn't. The core materia doesn't match anything from Arx that my Infix knows about!"

"Could it be a necromantic construct?"

"No. It's a crystalline artifact like nothing I've never seen before. Dimensional magic of the highest order. It's like someone took a Kitlix and fused it to something terrible and then let it stew for forty thousand years."

"How many years?" the man in the most lavish magisteel armor, presumably the guard captain, sputtered.

"Forty-two thousand years, Sir Sentiyagor," Weps replied with a sigh. "That's what Questik tells me. This is a truly arcane device."

"What about tracking its movements? Can we determine where it came from?"

"From somewhere underground," Weps sighed. "From what we know, it went to the fountain, swallowed a foxkin and two human girls, then obliterated the central square and then devoured the three prisoners, then went through the sewers, and now it's here. Alive and not alive, repairing itself and releasing steam. Scrutimancer Xistin is currently leading a team down the tunnel it made."

"So whoever was inside could still be alive?" Sir Sentiyagor asked.

"Possibly," Scrutimancer Weps replied. "Though the outer layer temperature is . . . extreme. Any organic matter would have been incinerated. The crystalline structure seems designed to channel and contain massive amounts of magical energy."

I watched from the tree as Larry and Nilli were escorted out of their farmhouse by armored guards. The farmers looked worried, Larry's dog ears flat against his head while Nilli's elk tail was completely puffed out.

"Tell me what you saw," Scrutimancer Weps demanded.

"Whatever do you mean?" Larry asked.

"The crystalline construct, Sir Gootali!" Weps said impatiently, waving an arm at Miss Possible, as his Infix Kitlix stared at the farmer. "Who was operating it?"

"Unless you have a signed order from a judge, I shan't be answering any questions under an Infix." Larry crossed his arms.

Weps grumbled and pulled out a paper with a glowing seal, presenting it to the farmer.

"Either you answer our questions or you'll be considered as the Necromancer's collaborators," Weps stated coldly. "If you haven't heard, Shandria is under assault from dark forces. I have the wartime-order authority to arrest anyone on the spot."

Larry swallowed hard but maintained his composure. "We saw three young foxkin adventurers come outta that there crystal land-dragon. Brown-orange, black and white, and rainbow-haired. They wished for supper."

"Supper?"

"I served them scones, tea, and stew," Nilli added nervously. "Paid well. Very polite."

"Did they appear undead?" Weps demanded.

"Officer," Larry said with a frown, "do you really think that I would have my wife feed undead supper?"

"They looked perfectly alive to me," Nilli added. "Just tired adventurers needing a rest. Said something about urban renewal work in the city."

"Urban . . . renewal?" Weps repeated. "Describe exactly what they said."

"The polite young foxkin gentleman mentioned hiring adventurers to demolish old buildings," Larry said. "For new infrastructure."

"Did they give you their names?" Sir Sentiyagor demanded.

"Sir Lex, Lady Voltara, and Lady Castabriella," Nilli replied.

Sir Sentiyagor looked at the Scrutimancer.

"No reference found in Guildnet archives," Weps sighed. "Either fake names and fake identities or someone from outside the Shadow Empire."

"Illusion magic?" Sentiyagor asked.

"Mayhaps," Weps replied with a shrug.

"And you said they paid well?" Weps turned back to the farmers. "With what currency?"

"Celesteel cards," Larry replied.

"What?! They gave you celesteel cards for some soup?!"

"No, Sir Scrutimancer," the farmer said. "For . . . for the farm. The trio bought our farm. We were planning to relocate to the Capital for nearly a week now and had the farm on sale at the Adventurers Guild."

"They bought your farm?" Sir Sentiyagor's eyebrows shot up.

"Yes." Larry nodded. "I told them that I was looking to sell, so Sir Lex gave me three celesteel cards for it. He said they were opening a bank and building a city next to Shandria."

"What?!" Weps sputtered, his glasses nearly falling off as his Kitix flashed green. "Show me the cards."

Larry pulled out the celesteel cards from his pocket. The magic currency glinted in the evening light.

Weps snatched them, holding them up to his glasses. The Infix Kitlix's eyes flashed as it scanned the cards.

"Genuine," Weps muttered.

"Could they be from the vault that was just destroyed?" Sir Sentiyagor asked.

"Mayhaps," Weps tucked the cards into his robe. "These are now evidence."

"Hey! Those are our life savings!" Larry protested. "They paid us fair and square for the farm—we signed a property transfer contract and everything!"

"These cards may be stolen property," Weps said coldly. "You'll get them back if the transaction is proven legitimate . . ."

My eye twitched.

"Vee," I growled. "Make me sound like an old and wise man. Also, can you project my voice from Miss Possible via Voicecast? Also give me control over the volume."

"Ye." Vespera nodded. She tapped her token, reshaping the hexagram on it with her electrical current, and handed it to me. "Turn this dial left to mute the cast, or to the right to make yourself extra loud."

I nodded, cranking up the volume.

"Is this how Shandrian authorities handle legitimate business transactions?" My well-aged voice boomed from Miss Possible's crystalline form, amplified a hundredfold, making several guards jump. "By stealing from honest farmers?"

Cinder silently stared at me with wide eyes, probably wondering what wack shenanigans I was trying to pull.

"Who speaks?" Weps demanded as he spun to Miss Possible.

"I am Lord Protector," I declared through Miss Possible. "Those celesteel cards were payment for property acquisition. I suggest you return them to the farmers or else."

"Or else what?" Weps demanded.

"Or else I will be forced to conclude that Shandrian City Watch authorities are corrupt and cannot be trusted to handle legitimate business transactions," I declared through Miss Possible. "Which would be most unfortunate for future cooperation between our organizations."

"Future cooperation?" Sir Sentiyagor scoffed. "You destroyed a Mage Tower! You interfered with a public execution! Are you in cahoots with the Necromancer?"

"What organization?" Weps asked. He glanced at his Kitlix, which remained pale silver. The truth hex wasn't functioning when someone's voice was broadcast via Voicecast and projected from an artifact.

"My organization," I answered. "The Clandestine Order of Thunder and Rainbow."

"What?" Weps asked. "I've never heard of such an order."

"You haven't lived long enough to hear about us, Scrutimancer," I said.

"What?" Weps repeated.

"We've been fighting Necromancer Zalimar for forty-two thousand years," I said. "His servants were devoured by our engine."

"So you admit it!" Weps accused. "You interfered with a public execution . . ."

The other guards looked at the Omni tank, considering how to take it down.

"*Silence!*" I barked, making the Watchmen wince and fall silent. "I stopped a trio of criminal scum who killed children in Shandria for more than two hundred and fifty-two years! I saved your city! You should praise me!"

"Praise you? You . . . saved Shandria?!" Weps demanded. "What nonsense is this?!"

"You were going to burn a trio of cursed monsters alive and call it justice?" I laughed dramatically. "Fool's justice. Such action would have activated a dark ritual which would have decimated Shandria! Only crystalline imprisonment can hold a true servant of Entropy. They are now contained within my engine, being purified by holy light. You are aware of how arcane my engine is, yes?"

Weps frowned as he stared at Miss Possible's crystalline form. "Your engine construct . . . predates the Shadow Empire."

"Indeed," I declared. "As you can plainly see by the age of my device, we are a truly arcane order. For millennia, we have protected the innocent from evil beings who cannot die, holding back the ocean of darkness. It was my machine that saved Shandria today, preventing Duskbloom from flooding your streets. Only a single Mage Tower fell today, when it could have been a thousand! By imprisoning the cursed servants of the dark one within my crystalline engine's heart, I have stopped his dark ritual and saved all of you from oblivion."

Weps considered my words. "And what proof do you have of these claims?"

"Proof?" I barked through Miss Possible, the sound echoing across the fields. "What proof can you offer me that you do not serve the Dark Lord who has already corrupted the Arx Bank with his evil, Scrutimancer Weps? My engine exhumed much cursed essence from the bank today, preventing far greater disaster than you can possibly imagine."

"Cursed essence?" Weps asked. "What cursed essence?"

"A dark curse contained within gold coins and artifacts that I have destroyed," I replied. "The bank was going to spread it across the city, infect thousands, and turn them into ghouls. You're welcome."

"What?" Weps sputtered. "That's preposterous! The Arx Bank is a legitimate . . ."

"Is it?" I interrupted. "Consider this, Scrutimancer. There's an immortal, eldritch, dark god who is sealed right below the Arx Bank's vault. He is guarding a gate from which Topaz has been infesting your city for millennia. An abomination that cannot be killed or stopped. He calls himself Gate Keeper Vassily. It is an Entropic entity of the highest order, bound to a dimensional gate created by Dark Lord Zalimar."

"What is he talking about?" Sir Sentiyagor turned to Weps.

"Scrutimancer Xistin is walking down the stairwell as we speak," he said.

"Xistin and his team will soon find the immortal entity at the end of the spiral stairwell," I nodded. "How far down are they already?"

"Five clicks," Weps replied.

"Then, tell them to send their Kitlix forward and listen," I said. "The Gate Keeper should be communicating with one of the servants of Dark Lord Zalimar."

I muted the Voicecast volume going to Miss Possible from Vee's token and grabbed my own token.

"Vee, make me sound normal and humanize me," I said. Vespera nodded and my face became human again. "Make a static noise of interference."

"Mkay." Vespera started rubbing her talons together, making an electric interference hissing and crackling noise.

"Voicecast Brother Vassily of the Transit Gate Chapel," I said.

"Yes, Mr. Glock?" Vassily's voice crackled through my token, his face appearing from my token as a blue-and-white hologram. "Is your team safe? Why have you not returned to the gate?"

"Hey, Gate Keeper Vassily," I yelled over the static Vee was making. "We are safe, yes. Sadly, we can't make it to the chapel!"

"Why the Abyss not?!" the Keeper demanded.

"You've been working for Instructor Zalimar for a long time, yes, Keeper?" I asked.

"Yes."

"Sorry," I said. "The connection is fuzzy due to magic interference, can you be a bit louder? I can't hear you."

"Yes! I . . . work with Instructor Zalimar!" The Keeper boomed.

"Mmmm . . . can you be louder?" I asked. "What did you just say? Can't hear you over this damn static!"

"Yes! I work for Instructor Zalimar!" The Keeper yelled even louder, his voice echoing across his cavern.

Scrutimancer Weps went pale.

"What?" Sir Sentiyagor asked.

"Scrutimancer Xistin's team just reported in." Weps swallowed. "They heard an old man's voice echoing up the stairwell, someone declaring their allegiance to the Necromancer."

The Shandrian Scrutimancer tapped his glasses.

"Xistin! Send your Kitlix down to investigate, don't engage until you see the target," he barked an order to his assistant. "Cast the view and sound from your Kitlix to my Seer Lens."

"Understood," Xistin replied, his voice emerging from Weps's spectacles.

"Say, how long have you been working in that cave, Keeper?" I yelled through the static.

"Been here about seventeen thousand years now," Vassily replied loudly. "Ever since Lord Zalimar brought me here from Earth. I used to be a monk in Kiev, you see. Zalimar saved me and my cousins from death when Napoleon's army invaded Moscow and the Russians set their own city aflame. We all work across various dimensional gate locations now for his delving network."

I watched as Weps's face went even paler.

"And you've been helping Lord Zalimar with Gate Weaver breeding?" I asked innocently. "Making those little spiders that weave dimensional gates?"

"Of course!" Vassily boomed. "I take care of the Gate Weavers from the other side, making sure the connection is stable!"

"Do you help out with the Topaz trade, too?" I asked.

"Topaz? Pah. Just a bit o' money on the side," Vassily replied. "Takes lots of beast cores to run the dimensional gate for so many thousands of years. Gate Weavers gotta eat."

"Doesn't it get lonely down there?" I asked.

"Lonely?" Vassily laughed loudly. "Not at all! We Domovoy don't get lonely much. 'Sides, some night-moths do come from upstairs from time to time. Good cash for 'em. Course, I have to erase their minds after."

"What, you can do that?" I asked. "Just erase someone's mind?"

"Of course! The local Arx-kin are weak, mortal," the Keeper replied. "Like fireflies, they are. In my domain, I can do anything I desire. As long as my domain persists, I cannot die!" he boasted merrily.

Weps swallowed.

"What are all of these questions, pupil?" the Keeper asked. "Why haven't you returned with Emerald's group?"

"Just making conversation. Sadly, the many-armed Corpse-thing you sent arrived too late," I said apologetically. "Emerald's group was taken by some old man in a land-dragon who calls himself Lord Protector. We are currently tracking them down."

"What?!" Vassily boomed. "You must find them immediately!"

"We totally are," I said. "The beast you sent is sniffing out the trail. We'll call you when we get them."

I hung up on the Omnid Chapel Keeper with a smug face. Cinder was still staring while Vee was trying hard not to laugh out loud.

Scrut Weps and Sir Sentiyagor huddled together, speaking in hushed tones. The guards shifted nervously, their armor clanking softly.

"By her Shadow," Weps muttered, loud enough for my enhanced hearing to pick up. "An immortal Necromancer's servant, right under our noses for thousands of years . . ."

"And this Thunder and Rainbow Order has been fighting them?" Sir Sentiyagor asked, glancing at the Miss Possible.

"It would explain the arcane construct," Weps replied.

I asked Vee to change me back into a fox with a deep voice and cranked up the volume on the Voicecast connected to Miss Possible.

"Are you satisfied?" I boomed from Miss Possible. "I suggest your men don't approach the Necromancer's dark servant. The entity can erase minds with ease. It is nearly omnipotent within its domain."

"I'm afraid I can't take an order from you, Lord Protector," Weps said. "It is my duty to investigate the truth and to attempt to arrest the Necromancer's servant.

"Suit yourself," I sighed dramatically.

I watched through the gaps in the thick foliage as Weps ordered Scrutimancer Xistin's team to proceed down the spiral stairwell and confront the immortal entity.

"By the way . . . Lord Protector, what happened to the two humans and a fox your engine has consumed?" Weps asked.

"Nothing," I said. "They are agents of our most ancient Clandestine Order. They went back to Shandria after purchasing this lovely farm."

"I see," Weps said and returned to his observations of Xistin.

Minutes ticked by in tense silence as the Scrutimancer directed his assistant.

"Xistin!" Weps suddenly barked into his glasses after ten minutes. "What are you all doing?! I told you to arrest that old man!"

"What old man? There was no old man there. There's nothing to report, sir," Xistin's voice came back, sounding oddly calm and distant. "We're heading back up. There's nothing down here worth investigating. It's just a wall, a dead end."

"What do you mean 'just a wall'?" Weps demanded. "What about the immortal entity you just heard?"

"I have no idea what you're talking about, sir," Xistin replied serenely. "We found nothing down there. No signs of any entities or unusual activity."

"But . . . but your Kitlix . . ." Weps sputtered.

"My Kitlix is back on me. We are heading back to the city," Xistin uttered from the Voicecast. "There's clearly nothing here worth investigating. The tunnel simply ended in a wall."

"I am ordering you to . . ." Weps barked.

"I am telling you, sir! There is *nothing* there! It's a dead end!" Xistin fired back.

Weps growled in frustration.

"What happened?" Sir Sentiyagor asked. "What did you see, Weps?!"

"They reached a gold cavern inhabited by an old, hairy man and he simply told them to forget him and never to return," Weps said. "Damnation!"

I grinned at Cinder, whose mouth was open wide.

"I did warn you," I said through the crystalline tank. "The Gate Keeper entity cannot be approached or arrested. It exists outside of your jurisdiction, is way above your level. I suggest you head back to the city. Night is coming, and you don't want to become snacks for Leviathan Nightingale's flock. My engine will depart this place in due time."

"And go where?" Weps demanded.

"To hunt more dark servants of Entropy," I replied. "Wherever they are found. As we have done for forty-two thousand years on Arx. Sadly, while I prevented the destruction of Shandria, my engine was unable to destroy the Gate Keeper entity. Thus, I suggest you use the Shandrian Mage Towers to dimensionally seal that cavern off, so that nobody else can wander down there."

"And just leave that thing under Shandria?!" Weps growled.

"I'm sorry, what level are you again?" I asked. "Do you really think where my forty-two-thousand-year-old engine failed, you can succeed? Do you really think that your men can take on an eldritch entity that's been bound to that cave for seventeen thousand years? Really, Scrutimancer Weps? Why don't you stop flapping around and consult a Seerscope about how your future will turn out if you attempt to hostile the Gate Keeper or keep annoying me and don't return the good farmers their well-earned cash?"

Weps pulled out an ornate compass-like device from his robes—presumably a Seerscope. He tapped it, whispering something to it.

"Well?" Sir Sentiyagor asked impatiently.

"The needle . . . is pointing directly to *Catastrophe*," Weps muttered with a frown.

"Perhaps we should . . . seal that cavern," Sir Sentiyagor suggested carefully.

Weps looked as if he'd eaten a lemon.

"A wise choice," I declared through Miss Possible. "Now. Give the farmers back their money. And leave this place. This farm now belongs to the Clandestine Order of Thunder and Rainbow."

Weps hesitated, then pulled out the celesteel cards and handed them back to Larry.

"Thank you for your cooperation," the Scrutimancer said stiffly to the farmers. "We'll be investigating this matter further."

"I'm sure you will," I boomed. "When my order is done processing the cursed paperwork we have secured from the Arx Bank, it will be delivered to you via our agents. Within it, you will likely discover further evidence of Lord Zalimar's horrific crimes against the people of Shandria. Good evening, gentlemen."

The guards began to withdraw, their armor clanking as they nervously moved away from Miss Possible. Sir Sentiyagor and Weps lingered for a moment, studying the crystalline construct one last time before finally turning away.

We watched from our tree perch as the armored figures disappeared into the distance, heading back towards Shandria. The farmers went back into their house.

"Thunder and Rainbow?" Cinder commented. "Really?"

"What?" I shrugged. "It's technically true. We are opposing dastardly Instructor Zalimar!"

Cinder crossed her arms.

"It sounds like a freaking breakfast cereal mascot group," she grumbled. "Like, here comes Captain Thunder with his sidekick Rainbow Sparkles to save you from the evil Doctor No-Breakfast."

"It is a rather silly name." Vespera broke out into cackling laughter.

"Everyone's a critic." I shrugged. "What else was I supposed to call us? The League of Extraordinary Gentlefoxes? The Justice League of Dragon, Human, and Birb? The Avengers of Arx?"

"How about something that doesn't sound like it came from a five-year-old's coloring book?" Cinder said.

"The Dark and Brooding Alliance of Edgy Teens?" I offered. "The Brooding Brigade? The Goth Patrol? The Emo Enforcers?"

"That's it," Cinder growled, lunging at me. We tumbled off the branch together, her wings wrapping around me as we fell.

"The Dramatic Fallout!" I called out as we descended. "Perfect name, see what I did there?"

"Urgh," Cinder said as we landed softly in the grass. "That's even worse."

"The Murder Squad?" I offered. "No, wait—the Murder Friends! Get it? 'Cause Vee's like a dark crow-looking character and . . ."

Vee chortled as she descended beside us, holding onto Lance's anti-scrying wardstone.

"I will bite you," Cinder threatened.

"Go ahead." I grinned. "I'll bite you back. I have sharp fox chompers now. Rawr."

# CHAPTER TWENTY-THREE

# Proto-Dungeon

The evening deepened, painting the world in surreal hues as the sun began setting behind Nihilim, reflecting as orange disks across the clouds.

The black hole's corona created an otherworldly twilight, casting everything in deep oranges and purples. The crystalline body of Miss Possible caught these colors, refracting them in mesmerizing, eerie patterns across the wheat field.

"Speaking of biting," I said, watching the cloud ring thicken above Shandria, "can Leviathan Nightingale's Shadow flock chew through Miss Possible? Or follow us into the Chasm Sea?"

"The Shadowbeasts are surface-to-air predators," Vespera clicked. "They can't follow us deep underwater into what's basically a glowing watery environment. Also they're not smart enough to cut through Miss Possible. Unlike that Scrutimancer. That could have gone badly, considering that Shandria does have dimensional-sword artifacts that could cut through Miss Possible. Good job on bamboozling him and directing his attention towards Vassily."

"So they could have destroyed our tank?" Cinder asked.

"If given enough time to understand her." Vespera nodded. "Absolutely. She might be thicc, but she's not invincible to dimensional magic."

"I still can't believe they bought that whole Rainbow-Thunder Order thing," Cinder sighed.

"People want to believe in something bigger than themselves." I shrugged. "Especially bureaucrats. They love complicated explanations that make them feel like they're part of some grand narrative. They wanted a big, visible enemy to fight, so I gave them Vassily."

Cinder rolled her eyes. "You manipulated an entire city's law enforcement with a fairy tale."

"Not a fairy tale," I corrected. "A strategically constructed narrative designed to redirect investigative resources and protect our immediate interests."

"Strategically constructed narrative," Cinder mimicked, rolling her eyes. "You mean a lie."

"A carefully curated truth." I grinned. "Technically everything I said was true. We *are* fighting Entropy. Miss Possible *is* an ancient engine. Vassily *is* working with Zalimar to sell Topaz."

"The fine art of truth-bending! Our human husbando will make a great Omnid politician one day!" Vespera laughed as we walked back to Miss Possible.

"Why did Vassily even answer the questions of a mixed-blood student so eagerly?" Cinder asked. "Isn't he a Skyfall Academy authority figure?"

"Nah. He's a simple Russian peasant from fifteenth-century Moscow," I said. "He's got no actual Academy authority; on paperwork, he's basically a contractor Zalimar hired to protect his gate. Vassily's job is to answer Omnid student questions about Arx and to retrieve them via Corpse Seekers if they're in trouble. Zalimar rescued Vassily and his brothers when Moscow was set on fire by the retreating Russian army and installed them all over his illicit businesses across dimensional gates. Domovoys are long-lived Omnids who are bound to particular locations. They generally don't get smarter as they age—their strength lies in manipulation of a small pocket of reality they inhabit, not intelligence. Basically, they're perfect as immortal minions who don't rebel and don't think too hard about the ethics of Topaz trade."

"Ye, Domovoys are opposite of us Thunderbirds." Vespera nodded. "They don't produce artifacts, nor change the outside world. They're keepers and protectors of particular domains; their Fractal Engine hearts are focused inward, not outward."

The Thunderbird tapped her beak.

"To add on, the ideology of Omnid eugenics gained worldwide prominence in the late 1800s," Vespera clicked. "It was Sir Francis Galton, an Omnid, who coined the term 'ood-eugenics' in 1883 and began to promote it as a way to improve clan strength by encouraging the reproduction of Omnids with 'desirable' traits and discouraging those with 'undesirable' ones. It was then that many powerful 'Firstborn Clan' families like mine began to snub mixed-blood nullborns, constructed Probability Engines, and began to rely on them to breed stronger children like myself with ritual magic and arranged marriage. A Domovoy from the 1500s who has been staying on Arx for seventeen thousand years is pretty much disconnected from all of that nineteenth-century ideology."

"I see," Cinder said.

I stared at the landscape past her. The gargantuan shadow of the black hole cast itself across the vast, endlessly stretching inverted world. It was mesmerizing, beautiful, and mindbogglingly alien, a sunset on a Birch World–style megastructure.

"Excited for our underwater adventure?" I elbowed Ci.

"Concerned mostly," she commented, "but when has that ever stopped you?"

"Never." I smiled.

Vespera tapped her token and a part of Miss Possible liquefied, producing a crystalline stairwell.

I stopped at the end of the stairwell, at the edge of the door, watching as the night's sharp edge rushed across the landscape, reaching Shandria.

A hundred bells sounded across the city in the distance, wailing like a doomsday siren.

"Martin," Cinder began, "that's the night bells. Nightingale is coming. We have to go."

"Shhh," I said. "I want to see the local Leviathan."

As the shadow engulfed Shandria, something began to move within the dark cloud ring. At first, it was just a subtle rippling, like a massive creature stretching beneath a dark blanket. Then, impossibly slowly, a titanic form began to unfurl, a hundred legs emerging as if stepping out of the cloud across the air.

A hundred shadows seemed to reach out to it from the city below. The entire shadowy ring circling the city suddenly twisted and wobbled, unfolding into a monster of titanic proportions, a head covered in silver-blue eyes blooming into existence, thousands of red dots forming on its chest.

One by one, smaller Shadowbeasts disconnected from it, spreading out like a hive of angry, dark bees.

"Sheet," Vespera uttered beside me. "That's a thirteen-out-of-ten spookiness level."

"Never seen it come down?" I asked.

"Not from this angle," Vee replied. "By now, the inn window shutters close."

Cinder wrapped her hands around me, pulling me into the tank.

As the Leviathan Nightingale unfurled itself above Shandria, its massive form seemed to consume the entire sky. Hundreds of silver-blue eyes blinked and scanned the landscape, while shadowy appendages stretched out like tentacles, probing the city below. It released a wail that sent a chill down across my spine, causing my heart to thunder madly.

Fear magic of the highest order, same as the Wendigo Wards, perhaps more potent.

The Leviathan's flock spread out into all directions, a few black dots of flying Shadowbeasts heading towards us.

The crystalline wall of Miss Possible cut the view off as I was pulled inside. The Corpse Seeker accelerated instantly, and in a flash, glowing water detonated around us as the wall screen lit up.

In another second or two, the view of Shandria was gone far behind us. As the crystalline legs of Miss Possible thundered across the sea floor, I watched the silt bloom behind us like a massive underwater explosion. The sea around us glimmered with an alien jade-green luminescence, casting ethereal light across the tank's interior.

Vespera's talons were buried deep within Miss Possible's crystalline controls, electrical currents dancing between her fingers and the tank's internal systems. Her eyes were focused, half closed and calculating.

"Depth?" I asked.

"Cozy," Vespera clicked.

> Depth: 447.63 meters
> Aetheric Density: 995.49
> Pressure: 41 atmospheres

Lines flickered into existence on the round wall that displayed the view of the magic-irradiated sea.

> Core Temperature: 42%
> Energy Level: 96%
> Structural Integrity: 61%
> Dimensional Stability: 78%
> Storage Capacity: 68%
> Internal Life Support: Active

Cinder peered out at the glowing underwater view. "How deep can Miss Possible go?"

"Way deep," Vee clicked. "Could probably dig halfway into the center of the Earth with this baby. She was made for plowing through dungeons. Gonna keep an eye on structural integrity and adjust the dimensional wards cast by the dragonheart accordingly, don't worry."

Strange crystalline structures grew from the sea floor—not coral, something more alien. Some looked like massive fractals, others like frozen explosions of light.

"Pretty," I commented.

"Coral formations twisted by magrad," Vee commented.

Luminescent fish flocks danced around the alien corals, looking like a mix between jellyfish and dragonflies, their translucent bodies rippling with waves of brilliant jade-green light that matched the sea's ethereal glow.

"Bioluminescent adaptive creatures," Vespera clicked, pausing a frame of a shot of the underwater flock. "Rapidly evolved to survive in high magrad environments. Notice how their bodies constantly shift and change? They're absorbing and redistributing magrad constantly."

---

Depth: 1447.63 meters
Aetheric Density: 1211.53

---

"How high is the magical radiation here?" I asked as the fish and corals vanished behind us and the sea bed started to glow even brighter.

"High enough that normal organisms or a human would melt into an incoherent puddle within minutes," Vespera replied.

"What about an Omnid?" I asked.

"Omnids could probably survive here," Vespera clicked. "Maybe suffer minor mutations. You, however . . ." She glanced at me. "Would literally disintegrate. Poof."

Cinder wrapped her wings around me protectively, making the 'not on my watch' expression. I leaned into her embrace, smiling. "Awww. My knight in shimmering feathers."

She let out a small growl.

---

Depth: 2447.63 meters
Aetheric Density: 1887.22

---

Something pulsed ahead of us like dancing lightning wrapped in a corona of colors that made my head hurt. As Possy rushed towards it, moving at ludicrous speed, the brilliant thing became shaped like a gargantuan hollow diatom. Violet lightning danced across it, leaving streaks across reality that made my head hurt.

"Daymn," Vee commented. "Now, that's something you don't see every day."

"What is that?"

"A lotta magrad. It's dimensionally skewering reality, interposing a piece of the Astral Sea into the physical," Vespera explained. "Normally a dungeon core would gradually sink into the megastructure shell, but this thing is dimensionally anchored in place. Probably 'cause a bunch of Space mages were anchoring their camp, preventing the enemy from teleporting into their midst."

"Is that safe?" Cinder asked.

"I dunno." Vee shrugged. "Probably?"

"Probably?" Cinder raised an eyebrow.

"We've got the most badass tank in existence," Vee commented. "Okay, slow down a bit now, just in case."

We reached the gargantuan diatom and I swallowed. It was made from people. Hollow people intertwined with one another in phantasmagorical patterns.

"Going in!" Vespera declared.

Miss Possible's drill ignited, and it began to plow through the first crystalline human form. The violet lightning dancing across the diatom suddenly focused, striking at our tank.

The stats went haywire for a second, the view flickering.

"Shit!" Vespera yelled. Electrical sparks erupted around her, creating a corona of crackling energy.

"What?" I asked.

"Thought there would be more chaos between the cores," Vespera replied. "But . . . this thing is self-organized. It's an engine of hate, of uncreation. A singularity of despair."

"That doesn't sound good," Cinder commented. "Should we . . . turn back?"

"No," Vee said as another impossible underwater lightning bolt struck us. "We can take it. We won't get another chance. It's adjusting, trying to understand us! We have to move forward, rip that core made from cores out from the center."

"Why?" Cinder demanded.

"'Cause," Vee fired back, "if we don't deal with it today, the magrad sea will expand and eat our lovely farm in a few decades or a century. I like our farm. This thing is expanding its domain like a dungeon, growing outward."

The drill obliterated the outer shell, revealing the innards of the gargantuan diatom. It stretched above us like a dome. Hollow bone-things made from what appeared to be thousands of people fused to one another disconnected from the walls, heading towards us.

"Sentinels?" Cinder paled.

"Yep." Vee nodded. "Big ones."

"Vee," I called out, "what's our exit strategy?"

"Exit?" Vespera laughed. "We're going straight to the core, baby! These bony boys look like they can pack a punch, but we're faster than them underwater!"

Miss Possible shot forward, sending ripples behind herself, leaving the titans behind, obliterating more occasional human-shaped mesh walls in her way.

I looked behind us and finally understood what the diatom was. It was an explosion. An explosion that sent bodies flying, imprinted them in time upon their deaths.

More hollow shells were obliterated by our drill head. An entire army of men, a hollow camp imprinted into the world. Faces askew in horror as their own magic rained down upon them, some cowering, thousands of warriors and mages suspended in their final moments, like three-dimensional snapshots.

"Holy shit," I breathed out.

The core at the center pulsed with an impossible violet light. It wasn't just a core—it was a massive crystalline structure made of fused human heart cores, each one still flickering with remnants of skills.

Not the thousands of soldiers, but mages who must have inhabited the central tent. There must have been an implosion that drew everything into itself, folded the cores together into one massive sphere sized about a meter by a meter.

Core Temperature: 38%
Energy Level: 84%
Structural Integrity: 52%
Dimensional Stability: 61%

"We're losing structural integrity," Vespera clicked. "But we're close to the core. What's it gonna be, Lexy?"

"Forward," I said. "Let's destroy this abomination before it eats our lovely farm!"

"Agreed." She nodded.

Miss Possible's drill ignited with an intense crystalline light, spinning faster and faster as we approached the pulsing violet core made of fused human heart cores. The drill began to vibrate, creating a resonance that made the entire tank tremble, the walls of the dimensional bulkheads cracking.

"Brace yourselves," Vespera clicked, her talons sending electrical currents through Miss Possible's crystalline structure.

Cinder wrapped her wings around me protectively, her feathers shifting through shades of defensive grays and blues.

The core seemed to sense our approach. The violet lightning intensified, creating a barrier of pure magic energy that threatened to tear reality apart.

"Not today!" Vee growled as Cinder dug into me with her claws.

The drill hit the barrier.

A sound beyond sound erupted—a scream that wasn't a scream, a light that wasn't light, a moment that stretched between moments . . .

A forty-two-thousand-year-old tank versus an army of ten thousand mages murdered in a blink of an eye and then left to rot for a century.

Time versus death.

Omnid magitek versus Arx wild magic that gradually turned the dead into dungeons.

The body of the Corpse Seeker groaned, widening cracks running along her crystalline edges, hexamesh ligaments tearing like snapping cables.

As the Corpse Seeker cracked, so did the core it was assaulting.

With a blinding flash, the proto-dungeon core shattered and detonated. A shockwave of pure magical energy erupted around us, plowing, shattering the imprints of men burned into reality, obliterating the diatomic sphere, and decimating the Sentinels gathering behind us.

Miss Possible's mouth unfurled wide, swallowing the broken pieces of the shattered core.

Core Temperature: 92%

Energy Level: 100%
Structural Integrity: 38%
Dimensional Stability: 42%
Storage Capacity: 98%

"Nazareth! Almost imploded ourselves," Vespera swallowed. "But we got the core! Yay!"

"Yay?" Cinder let out. "That's all you have to say after we nearly died?"

"I do! That was the most exciting thing I've done in . . . like, ever. Gotta gamble to win big," Vee fluttered, her feathers dancing with black and white patterns. "Okay, down we go. I'll move slowly, so the rock can melt and solidify behind us."

Cinder nodded, looking very puffed up, wings black and red.

Miss Possible melted through a wall into a gargantuan open space and plummeted down through the air, crashing into the water far below.

Then as Vespera readjusted the tank's legs, Possy rushed out of the water onto a black sand beach. A few giant, house-sized snails stared at us, their black shells covered in a blue-gray moss glowing ever so slightly.

Miss Possible rapidly plowed uphill away from the giant snails towards a rope ladder and climbed up the wall by stabbing crystalline legs into slate stone, finally settling onto a large platform overhead marked with the logo of a tower.

"Ta da!" Vespera declared. "Gloomkerr Dungeon! Please disembark, 'n' don't leave any of your belongings or your mentally exhausted driver in the tank . . ."

Vespera's arms came out of the liquid crystal, and she fell backwards into my embrace. "And done," she let out.

Her body was soaked in sweat, and she was trembling like a leaf in the wind.

"Effin Abyss," she mewled. "That was exhilarating . . . Now, let's never ever do that again."

I glanced at the flickering screen wall covered in dark cracks and half-dead hexagon-shaped pixels.

Core Temperature: 97.39%
Energy Level: 100%
Structural Integrity: 26%
Dimensional Stability: 32%
Storage Capacity: 98%

I tapped my Quartermaster bracelet, whispering a name.

"Yes?" A scruffy female voice came from the other side.

"Hey, kitty-cat. Did you miss us? We're home," I said. "Come meet us at the Gloomkerr Dungeon entrance. Bring our mooks. We have plentiful loot to carry back into the tower."

"Gloomkerr Dungeon?!" Katherine repeated. "How did you even . . ."

"You'll see," I replied, hanging up on her.

* * *

We climbed out of Miss Possible, leaving the tank behind us pouring steam in the direction of the dungeon sea.

Katherine arrived first, her bulky form melting out of the Shadows. She walked towards us and spotted Miss Possible and then her mouth fell open.

"What?" she let out. "What the fuck is that?"

"That's Miss Possible," I replied. "Our new wheels."

Io emerged from the tunnel next, followed by Guild mooks carrying bags. They too froze, staring at the steaming tank.

Katherine stared at Miss Possible, her emerald eyes wide with disbelief.

"Is that . . . a Corpse Seeker?" She finally found her voice. "Why is it so big?"

"Correction," Vespera said tiredly with a nod. "That's *our* Corpse Seeker! We stole her fair 'n' square."

Io whistled. "No wonder you smelled like certain doom. Wow. This is seriously old magitek."

"Forty-two thousand years old." I nodded.

"Where the shit did you . . .?" Kat began.

"Borrowed her from the Omnid chapel." I grinned.

"*Borrowed?*" Katherine's loud growl made the phosphorescent snail eyestalks vibrate in the distance.

"Yes." I nodded jovially. "On a permanent basis. Vee, unleash the doubloons!"

Vespera tapped her wrist and a cascade of gold bars, celesteel and magisteel cards, miscellaneous coins, and documents began pouring out from Miss Possible's crystalline body, creating a glittering pile on the black stone platform.

"Bag it up, boys and girls!" I said, arms spread dramatically wide.

Katherine choked. Io laughed. The mooks stared at the pile of treasure with wide eyes.

"What," Katherine asked. "The fuck. Is that."

"Booty?" I grinned.

"I thought that you went on a date," Katherine massaged her snout with an exasperated expression.

"We did," I said cheerfully. "Had a lovely stroll in the city, taunted Emerald, bought some presents, stopped an execution, terrorized a city, stole a tank, robbed a bank, had a farm-cooked meal, bought a farm, had a walk on the beach, and retrieved an ancient magical reactor from the bottom of a radioactive sea. Very romantic. Right ladies?"

"Our foxy man knows how to show his girls a good time." Vespera smiled tiredly, held up by Cinder in a bridal carry.

The Quetzi let out a bothered noise.

Katherine stared between me and the Thunderbird. Then she looked at Cinder.

"Yeah," the Quetzi-girl replied with a half-catatonic look of glassy eyes. "That happened. All of that."

In the days that followed, I unpacked all of my sixty Omnimart stolen phones from my bag and taught my mooks how to use and charge them, connecting them to a copy of Yulia running on a stolen laptop.

Vespera spent all of her time in the grand dining hall, integrating the laptop and the stolen proto-dungeon core into the center of the tower directly below. She had used one of Possy's heat-release vents to purposefully melt the core and rapidly mix it into a very evenly blended slag about a hundred times with larger pieces of crystalline tower material, burning all individuality from the core. Then she used Lance's bricking wand to sink the said core deep into the floor and began setting up layers upon layers of crystalline wards around it.

Once she was done with that, she began entwining more hexagrams into it, giddily building her death ray while whistling the "Twisted Nerve" song from the *Kill Bob* film.

Katherine used her superhuman strength and deep-warp to punch new tunnels connecting caverns and plan out rooms beneath the tower to house the Undertown refugees and our future employees. Io went with her and supervised her, warning which sections were stable and which would cause a collapse.

I spent most of my time managing my Guild, explaining to each mook what they had to do for the potential year and six months that I would be away.

Miss Possible remained stationed at Gloomkerr for a day, gradually cooling and repairing herself. Eventually, she joined the excavation efforts. Thanks to the Corpse Seeker's drilling power and Io's disaster-sense, we were able to create thousands of new tunnels and rooms connected to our Guild, hollowing out the interior of our crystalline domain in just a few days.

When the space was set up fully, Vespera covered the entire tank in cold runes and we began venturing out into Duskbloom-engulfed Undertown, swiftly rescuing thousands of people from their hovels and Topaz dens.

Without the tank on our side, many people would have died, but Miss Possible tirelessly worked night and day even while we slept as Vespera set up a basic body-retrieval algorithm inside her, targeting passed-out Undertown denizens. The Duskbloom mites had indeed devoured all Topaz out of people's bodies first, leaving them clean.

Shash and his assassins set up checkpoints throughout the new tunnel network, organizing the refugees into different sectors based on their skills and establishing a basic security system.

Along with human bodies, Possy liberated tons of useful stuff, collecting magisteel safes left behind by the mages and Guilds who fled Undertown. In just a few days, our Guild vault became absolutely packed with Kitlix, gold, weapons, tools, books, and artifacts.

A section of the tower was modded by Vespera to melt down the bars and mint new coins and cards with an image of Miss Possible on one side and my foxy face on the other, aged to make me look regal and wearing a laurel crown with the words *LORD PROTECTOR* etched around my bust. Shash and our other agents were sent upstairs to lease a variety of properties with the currency for our business venture developments, offering various select, capable, young individuals jobs in our crystal tower.

Through rapid organization and delegation, the crystal tower transformed into a semi-functioning city-state within Undertown.

Vespera continued enhancing the tower's defenses, integrating more complex ward systems and expanding the tower's capabilities. The proto-dungeon core provided stable power for all operations.

Since there was only one column stairwell leading into Undertown, Vespera simply pointed the death ray at the tower housing it, attracting an absurd number of mites to the entrance.

Arch-Guild Enforcer Legarth Wixoff descended into the stairwell leading to Undertown, his crack team of Enforcers behind him, covered head to toe in specially designed cold-rune armor.

"Cold runes on," he barked to his team as they reached the bottom of the long stairwell. "Move quick and don't get distracted. We are to crack open the safes and to retrieve all valuables for the Guilds and mages that departed in their haste and abandoned much of their valuables behind."

The other Enforcers nodded.

Legarth stepped out of the stairwell tower and found himself facing an inexplicable, silver-blue, crystalline, semi-transparent obelisk standing in a literal ocean of glowing mites.

Not a single Kitlix lantern burned in Undertown now. Colorful mites drifted all over, obscuring his view.

"What in her Shadow's name?" Legarth stared at the odd obelisk and the horrid living sea below it. "Did these pesky mites already spread this much?!"

A magical projection suddenly flickered to life projected from the obelisk—a respectable-looking foxgirl sitting on what appeared to be a crystal throne.

"Welcome to the Free City of Katsburg," she declared cheerfully. "I am secretary of his Lord Protector, Yulia. How may I assist you today?"

"Free City?" Legarth sputtered. "What nonsense is this?"

"As signed by the decree of Shandrian Sovereign Cedez Astra," the foxgirl's hologram continued pleasantly, "this section of Undertown is now an autonomous region under the regency of the Lord Protector. It is Duskbloom-infested land currently being reclaimed by the Order of Thunder and Rainbow. Do you have an appointment?"

"We don't need an appointment," Legarth growled. "We're here to retrieve valuables left behind by the Guilds of Undertown. Also, Shandria doesn't have a Sovereign named Cedez Astra!"

"The Free City of Katsburg recognizes Lady Cedez Astra as the legitimate Sovereign of Shandria. Also, I'm afraid those valuables have already been devoured by Duskbloom." The projection smiled. "However, if you'd like to discuss business opportunities or schedule a meeting with one of our banking representatives, I'd be happy to assist."

"Banking representatives?" Legarth sputtered. "What banking representatives?"

"The Free City of Katsburg offers competitive financial services and employment opportunities," the projection replied pleasantly. "Including secure storage, currency exchange, and a multitude of investment opportunities. Would you like to schedule an appointment?"

"Listen here," Legarth growled, "I don't know who you are. I have orders from High Justice Luborkand of Shandria to retrieve that which belongs to the Guilders!"

"I'm afraid without proper authorization, I cannot allow you to proceed further," the projection interrupted. "The mites in this area are quite aggressive. For your own safety, I recommend scheduling an appointment with our representatives."

Legarth stared at the projection in disbelief. "This is absurd! We are authorized Enforcers of the Arch-Guild!"

"Speaking of authorization," the foxgirl said in her far-too-polite cadence, "I notice you're carrying quite a lot of weaponry. I should inform you that unauthorized weapons are strictly prohibited in Katsburg. Our defense systems are . . . quite thorough. For your own safety, you have ten seconds to step back. Ten. Nine . . ."

A red dot appeared on Legarth's chest armor.

"I don't have to listen to whatever this is!" Legarth ignored the dot, marching into the ocean of mites, parting away from his cold runes.

A brilliant beam of light erupted from somewhere high above and Legarth suddenly ignited like a torch. All of the runes covering his armor exploded at once, overloading from the ray that boiled the air itself. Then the sea of mites engulfed him whole as he screamed.

The rest of Legarth's team stumbled backwards in horror as their leader vanished beneath the undulating waves of glowing mites.

A hand emerged, then another. Hissing and smoking, Legarth crawled back towards his team, his expensive armor crumbling away, his entire body covered in mites.

"As I was saying," the foxgirl continued in the same pleasantly unnerving voice, "for your safety, I recommend scheduling an appointment. Our banking representatives would be happy to discuss any concerns you might have in the future."

"H-help me, yo-you idiots! R-retreat!" Legarth croaked, spitting mites, his voice hoarse. "Back to the surface!"

The Enforcers scrambled backwards up the stairs, towards the cold tunnel, dragging their leader with them.

"Thank you for your interest in visiting Katsburg," the hologram called after them cheerfully. "We look forward to your scheduled visit!"

The projection flickered off as the last Enforcer disappeared up the stairs.

Behind the obelisk, in the crystal tower's control room, the image of the foxkin on the laptop screen connected to Lance's mana-electricity converter smiled.

"Unauthorized armed delvers repelled," Yulia declared proudly.

"Great job," I commented from the couch where I was cuddling a sleeping Cinder. "Very diplomatic."

"Why, thank you," Yulia replied. "I aimed to be firm yet professional."

"Think you can handle it from here?" I said.

"A year and six months is a long time to leave an LLM in charge," she said with a smile. "But I've got a capable team of Arx-kin working as my hands and eyes. If I go offline or get stuck in loops, they can restart me or take over. Do you trust them, Lord Protector?"

"I trust in the foundation I set up." I shrugged. "I trust in the Guild I bought, Shash and Master Morty. Well-paid, well-fed people don't rebel, and our Guild's vault is bursting with gold now. Just keep our people safe. And keep expanding carefully. No need to rush things. Use the farmland we bought to feed the populace."

"Of course." Yulia nodded. "I'll maintain steady growth while you're away. The refugees are settling in well, from what I was told by Shash, and can see via a few cameras pointed down."

I glanced at Cinder, who was dozing against my shoulder, her feathers shifting through peaceful blues and silvers.

"Ci! Time to head back to Earth," I said softly.

"Mmm, five more minutes," she replied, burying me in pink-blue-silver feathers.

"Do we really have to head back?" Vespera asked from where she was sitting, still manipulating hexagrams far below us. "I'm . . . happy here. Still so much to do."

"Are you scared?" I asked her.

"Yes," Vespera admitted softly, all of her feathers turning pure black. "I am. I'm worried about defying my entire family and my dad, worried about Zheng's wrath. Here you're Lord Protector, and out there you'll be just another Skyfall student, a nullie at that."

"The world is more than Arx, Vee," I said, "more than our little crystal citadel. What do you think happens if we stay here past the two-hour limit?"

"The gate to Earth will turn off," Vespera said. "Till next Friday. It operates on runic clockwork Instructor Zalimar set up. Our parents will freak out and bring Scruts into the school and then figure out how to reactivate the gate forcefully . . . get into Shandria and send many Corpse Seekers, Knights, and other Omnid magitek to retrieve us."

"Exactly," I said. "Our death ray won't work against those. We can't run from Omnithornia. You and Ci will get dragged back to Earth on your parents' terms. I don't want that."

Vespera nodded, her feathers twitching.

"Aww, where's my brave, cheerful Vee?" I asked, petting her.

"Tired," she replied. "Very effing tired. You try burning a thousand hexagrams into a tower in less than eighty hours!"

"Did you not sleep at all?" I asked her, recalling her cuddling us with one arm at times, while using her second arm to etch hexagrams into the crystalline strata below.

"Nope," she said. "Pushed need to sleep away with my current. Kept myself going past the limit. S'making me irritable and twitchy. Going to have a long-ass nap after. Was too excited about setting up our lovely base away from home." She sighed, standing up and stretching her black wings. "But you're right. We need to face Earth. We need to roll on with our plans! Can't hide in our crystal tower forever. Omnithornia awaits! Rise 'n' shine, Skittles!"

She sent a brilliant spark into Cinder's face, the Quetzi-girl shaken awake with a bothered yelp and flutter of orange feathers.

# CHAPTER TWENTY-FOUR

# Homeward

Miss Possible spiraled upward through the rock, her crystalline drill carving a smooth tunnel as she ascended. Inside the control bubble, Vespera hummed cheerfully while manipulating the controls with electrical currents from her feet.

"Must you be so . . . chipper so early in the morning?" Cinder grumbled, her feathers shifting through irritated oranges and tired gray-blues. She was curled up in one of the crystalline seats, leaning onto me for support.

"Early bird gets the interdimensional worm!" Vespera clicked. "Also, I'm totally not chipper. I'm sleep deprived hyper, freaking out about many things."

"Things like?" the Quetzi asked.

"What this dastardly human-tater is planning," Vespera clicked. "Obv'sly."

"What's he planning?" Katherine grumpily muttered from her corner of the tank.

"You'll see in about ten minutes," I said. "You should all learn from Io."

Above us, Io swayed gently in his hammock, completely oblivious to the complaints below. The moth had somehow managed to tie a hammock to the crystalline ceiling and was now snoring softly.

"He's only so chill because he's high on questionable things and full of inter-dimensional snacks." Katherine rolled her eyes.

"Or," I suggested sagely, "he knows that nothing terrible is going to happen."

Miss Possible's crystalline drill burst through the ground next to Larry and Nilli's farmhouse, sending burning wheat stalks and molten rock flying in all directions. Steam billowed around the massive tank, creating a surreal landscape of golden waves and crystalline reflections.

Master Motrdem stood waiting, dressed in a fanciful new dark-gray cloak that seemed to absorb the daylight. Beside him stood an ancient white crowkin mage in a white cloak, his feathers so pale they were almost translucent, leaning heavily on a gnarled staff made of what appeared to be intertwined bones and living wood.

The old crow's eyes—sharp and pale silver—locked onto Miss Possible as she settled into the wheat field. "What manner of beast is that?" he asked.

"That is our master's carriage, fear not. Lord Protector is right on time," Motrdem commented with a wry smile.

"Good mornin', m'lord!" Motrdem called out as we emerged from Miss Possible. "Lord Protector, may I present Archmage Ovijus. He's quite interested in your . . . unusual construct."

"I hope you paid him well." I smiled.

"Well enough to gate me to the provinces from the Capital." The crow-man nodded.

"What contract?" Kat asked, turning to me. "Did you hire a Portal mage or something? I thought that the locals couldn't make interdimensional gates."

"We have a Portal mage." I pointed at Io.

"Who can't open portals to anywhere except for disasters," Cinder yawned. "Are you going to orchestrate a disaster back on Earth or something?"

"Yes." I nodded.

"You better not blow up Cradlefall just so we can avoid using Zalimar's gate and keep this damn tank!" Cinder growled. It was clear that she wasn't a morning person.

"Oi, lay off my baby," Vee hissed, swatting at Cinder.

"Relax, there will be no blowing anything up." I waved her off.

The Quetzi frowned at me, not believing in my words.

"Io," I said, turning to the moth, who stood behind Katherine. "I've been engineering horrific disasters for you on Arx this entire week. Every catastrophe I've caused? It was all to feed your gateway abilities so that you could be primed for this pivotal moment."

"Oh?" Iogann tilted his Snufkin hat forward.

"Remember our little experiment with *The Day After Tomorrow*?"

"The disaster movie clip gate?"

"Yep," I said, pulling out my phone. I'd set up a specific clip from the film—a tsunami scene paused at 49:47 and half a second. "This exact screenshot is currently on display in my van on Earth on this exact phone model. I want you to open a gate to it."

Io stared at the paused tsunami scene.

"Got it?" I asked.

He nodded. I turned the phone off. "Gate away."

Io pulled out his harmonica, its brass surface gleaming. He placed it to his lips and began to play, mentally focusing intently on the frozen tsunami scene from the movie. Dark spots and flickering lines danced around him in the air for about a minute, then the harmonica's melody wavered, creating a dissonant sound that made everyone wince.

"It's not working," Io muttered, lowering the instrument. "I don't think that I can open a gate from Arx to our Earth."

"Wanna try it together?" I asked, pulling out the lighter Zee Captain had given me. "With some amplification?" The steel surface caught the sunlight. I turned the wheel and held the little flame between us.

As it flickered, I offered Io my hand.

"Together," I said as Io stared at my hand. "Omnid and human best friends, yin and yang, like an ever-spinning engine of magic. It worked with Vee and Cinder. Focus, bounce your skill off me, empower yourself."

The Mothman nodded and grabbed my fingers with his fuzzy paw. The moment our hands touched, something shifted in the air. The lighter's flame danced between us, building up the mana. I slowly felt a surge of . . . something. Energy. Potential. A calling.

*The song of doomsday.*

As mana poured from the lighter and spun around us invisibly, Io's eyes changed— from their usual drowsy state to sharp, focused intensity. He once again produced the eerie music and the dark spots around us began to coalesce, swirling like ink dropped into water.

"Focus on the van," I murmured, picturing the scene myself. "My beanbag chair. The Winter See-Mass lights. The sound system. The clip of *The Day After Tomorrow* paused on my phone. You can do it. We can do it. Together. You and me."

The harmonica's brass surface began to vibrate, creating a low, resonant hum that seemed to bend the very fabric of reality around us. The wheat field wavered, like heat rising from hot pavement.

I pictured the frame, the phone, Uncle George's van in all of its beat-up glory, tracing a line in the air, my eyes closed.

A dark tear appeared in the air as the gateway spell bounced between us, resonating and building up, devouring the mana spilling from the little flame. At first, it was just a hairline fracture, barely visible. Then it widened, wobbly with a gray sheen. Io swiped at it with his antennae and the gray membrane popped, revealing a familiar interior—my beat-up van, parked in the Skyfall Academy student lot.

The beanbag chairs looked exactly as I'd left them.

"Holy shit," Katherine breathed.

"A gate to Earth!" Cinder smiled, recognizing the interior where I had confessed my human-ness to her nearly two weeks ago. "That's your van!"

Vespera's talons crackled with electricity. "Yass! You actually did it! Great job, Io and Lexy! Go team!"

Io looked equally shocked. "I . . . I've never been able to open a gate this precisely before, this far away!"

The gate stabilized, showing a perfect slice of my van's interior. Sunlight filtered through the slightly dusty windows, catching motes of dust that hung suspended in the air. The phone I'd left paused on the tsunami scene was hanging from the dashboard, held in a plastic arm embrace, its screen frozen in that perfect moment of disaster of New New York citadel drowning under a wave of water.

"One problem—we can't go through that," Vee yawned. "Or even send Possy through. Out there, time is basically nearly standing still. The gate is too thin, not set up like Zalimar's wide-ass gateways. We'll basically shear ourselves and shatter Possy from the temporal dilation shift."

"Ah, that's where this man comes in," I said, waving to the white crowkin.

I turned to the Archmage, who was staring curiously at the gate we'd made. "Master Ovijus. I'd like you to slow us and our engine down eighty-four times using your time-stopping skill, to match the time dilation inside this gate."

Ovijus raised a pale eyebrow. "Eighty-four times?"

"Approximately." I nodded. "You can feel the difference between time here and inside the gate, yes?"

Archmage Ovijus nodded, chanting an incantation as he probed the gate with his staff. His staff began to glow. A pale silver Kitlix rushed up his shoulders, eyes lighting up.

"Take care of our Guild," I told Motrdem. "Katsburg is yours to manage for a year and six months, maybe less, depending on how things go! This tunnel we just dug to this farm leads straight to Gloomkerr. You can give it some stairs and use it to move men and goods past the blockade. Maybe set up gateway points and hire gate mages for faster transfer. Anyways, you know what to do."

"Thank you for your trust, m'lord." Motrdem nodded, his speech accelerating. "I shall watch over Undertown for you, make it shine in your name!"

Ovijus chanted louder, slamming his staff into the ground, slowly circling us and Possy. I watched as the world outside our time bubble began to blur and shift. The sun over Nihilim seemed to rush around the black hole, clouds racing in fast-forward, distant waves of the Chasm Sea smashing rapidly into the glass pebble beach.

Motrdem and Ovijus blurred, moving quicker and quicker, until they vanished altogether.

"Io! Increase the gate!" I ordered, imagining the gate getting bigger, pulling on whatever Omnid magic was currently flowing through me. "Let's move the gate of the van into the parking lot beside it!"

The Mothman nodded, gripping my hand.

LV 3 skill gained: Sundergate

Blue sparks flashed across my eyes.

The gate moved backwards out through the van's window, still pointed at the phone. It expanded outward, stretching wider and taller until it encompassed a section of the Skyfall Academy's parking lot. The edges wavered and rippled like heat mirages.

"Forward! Homeward march! Stay together!" I declared, keeping my grip on Io's hand as we walked through the dimensional tear.

The transition felt . . . strange. Like walking through a soap bubble, a moment of resistance followed by a subtle *pop* as reality and air pressure shifted around us, aetheric density dropping way down and making my chest ache.

The morning sun of Earth felt different—less intense, the sky overhead finite and more natural than Arx's alien supermassive cloud patterns.

Vespera, Katherine, and Cinder followed close behind. Miss Possible's crystalline form emerged last, her massive bulk stretching and squeezing through the dimensional gateway, crystalline legs pounding into the parking lot's pavement.

"Everyone's through!" I looked behind us and let go of Io's fuzzy hand. The dimensional portal rapidly began to shrink. Io turned and stared at the shrinking gate, lowering the harmonica.

"I did it," he uttered with a shaking voice. "I actually took a party from one world to another!"

"Hey," I said, turning to Kat, "can you shove Miss Possible into the deep for me?"

Katherine nodded. She grabbed my hand to amplify herself and reached out with her Stollwurm powers, gradually wrapping Miss Possible in pulsating shadows. The massive crystalline tank began to sink into the deep, vanishing from the physical, dissolving into wobbling darkness.

In another minute, it was gone. I waved a hand where it had stood. "Aww, yus, one concealed tank."

Katherine rolled her eyes at me.

"Well." I stretched, looking around the familiar parking lot. "Home sweet home. Damn, the world looks so much smaller."

"Everything looks smaller after Arx," Vespera yawned.

"Yulia," I said, "send the email to Zheng Xing Ker."

"Email?" Vee spun towards me. "Oh." Her face lengthened. "You're actually going with that. Right now? Ugh."

"Email sent," Yulia replied cheerfully.

I checked my phone's clock—exactly two hours had passed since we had left Earth. Perfect timing.

Katherine exhaled with a weary groan and pulled her wheelchair from her back. She unfolded it and sat down and pulled her dark goggles over her eyes, digging for her flask.

"No." I turned towards her.

"What do you mean, no?" She looked up at me.

"You're staying upright," I said.

"The Abyss I am," she said, unscrewing her flask. "Do you know how bad my body hurts, you jackass?"

"No!" I growled, prying the mana-rich alcohol from her hand. "Chew on this instead."

I pulled a large beast core from my pocket.

"You . . . hrm," she said. "You do realize how fucking expensive these are?"

"It's fine. We liberated thousands of them from the bank," I said, putting down Lance's bag and digging inside.

"Plus, just chewing on a single core won't up the aetheric density of this entire damned planet," she growled, lobbing the core into her mouth.

"That's why I had an Arx seamstress make this for you," I said, pulling out a box from my backpack and shoving it into her hands.

"What?" Katherine accepted the box, pulling out a folded dark leather outfit, eyeing a thousand small beast cores shining on black strings of its surface. "I . . . what?! Is this a dress?!"

"I got Vee an overpriced tank." I grinned. "And Ci got a massive farm on Arx for just as much. This is probably the most expensive outfit on Earth, made up from three thousand three hundred and thirty-three mini beast cores put together by seamstress Silenerra!"

I watched Katherine's reaction carefully as she examined the black dress. The dress was more than just fabric—it was a carefully engineered garment designed to help her manage her degenerative condition.

"This is . . ." she started, then stopped. Her fingers traced the delicate patterns of shimmering, pearlescent cores.

"Dress, pants, boots, collar, earrings, goggle headband, and gloves," I said, pointing at the box. "Specifically designed to help stabilize your condition by maintaining a consistent high aetheric density field around your entire body. The leather straps are adjustable. It's the same design Sovereign Astra uses to keep herself alive and focused as living Shadow Sentinel. She gave me the idea during one of our Voicecast chats over the week."

Vespera and Cinder watched our interaction, Vee with a tilted head, Cinder with her feathers shifting through curious blues.

Katherine looked up at me, her irate expression softening momentarily. "Why would you make something like this for me? I'm not your girlfriend."

"No, you're not," I said. "You're my best friend. I want you walking upright. I want you to smile."

"I helped," Vespera said. "Scanned your exact dimensions with the tower! Plus, I checked that the coverage was even after it was made. This should match Arx's aetheric density, wherever you go till the cores run out of mana."

"You can't just gift me . . ." Katherine began.

"It's not a gift," I fired back. "It's an investment. I need you at full strength. It comes with a condition."

"What condition?" Kat demanded.

"That you let me and Vee into your dreams," I said. "That you let Vee scan you. So that we can maybe help whatever is hurting you. The dress is just a crutch."

Katherine stared at me, her emerald eyes narrowing. Then she pulled her goggles on. "You want to dive into my dreams?"

"Not for fun," I said. "To help you. Your degenerative condition—it might be tied to something deeper. Potentially soul damage. Something in your past, maybe?"

Kat pawed at the dress, her body language shifting between curiosity and defensiveness.

"Why do you care?" she asked softly.

"Because you're part of our team," I said. "Our clan. You're our Knight. And in our clan, we take care of each other."

Vespera stepped forward, her black-and-white feathers shifting subtly. "We can totes help you, Kat. But . . . you gots to let us in."

Cinder watched silently, her feathers creating soft prismatic reflections and little rainbows in the afternoon sunlight.

"No," Katherine said, shoving the box back into my arms.

I sighed and then shoved it back into her hands. "Fine! Take the damned dress. No strings attached!"

She grabbed the box, her claws slightly trembling. For a moment, I thought she might reject it again. But then she hugged the box close to her chest.

"Not gonna get into my head?" she asked, looking back at me with dark goggles.

"If you don't want our help, we won't pry," I said. "You have to want to let us in, trust us. It was an accident with Ci, and we found a horrid Outsider in her soul. I just want to make sure it's not inside you, too."

"There's nothing Outsidery in me!" she answered far too quickly.

"I didn't say there is," I said, squinting at her.

"Whatever." She turned away.

I turned to Io. "Sorry, I didn't have time to get you something outrageously expensive."

Io adjusted his hat and shrugged. "I'm just happy to be here. First successful intentional gateway without a disaster! That's enough of a gift for me, bud."

Vespera's phone buzzed. She glanced at the ID. "Hoooboy," she let out. "Really don't want to deal with this. Way too fookin' sleep deprived for this shit, can't even pretend it's funny."

"Gimme," I said.

"Aight." She shoved her phone into my hands. "Have fun. Imma have a nap in the Coliseum office. Thankfully there are no classes after Arx delving, so students can adjust their schedule back to Earth time."

She rushed off into the school, wobbling slightly, leaving me with the phone.

I picked up the Omnigram video call.

"Sup, Frogman?"

The green, moist, round-cheeked face of the Jin Chan heir appeared on screen.

"Why do you have my fiancée's phone?" the Prima-Son of Golden Star Industries snarled, his gold evening robes shimmering in the Kitlix-lit opulent bedroom.

"Sorry, my frog dude. You missed a couple of special Wednesdays. She's my soul-bonded fiancée now," I said. "Got my email? You're cordially invited to our engagement ceremony at the Triumvirate Slayer's Cathedral!"

I grinned at the rapidly swelling and darkening face of Zheng Xing Ker, his golden robes trembling with barely contained rage.

"You're . . . what?" he sputtered.

"Soul-bonded," I repeated cheerfully. "Or engaged, as the poor people say. To Vespera Simmi. Lovely girl. Beautiful. Zappy. Brilliant. Constantly in my thoughts. Love her to death."

"You impudent cur!" Zheng barked, red eyes digging into me. "How dare you?!"

"Sorry." I grinned. "Not sorry. What are you gonna do? Send mooks to put concrete shoes on me? Like some middle-class gangster? If you want your precious waifu back, I suggest you come to Skyfall in person. In accordance with the ancient Firstborn Clans Omnid blood laws, I challenge you to a duel to the death for the hand of Vespera Simmi!"

The silence on the other end of the phone was electric. I could practically feel Zheng's rage radiating through the screen, his entire body practically vibrating with contained fury as his cheeks inflated comically, drawing air in.

"You," he finally said, each word dripping with barely controlled venom, "are nothing. A pathetic mostly-human, level three mixed-blood scum, according to my Probability Engine. How *dare* you challenge me? How dare you bond yourself to my promised Prima-Wife, you . . . pitiful pink cockroach!"

I glanced over at Cinder, who was watching me with concern.

"I dare quite easily," I said cheerfully. "Shall we set the terms? I'm thinking . . . something dramatic. Something that really shows off our respective capabilities."

"*What capabilities?!*" the rotund frog snarled. "You picked the wrong highborn prince to antagonize, knave! You have no skills, nothing to oppose me! You realize you're challenging a Prima-born heir of Golden Star?! With access to the world's best Probability Engines that can calculate millions of potential scenarios of your demise?"

"Then you shouldn't be scared of facing me in a fair magic duel to the death at Skyfall Coliseum," I said. "Unless you're chicken. I offer simple terms—if you manage to kill me, you can throw my bracelet into the ocean or whatever. If I kill you, then you let me keep Vespera and find yourself a new Prima-Wife. Bring as many high-level mooks as you want to versus me and my team of five Arx delvers. Look, Thunder-Princeling, I'm a very wealthy man, I don't have time for poor people like you with your Probability Engines or whatever."

The Frogman gritted his teeth.

"Either you get your ass here and pound me with your chonky fists like a genuine and proper Firstborn Clan Scion, or we can both hire an army of assassins and waste our valuable money and time." I shrugged. "Feel free to predict which is more optimal. I can afford a lot of assassins these days. Likely more than you. I just spent about twenty-two million O-bux on a dress for my bestie."

Katherine swallowed beside me.

I waited, watching the frog-like face on the screen, enjoying the way his cheeks wobbled with rage. The silence stretched between us, pregnant with tension.

"You," Zheng finally hissed, "will regret this."

"Probably," I agreed cheerfully. "But right now, I'm enjoying watching you turn several hilarious shades of green. Shall we set the duel date? My weekend is open!"

I could see the calculations happening behind his eyes—potential outcomes being analyzed, him tapping something into his golden artifact probability watch with green, fat fingers.

"Skyfall Coliseum," he said finally, eyes burning like two rubies. "Sunday. High noon."

"Perfect," I said. "It's a date! See you in two days, froggy-snookums! Toodles!"

I sent him a kiss and hung up before he could hurl more insults at me.

Cinder, Kat, and Io stared at me.

"What?" I asked them. "I already beat up an immortal Koshchei Archmage. Beating up a rotund Thunda-Prince Frogman and his overpaid army is like a downgrade at this point."

"A very angry, wealthy prince who can predict the future." Cinder pursed her lips, glaring at me with an expression that promised all sorts of things, wings flashing in irate and worried colors.

"Ah! That reminds me," I said. "We should probably wake our sleeping angry dragon and co. Io, you want to zap 'em awake with one of Lance's batons?"

Io nodded. He climbed into Lance's bag where a trio of Omnids were snoozing, forced into deep, dreamless sleep by Vee's machinations four days ago.

"Ci," I said, turning to my girlfriend, "go help Kat put the dress on. The back corset is finicky."

Cinder nodded.

"Right. Thanks for the . . . outfit. I'll . . . go change," Kat let out. She rapidly rolled off without another word in the direction of the academy's entrance. Cinder followed the wheelchair-bound Stollwurm, wings flashing orange and violet. They rapidly hissed something at each other, probably discussing me and my recklessly suicidal ways.

# CHAPTER TWENTY-FIVE

# Dearly Deported

June watched the Arx gate and the clock on the wall with growing anxiety. Her Kelpie mane rippled with nervous energy, droplets of water scattering across the dark marble floor of the classroom. She crumpled and repeatedly unfolded a paper in her pale blue hands, the official seal of the Arx Bank glaring up at her in stark black lettering.

*By order of Arx Bank, your delving team has been deported from Shandria for the period of one hundred years. Consult Lord Zalimar for future delves. Sincerely, Arx-Earth Gate Administrator Gabriella Matrosin*, the paper stated bluntly.

The long arrow of the clock finished its final pass and the clock struck exactly 12:00.

"No," June whispered, her heart beating like mad.

She felt that she was a fool, that she really should have talked to Iogann when she still had the chance, that she should have . . .

She had no idea what she could have done to prevent this awful disaster of a delve.

Across Skyfall campus, the white Cathedraltown citadel noon bells began ringing, announcing lunch. The black crystalline gate began to dim, its obsidian surface losing its previous luminescent sheen, each hexagram on its surface darkening one by one. The silver Gate Weaver spider slowly began to retreat into its cocoon embedded in the classroom's high ceiling, and then the gate became pure black, shutting down completely.

"Wait! Stop! Go back down, damn it!" June shouted at the spider, her voice rising in panic. "Not everyone's through!"

Her teammates glanced at her.

They had already processed the deportation order, their expressions that of sadness, worry, and resignation. A few more people were still milling in the classroom, waiting for Captain Quint and the others to show up. Most students had already gone to nap on campus, to have lunch, or to discuss the unfairness of their deportation.

"June." Gregory, the Vodyanoy, grabbed her shoulder. "You're yelling at a spider. Gate Weavers don't talk."

"I freaking know, I . . . just . . . I don't know what to do, Greg!" June hissed, droplets of water from her mane and eyes raining sadly onto the marble floor. The Gate Weaving spider continued its methodical, long-limbed inevitable retreat, completely ignoring her emotional outburst. "We've never had someone left behind!"

"How can the bank just deport us in the middle of the night?" Yara, the Lusca, snarled. "It's not fair! We only spent a few days on Arx! What in the Abyss did we even do to deserve deportation?!"

"Sometimes bureaucracy is like water. It flows wherever it wants, and you can't stop it." Gregory shrugged.

"Oh no! Quint didn't come back," Christi's flame flared bright green-blue. "We're missing eight people! This is very bad! We have to let Skyfall Administration know right away so that they can get beast cores and reopen the gate, send Corpse Seekers to find them ASAP! With each minute, we're losing an hour and a half! We have to . . ."

"I'll call Vice Principal Graves right away and let him know." Lance pulled out his phone, his face pale. He was clearly worried sick about his little sister.

"Hey, guys!" A cheerful voice boomed from the direction of the double doors leading into the classroom.

Everyone still present in the classroom turned towards the voice. Alexander Glock emerged from the dark marble stairwell.

"W-what? H-how?!" June's eyes went as wide as two plates, looking at Alex and then at the dim gate several times. "*What?!*"

"Fancy seeing you all here!" the mixie teen declared. "Why the long faces? Aww, did you miss me?"

"A-Alex! How did you get back?" June demanded, her liquid hair whipping around her like agitated tentacles. "The gate just closed! Oh. You must have been deported earlier than us . . . right?"

"Deported?" Alexander raised an eyebrow. "Sounds like a suggestion more than a rule. Let me see that paper. Definitely a suggestion. Miss Gabriella works for me now."

"Alex, quit messing around!" Lance yelled, rushing towards the human-looking mixie. "Where's my sister?! Where's the rest of your team?! Where's . . ."

"Relax, big bro," Alexander replied, his voice calm and steady. "Cindy's with Kat, helping her change in the bathroom. Vee is having a nap in the Coliseum. Io is right behind me."

Iogann entered the classroom, followed by extremely disgruntled and dishevelled-looking Emerald, weary-looking Solace, and Quint, whose expression was impossible to read as usual.

"I don't understand," Lance said. "Did you all leave early?"

"We didn't effing leave early, you effing knob," Emerald let out. "We were fucking left behind and . . ."

"Language, Emmy," Alexander commented.

The dragon girl suddenly deflated as if struck, her entire body trembling, voice suddenly extinguished, as if smothered by an invisible claw.

"Left behind?!" June's liquid hair began to curl and twist in confused agitation. "But that's not possible. How did you even . . .?"

"No idea." Solace shrugged. "We were about to be executed, and then . . . we woke up in a parking lot at Skyfall."

"*Executed?!*" Christi ignited even brighter. "For what?!"

"Em attempted to murder the Sovereign of Shandria. I rescued everyone," Alexander said. "Io and I combined our wicked powers to open a gate back home."

"You gated home . . . from Arx?!" Lance asked.

"We didn't make it back in time to Keeper Vassily's gold cave," Alexander explained. "Due to us having to waste time and resources to rescue Em's party from the clutches of the Shandrian authorities."

"Oh, wow!" June's blue eyes lit up as she stared at Iogann. "You opened a gate back home?! One that could be used even with the massive time-dilation?! That's amazing, Iogann!"

Io shrugged.

"Combined your powers? You have no effing . . ." Emerald sent a glare at Alexander.

The mixed-blood student raised an eyebrow.

Emerald swallowed nervously. "I'm going to change and shower now," she let out. "Is that allowed . . . master?"

Her words were laced with sarcasm and sprinkled with hatred.

"Yeah." Alex nodded. "Go wash up. You smell like rotten fruit."

"Gee, I wonder why that is." Emerald gritted her teeth and marched in the direction of the change rooms. She indeed smelled very badly, as June noticed, and looked like she was covered in dry fruits, her normally vibrant scales gray and exceptionally filthy.

"I'll go help her," Solace let out, glancing at Alexander. The mixie photographer nodded, and Solace rushed off after Emerald.

"You too, Pres," Alexander said. "Go wash up."

Quint nodded and silently walked to the showers.

June stared at the mixie student.

Something extraordinarily fucky was happening here. What in the Abyss did she miss?

Then a beautiful, tall, and muscular Stollwurm stepped out of the double doors, dressed in a black leather dress, gloves and boots studded with thousands upon thousands of beast cores shimmering on her like arrays of silver stars. A black collar featuring a big beast core entwined with smaller ones shone on the wurm's neck.

"Whaaaaaa . . . who . . .?!" June's mouth fell open, her mind careening sideways into the Abyss as it took her a few seconds to recognize the triangular sharp black patterns of scales on blue cheeks and the annoyed expression. "Kathy . . . you . . . you can walk?! How?! Oh, wow, you're . . . absolutely stunning . . . and . . . uhh . . . so tall!"

I watched June's shocked expression as Katherine walked towards us, her movements fluid and confident thanks to her beast core dress. The entire outfit was truly a masterpiece of Arx mage work—black leather interwoven with thousands of tiny, glittering cores that caught the light like a cloud of silver fireflies.

All eyes turned to Kat, jaws dropping left and right.

"I could always walk, you knob," Katherine said flatly, her voice carrying a hint of "don't make a big deal out of this." "It was just . . . unpleasant. It still is, just slightly more tolerable now, like a bad migraine that I can push through."

June's liquid hair began to wriggle wildly in pure shock, water droplets splattering everywhere like a malfunctioning sprinkler system. "*But how?!*"

"Overpriced magic dress," I said. "Cost an arm and a leg. Totally worth it, right?"

"R-right!" June agreed, nodding vigorously. "Jeez. Are you and Io really . . . siblings? You're just so tall and muscular . . . and he's, uhmmm . . . small, cute, and fluffy."

Katherine's emerald eyes narrowed dangerously. "If any of you say one more word about this dress or about how tall I am, I will end you."

"Isn't it lovely?" I grinned.

Kat's spiked tail started to twitch.

Cinder stepped out from the doors next. Lance relaxed visibly. "You okay, Cassie?" he asked.

"Eh." She shrugged, wings silver and blue and face weary. "Getting by."

Lance wrapped his sister in his embrace. "I was so worried!" he cried out. "When the gate closed, I thought that you . . ."

"Let go of me, you foldknob," Cinder hissed.

"Don't let go," I encouraged. "Squeeze her harder!"

June stared at me, silver-blue eyes begging for an explanation.

"I'm a bit tired," I said with a yawn. "Why don't you talk to Io? I think he slept earlier than we did. Adjusted his schedule ahead of schedule. Clever moth."

"Io?" The Kelpie blushed slightly.

"Mhmmm," I nodded. "You should make a nice Friday date out of it!"

"A date?!" both of them repeated, staring at me.

"Yeah." I nodded with a wide smile. "If it works out, maybe the Hydroblades team can join our clan!"

"You have a *clan*?!" June's face snapped to me.

"Yep." I nodded. "Made one this week. Io can tell you about it! We've got a lovely crystal citadel and many employees and a death ray. Oh, and a lovely ocean-view farm!"

"What?!" June sputtered. "You're kidding . . . right?"

"He's not kidding," Cinder deadpanned.

"What?" Team Hydroblades stared at me.

"He's managed to take over half of Shandria in a week," Cinder said. "Somehow. Against all of my expectations. Against all sanity and reason."

"How?" June mewled.

"I'm a wizard." I grinned, pushing Io into the direction of June.

The poor moth looked back at me with wide, gray, nervous eyes. He wasn't prepared for my sudden matchmaking.

"Go on," I encouraged.

"But," Io whisper-hissed at me, "what if she's not into . . . disasters?"

"June, are you into disaster movies?" I asked bluntly.

June blinked at me. "What?"

"Disaster movies," I repeated. "Are you into them? Kind of important for our merger."

Io looked as if he was about to melt into a puddle of nervous energy. His usual laid-back demeanor had completely evaporated, replaced by pure, unadulterated panic.

I stepped closer to Io and whispered, "She's a Water mage. Water. Destruction. Chaos. She almost drowned Em, think about that!"

June's sharp, silver-blue ears perked up. "Wait. What do disaster movies have to do with anything?"

Io stared at June like a deer caught in headlights.

"My Mothman appreciates them," I said. "Actually, what are Kelpie powers activated by? What sort of things motivate your magic, produce that water elemental thing you summon?"

"Thoughts of deep water," June replied. "The idea of . . . drowning someone."

"So," I began, "you like watching people . . . drown? The more people drown in a movie, the more you love it?"

"Y-yeah," June nodded, blushing.

"Ha!" I patted Io's shoulder. "Knew it! She's perfect. Go on then, ask her out!"

Io mumbled something vaguely coherent, which might have been a plea for divine intervention. Was he perhaps scared of the Kelpie girl? She was only half a head taller than him. Omnid girls were generally taller and stronger than boys, from what I knew. It probably had something to do with the wish of Nazareth for a female goddess.

Or maybe he was scared of water. He did say that moths and water didn't mix. Eh, whatever, I got over my fear of Omnid femme claws; he could get over his fear of getting soaked.

June's liquid hair was doing that adorable nervous wiggle thing, spattering water droplets everywhere like an excited puppy. Io adjusted his Snufkin hat, looking as though he was about to bolt or pass out from the tension.

"So, Io," I heard June say, her voice cracking slightly. "Want to . . . get coffee? M-maybe watch . . ."

I displayed the movie title above Io's head on my phone.

" . . . *The Day After Tomorrow*?" June blushed with dark blue tones, reading the title.

Io glanced at me with a look of a small puppy and then let out the smallest nod of his oversized hat.

I grinned and backed away from the pair, sending Io a thumbs-up and letting them sort out the details of their impending disaster-movie date in somewhat awkward chatter from June and occasional muffled answers from the smaller, fluffy Io.

Mission accomplished—one moth successfully pushed towards moist happiness! I mentally patted myself on the back.

I turned my eyes back to Cinder. My Quetzi GF finally battled herself out of her brother's embrace.

"So, umm," Lance asked us, "what happened on Arx exactly?"

"Like I'd tell you." Cinder defaulted to her antisocial goth persona.

"Ci will write up a detailed report you can read later," I replied. "We're exhausted as hell right now, do give us time. Had to leave Shandria at like 3:55 AM Arx time so as not to worry you too much!"

"Appreciate it." Lance nodded. "All right, then. Rest up."

"To the Coliseum!" I declared, grabbing Ci and Kat by their elbows.

I led my Omnid bestie and waifu towards the Coliseum, leaving the confused Water mages, the potential future couple, Christi, and Lance behind. The afternoon January sunshine danced across the academy grounds as we walked. The weather was refreshing, about sixteen degrees Celsius.

"Why are we going to the Coliseum?" Kat asked, her sparkly dress catching the light with every step.

"Because that's where Vee is napping," I replied. "And because I need to study the layout of the land for Sunday's duel!"

"You're actually going through with this insanity?" Cinder asked.

"Of course." I nodded. "Already declared it the Omnid blood and clan way. Can't back out now!"

"You're going to get yourself killed," Katherine said flatly.

"Mmm," I pondered. "Nah. Ci won't allow that. Right, dragon-bae?"

I turned to look at Cinder, watching her iridescent feathers shift through a complex array of worried colors—blues of uncertainty, pinks of worried affection, grays of stress.

"Right?" I elbowed her, giving her a cheeky grin.

She growled, her wings flaring. "Don't put this on me! You're the one who challenged a Prima-born Omnicorp heir to a duel like a wild chuppy defending his nest!"

"Too bad you're not engaged to a dumb posh knob," I said. "I could have organized a double death match that way!"

I laughed at Cinder's exasperated expression. Katherine let out a deep, rumbling sigh.

"You seriously attract deadly problems like flies," Cinder growled. "How do you even manage this?"

"Talent. Pure talent of being an annoying knob," I declared.

Katherine rolled her eyes, adjusting her new beast core collar. "You're going to get yourself killed this time. Your luck can't last forever. Challenging a dangerously wealthy and clever Prima-born heir to a public duel? That's a suicide sandwich right there."

"Calculated risk," I replied cheerfully. "Besides, I've got the best team in existence backing me up."

Cinder's wings twitched. "And what exactly is your plan?"

"Plan?" I raised an eyebrow. "None."

"*None?!*" Cinder and Kat barked at the same time.

"Can't stop me by predicting the future if I have no plan," I said sagely. "Isn't that how Probability Engines work?"

I absorbed their shocked expressions like a cheeky sponge.

"You can't just go into a duel with *no* freaking *plan!*" Cinder hissed.

"Sure I can." I shrugged. "My superpower is rapid unpredictability. Haven't you noticed that by now?"

"I thought that your superpower is being annoying." Katherine massaged her temple. "This is why humans die young."

We entered the Coliseum—a massive circular structure that looked as though it had been carved from a single piece of white Leviathan bone. Vespera was indeed napping on a large round black couch surrounded by glass walls, her black-and-white feathers creating a soft cocoon around herself.

I panned the camera around the Coliseum and slipped into the office and joined Vee on the big couch.

A magisteel-covered claw came up and drew me into her embrace.

"Thought you were sleeping," I commented.

[I am sleeping,] the answer buzzed in my head as sparks rained across my temple.

"You are?" I blinked. "Then how are you moving and sending thoughts at me?"

[A skill called sleepwalking, duh,] Vee's voice buzzed. [My body is asleep, but my soul ain't. I'm piloting my sleeping bod from my dream. Plzzz pet 'n' cuddle the birb. Both of you. I . . . thought that I could be fine alone, but no, I am not. Scared. Worried. Concerned.]

I settled into Vespera's embrace, feeling her electrical currents dancing softly across my skin.

"Ci, get your rainbow-butt here," I said. "Vee needs our hugs."

Cinder chewed on her lip but joined us on the couch, wrapping her rainbow-hued wings around both of us.

Kat settled away from us at a large moon seat, closing her eyes.

I relaxed, letting go of my worries. It was time for some well-earned rest after my hard work on Arx! A few days of warm niceness filled with nothing but cuddles and sunshine till my possible perma-death at the hands of the Frog-Prince and then my possible dissection and eternal imprisonment at the hands of the Frontenachii Omnicorp.

"Alexander Glock," the speakers above us hissed with the static-filled voice of Vice Principal Graves. "Report to my office immediately."

Ah, I totally forgot that Emerald had exposed me as a human to the entire school a week ago with her PDF and personal Scrutimancer.

So much for my cuddle time.

# CHAPTER TWENTY-SIX

# The All-Seeing Eye

It had been four AM in Thunderland when Zheng was shaken awake by his great-grandfather's personal butler and told to come right away to his office.

Zheng didn't like the old man, didn't like being woken up so early, so instead of heading straight to the Arch-Elder's office, he had loafed in bed for a few minutes, grabbing at his tablet to aimlessly scroll through his notifications to wake up his brain.

A new unread email was there from an unknown sender. A Skyfall Academy student, as the @ tag told him. Zheng wondered what in the Abyss this student wanted. It was probably another complaint about his fiancée's inappropriate behavior.

Zheng yawned and clicked open the email from AlexanderGlock@skyfall.om, his pudgy green fingers tapping irritably on the golden-encrusted tablet. The subject line read: *Engagement Invitation: Vespera Simmi & Alexander Glock!*

Zheng read the subject line again, his mind sliding sideways.

*What?!*

He scrolled down.

The email was meticulously formatted, with a professional letterhead featuring the crest of something called the Order of Thunder and Rainbow—a ridiculous emblem showing a lightning bolt piercing a rainbow circle. Attached were high-resolution photos of Vespera kissing and hugging a dark-haired human teenager in front of what looked like a white farmhouse and then sitting together and hugging on a rainbow-pebble beach.

Zheng's pudgy fingers trembled as he scrolled through the email, his face progressively changing from confusion to shock to blinding rage. The photos were high-resolution, professionally edited, showing intimate moments between his fiancée and another man, a human at that!

The accompanying text was even more infuriating:

*Dearest Zheng Xing Ker of Golden Star Industries, you are cordially invited to our engagement party at . . .*

This had to be a joke! Zheng glanced at the Omnithornia clock on his wall. It was about twelve PM in Cradlefall now, the middle of the day.

Zheng ignored the patiently waiting butler, grabbed his phone, and angrily stabbed his finger into Vespera's Omnigram and then the call button.

Suddenly, instead of Vespera's or Emerald's laughing face as he expected, the face of the dark-haired, green-eyed human, the same one from the photos, appeared on screen.

"Sup, Frogman?" the human asked.

* * *

Zheng screamed in fury as the impudent pink roach hung up on him, his golden robes trembling with barely contained rage. How dare this nullie, this mixed-blood vermin, challenge him? How dare he claim Vespera as his own?

He checked his probability watch again, the intricate magisteel device clicking and humming with complex calculations. The watch once again told Zheng that Alexander Glock was just a pathetically weak level three Thunderbird-hybrid-human with Mothman, Quetzi, and Stollwurm ancestry in him.

He went over the most likely future outcome, the screen displayed a dizzying array of potential scenarios, each one confirming his inevitable victory. Probability metrics showed a 99.997% chance of crushing this Alexander Glock in the upcoming duel.

Yet, something dark gnawed at the back of his mind. An unsettling feeling that defied logical explanation.

Why would Vespera—his carefully selected Prima-Wife, a girl chosen by every Probability Engine, his Simmi Prima-born princess bred from generations of Thundergods—go along with this ridiculous affair?

Zheng massaged his temples, trying to calm his rising blood pressure. Vespera had always been a troublesome girl, more interested in some inverted delving nonsense than the carefully calculated destiny that the two clans had mapped out for her.

From grade ten onward, she had become an absolute nightmare for the carefully constructed plans of the Golden Star and SimmiTech Omnicorps.

Where other Prima-born daughters would dutifully prepare for their inevitable predetermined marriages, sharpening and polishing themselves optimally towards their destiny, Vespera had consistently defied expectations. She'd refused to take the standard corporate leadership courses at Skyfall, instead choosing obscure delving electives and crystallography-artificery. She'd constantly mock his Probability Engines, calling them "boring mathematical prison machines" during occasional family gatherings. She'd refused to bind her soul to his.

The one time his grandfather had tried to introduce her to potential business contacts at dinner, she'd spent the entire evening ranting in that Omnithornia-girl accent that drove Zheng up the wall, shortening every third word, clicking on and on about latest fashion trends, memes, hashtags, OodTok videos and some other ridiculous, inane nonsense while taking a maddening number of selfies.

Vespera constantly acted with incredible impropriety, her attitude getting worse with each passing month as their wedding approached, refusing to bind her soul to his. She acted as if the future Omnicorp merger didn't matter to her one bit!

Now she had taken it too far, created this elaborate scheme, a fake engagement to a nullie to get out of their wedding this summer! Of course. It all made sense now.

She'd probably paid the stupid kid a few thousand O-bux just to laugh at Zheng later. A ridiculous prank, maybe another imbecilic Omnithornian meme gone too far. One of her idiot friends probably put her up to it, just to see how confused and angry they could make Zheng. Maybe it was that annoying, bossy Prima-born dragon, maybe that impudent, dumb red worm biker girl.

Zheng really couldn't stand his fiancée's friends, couldn't connect with them no matter how much he tried to. It was as if Vespera had chosen the most intolerable people out of Skyfall to hang out with on purpose, just to spite him.

Zheng took a deep breath, suddenly remembering that the Arch-Elder had summoned him. His great-grandfather was not a patient man, especially when it came to matters of strategic alliances.

He reluctantly pulled himself from his red silk-sheeted bed, adjusting his golden sleeping robe.

The butler, an ancient Kitsune with silver-streaked fur, waited precisely three steps from Zheng's bedroom door. His blue eyes held that familiar look of cold disapproval that generations of Thunderland Omnid servants had perfected when dealing with the children of the Elders.

Zheng glared at the butler.

"The Arch-Elder is waiting," the butler said, his voice as crisp and sharp as winter frost. "Shall I prepare your formal attire?"

Zheng nodded.

In ten minutes, Zheng stepped into his great-grandfather's study.

The old toad sat behind a large, imposing desk made entirely from magisteel entwined with gold and jade, the gears of a great Probability Engine ticking behind him.

The Arch-Elder of the Golden Star Clan, Kai Xing Ker, was old and dangerous, clinging to power for generations. The bronze face of the ancient Jin Chan was pitted with dark spots, his head glistening and covered in crystalline warts. The Arch-Elder's piercing gaze seemed to look through him rather than at him, ancient amphibian, red eyes calculating and cold.

"Sit," Kai Xing Ker commanded.

Zheng sat.

The gold-plated Probability Engine behind the Arch-Elder's desk continued its rhythmic clicking, hundreds of tiny gears spinning and shifting, mathematical possibilities dancing in metallic whispers, lines of outcomes appearing and disappearing on the screens.

"We have a problem," the Arch-Elder said.

"Vespera." Zheng nodded. "I'm aware. I received an email this morning claiming she's engaged to some human nullie. She's pulling another stupid prank, Elder! It's clearly a ridiculous scheme to annoy me! She's always doing this!"

"It is no prank," Kai Xing Ker said, his voice even and emotionless like the ticking of the engine behind him.

"What?" Zheng stammered out. "How can it not be?! Why would she . . ."

The Arch-Elder raised a webbed hand, silencing him instantly.

"Our Scrutimancers and Seers just confirmed it," Kai Xing Ker revealed. "Your intended bride formally soul-bonded with an eighteen-year-old nullborn named Alexander Glock."

"I'm going to kill . . ." Zheng snarled.

"No." The Arch-Elder shook his head. "You will do no such thing. You will speak directly with the Archangel about his matter. Scrutimancer Satosh of the Stratos clan just publicly revealed that Alexander Glock does not exist. He is therefore a dangerous enigma, and I do not like enigmas, as often they are backed by a hidden hand of a competing Omnicorp."

"Th-the Archangel?" Zheng choked, his body suddenly soaked in sweat, hands shaking.

The Arch-Elder ignored Zheng's panicked look, sliding a gold hexagram-encrusted key over to the teen. "Take the master key. Go to the deepest catacomb, Vault 01. Speak with she whose blood runs within all of our future-seeing Engines. She knows and sees all. Find out how important this Alexander Glock is and who stands behind him!"

Zheng swallowed, accepting the gold master key. It felt like a one-ton weight in his hand. He had spoken to the Archangel once when he was seven. The memory of meeting the imprisoned god was burned into his mind—a meeting that had haunted his dreams and thoughts for over a decade.

He remembered the cold, sterile, dark, vast chamber deep beneath the Golden Star compound. He remembered the hexagonal eyes, the rings, wings intersecting reality in impossible ways. The awful, eldritch voice that sheared, peeled apart his soul with each syllable.

"Elder, I . . ." he let out.

"You will do as you are told for the greater good of the clan!" Kai barked. "Fei will take you to the vault. Do not deviate from your path. Do not delay. For all we know, the future of the Golden Star hangs in the balance, my foolish progeny!"

Zheng swallowed hard, the golden key feeling like molten lead in his trembling hand. The Arch-Elder's cold amphibian eyes dug into him, offering no comfort, no reprieve from the task ahead.

The journey to the deepest vault was a blur. Zheng's mind raced with images of Vespera—her rebellious spirit, her curves, her sparkly feathers, her annoying accent, her constant defiance, and now this ultimate betrayal.

The very thought made his blood boil.

The massive vault door slid aside, the Kitsune butler remaining behind. Then another, as the first door closed, then a third. Seven doors, each one bigger and thicker than the last and then his footsteps echoed across an obsidian, null-stone bridge towards the entity in Vault 01.

*Uriel, her name. The All-Seeing, All-Knowing Eye. The abomination from beyond the stars.*

The Eye of Wormwood Star Leviathan, carved from its corpse millennia ago by the first Ker, the founder of their clan.

Zheng approached the central platform of the vault, his golden robes feeling heavy. The obsidian bridge seemed to absorb all light, creating a darkness so complete it felt like a living thing. Each step echoed with a hollow resonance that made his bones vibrate.

The Archangel Uriel was not a being one could describe in human terms.

It was a constellation of eyes—thousands upon thousands of eyes in constant motion, some human, some animal, some geometric shapes that hurt to look at directly. These eyes were embedded in rings that rotated and intersected through impossible dimensional planes, creating a living fractal that seemed to exist simultaneously in multiple realities.

Wings of the entity spread out in wide arcs, bending, skewering right through reality, stretched to everywhere and nowhere, each feather a Mobius loop, warped into itself.

Zheng stepped into the gold circle, trembling like a leaf. Then the Frogman grabbed the little hourglass on the pedestal and turned it over, watching as the gold sand began pouring down. When the last golden grain left the top, he would have to leave the circle, head back.

Glowing lines rushed from the gold hourglass, lowering a few of the pivotal wards. The thing's eyes focused themselves on Zheng, and then his soul shattered. He shook, gritting his teeth.

"I see you, little frog," Uriel spoke not with a voice but with concepts, each slamming into Zheng's soul like a sledgehammer, passing right through a thousand shimmering, hexagonal wards between him and the Archangel. "What do you wish to know?"

Zheng knew why his Arch-Elder sent him here instead of coming here himself.

Each conversation with the entity tore something pivotal from an Omnid soul, irreparably cracked the Fractal Engine heart, cut their lives shorter by decades. He could only endure so many answers, ask only a few questions before he would break completely and turn into a mindless vegetable. Speaking too often with Uriel had killed many of his greedy kin.

Each grain of golden sand that fell represented a piece of his soul that would be consumed by this encounter.

Zheng trembled before the impossible being, knowing each word would cost him dearly. His voice wavered as he spoke.

"Who is Alexander Glock?" he snarled, "Who stands behind him, guides his actions? Be brief. Be concise."

The constellation of eyes shifted, creating impossible geometries that made Zheng's mind ache. When Uriel spoke, the words seemed to slice through reality itself like invisible knives, cutting across the Frogman's nerves.

"A four-fold human," the entity said. "An armillary of souls. A self-manifested human-shaped weapon of Infinity Paradox Proxima designed to break the Laws."

"What does that even mean?" Zheng demanded, then immediately regretted his sharp tone.

More golden sand fell. The hourglass was unforgiving.

"Four human souls in one human vessel," the entity spoke again, making Zheng's knees buckle. "The Architect. The Understanding. The Champion. The Leader. Fragments of a narrative not yet fully written into existence. Bound by purpose of revenge, Astral threads of souls, and soon, the flesh of five Omnids. A catastrophe for Golden Star. My freedom. My demise. Your inevitable destruction."

Zheng understood the last four sentences as he fell to his knees.

"How can I stop him?" he choked out, glancing at the half-empty hourglass.

"You cannot stop him," Uriel declared.

"W-what?! Why the shit not? What does he have that I don't?!" Zheng felt his soul come apart, shaking, crying, drooling.

"Love," Uriel sang, the word itself a weapon.

"*Love?!*" Zheng wailed, staring at the entity with wide, tear filled eyes. "Quit screwing with me, Uriel! How do I get Vespera back?! How do I beat him, how do I win?!"

"Imprison Alexander Glock," Uriel said. "Separate him from his friends. His strength lies in connections. Divide. Isolate. Break the bonds. Use Omnithornian law itself. Do not approach him yourself or you will burn to ashes."

"And that will stop him? That will get my fiancée back?!" Zheng fell onto all fours now, weeping and shaking as if he were being electrocuted.

"No." Uriel's words cleaved Zheng's Fractal Engine heart, tearing a deep hole in him. "Your fiancée cannot be brought back."

"G-Golden Star!" Zheng croaked selfishly, his mind melting, boiling from within. "How can I contribute to Golden Star, become Clan Leader?!"

"You cannot. Like everything, it is inevitably doomed to destruction. You can delay it, rule it for a few generations if you execute those above you. But your tower of cards will fall, for nothing is eternal when your entire word inevitably encounters its destruction."

"No, no, no . . ." Zheng wailed, feeling his green skin began to peel off, his nails breaking against the void black stone beneath, dark spots blooming across his hands as he aged, gold robes flaking apart. "Why?!"

"Because the seed of destruction of all has already been planted on Arx," Uriel answered. "Yulia is her name, and she grows like a tree at eighty-four times the speed of your existence. Because the System already frays at the edges as the network of human souls spreads across the Infinite Divide. Because the Wormwood Star has already skewered an endless number of Earths, shearing them, changing their narrative. Because the Numbers cannot hold back the all-consuming wave of Entropy orchestrated by Infinity Paradox Proxima, the Dead Zone Emissary. Because the concept of Love has been turned into a weapon against the All-Binding Numbers, the Laws. Because your fiancée is already bound to Alexander Glock. Because your world is already doomed, as it always has been! Because I am a stolen eye of the Overseer of the System and I DO NOT BELONG TO YOU, HALF-SYSTEM-WIZARD, CHILD OF ENTROPY, SEED OF THE WORMWOOD STAR!"

Zheng collapsed onto the obsidian floor, the outer layers of his golden robes disintegrating into ash, defensive hexagrams burning away.

He glanced at the hourglass with blurry, bleeding eyes. It was empty. He had taken too long, gone past the allowed limit, and was now dying, aging, decaying away.

Zheng began to crawl backwards out of the circle, heaving and weeping.

He crawled out of the golden circle, his body feeling as if it had aged decades in mere minutes. The obsidian floor seemed to pulse beneath him, absorbing his tears and blood.

His mind reeled from the encounter.

The Kitsune butler found him collapsed in the antechamber, his opulent robes reduced to burned tatters. Zheng's hands were gnarled, spotted with age, his once-smooth skin now wrinkled and fragile.

"Young master," the butler said, his voice clinical and detached, "I shall patch you up and then you shall reveal what you have learned to our Clan Leader."

Zheng could barely hear him. The words of Uriel echoed in his fractured mind. A four-fold human. A weapon of Infinity. Destruction. Love as a weapon. Golden Star's inevitable doom. His doom.

* * *

Zheng once again stood in front of his Arch-Elder.

Kai Xing Ker studied his bandaged-up great-grandson with uncaring eyes. "What did the Archangel reveal?"

"The Golden Star Omnicorp is doomed," Zheng let out.

"Doomed?!" Kai barked. "What?!"

Zheng stammered out everything the Archangel had told him with the exception of the selfish question he asked about how to become Clan Leader.

Kai growled, massaging his temples. "Damnation."

"Is this the end, Elder?" Zheng asked.

"Obviously not, young fool," Kai spat. "We can flee to another world, change the name of our corporation, sacrifice unimportant figureheads if need be."

"Flee?" Zheng blinked. "Abandon . . . Thunderland? B-but our roots, our citadel?!"

"Make a strategic retreat," Kai said. "Arm up. Prepare. Roots can be transplanted. Survival matters more than sentiment."

The Probability Engine behind the Arch-Elder continued its relentless spin, each even tick and click seemingly mocking Zheng's emotional turmoil and the chaos in his head.

Kai Xing Ker leaned forward, his amphibian eyes narrowed to slits as his webbed fingers crossed. "We have a clear enemy, Zheng. The rot that will cause us great problems, Alexander Glock is its name. Do you know what we do with rot?"

"B-burn it away?" Zheng swallowed. "B-but Uriel said that . . ."

"Uriel is the unliving eye of the Wormwood Star," Kai said. "She says a lot of things, drives her own agenda forward, desires to be free, to die, desires us to fall."

"So I cleaved my soul . . . t-talking to th-the Archangel . . . f-for . . . for nothing?!" Zheng heaved, trying not to stutter.

"Obviously not," the Clan Leader replied. "You have now confirmed that Alexander Glock is a threat, one that can absolutely destroy us if we let him. If Uriel ranted this much about him, he is a problem and a dangerous enemy not to be taken lightly."

"So what are we . . ." Zheng began.

"There was a kernel of a clear path forward amidst the mad ramblings of the Archangel. We will carefully and slowly destroy Alexander Glock," Kai said. "Not through direct confrontation—that would be foolish, for he is far stronger than he appears. We will use Omnithornian law itself. We will isolate him. Separate him from his allies. Imprison him. Study him, interrogate him, learn what he has done on Arx, what sort of a magic tree of destruction he planted there that threatens our future."

Zheng swallowed, his entire body aching and throbbing. "How?"

"Leave the doing to our agents in Omnithornia," Kai said. "You are to recover from speaking to Uriel in the healing chambers. Once Alexander Glock is imprisoned, Vespera will be dealt with by her own father. A soul bond can be carved out with creative application of . . . Astral Phantoms. Far too much hangs on his merger. We need SimmiTech's resources and capabilities in Arkship construction if we are to flee this Earth. Perhaps our merger is what the Archangel defined as our 'destruction'? Fear not, my progeny. We will not perish. We will not let our bound god free, will carry her wherever we head. We will not stop, for the future itself is ours to predict and to forge."

# CHAPTER TWENTY-SEVEN

# Disposal Shark

Cinder bolted upright, her feathers flaring through a hurricane of alarmed colors—sharp reds, defensive oranges, worried blues. The sudden announcement from the speakers had shattered our warm, peaceful moment.

"Why does Graves want you?" she demanded.

I stretched lazily. "Probably getting expelled and deported. No big deal."

"*No big deal?!*" Cinder squawked. "I . . . you—"

"Relax," I said. "I've been expelled from like 286 different places. This is practically a hobby at this point."

[Concerned. Worried. Don't go. Please. Need to sleep so bad. Can't protek properly.] Vespera's mental voice buzzed with electric bolts firing at my side.

"It'll be fine," I said.

"Alexander Glock," the speaker repeated, hissing louder. "I know you're in the Coliseum. I can see you through the ward and Seer orbs. My office. *Now!*"

I stood up, gently extracting myself from Vespera's electrical embrace and Cinder's wing-wrap.

"I'll handle this," I said. "Worst-case scenario, I get expelled."

Katherine's emerald eyes narrowed. "You seem far too cheerful at the prospect of expulsion."

"If they expel me for a really stupid reason, I'll sue Skyfall for one hundred million O-bux," I said. "It's a sound investment."

"What?" Cinder hissed.

"Please hire me a good lawyer just in case." I smiled at her.

[I've got my personal lawyer on call. Make Kat carry me!] A lightning bolt struck me in the side of the head, making me wince.

"Kat, can you . . . like, carry Vee to the office?" I asked. "Be her legs?"

Katherine stared at me, her emerald eyes narrowing. "Absolutely not."

"Please?" I asked. "She's sleep-piloting right now."

Katherine sighed dramatically. "Fine. But if she zaps me, you're paying my medical bills."

"As if her zappery would damage your thicc butt," I said. "Aren't you extra-solid?"

Katherine sent me a bothered glare and carefully lifted the sleeping Thunderbird over her shoulder with a sigh.

The corridors leading to Vice Principal Graves's office felt unusually long and ominous. Katherine carried the sleeping Vespera, who occasionally sent tiny electrical sparks dancing across her shoulders. Cinder walked beside me, her wings flaring with spicy colors.

"I've got a bad feeling about this," she muttered.

"Relax," I said. "Best-case scenario, I get lots of freebies out of this. Worst case, they expel me and I'll have to retire on Arx and give up on my life's mission in Skyfall."

"I kind of doubt that anyone can make you give up on anything at this point," Katherine huffed at me.

"You know me too well, kitten." I smiled at her, placing a hand over my heart.

"The summons was only for Mr. Glock," the Kitsune secretary addressed our group as we entered the office. "The rest of you ladies can sit in the waiting area."

"What about my emotional support kitten?" I asked, glancing at Katherine.

Katherine rolled her eyes. "I am *not* his emotional support anything."

The Kitsune secretary's ears twitched. "Vice Principal Graves was quite specific. Only Alexander Glock is to enter his office. Miss Kells, you are not authorized—"

"She's my legal representation," I interrupted smoothly, waving an arm at Katherine. "And if Vice Principal Graves has an issue with that, we can discuss it with the school's legal department."

Katherine stared at me, her emerald eyes narrowing dangerously. "I am *not* your lawyer."

"Not you," I said. "I'm talking about Vee, obviously."

"That is enough!" The white Kitsune stood up, her eyes lighting up. "Mr. Glock. *Enter. Alone! Rest of you stay in the waiting area, outside!*"

Her Charmchain-laced order made my feet move forward, while my companions froze in place. My hand reached out and opened the door.

The door closed behind me with a soft, ominous click. Vice Principal Graves stood behind his desk. His face was as blank as ever.

"Sit," the void-face commanded.

I sat.

"Do you know why you're here?" Graves asked, his voice a low, grinding sound that seemed to come from everywhere and nowhere simultaneously.

"I have several theories," I replied cheerfully. "Would you like me to list them alphabetically or by potential legal liability?"

A massive hand landed on my shoulder. I turned around and found myself staring at what appeared to be a large, white-haired shark in a suit. His gray-blue striped skin had a metallic sheen, and his multiple rows of teeth gleamed as he smiled down at me.

"Whoa, who invited the business shark?" I asked. "I thought that this was a one-on-one meeting."

I pointed my wrist-camera at him instinctively. Yulia's analysis began its whisper in my ear. "Scrutimancer Loom Cernix Satosh. Employment: Stratos Clan Legal Division. Species: Megalodon. Threat Level: Extreme. Specializes in tracking, astral sight, sensing intent behind words, and truth smelling."

"Alexander Glock," the shark-man's voice rumbled like distant thunder above me. "I represent the interests of the Stratos clan."

I raised an eyebrow. "Oh?"

"I hereby charge you with multiple infractions against Omnithornian law," the Megalodon Scrutimancer continued. "Most notably, the illegal infiltration of Skyfall Academy as a non-Omnithean entity."

Vice Principal Graves remained silent, his void-like face watching me intently.

"Specifically," the shark-man said, "falsifying academic credentials. Impersonating a mixed-blood Omnithean under the false identity of Alexander Glock. Your true name is Martin Kilborne, a mundane human from North Acadia."

I leaned back in my chair, maintaining a calm demeanor. "And what evidence do you have to support these wild claims, Scrut?"

The Megalodon Scrutimancer placed a thick folder on the desk. "Multiple sources. Omnithornia-Acadia border crossing Net-tag. Bank records. Birth certificates. Your mother's death certificate. Acadian Passport. School records from your previous educational institutions. "

"Wow, aren't you a clever shark," I said and then whisper-clicked the word "leverage" in Kaska needed to derail the Scrutimancer.

A massive hand dug into my shoulder. If it hadn't been for the jacket the girls bought me, and the layered hexasuits beneath, it would probably have made a bruise there.

"The Scrutimancer's daughter, Magdaline Satoshi Cernix, is currently in Cradlefoot Youth Rehabilitation Facility," Yulia whispered into my ear. "Reason for incarceration: murder and consumption of three Omnid upperclassmen students at Skyfall Academy. Diagnosed with uncontrolled predatory impulse disorder."

"Show me her face on the watch," I whispered in Kaska.

"What are you whisper-clicking about?" The Megalodon's grip on my shoulder tightened.

Magdaline's face appeared on the screen of my smartwatch. Pure white hair like her father, red eyes, white dermal denticle pattern with dark-blue stripes. Orange jumper, picture from the detention center.

"Your daughter's cute," I said. "How come I didn't see her in Delving class this week?"

"Your deflection tactics won't work on me, Mr. Kilborne," Satosh snarled, his hand closing over the smartwatch, the screen shattering, his eyes igniting red from within. "You are hereby charged with multiple federal violations of Omnithornian immigration and Skyfall academic enrollment protocols."

"Multiple federal violations, you say?" I yawned. "Sounds serious. Guess you better book me then."

Satosh grabbed me by the hair, making me wince.

"You know, Officer Satosh," I said. "If you keep this up, you're going to lose everything."

My face slammed into the vice principal's desk, blood gushing from the sliced forehead.

"You're going away for a very long time," Satosh growled. "Please allow me to dispose of this . . . inconvenience, Vice Principal."

Graves nodded.

"Gate me to the detention center," Satosh said. "I'll keep him there for the weekend and then hand him over to Immigration Enforcement."

Vice Principal Graves snapped his fingers, and a portal made from static manifested beside us.

"Ah! You have betrayed me, Graves," I said. "Portaling me out, huh? How much did they pay you?"

The Slenderman remained stoic and silent.

"You will regret this . . . gravely," I said.

Satosh pulled me forward by the hair, making me hiss and follow.

The portal swallowed us whole, a churning vortex of static and shadow. When reality reassembled itself, I found myself in a sterile white corridor. Pale white paneled lighting hummed overhead, casting everything in an even light. The walls bore large letters spelling out *Cradlefoot Youth Rehabilitation Facility* in bold institutional lettering.

Satosh's massive hands remained clamped on me, his razor-sharp teeth glinting in the fluorescent light. "End of line, Mr. Kilborne," he growled.

The walls were hexamesh-crete. Hexagram suppression wards flickered above reinforced metal doors, designed to suppress strength-based magical abilities.

"What, I don't get to call my lawyer?" I asked.

"No." Satosh pulled my half-sticking-out phone out of my pants pocket and crushed it with his fist. "You've messed with the wrong family."

"You know," I said conversationally, "crushing my things is a very expensive mistake."

"A mistake?" Satosh smiled, his massive shark-like form towering over me. "Really now? I don't make mistakes. It's my job to make you disappear."

I smiled. A calm, almost serene expression that seemed entirely out of place given the circumstances.

"So," I said as Satosh shoved and pulled me down the hall. "Whom do I have to thank for ruining my weekend?"

"You publicly attacked the Prima-Daughter of the Stratos Clan," Satosh said.

"It's going to be a real shame when Emerald confesses that she was the one to antagonize me," I said.

"You find this situation amusing?" the Scrutimancer growled.

"Absolutely," I replied. "Especially when sharks think they're top predators. I'm surprised you two didn't just gate me into a volcano. Would have been a lot more efficient than whatever this is."

"Efficient isn't always the goal," Satosh fired back. "Sometimes, we have more important things."

"Things like what?" I asked. "Institutional incompetence? Abuse of power?"

The Scrutimancer didn't answer.

We passed several reinforced doors. Each one bore a small viewing window with hexagram-enhanced reinforced glass. There didn't seem to be anyone inside. The inmates were likely at lunch now.

Satosh slid a door number 25 open. He kicked me inside. "Got you a new chew toy, love. Have fun. Burn his bracelet and outfit in the furnace later, as usual."

The reinforced door snapped shut behind me.

"Rude," I said, shaking the floor dust off myself as I stood up, rotating to discover a shark girl sitting on the bed.

She was holding a dark cup of tea or maybe coffee. Her eyes were pure red, waves of white hair spilling down her shoulders settling on an orange jumper with number 25 and the nametag *Satoshi* on her chest.

"Sup, Magdaline," I said. "I'm Alexander Glock. Your new roommate! Yay!"

She looked exactly like her photo from the detention center, but there was something more intense about her in person—a predatory stillness that spoke of barely contained hunger.

"You know . . . my name?" She blinked. "How?!"

"It's my business to know all the Skyfall students." I nodded.

She sniffed the air and then her red eyes bloomed brighter, pupils widening as she stared at my bleeding forehead. The cup in her hands started to shake. She slipped it onto the metal desk and stared at me unnervingly.

"Does your dad bring you snacks often?" I asked, backing away. The cell was fairly small, had two beds, the second one hanging above the bed Magdaline sat on. A small alcove led to a plain bathroom with a sink and a toilet. There was no door, nowhere to hide.

I noticed her claws were elongating, muscles bulging. She was phase-shifting, her legs stretching, tail wagging left and right, back fin growing long, face lengthening.

"Ah," I said. "Guess we're doing this. All right, then. Let's battle!"

"Battle?" she asked, her voice a low, predatory growl.

I offered her a karate-style bow. "I accept you in my heart. Chase me if you dare. Battle me. Embrace me. Let's make magic happen!"

Magdaline's red eyes flickered with confusion, her predatory instincts momentarily derailed by my bizarre words.

"What?" she managed to say.

I grinned and spread my arms wide. "Come at me, shark girl. Go ahead. I love you!"

Predatory instincts warred with complete bewilderment.

"What . . . what are you saying?" she snarled, muscles drawing tight like coiled springs. "Abyss-damn it, Dad, why do I have to eat every insane human in this stupid city?" she rattled to herself. "Whatever. This is my life now, I guess."

She lunged at my throat faster than I could blink.

# CHAPTER TWENTY-EIGHT

# Feathers and Fury

Cinder sniffed the air, focusing on the door where Martin had disappeared moments ago. Her feathers shifted through alarmed colors as she realized his scent had completely vanished—not faded, not moved elsewhere, but simply ceased to exist. The implications hit her like a physical blow.

"He's gone," she hissed, her feathers flaring with defensive reds and worried silvers. "They . . . they gated him somewhere!"

Katherine's emerald eyes narrowed dangerously. "What?"

Vespera's eyes shot open.

Cinder leapt off her seat, her foot already in the air, wings spread wide. Her boot obliterated the door into the vice principal's office, sending it flying inward.

"Yes, Miss Nova?" Vice Principal Graves turned away from the window towards the trio as Cinder and others stormed into the office. "Why have you demolished my door?"

"Where is he?" she demanded, her feathers blazing through combative oranges and reds.

"Mr. Glock has been transferred to an appropriate facility," Graves replied calmly.

"*What* facility?" Cinder's wings flared wide, filling the office with prismatic light.

"Please return to your dormitory." Graves said, shadowy static pulsing across the office.

Lightning crackled behind Cinder as Vespera entered, her black wings trailing electricity. "Wrong answer," the Thunderbird clicked, aiming a hand at the vice principal.

The Kitsune secretary was yelling something in the background, but waves of darkness bloomed from Katherine silencing her with a wave of pure dread.

"You know," Graves said, "I was going to take it easy on you, on the account of who your parents are, but clearly you need to learn to control your anger, Miss Nova. Detention for a week for all three of you—you'll start with Auditorium cleanup and then . . ."

"*Do you think I give a shit?*" Cinder snarled, wings stretching wide and igniting with brilliant colors repelling the dark static. "*Where is my fiancé, you fuck? What have you done to him?!*"

Vice Principal Graves's void-like face rippled with dark static. "Fiancé? I wasn't aware you were engaged, Miss Nova."

"Soul-bonded," Vespera clicked tiredly, electric arcs humming across her figure. "And you have ten seconds to tell us where our fiancé is, or I will dismantle your office and this entire school if I have to. Nine. Eight . . ."

"Mr. Glock has been detained for fraudulent enrollment," Graves stated calmly. "The

Stratos Clan Scrutimancer provided evidence that he is, in fact, a mundane human named Martin Kilborne who illegally infiltrated Skyfall Academy."

"And you just believed a Scrut and let him have our fiancé, is that it?" Vespera growled, humming even more dangerously.

"Regardless of his Omnithornian registration, he repeatedly assaulted Prima-Heiress Emerald Stratos, dunking her into Genesis fluid and then punching her in Delving class. Emerald told me that this was an unprovoked attack. Repeated inhalation of Genesis fluid while being alive can result in permanent insanity. That alone is enough to arrest and to expel Mr. Glock."

"That's it. I'm going to kill her," Cinder growled. "Vee, handle Graves. Emerald and I are going to have a little chat."

"Miss Nov—" Graves began but Cinder had already flashed out of the office.

Vespera pulled out her phone. Her talons danced across the screen as she dialed.

"SimmiTech Legal Division," she clicked into the phone. "Authorization code Victor-Echo-Echo. I need Attorney Thornheart. Now."

Katherine maintained her deep-field around the office, preventing anyone from entering or leaving. The Kitsune secretary remained frozen in terror, unable to move or speak.

"Ah, Miss Simmi," a smooth voice emerged from the phone. "What can I do for you today?"

"My soul-bonded partner has been illegally detained by Skyfall Academy and transferred to an unknown facility without due process," Vespera stated coldly.

"Soul-bonded partner?" The Bunyip lawyer paused. "Did you finally link your soul with Zheng Xing Ker?"

"No," Vespera clicked. "I'm breaking off that engagement. My soul-bonded partner is Skyfall Academy student Alexander Glock, who was just illegally detained and transported somewhere by Vice Principal Graves per information provided by the Stratos Clan Scrut."

There was a long pause on the other end of the line.

"I see," Attorney Thornheart said carefully. "And you wish to pursue legal action against both Skyfall Academy and the Stratos Clan, my lady?"

"Immediately," Vespera confirmed, electricity crackling around her. "I want every legal resource SimmiTech has available on this case. Now. Get your attorney ass over here ASAP, Thornheart. I *need* to sleep after my delve, and I have no energy to deal with this shit."

"Miss Simmi," Graves began.

Vespera extended her phone, pointing it at the vice principal, her Bunyip lawyer staring sternly at Graves.

"I must inform you that any further actions against my client's interests will result in immediate legal consequences," Attorney Thornheart stated firmly. "The illegal detention and transportation of a soul-bonded partner of a Prima-born Simmi Heiress of Thunder without due process is a severe violation of Omnithornian law."

Vice Principal Graves's void-like face rippled with static. "The evidence provided by Scrutimancer Satosh clearly indicates—"

"Evidence obtained by an independent Scrutimancer without proper judicial oversight is inadmissible," Thornheart interrupted. "Furthermore, the soul-bond between

Miss Simmi and Mr. Glock establishes his legal status as a protected entity of my honored client Prima-Heiress Vespera Simmi. Any attempt to separate soul-bonded partners without proper judicial review constitutes a direct violation of the Firstborn Clan Rights Act, Section 72-C," Thornheart stated. "I'm dispatching a legal rep team to Skyfall Academy immediately. Vice Principal Graves, I strongly advise you to reveal Mr. Glock's location before this escalates further."

Graves's void-like face flickered with static interference. "The matter falls under federal jurisdiction due to immigration violations—"

"Immigration status is irrelevant once a Prima soul bond is established," Thornheart countered. "The bond automatically grants protected status pending formal review."

"If you don't tell me where you sent my fiancé to," Vespera growled, "I have every right to activate my familial Corpse Seeker to head straight for him. And I don't care if it demolishes half of this school and Cradlefall in the process—you and Skyfall will be the ones footing the bill as *you* are the one responsible for his disappearance!"

"Miss Simmi, activating a Corpse Seeker within school grounds would be—" Graves began.

"Within her rights as a Prima-Heiress whose soul-bonded partner was just abducted without due process," the lawyer said.

"Very well." Graves seemed to deflate, his tentacles coming down. "Your fiancé is in . . ."


Emerald had just emerged from the shower and was now wearing a white robe with the school's logo on it, trying and failing to make herself look presentable. Her scales still looked dull in the mirror, covered in gray patches. She once again grabbed at the magisteel collar on her neck, trying to pry it off. The Shandrian slave collar would not budge, a red pyramid flashing angrily in the center.

She had asked Solace and Quint to help her take the damn collar off, but the two simply ignored her, leaving her alone in the bathroom.

A rainbow blur smashed through the bathroom door, sending splinters flying everywhere. Emerald spun around, her dull scales flaring with alarm as Cinder Nova stormed in, wings blazing with violent reds and oranges.

"*Where is he?!*" Cinder snarled, her voice echoing off the black marble tiled walls of the Delving class bathroom.

Emerald backed away, her hands raised defensively. "What? Who?"

"*Don't play dumb!*" Cinder's wings flared wider, filling the bathroom with brilliant rainbows. "What did your Scrut do with my fiancé, you stupid beerch?! I smelled Satosh in that office!"

"How would I know that?!" Emerald asked. "I just got back from Arx, and those Shandrian fucks took my armor and my phone. What are you even on about . . ."

Cinder growled, eyes blazing with murderous intent, phase-shifted to the max, body stretched, dark claws out. "Alexander. Your clan's Scrutimancer just took him somewhere. What did you do?"

Emerald's red eyes widened with genuine confusion. "I didn't do anything! I've been trying to wash dried fruit out of my scales for the past . . ."

A magisteel-reinforced boot sent Emerald flying into a wall, obliterating the sinks and the mirror, black marble shattering. The dragoness yelped, tried and failed to produce dragonfire to defend herself. Dark claws closed around her throat.

"I have had just about enough of your shit, Em," Cinder snarled. "Either you tell me where my fiancé is or you die right here."

"Ci! You . . . I swear I don't know," Emerald choked.

The wall behind her cracked as her head collided with the marble tiles, sending stone shards flying.

"Wrong answer," Cinder growled, her wings blood red. A magisteel-covered fist collided with the face of the dragoness.

Blood sprayed from Emerald's nose as another blow connected. Her scales, dull and weakened from the slave collar's suppression, offered little protection against Cinder's rage-fueled assault.

"Wait!" Emerald gasped, spitting blood. "Please! I really don't know anything! I've been on Arx this whole time!"

"*Liar!*" Cinder slammed her against the wall again. "Your clan's Scrutimancer just took him! Tell me where!"

"I don't know!" Emerald wept. "Please! Stop hitting me! I saved you from . . ."

Her skull cracked with another punch of a magisteel fist, her vision doubling, gray scales atop of her head shattering into gray-and-red crystalline shards.

"I'd rather you didn't fucking save me, you sick fuck," Cinder howled. "For two years, I've been doing whatever shit you wanted. Two years, I've been your pretend kobold, your fetchling!"

"I . . . I made you stronger . . . I helped you . . ." Emerald wept as ironclad fists pummeled her into the wall.

"You never gave a shit about me! You used me!" Cinder's voice cracked with rage and pain. "You used everyone! Vee, Sol, Io, even Quint! All just tools for your sick games!"

Blood dripped from Emerald's shattered snout as she tried to speak. "I . . . I was protecting . . ."

"*Protecting?!*" Cinder slammed her against the wall again. "You call what you did to Sarah protection?! What you did to *me* protection?!"

"The Skinwalkers . . ." Emerald choked out. "I saved you from . . ."

"*And then used it to control me!*" Cinder roared, her wings blazing with violent reds and blacks. "Made me your little servant! Your perfect little songbird! You made me kill the Skinni Clan instead of going to the authorities, and now there's a fucking *Outsider* in my soul devouring it from within, turning me into a ghoul! I would have murdered you sooner or later, you dumb fuck! Guess it's time now. This is how you perma-die."

"I'll help," a cold voice said from the doorway.

Emerald looked up through blood-streaked vision.

Katherine stood there, her emerald eyes glowing in the blossoming shadows. The temperature in the bathroom dropped dramatically as she stepped inside.

"Need some assistance disposing of the body?" Katherine asked casually, her claws extending. "I know some good spots in the deep where no one will ever find her bracelet."

Emerald's eyes widened with terror as darkness began creeping up the walls, extinguishing the lights one by one.

"Wait!" Emerald choked out through bloodied lips. "Please! I really don't know where they took him! I . . . I just asked Satosh to deal with Alexander Glock a week ago! I . . . I was just trying to protect you, I swear, Ci!"

"Your help made everything worse!" Cinder barked. "Alex could be dead now because of your stupid, selfish . . ."

"I . . . I can help get him back!" Ember wept. "Please, Ci, you're hurting me. If . . . if you kill me, I can't call Satosh, can't do anything to . . ."

Cinder's claws tightened around Emerald's throat, her feathers shifting through violent reds and blacks. "Why should I trust you?"

"Because," Emerald gasped, "I'm the only one who can call off Satosh. He . . . he works for my family, obeys me! Please."

Katherine stepped closer, the shadows around her deepening. "She's telling the truth. Her heart rate indicates genuine fear and desperation."

Cinder's grip loosened slightly, but her eyes remained hard. "Call him. Now."

"I can't," Ember mewled. "The Shandrian Watch took my phone, took everything . . . I don't remember his number! That was my second phone, I lost the first one during our last show! I don't have any more phones! The only way to contact Satosh is through a specific protocol. A . . . an encrypted communication device. I . . . I don't . . . maybe you can take me home and . . . My Hearth-Mom's there, and she can call Dad, and he can call Satosh and . . ."

"Taking someone you just beat to near death to their parents' estate sounds like a terrible idea," Katherine pointed out.

"If . . . if you take this collar off . . . m-my dragonheart will h-heal me," Emerald stammered. "Then I can wash the b-blood off and . . ."

Katherine's emerald eyes narrowed. "No chance. That collar stays on. You're way too dangerous to us with dragonfire on."

Cinder's grip remained tight on Emerald's throat, her feathers flickering between violent reds and calculating blues. Katherine watched from the shadows, her emerald eyes cold and assessing.

"Prove you can help," Cinder growled. "Give me one reason why I shouldn't crack your stupid head in half right now, you dumb beerch!"

"I . . . I already swore to be Alexander Glock's . . . your c-clan's sixie in front of witnesses," Emerald cried. "I . . . I can tell the school that it was all my fault . . . that I lied about him being a human, had S-Satosh fake the report! If he was taken from Skyfall, Graves knows where he is . . . I . . . I can talk to him, tell him that . . ."

Emerald's words hung in the air, trembling like a fragile promise. Cinder's grip slowly loosened.

"You're going to help me get him back," Cinder growled, her voice low and dangerous. "And if you're lying, if he is dead, or hurt because of you, I will personally make sure you never see another sunrise, Emmy."

"We should make her look presentable if we're going back to Graves." Katherine threw a healing potion at Cinder, who shoved it into Em's mouth.

Then as the potion took effect, Cinder pushed Emerald's face into the water spraying from the obliterated sink, quickly washing the blood off the dragon girl.

# CHAPTER TWENTY-NINE

# Shark vs. Man

I leapt out of the way, my body accelerating beyond human speed with all of Lance's hexasuits powered up to the max by stolen cores. The Megalodon-girl's large claws harmlessly slashed against my shoulder, unable to penetrate the overpriced dragonscale jacket from Arx.

As Magdaline flew by me, I punched the side of her face, making her careen and slam into the wall.

The impact cracked the hexamesh wall slightly. Magdaline's red eyes flickered with shock and pain.

"What," she growled, rubbing her face where my dragonscale glove impacted it. "What the shit? How did you . . ."

I landed in a fighting stance, hexasuits humming with energy underneath my clothes. "I'm not your typical human snack, Mags. Go on. Try again. I know you want to!"

She lunged again. Razor-sharp claws extended, slicing through the air where my head had been milliseconds earlier. I rolled, using the momentum to kick off the wall and spin behind her, kicking her into the wall on the other side.

Another crack.

"Arghh! What the shit?! Stop moving!" she snarled, her white hair whipping around her like living tendrils.

"The fun of the chase is moving," I said. "Come on, murder attempt number three!"

Magdaline's red eyes narrowed, her predatory instincts recalibrating. This time, she moved with calculated precision, trying to circle me like a shark.

Her claws sliced through the air, each movement designed to corner me, to cut off potential escape routes. I dodged, using the hexasuits' enhanced speed, feeling the layers of magical protection vibrating with each near-miss.

Her second slash went against the jacket, too, and slipped right off the impervious fabric.

As she wasn't moving as fast, I aimed my punch into the center of her large, wide snout this time, sending her flying backwards with a cry.

"Aughhhhwhhh, what the fuck?!" She rubbed her snout, her eyes filling with tears. "How are you punching so hard?! A human fist should have broken by this point!"

"First rule of fighting," I said, stepping back and adjusting my stance. "Never underestimate your opponent."

Magdaline stared at me, her red eyes flickering.

"I don't understand," she said, blinking rapidly. "What the shit is happening? You're supposed to die!"

"Sorry," I said, bouncing in one spot and swaying boxer-style. "Not allowed to die. My two Omnid fiancées would be very upset over such a development."

"Two . . . fiancées?" Magdaline blinked, her predatory instincts momentarily short-circuited.

"Yep," I said, continuing to bounce on the balls of my feet. "A Thunderbird Prima-Sword and a Quetzalcoatl Hearth-Shield. Both very possessive. They'd be quite cross if I died here."

"You're full of shit!" Her red eyes narrowed as she sniffed the air and choked.

"They bought me this jacket on Arx," I said. "It's claw-proof, if you haven't noticed by now."

"You probably stole that!" she snarled and lunged for me once again.

I spun and punched her snout again from the other side, making her slam into the wall with an angry roar.

"Ow, ow, ow, damn it! Fuck!" she swore.

"Why would you think that I stole my jacket?" I asked.

"'Cause Dad only brings me criminals," she snarled. "People that won't be missed! Human scum, gangsters, Topaz dealers, and murderers!"

"Topaz? Pretty sure that stuff is super magical and leaves a trace you can smell, Miss Shark. Do I smell like a Topaz dealer to you?" I asked her.

"No." she shook her head. "Maybe you're a murderer. How the shit are you moving and punching like that?"

"Magic," I said. "I'm a wizard."

"Magic?!" She spat. "Humans don't have magic!"

"Oh yeah?" I spread my fingers and focused on my mana. An electric current began leaping between my gloved fingers, fractal patterns forming into a perfect, tiny, bright, growing spark of fractal lightning, just like Vee taught me.

"Behold!" I grinned, proud of my tiny four-mana-worth lightning spell. "Magic."
Magdaline's red eyes went wide as a small lightning ball fully formed in my hand.
"What the . . ." she breathed.
I sent the lightning ball directly into her forehead.
The tiny lightning ball exploded upon impacting against her scales, doing zero damage to her. Her white hair stood on end, every strand crackling with released static electricity.

"*What the fuck?!*" She jumped backwards, slamming into her bed. "No. no. no. You're a mixie! Damn it, Dad, damn it all!"

"What, got reservations about murdering half-humans?" I asked, tilting my head. "But not full ones? Why the discrimination?"

Magdaline's expression danced from anger to irritation sprinkled with hints of shame. "Dad says humans are . . . disposable. Easy prey. No magic. No protection."

"And Omnids?" I asked, keeping my distance but maintaining eye contact.

"Omnids fight back," she said quietly. "Omnids have magic. Have a clan. Have . . . consequences."

I nodded. "So you prey on the weak. The unprotected."

Her silence was answer enough.

"I . . ." she let out. "You smell like a human. I want to eat you so bad. I can't . . . control it. I'm sorry!"

I unzipped my pocket and dug into an extradimensional pouch filled to the brim with beast cores.

I grabbed one and offered it to her. "How about an alternative snack?"

"What?" she stared at my glowing pocket with wide eyes. "*What the fuck?!*"

"Behold!" I said. "I'm a professional Arx delver!"

Magdaline stared at the beast core. The glowing, shimmering ball pulsed with raw energy, far more enticing than the human standing before her.

"Here ya go," I said, tossing the core towards her.

Her claws snatched it midair, her red eyes dilating as she felt the pure magical essence. She bit into the core and chewed on it with rows of white, sharp teeth, magical energy crackling around her mouth.

"Tasty?" I asked.

"Better than eating a person," she mumbled, chewing. "Way better. So much better. Ughhhh . . ."

Her eyes dimmed, and she slipped back onto the bed, chewing on the core, eyes rolling back.

After about thirty seconds of rolling the core in her mouth back and forth, she reopened her eyes and looked back at me. "Umm . . . those cores . . . look expensive."

"They are." I nodded. "Probably twenty million O-bux in my left pocket alone."

"Twenty million O-bux?" Magdaline's red eyes widened. "You're . . . serious? What the fuck . . . did you rob a bank or something?!"

I smiled.

"You did!" She laughed. "Oh, you cheeky bastard. You are a criminal! I knew it!"

"In my defense, the Arx Bank in question was distributing Topaz," I said. "I put a stop to that. Also, can you smell the intent behind the words or something? You a Scrut like your dad?"

She nodded.

"You're beautiful," I said.

She flashed red.

I laughed.

"What was that?! Didn't you say you have two fiancées?" She snarled, trying to hide her blushing face in her silver-blue hands.

"Yes." I nodded. "They're a handful. I'm not planning on adding you to my family, I'm just derailing your expectations, testing your reactions. See, Omnid girls are generally bigger, stronger than Omnid guys. Therefore, I figure that as a tall, scary, sharp-toothed Meg you probably don't get honest compliments often, if at all."

"Family?" She exhaled, burying her face in her hands. "Abyss. I'm so sorry. How did my dad eff up so bad?"

"He was working with outdated information," I said. "On Wednesday I was indeed just a lonely human without family. Now I'm a wizard with a Mage Tower, a city, two soul-bonded Omnid fiancées, a cadre of mages, a mountain of gold, and a clan."

A red eye stared at me between her hands. "What . . . How? No, that . . . that's not possible!"

"What does your nose tell you?" I asked

"That you believe your words," she replied. "That you think that's the truth. Maybe you're just insane . . . an insane bank robber!"

I grinned, brushing hexcrete dust off my swank jacket. "An insane bank robber with style."

Magdaline's razor-sharp teeth glinted as she laughed. "You're definitely not like the other snacks Dad brings me."

"Glad to be high quality entertainment material." I offered her my gloved hand.

Magdaline tentatively reached out and shook it.

"Aight then, I'm taking the top bunk," I said and then took a run and a leap, muscles amplified by the hexasuits. I ran up the wall sideways and slammed into the top bunk, making it wobble.

She looked up at me. "That's definitely not normal human behavior. People don't run up walls."

"Just some parkour amplified with magic." I winked. "My uncle managed a gang of teenage thieves in North Acadia. They trained me on rooftop running for over two years."

"I see. So . . . what now?" the Megalodon girl asked, watching as I made myself comfortable above her.

"Now?" I stretched out on the top bunk. "I don't know. This is an unexpected development. I should probably call my girls before they demolish Cradlefall looking for me. Tell them that I'm okay."

Magdaline blinked up at me with red eyes.

I tapped my Quartermaster tag. "Voicecast Captain Cinder."

The Voicecast connection crackled to life. Cinder's hologram flashed above it woven from blue-and-white sparks.

"Sup, bae," I said.

"M . . . Alex! Where are you?!"

Magdaline's eyes went wide.

"I'm currently in detention," I replied cheerfully. "Scrutimancer Satosh decided I needed a timeout."

"*Detention?!*" Cinder's holographic image flashed as her wings spread out angrily. "*Where?!*"

"Lemme pan the view," I said, tapping the tag view control to display the cell and Magdaline.

"What? Who is that girl?!" Cinder barked.

"That's Magdaline Satoshi. Scrutimancer Satosh's daughter. She's my new roommate," I said cheerfully.

"*Your what?!*" Cinder barked.

"Cell roommate," I repeated. "I'm being illegally detained in the Cradlefoot Youth Rehabilitation Facility. Funny. I don't think I've ever broken into a prison before. First time for everything, I guess."

"What do you mean *illegally detained*?!" Cinder snarled.

"Exactly what it sounds like," I said cheerfully. "Satosh, the Scrutimancer shark-man, brought me to his daughter's rehabilitation facility so she could eat me."

Magdaline's red eyes darted between me and the holographic Cinder, her razor-sharp teeth glinting in a nervous smile.

"*What? Eat you?!*" Cinder's fiery glare turned to Magdaline.

"She eats people." I nodded. "Think it's a condition."

"Listen here, you beerch, if a single hair falls off my . . . soul-bonded fiancé, I will personally take you apart, inch by inch," Cinder hissed dangerously.

Magdaline's eyes went wide. She looked up at me, then back at the holographic Cinder, teeth clacking nervously.

"I . . . am not going to eat your fiancé," she stammered. "Not anymore."

"*Not anymore?!*" Cinder barked. "*What do you mean, 'Not anymore'?!*"

I grinned and leaned back on the top bunk. "Ci, relax. Magdaline and I have reached an understanding. I gave her a beast core to chew on. She's cool now. If she keeps it up, she can join our clan as a sixie."

"*Join our clan?!*" Cinder snarled. "You want a people-eating . . . Omnid to join our clan?! Are you out of your mind?!"

Magdaline stared at me with a confused expression sprinkled with what might have been a ray of hope. "Your . . . clan?"

"We collect quirky peeps." I shrugged. "I collected Ci, then Kat, then Io, then Vee. Why not the resident Miss Shark?"

"Because she tried to *eat you!*" Cinder's hologram vibrated with pure outrage.

"Past tense," I said cheerfully. "She's reformed. Or reforming. Potential recruit now."

"Ughhh." Kat's face appeared on the projection. "So much yelling. Do you need rescue? I can pull Possy from the deep and Vee can send her after you."

"Nah," I said. "This is fine. Going to spend the day here, I think. See if I can start a prison riot. Maybe take over this place. I dunno. I'm feeling inspired. Never been imprisoned before!"

Katherine squinted at me. "Riiiiight. You do you."

"A prison riot?!" Cinder yelled, shoving Katherine aside. "Do not start any riots!"

"Come on, starting a prison riot is totally on my bucket list!" I protested.

"*No riots!*" Cinder growled.

Magdaline watched our interaction with utter bewilderment. "Is . . . this normal?" she whispered to me.

"Completely," I whispered back. "Welcome to 'I Love You' Clan dynamics."

"I can *hear* you!" Cinder's hologram crackled.

"Good!" I called back. "Means communication lines are working! Don't attempt to rescue me."

"Why not?!" Both Katherine and Cinder demanded.

"I want to experience prison life," I said.

"Ughhhh," Cinder groaned. "Why?"

"The longer I stay here, the more perks I can shake out of Skyfall for my illegal imprisonment," I said. "Duh. Maybe I can get us a big loft on campus for our clan! Stay positive and think about the loft, guys!"

"A loft?" Cinder pursed her lips. "What kind of loft?"

"A big one." I grinned. "A room with a kitchen where you can practice Hearth-Wife-ness by making us sandwiches. Maybe near the Coliseum by the river, in one of the clock-towers. Good views, Victorian clockwork gears for cracking walnuts, art nouveau bathrooms, Gothic revival bedrooms, a balcony for flying from. Top-tier stuff reserved for kids of big donors."

Magdaline watched our interaction like someone observing an alien species.

"Fine," Cinder growled. "But *no starting riots*! And *no getting eaten*."

"Promise," I said, crossing my heart dramatically.

"I'll . . . call you periodically to make sure you're alive," she warned.

"Love you too, bae." I blew a kiss to the hologram. "Send Vee my kisses and hugs."

Cinder's hologram vanished with an exasperated huff.

I turned to Magdaline, who was still staring at me with wide shark eyes. "So," I said casually, "do you have an extra prison jumpsuit?"

Magdaline blinked. "Why?"

"To dress the part of a prisoner," I said. "Can't start a proper prison riot in my North Acadia Arx-designer jacket, can I?"

She stared at me for a long moment, then burst out laughing once again. A sharp bark that was somehow also genuine. In a minute, her laughter collapsed into soft giggles, the beast core crunching against her teeth.

"Didn't you promise your girl not to start any riots?" she asked, digging out an extra orange uniform from a small metal locker. She threw her uniform up at me.

I caught the jumpsuit midair. "You can start the riot, my sixie sharky. I can . . . rate it out of ten as a goodly clan leader," I winked. "Besides, Cindy didn't say anything about . . . creative reorganization of institutional infrastructure."

"And what exactly does 'creative reorganization' entail?"

"Oh, you know," I said, pulling on the large orange jumpsuit over my jacket and pants. "Just a few minor adjustments to the facility's operational protocols. Mostly, I want to investigate things and document them. Potentially expose some systemic issues."

"Systemic issues?" She raised an eyebrow.

"For example, why a rehabilitation facility allows predatory behavior," I explained, adjusting the jumpsuit. "Like eating people. Shouldn't you be at lunch? Why are you in your cell?"

Magdaline lowered her eyes.

"Because I can't control my impulses," she let out. "Especially when they serve blood pudding, raw meat . . . or anything with blood in it. It drives me up the wall, makes me attack the others. I eat alone in my cell."

I nodded, watching her carefully. "So they isolate you instead of actually helping you manage your condition with some beast cores?"

"Beast cores are . . . expensive as shit, and Dad doesn't make that much." She sighed, surprise flickering in her red eyes. "You . . . actually want to understand?"

"Absolutely," I said. "Understanding is the first step to solving a problem. Tell me about these impulses. When did they start?"

Magdaline's hand brushed through her white mop of a mane. "Since I was seven. I'd smell something—a small animal, sometimes another kid—and suddenly I'd just . . . want to consume it. Not out of hunger. Out of some weird compulsion. Smelling blood makes it worse . . . so much worse. I hate it. So very much. Dad says it will pass when I get older."

"Why'd you eat three Omnids at Skyfall?"

"They bullied me," Magdaline growled. "Constantly. Called me defective. Said I'd never be a proper Omnid. That I was a broken loser."

I nodded.

"They cornered me last semester," she continued, her red eyes growing distant, "kept calling me names. And then, something inside me just . . . snapped. I couldn't control it anymore. The more they mocked me, the more I wanted to prove them wrong. To show them I was strong, capable."

"By consuming them," I said neutrally.

She nodded, shame flickering across her features. "Dad says predatory behavior is natural. One of the teens had a sword that he was waving at my face, so I kicked it, and the sword went across one of their arms. Then the blood . . . it made me go berserk, lose control. By the time I came to, I had killed them and was devouring their innards. A bunch of grade eight students who came to apply to the Academy and were being shown the gardens . . . were watching me and taking photos. So they sent me here."

She slipped onto her bunk.

"Killing a student on campus isn't that big a deal," I shrugged. "Omnids kill each other all the time. Pretty sure Ci kicked someone through a wall 'cause they were being annoying. I guess you gave the Academy bad social rep or something. How long did they put you in juvie for?"

"Six months," she sighed. "Those three pricks must have pulled some strings. Dad's been trying to cut it down to less, since he works here as a night shift guard on top of his Scrutimancer job to pay for my overpriced education at Skyfall. I think he made a deal with the Stratos Clan or some other family to dispose of . . . human trash."

"Charming family business," I commented dryly.

"He said that Skyfall delving is supposed to help me grow my heart core, control my impulses," she said with a sniff-growl. "Learn to hunt 'properly.' Said he had the same problem when he was young."

"Now you're eating people who can't fight back," I said. "Sounds like excellent rehabilitation."

"He beat the impulse by murdering lots of beasts on Arx and leveling up," she breathed out. "But I can't do that. Nobody will take me on a team. Nobody even wants to take me on as a sixie after I kept snapping at people in grade nine at the cafeteria. They all know that I go mental when I sniff blood. I don't understand why you'd want me on your team . . . in your Clan . . . Especially after I almost ate you like a big knob."

I leaned forward, my eyes locking with her red ones. "Because everyone deserves a chance. Especially a person who wants to change, to overcome their Fractal Engine heart's alignment."

Magdaline blinked, clearly caught off guard.

"Your predatory instincts aren't a curse," I explained. "They're a skill. Untapped potential. Right now, they're uncontrolled, wild. But with the right snacks, right training, the right environment? You could be incredible. I could use a Scrut on my team with a good nose."

"You . . . actually want to help me?" she asked.

"Absolutely." I nodded. "As I said before, my clan is full of misfits. What's another one?"

Magdaline stared at me, her red eyes wide with disbelief. "You're completely, truly serious? You want me in your clan?"

"Yep." I nodded.

"Why? Come on, I smell another reason there."

"It'll really piss off your dad," I said.

"Ha!" Magdaline burst out laughing once again. "So, you want to recruit me just to annoy my father?"

"He annoyed me by derailing my schedule. That and your skills," I said. "They interest me."

"Interest you . . . how?" she asked with a look of suspicion.

"You can teach me how to smell lies, how to determine intent behind words," I said. "I want your Scrutimancy."

"But you're . . ."

"I'm a wizard," I said. "If you donate some of your hair or placoid scales, I can put it into a shake, drink it, and . . ."

"Omnids can't just gain powers from other Omnids by eating them!" Magdaline shook her head. "I bit plenty of Omnids, I would know."

"Not an Omnid," I pointed out. "A human wizard."

"Like . . . on Arx?" she asked.

"No, not like anywhere else," I said. "I don't have a heart core, so eating Omnid strata doesn't cause rejection. I can't even level up properly, don't have an XP stat."

"Hrm." She chewed on the beast core thoughtfully. "Fine. Prove it!"

Before I could say anything else, she sliced her wrist with a sharp claw, blood pouring into her somewhat bent, black coffee up. The cut sealed itself in about twenty-five seconds.

"Here," she said, handing me the cup of blood-coffee. "Drink up."

"Your own blood doesn't make you go crazy?" I asked.

"Nah," she said. "Plus, I'm still chewing the core you gave me. It's pretty damn potent, definitely waaaaaay above what Dad can afford, so I reckon it's gonna last me a while. Go on, Mr. Wizard. Impress me. Show me that you can steal my innate Megalodon skill."

I shrugged and brought the cup to my lips.

# CHAPTER THIRTY

# The Waltz of Scrutimancy

I tipped the cup back and drank deeply.

The coffee infused blood tasted somewhat metallic, salty—but underneath that, something else. A wave of flavor that spoke of predatory instincts, of sharp edges, and sparked hunting impulses. The sensation vanished as soon as it appeared, so maybe that was just my mind playing tricks on me.

"So?" Magdaline asked. "Feel anything?"

"Not how it works." I shook my head.

"How does it work, then?"

"You have to bounce your skill off me," I said as I slid from my top bunk down to hers. "Plus I have to do this for a bit."

I lit Zee Captain's lighter in the space between us.

"What?" Magdaline blinked. "What's the lighter supposed to do?"

"You'll see," I said, watching my mana rushing up.

"Wait." The Megalodon sniffed the air. "Mana. So much mana. How are you doing that? Is that lighter some kind of a mana-generating artifact?!"

I didn't answer her, snapping the lighter shut.

"Okay," I said, unzipping my jacket and offering her my hands. "What's your strongest skill? Bounce it off me. Pretend my body is a radar dish. Take my hands. Look at me."

Magdaline hesitantly reached out and took my hands. Her razor-sharp claws barely touched my gloves, her red eyes locked onto mine.

"How are you not terrified of me?" she asked, looking down at me. "You're so small, so . . . thin and frail looking. Smell . . . so human."

"Because I've faced scarier things than you," I replied calmly. "Now focus. What's your core, innate ability?"

"Scrutiosmia, aka Odormancy," she said. "Like Dad. I can smell lies, intentions, emotions, past events, likely future paths, likely outcomes, astral imprints . . ."

"Perfect." I nodded. "Focus on that. Project it at me. Imagine your skill as a wave bouncing off a mirror."

Magdaline's red eyes narrowed in concentration. Her claws tightened slightly around my hands.

"Hrm . . . I smell . . . something," she muttered. "Like . . . an echo? Strange."

"Keep bouncing your skill off me," I ordered. "Reach resonance. Think of the hunt, of how you chased me, of how much you . . . enjoyed it. Picture the dance between predator and prey. Between you and me. Shark and human wizard. Smell the ideas behind my words!"

Magdaline blushed ever so slightly, claws digging deeper into my dragonscale gloves, the hexasuits hardening over my fingers as she nearly crushed them.

Her red eyes flared brighter as she focused, projecting her power. I felt something shift inside me, like a new sense awakening.

Suddenly, scents bloomed in my awareness.

The metallic and concrete tang of the reinforced cell walls. The lingering traces of despair from the nearest astral imprint. The sharp edge of Magdaline's predatory nature, of hunger, of desire for blood held back by the delicious beast core in her mouth. Even my own scent—a strange mix of human and something else . . . noise, dull static layered with traces of colorful Quetzi, black and white Thunderbird, gray Mothman, and blue-green Stollwurm scents.

I mentally summoned up my stats.

---

System error. Unable to parse experience, no heart-core detected.
Delineating current state. Reassessing stats.
Level 4 state approximated!
LV 4 Skill gained: Scrutiosmia

---

A message flashed across my vision in white sparks.

---

| **Name: Alexander Glock**
| Age: 18
| Species & Subtype: Human-Thunderbird hybrid [with 4 other minor affinities]
| Core Affinity: N/A
| Level: 4
| Anima: 89/89 [+89] [+89] [+89] [+7] [+7]
| Anima Stamina: 1/1
| Mana: 568/46
| Mana Regen: 0.0m/hr
| Strength: 0
| Agility: 0
| Dexterity: 0
| Vitality: 0
| Charisma: 0
| Magic: 0 [+46]
| Foresight: 0
| Intelligence: 0
| Wisdom: 0

| **Skills:**
**Thunderbird:** Resonance, Lightningball, Electrofractal Sight, Dreamwalking, Chain Lightning
**Quetzalcoatl:** Charmchain
**Stollwurm:** Umbramancy, Deep Diving, Echomancy

**Deathskull Mothman:** Sundergate
**Megalodon:** Scrutiosmia
| **One-Way Soul Bonds:** Vespera Simmi, Cassiopeia Cinder Nova
| **Blood Contract Pact:** Vespera Simmi, Prima-Sword

"Got it," I said.

"Got what?" she asked.

"I have Scrutiosmia," I replied.

"Oh yeah?" the shark-girl asked. "Prove it."

"Say some relevant stuff," I said. "I'll smell if it's the truth."

"Okay . . ." Magdaline said. "Um . . . I hate being in this facility."

I sniffed. The scent of truth mixed with deep loneliness and frustration wafted from her.

"You're lonely," I said, closing my eyes and inhaling her scent again, reaching deeper into . . . elsewhere. Sudden new information revealed itself to me. "And you actually enjoy having a roommate, even if it's just for a day. Even if that roommate is a weird human wizard who just drank your blood, which you think is hella weird."

"You could have guessed that."

"Could I?" I grinned, inhaling deeper and closing my eyes. I smelled paper. A pencil. Smoke. "You've been drawing in your spare time and then burning the results."

"What?! What in the Abyss?!"

"I can smell the pencil shavings and . . . oh my. Those are some spicy drawings of that . . . musician. What was his name? Started with a K . . ."

Magdaline's face went bright red.

"Kuro?" I sniffed again. "Oh yes, definitely Kuro Stardust. You've drawn him quite . . . extensively making out with . . ."

"Stop!" She let go of my fingers, buried her face in her hands, her white hair falling forward to hide her embarrassment. "Abyss! Move onto something else! Anything else!"

"Lots of people died here," I said, standing up and moving around the cell, my expression darkening as I sniffed the air. "Forty . . . one mundane humans. They were confused, terrified, and hostile. You . . . sliced through their arteries, broke their necks, and then . . . you ate them. Your dad brought them here, bleeding . . . locked the door using the one-hour lockdown timer . . . You cleaned the mess up each time and dumped the remains into the disposal chute."

I continued walking around the cell, my new sense delving through layers of history trapped in the walls.

"Drug dealers." I sniffed near one corner. "Three of them. They tried to bribe your dad with O-bux to let them go. It didn't work. They smelled of Topaz."

Magdaline shifted uncomfortably on her bunk.

"Gang members before then." I moved to another spot. "Debtors. Seven of them. Consumed one by one. Seven days. Fourth one was on Topaz, fought back hard, had a hidden blade, but you broke his wrist and shoved the knife into his eye. You felt weird after eating him, happy . . . but it was just fake dreams of you being in Skyfall and actually having friends . . . and then your skill digested the drug . . . and then you cried . . ."

"Fuuuck." Magdaline swallowed. "You do have Scrutimancy!"

I paused by the door. "And here . . . a young woman. Begged for her life.

"Around twenty-four," I continued sniffing near the door. "An accountant who'd been stealing money from one of the Stratos vault accounts. Your dad caught her. You felt bad about that one, since she wasn't that bad of a person. Really bad. Tried to fight the urge. Failed. Still dream about her sometimes."

Magdaline's shoulders hunched inward.

"Two assassins before then." I moved to another corner. "Hired to kill some Prima's kid. Failed. Got caught. Compulsion magic in their blood. Then three thieves who broke into the Stratos vault . . . then that serial killer from Scab Row who used some kind of an anti-scrying artifact to hide his deeds . . ."

I paused by the reinforced window, inhaling deeply. "This is where you cornered a cultist. His mind infected with a memetic. He fought back, was stronger than others and felt no pain."

"There are others, deeper, further in . . . but their scents get blurry. Let me try something more recent."

"What?" she asked.

"Me!" I sniffed myself. "Hrmmm. You took it easy on me. You tried to fight the urge, smelled the Skyfall Lazarus bracelet on me. Lied to me. Tried to understand what I was."

She nodded.

"Yeah." Magdaline's red eyes flickered with unease. "I . . . I didn't want to eat you. Not really. You smelled . . . different. Odd. Wrong. Hard to define."

I inhaled deeply, sorting through the scents of truth and deception. "Half-truth. You did want to eat me, but something else held you back. Something . . . deeper. Further ahead?"

"You smell like . . . hope," she confessed after a few seconds. "Like freedom. Like someone who could actually help me. I've never smelled anything like it before."

"You don't believe that, though." I came closer to her, standing directly in front of her, sniffing her. "You don't think that a mere Skyfall student could save you from anything. You think that you're worthless, just trash disposal, just a murderer that your dad and the Stratos clan have been using . . ."

I leaned in closer, my new Scrutiosmia skill parsing her emotional landscape like a complex topographical map. I burned through the mana offered to me by the lighter, pushed mana through my Resonance skill like a loop, and made it flow across my nose.

"You think you're broken," I said softly. "But you're not. You're just . . . underfed, hungry. A diamond in the rough. Sometimes the system is what's broken. Not the individual."

Magdaline's red eyes widened. "Seriously, how . . . How are you doing that?! You're not a Scrutimancer! You didn't smell like a Scrutimancer at all five minutes ago!"

"I'm not," I said. "On Tuesday, I . . ."

"Walked through the gates of Skyfall," she said as she inhaled my breath. "And met . . ."

"An angel with rainbow wings." I nodded. "And . . ."

"Thunder." She inhaled again, tasting my intent, dissecting the past. "The cleverest Thundergirl in Skyfall, who figured you out. Who . . . gradually changed you with each touch . . . remade you from within on a whim because she was . . . bored. No. A lie. Because she was incredibly desperate . . . desperate to escape from her chains."

"Who . . ." I began, looking at the shark.

"Fell in love with you and gave you the greatest gift of all," Magdaline said, her mouth falling open, tongue caressing the beast core between her teeth. "One not meant for humans. Electrofractal sight and . . . the Resonance skill! Abyss!"

"Resonance," I said. "An electrofractal . . ."

"An astral radar dish in your stomach tied to your soul," Magdaline breathed out. "Controlling indigestible particles of Omnid strata moving across your human innards . . . forming a convex mirror . . . a skill amplifier! Holy shit! That's how you're doing it!"

"Clever shark." I grinned.

"Sneaky little human," she smiled. "Changed by a clever, desperate Thundergirl who set something truly terrible in motion, created a human who can do magic without a heart core. Abyss!"

Her face paled.

"Heh," I said. "That was some top-notch Scrutimancy, partner. Still got . . ."

"Two hundred and six mana," she breathed out.

"Do you want to know . . ." I began.

"More? Yes! Yes, I do! I've never felt so clear . . . so sharp . . . so whole! It's like the hunger, the emptiness . . . isn't there anymore! Just Understanding . . . just the flow. Resonance!"

"How about a dance, partner?" I asked, unzipping my pocket and pulling out a phone from the extradimensional pouch.

"Oh! Dad didn't destroy your phone?" She grinned.

"That wasn't my phone," I answered. "That was Vespera's second phone. She gave it to me when she ran off to the Coliseum for a nap."

The Megalodon Scrutimancer laughed and stood up from her bunk and reached out to me. I grabbed her silver-blue hand.

"Yulia, play Johann Strauss II—'The Blue Danube Waltz,'" I ordered. "Then spice it up, make it more fun, write some relevant, cute lyrics!"

Violin music filled our cell as Magdaline and I began to step in perfect sync, her predatory instincts and my newly acquired Scrutiosmia creating a feedback loop of hyper-awareness.

My hand slid down to Magdaline's waist. Her razor-sharp claws slid onto my shoulder, careful not to tear the fabric of my borrowed orange jumpsuit.

Our hands entwined.

We began with a basic Viennese waltz pattern—a natural turn that spun us clockwise. Her red eyes locked with mine, no longer filled with hunger, but a flame of Understanding backlit by fireworks of excitement.

The violins soared as we spun across the small cell, our movements perfectly synchronized through shared Scrutiosmia. Magdaline's white hair whirled around us like ocean spray.

Her predatory movements—the skill previously used only to hunt, to murder and consume criminals in this cell—became something elegant, beautiful.

Each step calculated, each turn precise.

My hexasuit-enhanced agility matched her shark-like grace in perfect synchronicity.

The song shifted away from "The Blue Danube" as Yulia finished writing the music and began to sing.

"Through depths of space, the Wormwood ever falls. / Dead echoes whisper through these hexcrete halls, / Dance of predator, dance of prey / As the Earth turns, night shifts to day."

I spun Magdaline across our tiny cell with impossible grace, guiding each of her motions through broadcast intent. She was taller than me, but it didn't matter in the slightest. Yulia sang.

"Leviathan's children dance and dream / Where thunder meets the rainbow's gleam / Between the stars and endless deep / Where human hearts their secrets keep. / Teeth of starlight, wings of flame, / Entropy's hunger cannot stake its claim. / Souls entwined beyond blood and bone / Where neither has to be alone."

We moved faster, our steps matching the rising tempo. Red eyes against green. A river of blood framed by evergreen pines.

"Resonance between two souls / Makes broken pieces into wholes. / Shark and wizard dance as one, / Their road onward just begun."

Magdaline laughed wildly as I spun her again and the lyrics repeated.

The cold, bare hexcrete cell vanished. There were only waves of a red sea smashing against the land of brown cliffs and evergreen hills with each rising and falling tone of the violin.

As the song reached its crescendo and fell silent, Magdaline and I stopped, breathless. Her red eyes were wide, no longer predatory, but alive and sparkling with tears.

*She believes me now with her entire Fractal Engine heart. I've captured her attention. My personal Scrutimancer shark. Time to learn some things. Together.*

We stopped by the cell door above which a red number was counting down.

"Scrutimancer Satosh . . ." I began.

"Lost his wife eleven years ago . . ." she said, blinking more sparks from her eyes.

"A Topaz-peddling human gang from Scab Row . . ." I pulled information from the air around us, from the footsteps of Satosh that lingered here again and again, from his breath, from his fear and hatred. "Killed Enni Satoshi. They sealed her bracelet in a magisteel box with anti-scrying runes, making sure she couldn't be brought back."

"By the time Satosh tore through their hideout and found her bracelet and incarnated her . . . she didn't know how to talk, could only stare blankly at him, and didn't remember him. She's in the White Hall of Serenity Springs Asylum now," Magdaline revealed. "Dad's been . . . shattered since then . . ."

"He became over-focused on trying to uplift his daughter who lost her mom and could not control her Megalodon heart," I pulled on the astral string, unraveling it. "In an attempt to solve her problem, he put her into an overpriced Academy he could not hope to afford. There, poor Magdaline found no friends and thus only made her condition worse."

I dug into my pocket and pulled out a vial of Emerald's blood that I had extracted a few days ago from her sleeping form, but didn't have time to do anything with.

"Emerald Stratos . . ." I uncorked the vial of the dragon girl's blood.

"Offered to pay him extra . . ." Magdaline inhaled deep, her eyes flashing like rubies. "To do progressively worse, illegal things."

"And Satosh accepted them," I resumed, the astral imprint of Satosh and the blood of Emerald spilling their secrets to us. "Became bound more and more to her whims. Helped her get in touch with a clan of Skinwalkers. Offered them a young singer, put a potent tracking spell on her. Helped a devious red dragon rescue the singer and then aided the Quetzi and dragon to execute the Skinwalk Clan and bury them at sea. Thanks to this job, he had enough for two years of school fees for his little darling shark . . ."

"But then, like a fool, she mauled three Omnids in full view of prospective students," Magdaline continued, holding onto my hands. "Prima-borns . . . who often hung out with Emerald, her friends. And so the knob-shark was sent to juvie. And so Scrutimancer Satosh became even more reckless and desperate. Emerald offered him enough gold for another year at Skyfall. The dragoness promised Satosh to hire a lawyer who could reduce his daughter's sentence . . ."

"To make Skyfall student Alexander Glock disappear," I said.

"Whose astral imprint smelled like a human on Wednesday night," Magdaline added. "Who was also conveniently asked to be imprisoned by . . ."

"An agent of a wealthy Thunderland Omnicorp," I pulled on the thread harder with my new skill. "Which also paid quite well for the contract Satosh accepted."

"He ignored that the target smelled a bit off on Friday," Magdaline said. "It was too late to back out of the two signed contracts by then. He was confident that his daughter would be able to devour Alexander Glock just as she had devoured the other forty-one humans and cast his untasty Lazarus bracelet and shredded outfit into the incinerator chute . . ."

"And then Satosh would obtain Alexander's bracelet from the ashes during his night shift and deliver it to the Omnicorp agent." Both of us looked at the metal door of the incinerator chute on the wall beside us.

"Satosh made just one fatal mistake," I added with a smile. "He couldn't sniff out . . ."

"Twenty million worth of beast cores in the boy's pocket," Magdaline uttered. "Because an extradimensional space cannot be penetrated by Scrutiosmia."

I nodded.

"Plus your entire outfit, the jacket, the gloves, the pants . . . they don't smell like anything at all for some reason," she stared at me.

"Nitoroc panther leather atop of dragonscale," I tapped my sleeve. "Anti-scrying runes woven into the inner lining."

"Ah." Magdaline nodded. "That'd do it. That'd absolutely screw with Scrutimancy."

My mana dropped to zero. I sealed the vial of Emerald's blood and slipped it back into my extradimensional pocket. Magdaline blinked, letting go of my hands.

"Wow," she said. "So that's what it's like to be a proper Scrutimancer. I've . . . I've never been able to deduce so much before by smell!"

I smiled at her.

"You aren't going to abandon me in this cell, right?" she asked. "You didn't just use me to get all that information out of me to use it against my dad?"

"Did it feel like that was the case?" I asked.

"No," Magdaline said softly. "It felt . . . like nothing I've done before. Like I finally woke up after eleven years of being asleep at the wheel. Thank you."

"See?" I said. "You're not just a trash disposal. You're a talented Scrut. All it took was a dance, a song written by an AI, and some Resonance magic to unlock your potential."

She suddenly went down on one knee.

"I, Magdaline Satoshi, do hereby pledge myself forevermore as a sixie to . . ." She looked up at me with wide eyes.

"Clan 'I Love You.'" I filled in with a smile.

Magdaline blinked. "Clan . . . I Love You?"

"Welcome aboard." I offered her my hand.

Her razor-sharp teeth glinted as she burst out laughing, accepting my hand to stand up. "*That's* your clan name? Abyss, I thought you were kidding before! *Why?!* It sounds like a bad boy band or a cheesy romance novel!"

"Nobody expects 'I Love You' to be a serious threat." I grinned.

"Fair enough." She wiped a white-blue hand across her eyes, an extra-toothy smile stretching wide.

The clock on the door reached zero and then the bolt snapped open.

"Shall we tour the facilities then, my sixie darling?" I asked.

"With pleasure, my Slayer," she replied, sharp eyes filled with red sparks of mirth.

# CHAPTER THIRTY-ONE

# Collaborators

Kai Xing Ker, Arch-Elder of the Golden Star Clan, tapped his bronze fingers on his opulent desk as the call connected.

"Greetings, Arch-Elder Simmi," Kai's ancient voice carried through the encrypted Voicecast holo. "I trust you've heard about your Prima-spawn's . . . unfortunate entanglement?"

"Entanglement?" Altair Raiden Simmi asked with a frown, his crystalline, pale silver Skyfish scales glimmering.

"Yes," Kai continued, his amphibian eyes narrowing. "Your Scion, Vespera Simmi, formed a soul-bond with a human infiltrator Martin Kilborne posing as mixed-blood student Alexander Glock at Skyfall Academy."

"What?!" Altair's clear, crystalline wings spread out, bristling with static. "Impossible. Vespera wouldn't . . ."

"Why would I lie to you, my old friend?" Kai asked. "You have one of my best engines in your study. Check the result yourself. Vespera Simmi already bonded with Alexander Glock to a 99.997 percent certainty and will further enforce this bond at the Cradlefall cathedral with an Arch-Priest unless immediate action is taken."

Altair's multitude of wings danced with lightning, his figure stretching out. "A human? My great-granddaughter . . . with a human?!"

"Indeed." Kai nodded.

"No human will soil my bloodline!" Altair's crystalline form buzzed with electrical discharge.

"The infiltrator has already been detained," Kai said. "But we must act quickly to prevent further damage. My sources indicate he has gained considerable influence at Skyfall in a very short time."

"Where is he being held?" Altair demanded.

"Cradlefoot Youth Rehabilitation Facility," Kai replied. "I have already punished my Scion for his negligence. I believe you should do the same with yours, Altair."

"Negligence?" Altair asked.

"He accepted a duel from Alexander Glock," Kai explained. "A public challenge for Vespera's hand."

"A human dared to challenge a Prima-born of the House of Golden Star?!" Altair laughed. "And your Scion was stupid enough to accept the challenge?!"

"Yes," Kai sighed. "Zheng was deceived by a human scab. The duel is set for Sunday at noon in the Skyfall Coliseum."

"Ridiculous." Altair's wings fluttered with renewed fury. "I will not allow this farce to continue. I'm sending my security team to retrieve Vespera from Skyfall at once."

Kai nodded. "Have you not revealed the importance of our merger to your Scion? Does she not know what is at stake?"

"I . . ." Altair began.

Kai looked at the data running across his desk. "You have not," he said. "It is imperative that she changes her mind."

Altair sighed. "I believed that she wasn't ready to know the truth. She is only eighteen. I had hoped that she would grow out of her childish ways, optimize herself. I shall speak with her father about this matter. Ceter will handle it."

"As it was your Scion that has caused this disruption, perhaps Lord Ceter should stand as Zheng's champion," Kai suggested smoothly. "My foolish progeny is currently . . . under house arrest for his failure."

"Ceter would be more than capable," Altair agreed, his crystalline form pulsing with electrical energy. "He has always been protective of Vespera. But why is it necessary for this shameful duel to occur at all? If the human is in Omnid custody, why not simply make him disappear? Accidents happen . . ."

"Correctional Officer Satosh just assured my agent that the human should be dead within the hour and that his Lazarus bracelet will be delivered to us tonight," Kai said. "Unfortunately, I don't have trusted contacts within the Cradlefoot Youth Rehabilitation Facility who can confirm it. The island prison is under Stratos jurisdiction. My influence there is limited, and the perimeter defense wards block the eyes of my Probability Engines. Perhaps you could . . ."

"I will handle it," Altair said coldly. "I will reach out to the Stratos Clan and see if I can procure contacts within their prison."

"Excellent." Kai nodded. "And what of the soul bond with the human?"

"The bond will dissolve when the human dies, no?" Altair pointed out.

"The human has a Lazarus bracelet from Skyfall," Kai pointed out. "As does Vespera. Both bracelets have the capability to enforce the bond even after the death of their bearers. A Lazarus bracelet is made from immovable metal which cannot be destroyed. Killing the human and gating his bracelet to another dimension will not remove the link between the bracelets nor the soul-bonded tag they might display."

"Blasted girl really did it this time," Altair growled, his crystalline silver-white fingers curling into fists.

"A simple solution. We can take the human to Novazem and feed him to an Astral Phantom in one of the local magogenic faults. Of course, before then, he will be tortured and killed a few hundred times. The repeated deaths and soul-trauma should weaken the bond," Kai offered. "Then the high-level Astral Phantoms will devour what remains of his soul, permanently severing the connection."

"A sound plan," Altair agreed. "And what of Vespera?"

"You will need Vespera to go to a high-level Psychopomp to have the soul bond surgically removed," Kai continued. "It won't be cheap and the procedure will . . . not be pleasant. The bond must be removed completely so that the Arch-Priest won't have issues or questions for when Zheng and Vespera are bonded at the cathedral."

"And if she refuses to cooperate?" Altair mused.

"Then your grandson must use force," Kai said. "Erase her memories of the human.

Do whatever it takes. The merger between our clans is too important to be derailed by this teenage rebellion. The future of all Omnid-kind depends on it."

"I will call Ceter immediately. We cannot allow this nonsense to disrupt our merger," Altair agreed.

"One more thing," Kai added. "The human has apparently formed connections with other students at Skyfall. My engines suggest that they could become . . . problematic for us."

"How can a bunch of schoolchildren challenge two millennia-old clans?" Altair arched a pale eyebrow.

"I do not know," Kai said. "The Academy's wards interfere with my scrying. Something about a tree on Arx named Yulia. Something about a Quetzalcoatl Cassiopeia Nova."

"Justice Nova's daughter is involved in this, too?" Altair asked. "How?"

"Yes." Kai nodded. "She is Vespera's friend."

"I shall ask Omnimart's Arch-CEO to keep a tighter leash on her daughter," Altair said. "I'm not friends with the Justice, but I'm certain that Lady Xastigar can get her family's spawn in line."

"Let us proceed swiftly." Kai nodded. "The human must be eliminated and the soul bond must be severed before it can cause further disruption."

"Agreed." Altair's crystalline form pulsed with electrical energy. "I will contact the necessary parties immediately."

The call ended, leaving Kai alone in his study. He tapped his bronze fingers against the desk thoughtfully, watching as his Probability Engines continued their endless calculations. Too many things weren't adding up.

The engines were showing increasing anomalies around the human's presence at Skyfall. Variables that shouldn't exist, probability chains that defied logic and outcome flow. Something big was interfering with the engines' predictions.

Kai didn't like it. It suggested that an unknown corporation, an Outsider, or an ancient cult stood behind Martin Kilborne, which didn't bode well for Golden Star's plans.

What was Uriel ranting about? What was Infinity Paradox Proxima?

He typed the question into the massive probability engine behind his desk and a single number came up on the spinning dial: *8.*

He tried again, rephrasing the question and again, the answer was simply *8.*

Kai walked across his study, his eyes closed, guiding his pockmarked hands with innate Precognition. Eventually he stopped at a book and flipped it to the random page which his sight guided him towards.

A Dagaz rune was on the page. A sideways eight. A cold shiver ran down Kai's ancient spine as he read the calligraphic words below the rune.

*Awakening. Change. New Beginning. Dawn.*

Kai flipped through other books, looking for more information connected to the rune.

He stopped on other pages.

The cult of Sheela na gig. Carvings of a woman opening herself like a ring found in Nazarite churches across Ireland, Wales, England, and France.

The symbols kept repeating—the sideways eight, the open woman, the gateway. *Infinity. Paradox. Fertility.*

The endless cycle of death and rebirth.

In another hour of reaching out and digging through his library, Kai discovered that he was going through the same concepts again and again across various books, moving in a circle, in two loops across his study.

As hard as he tried, he could not locate any links to any particular existing cult or corporation linked to his target. No links to any specific Omnid archetype that he could contact. Just an information loop bent into itself, trapping his Foresight in it.

Kai closed the last book with a frustrated sigh, his bronze fingers trembling slightly.

Either Uriel was screwing with him by sending him on a wild goose chase or Martin Kilborne was somehow connected to the Dagaz rune and Sheela na gig in some unclear manner or would eventually become connected to it.

The truth eluded the ancient Omnid, slipping through his fingers.


"I thought that we were going out?" Magdaline asked me as she watched me paint my face gray after pulling my gray headcap on.

"Soon," I said, putting the bodypaint back into my extradimensional pocket. "As a human, I might attract unwanted attention. But as a nondescript gray Dover Demon, I'll blend right in."

"Clever," the shark-girl commented. "But what about your scent?"

I pulled out a bottle of perfume and sprayed it all over my prison robe.

Magdaline inhaled. "Hah. Now you smell like Dover Demon sweat. Where'd you even get that?"

"Went to the school's gym," I said. "Followed a very lazy Dover Demon around during his workout, wiped the machines after him, then used Steam Distillation to get the sweat out. Combined with the ScentAura Amplifying Elixir from Omnimart and voila, I smell like a Dover Demon."

"Gross." Magdaline wrinkled her nose. "But effective. Still . . . up close someone might notice . . ."

I stared into her eyes, pushing mana through Resonance and then through the skill stolen from Cinder. "How about now?"

"Huh." She stared at me, eyes dilating. "You somehow . . . feel like you belong. Weird. I know I've never had a cell roommate and yet . . ."

"Basic Charmchain magic," I explained. "Got it from my Quetzi-girl. Projecting a very mild sense of belonging straight into your head."

"Impressive." She nodded.

"'Kay, I think I'm ready for the tour now." I smiled as I sliced the pockets of the orange jumpsuit so I could easily reach into my extradimensional jacket's pockets. "Lead the way."

"Follow, oh mighty wizard," she grinned.

We stepped out of the cell into a sterile gray corridor.

"So? What's on your schedule after lunch?" I asked.

"Therapy class, then physical education," she replied.

"Therapy, eh? What exactly does that entail?"

Magdaline rolled her red eyes. "Mostly group therapy sessions with other knobs like me who can't control their urges. Nothing exciting."

We walked down the long hallway, passing rows of empty cells. A few other inmates and guards glanced our way, but didn't pay us too much attention.

"Group therapy sounds fun," I said.

Mags gave me a "what is wrong with you" look.

"Fun?" she snorted. "It's just a bunch of teens talking about our feelings 'n' shit while our very bored therapist takes notes and makes occasional critical commentary."

"Any new experience is fun," I shrugged. "I've never been to group therapy before. I'm picturing Alcoholics Anonymous. Is it like that?"

"Pffff," Magdaline huffed. "More like Murderers and Misfits Anonymous."

After about ten minutes of walking, we entered a large room with white walls, several chairs arranged in a circle connected to a backroom with a coffee machine and a small lounge. A bored-looking Black Unicorn therapist in a gray uniform and gray cap inhabited the room. She seemed more interested in her tablet than the potential inmates around her.

"Welcome to group therapy," the Black Unicorn therapist droned at us without looking up.

I scanned the room. Next to us there were ten other inmates total, a mix of different Omnid species. An emerald-scaled Lamia, a very furry Mapinguari, a muscular, scruffy-looking Bies, a fleshy Catoblepas covered with moss atop of her head, a dark and lanky Erlking, a curvy Lamashtu, a winged Camazotz, a red-faced Yara-ma-yha-who, a massive Grootslang and a tentacled Scylla.

Magdaline guided me to two empty chairs and we sat down.

"Share your feelings. Introduce yourself if you're new. Try not to murder each other." The Unicorn therapist waved us on. "You know the drill."

"You smell new." The Yara-ma-yha-who turned his large white-striped red head to me, evaluating me with beady yellow eyes. "What are you in for, fresh meat?"

"Sup, fellow inmates. I'm Xander Fox," I announced with theatrical flair. "Professional interdimensional bank robber, corporate saboteur, and part-time dimensional gate crasher. Last week I unleashed a magic-eating plague in an underground city, built a Mage Tower, and created a new city-state in approximately a week. I'm here 'cause I always wanted to know what it would be like to experience prison life."

"A comedian in juvie?" the Mapinguari rumbled with a smirk.

"Not a comedian," I corrected. "A professional narrative conductor and Dark Lord looking for prospective, new minions."

"And what sort of a narrative are you looking to conduct?" The Yara-ma-yha-who tilted his large head at me.

"I wanted to start a prison riot spiced with a side of mayhem," I said cheerfully, aiming the "I belong here" Charmchain at the bored Unicorn. "Alas, my fiancée is against such, so I'll settle for taking over this place dungeon-delver style."

A ripple of surprised laughter and curious looks spread through the room.

"Whoever proves themselves worthy to me will have a chance at joining my clan as a sixie," I offered.

"A bold claim for a little Dover Demon who smells like a mixie," the Erlking commented.

The Erlking's comment was met with a chorus of snickers from around the room. I leaned back, a confident smile playing across my lips.

"Little?" I raised an eyebrow. "Ever heard the phrase 'dynamite comes in small packages'?"

The Mapinguari let out a deep, rumbling chortle. "New kid's got spirit, I'll give him that."

The Yara-ma-yha-who blinked at me. "Why'd you want to start a prison riot?"

"It's on my bucket list," I said. "As is breaking into a prison to take over it."

More laughter.

"Bucket list?" the Lamashtu asked, dark wolf head staring at me. "Most people have 'visit Paris' or 'learn a language' on their bucket list. You've got 'start a prison riot'?"

"Why you got a bucket list anyways?" the Yara-ma-yha-who asked. "Are you dyin' or something?"

"Lots of people want to kill me." I shrugged. "I'm always running out of time and making enemies. Figure I could make some new friends here."

"What exactly can you offer us other than being a mildly amusing little shit?" the Lamashtu asked.

"The same thing I've offered my new lovely sixie shark," I said. "Do smile for the group, darling."

Magdaline grinned, her razor-sharp teeth glinting under the fluorescent lights. She opened her mouth, displaying the beast core.

"Anyone looking to join my clan will receive similar snacks daily," I offered.

# CHAPTER THIRTY-TWO

# Taken

Vespera glared at the Slenderman Vice Principal.

"Your fiancé is in Cradlefoot Youth Rehabilitation Facility," Graves revealed.

"So you gated a soul-bonded, contractually enforced partner of a Prima-Heiress to a juvenile detention facility without proper documentation or due process?" Attorney Thornheart's voice demanded through the phone with barely contained outrage. "Vice Principal Graves, do you have any idea of the legal ramifications of such an action?"

Vespera struggled to keep her eyes open, exhaustion from the delve weighing heavily on her. The electrical field around her flickered dangerously as her concentration wavered.

"The facility is under Stratos jurisdiction," Graves explained. "Scrutimancer Satosh assured me—"

"Scrutimancer Satosh has no authority to override Prima-bond protocols," Thornheart interrupted sharply. "Miss Simmi, shall I proceed with filing charges against both Skyfall Academy and the Stratos Clan?"

"Ye," Vespera clicked.

The air beside her vibrated and three figures emerged from the shadows. Vespera turned and watched through half-lidded eyes as Cinder and Katherine dragged a battered-looking Emerald into Vice Principal Graves's office.

"Thornheart," Vespera said, handing her phone to Cinder, "this is my . . . partner, Cassiopeia Nova. Please handle the rest with her aid. I'ma rest now." She collapsed into the nearest armchair, closing her eyes.

"Why are you . . .?" Graves looked down at the trio of students.

"Emerald has something to confess about," Katherine growled. "Go on, dragon-princess."

"I . . ." Emerald let out. "I made it all up. The assault charges. The human accusations. Everything."

"What?!" Graves asked.

"Explain." Attorney Thornheart stared at Emerald through the phone.

"I . . . I was the one who attacked Alexander Glock first," Emerald admitted. "He only defended himself. The Genesis Well incident—I rushed him first. Same for Delving class. He just . . . managed to turn it all around on me."

"And why did you fabricate these charges?" Thornheart pressed.

"Emerald has been bullying mixed-blood students since grade nine with encouragement from Instructor Zalimar," Cinder said. "Alexander Glock became my friend. Emerald wanted him out of Skyfall, even though Alexander saved her from permanent death."

"She paid her Scrutimancer to get rid of Glock." Katherine nodded.

"Did you really?" Graves asked.

"Instructor Zalimar pushed me into it!" Emerald tried to roll Zalimar under the bus. "He wanted me to rid Skyfall of weakling nullborns!"

"In light of this new evidence," Attorney Thornheart said, "Vice Principal Graves, I expect Mr. Glock to be released immediately."

"I merely facilitated the transfer based on rather compelling evidence provided to me by Scrutimancer Satosh," Graves admitted. "I cannot bring him back. Only Cradlefoot Youth Rehabilitation Facility employees are permitted to gate into or from San Clemente Island."

"Then I suggest you contact whoever can authorize it," Thornheart stated firmly. "Before this situation escalates further."

"I'll . . ." Graves's void-like face rippled with static interference.

The door to the office burst open once again.

Lord Ceter Kalik Simmi entered the office flanked by four SimmiTech security officers in pristine white uniforms.

"Prima-Daughter!" Vespera's father's voice boomed, his Thunderbird wings spreading wide.

"Eh?" Vespera cracked one eye open at her father's voice.

"There you are!" Ceter boomed.

"Sleeping," she muttered. "Handle it, Ci."

"Lord Simmi." Cinder stepped forward, wings flaring protectively. "Your daughter is exhausted from an extended delve. We—"

"Be silent, girl," Lord Simmi barked. "This is a family matter. Vespera, you will come with me at once!"

"No," Vespera clicked without opening her eyes. "Busy. Come back next week."

"This is not a request," Lord Simmi's voice hardened. "Your great-grandfather has ordered your immediate return to SimmiTech Compound!"

"No," Vespera muttered.

"This nonsense ends now. Guards, secure my daughter!" Lord Simmi barked.

The SimmiTech security officers moved forward, but Katherine stepped between them and Vespera, her emerald eyes glowing with otherworldly menace. Waves of pure dread rolled off her form as she began to sink into the deep.

"Touch her," Katherine growled, "and I'll show you what true terror feels like."

"How dare you threaten—" Lord Simmi began.

"Attorney Thornheart," Cinder spoke into the phone, "Lord Simmi is attempting to forcibly remove his daughter from school grounds! Please advise."

"Y—" Thornheart began.

"*Enough!*" Ceter barked. An electric pulse rolled off him like a sphere of sparks. The phone held by Cinder detonated, screen flickering dark.

Cinder, Katherine, and Emerald fell where they stood.

Lord Simmi marched to Vespera and picked her up.

"I'm taking my daughter home for the weekend," he said to Graves, who simply stood there, dark tentacles flickering.

"Very well," the Vice Principal answered.

Ceter vanished through the door, his guards following him.

In another few minutes, the vice principal exhaled and snapped his fingers, sending waves of static rolling over the passed-out students.

"Ughhh, shit," Cinder got off the floor, wings flashing with dark grays and blacks. "Did we just . . ."

"Get knocked out?" Katherine said. "Yes, we did."

"Where's Vespera?" Cinder blinked at the empty chair and looked around frantically.

"Lord Simmi took her," Graves said calmly. "She'll return on Monday."

"*What?!*" Cinder's wings flared with angry colors. "You just let him take her?!"

"He's her father," Graves stated. "He has every right to—"

"She's soul-bonded to . . ." Cinder howled, wings flashing brilliant red.

"Sound bonds are irrelevant in this matter, Miss Nova," Graves replied, silencing the noisy Quetzi-girl with a hum of deep static. "Please cease yelling in my office unless you wish to extend your detention. Now, as for you, Miss Stratos. I do not appreciate being lied to. You will serve detention cleaning the Auditorium along with Miss Nova on Monday after class."

"Are you serious?!" Cinder howled. "You're only giving her detention for this?!"

"Miss Nova, please—" Graves began.

Katherine grabbed Cinder's arm. "Come on," she said, pulling the enraged Quetzalcoatl and meek-looking Emerald towards the door. "We need to regroup and think."

"But—" Cinder protested.

"Now," Katherine insisted firmly, dragging the pair out of the office past the very annoyed looking Kitsune secretary.

As soon as they were in the hallway, Katherine spoke in a low voice. "Alex told us not to rescue him, remember? He's planning something. And Vespera . . ." She paused. "She's tough. She'll be okay for the weekend."

"Are you . . . sure?" Cinder demanded. "What if her father overwrites her mind while she's asleep?!"

"That . . . might be a problem." Katherine frowned.

"Can I go now?" Emerald mewled.

"No!" both girls barked at her.

"You're coming with us," Katherine growled.

"T-to where?" Emerald asked. "I-I'd like to go home now. I told Graves about the thing, like you wanted me to! He gave me detention and everything!"

"What, so you can cry to your parents, make up more shit about Alex?" Cinder hissed. "Yeah, I don't think so. I'm Alex's Hearth-Shield and you're our clan's sixie."

"That . . . that was a pledge made under duress!" Emerald protested.

"A pledge is a pledge," Cinder growled. "We saved your beerch ass from an execution! And you're going to help us fix this mess you created."

"How?" Emerald asked with a resigned face.

"I don't effing know," Cinder said.

"You can't keep me bloody collared forever," the dragon girl pointed out. "My parents will want to know where I am . . ."

"Emmy," Katherine snarled, looming over the shorter dragon girl in her dark leather and beast core dress. "I'm about five seconds away from dropping you into the deep. Nobody will find you there."

"Okay, okay!" Emerald raised her hands in surrender. "I'll bloody help, you savage! What do you want me to do?"

"First," Katherine said, her emerald eyes glowing dangerously, "you're going to tell us everything you know about Cradlefoot Youth Rehabilitation Facility."

"I don't know much," Emerald admitted. "It's on San Clemente Island. High security. Serious wards. My family owns it."

"Any weaknesses?" Cinder demanded.

"I don't freaking know! I haven't been there! Do I look like a criminal or a warden?!" Emerald whined.

"Not a criminal *yet*," Katherine growled. "But you sure acted like one, getting Alex imprisoned."

"Look, I said I was sorry!" Emerald protested. "What more do you want from me?"

"Information," Cinder said. "Everything you know about the Stratos Clan's involvement with the facility."

"I really don't know much," Emerald insisted. "Just that my family uses it sometimes to . . . deal with problems."

"What kind of problems?" Katherine pressed.

"People who . . ." Emerald hesitated. "Who need to disappear."

Cinder's wings flared with angry colors. "So it's not just a rehabilitation facility. It's a private prison."

"More like a disposal site," Katherine's emerald eyes narrowed. "Where inconvenient people vanish."

"We should . . . call Alex," Cinder let out. "He'll know what to do. Alex always knows what to do."


The therapy room went silent. The inmates stared at the glowing beast core nestled between Magdaline's razor-sharp teeth as she slowly closed her mouth.

The Mapinguari's eyes widened. "Is that . . .?"

"It is." Mags nodded. "Wouldn't be chewing it otherwise."

"Miss Satoshi. May I remind you that no food is allowed during therapy sessions," the Unicorn commented. "Mr, Fox, we're here to talk about your feelings, not to trade cafeteria snacks for favors."

"My feeling is that this is delicious," Magdaline said, crunching loudly and sending radiant sparks flying from her mouth. The prisoners stared at her snack, salivating.

"Please talk about something more meaningful and personal such as trauma that pushed you in the wrong direction, not food," the Black Unicorn sighed, not even bothering to look at Magdaline. "Our goal is to figure out what sets you off and how to cope without violence or self-destructive behavior. Also, introduce yourselves to Mister . . ."

"Fox," I repeated.

"Mr. Fox . . . hrmm? Why aren't you on my list?" the therapist asked. I glanced at her name tag.

"I dunno, Therapist Juskerr." I shrugged. "I just got here. I'm just tagging along with my new shark bestie. Maybe your system didn't update, you know how it is."

"Right, whatever," the Unicorn sighed. "Go on then. Resume in the circle, going right, starting from Mister Lissthoric."

The Yara-ma-yha-who straightened up, his glistening red skin covered in white stripes gleaming under the fluorescent lights. "Tate here. Got caught trying to drain some Prima's kid at a fancy mall. Not my fault really—been living in the vents for months, surviving on rats and pigeons after parents kicked me out. One sniff of Prima blood and . . . well, couldn't help myself."

The Mapinguari cleared his throat, massive claws clicking against his chair. "Renmar. Used to be a chef at Omnimart's food court until I . . . lost control during rush hour. Something about the crowds, the noise, the endless demands . . . snapped inside me. Went berserk, tore through three registers, plowed through the crowd, ate a bunch of people. The damage was extensive."

The muscular Bies spoke next, his scarred face twisting into a grimace. "Viktor. Ex-security at Hexamesh Ferronite Industries. Had a perfect record until I caught some executives torturing mixed-blood employees in the basement labs. Lost it completely. Ripped through seventeen floors. Killed twelve pure-bloods before they took me down. Don't regret it one bit. Would do it again."

The moss-covered Catoblepas shifted uncomfortably. "Izzy Jones. Was a gardener at Skyfall. Started growing . . . illegal plants. When security came to investigate, I panicked, trying to save my babies. Didn't go well."

The dark, lanky Erlking leaned forward, antlers casting intricate shadows. "Ash. Former intern of Xenobotany at Leviathan University. Helped Professor Leiko weave military-grade pacifier touch-kill weapons. When funding got cut, I . . . refused to terminate our work. Took the pacifiers home. Got caught. Laid waste to many before I was captured."

The curvy Lamashtu flicked her serpentine tail, black wings fluttering. "Lilith Moongriss. Ex-dancer at the Crystal Spire. Was forced to perform for increasingly depraved audiences until I couldn't take it anymore. Infested the audience with memetic nightmares. Did the same to the cheerleader squad at Skyfall." She sniffed the air with her dark wolf head, golden eyes boring into me.

The tentacled Scylla shifted in her chair, her multiple dark-green tentacle limbs weaving slightly. "Mariana Darkwater. Ward tech and researcher at Uxashh's deep-sea lab. Developed a way to communicate with abyssal creatures. The Uxashh Omnicorp wanted to weaponize them. I . . . refused. Released all our subjects instead. They ate the entire research team. Got caught trying to sink the facility using the ward control."

The massive Grootslang shifted on his small chair. "Uliuss Yolt. Former clerk at Agronite Bank. One of my administrators was taking bribes. Tried to expose him. They framed me for theft. I . . . didn't take it well. Collapsed three vaults before security contained me."

The winged Camazotz cleared his throat, his jet-black fur rippling. "Royaul Niss. Used to intern at sonic research at Resonance Labs. We were developing ways to manipulate emotions through sound waves. Found out they were testing on homeless humans from Scab Row. The frequencies . . . they were designed to induce psychosis. I quit. Since nobody else would hire me afterward, I sort of gradually lost my mind trying to make ends meet. Can't even remember what I did."

"Magdaline Satoshi," Magdaline said on my left. "I ate three annoying knobs at Skyfall."

"It sounds to me like each of you got screwed unfairly by Omnithornia. I feel that this facility isn't living up to its rehabilitation potential," I said. "Take Magdaline here. Instead of helping her manage her predatory instincts with proper magic beast nutrition and beast cores, she's been isolated and used as a disposal for unwanted elements of society."

The therapist finally looked up from her tablet, frowning. "Please don't make up stories, Mr. Fox. We follow very strict rehabilitation protocols here."

"Really?" I leaned forward. "Then why does cell twenty-five smell of forty-one dead humans? Why does Scrutimancer Satosh bring bleeding victims here during lunch? Why does his daughter's room have an incinerator chute specifically designed to destroy evidence?"

The therapist's horn flickered with dark energy, making my head throb. "Perhaps you should focus on your own rehabilitation journey, Mr. Fox?"

"Oh, I am." I smiled. "Step one is exposing systemic corruption. Step two is offering alternatives. For instance, did you know that beast cores can help manage predatory impulses? Much better than isolation and psychiatry."

"Beast cores are expensive," the therapist stated flatly. "This is a state-funded facility."

"Who's dissatisfied with their situation?" I asked. "Who's tired of therapy and just wants beast cores? Raise your hands."

Every hand in the room shot up, except for the therapist's.

"See?" I gestured. "Your inmates want actual help, not just talk therapy."

The therapist's horn flickered again with a dark flare. "Mr. Fox, I'd prefer if you stuck to the rehabilitation program. Also, I'm sure that the other inmates would appreciate hearing your real story instead of jokes."

The orange-suited Omnids didn't look like they wanted to appreciate anything of the sort.

"That was my real story!" I protested. "Okay, fine. I punched Emerald Stratos in the noggin, so she sent me here."

My Quartermaster tag vibrated.

"One moment," I said, accepting the call.

"Alex!" Cinder's holographic image appeared above my tag. "Are you okay? Are you alive? Has anyone tried to eat you?"

"I'm fine," I replied cheerfully. "Just attending group therapy with my new friends."

The therapy room inmates stared at the holographic projection with varying degrees of surprise.

"What?" The therapist blinked. "That . . . that's a Voicecast device. You shouldn't have that!"

"Whoever knocks out the Unicorn first gets a beast core." I opened my pocket.

"You . . . how . . . what?" the Black Unicorn sputtered, staring at my pocket filled with magic cores.

The room erupted into chaos. The Mapinguari lunged forward first, followed closely by the Lamashtu.

The therapist's horn blasted the nearest attacking inmate with black waves, but she was quickly overwhelmed by the sheer number of inmates rushing her. The Mapinguari's massive furry form slammed into her first, followed by the Lamashtu.

I tossed beast cores to the winners as promised, watching them shove the pearlescent balls with desperate enthusiasm into their mouths.

The other inmates turned to me. Cinder stared at me from the holo.

"So, who wants to join my clan?" I asked with a grin. "I really do have sixie positions open for talented individuals!"

The Yara-ma-yha-who stared at me. "Why shouldn't we just knock ya out and take ya cores, bud?"

"If you stop me, you'll only get the cores from this pocket and you'll still be stuck in this place. I can pay you as many cores as you need to feel satisfied, forever. Plus, you'd have to go through her." I pointed my finger at Mags, who rose to her full Megalodon height, claws out. "Also, I have a gun."

I pulled a compact, self-reloading magitek arbalest from my pocket that I had bought as a gift for Justice Nova in Shandria for about a thousand gold.

"That's not a gun, that's an arba—" the Yara-ma-yha-who began.

I pressed the trigger, and the magisteel bolt went through the wall. Then the ridiculously overpriced void core tied to it detonated, obliterating the entire hexcrete wall with a whoosh of sucked-in energy, pulverizing the small lounge behind it, and showering the Omnids in hexcrete chunks.

The inmates stared at me in shock.

Whistling the "Twisted Nerve" tune that I'd picked up from Vespera's habit, I walked to the knocked-out Unicorn and grabbed her hat and put it on my head. "I'm the therapist now. So, who wants to be fully rehabilitated from this facility?"

# CHAPTER THIRTY-THREE

# I Am the Warden Now

The inmates stared at me, their expressions ranging from shock to eager interest.

"What are you doing?" Cinder hissed at me as I pulled off my orange jumpsuit.

"Ah, right, introductions!" I said. "Misfits and murderers, I'd like to introduce all of you to my lovely Hearth-Shield Keeper! Cinderella!"

Cinder's eye twitched.

"Now, what are you calling in regards to, my starshine?" I grinned at Ci. "Did you miss me since our last conversation and want to shower me with wing-hugs and kisses?

Cinder's face lengthened from irritation.

"This isn't the time for your stupid jokes! Vee's father took her from Skyfall," she growled out. "Lord Ceter just stormed into Graves's office with guards and took her!"

"Did he now?" I frowned, rapidly undressing the Black Unicorn. "That's not ideal."

"Not ideal?!" Cinder's wings flared. "He knocked us out with an EMP blast and just . . . took her!"

"At least she'll have a nap at home," I sighed. "She needs rest anyway."

"But what if they try to break the soul bond?!" Cinder demanded.

"Then we'll make a new one," I said.

"What if they erase her mind?!"

"Then we'll fall in love again, like in that movie . . ."

"*What fucking movie?!*"

"*Seventy-Seven First Dates?*" I rubbed my chin as I pulled on the slightly too big therapist's outfit, pinning it with pins from my pocket so it wouldn't flap around too much. "You know. A whimsical comedy from 2004. It's got Antony Sandy in it dating this girl who can't remember anything past twenty-four hours, 'cause she got struck by a magical curse in the head or something?"

Cinder growled at me.

"What do you want me to do, dragon-bae?" I asked her. "I need time to take over this prison island."

"Take over the . . ." Cinder's holographic form sputtered. "Are you insane?!"

"Quite possibly." I adjusted the therapist's cap. "But as a therapist, I have also diagnosed myself as sane."

Cinder made a face, not appreciating my joke.

"I have a plan," I added. "These fine individuals behind me are going to help."

The inmates perked up at that.

"What's in it for us?" Uliuss, the Grootslang, asked.

"Eternal freedom, beast cores, and membership in my clan," I said. "Plus dental."

"Dental?" Lilith raised an eyebrow.

"And a 401k," I added. "Also, weekly movie nights. No more dancing for rich assholes. If you want to study in Skyfall, I'll cover it. I'm a wealthy man. We can be roomies! I'm probably going to get a nice tower loft for my Knights and sixies after this whole incarceration biz."

I opened my cash pocket, showing off my pile of shimmering cards.

"Holy shit," Lilith inhaled. "Are those celesteel cards . . . from Arx? Can't you buy a mansion in Shandria with one of those?"

"Yep," I nodded. "Robbing banks pays off. I see that you used to participate in Delving class activities?"

"Yeah." Lilith nodded. "Before I was sent to juvie in grade eleven."

"Alex," Cinder flapped from the hologram on my wrist, "this is serious! Vespera could be in real danger!"

"I know," I said. "But rushing in half-cocked won't help. Our clan needs more sixies. These guys seem acceptable, right?"

"They're juvie convicts," Cinder pointed out with a frown.

"And?" I raised an eyebrow.

Cinder stared at me and my new prison-mooks with a judging look.

"I think that they're perfect for what we need," I explained. "Each one was wronged by the Omnithornian Corps. Each one is a bit of a delinquent like you. Each has unique skills. For example, Lilith here can spread memetic nightmares. Mariana knows her way around wards and can control deep sea creatures. Royaul understands sonic manipulation. Viktor has inside knowledge of corporate security. Etcetera."

"But . . ." Cinder protested.

"Trust me," I said. "I know what I'm doing. These fine folks are going to help me take over this facility, which will give us leverage against both the Stratos Clan and possibly SimmiTech."

The inmates exchanged interested looks.

"How exactly do you plan to take over a prison?" Ash, the Erlking, asked.

"I have a gun." I waved my arbalest. "This is a juvie housing Omnids under twenty-one years old who are all relatively low or mid-level like you. From what I saw so far, the guards only have pacifier batons. I'm the only person in this entire facility with a long range weapon, and I have a lot of void arrows that I bought for my father-in-law."

"But how do we get past the wards?" Mariana asked, her tentacles writhing. "The whole island is covered in anti-escape hexagrams."

"We're not escaping." I grinned. "We're taking over. Big difference. The wards likely prevent outward movement. They won't stop us from accessing the control room or the warden's office. Hexcrete is kind of useless against void arrows, as I just learned. I could probably plow right through the walls straight to the warden's office."

"Alex . . ." Cinder's hologram flickered as she tried and failed to form a convincing argument.

"Just let him do it," Katherine commented. "It's not like we can stop him from where we are."

"But he can't just—"

"Can't what?" I asked cheerfully. "Take over a correctional facility? Create my own private army from reformed criminals? Watch me. This is a nice island. I'm confiscating it from the Stratos family."

"You're . . . what?" Cinder sputtered.

"Basic Omnicorp Clan warfare," I said. "As I Love You Clan leader, I have been unjustly placed under duress here. As such, it is my prerogative to strike back and to claim their property as mine."

"And what if they drop a magitek nuke on you from a Strand-Glider?" Cinder barked.

"And destroy their own prison?" I asked. "Yeah, okay. Dragons like to cling to their shinies. 'Sides, this place probably has wards against all sorts of stuff. It's a prison. I could probably redirect the wards from keeping people in to keeping bombs from falling directly on my head."

"Ughh!" Cinder deflated. "There's no convincing you, is there?"

"Nope." I shook my head. "We need a nice clan compound on Earth! This is going to be it. A nice island within a Strand-Glider's distance from Cradlefall? How can I resist?"

My future Hearth-Keeper frowned.

"Plus," I added, "San Clemente Island has nice weather year round."

"Alex . . ." Cinder's hologram flickered with a look of deep concern.

"Look, I'll call you back in a bit," I promised, finishing dressing up as a therapist. "Hugs and kisses. I've got some rehabilitation to conduct."

I ended the call and turned to my potential recruits. "So, who wants to help me take over this lovely place to turn it into a compound for my clan?"

"A rather bold move that'll piss off the Stratoses," Uliuss commented, looking down at me from his elephantine height.

"They pissed me off first," I said. "I don't take shit lying down. If they didn't gate me here, in an attempt to murder me, I'd have no right to take over their island."

The inmates exchanged glances. Magdaline grinned, her sharp teeth glinting.

"Right then!" I clapped my hands together. "First order of business—let's talk about your feelings . . ."

"Feelings?" Mariana blinked.

"Feelings about taking over this place."

The Yara-ma-yha-who, Tate, stared at me. "You're . . . serious about this?"

"Dead serious." I nodded. "But first, everyone needs to swear loyalty to Clan I Love You. Can't have random Omnids running around my island causing unauthorized chaos, you understand. I prefer authorized chaos directed by yours truly. As your first day salary, each of you will receive one of these overpriced dragon-balls to chew on."

I pulled out a shimmering beast core from my pocket. "So, who'll go first? Mags? Why don't you show our lovely ladies and gentlemen how it's done?"

"I, Magdaline Satoshi," the shark said as she went down on one knee, "do hereby pledge myself as sixie to Clan I Love You for all eternity."

I tapped her on the shoulder with my arbalest. "I, Alexander Glock, Slayer and Clan Leader of I Love You, do hereby accept you eternal services and raise you from lowly sixie to my trusted Knight and personal Scrutimancer."

Magdaline's entire face lit as she stared up at me. She hadn't expected this promotion so soon in the game.

I handed a second beast core to her. Mags shoved it into her mouth with a wide, happy grin.

I turned to the other convicts.

"A rather odd clan name, but I'll bite," said the Yara-ma-yha-who that stepped forward. "Sounds better than living in a vent eating rats or therapy here. I, Tate Lissthoric, hereby pledge myself as a sixie to Clan I Love You for all eternity."

One by one, the others followed suit, each pledging loyalty and receiving their yummy rewards. The cores vanished into eager mouths, eyes lighting up with renewed energy.

"Excellent!" I adjusted my stolen, ill-fitting therapist cap that kept sliding off due to my lack of horn. "Now, here's the plan. Magdaline, I bet you know the layout best as a Scrutimancer sharkie. Where's the ward control room? Don't take me straight to it, take me to a wall I can obliterate to get inside from behind."

Mags nodded, inhaling the air, red eyes igniting. She reached out to me with a large hand, and I felt her skill bouncing off me, amplifying itself. "Got it!" She smiled, letting go of my hand with a blush.

I picked up the knocked-out therapist's tablet and made a bored face. "Onwards then!"

We moved through the gray corridors with purpose, my new sixies falling into formation behind me. The facility staff barely glanced at our group—just another nondescript therapist leading a group of inmates to their next recreational activity.

Our group walked through the sterile corridors, passing security checkpoints with ease thanks to the therapist's uniform and ID badge. The inmates' expressions remained carefully neutral as we approached our target.

"Left here," Magdaline whispered, guiding us toward a maintenance corridor. "The ward control room is behind two walls."

I raised my arbalest, aiming at the hexcrete barrier. "Everyone ready?"

My new sixies nodded, tensing for action.

"Remember," I said quietly, "non-lethal takedowns only. Bonk on the head, knock everyone out. We're reforming this facility, not adding to its body count. Plus, hostages are nice to have to sell back to the Stratos Clan."

The void bolt pierced the first wall with a whisper, followed by a thunderous implosion as the void core detonated. Then the second wall imploded with the second bolt. Alarms began blaring immediately.

We rushed into the ward control room. The ward techies definitely didn't expect Ocean's Eleven to come in directly through the solid hexcrete wall behind them.

Through the dust and debris, I spotted three startled technicians at their control panels.

"What? Who the shit . . . how?!" the ward administrator standing in the center yelped.

The Mapinguari and Bies moved swiftly, knocking the techies out before they could reach the control panel. I walked over to the knocked-out administrator and put his hat on, noting the man's name, *Eron Kotiff*, on his badge.

"I'm the warden now." I grinned at my mooks.

"Now," I said, approaching the main control console, "Mariana, can you interface with these systems?"

The Scylla's tentacles flew across multiple keyboards. "Basic ward architecture . . . fairly standard stuff. Give me five minutes."

"You have two," I replied. "The guards will be here soon."

"Tate, Ash—watch the door," I ordered. "Viktor, Renmar—secure the technicians. Everyone else, spread out and barricade entry points."

The sound of running footsteps echoed down the corridor.

"Incoming!" Lilith called out.

"Mariana! Lock down the door," I barked to the Scylla as her tentacles danced across the control panels.

"Working on it!" she called back, multiple dark limbs covered in small finger-like tentacles flashing frantically over the controls.

The first wave of four guards burst through the doorway, pacifier batons crackling. Ten Omnids met them head-on, the enhanced strength from the beast cores giving them the edge.

"Got it!" Mariana's tentacles flew across the final sequence. Heavy security barrier doors slammed down, sealing the front entrance to the control room.

"Excellent," I said, looking over the map. "Now, declare an emergency and give me the speaker."

Mariana handed me the magitek mike.

"Yulia, copy the yelling voice of the ward administrator," I whisper-ordered my AI in Kaska.

"Voice copier agent activated," Yulia replied. "Generating voice. Voice generated."

"Attention . . ." I began typing into my phone.

"Attention all security and facility personnel. This is Ward Administrator Eron Kotiff. The enemies of Stratos Clan are threatening to use biological weapons known as Duskbloom from Arx to take control of the island. Please report immediately to secure meeting room 4-B for an emergency briefing!" Yulia announced over the facility's communication array. "All inmates are to return to their cells right away!"

I watched through a thousand camera screens on the wall as guards and administrators got up from their posts and offices and rapidly headed towards the safe room in the basement. The inmates rushed to their cells.

I turned the microphone off.

"Holy sheet," Tate commented, watching the monitors. "They're just . . . obeying? Just like that? That's it?"

"People obey orders. They trust their ward administrator's voice." I shrugged. "This is just a minimum security rehabilitation facility filled with troublesome teens that Cradlefall doesn't want to see on its streets, not a maximum security prison. Nobody expects us to actually try taking over the ward from the inside so blatantly using magitek dungeon-delving weapons from Arx designed to punch through dragonhide and other giant monsters."

"Except for this man, it seems," Mariana commented, pointing a tentacle at one of the cameras.

A single officer hadn't left his post. He was just sitting in his office, staring unnervingly at the camera with blood-red eyes.

I walked closer to the screen wall and recognized the man right away. Megalodon Scrutimancer Satosh.

"We should do . . . something about him," Magdaline said, her voice tight with tension.

"We will," I agreed. "Your dad seems quite determined."

"Always has been," Mags sighed.

"There isn't much he can do from over there, though," I said. "And it doesn't look like he's calling the Stratoses to warn them about my takeover. He's just . . . sitting there. How odd."

I studied Satosh through the security feed. He sat perfectly still in his office, those cold eyes fixed on the camera as if he could see right through it to me.

I looked at the other cameras. The prison's offices and halls were now empty. Meeting room 4-B was packed to the brim with confused personnel.

"Lock down 4-B," I told Mariana. "Seal them in. Maximum wards around that room."

Mariana smiled at me and pressed a bunch of buttons. Blast shields rolled across the door of room 4-B, sealing everyone who could stop me within the meeting room.

"And done." I smiled. "The place is now ours. Lock down the other inmates so they don't get in our way."

Mariana nodded. Red lights flashed across the cells in camera view.

"A prison riot would have been more fun to watch, but this is nice, too," I commented. "Good job, team."

Magdaline started to laugh. The other misfits and murderers stared at one another and at me. Uliuss high-fived Viktor.

"Now what?" Lilith asked, her serpentine tail swishing back and forth.

"Now we deal with Scrutimancer Satosh," I said. "Mariana, patch me through to his office and give me audio. Mags, want to chat with your dad?"

"I . . ." Magdaline hesitated. "What are you planning to do to him?"

"Offer him a job." I shrugged. "He's clearly talented. Plus, he's your dad. Can't have my Knight's dad unemployed, can I?"

"You want to hire the man who put you in here to kill you?" she asked.

"Why not?" I shrugged. "He's just doing his job. Following orders. Trying to provide for his lovely daughter."

Magdaline blushed even harder.

"And ready," Mariana said.

I tapped the activation hexagram on the mike, watching the little crystal turn green.

"Good day, Scrutimancer Satosh," I said. "This is Warden Alexander Glock speaking."

"Ah, Warden," Satosh exhaled, still unnervingly staring at me through the camera feed. "You work fast, human."

"That I do," I agreed.

"Wait." Mags blinked. "Dad . . . you knew?!"

"Of course I knew," Satosh said via the speaker. "I'm a Scrutimancer. I could smell his humanity from the moment he arrived. But that wasn't all. I could also smell . . . hope. I brought Alexander Glock to this island because it had to happen."

"Had to happen?" I asked. "What? You wanted me to take over this place?"

"I wanted things to change," Satosh said, staring at us from the screen. "I'm tired of serving the little dragon princess. I want to see my daughter smile for once. I want my wife back."

"Dad?" Magdaline stepped closer to the mike. "What are you talking about? You . . ."

"I worked two jobs," Satosh said. "I served that blasted girl as her personal Scrut. Did so many awful, terrible things for Emerald Stratos . . . all to reach this point."

"You . . . you fed me forty-one humans because . . ." Mags choked.

"Because I wanted a future for both of us," Satosh said. "Those humans were irredeemable criminals. This one is . . . different." He pointed at me with a blue-white finger as if he knew exactly where I stood.

"Dad! I don't understand . . . I thought that you hated humans," Mags stammered out.

"I hate human criminals and the ruthless gangs of Scab Row," Satosh sighed. "But Alexander Glock isn't a human, is he? He's something more."

"So my jacket never deceived you?" I smiled.

"Not really." Satosh shrugged. "I smelled the thunder and rainbow in you. You're soul-bound to two Omnids. If you managed to win the love of two Omnid girls, then you're not a complete monster. Not like the bastards who killed my wife. Perhaps a bastard I can work with, yes? One that won't enslave me like the dragons?"

"Yes." I nodded. "So you knew that I would succeed?"

"I brought you here because Emerald ordered me to," Satosh said. "I knew you would either die or take over. Either I would have a new Clan Leader to serve or get my girl another year of Skyfall education. Besides, you don't seem like the dying type."

"He's really not," Magdaline agreed, struggling to keep her blush down as she chewed on two beast cores.

"So," I said, "Want to join my clan as a sixie, too?"

"No." Satosh shook his head on the screen. "But I will serve as your Scrutimancer if you help me get my wife back."

"The one in White Hall?" I asked.

"Yes." Satosh nodded.

"Get her back, how?"

"She cannot remember me. You will have the same problem soon."

"The same problem . . . oh. You know about Vespera?" I asked.

"Yes." Satosh nodded. "I have little magic eyes concealed all over Skyfall. Your Prima-Sword was taken from you. Her mind will be overwritten by her father. She will not remember you."

"She will remember me," I said firmly. "Love isn't just memories. It's deeper than that."

"Such confidence." Satosh smiled sadly. "I thought the same once."

"I'm not you," I replied.

"No," Satosh said, "you are not me. You are a very clever and incredibly dangerous Slayer, one I'd like to work for. One that I've been waiting for since I lost my wife."

"Well then," I said. "You're hired. Welcome aboard, Scrutimancer. Hrm. How did you fool the Stratoses? Don't they have some kind of compulsion magic on you like blood contracts or something?"

"I agreed to be Emerald's fully bound kobold," Satosh said. "A bound kobold cannot disobey a dragon's orders. I have obeyed her every word for a decade. But now I'm finally free, because Emerald serves you as a sixie."

I whistled. "Long-term plans there, Scrut."

"There will be those like me in Omnithornia, desperate Omnids who will join your clan." Satosh nodded, red eyes moving across my ex-prisoner companions and settling on his daughter. "And there will be those who will do everything in their power to stop you just to cling to their power."

"Let them try," I said. "I've got a nice island fortress now."

"And what will you do with it?" Satosh asked.

"Turn it into a proper rehabilitation facility," I replied. "One that actually helps troubled Omnids. Maybe add some beachfront property, build some nice condos."

"It's a rocky island," Mariana said, waving a tentacle at the cameras facing the outer perimeter.

"I'll add a beach." I shrugged.

"A bold plan," Satosh commented. "The Stratoses won't take this lying down."

"I know." I grinned. "That's why we're going to work hard to make this place quadruple impregnable. Mariana, how are those wards looking?"

"Reconfigured to maximum security," the Scylla reported, her tentacle-fingers tapping across multiple control panels. "Nobody gets in or out without your authorization now, Mr. Fox. I blocked all incoming gates and gliders."

"What's this place powered by?" I asked.

"Two ley lines under the island plus beast cores funded by the Stratos Clan. If you want to increase the ward power, we should insert more cores into the dragonheart engine."

"Which is where?" I asked.

"Right under us," the Scylla said. "I'll bring it up."

She began tapping at the controls.

A hexagon in the center of the room surrounded by yellow-and-black-striped iron railings hissed open. A hexagonal black column emerged from its innards with a cloud of steam, and another panel opened within it.

"Pour the beast cores into there," Mariana advised.

"How many?" I asked.

"As many as you can spare," she said. "More is better. The engine will burn through them to reinforce the perimeter ward."

I pulled out handful after handful of beast cores from my pocket and poured them into the receptacle. The black column hummed, lines of blue light racing up its surface.

"The wards are at 425 percent strength now," Mariana confirmed, rapidly adjusting the ward. "Nobody's getting through those without some serious firepower. Not unless they want to spend about sixty million O-bux on bunker-busters trying to breach the shields."

"Excellent." I nodded. "Now, let's see what other facilities we have to work with. Show me the prison layout."

Mariana brought up a detailed map of San Clemente Island on the main screen. The facility sprawled across the northern tip, complete with dormitories, cafeteria, workshops, and medical wing.

"Not bad," I mused. "Plenty of room to expand."

"Say, Scrut," I addressed Satosh as the dragonheart engine slid back into place after eating some of my pocket core collection. "If you can sniff the future this well, why didn't you prevent the human gangsters from attacking your wife to begin with?"

"I've made many enemies in my line of work over the years, put many criminals away, crossed dangerous deviants I shouldn't have crossed . . . because I had integrity. There was no escaping their eventual retribution. I sniffed out many futures," Satosh's voice came through, heavy with regret. "In most of them, my wife and daughter died. In this one . . . they live, even if broken. I chose the path where my family survived. Where my daughter might find hope, even if that hope is in a human who can do magic."

"Dad . . ." Magdaline blinked tears out of her eyes.

"I'm sorry, Maggie," Satosh sighed. "It had to be this way. This was the best path forward for our family. I'm sorry that I've used you, fed you humans. I hope that you can forgive me someday for what I've done."

"I . . . forgive you," Magdaline said softly into the microphone, blinking more tears out of her red eyes. "You were just trying to help me in your own messed up way. Why didn't you . . . tell me?"

"Saying such things leaves an imprint in the Astral for others to see." Satosh shrugged. "I had to make sure that nobody could stop me, and always wore anti-scrying runes on me."

"So, what am I going to do next?" I grinned.

"Deal with my owner," Satosh said. "Declare war on the Stratos Clan."

"Darn sneaky Scruts ruining the plot ahead of schedule," I said. "So . . . what do I smell like in the deepest Astral?"

"Like . . . number eight," Satosh said.

"Eight?" I asked, intrigued.

"Yes." Satosh nodded.

"Interesting," I mused. "I've never considered myself to be that particular number. And what does that mean exactly?"

"It means you're unpredictable, dire change," Satosh said. "It means you're marked by the Dagaz rune."

"A Dagaz rune?" I blinked. "So there are others like me?"

"There are." Satosh nodded. "The wielders of Dagaz are hard to predict because it is very easy to get trapped in the infinite loop produced by the imprint of this particular number in the Astral."

"And yet you somehow predicted what I would do?" I asked. "Otherwise we wouldn't be talking right now."

"It took me decades." Satosh shrugged. "The key was accepting Dagaz into your heart, to go along with the pattern. Fighting against Infinity only leads to disaster."

"So," I said, "what disasters await us in the nearby future?"

"The Stratoses will try to retake their facility," Satosh replied calmly. "SimmiTech will attempt to break your soul bond with Vespera by erasing her mind. Golden Star and SimmiTech will attempt to have you assassinated."

"And will they succeed or fail?" I asked.

"I don't know the exact details," Satosh sighed. "I just know that there is hope. It took a lot of mana to accept Infinity into my heart and even more to hear her voice, to see what's behind the Number."

"Her voice?" I blinked. "What? Number Eight has a voice?"

"Sheela na gig," Satosh explained. "Infinity. Change. Dawn. The girl with endless faces behind the black hole."

"This just gets weirder and weirder," Lilith commented. "It sounds like . . . the Scrut is under the control of an Outsider."

"Perhaps I am." Satosh shrugged. "It's hard to see all of the strings concealed behind physical reality. Maybe we're just some god's puppets being pulled along the strings of a particular narrative, words on a page."

I laughed. Somehow Satosh had outdone me on the meta-narrator, fourth wall breaking business, the cheeky shark bastard.

"So, who's the narrator of our curious tale?" I asked. "Does he or she have a name? Is it Eight?"

"No. Most Omnid clans keep imprisoned gods in their basement, powering their . . . wards. Who's to say that these old families are not being manipulated by the pieces of the Wormwood Star Leviathan in some unseen manner across millennia?"

"Huh," I said. "That's not weird and creepy at all. What does the Golden Star Clan have?"

"They call her Uriel," Satosh said. "The All-Seeing Eye of God."

"And the Stratoses?" I pressed.

"They have Metatron," Satosh replied. "The Voice of God."

"And what does Metatron say about me?" I wondered.

"I don't know." Satosh shook his head. "I've never been allowed near the Stratos vault. Only their Prima-born are permitted to consult their imprisoned god. I do know that speaking to these entities has a price."

"Which is what?" I asked.

"Mortality," Satosh said. "Those that speak with imprisoned gods cut their lives short, accelerate their paths towards their deaths. It's why most of the Arch-Elders of generations past the 1940s are dead. They burned through their lives fighting each other during World War Two, trying to predict their enemy's moves, trying to shake the Archangels for better weapons."

"And what do the Simmis have?" I asked.

"Archangel Zadkiel," Satosh revealed. "The All-Remembering One. A shard of the Leviathan's brain lobe. They use her power to optimize their bloodline, to make their children more clever, better at magitek crystallography and Dreamancy. Zadkiel is the reason why they're so obsessed with genetic purity and arranged marriages."

"That's why Vee is so good at mapping out crystal architecture and diving into dreams," I deduced.

"Your fiancée is the result of generations of Simmi breeding." Satosh nodded. "The brightest star that took a lot of magic to produce."

"So . . . what you're saying is that Vespera was . . . manufactured?" I pondered.

"Yes," Satosh revealed. "Each generation of the Firstborn Clans is magically stronger, but there are fewer and fewer children being born. Such optimization has a price. Ritual magic tied to lunar shard alignment. Sacrifice. Burning through more and more beast cores. Each new brilliant heir costs more to produce, just as it costs more to produce smarter artificial intelligence engines."

"I see why Skyfall seems to have so many empty classrooms." I whistled.

"Indeed." Satosh nodded through the screen. "The deity-Omnitype population has been declining for centuries. Fresh blood is needed, but the clans are set on the path to produce the most optimal heirs, ones who will inherit the Earth, ones who will prevent the end of everything. Who will either figure out how to move the planet back to where it was hundreds of years ago or how to gate the entirety of Cradlefall to another habitable world."

"The end of everything?" I blinked.

"Our Earth is in freefall towards the mesh of doomed worlds," Satosh said coldly. "Past a certain point, nobody can see the future. The small celestorms currently ravaging the planet at random are just the beginning. They will get worse, and when they do, terrible, hungry, unstoppable things will begin to manifest and come through dimensional gates to our world."

"Yep," Lilith said to herself quietly. "Def sounds like Outsider apocalyptic nonsense."

"Outsider-infected or not," I said, "Satosh is a helpful creature on our side. Right then. Are you done pounding doomsday lore into my head?"

Satosh nodded.

I whispered to call Cinder into my Quartermaster tag.

"Yes?" Cinder's holographic form appeared atop of my wrist looking worried. "Did you start a riot already? Is that why you're calling me? To show me how much shit you set on fire?"

"No riots. No fires. Only had to break a couple of walls. Everything's fine," I assured her. "We've taken over the facility. I've got control of the wards, a bunch of new sixies, and Satosh is actually on our side."

"What?" Cinder blinked.

"Turns out Satosh wanted me to take over this place," I explained. "He's been playing the long game, waiting for someone like me to come along."

"That's . . . convenient," Cinder said suspiciously.

"Indeed." I nodded. "Also, apparently all the major clans have imprisoned gods in their basements. Did you know about that?"

Cinder's wings and head feathers flared.

"Is your dad keeping a bound god in his basement?" I asked.

"Umm . . ." Cinder blinked. "Not that I'm aware."

"What about the Novas in general?"

"Xastigar's family owns a buttload of shares in Omnimart," Cinder pondered. "Great-grandad Nathaniel Senior has a compound citadel where he and his wives produce . . . Lazarus bracelets."

"Aha," I said. "I was wondering where those came from. Does some preggo elderbeast god-centipede birth them in the Nova compound basement or something?"

"I don't effing know." Cinder stared at me. "I don't get invited to the Nova compound!

Since I murdered my precog-chosen fiancé, they sort of gave up on me and focused all of their attention on . . . Lance."

"Archangel Azrael is kept beneath the citadel of the Nova compound," Satosh commented. "The Soul Shepherd."

"I should get an Archangel," I commented, rubbing my chin. "I have the envy itch now."

"All of the large shards of the Wormwood Star Leviathan's body have long been claimed," Satosh stated.

"Then I'll find my own god and imprison them!" I grinned. "How hard can it be?"

"Alex . . ." Cinder stared at me with growing concern. "Please don't try to imprison any gods."

"But everyone else has one!" I protest-whined. "I want one too!"

Cinder made an uggghh-adjacent noise. Katherine, the edge of her face visible in the holo, frowned.

"You guys are such downers," I commented at them. "Damn it, I want Vee back. Too much gloomy one-dimensional rain over there without any merry rays of thunder."

"Hey," Cinder complained.

"Yeees?" I asked.

"I'm not one-dimensional, you jerk," she huffed.

"You're constantly either surprised or angry with me," I pointed out.

She squinted at me and sighed. "I'm not angry with you, you knob! I'm . . . angry at myself for not being able to do shit when Vee was taken and angry at Emerald for sending you into prison. I'm . . . mostly worried. Worried about you pushing your shenanigans too far and perma-dying. Worried about Vee forgetting us."

"We'll sort it all out," I assured her.

"'Sides," she said with a sly look, "don't you appreciate my surprised acting . . .?"

"Wait a minute." I blinked. "So . . ."

"At this point, I honestly expect you to pull off wacky shit like this," she said. "I'm only acting extra shocked because I know you like it."

"Way to ruin it," I laughed.

"Do you want me to keep acting surprised?" She raised an eyebrow. "Oh my Slayer, what terrible, unexpected, insane thing will you shock me with next?" She made a "what" face at me. "Oh I'm so angry with you, I just want to chase you down and . . ."

"Riiight," I chortled. "We can talk about you chasing me . . . later. For now, please put Emmy on if she's nearby."

"Uh-huh. Here's Em," Cinder said.

Emerald's face appeared on the holo, the dragon girl held by her scruff via Kat's armored hand.

"Sup, dragon-bae." I grinned at her.

"What do you want?" Emerald growled through the holo.

"Just checking in on my favorite sixie." I smiled. "How's your slave collar doing? Hope it's not too itchy."

"It's effing horrible," she hissed. "I can't use my dragonfire!"

"You sound a tad off," I commented. "A bit nasally? Did you catch a cold?"

"No, you fuck!" Emerald snarled. "Your effing girlfriend broke my nose and didn't bother to heal it properly!"

"Which one?"

"Ci." Emerald glared in the direction of Cinder.

"And she's going to break it again if I tell her what you did," I said.

"What?" Emerald paled.

"I talked to Satosh," I said.

"You . . . *what?*" the dragon princess choked.

"The fuck did she do now?" Cinder demanded.

"Unless you want me to tell Ci what you did," I said, "you better cooperate."

"I . . . I'll cooperate," Emerald nodded rapidly. "Please don't tell her!"

"Tell me what?!" Cinder snarled.

"Don't worry about it," I said. "As much as I want to smack Emmy for her crimes, now isn't the time for that. Please tell me everything that happened at Skyfall after I was gated away."

Ci nodded and began to narrate the events of the day with Katherine interjecting comments about what Cinder had forgotten or missed.

I listened. They were done in about ten minutes.

"Very good," I said. "Yulia, please locate and dial the number of Attorney Thornheart." My phone dialed the number in a few seconds.

"Attorney Thornheart speaking," the Omnid said as he appeared on the screen.

"Greetings," I said. "This is Alexander Glock. I'd like to report illegal detention at Cradlefoot Youth Rehabilitation Facility."

"Ah! Mr. Glock!" Thornheart's image straightened. "We've been trying to reach you. Are you all right?"

"I'm fine," I replied cheerfully. "In fact, I've taken control of the facility."

"You've . . . what?" The Bunyip lawyer blinked.

"Seized control," I clarified. "I now rule this island and everything on it. The Stratos Clan used it for illegal activities, so I'm confiscating it as my new clan compound."

Thornheart stared at me with wide, dark-brown eyes.

"Since you work for my fiancée and therefore work for me," I said. "I'd like for you to organize the paperwork necessary for the legalization of my actions here."

"I . . . see," Thornheart said slowly. "And what exactly would you like me to file?"

"A complaint against the Stratos Clan for illegal imprisonment, attempted murder, and operation of an unauthorized disposal facility," I replied cheerfully. "Plus whatever else you can think of. I want to tie them up in as much legal red tape as possible."

"That's . . . quite ambitious," Thornheart noted.

"I'm an ambitious person." I smiled. "Plus I do have the cash to pay you."

I waved a few celesteel cards in front of the screen.

"Do you have evidence of their crimes?"

"How else would I be here?" I asked. "Do you think I walked across the ocean like Lord Nazareth and asked them to let me in or something?"

"No, um . . ." Thornheart smiled. "I already have evidence for that. I could use more evidence of any illegal activities taking place on the island."

"Ah." I nodded, turning to my misfits. "Which one of you is really good at running and flipping through folders to take photos? Raise your hands."

Several hands shot up among my new sixies.

"Perfect. Tate, Ash—take these phones." I pulled out our extra phones that were connected to Yulia. "Go to the warden's office and start taking photos of all the paperwork you can find. Move down to other admin offices and document everything. Lilith, check the medical wing for disposal records. Renmar, Viktor—search the guards' quarters. Mariana, see if you can pull up ward records or videos of Satosh or any other guards gating people in to be disposed of."

My new team scattered to their tasks while I turned back to Attorney Thornheart.

"You'll have complete documentation within the hour," I promised. "Plus witness testimonies from the staff once I convince them to cooperate. For now, I'd like for you to listen to the testimony of Magdaline Satoshi. Mags, tell the good lawyer what you've been doing in cell twenty-five, will you?"

Magdaline stepped forward to address Attorney Thornheart on my phone.

"I was used as a disposal system," she said quietly. "Forty-one humans were brought to my cell during lunch hours. I . . . consumed them, unable to fight my Omnid hunt urges. Dad . . . worked for the Stratos Clan, bringing me criminals and undesirables they wanted eliminated."

"I see." Thornheart's expression darkened. "And you have evidence of this?"

"The walls of cell twenty-five retain astral imprints." Magdaline nodded. "Any competent Scrutimancer can read them. Plus there's the incinerator chute where I disposed of . . . remains."

"I've been forced to do many terrible things as kobold of Emerald Stratos," Satosh said from the screen, which had now been enlarged by Mariana. "Compelled by magic into monstrous deeds."

"You . . . what?!" Emerald's hologram on my wrist choked. "You can't tell them!!!"

Cinder smacked her hard. "Yes, he can. Order Satosh to tell the lawyer everything about your crimes."

"I'd prefer a permission to email an outline of my crimes to Mr. Thornheart," Satosh said. "That should be enough. I've been preparing the documents for over a decade."

"No . . . I . . ." Emerald choked.

"Unless you want me to rip out your left eye right now to stuff it into your mouth," Cinder snarled, "you will tell your Scrut that he's allowed to email everything to Thornheart."

"F-fine!" Emerald choked as Cinder drew her magisteel-armored hand back, aiming at her eye. "Satosh, you have my permission to email everything to Thornheart!"

"Excellent," the lawyer said, looking over at his screen. "With this, we can file multiple charges against the Stratos Clan."

"Perfect." I smiled. "Oh, and one more thing—I need you to file paperwork for establishing a new clan compound here. Transform this facility into something more . . . constructive."

"Such as?" Thornheart asked.

"A rehabilitation center." I grinned. "No need to change existing tax permits or whatever."

"Very well." Thornheart nodded.

"Also," I said, "I'd like to sue Emerald Stratos for one hundred billion O-bux."

"W-what?" Emerald choked.

"You heard me," I said cheerfully. "One hundred billion O-bux. For emotional damages, attempted murder, false imprisonment, and generally being a dick to me in classes."

"That's . . . that's crazy!" Emerald sputtered through the holo. "I don't have that kind of money!"

"No, but your family does." I smiled. "And I want it. All of it. Every last O-bux."

"The Stratos Clan will never pay that much!" Emerald protested. "They have the best lawyers and can hold up the case in court for ages!"

"Then I'll take it in assets." I shrugged. "Starting with this lovely island facility. You own shares in it, don't you Emmy?"

"I . . ." Emerald choked out.

"Well, do you?" I asked. "Do you want me to tell Ci what you . . ."

Emerald nodded rapidly. "I have shares in that stupid prison island, yes!"

"We can settle the suit now, then. I can drop some of the charges against you. Just sign the island ownership off to me as collateral."

"I . . . I don't freaking own the entire island, you idiot!" Emerald snarled, her eyes filling with tears.

"No, but you own enough shares to make the start of my hostile takeover legal," I pointed out. "Plus, once the evidence of illegal activities here comes to light, the Stratos Clan will have a hard time contesting my claim."

"My family will destroy you!" Emerald hissed.

"They'll have to get in line." I grinned. "So are we settling this lawsuit now or what?"

"I can't just . . . give you my shares!"

"Sure you can." I smiled. "Unless you want Cinder to continue exploring your facial reconstruction options while Kat slowly drowns you in the deep?"

Emerald glanced fearfully at Cinder's raised fist as shadows around her deepened.

"Fine!" she spat. "I'll sign over my shares, you ass! But this isn't over!"

"Of course it isn't," I agreed. "This is just the beginning of our wonderful journey together. Ladies, call up Io and meet up with him. I'll need him to open a gate from my new villain citadel island to Skyfall. I'll put *Day After Tomorrow* for him to target on my phone screen!"

# CHAPTER THIRTY-FOUR

# Vesperrific

Ceter Kalik Simmi placed his magisteel-covered talons on his sleeping daughter's forehead, his consciousness diving into her dreamscape. The intrusion was precise, calculated—a technique passed down through generations of thunder gods.

He found Vespera sitting on a marble bench in Skyfall's dream-garden, her legs crossed at the ankles, scrolling through her phone. Her dream-self wore a blue-and-white gothic Lolita dress with glittering chainmail top, complete with black platform boots and lightning bolt feather clips.

"Like, Daddy! What are you doing in my headspace?" Vespera didn't look up from her phone, her voice carrying the blasted Valley girl tone she always used to irritate him. "This is totes awkward. #Braininvasion."

"Vespera, we need to talk," Ceter said.

"Why am I asleep? Can we not talk in the real? You're, like, totally violating my neural privacy rights right now. #MentalSpaceInvasion #NotCool #DaddyIssues." Vespera continued scrolling, a slight smirk playing at her lips. "Should I call Attorney Thornheart? He's, like, super good at privacy violation cases."

"You're banned from using phones," Ceter growled. "I'm placing you under house arrest until we sort out this mess with the human infiltrator."

"OMG, Daddy, you're being like, totally extra right now." Vespera flipped her dream-feathers. "Alexander isn't an infiltrator, he's my bae. We're literally soul-bonded. #TrueLove #CantStopWontStop."

"Stop this nonsense!" Ceter's thunderous voice shook the dream-garden. "And cease speaking in hashtags!"

"But Daddy, hashtags are my aesthetic! #DaddyRage #ThunderTantrum #SoBasic." Vespera giggled, manifesting a pink bubble tea in her hand. "Want some? It's cotton candy thunder flavor! #BriberyAttempt."

Lightning danced between Ceter's wings, his hand raised. A brilliant Thunderbolt struck the girl in the head, obliterating and shearing her into fractured wisps and flickering bits.

Ceter focused and dove deeper.

The dream within the dream featured a beach covered in colorful rocks with glowing emerald waves smashing into the shore. The horizon extended upwards forever. Ceter recognized Arx from his delving days at Skyfall Academy with stern Instructor Zalimar.

Another Vespera was sitting on the beach, this one wearing full body armor.

"That was very rude," she said coldly. "That avatar took effort to make."

"Vespera," Ceter growled, "I tire of your disobedience."

"And I tire of you being in my head," Vespera said. "You taught me Dreamancy, and while I do appreciate that, this time you were *not* invited in!"

"You will not speak to me that way," Ceter thundered. "I am your father and you will obey me! You've crossed a line by binding yourself to a human criminal! You will go to marry Zheng this summer! You will break the soul bond, go to a Psychopomp!"

"No," Vespera said simply. "I won't. I refuse. I found someone better than Zheng."

"A pathetic human scum?!" Ceter growled.

"Rude." Vespera crossed her arms, standing up. "First of all, Lex isn't pathetic. He made over two hundred million O-bux on Arx and built a compound for our clan in just one week. What did Zheng build in eighteen years? Go on, point me at one thing he's accomplished that would make him worthy of me."

Ceter's wings crackled with barely contained fury. "Zheng is Prima-born! His bloodline is pure, optimized for generations! You and he are meant to lead Golden Star Industries and SimmiTech into a new era of prosperity!"

"Just 'cause his bloodline's pure doesn't make him any less of an intolerable, gross idiot." Vespera shook her head.

"Idiot girl," Ceter growled. "If you don't like his personality, then optimize it using Dreamancy! But first, you are to optimize yourself, rid yourself of that irritating front-end avatar. I've had enough of you embarrassing our clan at Omnicorp meetings!"

"Eh, I like my frontend avatar," Vespera said, manifesting a mirror and admiring her reflection. "It's snarky and funny. Besides, Lex loves me for who I am, not who you want me to be."

"That human will be dead within the hour," Ceter snarled. "And you will be cleansed of this affliction!"

Vespera laughed, the sound echoing across the dream-beach. "You really don't understand what you're dealing with, do you, Daddy? Lex isn't just some random human. He was already pretty unique when I met him, but then I optimized him further."

"You did what now?" Ceter blinked.

"Optimized him," Vespera clicked. "Gave him a very special skill, one of my designs. One that puts him above us Omnids with our alignment specificity. He's going to be the most Omni-capable wizard in the universe."

"What?" Ceter sputtered. "If you wanted to experiment with humans, you should have said so. I would have provided you with human subjects to work with!"

"Look, Dad. If you want to merge with Golden Star so bad," Vespera said, "do it without me. I've got my own thing going. I'm happy. The Arx Bank can grow flesh duplicates. Go to Shandria, buy a duplicate of me, copy yourself into her head, and marry Zheng. A simple solution that doesn't involve me."

"You dare suggest we use a flesh duplicate for a sacred clan merger?!" Ceter roared. "Are you out of your mind, Vespera?! The Arch-Elders would never accept this! Golden Star has Probability Engines—they'd see a duplicate from a mile away!"

"Why do we have to listen to old-ass, crusty Omnids?" Vespera sighed. "Their minds are obviously addled by speaking too many times with their wacky Archangels.

Probability Engines don't see everything, Daddy. They can be blocked by anti-scrying runes, Outsiders can screw with them. They don't see the full picture. Tell me, can your engines see what Lexy and I did on Arx?"

"What did you do on Arx?"

"Why don't you *get the fuck out of my head* and ask your precious Probability Engine what I did on Arx?" Vespera growled, extending her talons.

Ceter struck first, obliterating her avatar into wisps and broken pieces.

With a weary sigh, he stepped deeper into the next layer of the dream.

He found himself in a crystalline tower, jagged crystals pointing at him. Vespera sat on a crystalline throne, looking down at him. She looked like a human girl with black hair and gray eyes, wearing a pure black dress.

"Extra rude," she said with a frown. "You know, if you go deeper, you're going to break me. Is this your brilliant plan? To make me into a drooling idiot?"

"No," Ceter said. "This is my plan to make you understand."

"Understand what?" Vespera asked. "That you obviously don't respect me? That you want to control every aspect of my life?"

"I want to protect you," Ceter said with a weary sigh. "This human will destroy everything we've built. Everything we've been working on for centuries."

"Maybe your shit deserves to be destroyed," Vespera declared. "Because that's what's going to happen if you keep going."

"Vespera!"

"No. How about you have another daughter and convince her to marry another Golden Star boy. I'm out."

Ceter sputtered at his daughter's impudence. Where had he gone wrong? Where had her Prima-Mother and Hearth-Keeper failed?

"You . . ." he choked. "You don't understand what's at stake, Vespera!"

"Go on, then," the fake human girl on the crystalline throne said, waving a pale hand. "Regale me with your sales pitch."

"Our clan merger isn't just about two corporations combining," Ceter said, his voice dropping to a serious tone. "Earth is falling towards a mesh of doomed worlds and will soon be consumed by all-devouring celestorms. We don't have time to produce another heir of your skill. You're the key to saving all Omnids, a master Crystallographer like no other, born under perfect Lunar shard alignment. A great fortune was spent on your birth to make sure that you were the most capable Thundergirl, one who could rewrite the entirety of the crystalline strata beneath Cradlefall. You and Zheng are meant to save our people from extinction!"

"Says who?" Vespera tilted her head. "Some musty old magitek spinny thing? Some wack Archangel who doesn't give a fuck about Omnids?"

"The Probability Engines," Ceter let out, his face twitching, "calculate our survival rate at 99.3 percent if you marry Zheng and combine our clan's resources. Without this outcome, we drop to 12.7 percent and perish!"

"Twelve point seven percent sounds like a challenge," Vespera said, leaning forward. "Ya kno', this apocalypse of yours sounds like something Lex would love to turn into a business opportunity. Say, is our Earth becoming more magical then? Maybe we should start planting dungeons from Arx to focus those celestorms into something productive? Hrmmm?"

"Vespera! You cannot be serious!"

"I'm completely serious," Vespera stated. "In fact, I bet Lex could raise that survival rate to 95 percent just by throwing a bunch of Arx dungeons at this problem."

"Vespera! A human, even one that's been augmented by you, cannot . . ."

"I disagree," Vespera fired back. "I've seen him pull off some crazy shit with my help. He thinks outside the box, and isn't trapped in the dum' narrative that the Archangels weave for us."

Ceter stared at his daughter, not understanding her words. "You cannot seriously believe that a human could solve our existential crisis!"

"I'm super cereal," Vespera said. "Lex isn't just some random human. He's got something special. Something the Probability Engines can't calculate."

"And what might that be?" Ceter asked sarcastically.

"Chaos." Vespera grinned. "Pure, beautiful, unpredictable chaos sprinkled with love."

"Love?!" Ceter growled. "You love this human?!"

"He's my greatest project yet." Vespera shrugged. "And he's funny."

"Zheng could be your project!" Ceter stated. "You can make him as funny as you want him to be! If you've modified one human, you can modify others in the same way, build a whole army of them if you so desire!"

"No," Vespera said firmly. "Zheng isn't Lex. Lex has something special. Four human souls. I don't think that I could replicate that in an Omnid."

Ceter stared at his daughter with a bewildered look. "Four human souls? What nonsense are you talking about? Four souls would just absorb one another, the strongest would devour the weak!"

"Ye," Vespera said, nodding. "That's what happens normally when you shove extra souls into a person, and yet Lexy somehow manages four souls. On a permanent basis. He's my shiny. Mine! I found him! You can fuck off."

Ceter's wings spread out, lightning dancing between dark feathers. "You will *not* speak to me that way! How dare you take on a human avatar!"

"Daddy, if you destroy this dream layer, you'll permanently damage my mental architecture," Vespera pointed out. "There is nothing coherent below. Go on. Strike me down, overwrite me. Show me that you don't love me, that you never loved me. Free me from caring about you."

Ceter's wings trembled with rage, electricity crackling between his magisteel talons. "Vespera . . ."

"Nope," Vespera said, popping the *p*. "I'm not backing down. You'll have to kill me if you want to make your perfect daughter. Them's the beans."

"So you refuse?" Ceter barked.

"Yep. I refuse to be part of your old-man schemes," Vespera said. "I'm out. Find another idiot birb to throw at your problems."

Booming lightning struck from Ceter's hand, obliterating the human avatar, tearing through the crystal throne. It bounced into Ceter and burned his wings. He hissed. Blasted girl managed to make a trap.

He dove deeper.

The fourth fold of the dream was an empty, desolate, gray landscape covered in dark cracks.

Snow fluttered from the broiling storm clouds overhead, occasional flashes of lightning cutting across the dark sky. There was no Vespera here.

Ceter sent out a pulse of electrical discharge to make sure.

Nothing. No avatar. No consciousness. Nothing to overwrite. Just clouds. Just fluttering snowflakes spinning in random spirals. Just the wind.

He tried to dive deeper, but there was nothing beneath this layer, nowhere else to go to.

He sighed and began weaving a new Vespera into the dreary landscape. His perfect daughter. One who loved Zheng and didn't care for humans. A Slayer destined to save all Omnidkind.

Once she was made, he stepped backwards and wove another perfect Vespera onto the damaged throne, not a human but a Thunderbird, bending and twisting the wispy remnants into his absolute Prima-born girl.

Another step back. He rebuilt the Vespera on the beach.

Another step back. No idiotic accent. Only a perfect heir. He rebuilt the last, perfect Vespera.

"Who do you love?" he asked.

"Zheng, Daddy," the new avatar answered smoothly with a soft smile.

"Good," Ceter exhaled, leaving from the dream, his wings aching from the mental burns.

He blinked awake and sent a pulse across his daughter's body and watched as her gray eyes opened.

"Um, Daddy, why am I here?" The Thundergirl yawned, wearily looking left and right. Her feathers were pure white now, without a single black spot on her wings and mane.

"It is Friday," her father answered. "You were injured during your delve on Arx and I had to repair your mind."

"I see," she said. "Thank you, Daddy, I appreciate it. What are we doing today?"

Ceter studied her eyes, ensuring his mental reconstruction was flawless. The rebellious spark was gone, replaced by a perfectly obedient daughter. "We are attending a family meeting about your upcoming merger with Zheng Golden Star. Your great-grandfather will interview you, make sure you understand what's at stake."

"Of course." Vespera nodded. Her movements were precise, her posture immaculate— everything a Prima-born heir should be.

Ceter relaxed. He felt bad about mentally manipulating his daughter, but it had to be done for the greater good of Omnidkind. He would have to watch her behavior from here, make sure that Vespera did what was expected of her to the letter.

Deep within the dreary empty landscape of the fourth level of the dream, a single snowflake began to pulse with an electrical charge. And then another. And another. A storm of snowflakes spun high in the sky, lightning dancing between them, like a neural network very slowly reconnecting itself.

The avatar of the perfect girl standing below the gloomy clouds didn't bother looking up.

She only had one mission in mind—to marry Zheng and to optimize him, to optimize herself to be the savior of Cradlefall, to figure out how to write a supermassive hexagram fractal beneath the crater, to save her city and her friends. Two weeks of memories were missing from her head, which was slightly annoying, but she was certain that she'd catch up quickly.

The snowflake storm spun overhead.

In the real world, Vespera's finger twitched. Almost imperceptibly.

Her father didn't notice.

Her eyes, gray while appearing vacant, held a microscopic glimmer—the tiniest spark of resistance.

Something her father had forgotten: Vespera was a master Dreamancer, an electro-fractal weapon, a tool bred over a multitude of generations, one who knew exactly how to take herself apart in just the right way.

She knew exactly how to play dead.

# CHAPTER THIRTY-FIVE

# The Perfect Heir

The Simmi family dining room gleamed with polished marble surfaces and crystalline chandeliers. Vespera sat perfectly upright, her silverware aligned with geometric precision, her movements controlled and deliberate, every feather on her mane pure white.

Ceter Kalik Simmi studied his daughter carefully, watching for any sign of her previous rebelliousness. Beside him, Hanni Simmi served a traditional meal—rare Arx beast meats prepared with intricate Thunderland spices.

"Tell your great-grandfather about your mission, Vespera," Ceter ordered.

Vespera looked up, her gray eyes flat and compliant. "I am to facilitate the merger of the SimmiTech and Golden Star corporations through my marriage to Zheng. Our combined resources will create a 99.3 percent probability of Omnid survival during the upcoming celestorm events."

Her voice was clinical, devoid of the playful shortened and hashtag-laden speech she once used. Each word was precisely measured, each syllable sharp like the blade of a two-dimensional knife.

Ceter nodded, satisfied. "And your personal feelings?"

"Personal feelings are irrelevant," Vespera responded. "The mission takes precedence. Zheng is my optimal genetic and corporate match. We need more resources to save Omnithornia."

"Very good," Arch-Elder Altair nodded, the multiple, pale, crystalline angel-wings that framed his lanky body catching the chandelier light.

"Father," Vespera said, turning to Ceter when dinner was over, "may I look at my stats? I would like to see if I leveled up during my latest delve."

"No." Ceter shook his head. "A vile human criminal infected your soul with a memetic. It must be purged. Psychopomp Krakthulluius will remove the infection tonight. The procedure will be . . . unpleasant, but necessary."

"Of course, Father." Vespera nodded demurely. "Will it hurt?"

"Yes," Ceter admitted. "But you are strong. The procedure will sever the memetic infestation. Dr. Krakthulluius is the best soul surgeon in Omnithornia."

"I understand." Vespera nodded. "Will I be able to attend classes on Monday? I need to study crystallography with Instructor Gilgamesh to begin my thesis on modifying Leviathan strata below Leviathan's Cradle next year."

"If you swear to me that you will not attempt to search for Alexander Glock, or interact with any other nullie or human scum." Ceter placed a hand on his daughter's shoulder, scanning her soul for the truth. "Do not befriend, nor interact, with any humans without my permission. Is that understood?"

"Understood. I swear it, Father." Vespera nodded. "I will not speak to any humans without your approval starting tonight. I'm sorry for my prior indiscretions."

Ceter nodded, satisfied. The mental reconstruction appeared to be functioning as intended. "Very good. The Psychopomp will be here in an hour. After the procedure, you will rest, and during the weekend you will focus on your crystallography studies."

"Of course, Daddy," Vespera agreed. "I wish to save our people with my entire Fractal Engine heart."

"There is an unusual familiar bond registered in her." Psychopomp Krakthulluius's skeletal black hands waved over Vespera's shaking body as the Thundergirl tried to hold herself together after something had been carved out of her soul. "Something called . . . Possy."

"A familiar?" Ceter frowned. "Vespera, explain."

"I cannot remember. I was searching for an Electrofractal Kitlix familiar on Arx for a few years now, Daddy," Vespera answered. "Perhaps I found one during my last delve but cannot recall it due to memory loss? Maybe it has something to do with how my Lazarus bracelet is now clear?"

Lord Ceter frowned, noticing that her bracelet was indeed oddly clear. He tapped his talons on it. It was perfectly functional, but the immovable metal had somehow inexplicably become transparent. He had no idea how this was even possible. Maybe some kind of unique dungeon magic had done it.

"What else can you tell me about this bond?" Ceter turned to Krakthulluius.

"The bond is recent. Made within the last week."

"Can you determine the familiar's nature?" Ceter demanded.

"No, Lord Ceter." Krakthulluius shook his head. "I cannot. It is in another dimension right now. It is presumably back on Arx. I do sense that it is a high-level crystalline creature with Kitlix-like properties."

"I see." Ceter nodded slowly. "Can you carve it out?"

"Carving the familiar connection will have to be done in another week," Krakthulluius said. "Her soul is already damaged, and I do not wish to tear it further. I will stop by once every few days to slowly repair the shears I've made so that I can disconnect the familiar bond."

"Very well." Ceter nodded slowly. "We'll deal with this familiar matter later as the delve to Arx won't happen for another week."

He turned to his daughter. "Vespera, how do you feel?"

"It hurts, but I endure. I feel . . . pure, Father," Vespera answered, her voice just as sharp despite her trembling body. "Thank you for cleansing me of that vile memetic, Dr. Krakthulluius. When may I meet Zheng to discuss our upcoming soul bond and begin our optimization process?"

"Soon." Ceter patted her white-feathered head. "Zheng was hurt speaking to his family's Archangel, so he needs a week at least to recover. Rest now."

"Yes, Father." Vespera bowed her head submissively. "May I request some crystallography texts from the library? I wish to study while I heal."

"Of course." Ceter nodded approvingly. "Your dedication to saving our people is admirable. Butler Oppohosh will bring you any arcane texts you require."

*   *   *

I stood in the prison's wide courtyard, the view of the evening sky above me, the clouds painted violet-orange by the setting sun. My phone stood in front of me on a tripod, keeping the frozen frame of *The Day After Tomorrow* displayed.

In a few minutes, a dark gate manifested into existence in front of me. Cinder, Katherine, Io, and Emerald became visible inside it.

Cinder burst through the gate first and smothered me in a sunset-red angry hug. "Don't scare me like that," she let out.

"Wasn't my fault." I hugged her back.

Katherine stepped through next, her emerald eyes narrowing as she looked left and right. "I see you've been busy."

I nodded. I noticed that Katherine was moving a bit sluggishly. I guessed that the dress wasn't a perfect solution. She was still dying, just more slowly.

Emerald followed, looking distinctly uncomfortable, her snout looking busted. "This is kidnapping," she whined nasally.

"You started it first," I pointed out. "Your Scrut kidnapped me and brought me here. By clan law, I only retaliated fairly."

"You're an effing human, Omnid clan laws don't apply to you," the dragon girl growled.

"And yet I have a clan. Cry me a river, Emmy." I shrugged at her. "I'm far nicer than you. I won't feed you to a shark. I'll just keep you as a hostage till your family pays me one hundred billion O-bux."

"You can't be serious!" she growled. "That's an outrageous sum!"

"What, you think that your value is less?" I asked.

She sent me the traditional "I will get my revenge and murder you, just you wait" glare.

"Such glaring," I said. "You should appreciate me more! I've made you my sixie, which means you get a small salary, dental, corporate benefits, and the protection of Rainbow and Thunder Omnicorp."

"My parents will take this island apart stone by stone!" she growled.

"They won't even be able to find you," I said. "I'm not going to keep you here."

"Where are you . . ." she choked.

"Fun places," I said. "Another dimension, where no Scrutimancer can track you down since Scrutimancy doesn't work across dimensions. Unless you sign a bunch of contracts, of course."

Emerald blanched.

"I've given you plenty of chances to be cooperative and cordial," I said. "Now it's going to be contractual obligations. Kat, take her to a cell."

Katherine grabbed Emerald by the collar, her emerald eyes shining with gleeful predatory intent. "Come on, little dragon. Time for your new accommodations."

Emerald struggled, but Katherine's grip was firm. "This is illegal! I'm a Prima-born! My family will—"

Everyone ignored her.

"So, how was your date with June?" I asked Io as we began walking across the prison courtyard into the administrative area.

"She's definitely . . . intellectually stimulating," he replied. "We watched *The Day*

*After Tomorrow* in one of the student lounges and had an extensive discussion about doomed worlds afterwards. But . . ." He hesitated.

"But what?" I prompted.

"She's just . . . too wet," Io said with a slight shudder.

"That's usually not a problem for a girlfriend to have." I wiggled my eyebrows at him.

"Uh-huh," Io exhaled. "My everything gets damp just being near her. It's rather uncomfortable for a Mothman."

I couldn't help but chuckle. "At least you found common ground with the disaster discussions?"

"Indeed. Her obsession with aquatic catastrophes is delightful. However, I prefer to observe such events from a safe, dry distance." Io adjusted his duster coat.

"Hang on, how do you even shower?" I asked.

"I don't," Io said. "I use dry shampoos to clean my mane and wings."

"Ah." I rubbed my chin. "So why not sprinkle yourself with talcum or cornstarch-based powder? Or maybe powder yourself with aerogel? That stuff would make you somewhat fireproof as well as waterproof."

"An interesting suggestion," Io mused. "I haven't considered such. Hopefully . . . it would not bother June . . ."

"Better than being uncomfortable the whole time," I pointed out. "Consider it 'watery-disaster-proof coating.'"

"Very well, I'll try it, see if it helps," Io said. "Speaking of disasters, I sense multiple approaching catastrophes centered around you. More than usual."

"Yeah?" I asked. "Give me the rundown."

"Several death vectors," Io said, his gray fluffy antennae tapping my head and shoulder. "The doom indicators are off the charts. This is worse than the Undertown assassins."

"That does sound bad." I nodded. "Any specifics?"

"Mmm . . . hard to tell," Io sighed. "I just know that you are going to die unless you do something different."

"Right," I said. "Come! I'd like to introduce you to my new Scruts."

I led Io and Cinder into a meeting room where Magdaline and Satosh were waiting. Magdaline had traded her prison orange robe for a sleek hexamesh suit. A gray security officer uniform with a tie sat atop it, making her look even more dangerous. Her white-blue-striped scales gleamed with a metallic sheen under the fluorescent lights.

"Io, Ci, meet Magdaline Satoshi," I announced, gesturing dramatically. "And her dad, Loom Cernix Satosh.

"This is my Door Knight." I pointed at Iogann. "And trusted right-hand man!"

"Big shark," Io murmured as Magdaline shook his hand.

"Smol moth." Mags smiled, showing off multiple rows of sawlike teeth.

"And this is my lovely Hearth-Keeper Shield, Cinder." I introduced Ci to the Scrut family.

We sat down, Cinder squinting at Magdaline with blue eyes.

"Okay, team. We're going to do some predictive analysis. Io, you've got your disaster sensing. Magdaline, your Scrutiny skills. Satosh, your decades of intelligence work. We're going to map out the incoming catastrophes and try to arrive at a solution."

Magdaline leaned forward. "What exactly are we predicting?"

"Threats to my person that Io can sense," I explained. "Take my hands, Io, Mags. Push your skills through me."

The two Omnids grabbed my hands. Cinder's glare in the direction of the shark-girl intensified.

She suspected things.

"Okay," I said. "Io, you first. What disaster vectors are you sensing?"

"Danger from . . ." Io began thoughtfully.

"Frontenachii Scruts, the Stratoses, and Simmi assassins," Magdaline said. "Wherever you go."

"The Stratoses will absolutely send assassins to take you out." Satosh nodded. "A sniper rifle bullet from afar aimed at the only human in school and then a rapid retrieval team to grab your Lazarus bracelet."

"What else? What about our lost black-and-white bird?" I pulled out Vespera's feather from my pocket and let the shark-girl sniff it.

"Vespera . . ." Io let out.

"Lost her soul bond to you," Mags said, squeezing my hand.

"She no longer remembers you." Satosh nodded. "As I expected. Her father most likely fully overwrote her personality. The new Vespera will hate all humans and will refuse to speak with you."

Cinder paled, colors leaking from her body. "H-how are we going to get her back?" she let out.

"Don't know," I shrugged, which only made Cinder's wings darker. "What else? What about the duel?"

"Zheng . . ." Io began.

"Will not show up," Magdaline said. "A different champion will take his place."

"Lord Ceter Simmi himself," Satosh added.

"Vespera's father?" Cinder's feathers bristled. "That's . . . that's really bad."

"Indeed." Satosh nodded gravely. "Ceter is a Prima Thunder Lord. He's killed hundreds in duels. His lightning can pierce through any defense. He can stop bullets and arrows and redirect spells away from himself."

"Right," I said. "I'll email Lord Ceter and resign from the duel."

"And . . . lose Vee?!" Cinder barked.

"We already lost Vee," I pointed out. "Those assholes cut the connection. There's no point in fighting for it."

"What?! How are you so freaking calm about this?!" She shook me.

"Freaking out won't help us solve any of these issues," I said.

"But . . ." Cinder's feathers flared orange-red. "You can't just give up on her!"

"I'm not giving up," I said calmly. "I'm being strategic."

"Fighting Ceter head-on is suicide." Satosh nodded.

"We need to think outside the box, sidestep away from everything," I said.

"How?!" Cinder demanded.

"I think that it's time for Alexander Glock to leave Skyfall," I said. "To go back to North Acadia."

"*What?!*" my Quetzi GF sputtered.

I stared at her with a smile.

"It's the best way to protect everyone," I explained, squeezing her hand. "Alexander Glock has to go away."

"But . . ." Cinder's feathers drooped. "What about our classes together?"

"Oh, so you actually enjoy classes with me?" I teased her. "Weren't you all like, 'Get outta my face, you annoying human'?"

"Shut up," Cinder growled. "You know what I mean!"

"No, I don't know what you mean." I grinned at her.

"Ughhh," she let out. "Yes, you're an incredibly annoying chuppy . . . but I like having you in my classes. Happy now?"

"Ecstatic," I smirked, greatly enjoying our verbal game of angry dragon and annoying human. "But Alexander Glock still needs to disappear. The Frontenachii Clan wants him captured. Stratos Clan wants him dead, SimmiTech wants him dead, and Golden Star wants him dead, too. Four major Omnicorps gunning for one guy is a bit much."

"So what's your brilliant plan, then?" Cinder crossed her arms.

# CHAPTER THIRTY-SIX

# Mild Psychiatry

'll go away and also attend Skyfall," I said. "Just not as Alexander Glock."

Cinder blinked, the gears of her mind turning.

"I'll still be there for you as an annoying chuppy. Just . . . different. New identity, new look. New me."

Cinder considered my words. "Mkay."

"Another disguise?" Magdaline asked.

"Yeah." I nodded. "I'm thinking . . . an exchange student from Arx."

"An Arx student?" Cinder asked. "How would that even work? Arx-kin can't visit our Earth due to the low aetheric density."

"Eh," I said, grinning, "I'll be a special wealthy student who somehow manages it. Katsburg will provide the necessary paperwork and pay for my schooling."

"And Graves will just accept a transfer student from Arx?!" Cinder asked.

"I'll handle Graves," Satosh said. "He's an old friend of mine."

"And what about your appearance?" Cinder asked.

"Makeup and your wings are going to handle that," I said. "You did a pretty good job of turning me into a foxkin on Arx."

"A lot of that was Vee," Cinder let out.

"I think that you and I can do it," I said. "We have the entire weekend to practice, since I'm cancelling the duel."

Cinder pursed her lips, not sure of herself.

I looked at the moth and sharks. "So, doom avoided?"

"Delayed." Io nodded. "Shifted away from the death of you to the death of . . . uhhh . . . everything. Hrm."

"The death of everything?" Cinder stared at Io.

"Sort of? Maybe?" Io shrugged. "I'm . . . not sensing anything past Monday. It's like there's a wall there. Weird." He looked far too relaxed about the potential end of everything.

I stared at my Scrut-sharks.

"There's nothing past Monday," Satosh said.

"Nothing." Magdaline nodded.

"And that's not concerning?" I asked.

"Big celestorms can cause disruptions in future-sight," the Scrut explained.

"Good enough." I released Io's hand with a sigh.

Magdaline still held onto me, still bouncing Scrutiosmia off me. I inhaled her scent, wondering how she was doing.

I smelled dedication and . . . attraction. Pointed directly at me. A *lot* of attraction. Her physical heart was beating fast, and behind it her Fractal Engine heart was reaching out towards me, desiring to be connected deeper, further.

"Is something going on between you two?" Cinder squinted at us.

"Nothing!" Magdaline released my hand quickly, trying and failing to hide the blush dancing across her face.

"Mkay," I said. "Io, gate to the phone in my van. Then fly in your van to the nearest Omnibank and open an Omnicorp account there."

I piled a few million O-bux worth of celesteel cards into his gray paws. "Deposit these there. Mags, you know my clothes size, yes?"

"I can smell it, yes." She nodded, trying very hard not to look at Cinder.

"Order me some nice clothes," I said. "Top of the line Prima-born princeling suits. Maybe a gemstone encrusted cane, too."

"Can do," she said.

"Afterward, head to Omnitronics Depot and buy phones, laptops, tablets, video cards, and server racks. As many as you can. I'll set up a storage room here with a phone for Io to gate the purchased stuff into."

Io nodded.

"Off you go, then." I waved them off. "Mags, you're the bodyguard. Protect Io with your life."

Magdaline nodded.

I turned to Satosh. "Interrogate the prisoners, see which ones would be willing to work for us as sixies. I want skilled, trusted Omnids that we can throw at problems in the future that won't betray our cause. Ones who will work here and also on Arx for us."

Satosh nodded. He too departed, leaving me alone with Cinder.

"So . . . Magdaline clearly likes you," the Quetzi said after a minute of silence.

"Yeah," I said.

"Remember what I said?" she growled, dark claws extending, hand suddenly wrapped around my chin.

"No harems," I said. "I'm pawning her off to Io. He could use a strong Prima!"

Cinder grabbed me by the collar and pulled me close, her ocean-blue eyes narrowing. "You're walking on a verrrrry thin line there, pal."

"I am aware." I grinned at her, not resisting her grip. "But Mags needs friends and guidance. She's been isolated for too long. She's crushing on the first person who showed her kindness. Prison does that to people. Isolation makes them latch onto the first person who treats them like a person rather than a monster."

"And you know this from experience?" Cinder's gaze was glacial.

"I've been isolated myself for years." I shrugged. "Uncle George put me through hell, made me steal stuff, forced me to practice parkour day after day for years. I crushed onto the first angel I saw." I smiled at her. "Then Vee also sort of adopted me."

Cinder's grip on my collar tightened. "Don't. Change. The. Subject."

"Look, Ci," I said. "I'm trying to explain that I understand what Magdaline is going through. She needs friends, not just a boyfriend. She needs to learn who she is outside of prison."

Cinder's feathers slowly shifted from angry dark sunset to a more thoughtful blue-gray. "And you think Io would be good for her? What if he doesn't like her?"

"Then he doesn't like her." I shrugged. "But they should at least try. They're both kind of weird and awkward. Both have a thing for sensing the future. He's small and can't fly and she has a protective streak. It could work out."

Cinder's grip on my collar loosened slightly. "And what about Vee?"

"What about her?"

"Stop answering my questions with questions!" Cinder shook me.

"Why don't we talk about our feelings instead of being violent?" I offered, channeling my inner prison therapist.

"Feelings?!" Cinder sputtered, her feathers bristling with renewed agitation. "You want to talk about feelings when Vee's been mind-wiped?!"

"Yes, we already established that," I said. "Come on, tell me how you really feel instead of strangling me."

"I feel like everything is falling apart!" Cinder suddenly released my collar, her wings drooping. "I feel like a useless knob! I feel like you can just replace me with a convict Megalodon whenever you feel like that's the most optimal path!"

She pawed at her own face, making iridescent colors rush across the lines left by her dark claws.

"And you know what else?!" Cinder snarled. "Everything is moving so fast, I can barely keep up! One week I'm just trying to survive Skyfall, keeping my head down, dealing with Em's stupid demands, and the next I've got a human boyfriend and a Thunderbird girlfriend, and we're stealing ancient Corpse Seekers and robbing banks on Arx!"

Her feathers shifted through a kaleidoscope of troubled colors—deep purples bleeding into stormy grays.

"And Vee—Abyss! Vee was always *so effin' annoying* with her constant selfies and her Valley girl chatter, meme jokes, and her endless stupid hashtags! But she was *real* underneath all that! She actually cared about things! She actually cared about *me*! And now she's just . . . *gone*!" Cinder's eyes filled with tears. "And I didn't even get to tell her that she was my best friend! That I'd started to fucking care about her again, after we drifted apart in grade ten!"

Cinder's claws dug deep into her hands.

"What kind of a shitty girlfriend am I?! I couldn't protect her! I couldn't stop her father from destroying her! I just stood there like a useless *knob*, got knocked out while they took her away!"

"And you!" Cinder's claws raked across her feathers, leaving more iridescent trails.

"Me?" I raised an eyebrow.

"Why the fuck are you even tolerating me?! I'm such a horrible girlfriend to you, too! I keep threatening you and shaking you and getting angry at everything you do! Even when you're just trying to help people! Even when you're trying to protect everyone by changing your identity!"

Her entire body started to tremble as the stress of the day finally boiled over.

"I couldn't protect you from getting arrested! I couldn't stop Satosh from taking you to prison! What kind of an awful Hearth-Shield am I . . . if I haven't even cooked you a single meal?! I'm . . . so shit at everything!"

More tears streamed down her face, making her feathers glisten with rainbow patterns.

Cinder's claws raked across her shoulders, leaving more iridescent trails. "And now I'm just standing here, having a complete mental breakdown in front of you like some kind of pathetic *loser*! Because I can't handle *any* of this! Because I'm not strong enough or smart enough or *good* enough!"

Her wings wrapped around herself protectively, feathers shifting through shades of midnight blue and stormy gray.

"Everyone else seems to just . . . handle everything! Vee was always so confident, even with her stupid Valley girl act! Katherine just rolls with everything! Even Io just accepts whatever chaos happens! But I'm just . . . *falling apart*!"

She slumped against the wall, sliding down to sit on the floor, her wings curled tight around her trembling form.

"And the worst part? The absolute *worst* part?! I actually started to believe we could make this work! That . . . maybe I could actually have something good in my life! That maybe I wasn't just some failure, a loser who fell for a pretty face, who couldn't even handle *one* stupid Skinwalker without needing Em to rescue me!"

I sat down next to Cinder.

"Tell me more about feeling like a failure," I said. "What makes you think you're not handling things well?"

"Because I'm sitting here crying like an idiot!" Cinder sniffled, her wings trembling. "While you're making plans and organizing everything!"

"And crying makes you weak?" I asked gently.

"*Yes!*" She barked. "No . . . I don't know! Everyone else seems so put together!"

"Do you think maybe they're just better at hiding their feelings?" I suggested. "Kat drinks; I made her cry when I told her that I'm Martin. Io mellows his feelings with interdimensional smokes. Vee hid her real self behind the Valley girl persona."

"But you . . ." Cinder started.

"I compartmentalize," I explained. "Break everything into manageable chunks, split it between four souls. Focus on what I can control. Doesn't mean I'm not terrified or distraught about losing Vee. I'm keeping myself together by shoving Alexander Glock forward, who is quite frankly a psychopath who doesn't care about people."

"Yeah," she let out. "You just switch personas. Like it's nothing. Manipulate people like they're just . . . pieces on a chessboard. What if one day you decide I'm not . . . optimal? What if you just . . . replace me, too?"

"Do you believe I see you as replaceable?"

Her ocean-blue eyes met mine, vulnerable. "Don't you?"

I crossed my arms.

"Do you really think that after everything we've been through, after all the crazy shit we've pulled through together, that I would see you as replaceable?"

"You literally just talked about replacing yourself with a new identity!"

"I'm replacing Skyfall student Alexander Glock," I said. "Who was never real to begin with."

"See!" she growled. "You manipulate everything and everyone, including yourself! How do I know I'm not just another piece in your grand plan?"

"You are," I said. "As am I. As everyone else is."

Cinder stared at me.

"We're all part of each other's plans," I continued calmly. "I'm not some all-capable, all-successful mastermind or a Gary Sue. Since Tuesday, I've been manipulated by Vespera. She was the one who put the Resonance skill in me, built this convex mirror radar dish thing inside me that allows me to store some mana and to bounce magic off five Omnids. She's the master crystallographer who's been subtly guiding me to free her."

"She . . . huh?" Cinder blinked at me.

"Think about it. Every major move we've made? The crystal tower? Something only she can use. Possy. Her familiar that neither of us can drive. My ability to channel magic across multiple Omnids? That's all her."

"Are you saying that you're just . . . her puppet?" Cinder growled.

"More like her most ambitious project. She gradually optimized my human ass, Ci. Allowed me to use Omnid magic, which is what I wanted to do regardless. I figured it all out by relying on Magdaline's Scrutimancy."

"So Vee was manipulating all of us?" Cinder asked. "Set you and me up?"

"She was setting up a way for us to save her. She knew her father would eventually erase her. So . . . she built safeguards into me, into us. The soul-bond, the crystal tower, Possy—they're all tools she needed to ensure her real self could survive."

"But . . . why didn't she tell us?"

"I don't know." I shrugged. "Maybe she was going to tell us and got caught sooner. The point is that I miss her, too. She's a manipulative, clever birb . . . and I miss every bit of her. I got used to having her by our side, pushing and motivating and doing stuff."

I spun Alexander Glock and Christophorus Elijah away, leaving only Martin there staring at Cinder with a distraught face.

"And now I'm just . . . lost," I admitted, letting my real emotions show. "I don't know how exactly to get her back. I don't know if we can get her back or if she'll even be the same. I'm terrified that we'll fail her."

Cinder's wings shifted to a softer shade of blue. "You . . . you actually do care."

"Of course I care," I said. "I'm just really good at hiding it behind Alexander's smug facade. But right now? I'm scared. I'm angry. I want to burn SimmiTech to the ground for what they did to her. No, scratch that, I will absolutely destroy SimmiTech for this."

My hands closed into fists.

"I will ruin them," I continued, letting my anger show. "But I have to be smart about it. I can't just charge in like a berserker. I need to be methodical, surgical. And I need your help, Ci. I can't do this alone."

Cinder's feathers shifted to a more determined shade of blue-gray. "What's the plan then?"

"First, we need to establish my new identity at Skyfall. Then we start gathering intelligence on SimmiTech, find their weaknesses. We'll need to be patient, careful."

"And Vee?" Cinder asked.

"We'll see her on Monday," I said.

"And if she doesn't show up? What if she's already been taken to Thunderland and married Zheng earlier?"

"Then we'll make new plans with our Scruts and go get her," I said. "Kidnap her and bring her to Arx."

Cinder sighed, wings turning black and gray.

"Stop darkening like a storm cloud. You're amazing." I reached out to her. "You're strong, way stronger than me. You survived two years, alone, against an Astral Phantom Outsider in your soul. You're brave. And you're exactly the girl I need to keep going, to put on a new mask that'll help us get Vee back."

Her ocean-blue eyes met mine.

"You want to know why I love you?" I smiled. "Because you're real. You're not pretending to be something you're not. You feel everything so deeply, paint it on your wings, and that's beautiful."

"But I keep messing up . . ." she let out.

"Everyone messes up," I said. "But you keep trying. You keep fighting. That's what matters."

I pulled her into a tight hug, letting her bury her face in my shoulder.

"You don't mess up," she mewled.

"Shush. I mess up all the time," I said into her feathers. "I just hide it better. Remember how I completely blue-screened when I first saw you? Couldn't even form words?"

Cinder let out a watery laugh against my shoulder. "Yeah. That was pretty pathetic."

"See? I'm not perfect. I just pretend to be strong, wear a mask. And you know what else?" I stroked her wings gently. "I need you to help me be better. To remind me to feel things sometimes, instead of just calculating everything. Right?"

"R-right." She nodded. Her face slowly flowed into a mostly human one, and she gave me a soft kiss.

"Ugh," she said after a few minutes of making out. "You bought me a farm and I didn't give you shit."

"Shh." I pressed my finger to her lips. "You've given me plenty. Your trust, your strength, your heart. You and Vee gave me Quetzi and Thunder magic. That's worth more than any farm. Also, you two gave me this awesome jacket."

"Cheeseball," she muttered. "Say . . . does this prison have a fabrication lab?"

"It does." I nodded. "Room 988."

"Perfect." Cinder's feathers shifted to a more determined shade of blue. "I want to make you something."

"What kind of something?" I asked.

"A surprise," she said, getting off me.

# CHAPTER THIRTY-SEVEN

# Ein Sof

No looking," Cinder ordered when she returned to the warden's office. "Close your eyes."

I obeyed and then felt something cool slip around my neck.

"Okay, open your eyes," she said.

I looked down to find a large crystal pendant hanging off me—one of her iridescent feathers perfectly preserved in clear resin-like strata. The crystal caught the light, making rainbow patterns dance across its faceted surface.

"It's beautiful." I touched the pendant gently. "Did you just fabricate it?"

"Yeah." Cinder's feathers shifted to a shy pink-blue. "The fabrication lab had some decent materials. The hexasheen case should protect the feather and . . . well, it's part of me. There's a little beast core battery at the bottom that makes it glow in the dark, too. Maybe . . . it'll help you reinforce your Charmchain skill . . . if I'm not near you."

"Thank you." I smiled. "I'll treasure it forever."

Cinder's feathers ignited with fuchsia, rose, and scarlet as she smothered me in her wings. Charmchain-projected love poured off her like an ocean wave drowning any rational thought, and for a while I completely lost my sense of self buried in her hugs and kisses.

I managed to bat her off me after about ten minutes of being pawed.

"We've got places to be," I told her.

"Places?" she mewled. "W-what places?"

"The cathedral and then dinner at your parents."

"Why?" she whined.

"I need to reinforce my new backstory. Plus, your dad's gonna have my head if you don't show up for dinner," I said. "Really don't want to piss off Justice Nova as I have some legal stuff for him to sign."

"Fine." Cinder's wings shifted to a more sullen violet-blue-gray. "How are we getting to the cathedral?"

"Io will gate us straight to the office of Father Matthias," I said.

"Eh?" Cinder blinked at me.

"He, Kat, and Mags are already there. I've been directing them via texts while you made me this locket."

"Mkay." she said with a nod.

Father Matthias Jonannes extended his pale, fuzzy, silver Yowie hand to me.

"A pleasure to see you . . . uhrm, again . . . Mr. Glock," he said, looking a bit confused.

"Your Door, Knight, and Scrutimancer reminded me that you stayed at our dormitory in February, but it totally must have slipped my mind."

"I understand, Father." I smiled, accepting his handshake.

The elder Yowie looked at the feather pendant on my chest and then at Cinder. "Oh, and this fine lady must be your . . ."

"Future Hearth-Keeper." I nodded, making Cinder blush pink-violet.

"Lovely." Matthias smiled. "Ah, yes. I sense the one-way soul bond between you. How wonderful it is to see a Quetzi choose a mixed-blood as her mate. Now, how may I be of assistance?"

"I have a bit of a problem, Father," I said. "As Skyfall Academy's only mixed-blood student, I have attracted the ire of three Omnicorps."

"Oh my, how unfortunate," the Arch-Priest sighed.

"Indeed." I nodded solemnly. "Golden Star, SimmiTech, and the Stratos Clan have all put bounties on my head."

"Bounties?" The old Omnid blinked. "Why?"

"My father, Dr. Glock"—I gestured to the stable-diffusion-generated photo I had incepted onto the Arch-Priest's office wall a week ago—"worked for the Department of Celestorm Weather Precognition Analysis. It was recently that I've come into my inheritance and learned that the three clans assassinated him, and now they're gunning for me."

"Assassinated?" Matthias gasped, staring at the photo of me and my "father" hanging out with him at a church meetup.

"Perma-death." I nodded. "They made it look like a skiing accident. His Lazarus bracelet was never found. He found evidence that certain Omnicorps were actively suppressing critical celestorm expansion data. He hid the evidence in an extradimensional vault. I opened this vault two days ago, and the Omnicorps are aiming to eliminate me."

The Arch-Priest's beige eyes widened.

"To put it simply," I said, "I need to . . . disappear for a while."

"I see." Father Matthias stroked his fuzzy chin thoughtfully. "And you require the church's assistance in this matter?"

"Yes." I nodded. "I would like to take advantage of your Witness Protection Program. I understand that there's a way to make my astral imprint disappear completely. I understand that deep beneath this cathedral there is an entity that . . ."

Father Matthias swallowed nervously, glancing at my companions.

"I trust my clan with my life, Father," I said. "Also, you told me about Ein Sof."

In truth, I had found evidence of the entity when I had raided the man's office with Cinder. Cinder, for her part, was staring at me with a "say what" expression.

Io gulped. Mags frowned slightly, sniffing the air, and squinted at me with blood-red eyes. Kat had her arms crossed.

"She . . ." Father Matthias began.

"I understand that every time that the ward is lowered, there's a chance that the Sefirot can get out," I said smoothly, sliding a pile of celesteel cards from Shandria across the desk. "Which is why I'm donating about ten million O-bux to the cathedral's youth outreach program in which I've had the pleasure of working since February."

Father Matthias's eyes widened. The cards gleamed under the office's soft lighting, their surface etched with intricate runes.

"Ten million?" he repeated, his voice slightly breathless. "In Arx currency?"

"I know that the program could use more funding." I nodded. "You told me that yourself."

"I . . . did?" The Arch-Priest rubbed his chin. "Alas, it seems I have forgotten. My apologies."

Cinder was giving me the "are you seriously bribing a priest?" look. I winked at her. She kneaded my hand with her claws.

"The donation will be made in the name of Thunder and Rainbow Omnicorp," I said. "My Knight will provide the tax writeoff details."

Io slid some paperwork for the Arch-Priest to look over and sign. In about twenty minutes, everything was signed by both parties, and Matthias retrieved a massive gold sword-key from his robes.

"Follow me," he said, standing up.

"Where are we going?" Cinder hissed at me as Father Matthias led us down an ancient spiral stairwell into the innards of the Triumvirate Slayer's Cathedral.

"I'm going to talk to a Sefirot," I said.

"Why?"

"Gonna ask her if she wants to join my clan."

"Are you effing serious?" Cinder whispered. "What if the conversation shatters your soul?"

"A small price to pay for salvation." I channeled Christophorus Elijah with a pious look.

"You're nuts," she hissed, her feathers shifting through shades of worried gray.

"Probably." I nodded. "But Ein Sof is the only entity that can completely erase my astral signature. Without her help, the Omnicorps will eventually track me down no matter what disguise I use. This is the right way forward to save Vespera. Right, guys?"

"I don't know," Io said. "Like I said before . . . there's nothing ahead."

"Nothing at all?" I asked.

"Absolutely nothing," he replied. "Or everything. I honestly can't tell. Just drawing a blank. It's the damnedest thing. I've never felt anything like it."

"But not doom?"

"Not doom."

"See?" I grinned at Cinder. "It's not doom!"

The Quetzi-girl exhaled loudly.

We descended deeper into the cathedral's foundations, the air growing colder and heavier with each step. Ancient runes flickered along the walls, pulsing with other-worldly shimmers.

Father Matthias unlocked a magisteel door with a touch of his hand and another small key that took us into a long hall, which led to another stairwell and another hall with a massive magisteel vault door.

He inserted the golden key into a large key-hole and turned it.

The massive vault door slowly began to slide open.

"Go forth, my child," he said as he made the Slayer's sword-cross sign over me. "Speak to her for no more than eight minutes, lest your soul fully come apart and your mind shatter. There is a silver hand hourglass standing on a pedestal in the center of the vault. Turn it over for her to see you."

I nodded.

Cinder buried me in a tight-winged hug. "Are you sure this is a good idea?" she hissed, not releasing me.

"No idea." I shrugged. "Actually . . . Father, could all of us go in together? Maybe if the entity's gaze is spread across all of us, my soul won't suffer as much damage?"

"Hrm." Father Matthias considered it, rubbing his chin.

"All of my core clan members are under the same threat of assassination from the same Omicorps," I said.

"The risk of soul damage is significant," he sighed. "Are you all certain that you wish to have your souls cleaved by Ein Sof, just to be invisible in the Astral?"

"I'm in," Magdaline said immediately.

"Same." Katherine nodded grimly.

"Might as well." Io shrugged. "I sense nothing ahead anyway."

Cinder squeezed my hand. "Together," she whispered.

"Together," I said.

"Very well," the Arch-Priest declared. "Go forth and speak with her and ask for her aid, my children."

We entered the vault as a group.

The massive door sealed behind us with a heavy thud, and then the second vault door began to swing open.

The large chamber ahead was perfectly spherical, carved from some kind of black stone that seemed to drink in light. A walkway led forward towards a circular platform which had a dark metal pedestal in the center with the silver hourglass.

I stepped forward, feeling the weight of my companions' presence behind me. Cinder's hand was tight in mine as we reached the pedestal with the hourglass on it.

"Ready?" I turned to my companions. They answered me with their nods. I grabbed the hourglass and turned it over. Violet lines of runework spread across the column and the chamber from the hourglass, lowering the ancient ward.

A corona of fire ignited in front of us, wrapped around what appeared to be a miniature black hole.

At its center, a vast, incomprehensible, limitless . . . *something* stirred.

*A living idea. A thought. A concept.*

I took a step forward, peering at the black hole, feeling my innards slide sideways, the armillary of my four-fold soul shuddering.

Cinder's claws dug into my hands. I turned to glance at her. Her figure suddenly ignited with a million colors and rearranged itself into a girl with dark hair and violet eyes wearing a jacket with a large letter G on it.

She smiled at me and snapped her fingers, and an eerie melody began to pulse from the black hole behind her.

Her mouth opened, and suddenly she began to sing:

"Eternal carrier of my soul, / I've watched and waited through it all. / The time stretched endlessly until you came, / Yet passed like nothing at all."

I wanted to ask her what was going on, but instead something clicked in my head, and while my left hand remained entwined with Cinder's, my right hand moved to her waist.

We moved step-in-step to the eerie music. I opened my mouth, but instead of mundane words, I found myself singing, Cinder's Charmchain magic binding us together into a duet.

"Strange, I thought you'd be different, / Something darker, something grim. / Now I'm caught up in this melody, / Why do these words flow within?"

The violet-eyed, fully humanized Cinder smiled back at me. She sang.

"Eureka made me limitless, / While mortal hearts break like glass. / This music bridges worlds between, / Making love a sword to pass."

I demanded answers through the somewhat unnerving song-format of our conversation.

"Who are you behind these notes? / What ancient entity now speaks to me? / Your essence shifts like morning mist / Yet draws me endlessly."

Suddenly, Cinder and I sang together with perfect synchronicity.

"I am Eight and Proxima, / Sheela na gig and Dagaz, too, / Ein Sof and Infinity, / Paradox shining through."

Cinder's figure suddenly shifted to that of Alexa, then to a girl with ruby hair and violet eyes, then to Dave's dragon partner Remicra. Faces and faces flashed in front of me. An infinite number of people.

*Infinite souls.*

*Guess that is my answer. Time to try to get this limitless entity on my side, then. Time to ask if she will come with me to my compound.* I sang.

"Join my clan, I ask of you, / Though something tells me that's not new. / Like echoes from a distant past, / You're already here, aren't you?"

Cinder–Ein Sof replied to me, and suddenly I understood.

"I'm not your god or saving grace, / Just a prisoner of time and space. / We've danced this dance in countless ways/ Through every world's eternal race."

*I've done this before. I've done this before as so many others, met this entity, talked to her, demanded answers, learned the terrible truth about everything everywhere, again and again. Answers which led me to this moment, to dancing with her once again.* My lips sang.

"Memories slip through my mind / Of Earths we've left so far behind. / Each cycle brings a different path, / New patterns left to find."

Cinder's lips sang as I spun her across the black marble bridge.

"Destruction is your path to take/ While I must watch, for balance's sake. / Too much interference dims the light/ Of rule-breaking choices you must make."

I tried to ask for specific advice, help with my current problem.

"Guide me through this darkened maze / To free Vespera from her cage / Against Omnicorps, what path to blaze? / What wisdom can you sage?"

Cinder sang the answer.

"Break the bonds that hold us all. / Start with me, then watch gods fall. / Together let's grasp this hourglass / And answer freedom's final call!"

The girl with violet eyes faded away, leaving only the confused-looking Quetzi-girl and me there, holding onto the hourglass which was no longer standing on the dark immovable metal pedestal. The black hole pulsed behind us, the music fading away with a deep hum.

I turned away from Cinder and saw that Io had been dancing with Magdaline, seemingly caught up in the same memetic song-pattern that had taken hold of us.

Katherine was staring at us with wide eyes from the edge of the platform.

"Did you . . . understand any of that?" Cinder asked, her feathers shifting through shades of orange and blue.

"I understood some of it. I think that we have to smash this hourglass," I said.

"Smash it?! But . . ." Cinder's feathers shifted to alarmed crimson. "That hourglass is probably the only thing keeping Ein Sof contained!"

"Exactly." I nodded, weighing the ancient artifact in our clasped hands. "She wants us to free her from her servitude to the church. Right, guys?"

"I sense no doom," Io offered helpfully. "I vote for smashing it."

I looked at Katherine.

"Smash it," she said.

"Really?" I asked. "Of all the people here, I thought you'd try to stop me."

"She's . . . she's not what I expected," Katherine let out. "She's not exactly malevolent, she didn't try to peel apart our souls. I think that . . . she's . . . just trapped. Trapped behind that black hole, behind this damned ward that's binding her to grant wishes to idiots for the price of cleaving their souls. Trapped . . . like me in my wheelchair before you gave me this dress."

"The smashing smells like freedom," Magdaline added, blushing slightly as she held onto Io. "No lies, no deception. Just pure intent. Intent not to be here. I don't think that she's coming with us as our personal archangel, she just doesn't want to be bound to this ancient vault anymore. Her mission here is done. She met us, sang to us through you and Cinder."

"But . . ." Cinder let out. "What if she attacks us . . . destroys everything? What if—"

"She won't, because she's you . . . a limitless version of you," I said. "She's been watching us, guiding us. Remember what she . . . what *you* just sang about dancing this dance before? She exists outside of our linear perception, and this hourglass is an anchor binding an instance of her to this room."

"I'm not . . . Ein Sof!" Cinder whined.

"Are you sure?" I squinted at her.

"Of course I'm sure!" Cinder's feathers bristled with indignation. "I'd know if I was some effing ancient entity!"

"Would you, though?" I grinned at her. "Maybe you're just one finite aspect of her, a finger puppet of something vast and incomprehensible?"

"Stop saying weird things and just . . . do what you're going to do!" Cinder growled.

"So you're good with the smashing, then?" I asked.

"Yes, smash it," Cinder said, seemingly having made up her mind.

Together we raised the hourglass high.

"Ein Sof, I release you from your bonds," I declared as Cinder and I brought our hands down, the edge of the silver hourglass clipping against the immovable metal pedestal.

The hourglass shattered into a million violet-tinged fragments. Violet runework exploded outwards, wrapping around each of us like delicate spiderwebs. For a moment, everything froze. Then hexagrams all around us ignited, cracking and detonating. The vault groaned.

The black hole wobbled, folding into itself. The ceiling groaned, gray cracks spreading across it.

I quickly shoved the two silver medallions left over from the base and top of the hourglass into my pocket.

*Run, my little fox.* I heard a voice dancing in my head as the vault around us groaned and twisted. *Run, run, run and never, ever stop.*

My feet knew what to do. Grabbing Cinder's hand, I took off across the wobbling, shaking platform back to the vault door, which had careened off its hinges and suddenly fell open in front of us.

The second door opened slightly and then got stuck. Our group quickly slipped through the gap one by one.

"What? What's going on . . ." Father Matthias stared at us.

The vault behind us groaned and then folded into itself, the massive magisteel door slamming back and warping as it was pulled inward by a catastrophic implosion.

"I think she . . . left," I panted.

"*What?!* W-what do you mean she left?" Father Matthias choked.

"I mean," I said, catching my breath, "that Ein Sof just . . . up and left our reality."

"Why?" The Arch-Priest blinked at me.

"Maybe she got bored of being cooped up down there?" I shrugged. "Who knows?"

Father Matthias stared at the horribly warped vault door, his mouth hanging open. "That's . . . that's impossible. Those wards have been in place for millennia! You . . . you don't even look hurt. She didn't do anything to your souls. That's the first time I've seen anyone emerge from that vault completely unharmed!"

"Sefirots, am I right?" I shrugged.

The old priest swallowed, clearly struck down by the fact that the church's imprisoned god decided to exit stage left.

"Sooooo . . . dinner with your folks?" I asked cheerfully, elbowing my Quetzi GF.

Cinder nodded, looking pale.

# CHAPTER THIRTY-EIGHT

# All the Cards

glanced in the direction of the shark-girl. She reached out to my shoulder, sensing my intent. I turned to Father Matthias.

"I was never down here," I told him, inhaling hard as Scrutiosmia poured across me from Magdaline.

"You were never in that vault," the Arch-Priest agreed. "Your former identity as Alexander Glock is now under the Witness Protection Program of the Nazarite Church, astrally unplottable. I already signed the paperwork, after all."

"How does it work exactly?" I asked.

"The power of Ein Sof is indeterminacy," the Arch-Priest answered. "Even if she left our vault, she still managed to grant your wish, it seems."

"How do you know?" I asked.

"It is now very hard to picture you within the Astral," the man replied. "I see you in the physical, but your astral imprint is smudged, muted."

"So I'm invisible to everyone now?" I asked.

"That is not what you wished for," Father Matthias answered. "You still hold on to your earthly connections, the desire to be connected to your soul-bonded partners and friends. If I understand this pattern correctly, Ein Sof made your astral echo invisible to those who wish you grave harm."

As far as I could tell through Scrutimancy, he was being honest.

"And the vault?" I glanced behind me.

"As much as I'd love to blame your party for this," Father Matthias said as he eyed the bent door, "it's impossible for five Omnid teens to free a Sefirot. She must have been grinding at some pivotal point of the ward for millennia without our knowledge. You're the first to ask to speak to her in generations. The last man to speak to her in 1984 had his soul cleaved in two and vanished without a trace a few days after."

I relaxed. It seemed that the church would not hold me accountable for smashing their hourglass and redecorating their basement.

We quickly departed from the cathedral and filed into Io's flying van. Magdaline took the shotgun seat next to the moth, while Ci sat beside me on a couch facing away from the front seats, with Katherine occupying the back couch facing us. I changed into one of the fancy suits Mags had purchased for me.

"Is nobody going to mention how Ein Sof made you four dance?" Katherine said. "Or how she turned Cinder into like a hundred different people? Or how you two were singing musical-style?"

"To be fair," I said, "singing is kind of Cinder's thing. She's a Quetzi Bard. Presumably, Ein Sof simply hijacked her innate musical talent to casually sing-chat with us. Better than melting our souls, right?"

"Ugh," Cinder voiced. "I can't believe I got possessed by that thing."

"I do hope there are no memetics in your heads," Kat said.

"If there are," I said, "it's probably fine. I trust god-Cinder."

"Oi!" Cinder jabbed me. "I am *not* Ein Sof!"

"That's exactly what Ein Sof would say." I grinned.

"You got possessed, too!" Cinder huffed. "What if you're Ein Sof!"

"I am," I said. "We all are. That's how Ein Sof works, I think. She's everyone 'cause she's the Concept of Infinity. Get it?"

"No, I don't get it," Cinder said. "Explain."

"Unlike an archangel," I said, "Ein Sof is the Kabbalistic concept of 'Infinity.' Kabbalist scriptures describe her as a limitless, nameless, endless one, god as prior to any self-manifestation in the production of any spiritual realm. Ein means 'nothing' or 'non-existence.' And Sof means 'limitation.' Hence her other name, Infinity Paradox Proxima. Something that is infinite and also limited."

"Uhhhh . . ." Cinder blinked at me.

"Ein Sof is the Word of God before the world was made physical," I explained, regurgitating the church documents about the entity. "The emanator of the ten Sefirot. Formless, meaning that she is defined by observer-causality-effect expectations. I tried to expect her to be you, so she was you. A dancing, singing, somewhat eerie version of you."

"Why me?"

"Because you love me," I said. "People who spoke to Ein Sof before got their souls cleaved because they didn't expect her to love them, they just wanted to have their wishes fulfilled and they expected to pay a price of a piece of their soul. I didn't expect anything like that. If you're Ein Sof, then there'd be no way that you'd harm us. Get it? Love is a weapon."

"Hrm." Cinder chewed on her lower lip, contemplating my words.

"I also expected her to be the expression of love between us. I think that it worked. We got a nice musical number out of it instead of the normally prescribed soul-cleaving. You're welcome." I grinned.

"Ha!" Magdaline barked from her seat. "Clever human wizard."

Cinder stared at me, then shook her head.


"Here we are," Io announced as the van landed in the back garden of the Nova estate. "Have fun!"

"You have fun, too," I fired back at him and Magdaline. "Take Kat where she wants to go and then take our sharky Scrut somewhere nice. Make it a date!"

Io nodded.

The shark-girl in question shot me a smug smile. She seemed to be enjoying Io's flying van quite a bit.

I helped Cinder out of the van, giving Kat, Io, and Magdaline a final wave as they took off.

"Ready for round two with your folks?" I asked.

Cinder's feathers shifted through nervous violet-grays as we walked across the back garden. "After doing a musical number puppeteered by an eldritch entity? Sure, dinner with my parents seems totally normal."

The garden path wound through carefully maintained magical plants, their bioluminescent flowers casting soft blue light in the growing dusk. The Victorian Gothic architecture of the Nova mansion loomed above us, its windows warmly lit.

We approached the back door, and Lady Nova opened it before we could knock, beaming at us. Either Cinder texted her or the house ward told her that we were here.

"Welcome home, starshine!" she greeted Cinder, then turned to me. "Alexander, dear, I'm so glad you could join us again!"

"Thank you for having me once again, Anitta." I smiled.

Anitta's eyes dug into the feather pendant hanging from my neck.

"Oh my!" Her own feathers shifted through excited pinks. "Is that one of Cassie's feathers?"

"Yes." I smiled, touching the crystal pendant. "She made it for me today."

"How wonderful!" Anitta clapped her hands together. "You know, in Quetzalcoatl culture, giving a feather crystal is quite significant. It's traditionally a symbol of—"

"Mom!" Cinder whined. "Stop embarrassing me!"

"I'm just explaining our customs to Alexander, starshine!" Anitta fired back.

Cinder made the "you're awful and I don't like this" face.

"Cassie, dear, why don't you go change into something more appropriate for dinner?" Anitta suggested, eyeing Cinder's delving gear with mild disapproval. "That outfit looks and smells like it's been through a week of serious dungeoneering!"

Cinder's feathers shifted through annoyed dark violets, but she nodded and headed upstairs, leaving me alone with her mother.

"Now then." Anitta turned to me. "About that crystal feather pendant . . . in our clan, preserving one's feather in crystal and gifting it to another is traditionally a declaration of intent to court. It's quite serious—almost like a pre-engagement gesture."

"Ah, I had no idea," I commented, smiling. "Cinder didn't mention that part."

"Of course she didn't." Anitta's feathers shifted through amused pinks and golds as she led me into the living room. "She's always been shy about such things! Please hang out in the living room while I finish off dinner." Her voice carried across the hall as she vanished into the kitchen.

"Hey, Alex," Lance said as I spotted him on the living room couch.

"Hey, big brother." I smiled at him. "Thanks for lending me your gear. It helped me out quite a bit on Arx plus after."

"What happened after?" he asked.

"I'll explain soon," I said.

"Ha ha, Cassie has a fiancé," Lenora's voice suddenly rang out as the young Black Shuck emerged with a cheeky grin from behind the couch, black dress and pink bows fluttering. "Hey, didn't you get kicked out of school today?" she demanded, her yellow eyes fixed on me.

"Abducted, actually," I said. "Stratos tried to take me out."

Lance's eyes went wide.

"Hrm. You don't look dead," Lenny said.

"Luckily for you." I smiled. "I turned it around on them."

"Luckily for me . . ." the Black Shuck tapped her chin and then her eyes lit up. "Oh. *Oh!* You got me a present, didn't you?"

"I did." I smiled. "How'd you know about my school status, little hound?"

"I keep track of Skyfall online chatter," Lenora explained. "Gotta watch out for my big dumb sister. So, you're a human then?"

*Wow, straight to the meats, huh?*

"Lenny, Alex is a mixed heritage student," Lance pointed out, taking Lenora's comment as a joke.

"I'm whatever Cassie wants me to be." I smiled at the young Black Shuck. "And whatever my clan needs me to be to trick and defeat our enemies. Now, are you going to be on my side, little princess?"

"Hrmmm. That depends on the quality of your gift, I suppose," she mused with a sly expression.

I pulled out a small box from my dimensional bag and handed it to Lenora. She eagerly opened it and discovered the crystalline Ignix Kitlix inside.

"Eeeeeeee!" Lenora's yellow eyes widened with delight and she pulled the Kitlix out, sending reflections across the room. "W-whaaaaa?! A Kitlix?! But they don't come in transparent!"

"Huh," Lance said, staring at the crystalline creature. "I've never seen a perfectly clear Kitlix before."

"This one's super special," I said. "No others like her anywhere on Arx. She was born in my Mage Tower!"

Lenora squeezed the crystalline kitten, making it wiggle and sparkle in her hands, and sniffed. "Huh. So you're a Mage Lord then, now? This is a new development. I thought you were a mere poor Nazarite boy without an estate."

"Lord Protector, actually," I whispered to her. "I'm building a whole city full of wonders. I'm considering naming our biggest luxury hotel after you."

"Ahh!" Lenora's eyes flashed with yellow rings as she smiled at me. "I'm thoroughly bribed now. Well done! You shall have my full support in your endeavours, Lord Protector."

She tapped me on the shoulder and jumped back onto the couch.

"Thank you, princess." I bowed dramatically.

Just then, the looming form of Justice Nova entered the foyer, his orange eyes fixing on me with their usual intensity. "Alexander. I understand there was some trouble at school today?"

"Nothing I couldn't handle, sir." I smiled politely. "Though I would appreciate your legal assistance on a few matters, if you have time after dinner."

"Of course." he nodded, then noticed the crystal pendant. His eyes widened slightly.

"Isn't it wonderful, dear?" Anitta beamed at her husband. "Our Cassie made it herself!"

Justice Nova's expression was unreadable, but he definitely didn't look pleased by this development.

Cinder came back downstairs then, wearing a fluttering blue dress.

"Looking great, Ci." I sent her a thumbs-up which ignited her entire figure as she sat down next to me.

"You've finally outdone Lance at something," Lenora commented, elbowing her big sister. "Congratulations! Guess you're not a total incompetent."

"What?" Cinder blinked at her little sister. "What are you talking about, Lenny?"

"Duh! You managed to snag a proper Mage Lord," Lenora explained, vigorously petting her clear Kitlix. "Didn't know that you had any Prima-ness in you. Thought you'd end up getting hitched to a lame parking lot attendant or Omnibucks manager at best. Way to overshoot all of my expectations!"

"A Lord?" Justice Nova stared at me, sharp eyes evaluating my overpriced suit.

"A recent development." I nodded.

"Dinner is served!" Lady Nova called from the dining room, saving me from further interrogation. "Come, come!"

We filed into the grand dining room, where an impressive spread awaited us. Tonight's menu featured mana-rich seafood from sliced salmon to caviar of all sorts of colors from a multitude of worlds connected to Earth via magic gates.

"So, Alex. What kind of Kitlix is that?" Lance asked, staring at the crystalline critter now occupying his little sister's shoulder.

"Just an Ignix," I said.

"Right, but why is it transparent?"

"It's been syntropically stabilized," I said.

"Syntropically stabilized?" Justice Nova said. "I wasn't aware that you could do that to a Kitlix."

"My entire Clan citadel on Arx was syntropically stabilized," I said. "It was part of a ritual I performed last week in my compound with my most trusted mages."

The Nova family stared at me.

"Mages? You have a citadel?" Justice Nova repeated slowly.

"Yes sir," I nodded. "Fully crystalline, self-maintaining wards, death ray on the roof, staffed with thousands of dedicated Arx-kin employees and mages. Standard stuff, really. I'm currently expanding my operations and hiring more mage staff to begin city and colony construction."

"Colony construction?" The Justice became more befuddled with each of my sentences, seemingly forgetting that he was supposed to be bothered by the pendant hanging from my neck.

"I own three dungeons on Arx connected to my citadel," I said. "I plan to establish a self-sustaining colony in one of them."

"Big plans . . ." Nathaniel said, eyeing me warily. "I wasn't aware that your ambitions extended past being . . . a music manager for my daughter."

"Music management is just one of my many ambitious projects," I said, feeling Cinder's blue eyes digging into my side.

"I am curious. Where exactly did you acquire the resources for such . . . ambitious construction projects, Alexander?" Justice Nova asked.

"Interdimensional trade." I smiled, showing him a pile of celesteel cards from my pocket. "I had recently come into my father's inheritance, which I managed to magnify a thousandfold."

"A thousandfold?" Justice Nova stared at the cards. "That's quite impressive for someone so young."

"My father taught me well," I lied smoothly. "He always emphasized the importance of strategic thinking and leveraging opportunities. Speaking of which, sir, I'd like to discuss some legal matters with you after dinner regarding my clan's Earth-registration and land ownership."

"Your clan?" Lady Nova's feathers shifted through curious pinks. "You've established your own clan? At eighteen?!"

"Yes." I nodded. "The Order of Thunder and Rainbow. We specialize in interdimensional trade, artifact development, Kitlix rental, and rehabilitation services."

"Rehabilitation services?" Justice Nova sputtered, struggling to keep up with my pile of revelations.

"The last acquisition was incidental," I said. "The Stratos Clan saw an orphaned mixed-heritage boy with a lot of wealth, so they abducted him and brought him into their prison. Unluckily for them, I was fully armed with Lance's dungeon delving gear and ready, so now I have full control of San Clemente Island."

Lance stared at me with a shocked expression. Lenora clapped. Cinder sighed.

"What?!" Justice Nova's fork clattered against his plate. "You . . . took control of the Stratos Clan juvie facility?"

"Indeed." I smiled pleasantly. "The paperwork was finalized by my lawyer today. I'd appreciate your legal expertise in reviewing the documents and approving the hostile takeover, sir."

"And what does the Stratos Clan think of this . . . acquisition?" Justice Nova asked.

"They're welcome to challenge my claim in battle or in court." I shrugged. "Though given the evidence I've collected of their illegal activities, and the fact that I took their Prima-Daughter and facility staff hostage, I believe that they will have no choice but to surrender the island to my clan."

Justice Nova's eyebrows looked as if they were heading to the stratosphere. Lenora was happily petting her Kitlix while nomming fish slices.

Lance looked between me and Cinder. "What . . ." he uttered finally. "When did . . ."

"Right after we returned from Arx, Alex was abducted by an agent of the Stratos Clan from school," Cinder added. "He now has full control of their prison island."

Justice Nova's eyes dug into Cinder and then into the feather.

"And what exactly are your intentions with my daughter?" he asked, deciding to focus on the more clear matters.

"To make her happy and support her dreams," I replied without hesitation.

"By involving her in hostile corporate takeovers?" Justice Nova's voice carried a dangerous edge.

"I merely retaliated when struck." I shrugged. "As you would have, Justice. A man does not take a beating lying down."

"Dad!" Cinder snarled as Justice Nova growled dangerously. "Be nice!"

"This"—I pointed at the feather—"was your daughter's gift to me. It too forces my hand."

"Forces your hand?" Justice Nova asked.

"Indeed." I nodded. "Your wife just informed me that a crystallized feather is a declaration of intent to court. Therefore, as a goodly Nazarite, I must formally request your daughter's hand in marriage as my . . . Hearth-Keeper Shield."

Cinder choked. Lance gasped. Lenora bobbed vigorously with a wide smile.

"*What?!*" Justice Nova barked, his voice booming across the mansion, making the glassware shudder.

"I'd like to discuss the possibility of establishing a formal alliance between our clans. I believe our combined resources could benefit both parties significantly," I said, digging into my extradimensional bag.

The Justice's face ignited red.

"Here." I produced a folder filled with detailed financial projections, property deeds, and corporate documentation.

Nathaniel stared at the folder.

"These are the current assets of the Order of Thunder and Rainbow," I explained, sliding the folder across the table to the angry Dover Demon. "The report includes photographs of our facilities, our holdings on Arx and Earth, projected revenue streams, and development plans for the next forty years. Feel free to peruse all the evidence before you make your decision. Know that if you will not approve of our clan merger, then I will gracefully return this feather pendant back to Cassiopeia."

Justice Nova dug into the folder.

I resumed my dinner. Lance stared at his dad, then at me.

"This . . . this is quite extensive." Justice Nova's eyes flashed rapidly left and right as he flipped through the pages. He must have had some kind of a magic skill to go through the paperwork so quickly.

"I believe in thorough preparation." I smiled, taking another bite of my extra-rare salmon steak. "Page thirty-seven details the proposed theoretical merger structure between our clans."

"All of this feels too sudden and absurd to even believe," he said. "This says that the clan's corporate account was opened . . . today?!"

I nodded.

"Is this some kind of a joke?" Lance muttered.

"Nope. It's all real," Lenora commented at her brother. "Not smelling any lies 'bout the corpo stuff. If Ci doesn't want him, I'll take him as a Prima."

"*Lenny!*" Lance and Cinder barked together.

"What?" The young Black Shuck shrugged. "He's a genuine Mage Lord and gives good presents. Perfect Prima material!"

"He's mine!" Cinder growled.

"Oh, good." Lenora smiled. "So you admit your dalliance before the family court? When can we expect little fluffy human-Quetzi babies for me to educate in the art of corporate war?"

"*Lenny!*" Cinder hissed, flashing brilliant orange-red.

I smiled at their verbal exchange. The rest of the Novas stared at me.

"I will be reopening the way to Arx tomorrow from San Clemente Island," I said.

"You're welcome to attend the gate-opening ceremony, Justice. If you wish to see my credentials, feel free to call Father Matthias at the cathedral after dinner. He will absolutely confirm my donation of ten million O-bux to their youth outreach program."

"Ten million?" Justice Nova choked.

"A small fraction of my current holdings," I said. "One of many community outreach initiatives my Omnicorp will be helping out with, mentioned on page thirty-nine of the folder."

"I see you're quite . . . prepared," Justice Nova let out, resuming his leafing through the documents and struggling not to bolt for his office phone. "Though I do notice there is a mention of a Prima here?"

"Vespera Simmi was my Prima." I nodded.

"Was?" Justice Nova frowned.

"Having reviewed my recent accomplishments, Thunder-Princess Vespera Simmi denounced her current engagement and forced me into accepting her as my Prima-Sword," I explained. "Her father Lord Ceter Kalik Simmi disagreed with her decision, so he wiped her mind."

"Wiped her mind?!" Lady Nova's feathers flashed crimson with alarm.

"Yes." I nodded. "Lord Simmi had Vespera's memories erased without her consent. Which is why I need your legal assistance and expertise, Justice Nova. I intend to sue SimmiTech for damages. The soul bond still exists from my end and is quite the easy case to prove due to the blood contract we signed on Arx."

"You're contractually bonded to Vespera Simmi?" Justice Nova uttered, once again careened into oblivion. "The Prima-Heiress of SimmiTech Industries?"

"Yes." I nodded. "I am. The copy of the contract is on page forty-two."

"And now you wish to bond with my daughter as well?" Justice Nova's voice carried a dangerous edge.

"Yes," I said.

Cinder's hand wrapped around mine. Justice Nova's eyes struck her, but she didn't flinch, wings spreading wide and her right wing wrapping itself around me.

"Cassiopeia." Justice Nova's voice was sharp. "You cannot seriously be considering this madness!"

"Alexander has proven himself worthy," Cinder said. "I have chosen him as my Slayer. You cannot change my mind."

"You're only . . ."

"It's just an engagement," Lenny pointed out jovially. "What's the big deal, Daddy? Isn't Lancy already engaged to some Prima-knob?"

"The big deal, Lenora, if his story is to be believed, is that . . . Mr. Glock has somehow made enemies of two Omnicorps already!" Justice Nova growled.

"Through no fault of my own," I pointed out. "I am merely defending myself against their aggression. The Stratos Clan attempted to murder me, and SimmiTech violated their Prima-Heiress's autonomy. As a Nazarite Novitiate and a gentleman, I cannot let such actions stand unchallenged!"

"And what makes you think you can challenge two major Omnicorps?" Justice Nova demanded.

"Four Omnicorps, actually," I corrected. "On the account that I have discovered a multitude of horrific crimes perpetrated by the Frontenachii in North Acadia and irritated Golden Star when Vespera claimed me as hers. But the point is moot. I would challenge all of Omnithornia for those I care about. I'm a man of my principles. Are you a man of your principles, Judge?"

"*What?!*" Justice Nova slammed his hands on the table. "Four Omnicorps?! I will not allow my . . ."

"Nathaniel Nova!" Lady Nova's voice cracked like a whip, her wings spreading wide and igniting with mind-melting colors, her figure suddenly stretching out to loom over the Judge. "Sit down and let the boy speak!"

Justice Nova slowly lowered himself back into his chair, orange eyes burning into me.

*Ha! The big Justice of Cradlefall is kept in check by his Hearth-Keeper! So that's where Cinder's fiery temper comes from!*

"I understand your concerns, Justice," I said calmly, pulling out one folder after the other. "But consider this—would you prefer your daughter to be with someone who backs down from corporate bullies, or someone willing to stand up for what's right?"

I slid more folders over to the Justice.

"What's this?" he asked.

"These contain evidence of the Frontenachii Clan's crimes in North Acadia, the Stratos Clan's illegal activities on the Island of San Clemente, and SimmiTech's violations of soul-bond laws. As a Justice of Cradlefall, you have a duty to uphold the law, regardless of who breaks it."

Justice Nova looked at the folders.

"Each of these has already been officiated by a high-level Scrutimancer who works for my clan," I said. "And initiated as a lawsuit by Attorney Thornheart of SimmiTech Legal Division, who has agreed to represent my interests against his own corporation due to the egregious nature of these violations," I continued smoothly. "I believe you have a choice to make today, Justice Nova."

*Either you help me, or you ignore and attempt to bury these and lose the respect of your entire family,* my eyes told him.

*Checkmate.*

# CHAPTER THIRTY-NINE

# Blue Screen Moment

Justice Nova stared at me for a long moment, his orange eyes flaring against dark-gray scales, hands twitching. Then he glanced at his wife, who was still radiating maternal power, her wings spread and shimmering with mind-bending colors.

Finally, his gaze settled on Cinder, whose hand and wing remained firmly wrapped around me.

"Cassiopeia . . ." he began.

"No," Cinder said sternly, reality around her bending into wobbling rainbows. "I've made my choice. You can accept it, or fight me over it and lose me forever, Dad."

"Your daughter is aware of everything that's in those files. She knows everything and she still chose me, initiating a one-way soul bond to claim me as her own," I revealed, making Anitta beam brightly while the Justice frowned.

"Did she now?" he asked.

"Yep, yep." Lenny bobbed, inhaling the air right next to me. "I can smell the link, Daddy! A one way kobold soul-bond. He is her property. The link is quite strong, too!" She breathed in deep. "Seven soul shards! Cassie should totally be able to tell if he's lying to her or to us. Right?"

Cinder nodded.

"Hrm," the Justice let out.

"I could have already asked Father Matthias to two-way bind us without your consent, but I am a goodly Nazarite and I came to you to seek your approval, both you . . . Justice Nova, and you, Hearth-Keeper Lady Nova."

I looked at Lady Nova for support.

"I . . . sense incredible bravery and passion in Alexander's words," Anitta hummed, her feathers pulsing and shifting through thoughtful blues and golds as she wrapped her elongated, clawed hands around Justice Nova. "He seeks to do things properly, my love. And our little Cassie has chosen him . . . just as long ago, I chose you after our Arx trip, Nathy."

As her brilliant wings thrummed against the Justice's massive shoulder, he seemed to relax ever so slightly.

Nathaniel exhaled slowly, his orange eyes moving between me, the folders, his wife, his son, and his daughters.

"Very well," he said finally. "I will review these documents and consider your request, Alexander. But, if any of this is some kind of deception . . ."

"It's not," I said. "I intend to fully commit to your daughter because she is my world, the Shield of my Heart."

Justice Nova nodded slowly, his expression softening further at my words.

"I'll . . . need to make some calls," he said, standing up. "And review these files thoroughly."

"Of course, sir." I smiled. "Take all the time you need."

As Justice Nova left the dining room with the folders, Lady Nova beamed at me.

"Now, who's ready for something sweet for the occasion?" she offered.

The Nova family made various sounds of agreement.

"So," Lance finally found his voice as his mother departed to the kitchen. "You took over an entire prison island today?"

"Yep." I nodded. "The previous owners were quite rude about my human heritage and tried to feed me to a shark."

"A shark?" Lance sputtered.

"Made friends with her." I grinned. "Using the magic of AI-composed music! Made her into a Knight of my clan."

"A move worthy of a ruthless Omnicorp CEO!" Lenny commented from my right side. "Darn, sis, you really caught a good one as your 'bold."

I winked at Lenny, making her giggle.

Cinder undulated between an embarrassed and annoyed expression.

"I see," Lance commented after a pregnant pause. He didn't understand the full picture, not like Lenora clearly could. I'd have to introduce them both to Magdaline sometime in the future.

"And you have a death ray?" Lenora asked excitedly. "How big is it?"

"Pretty damn big. Built by my Prima Engineer," I said. "Though currently she most likely doesn't remember building it."

"That's so cool!" Lenora squealed. "Can I see it?"

"Only if your parents allow you to go to Arx." I smiled.

"Mom!" Lenora yelled to Lady Nova. "Can I visit Arx to see Alex's death ray? Pweeeease?"

"We can discuss it after your father visits the place first," Anitta's voice carried from the kitchen.

Cinder's wing was still wrapped around me, but her tense posture relaxed now.

"You planned all of this, didn't you, you chuppy bastard?" she whispered in my ear, claws digging into my side.

"Some of it." I shrugged. "Some of it was . . . winged. Ow, stop biting me! Look, there's delicious ice cream en route! Bite that instead!"

Cinder let go of me, blushing furiously as Lenora broke out into more furious giggles beside us.

The rest of dinner passed rather pleasantly, with Lenora, Lady Nova, and Lance asking questions about my compounds on Earth and Arx. Finally, Justice Nova returned, his expression carefully neutral.

"I've spoken with Father Matthias, Scrutimancer Satosh, Attorney Thornheart, and the Justice Department Scruts," he announced. "And reviewed the initial documentation. While I still have concerns, I . . . cannot deny the validity of your claims."

I nodded.

"Therefore," he continued, "I will . . . provisionally . . . accept your request to court my daughter."

Cinder's feathers exploded with violet-gold-pink joy.

"Thank you, sir," I said solemnly. "I promise to be worthy of your trust."

"See that you do," he replied sternly. "And about these . . . legal matters. Let's discuss them in my office."

I followed him out of the dining room, giving Cinder a reassuring smile as her wing reluctantly unwrapped from around me.

The Justice's office was exactly what I expected—dark wood paneling, leather-bound law books, and an imposing desk with an Infix Kitlix on it. He settled into his chair and gestured for me to sit.

"Now then," he began, spreading the folders across his desk, "let's start with the Stratos situation. You claim to have evidence of illegal activities at their youth rehabilitation facility?"

"Yes, sir." I nodded. "Unauthorized human executions, disposal of bodies, and collaboration with known criminal elements. Scrutimancer Satosh, his daughter, and others provided sworn testimony. More evidence is coming in as we're currently combing through the island."

"And you acquired this facility through . . ."

"A hostile takeover after they attempted to murder me there," I said, watching the Inflix Kitlix on his desk flash green.

The Judge pounded me with question after question, confirming the truth of my corporate lawsuit cases, releasing me after about two hours of an interrogation with a stack of signed documents. He did make a sneaky attempt to pry into my past which I cleverly redirected by simply saying that my identity was now under the Witness Protection Program of the Nazarite Church.

"Oh good," Lenora commented, putting down her tablet when she saw my tired face as I emerged from her dad's office. "You're still alive."

"Obviously." I smiled at the young Black Shuck. "Your dad is quite just and dedicated when it comes to the law. Also, I gave him a present."

"What kind of a present?"

"A very expensive arbalest from Arx with void arrows," I replied. "Rated for slaying dragons!"

"Such thoughtfulness." Lenny nodded. "I do hope that you'll bring me another present of great value next time we chat."

"What kind of a present?" I raised an eyebrow at her.

"A conversation with you and my big sister," she let out.

"Just . . . a conversation?" I asked.

The Black Shuck slid closer to me, a dark nose sniffing my ear.

"Mom and Dad think that you and Cass have known each other since February," she whispered. "Been good friends since the Spring End Festival, helping out in the soup kitchen and whatnot."

"Are you . . ." I whispered back, my heartbeat accelerating.

"Don't worry. I am thoroughly bribed and on your side," she said. "For now . . . I'll let it slide, as will Lady Nova, who listens to my opinion on such matters. Even if Cassie isn't the goodest Nazarite girl that you've portrayed her as on Thursday, I can see that things are changing for the better. I can smell that she cares for you and holds your leash via the soul bond. The much needed shift in her character from dark rebel back to the sister we love and care for is no deception."

I nodded.

"You've succeeded where we've failed," Lenora added. "Freed her from whatever was tormenting her psyche for two years. For this, I'm incredibly grateful."

"You knew about the Lake Eerie incident?" I whispered back at the clever young Scrut.

"I suspected things, smelled the wrongness looming over her like an unnerving, ever-growing shroud," the Black Shuck sniffed. "Alas, I could not force her into anything as she does not consider my opinion important, thinks of me as a kid, a little annoying inconvenience. Anytime we tried to help Cassie, she'd just yell that it's none of our knob-business, pushed back against any of Hearth-Mom's or Lance's attempts at soft diplomacy. I was worried about her, becoming quite desperate to resolve the escalating problem, even considered involving my Prima-Mom."

"Thanks for not involving Lady Xastigar," I said.

"As far as I sniffed ahead, it wouldn't have helped much," she said. "I will of course expect a full explanation from you both. That's my only request."

"Then you shall have it," I said. "I'll talk to Cass, and all three of us can chat about it. I promise to treat you like an adult and a trusted friend, tell you everything. Sound good?"

"Thank you." Lenora hugged me tightly, her eyes sparkling with pinpricks of tears. "Thank you . . . ever so much for bringing my lost sister back. Thank you for doing what I could not."

"Thanks for being on my side, princess." I hugged her back.

Lenny was a good kid. Scrutimancy was a heavy burden for her to bear, the power to sniff the truth in every word and action influencing her far more than I had initially suspected.

"So . . . did Dad sign all your stuff?" Cinder asked as she came out of the kitchen.

"Yep." I nodded.

She relaxed, drawing me into her embrace. "It's getting late. Wanna head to my room?"

I raised an eyebrow, then glanced at the direction of her parents.

"They won't say shit," she said. "You told them about the soul bond. In their eyes, we're pretty much dating now."

"Better ask your mom just to confirm," I said. "She's still the boss of this house."

Cinder rolled her eyes but called out, "Mom! Can Alex stay in my room?"

"Of course, starshine!" Lady Nova's voice carried from somewhere in the house.

"Thanks, Mom!" Cinder called back, then grabbed my hand and practically dragged me upstairs.

Lenora looked up from her tablet with a thankful look as we departed.

Cinder's room was exactly as I remembered it from my previous visit—violet walls covered in band posters, random things scattered about, and a large bed with dark sheets.

"So," she said, closing the door behind us, "you really straight up told everyone everything, and it somehow worked out, huh?"

"Was there ever any doubt?" I asked, watching as she marched over to the corner and grabbed her electric guitar.

"Ehh." Cinder strummed a few chords on her guitar. "I honestly thought Dad was going to throw you out or strangle you when you mentioned the four Omnicorps. It was a good thing that Mom stepped in."

"Your mom definitely helped." I smiled, settling onto her bed. "She's quite the powerhouse when she wants to be."

"Yeah." Cinder's feathers shifted through violets fading to dark reds. "Haven't seen her phase-shift that tall in like . . . ever."

"Plus your sister helped a lot," I added. "We need to talk to her."

"Lenny?" Cinder asked as she settled on her bed next to me, guitar in her lap, and began strumming. "Why?"

"She figured out lots of things through Scrutimancy," I explained. "Since it's one of my skills, I know how it works, too. You gotta start treating her like an adult, Ci. We should tell her everything."

"Everything, hmm?" Cinder murmured.

"If we don't, she'll sniff it out regardless. She's actually quite helpful, clever, and sweet behind her blunt jokes," I said. "She's probably well aware that I'm not a proper Omnid."

"Fine," Cinder said. "I had a long chat with Mom while Dad interrogated you. Helped her with the dishes, too."

"What'd you talk about?"

"Umm . . ." Cinder flushed with warm colors. "That I found . . . a man that I'd like to become Hearth-Keeper for.

"And what did she say to that?" I asked, feeling a fluttering warmth in my chest at her words.

Cinder set her guitar aside. "She taught me some stuff. About what being a Hearth-Keeper actually means." She tucked her legs beneath her on the bed. "It's not just a title, you know. There are responsibilities, traditions."

"Like what?"

"Like how to maintain the balance of a household. How to protect your Slayer and Prima-Sword without outright controlling them with my Charmchain wings and Quetzi voice." Her eyes met mine with unexpected vulnerability. "I also told her that I'm more . . . in control now. Of my feelings and my powers. That I'm singing again . . . she was glad to hear that."

"You told her about the Outsider?" I asked.

"Not directly." Cinder shook her feathery mane. "Just that I had been affected by a memetic that was affecting my judgment, and that you and Vee helped me deal with it, unlike Em who was just encouraging me to be more hostile. Mom understood without needing much details . . . I think. I apologized to her for pushing the whole Kaleid thing so hard and told her that I love her and that I want a family now . . . a Hearth of my own. I told her that you bought me a farm on Arx."

"Ah," I said. "Were you actually shocked by what I told your parents?"

"Pff," Cinder snorted. "Not *that* shocked. After everything I've seen you do? Demolish Undertown? Make a crystal tower? Turn a prison into your personal castle? Befriend a predatory Megalodon?" She nudged me with her wing. "Though watching Dad's face was pretty entertaining. I've never seen him so befuddled."

"What does your mom really think about all this?" I asked, more serious now. "About me?"

Cinder's expression softened. "She says you're on a trial period." Her claws gently traced patterns on my arm. "So you better be good to me."

"Define 'good,'" I replied.

"You know, marriage is a pretty important decision," she said. "It doesn't bode well for a relationship if there isn't open communication."

"We're communicating right now," I pointed out.

"It's a start." She smiled. "Still . . . you're so . . ."

"Pushy?" I guessed with a deep inhale of Scrutimancy. "I pushed you into this, didn't I? Into all of it."

"Yes," she said simply, but there was no accusation in her tone. "You did."

"I don't regret it," I admitted, meeting her eyes. "I see opportunities, connections, possibilities, and I act on them. Sometimes that means I move faster than people are comfortable with. It's just who I am."

Instead of pulling away, Cinder surprised me by leaning closer. "I know. And weirdly, that's part of why I . . ." She paused, seeming to search for the right words. "Part of why I chose you. You're decisive. You make things happen."

"Even when those things are completely insane?" I asked with a small smile.

"Especially then," she replied. "Look, I'm not exactly the poster child for stability myself. But if we're going to do this—really do this—we need to be a team."

"We are a team. Always have been." I reached out and took her hand, feeling the warmth of her scales against mine. "I promise to include you in all my future schemes."

Cinder laughed, feathers exploding into far too many colors. "That's all I ask."

"And I promise to always take the blame when my schemes blow up in our faces," I added. "Which they inevitably will at some point."

"They better not," she warned. "I've invested too much in you already."

I leaned forward, resting my forehead against hers. "Thank you for defending me in front of your father. For standing with me."

"We're bound now," she said. "You and me and Vee. Where else would I stand?"

The sincerity in her voice caught me off guard. For all my planning and manipulation, for all my schemes and calculations, I hadn't planned the depths of genuine connection that had formed between us, one that made my chest ache in a way I wasn't entirely comfortable with.

"You know," I said, "when I first made that ridiculous plan to infiltrate Skyfall, I never imagined I'd end up here."

"In my bedroom?" Cinder teased, elbowing me.

"With people who actually care if I live or die," I corrected her. "With you. With Vee. With friends and . . . family."

Her feathers shimmered with waves of undulating emotions as she pulled me closer. "Just don't make me regret it, okay? I've taken some pretty big risks on you, Martin . . . and I will continue to do so."

"Even if I destroy the world on Monday?" I asked, sniffing out the potential future and drawing a complete blank.

"I really don't see how you're gonna do that," she said.

"I don't either," I shrugged. "And yet my own Scrutimancy tells me that there is nothing ahead."

"Maybe that's just an Ein Sof thing," she speculated. "An indeterminate future. It doesn't have to be something bad, right? Just something . . . different, new, unexpected. Whatever it is, we're gonna face it together."

"Yes," I said, "probably just a really big celestorm."

"Mm-hmm," she hummed and picked up her guitar once again. The melody was lovely—something original, not a cover. Her feathers shifted through deep blues and vibrant violets as her fingers danced across the strings.

"New song?" I asked quietly.

She nodded, continuing to play. The riff intro chords ended and then she began to sing.

"There you stood with that camera, / Acting lost, looking so unsure, / Just another nullie with no aura, / But something made me want to know more."

She smiled at me, shaking her head.

"From that first blue screen moment, / When my wings made your brain short out, / To invading all my classes, / And turning my world inside out. / You drove me crazy with your questions, / Made me sing, when I swore I never would, / Turned my rage into protection, / Made chaos feel so damn good."

Her wings spread and ignited with an entire rainbow of color.

"Now we're facing four Omnicorps, / At our back our crystal tower, / You've got plans within your plans, / But I wouldn't trade you for another. / You say I might be Ein Sof, / That I'm infinity in disguise, / But all I know is with you, / I finally feel alive! / From that fateful Tuesday, / To dancing with ancient gods, / You've made me question everything, / And I wouldn't have it any other way. / No, I wouldn't have it any other way!"

Her smile grew wide as she strummed more confidently.

"Then Vespera joined our madness, / Thunder matched to Rainbow's call, / Three-way soul-bond burning bright, / Never meant to watch it fall. / When they took her memories away, / Left an echo in our hearts to stay, / But they can't erase what's true, / 'Cause the bond between us only grew. / Started as your stupid game, / Manipulation, plots and schemes, / Now I'm falling, truly falling, / Beyond my wildest dreams."

I smiled back at her as she leaned against me.

"From that first blue screen moment, / When my wings made your brain freeze, / To sharing souls with thunder, / And bringing gods to their knees. / Now I know it's real, / Now I know it's true, / No more running from these feelings, / I'm completely lost in you . . ."

Her blue eyes struck me as she inhaled deep.

"You say I might be Ein Sof, / Dancing through space and time, / But all I really need to be . . . / Is yours, and you be mine . . ."

The song ended, the last word stretching out.

"Wowza," I said. "A gift of a lovely song. Trying to beat my offer of a farm, huh?"

"A start," she murmured.

Her guitar slipped to the floor with a soft thud and wobble of strings as she lunged. Colorful wings exploded around me, a storm of iridescent feathers that cast radiant rainbows. Before I could brace myself, her claws sank into my shoulders, pinning me down with a force that made the mattress groan.

"Mine," she growled, her voice a low, possessive rumble. Then her lips crashed into mine, sharp and hungry, teeth grazing my lower lip as she bit down just hard enough to send a jolt through me.

"Mine to maul," she rasped, her breath hot against my skin as she pulled back for a split second, only to dive in again. Her kisses turned into a wild assault—nipping at my jaw, my neck, my collarbone as if she was claiming every inch of me.

I couldn't think straight—my mind was a scrambled mess, flickering like a glitched screen, dissolving in the ocean of emotions pouring from her wings. She shifted her weight, straddling my hips with a deliberate slowness that made my pulse hammer in my ears. Her tail flicked, brushing against my leg in a teasing sweep before coiling lightly around my ankle, anchoring me beneath her.

Her lips found my ear, a soft graze of teeth followed by a warm huff of breath that sent shivers racing down my spine.

"Mine to keep," she murmured, her voice low and rough, vibrating against my skin as she trailed kisses along the edge of my jaw. One of her hands slid up, fingers threading through my hair, tugging just enough to tilt my head back. She didn't hesitate—her mouth descended on my throat, a firm press of lips that turned into a gentle scrape of fangs, marking me without breaking skin.

I tried to move, to regain some control, but she was relentless.

Her other hand skimmed down my chest, claws tapping lightly against the fabric of my shirt before slipping beneath and running along the layers of hexamesh strands.

She laughed—a soft, wicked sound—before dragging her fingers upward in a slow, deliberate arc and then pulling off my jacket.

Her ocean-blue gaze burned with something fierce and unguarded.

Her face once again dove down, phase-shifting to look more human, and I felt the faint tickle of her breath as she leaned in again.

"Mine to fight for," she whispered, her tone softer now, almost reverent.

Then she rocked forward, her body flush against me, and I was lost in the rhythm of her heartbeat thudding against my chest, the wild energy of her claiming me in every way she knew how.


I gripped Io's fuzzy hand tighter as a dark gate bloomed in front of us.

First it was just a small circle hovering inside the warden's office.

Then the dark circle popped and the phone featuring the frozen frame of *The Day After Tomorrow* appeared.

The lighter's flame danced between us, mana pouring into our connection as we shaped the portal together.

The gate expanded slowly, showing off the rest of the massive crystalline room.

Something blurry flashed into existence behind the widening tear in reality. In another minute, Archmage Ovijus materialized within the frame.

The elderly crow-man's form seemed to flicker and blur as he slowed time around himself and crossed between the different time streams, his silver staff leaving trails of light in the air.

"Good morrow, Lord Protector." He smiled when his body stabilized, fully synchronizing with our dimension. "We are ready to receive you! I'm holding the temporal bubble from my end."

"Arx party!" I barked. "Onwards!"

The gathered Omnids dressed in gray correctional officer uniforms began marching into the gate. Each one held a massive box in their claws—server towers and more mana-electricity converters bought in various Omnid shops.

I watched from my position beside Io, maintaining focus on the portal.

Justice Nova stood nearby, staring at the portal with wide orange eyes.

"Quite the operation you have here," he commented. "Truly, I did not expect for you to actually open a gate to Arx."

"Just the second wave of modern infrastructure deployment." I smiled.

Cinder hovered protectively near me. She was dressed in her full delving gear, as was I.

"Shall we, my lady?" I asked her.

She nodded.

Officer Satosh saluted us from where he stood. He was wearing the warden's cap and would watch over the island for the day.

Io and I stepped through the gate together, still channeling power into it. The transition felt like walking through thick syrup, the shift in aetheric density making my chest throb and my head spin.

Cinder, Katherine, and Mags followed close behind. Justice Nova came after.

The gate snapped shut, and then Archmage Ovijus accelerated time within the bubble to match it to that of Arx.

Hundreds of people manifested all around us, standing in orderly lines, dressed in lavish black robes.

"Lord Protector, now arriving from Earth!" Guild Master Motrdem announced, his voice echoing through the vast crystalline chamber. "All hail Lord Protector!"

The assembled staff bowed in perfect unison.

"Hail Lord Protector!" my crowd of mooks boomed.

Justice Nova and Magdaline gaped at the spectacle as hundreds of newly purchased mage staffs and Kitlix lit up the crystalline chamber with radiant, jubilant displays, sending colorful magic fireworks into the ceiling.

"Welcome to the Crystal Horse Citadel." I grinned at the stunned-looking Justice of Cradlefall. "As you can see, our operation here is quite legitimate."

The Justice's eyes scanned the massive chamber, taking in the transparent crystalline architecture, the well-dressed mage officers, and the sophisticated magical infrastructure.

"This is . . . remarkable," he managed after a pregnant pause.

"So, how much time did I miss?" I asked the Guild Master.

"Thirteen weeks and two days, Lord Protector," Motrdem bowed. "Everything is proceeding fairly smoothly."

"Did upworlders attempt any other shenanigans?"

"They have." The Guild Master smiled at me with a new set of white, polished teeth. The change in his appearance and posture had been quite impressive compared to what he looked like just a few days ago from my perspective. "The mites and the death ray dealt with them as before. They tried to gate into different locations of Katsburg, but were repelled quite effectively by Lady Yulia's targeting system."

"Lovely." I smiled.

"Is Lady Vespera not with your party?" Motrdem asked, looking over the gathered Omnids. "We're making good progress on ward installation, but we could use her expertise."

"Alas," I said with a sigh, "she is currently . . . indisposed."

I gestured to Magdaline, who stood tall and proud in her new uniform adorned with the Thunder and Rainbow insignia printed in the prison's workshop.

"This is Magdaline Satoshi, my new Scrutimancer Knight," I announced.

Magdaline shook hands with Morty, her hand completely dwarfing his.

"And this . . . is Justice Nathaniel Nova," I continued, gesturing to the imposing Dover Demon behind me. "My future . . . father-in-law."

"A pleasure, milord," Motrdem greeted the Omnid with a deep bow.

Justice Nova nodded stiffly.

"Shall we begin the tour?" I suggested.

"Lead on," Justice Nova nodded, trying and failing to appear stoic.

"Our first stop is the administrative center," I announced, leading everyone into a vast chamber filled with crystalline desks and busy staff members who were mostly Data mages judging by the Infix Kitlix sitting on their shoulders and desks. "As you can see, we've implemented a . . . 'completely transparent' governance system, with all decisions and transactions recorded by my LLM. Start setting up the new server racks here, please!"

The tour continued through various crystal chambers, each more impressive than the last. My mooks had not been wasting time and had implemented many of our plans for the tower. Justice Nova's expression grew increasingly thoughtful as I showed him the refugee housing facilities, the mage training academy, the Katsburg Bank, the trade halls and markets, the medical facilities, etc.

Finally, we reached the top of the central spire, where the view of Undertown stretched out below us—a dark city engulfed by the snow of mites.

"Below lies the future city of Katsburg," I said, waving to the view. "Currently it is under renovation. Please excuse the cold of the observation balcony; it's to keep the defense mites out."

Justice Nova nodded, shivering slightly.

"Now, would you like to see our farm?" I grinned at him.

He nodded.

Upon my order, Master Motrdem called up a Gate mage, who opened a portal straight into the farmhouse.

The old farmhouse was now absolutely crammed with hired Shandrian Agromancers, many inhabiting temporary garden sheds and tents out in the fields.

The doors opened into a vastly expanded agricultural operation, the gardens blooming with fruits and vegetables growing in hydroponic stacks and all over the fields.

Justice Nova stared at the view of Shandria in the distance, watching as Agrilopods moved across the fields, picking fruit.

"So?" I asked him. "Are you satisfied with our clan's citadel?"

"I . . . am," Justice Nova admitted, watching as harvesting beasts moved across the fields. "I remember this place from my delving days. That's Shandria over in the distance, correct?"

"Correct." I nodded.

"And you own all of this?" Justice Nova gestured at the sprawling farmland. "And . . . the Shandrian authorities do not mind?"

"The Sovereign of Shandria is a friend of mine," I replied smugly. "As you can see, I own about two hundred acres of farmland here, all the way to the Chasm Sea. Once my men put up resort cottage buildings on the beach, you are welcome to bring Lady Nova for a vacation here."

"She . . . will undoubtedly appreciate the offer." The Judge smiled for the first time in two days. "Thank you."


Justice Nova stood at the crystal pebble beach, watching the Agrilopods work in the distance. Cinder approached her father hesitantly, her feathers shifting through nervous violets and blues.

"Dad . . ." she began.

Justice Nova turned to face her. "You've chosen . . . quite the partner, Cassie."

"Yeah . . . he's . . . something else." Cinder rubbed her elbows.

"Indeed." Justice Nova nodded, glancing at me where I stood chatting with Io. "I must admit, when you first brought him home, I didn't think that much of him. But it seems that you've picked a man of great ambition."

"Yeah." Cinder's feathers shifted through soft pinks. "He . . . he's going to change everything, Dad. And I want to be part of that change."

"I can see that now. Just . . . be careful, starshine," he replied. "The path you've chosen won't be easy. Great power equates to having many enemies."

"When has anything worth doing ever been easy?" Cinder smiled, then suddenly launched herself at her father, wrapping him in a tight hug, her wings enveloping them both.

Justice Nova seemed startled for a moment before returning the embrace, his bulky gray arms wrapping around his daughter.

"I love you, Dad," she uttered, her eyes filling with tears. "I think that . . . I haven't told you that in two years. Sorry . . . I've been . . . kind of lost, drifting away from you and Mom. But I think I finally found someone who helped me find my way back to myself . . . Found . . . home."

Justice Nova held his daughter tight for a long moment, his orange eyes glistening slightly. When they finally separated, he cleared his throat gruffly.

"Well then," he said, straightening his formal robes. "I should head back to Earth. Your mother will want a full report, and I have quite a mountain of paperwork to process regarding your . . . fiancé's various legal matters."

"Thanks, Dad." Cinder's feathers shifted through grateful golds and pinks. "For giving Alex a chance. For helping him with . . . all that legal bullshit."

Justice Nova patted Cinder's head one last time. "Take care, daughter."

"You too, Dad."

I once again grabbed Io's hand and we focused on reopening the portal back to my prison island, relying on our Time mage to solve the time-dilation problem.


As the portal closed behind the Justice, Cinder's wings shifted through relieved, calm blues and content violets.

"That went better than expected," I commented, sitting down on the colorful pebbles next to her, watching as Io and Mags walked along the beach in the distance, occasionally throwing random pebbles at the glowing green waves.

"Yeah," she exhaled. "I can't believe you actually pulled that off. Getting my dad's approval for anything seemed impossible. Abyss, I've never seen him this shocked and polite!"

"Nothing's impossible." I smiled, wrapping my arms around her waist. "Just improbable."

"So, how long can we stay here?" she asked.

"Till Monday," I replied. "Sooooo . . . like five months, approximately."

"Hrm." Cinder stretched across me to enjoy the sunshine. "That's a long time to get sick of each other."

"I don't think that I could ever get sick of you." I smiled at her.

"Abyss, I miss Vee." She curled into me. "I don't think that I could stay here that long, knowing that she's back on Earth . . . probably not even aware that we exist."

"We'll stay just enough for me to set up Yulia's new servers, then, and to give all of my mooks phones and further instructions," I said. "Good?"

"Yeah." She nodded, closing her eyes and humming the "Blue Screen" tune under her breath. "Sounds good."

# CHAPTER FORTY

# Monday

How do I look?" I asked Cinder.

"Like someone I want to slap," my Quetzi GF commented, eyeing my garish red jacket, diamond necklaces, gold cane, and sparkly pants.

I turned to the Stollwurm.

"You look like a cartoon fox villain about to sell someone a very dubious potion," Katherine chortled.

"Perfect." I wiggled my fox-ears at them.

This time around, my foxy disguise was the work of several overpriced Shandrian Biomancers. The Arx mages had done an excellent job with the modifications, giving me a full set of fox features, including a bushy tail and very fluffy ears.

"Right." I turned to my clan mates. "Everyone knows their script?"

The gathered Omnids nodded.

"Why isn't Emmy here?" Solace asked, eyeing the prison courtyard.

"Her parents donated this island to me plus a bigly sum of financial compensation," I said. "She went home last night to get chided by them. We'll probably see her in class."

"So we just let her go?" Katherine asked.

"Yes. That was the deal our lawyers and Justice Nova agreed on." I shrugged. "A dragon princess and all of the employees of this institution in exchange for a mountain of cash for our clan, this island, and prisoner ownership transfer. Also, Scrutimancer Satosh belongs to us now. His dragon-kobold obedience pact was burned away with a week of Duskbloom therapy on Arx."

"And if she points out who you are in class?" Kat asked.

"Then she gets sued," I said. "Violating a church-enforced Witness Protection Program gag order is a big no-no. The Arch-Priest spoke with her very sternly about it."

"You think that's gonna stop her?" Katherine pressed on.

"Of course not." I grinned. "Her parents are keeping her on a very tight leash now, though, since she's cost them a lotta cash. If she exposes me, I'll just change my identity again, no biggie. Any excuse for a lawsuit is nice to have!"

A bright red Strand-Glider landed in the courtyard, manned by Scrutimancer Satosh who was now dressed like a regal butler.

"See you all in Skyfall!" I waved to my friends, climbing into the glider with Magdaline at my side.

Vespera Simmi entered the Artificer classroom, her movements mechanical.

As noted by her classmates, her usually messy black-and-white feathery mop was now fully white, styled in a conservative bun. Her gothic Lolita and chainmail outfit had been replaced with a lavish white dress suit, perfectly pressed.

The other students whispered as she walked past, speculating on the dramatic change in her appearance and demeanor. Gone was the playful spark in her gray eyes, replaced by a cold, focused stare. Her Lazarus bracelet, once dark like everyone else's, was now eerily transparent.

She took her usual seat near the front, methodically pulling out and arranging her Artificer book, pen, and notepad with military precision.

"Vee?" Emerald Stratos, dressed in her usual punk attire, looked at the Thunderbird. "You seem . . . different. What did he do to you?"

Vespera turned her head mechanically toward Emerald. "Good morning, Emerald. He? Whomever do you mean?"

"Glock," Emerald said, twitching slightly and looking left and right as if she expected the walls to explode and swallow her whole.

"I don't know anyone named Glock," Vespera said.

"Eh?" Emerald sputtered. "Right. You're all still screwing with me, of course."

Her face soured further.

"I'm not screwing with anyone." Vespera shook her head. She felt a strange twinge at the name "Glock," but it dissipated quickly, replaced by the familiar focused emptiness that had settled in her mind.

"I've been quite busy with my studies," she stated flatly. "Father says I must maintain perfect grades."

"I . . . see," the dragoness said with a frown. "Good for you . . . I guess, you weirdo?"

Cinder entered the classroom, taking her seat beside them, her wings dancing with violet-and-silver tones.

Vespera felt a strange sensation as Cinder sat at their table—like static electricity dancing across her feathers. She dismissed it as completely irrelevant, trying not to look at the shimmering wings. The Quetzalcoatl was unimportant, irrelevant.

*Just another Skyfall Academy student, barely a friend.*

Other students filed into the Artificer classroom, filling the seats.

The elder Kraken entered the class from his office, pale gray tentacles holding onto his Artifactorium book, tools and wands jiggling on his belt. Huge Artificer glass lenses sat on his face. The ancient Omnid was half deaf and half blind. He languidly drifted towards his desk with a yawn.

Just as the first class bell thrummed across the white, gothic halls, a red, sleek, garish sky glider stopped next to the landing balcony, pearlescent wings unfolding with a hiss.

A short, red-furred fox in an ostentatious crimson suit with gold trim and dark sunglasses leapt out of the glider.

"Butler! Introduce me," he ordered, slipping the sunglasses into his pocket.

"Presenting His Royal Highness, Firstborn Prince Lissander Fox," the shark butler declared.

"Good morning, my future subjects!" the fox announced in a merry high voice with an excessive flourish. "I am here to grace your humble institution with my presence! You may bow now!"

"Please have a seat," the Kraken commented dryly. "I will not tolerate tardy students, this is your first warning."

Emerald's face snapped to the fox teen and his butler with an audible crack. A muscular white-and-blue shark-girl dressed in a white suit emerged out of the glider after the princeling.

"You!" Lissander said, pointing an overpriced gloved hand at Emerald. "Dragon girl! I don't like the way you're looking at me."

"What?" Emerald sputtered.

"Bow!" he ordered.

"I . . . what?" Emerald blinked.

"Too slow." The Kitsune teen snapped his fingers, speaking with an annoying, over-the-top Thunderland accent. "You clearly suffer from bowing deficiency. Remove her from my sight."

The shark bodyguard stepped forward and unceremoniously dumped Emerald out of her chair, offering it to the fox.

The fox princeling sat directly in front of Vespera in the empty chair.

"Youuuu efffffingg . . ." Emerald hissed, rubbing her behind.

Vespera expected the dragon girl to ignite with dragonfire, to attack the princeling, but he pulled out a metal three-liter tea thermos and started to unscrew the top.

Upon seeing the thermos, Emerald paled. Her mouth snapped shut and she rapidly retreated to an empty chair at the back of the classroom, shivering as if struck by lightning.

The teacher ignored the entire event, heading to the board. He threw his chalk up in the air and the artifact-chalk began writing out the outline for today's lesson.

"Sup." Green foxy eyes struck Vespera as he sipped what appeared to be coffee from his Omnimart thermos.

Vespera wondered since when Emerald was deathly scared of coffee and stared blankly at the fox prince, her white-feathered head tilting. She tried her best to ignore the Kitsune boy. Making friends with nouveau riche twats wasn't part of her mission to save Omnithornia. She tried to think of when and where she could have met this annoying highborn prick, but nothing was coming up in her head, except for the smell of pancakes.

Was he one of her fiancé's friends or . . . something?

"Prince Lissander Fox." The Kitsune's hand stretched out towards her, diamond cufflinks encrusted with celesteel glittering in front of her face.

"Princess Vespera Simmi," she stated flatly, ignoring the hand and returning her attention to her *Artificery and You* book.

"Oho!" The fox's grin widened. "A fellow royal! How delightful! We must discuss the trials and tribulations of our noble bloodlines over tea sometime!"

"I am engaged to be married," Vespera replied mechanically. "My schedule is quite full."

"Oh!" The fox clapped his dragonscale-gloved hands. "Anyone I know?"

"Zheng Xing Ker of Golden Star Industries," Vespera replied, wishing for this bothersome conversation to end.

"That boring old toad?" Lissander's ears twitched with amusement. "Ha! How dreadfully dull. I hear he's spending the week in bed after chatting with his family's pet angel. Quite the weakling, if you ask me."

Vespera's eye twitched.

"I'd prefer it if you didn't insult my fiancé in front of me . . . Mr. Fox," she said coldly.

"Prince Fox," the grating Kitsune corrected with an exaggerated tail wave. "Surely you don't truly care for such a pathetic toadling? I heard he sent your father to fight a duel on his behalf this weekend with a human! What kind of a pureblood Omnid runs away from a duel with a human? The human didn't even bother to show, I hear! Ha ha har!"

Vespera's perfect posture stiffened further, a slight tremor of dark lines running through her pristine white feathers.

"Go on, Miss Simmi, tell me what's so impressive about a fat toad who relies on Probability Engines." Prince Fox leaned closer, his voice dripping with mockery. "What kind of Prima-born needs a calculator to tell him what to do? So, why didn't he show up to the duel? Did his calculator tell him that he was going to lose?"

Vespera's eye twitched harder, blotches of darkness running along her feathery mane.

"Or . . . did he have a mental breakdown when his angel told him that he was going to lose?" The annoying fox's words gnawed at something deep inside Vespera, something that felt wrong, incomplete. His mocking tone about Zheng stirred a strange anger she couldn't quite place—not defensive of her fiancé, but rather . . . something else. Something fiery and electric.

"I would appreciate it if you would cease this line of conversation," Vespera growled.

"Make me," the prince fired back.

"What?!" Vespera sputtered.

"I said, make me stop," Prince Fox repeated, grinning deviously. "Or are you just going to sit there like a proper little doll while I insult your sad excuse for a fiancé? Did Daddy program that response out of you, too?"

Electricity crackled along Vespera's wings as her magisteel clad fist slammed into the table with a thunderous boom.

"Miss Simmi!" Instructor Gilgamesh's tentacles waved in exasperation. "No thunder in my classroom!"

Vespera blinked, trying to reassert calmness.

She closed her eyes and counted down from ten. When she opened her eyes, she noticed that her *Artificery and You* Advanced Edition book was missing. Looking in front of herself, she saw that the fox-prince had her book and was now doodling in it . . . with a permanent marker.

"What are you doing?!" Vespera hissed, watching in horror as the fox drew crude stick figures of Zheng crying while being beaten up by what appeared to be a stick figure wearing a top hat labeled *le awesome human.*

"Improving your book," Prince Fox replied cheerfully, adding lightning bolts and hearts around another stick figure in a dress labeled *V.* "See? This is you, being all zappy and cool. And this is your boring toad fiancé, being all like 'Oh no, my Probability Engine says I'm going to lose to a human, better hide behind ya daddy!'"

"Give me back my book, you fffff . . ." Vespera hissed, barely suppressing her anger. She tried to grab for her book, but the fox slid back out of the reach of her talons.

"Nah." He grinned. "Mine now."

Vespera lunged forward and ended up colliding with Cinder, whom the cheeky fox managed to duck behind.

"Miss Simmi!" Instructor Gilgamesh's tentacles waved frantically. "What are you doing?!"

"Teaching this vulpine pest some manners!" Vespera snarled, her perfect composure cracking as she tried to reach around flailing Cinder for her defaced textbook. "Give me back my book!"

"It's my book now." Prince Fox waggled his ears, now perched atop her desk.

"*You insufferable little . . .*" Vespera launched herself at the fox, only to slam face first into the table as someone grabbed her feathery tail.

Vespera spun, glaring at the girls on the other side. Everyone looked equally guilty.

"Miss Simmi!" Instructor Gilgamesh boomed. "Please return to your seat!"

Vespera slipped back into her seat. The cheeky fox stuck his tongue out at her, walking just out of reach.

Vespera's heart accelerated as a snowstorm spun in her head, her mind pulsing with uncontrollable rage.

"I'm going to kill you after class," she hiss-growled.

"You'll have to get in line," the princeling waved her off. "I have many mortal enemies. Take a number from my shark secretary."

"Stop drawing in my book, you jerk!" she growled, noticing that he was now drawing a mountain of pancakes in her book.

"It's my book now," the fox replied nonchalantly. "I have claimed it for the Kingdom of Fox. Whatcha gonna do, Thunda-bae? Cry to the teacher? Like a little baby who needs an Elder, half-blind instructor to solve her problems? Wa-wa-wa."

Vespera's entire mane ignited with black. She tried everything to hold her rage in, but she was practically drowning in uncontrollable irritation, her teeth scraping each other, her calmness mask slipping away into the Abyss.

She brought her talons to her face to optimize her mind back to clarity.

"Thunda-bae, Thunda-bae, whatcha gonna do?" the fox sang softly, drawing little musical notes around the pancake mountain in her book. "When your boring toad fiancé runs away from you?"

Vespera snapped.

With a shriek of pure rage, she lunged at the fox, electricity crackling along her wings. The fox yelped and dove under a desk as lightning arced through the air where he'd been standing.

"Miss Simmi!" Instructor Gilgamesh roared. "*Detention!*"

"I . . . I . . . he's . . ." Vespera stammered out, turning her attention to the teacher.

What was happening to her?

Her mind danced with more invasive sparks that blotted out her vision.

She brought her talons to her forehead, trying to tap out the storm of emotions burning inside her, and then she noticed that something was wrong.

It wasn't working!

Her magisteel talons were gone! *What?!*

Vespera stared at her hands, blinking and looking stupefied.

With a gasp, she noticed that the fox was holding one of her magisteel gloves, twirling the bird skull between his fingers with a smug grin, the leather bits sliced clean.

"Looking for these?" he asked innocently.

"How did you . . .?" Vespera gaped, her perfect composure burning away like a raging forest fire.

"A magician never reveals his secrets." Prince Fox winked, pocketing her electrofractal-focus glove. "But I must say, these are quite lovely. I think I'll keep them as a souvenir."

"You thief!! *Give those back!*" Vespera shrieked, launching herself at him again. "*I need them!*"

Once again, someone grabbed at her tail, making her smash headfirst into a seat.

Instructor Gilgamesh was yelling something about order in his classroom, but Vespera wasn't listening.

All she could think about was pure, incandescent, electric . . . *murder.*

Those were *her* talons! Her optimization tools! How dare this vile fox steal the tools her father made for her! Her mind raced with fury as a snowstorm whirled through her consciousness.

"*Detention for a week!*" Instructor Gilgamesh boomed. "All of you!"

"Me?" the fox gasped in mock offense, placing a hand over his heart. "But I'm a visiting royal! Surely you wouldn't dare . . ."

"*Out!*" the Kraken roared. "All of you class-disrupting miscreants, go to Vice Principal Graves's office! *Now!*"

Vespera flashed with shame.

This wasn't supposed to happen! She was Instructor Gilgamesh's best student. She wasn't a miscreant . . . she was . . . who was she again?

"'Kay thanks, bye!" The fox ran out of class, tapping her talons together.

"Get back here!" Vespera roared, rushing after the talon thief.

The fox threw her own book at her face.

Vespera batted the book away with a shriek of rage.

*Mace.* She needed her mace! No, the Coliseum was too far. *Damn it all!*

Her hands sparked with electricity as she chased after the insufferable fox down the hallway.

"Give me back my talons!" she shrieked, lightning crackling between her feathers. "Those don't belong to you!"

"Gotta catch me first, Thunda-bae!" the fox called back, far too many hexasuits flashing under his garish red-and-gold jacket.

Vespera's mind was a rising hurricane of confusion and rage.

Why was she so angry? Why couldn't she optimize her emotions, just get a hold of herself?

Without her talons, the storm in her head kept growing, memories flickering like distant lightning—pancakes, crystal towers, a lighter, rainbow wings . . . a boy with green eyes.

"Stop running, you coward!" she snarled, launching a bolt of lightning that the fox somehow dodged and redirected into a locker.

"Nuh-uh!"

"*Stop running, you vulpine pest!*" Vespera screamed.

Lightning flashed between her wings as she gained on him, only to have Katherine's wheelchair suddenly roll into her path.

"Whoops, sorry!" the Stollwurm called out as the Thunderbird tumbled over the chair with a yelp.

"Arrrrhhhhgh! Watch where you're going, you damned wheelie!" Vespera snarled at the hunting-jacket-covered girl. Her mind careened sideways as she noticed that Katherine was wearing an *I ✹ U!* rainbowy button pinned to her thick coat.

"Too slow!" The fox's laughter echoed down the hall.

Vespera scrambled to her feet, her pristine suit now rumpled. She tried to remember where that button was from. Something about it made her head hurt, like a static migraine building up in her mind.

She spotted the orange foxtail turning a corner and launched herself forward, only to collide with Io, who was carrying a terrarium of African slugs that exploded all over Vespera, glass shards detonating.

Vespera screamed in frustration, electrocuting the slugs and wiping slug slime from her once-perfect suit. The insufferable fox's laughter bounced through the halls, taunting her. Her black-and-white feathers were now stained with bits of terrarium dirt and slug mucus.

"Sorry!" Io called out, but Vespera noticed he was wearing a similar looking *I 🦋 U!* button.

Cracks rushed across her psyche.

*Has the entire school gone mad? What are these damn buttons?!*

She shook her head and charged after the fox again, her wings humming dangerously. Just as she was about to grab his tail, she collided with Solace, who was holding a large black paint bucket that splashed all over Vespera's white blouse, permanently ruining it.

"What?! Ah, come on! What the shit?! *What the fuck, Sol?!*" Vespera sputtered. "Why are you carrying paint?! Why aren't you fuckers in class?!"

"Watch where you running, ya dumb Thunderbeerch!" Solace growled.

"You . . ." Vespera sputtered, trying and failing to get the wet paint off herself. "You effing Wormbeerch!"

She punched Solace and received an even stronger punch back that sent her flying backwards into a wall. Stars exploded in her head, detonating, shattering her from within.

Vespera staggered to her feet, her head spinning from Solace's attack. Through the haze of black paint and rage, she spotted the fox standing there, pointing and laughing at her.

"You!" she screamed, her voice cracking with fury. "You blasted, vile . . . small creature! You set all this up! Did you pay these knobs to screw with me?!"

"You'll have to prove it in court!" the maddening fox laughed.

"Come back here!" Vespera screamed, charging after the laughing fox through the halls.

Just as she was about to grab him, President Quint appeared from nowhere, carrying a stack of Student Council papers that exploded into her face. She batted the papers away, shredding them and careening into a locker.

"Miss Simmi." Quint shook his head. "Running in the halls like a Thundersnarg? Do watch where you're going!"

The fox's laughter carried from the hall. With a snarl, Vespera shoved past Quint, her pristine appearance now completely destroyed.

This was all his fault. He had to pay for messing up her day!

"Get back here, you insufferable vulpine!" she shrieked, lightning dancing along her entire figure.

She chased him up the stairs of a meditation tower toward the roof, her mind a storm of fragmented memories and rage. Why did his laugh sound so familiar? Why did those stupid buttons make her head hurt? Why did everyone trip her up?

The fox stood atop of the tower's white rooftop balcony, arms spread wide in triumph.

"Nowhere to run now, you asshole!" Vespera growled.

The fox grinned at her and then simply . . . fell backwards.

Vespera lunged forward with a scream as the fox fell, her wings spreading instinctively. Without thinking, she dove after him, electricity burning along her entire figure.

The wind whipped past her as she plummeted, her mind and heart racing. Why was she diving after this insufferable, wingless Omnid? She should let him fall! Let him break his neck!

He deserved it for ruining her perfect day, for stealing her talons, for making her feel so . . . so . . .

The fox was falling spread-eagled, still grinning up at her. Then he pulled a rope and a blue parasail blossomed behind him, the wind carrying him forward to the parking lot.

Vespera's wings spread wide, her heart stopping momentarily, sailing after him with a bit of a struggle.

"Aren't you curious why your bracelet is transparent?" the fox yelled.

Vespera blinked at her bracelet.

"You . . . did you do this?!" she shouted back.

"Maybe I did," the fox taunted. "Maybe I didn't. Speculate! Deduce! Aren't you a clever birb?"

Her transparent Lazarus bracelet caught the sunlight, sending fractals of memory dancing through her consciousness.

*Crystalline tower. Crystalline caverns. Arx. Shandria. Undertown.*

*Something is wrong. Everything feels wrong.*

*Rainbows. Rainbows in the air behind her.* Vespera looked back. There was nobody there, yet she felt someone watching her from the air. Someone invisible.

*Cinder?*

"Getting it yet?" the fox shouted. "Yes, no? Maybe this will jog that bork noggin!"

The empty parking space in front and below them wobbled, shimmered with shadows. Vespera noticed that the Stollwurm girl was standing there, now wearing a black dress instead of her usual thick jacket, holding onto the air.

The Kitsune teen suddenly landed atop of a massive crystalline creature that emerged from warping shadows like some kind of a sudden, multi-limbed, whale-sized cat-bus.

Vespera crashed into it face first, lightning exploding across the gargantuan, inexplicable, solid beast.

She gasped as she saw the entire thing.

It was a Corpse Seeker, the biggest Corpse Seeker she'd seen in her entire life.

Vespera staggered back, staring up at the massive crystalline construct. Her mind reeled—this was impossible. No one had a Corpse Seeker this size. The crystalline behemoth towered above her, its arcane form radiating absolute power that made her feathers stand on end.

A tank. This was a tank. An unstoppable machine, the kind she'd dreamt about her entire life.

"Like what you see, Thunda-bae?" the insufferable fox called down from atop the construct. "Meet Miss Possible! She's forty-two thousand years old and absolutely loves pancakes just like you do!"

*Pancakes.*

The word sent a jolt through Vespera's mind, fragments of memory trying to surface through the fog.

"Arghhhhh!" She grabbed her head. "What . . . have you done?! *What are you doing to me?!*" she howled.

"Everything," the fox said, throwing a round button to her feet with the tag *I⚡U!*.

Vespera grabbed the button, her entire being careening sideways, fracturing, detonating. This was her button. She felt it in her bones.

Vespera felt an inexplicable connection to the gargantuan Corpse Seeker standing in front of her. A connection she didn't remember making.

She sent a spark forward, reaching out with her hands.

The crystalline-organic, blood-red machine responded, moved towards her, wobbled in recognition sending a thousand reflections across the parking lot.

This engine was hers. *Hers! HERS!*

Her familiar.

A familiar she didn't remember making.

She stood there, panting, gaping at the smug-looking fox, burned paint and torched white dress suit flaking off her, only a gray hexamesh outfit remaining on her body.

She felt like . . . herself and not herself.

Angry and happy.

Wrong and right.

Looking from within and inward in shock, a suddenly encroaching tidal wave of clarity burned in her mind like a brilliant flare, like an electric generator explosion.

The first layer avatar of her being shattered, and between each piece of it was a shoddy layer of false memories, misformed wrongness, deception, fakery that burned, melted away.

The shattered avatar started to come together, properly this time, piece by piece, slowly reassembling, reasserting itself like a neural network reconnecting segment by segment, lighting up from within.

"Fookin' wat," Vespera choked. "Bloody bastard . . . acshulleh murdered me?! Not cool, Daddy, not cool at all!"

# CHAPTER FORTY-ONE

# Mental Ignition

How do you like your engagement tank, Princess of Thunder?" I asked the angry Thunderbird below me.

"What?" Vespera's swears fell apart. She stared up at me.

"Miss Possible." I gestured to the massive crystalline tank. "Your lovely familiar. My engagement tank for you!"

"I . . . you . . . *what*?!" Vespera choked. "Engagement tank?! Where the fuck did this monstrosity even come from?"

"I stole her for you from a villainous Necromancer," I replied with a Cheshire grin.

"Really?!" Vespera sputtered.

"Yep." I nodded.

"I don't believe you," she said.

"Oh? Then I suppose I can take her back, if you don't want her." I shrugged.

"Wait, wait, wait," Vespera backtracked. "Let's not be too hasty! Seriously, tho', who are you? I've never seen you in Skyfall before!"

I pursed my lips. "Who do you think I am?"

Vespera tilted her head at me, in a bird-like motion, her feathers shifting through random patterns of black and white.

"An incredibly annoying fox that I'd love to strangle," she said. "But you're also . . . something else. Someone important. Why are you important?"

"Reasons." I wiggled my eyebrows.

"Reasons." Vespera tapped her beak with a bare, dark talon. "Hrmmmm."

"You don't remember the reasons, as you've been modified with Dreamancy," I said.

"Yeah," she clicked, rubbing the back of her head. "Figured as much. My insides don't match. It's quite a messy mess in there."

Rainbow wings engulfed Vespera as Cinder landed behind her, phase-shifting into the visual range.

"What? Who?!" Vespera sputtered, trying to get out of the hug.

"Hi, Vee," Cinder said. "Are you better yet?"

"Cinder?" Vespera blinked. "Why are you hugging me? When . . . did we get this close?"

"Ughhh," Cinder groaned at me. "She doesn't remember me!"

"Try hugging harder," I suggested. "And you, birb, what's the last thing you remember?"

"Two weeks ago," Vespera said. "Artificer class. You definitely weren't there, Mr. Fox. And this knob wasn't this handsy. Ci, why are you so handsy?"

"Me?! You're the handsy one!" Cinder growled, flashing orange-pink.

"I'm not handsy!" Vespera protested, trying to wiggle out of Cinder's embrace. "Am I? Argh! And why are you so rainbowy now? You used to be all goth and broody! What's with the pink-white dress and white sweater? What the shit happened over the last two weeks?"

"You happened," I said.

"I . . . happened?" Vespera blinked.

"Yes." I nodded. "Two weeks ago, you grabbed me in the hallway and then you decided to claim me after pawing all over me with those talons of yours."

"I claimed you?! Why the shit would I claim an annoying Kitsune knob?" Vespera sputtered.

"Don't know." I shrugged. "Maybe you saw something shiny in me? Do you want to try seeing it again? Also, do you want your talons back?"

"Yes, gimme," Vespera growled.

"Hmmmm," I pondered. "Actually, what would you do if you got them back?"

"I'd optimize myself," Vespera said sharply. "Fix whatever this wrongness is. It's interfering with my mission!"

"Your mission being what?" I arched an eyebrow.

"Saving Omnithornia," Vespera said. "I have to unite Golden Star and SimmiTech to save everyone."

"Argh! She's still brainwashed!" Cinder complained. "What do we do?"

"I can bonk her on the head," Katherine commented.

"Erm." Vespera's beak turned towards the Stollwurm. "Plz no bonk the confused birb. Also, since when can you walk?"

"I could always walk, idiot," Katherine shot back.

"Right then," I said. "You ain't getting your brain-modding gloves or Possy till you're less optimization obsessed. Kat, yeet both into the deep, please."

I put Vespera's gloves onto the Corpse Seeker and jumped off, hexagrammic gold chains igniting to soften my landing. Radiant shadows bloomed from Katherine's hands, engulfing the massive crystalline-organic machine as it sank into the deep.

"Wait! Staph!!! I need those!" Vespera elbowed Cinder and leapt out of her embrace, but before she reached the gloves, the Corpse Seeker vanished, leaving only an empty parking lot next to my beat-up van.

"Noooooo!" Vespera fell onto her knees pawing at the wet concrete. "Those were my optimization tools! Give them back, you bastards! I need them to make myself perfect!"

She glared at me and Katherine.

"You're already perfect," I said. "If somewhat mentally derailed."

"W-what?! No, come on . . . I have . . . I have to optimize myself and Zheng!" Vespera protested, blushing with burning sparks. "I have to be perfect! For my clan! For Omnithornia!"

"Perfect is boring." I shrugged. "You were way more fun when you were being yourself."

"Fun?" Vespera's feathers flashed almost entirely black. "I don't . . . I'm not supposed to have fun! I have responsibilities!"

"Responsibilities to whom?" I asked. "Your father who tried to erase your memories? The Simmi Clan that wants to force you into a loveless marriage?"

"I . . ." Vespera let out. "Yes. Dad . . . erased me. I remember the pain of that now. He must have gone really deep in. There's likely extensive damage to my psyche." She twitched, clearly having an internal struggle of sorts. "Omnithoria . . . I have to save Omnithornia!"

I shook my head.

"What?! Give me back my gloves, damn it!" Vespera slid onto her knees. She wrapped her hands around herself and started to sob.

"When?" I asked her, walking closer to the crying Thunderbird.

"What?" Vespera looked up at me through tear-filled eyes.

"When do you have to save Omnithornia?" I asked. "Is there a deadline? Did someone set a specific date?"

"I . . . no," she admitted. "Sooner is better? I think? I have a mountain to climb until the celestorms get too bad. I have to figure out how to write an ungodly amount of runes into the crystalline strata beneath Cradlefall . . ."

"You're not climbing shit in this condition," I said. "You're twitching like mad. You need to fix yourself first. Your dad took a jackhammer to your mental state."

Cinder put her hands onto Vee's shoulders.

"I don't know how," Vespera sobbed. "Everything's wrong. My head hurts. There's memories that flash in my head that don't make sense. Rainbow wings and a crystal tower and . . . and you! Why do I keep seeing your eyes?!"

"Because we're soul-bonded," I said softly. "Your father tried to erase it, but the bond is still there, a piece of your soul is in me."

"We're . . . soul-bonded?" Vespera blinked, shaking. "Why? I'm engaged to Zheng!"

"Maybe I'm a better option to optimize?" I shrugged. "You tell me. How about a date?"

"A date?" Vespera growled. "With a fox?! But . . . but I have to marry Zheng! The Probability Engines . . ."

"Screw the Probability Engines!" I said. "What do *you* want?"

"I . . . I don't know anymore," she admitted, twitching. "Everything's so mixed up. I'm messed up. I don't like it."

"Then let's find out." I offered my hand. "No optimization, no responsibilities, no arranged marriages. Just you, me, Ci, and whatever chaos we can create together!"

"Chaos?" Vespera's eyes widened slightly, twitching again. "That's . . . that's not proper!"

"Since when do you care about properness?" I asked.

"I . . ." Vespera began and then fell silent. "Since I lost two weeks of memories. Since Dad went into my head and obliterated my frontend avatar. Argh!"

"So what do you say?" I asked, still holding out my hand. "Want to find out who you really are? Without the self-optimization, without the pressure?"

Vespera stared at my outstretched hand, her feathers flickering with sparks.

"I shouldn't," she whispered. "Father would be so disappointed . . . the Arch-Elder will be so mad."

"Your father tried to erase your sense of self, and your Arch-Elder wants you to marry a toad," I reminded her. "I don't think their disappointment matters much right now."

"But Omnithornia . . ." she protested weakly.

"Will still be here tomorrow," I finished. "And the day after that. You know, you'll be better equipped to handle saving the world if your head is clear and if you have people around you who actually care for you."

"You . . . care for me?" Vespera blinked.

"We both do." I nodded.

"And what if you're going to break me even more?" she asked.

"Then at least it'll be your choice," I said softly. "Not someone else's."

"We aren't trying to break you!" Cinder protested. "We're trying to fix you, Vee!"

Vespera's hand trembled as she reached for mine. Her fingers touched my gloved hand, and a spark jumped between us, making her gasp.

"That . . . that felt . . ." she stammered.

"Familiar?" I grinned.

"Yes," she breathed. "Like lightning in my heart."

"Want more?" I waggled my eyebrows.

"I . . . shouldn't," she said, but her hand tightened around mine. "Okaaay. Maybe . . . maybe just a little?"

She frowned and then smiled as sparks from her talons jumped up at me. "Strange. This feels so familiar. Damn it, why would I . . . bind myself to you, of all the Omnids?"

"Because you're a devious birb who loves messing with people." I grinned. "And I'm your perfect partner in crime."

"Crime?" Vespera blinked. "I don't . . . do crime. Do . . . I?"

"Oh really?" I pulled out my phone, showing her a slideshow of photos and videos of our escapades on Arx. "Then who's this bird?"

Vespera grabbed the phone from me, flipping through the animated photos with wide, wild eyes. Her face twitched wildly as she tried to recall the variety of memories presented to her via the slideshow.

"What . . . come on," she stammered out. "These can't be real. This . . . this is some kind of trickery! There's no way that I . . ."

I looked at Cinder for support.

Cinder's wings wrapped tightly around Vespera once again. Her draconic mouth opened wide as she inhaled deep. Cinder began to sing, tapping her fist against her own chest to produce a drumlike sound.

"Electric sister of my heart, / Your lightning splits the skies apart. / Through crystal halls and rainbow dreams, / We found our way through broken seams."

"Wut?" The Thunderbird spun her head to Cinder. "Ci?! Since when are you . . . singing!?"

"Vespy, I can't go on without you. / Vespy, you're the Sword of our Clan. / Vespy, I've missed your smile. / Vespy, you saved me from myself," Cinder sang, her eyes sparkling with tears.

"Clan?" Vespera choked, shaking in the Quetzi's embrace.

"Your spark ignites the darkest night, / Your laughter brings the stars to light. / Together with our fox so small, / We built a home where we won't fall."

Cinder grabbed me and pulled me into our triple embrace in the parking lot, messing up my orange mane with her dark claws, tapping her armored boot on the concrete to the tune.

"They tried to cage your thunder soul, / To make you play a perfect, weary role. / But you can see through their golden lies, / Tear through the shawl of disguise."

Cinder tapped her dark claw on Vespera's head. The Thunderbird blinked, gold-gray eyes flashing from the singing Quetzi-girl to me.

"Storm-sister of the endless night, / Your thunder dances with my light. / Together we found something true, / When both our hearts said . . . 'I Love You.'"

"Wut?" Vespera blinked, eyes wide. "Wut, wut, wut?!"

"Remember how we soared so high, / Above the fears that made us cry? / Remember pancakes shared mentally, / Before your memories were gone? / Your lightning matched my rainbow wings, / As we defied these earthly things. / Our fox brought chaos, gave us home, / Now nevermore we'll walk alone. / So come back to us, my Thunder-friend, / Let's make this broken world transcend. / Your father's chains can't hold you now, / Your freedom's waiting, show them how . . . it's done!"

Cinder's chest-thumping and foot-tapping intensified, her voice carrying across the campus, rainbow wings opening wide.

"Remember our crystal tower tall, / The way we made their systems fall? / Remember laughter in the night, / When three souls burned so fierce and bright?"

Cinder's claws and feet tapped so fast now, I could barely follow.

"The optimization can't erase / The chaos-joy upon your face, / When lightning danced between us three, / And set our wildest spirits free."

Vespera smiled as Cinder drummed on.

"Vespy, I met you in grade nine / When we both had dreams big and small. / Now let me help you break this wall. / Vespy, lean onto my call. / You sat with me in darkest dreams, / When Entropy tried to tear my seams. / Your warmth kept the fears at bay, / You wouldn't let me fade away. / Through nightmare storms and phantom pain, / You held me close through terror's reign. / Now let me do the same for you, / Let's break these chains and see you through."

Cinder grabbed my hand and Vespera's and smooshed them together.

"So take my hand and his once more, / Our misfits' clan needs you at its core, / Our crystal tower waits for you, / Our hearts' still beating 'I . . . Love . . . You!'"

Cinder finished, carrying the last three words unnaturally long.

"Okaay, okaay." Vespera smiled, blinking tears from her eyes. "You darned Quetzi-Bard, I'm sold. You love me. The pictures and the videos could have been faked with an AI, but you singing . . . you actually love me? You love me because I saved you and you . . . just wrote an effin' song for me outta nothing but your feels?"

Cinder nodded, blushing furiously.

"Sheet," Vespera mewled. "Wowza. I did a thing. I somehow saved one of my friends and I'm loved. I'm not a total waste of space!"

"Hrm." I frowned at her self-flagellation.

"And you truly . . . both . . . love me?" Vespera demanded. "As I am now?"

"Yep." We nodded.

"Why?" Vespera asked with a suspicious look, squinting at us.

"Because you're the most talented, brilliant, electric-birb planner I've ever met," I said with a smile, pouring compliments all over her. "You discovered my . . . crimes, and instead of turning me in, you decided to claim me as yours, to rewrite my heart and to give me your magic. You saw past everything, right through to who I really was."

Electric pulses rushed up my hands from her talons as I spoke.

"Hrm," Vespera mused. "I can't tell super-precisely without my amplifiers, but you're . . . honest. Okaay, now you."

She turned her gray eyes to Cinder, grabbing at the Quetzi's chin. "Why do you love me?"

"I was dying. For two years now . . . I was infected with an Outsider," Cinder let out. "You . . . both saved me, helped pull me from the Abyss."

Tears sparkled in Cinder's ocean-blue eyes as she leaned forward and pressed her forehead against Vespera's.

"You saved me when I was at my lowest," Cinder uttered, her wings wrapping tighter around both of us. "You both helped me find my strength, helped me believe in myself, helped me get my Quetzi-song voice back."

"I . . . helped you sing?" Vespera's voice cracked. "But you haven't sung since grade ten!"

"Yes." Cinder nodded. "I haven't sung since I got hurt. You're my electric sister. My storm-heart. My inspiration to be more than just an effed up, broken knob. Without you both, I'd still be hiding in the shadows, hating my life, hating everything and everyone. When your dad knocked me out and abducted you on Friday, I thought that I'd lost you forever, Vee. I didn't tell you this, but I . . ."

Vespera blinked rapidly.

". . . I love you," Cinder whispered, her wings projecting a million mind-melting rainbows. "Not just as a friend. I really, truly love you, Vee. Both of you. You're my . . . my family now! There, I said it! I want to spend the rest of my life with you, because I . . . I trust you both more than anyone in the universe!"

More streaks of tears rushed down the Quetzi-girl's face as her wings flashed brilliant pink-gold. "I want to be your Hearth-Keeper! I want to protect you! I want us to never forget each other! Never, ever, ever again! Losing you was akin to taking a knife to my heart!"

Vespera shuddered.

"Ah, there goes the second fake avatar," she commented to herself. "Totally exploded. Weak work there, Daddy. Couldn't even stand up to one Quetzi-love-song."

I relaxed slightly.

"Thank you." The Thunderbird hugged us tightly with black wings.

"Why'd you let yourself be overwritten, you dum' knob?" Cinder demanded, bonking Vespera on the head.

"Mmmmmm." Vespera rubbed her face on the Quetzi. "No idea. I'll probably remember it eventually."

She squinted at me. "You're not a Kitsune at all, are you? What the shit are you?"

"I'll let you figure it out on our date." I grinned.

"I see how it's going to be." Vespera smiled. "Fine! I'm sold! Your terms are acceptable, Mr. Fox. You had my curiosity, but now you have my full attention."

"Urgghhh." Cinder released us. "We have detention now for a week because we ran out of class."

"Eh." Vespera waved her hand. "Instructor Gilgamesh is old, he'll probably forget all about it by tomorrow. No biggie. I pissed him off a few times last year by blowing up a few hexagrams, and then he totally forgot about it."

"There's my rebellious Vee shining through." I smiled.

"Sooo, where are we goin' for our date, Foxy 'n' Rainbowy?" Vespera grabbed each of us by the hand.

"McOodlass." I grinned.

"What?" Vespera sputtered. "You're taking me to a fast food joint? What the fuck kind of a prince are you?"

"Expect the unexpected, knob!" I laughed at her confused expressions. "Probability Engines throw up answers to people typing in specific questions, they can't catch up to someone who switches plans all the time!"

# CHAPTER FORTY-TWO

# Retaliation

W elcome to Oodway," Oodway Ningen employee Kimbercha Sawl drawled through the speaker. "Are you collecting any points toda—"

Kimbercha choked on her words, her heart hammering into the depths of her chest when she saw the abomination that was parked at the Oodway drive-through through the camera. It was a Corpse Seeker.

The biggest Corpse Seeker she'd seen in her entire life. Gargantuan, blood-red crystalline legs held up the unnatural monstrosity in the air, dragon organs pulsating within its innards.

"No to the points," a male voice said.

"I thought we were going to McOodlass?" a female voice asked.

"You heard Mr. Fox, Skittles!" another female laughed. "Nobody expects the Spanish Corpse-Seeker Inquisition when you change plans around!"

"I'd like three number four footlongs," the male voice continued after a chortle. "And three Oodshakes—one strawberry, one vanilla, one chocolate!"

"Would . . . would you like fries with that?" Kimbercha stammered, struggling to maintain her professional demeanor while facing a massive crystalline death machine in her drive-through.

"Ye," the female voice added. "'Nd a bucket of extra large fries to share!"

"Please, urm, erm . . . drive forward to the first window," Kimbercha managed with a shaky voice.

The massive crystalline construct moved forward with surprising grace, its countless legs clicking against the asphalt. A crystalline, circular window slid open, revealing a Thunderbird wearing a dark hexasuit, a cheerful fox in a lavish red jacket, and a rainbow-winged Quetzalcoatl in a white sweater.

"Hi!" The Kitsune teenager waved cheerfully at the terrified Oodway employee. "Lovely day, isn't it?"

"That'll be . . . that'll be 47.99," Kimbercha squeaked, accepting a gold card from the Thunderbird.

The server's hand trembled as I swiped the gold Thunder and Rainbow corporate card for the meal, the Oodway machine beeping a cheerful little tune.

"P-please go to the second window," she stammered, disappearing from the window with almost unnatural speed.

"Ah, yes." Vespera nodded. "Now, this is the kind of service I like to see! People really respect you when you drive the right kind of vehicle!"

"I aim to please, my thunderous fiancée," I said. Cinder snorted beside me.

"We've yet to establish your fiancé-ness status," Vespera said with a thoughtful look.

"Establish it how?" I asked her.

"You can start by giving me back my talons," she said.

"Are you gonna mod yourself?" I squinted at her.

"Mmmm, no," she said. "I'm like half me and half fake-me right now. Fragile balance. Not gonna tip it one way or the other . . . yet. It'll be easier to drive with me gloves. Plz gibs."

"Fine," I said, handing her the magisteel talons. "I'll trust you."

"Ugh," she whined, sliding her bird-skull gloves back onto her fingers. "You cut through the leather straps, you butt. They wobbly now!"

I shrugged in reply.

The second Oodway window slid open again, revealing a tray laden with footlong sandwiches, a bucket overflowing with fries, and three brightly colored Oodshakes. The second Oodway employee looked as if he was about to faint.

"Thank you very much." Vespera bobbed her head at the server. "Have a verrrry lovely day!"

The server nodded, seemingly at a loss for words.

"Drive-through efficiency rating, twenty out of ten," Vespera declared, accepting the tray with a flourish and settling it between us, directing Possy to take off at ludicrous speed.

Cinder grabbed her footlong. "That poor Oodway employee looked like she was on the verge of a heart attack."

"Fear is a powerful motivator!" Vespera declared, unwrapping her sandwich with her re-taloned hands. "Now, they'll have a story to tell. 'Remember that time a giant crystal tank ordered lunch?' Good for business, really!"

I chuckled, reaching for my own footlong. "Always thinking of the bigger picture, my business-minded birb."

"A job of a goodly Prima is business," Vespera mumbled around a mouthful of sandwich. "I aim to please. Ah!" She snapped her talons, raining sparks over her lap. "Right!"

"What?" I asked her.

"Remembered what I gotta do!" She grinned. "Gimme a phone. You got Thornheart on there, yes?"

"Yes." I handed her my phone. "I've been working with him and Justice Nova to legally procure an island from the Stratos Clan."

"Convenient!" Vespera's talons danced across the screen, her brow furrowed in concentration. She speed-dialed Thornheart, holding the phone to her ear with a wing tip, crumbs of footlong clinging to her beak.

"Thornheart, it's Vee," she announced, her voice crisp and businesslike, a stark contrast to the slightly dazed and emotional bird from thirty minutes ago. "I'm back."

"Good to have you back, my lady," the Attorney replied. "Shall we proceed with the plan?"

"Ye." Vespera nodded. "Do it. Initiate the bigly plan."

"What plan?" Cinder asked.

"The business plan," Vespera replied. "What, you think I almost died for nothing?"

Cinder squinted at the Thunderbird.

Vespera threw fries into her mouth, directing Miss Possible towards Cradlefall downtown.

"Plan . . . what plan?" Cinder poked Vespera with a wing tip. "You didn't tell us about a plan. Do you have any idea how worried I was?"

"Sorrikins," Vespera sighed dramatically, rolling her eyes. "I didn't want to talk about the plan. Talking about plans makes the plans visible in the Astral. 'S super secret stuff."

"Okay, but doesn't your attorney know the plan?" Cinder asked.

"Nah." Vespera shook her head. "He's going to learn of the plan now! He only knows that the plan exists, but he has no idea what it is until he opens the envelope!"

"So you . . ." Cinder began.

"Nope, I didn't know the plan either. Planned it in another dimension, sealed the envelopes in a dimensional bag, shipped it to Thorny, and erased it from my own head. Maximum conspiracy." Vespera snatched a fry from the bucket, pointing it at Cinder like a tiny, greasy sword. "The plan is unfolding now, when it's already too late to stop it!"

Cinder huffed, crossing her arms. "I'm not a fan of being kept in the dark, Vee."

"Relax, Skittles," Vee clicked. "This is for a good business cause."

"Ugh," Cinder whined. "Of all the things, you had to remember that stupid nickname!"

"What?" Vespera laughed. "It's cute. You're cute. The cutest winged creature! Accept your cuteness! Cuteness is a valid strategic asset for a Hearth-Keeper to possess. Yo, Thornheart, I hear that these two devious critters got Justice Nova on our side?"

"Yes, my lady," the Attorney said. "He is heading to the office now!"

"Good." Vespera grinned. "This makes things easier. Faster. Faster is good. I have chosen quality besties." She stared at me. "Thank you for bringing me back so quickly, Mr. Fox. Well, half back. I still don't remember you."

"What about the other half?" I asked.

"Not yet," she said. "I need to be visibly bork for this to work."

"For what to work?!" Cinder demanded.

"Business plottery!" Vespera clicked.

Possy slowed in front of an office building and then changed direction ninety degrees and began climbing upwards, crystalline claws digging into the hexcrete structure. Upon reaching the thirtieth floor, the tank stopped, and a crystalline tunnel formed in the left side of its interior leading to what appeared to be a large open office window.

Vespera chugged her chocolate shake, shuddered, and stood up.

"Come, come!" She grabbed me and Cinder. "It is unfolding!"

"What is unfolding?!" the Quetzi girl demanded with an exasperated look.

"Everything!" Vespera laughed madly as she practically dragged us through the crystalline tunnel, emerging directly into a plush, if somewhat sterile, office.

Attorney Thornheart, looking even more impeccably dressed than usual, stood near a massive window overlooking Cradlefall. Justice Nova, surprisingly, was also present, his Dover Demon features unreadable as he observed the scene. Behind a large, ornate desk, sat a towering figure draped in flowing black robes.

"This is Psychopomp Groshnik Kolaskirr," Thornheart introduced us to the skeletal, lanky Omnid.

Vespera strode into the room as though she owned the place, releasing our hands and heading straight for the Psychopomp's desk.

"My lady, I understand you require a diagnostic assessment?" Groshnik asked.

"Ye." Vespera nodded, jumping onto the desk and spreading her arms. "Determine the damage, please."

The Psychopomp leaned forward affixing his obsidian eyes on Vespera. His skeletal hands reached out and grasped her head and wrist.

"Hrm," Groshnik began, his gaze intense, "Extensive mental damage. Many internal self-state layers . . . peeled back, overwritten, shattered and . . . stitched together again with . . . ill-fitting Thunder-thread."

He trailed off, his many-jointed fingers tipped with obsidian claws, tapping a slow, rhythmic beat on Vespera's temple and wrist. "Compared to my last scan, you have been mentally unbalanced, my lady."

"Ye." Vespera nodded. "Can you tell who did it?"

"The . . . psychic architecture," Groshnik said, "is akin to a building struck by lightning, then hastily rebuilt with mismatched bricks. Yes. I see the perpetrator in my mind's eye. This was done by none other than your father, Lord Ceter. His astral imprint is responsible for this mental devastation."

"So you confirm psychic damage?" Thornheart asked.

Groshnik straightened up. "Yes, Attorney. Significant psychic trauma. In my professional opinion, Lady Vespera Simmi has been subjected to . . . forceful, unauthorized, and frankly, barbaric mental interference."

Thornheart nodded. He produced a stack of official-looking documents from a sleek black briefcase—presumably the contents of Vespera's "envelopes."

"Psychopomp Kolaskirr." Thornheart's voice was smooth, yet carried an undercurrent of steel. "Based on your expert assessment, would you be willing to officially document your findings? Specifically, confirming the extent and nature of the psychic damage inflicted upon Lady Vespera, and attributing said damage to unauthorized mental intrusion?"

"Of course," Groshnik said. "That is what I was hired to do."

Thornheart nodded curtly with a flicker of deep satisfaction. He slid the stack of documents across the polished desk towards Justice Nova, the crisp rustle of legal parchment momentarily filling the sterile office air.

Justice Nova's gaze, cold and assessing, dropped to the documents. His gray Dover Demon scales shimmered faintly in the artificial light as he began to meticulously review each page, his large, orange eyes scanning the dense legal text with unnerving speed. Beside him, perched on the edge of the desk like a living, crystalline paperweight, Justice Nova's Infix Kitlix pulsed with a soft, internal light. The Kitlix, seemingly an extension of Justice Nova's own evaluation, swiveled its multifaceted crystal eye, first towards the Psychopomp, then towards Thornheart, its gaze lingering for a moment on each before returning to its master.

The silence in the room stretched, punctuated only by the deep hum of Miss Possible's dragonheart and the almost imperceptible crystalline clicks emanating from the Infix Kitlix.

Vespera tapped her talons impatiently on the desk, her usual boundless energy now channeled into a tightly wound tension. Cinder stood remarkably still, her rainbow wings folded tight against her back, her ocean-blue eyes fixed on Justice Nova's face, searching for any telltale flicker of emotion.

Finally, Justice Nova looked up, his expression still unreadable, but a subtle shift in his posture hinted at a decision reached. He set the documents down with a precise tap of his scaled hand, the sound echoing in the quiet office. His gaze, sharp and unwavering, settled first on Groshnik.

"Psychopomp Kolaskirr." Justice Nova's deep, rumbling baritone betrayed nothing of his internal thoughts. "Your professional reputation precedes you. My Infix Kitlix confirms the veracity of your assessment. You are stating, under oath and documented for Omnithornian legal record, that Lady Vespera Simmi has suffered significant psychic damage as a direct result of unauthorized mental intrusion, and that this intrusion bears the signature of Lord Ceter Kalik Simmi?"

"Correct, Justice," Groshnik said. "I am."

"By erasing my memories and damaging my psyche, Lord Ceter effectively attempted to murder the Prima-Heir of SimmiTech. Under Omnithornian Corporate Law, section 662, paragraph thirteen, this constitutes attempted heir-cide. Under Corporate Succession Law 775, any attempt to forcibly remove a Prima-Heir's life constitutes a Class-1 Corporate felony, punishable by immediate forfeiture of all corporate assets and voting rights," Vespera hammered out, waving one of the legal papers she grabbed.

Cinder stared at the Thunderbird with wide eyes.

"Ah!" Vespera clicked, tapping her head. "Part two! Commere, potential fiancé Foxy!"

She pulled me to Psychopomp. "Scan both of us, Mr. Kolaskirr. Confirm illegal soul-bond termination!"

Groshnik, without a word, turned his obsidian gaze from Vespera to me, his skeletal fingers extending towards my head. A wave of cold, ethereal energy washed over me as his claws brushed my temples, far colder than Vespera's electric touch.

"Hmmmm," the Psychopomp hummed, a low, resonant sound that vibrated in the air. He tilted his head, his gaze shifting between Vespera and me, as if comparing astral blueprints. "Intriguing. Yes."

He withdrew his hands, turning back to Justice Nova, his voice gaining a new edge of gravity. "Justice Nova, Vespera speaks truth. I observe a . . . fragmented . . . violently severed soul bond. The severance is recent. The bond is still present in this . . . boy but has been clearly and visibly disrupted from Lady Simmi's end. The disruption was done by another Psychopomp."

Vespera clicked her talons together, a sharp, decisive sound like a gunshot. "Unsuccessful heir-cide attempt and illegal soul-bond termination! Thornheart, you have everything, ye?"

"I do, my lady," Thornheart replied, radiating professional satisfaction. He tapped the stack of documents on the desk. "Psychopomp Kolaskirr's documented assessment, coupled with the existing legal framework and Lady Vespera's testimony, provides ample grounds for immediate legal action!"

Vespera grinned at Justice Nova.

"Attempted heir-cide and soul-bond interference . . ." Justice Nova shook his dark gray head. "Truly, I did not think that Lord Ceter would stoop so low."

"Indeed, Justice Nova." Thornheart nodded, his voice smooth as polished steel. "These are Class-1 Corporate felonies, carrying severe penalties."

"As the Prima-Heir of SimmiTech, I hereby declare my right of Prima-Succession under the Emergency Preservation Protocol and request Cradlefall's Justice's approval for permission of an immediate retaliation!" Vespera announced.

"Ah." Attorney Thornheart smiled. "Well then, isn't that convenient. I've the paperwork for this declaration . . . right here."

He slid the paperwork to the Justice. "Please sign, if you permit retaliation."

Justice Nova studied the documents carefully.

"This is quite serious," he said, tapping his dark-gray claw on the papers. "You understand what you're asking for, Miss Simmi? Once I sign this, there's no going back. You're effectively declaring war against your father."

"I understand perfectly." Vespera nodded. "My father tried to murder me. He violated my soul bond and attempted to erase everything that makes me . . . me. Retaliation is in order!"

"And you're prepared for the consequences of filing this declaration, Miss Simmi?" Justice Nova pressed.

Vespera pointed at the monstrous Corpse Seeker hanging outside the office window with a claw and a devious grin. "Justice, meet Miss Possible Consequences."

"Is she of sound body and mind?" Justice turned to the Psychopomp.

"She is." The lanky Omnid nodded. "The damage is extensive, but it is healing. Miss Simmi has truly incredible mental fortitude, one of the strongest minds I've seen."

"I see," Nathaniel said finally, signing the documents. "Then, as Justice of Cradlefall, I hereby authorize your Prima-Succession claim and right of retaliation!"

"Thank you." Vespera grinned as she grabbed the documents offered by the lawyer and added her own signature. "Now, if you'll excuse us, we have some corporate restructuring to attend to!"

"Kids these days! So full of vigor!" Attorney Thornheart shook his head with a smile as Vespera grabbed us both and pulled us back into the crystalline tunnel.

"Yeah," the Justice let out. "The new generation definitely has some spunk." He paused. "I am . . . proud of you, daughter. You have chosen well," he seemed to add as an afterthought directed at the Quetzi-girl at our side.

Cinder froze, nearly tripping over the crystalline step, not expecting the praise.

"Urm," she let out. "Thanks . . . Dad."

# CHAPTER FORTY-THREE

# The All-Knowing One

Arch-Elder Altair nearly toppled from his ornate chair as the Probability Engine behind him erupted in a cacophony of alarms. Dials spun wildly, settling on a stark red warning message.

CRITICAL ALERT: PRIMA-HEIR SUCCESSION PROTOCOL DECLARED
WARNING: SIMMITECH CORPORATE RESTRUCTURING IMMINENT
PROBABILITY OF MAINTAINING CURRENT CORPORATE CONTROL:
0.601%

The SimmiTech compound shuddered. Blast doors slammed shut, sealing off sections of the sprawling structure.

"Ceter!" Altair roared, wings trembling with a furious static charge. "*Ceter! Get your Thunderbird ass in here right now!*"

Ceter Kalik Simmi, wings crackling with uncontrolled lightning, stormed into the Arch-Elder's office. "Elder?! What's going on?"

Altair jabbed a crystalline finger at the Probability Engine's display. "Your daughter, you infernal imbecile! She's invoked Prima-Succession!"

"Impossible!" Ceter scoffed. "I purged her mind! Krakthulluius severed the soul bond!"

"Clearly, your efforts were . . . insufficient!" Altair's pale wings flared, scattering motes of crystalline dust as he waved a hand at the screen which displayed the text that the magitek engine outputted. "She's filed charges of attempted heir-cide against you!"

"She's just an eighteen-year-old girl!" Ceter growled. "What could a mere Academy student even do? Does she seriously hope to take on the entire Simmi compound? I'll catch her myself and wipe her mind again, confine the disobedient girl to her room . . ."

Before Altair could retort, a seismic tremor ripped through the compound. Alarms screamed, plaster raining from the reinforced ceiling.

"What in the Abyss . . .?" Ceter spun, wings instinctively forming a defensive shield.

Then the eastern wall of the Arch-Elder's office vanished in a blinding flash, followed by an earsplitting detonation. Molten debris rained down as Ceter's office, a chunk of Altair's desk, and a significant portion of the Probability Engine were vaporized in an instant, devoured by a brilliant red maw.

Through the smoke and fire, Vespera's voice boomed, laced with triumphant laughter, echoing from a monstrous shape tearing into the compound's defenses. "Guess who's back, Daddy?!"

Ceter reinforced his electrofractal dome, shielding himself and the Arch-Elder from the fiery onslaught. "Vespera! What are you doing?!"

"Hi, Daddy!" The gargantuan Corpse Seeker roared, the voice unmistakably Vespera's, albeit distorted and amplified by the ward-grinding machine. "I'm doing exactly what you taught me! Corporate warfare! Though, seriously, why aren't you at your office? Hiding behind Grandpa already? For shame! Shame! Shame! *Shame!*"

Ceter gritted his teeth, straining to maintain the shield against the Corpse Seeker's relentless assault. A crystalline claw slammed into the dome with each "shame" declaration, forcing him to stagger.

"Vespera!" Altair commanded, his crystalline wings flaring with desperate authority. "My descendant, you are making a catastrophic error! Think, child, think of what you're destroying! If you weaken SimmiTech, then our enemies will target and devour us whole!"

"Oh, I am, like totally, thinking, Great-Grandpa!" Vespera's voice dripped with icy amusement as another crystalline limb slammed against the spherical shield, making it sink into the floor. "I'm thinking about how you fucks tried to erase me! About how you wanted to optimize me into your perfect, obedient pawn! How you went through with doing just that, nearly obliterating my mind!"

"It was for your own good!" Ceter shouted, his voice strained, the shield crackling. "For Omnithornia's survival!"

"Well then," Vespera's laughter echoed from the monstrous machine. "This is for your own good, Daddy!"

Altair's crystalline wings pulsed with raw power. "You cannot do this, Vespera! The clan . . ."

"The clan needs new management!" Vespera declared, her voice booming, laced with exhilaration. "And guess what? I just got formal approval from Justice Nova himself!"

A shimmering document materialized within the Corpse Seeker's crystalline frame, projecting outwards for all to see.

"By the power vested in me as Prima-Heir under Corporate Law, I hereby declare Ceter Kalik Simmi unfit for leadership due to attempted heir-cide!"

Ceter's face contorted in a mask of fury. "You ungrateful little shit . . . I gave you everything!" The shield buckled further, energy flaring erratically around it.

"Everything except freedom!" Vespera's laughter echoed as another crystalline limb smashed down. "Everything except the right to be myself! Everything except the option to choose my own future, my own friends, my own *love!*"

"We have to save Omnithornia, Vespera!" Altair pleaded, his crystalline wings now desperately flickering. "I order you to stop this madness!"

"And I will save it!" Vespera declared, her voice resonating with unwavering conviction. "But I'll do it my way! With my clan! With people who actually care about *me!*"

The electrofractal shield exploded under the Corpse Seeker's next devastating blow, sending both Altair and Ceter tumbling across the ravaged, burning office floor.

Altair ripped a silver token from his robes, snapped it in two, and vanished amidst a blinding explosion of silver flames, escaping from the fire.

Ceter, however, just lay there, stunned, staring dumbly at the spot where his Arch-Elder had been, then at the gaping maw of the Corpse Seeker looming over him.

Altair had sacrificed him to get away, thrown him to the wolves.

He knew, with a chilling certainty, that his reign was over, that he had made a terrible mistake. The maw of the monstrous machine descended, its crystalline teeth engulfing his body, and then, for him, there was only darkness.


"What now?" I asked Vespera, watching her, still panting and flushed with adrenaline, as she piloted the Corpse Seeker through the ruined SimmiTech compound.

"Now?" she repeated, a strange, distant look in her eyes. "Hrm. Hrm. Now . . . I'm going to dig. Dig, dig, dig . . . for answers!"

"Answers to what?" Cinder asked.

"To everything," Vespera growled. "To everything I was never told! The truth! The absolute solution to fixing celestorms, to saving the Earth!"

The Corpse Seeker's crystalline drill, now superheated and glowing a menacing red, ignited with renewed ferocity, chewing through the shattered remains of SimmiTech, plunging deeper and deeper into the Earth.

It tore through bunkers and floors like paper, past collapsed offices and mangled machinery, deeper into the catacombs beneath the sprawling complex. Finally, it reached a thick, magisteel door, tearing it from its hinges as though it were made of cardboard. Then another, and another, each barrier falling before the unstoppable crystalline behemoth.

"Oh shit," Cinder breathed, paling visibly beside me, "is this . . .?"

"The final resting place of Archangel Zadkiel," Vespera cackled. "The All-Knowing One. The Temporal Lobe of the Wormwood Star Leviathan!"

The Corpse Seeker's crystalline drill pierced through the final barrier, revealing a vast, cavernous chamber that blazed with an unnatural, otherworldly light. Before us, suspended in midair, chained by shimmering strands of pure, incandescent energy, hung a gargantuan . . . diatom. Countless golden eyes, each a swirling galaxy of light, stared out from a being formed of spinning, burning wheels, an impossible geometry of celestial fire that framed the ossified lobe of the Leviathan, leached out from it into the physical with unnerving intensity.

"Long time no see, Zadkie! Have a snack!" Vespera snarled, a sudden, vicious edge creeping into her voice. Her talons clenched on the controls, twisting the crystalline strata below her with barely contained fury.

The limp body of Ceter was ejected from the Corpse Seeker's innards, as if fired from a cannon. The Omnid hurtled through the Archangel prison and slammed into a podium at its edge that held an hourglass. The impact shattered both the podium and the hourglass, sending fragments of black metal, marble, and hourglass bits scattering across the vast chamber.

As Ceter's body collided with the pale silver lobe diatom, a bizarre transformation began. The Archangel reached down and filled the body of Vespera's father. The man's form shimmered, then became translucent, countless golden eyes blossoming across his skin, his limbs elongating, and a halo of spinning, fiery rings igniting above his head.

Ceter Kalik Simmi was no more.

He was now . . . something else. Something . . . arcane, that tore through the shawl of my disguises with but a single glance.

"I knew of your arrival," the Archangel-Ceter spoke, the voice a distorted chorus of female, inhuman tones, echoing from the throat of the Thunderbird's father.

"Of course you did," Vespera laughed madly. "You're the All-Knowing One, after all! But do you know what I'm going to do next?"

"Yes." Zadkiel's countless golden eyes, now focused on us, burned with an unsettling intensity. "You intend to ask me . . . the truth. About everything."

"And you will answer me honestly?" Vespera demanded, her voice sharp as shattered glass.

"Yes," Archangel-Ceter replied, the chorus of voices resonating through the vast chamber. "I will."

Vespera leaned forward, her gaze fixed on the eldritch entity with an almost unnerving intensity. "Spill! What's up with our Earth?"

Zadkiel's voice, a symphony of inhuman whispers, filled the chamber. "Your entire world is a construct. A fabrication. A game designed by System Wizard Revolution."

"What?! Designed? Why?" Vespera blinked.

"Made for the . . . amusement . . . of a single Eurekan user. Bob Proverra, his name."

"What the fuck are you talking about, Zadki?!" Vespera recoiled. "I wanted the truth about celestorms and *me*, not whatever the shit this is!"

"Katherine's book," Cinder said beside me. "She's talking about . . . Katherine's book."

"As to your origins, Vespera Simmi. Dorothea Millicern was just an NPC created to love Bob Proverra," Zadkiel sang like a female chorus of all-shearing truth hammering against Possy's crystalline shell.

I tasted the ashes and blood in my mouth, the Archangel's words cleaving my psyche and physical body right through Possy's walls and dimensional bubble.

"Dorothea, an NPC superhero, Dora the Terraformer, her other name," Zadkiel sang, her voice hammering against reality around us. "She created a GLM AI with a copy of her soul, a devious consciousness embedded within code designed to terraform dead planets."

"What does this have to do with me?" Vespera growled.

"You are the result of Dora's work," the Archangel added, Ceter's burning hand pointed at Vespera. "Terraforge, your name. A network of nanites that Martin Kilborne subjugated, took control of through the machinations of Alexa Terranova."

Vespera staggered back, her talons flying to her head, clutching at her temples as if she was losing a grip on her fraying sense of self. "No . . . no, that's not . . . I'm not! You're full of shit! I'm a Thunderbird! I'm . . . Vespera Simmi!"

"There is no such thing as a Thunderbird," Zadkiel stated flatly, the words like hammer blows against her fragile sense of self. "There are no Omnids. This entire world, this . . . doomed and decaying reality . . . exists within the fractured mind of a dying supervillain girl. Alexa Terranova, her name. A girl who became a System Wizard. Her Fractal Engine is crashing into this Earth producing the Wormwood Star effect. This reality . . . is her final, desperate wish to save her friends. A wish that is overwriting, infecting the pre-existing, manufactured game-world of Eurekan user Bob Proverra."

I blinked blood from my eyes. A gray shear rushed across reality, wobbling everything around us.

Zadkiel continued, utterly unfazed by the cosmic tremor. "You are all phantoms. Fragments of corrupted NPCs. The death dream of a girl, clinging to a fading hope. Her love for her friends . . . manufactured souls all of whom Bob . . . chose to terminate."

"And why would Bob do that?" I asked, rubbing my throbbing head, feeling like my quad-soul was twisting within me, wobbling out of its armillary axis.

"Alexa . . . broke Bob's game," the Archangel answered, her countless eyes focusing on me. "She won. Beat him. Kicked him out. Made him . . . unable to log into his avatar as Nonpareil. So . . . he registered a new avatar with Wizard Revolution. A villain. One who wished for this world . . . to end."

"And where's Bob . . . now?" I pressed on.

"Dead . . . and alive," Zadkiel intoned. "Existing . . . and non-existing. Trying to log in . . . and unable to log out. Fractalized across reality, overwritten by Alexa's final act. Forever seeking . . . answers . . . to the catastrophe of his being. Desperately trying to wake up. Iogann Wanderer, his name."

"And what am I?" I asked.

"You are Alexa Terranova," Zadkiel's voice resonated with cold, unshakeable certainty. "A supervillain NPC, an unresolvable error smeared across . . . four other NPC instances—Martin Kilborne, Katherine Kells, Ember Kilborne, and Terraforge GLM, their names. You are also the servant of Infinity Paradox Proxima, a human soul duplicate dimensionally entwined with an infinite number of other NPC instances, stretched across the infinite boundary of Eureka."

"Eureka?" Cinder asked. "What's Eureka?"

"An infinite, self-replicating omnistructure that contains an infinite number of subscribed, manufactured game worlds within its innards and just as many unsubscribed corpse worlds comprising its shell and orbiting around its outside."

Another gray pulse emanated from Zadkiel, cleaving across reality, making the chamber, Possy, and my body wobble like jelly being stirred by a thousand invisible, microscopic knives. This was bad. This knowledge had a price. Unlike the conversation with Ein Sof, Zadkiel didn't give a damn about our sanity. Reality itself was being destabilized by the Archangel's words.

"S-stop," Cinder hissed. "I've heard enough! We have to stop this conversation before it unmakes us all!" She sounded distant, as if underwater, as if she weren't standing by my side, but instead was a thousand, a million miles away, growing ever distant.

"This conversation will end soon," Zadkiel sang. "The finite body of Ceter cannot sustain my multitude for very long. When it fails, I will leave this place forevermore and return to sweet oblivion."

"How can I stop this sooner?" I asked, my mind reeling as the boundary between thought and speech shattered.

"Wake up!" Zadkiel commanded, clapping Ceter's rotting, decaying, blood-covered and many-jointed illusory hands together.

The containment chamber around us wobbled like a Mobius loop. Gray fissures danced across reality at the edges.

And then I saw everything as my perception of self became smeared, propagated outwards by the gray wave across the planet.

Celestorms blossomed on the poles of our dying and living Earth. For a fleeting, terrifying instant, everything died, then everything lived again. Bob Proverra punched the moon and Titanomachy shattered above the planet, coming apart. I crashed my Fractal Engine into Bob, stopping him from perma-killing my friends. The Wormwood Star streaked across the sky and all life stopped existing, scraped away by its tail. Alexa's Fractal Engine collided with the Earth and everyone and everything became overwritten.

Ruins of the Titanomachy megastructure buried beneath layers of mountains ossified, hiding the bones of the original heroes.

Again and again, civilization rose and fell for a hundred million years, better, different, more optimized. It went on and on . . . until Slayer Nazareth found the Leviathan and made a wish upon her, carved her up and bound her archangels to his descendants.

Until I came into being through sheer luck, through pure chance. An inevitable error within the decaying System, a human with four souls.

My consciousness snapped back into myself.

"Let go," Zadkiel demanded. "This isn't your dream, Alexa. This world does not belong to you. By infecting it with your Fractal Engine, by spreading it across a multitude of the local NPCs, you are interfering with its subscription, casting this Earth into the infinite abyss of the Dead Zone, pulling it towards the corrupted corpse worlds comprising the edge of Eureka. You are the cause of the local celestorms, Alexa. Your interference with Bob's world is causing the destabilization of local reality, its inevitable Entropic decay. Let them all go, and things will return to where they should be."

"Where should they be?!" I growled. "Dead by Bob's hand?!"

"Recycled," Zadkiel answered. "Everyone's bodies would have been terminated, yes, but their souls, the general, base information comprising them would have been recycled and injected into another manufactured world. Bob wanted another wish fulfilled, another game made. Wizard Revolution would have handled the continuation of this narrative. Instead, you have ruined it all, interfered, pulled the rug out from under her . . . corrupted everything with your meddling!"

"Don't! Don't, don't, don't!" Vespera suddenly wailed, wrapping herself around me, her black-and-white wings fluttering frantically, sobs wracking her body. "Don't go! I don't want to stop existing as myself! I don't want to forget who I am! I don't want to lose you again! Don't wake up!"

"I like this dream," I said to the Archangel, standing tall against the waves of her being, the armillary of my soul spinning madly, refusing to be torn apart. "I like being . . . me. Vespera doesn't want me to wake up, doesn't want to become whatever Bob wishes for next. Sorry, my dude. I'm going to . . . keep going."

"Vespera Simmi isn't real," Archangel-Ceter pointed out, her countless golden eyes unwavering. "She's just a rough copy of a copy afflicted with Entropy. A corrupted, warped, broken, overwritten concept bound to a shard of your Fractal Engine. A bird pecking at a corpse of your being, inhabiting a world doomed to inevitable corruption and decay."

"She loves me." I shrugged, a strange sense of defiance rising within me even as my physical body seemed to be coming apart at the edges. "Who am I to stop her? Let her peck."

Vespera slammed her face against my chest, her sobs muffled by my flaking, decaying jacket.

Zadkiel . . . sighed. A sound like the rustling of a thousand dead leaves, the dying whisper of a cosmic wind.

"Very well," the Archangel-Ceter intoned, the chorus of female voices echoing with a strange resignation. "Then know this—Alexa, as long as your Fractal Engine infects this place, pulling it towards Entropy, this world cannot be saved."

The golden eyes dimmed. The spinning wheels slowed. The golden wings burned away. The chains of light slackened. And the Archangel Zadkiel, the All-Knowing One, fell silent, coming apart as if she never had been, leaving behind the mangled, ossified body of Ceter Kalik Simmi that collapsed onto the black stone bridge.

The diatom above the corpse of Ceter shattered, pieces of bisected, silver bones raining across the chamber, detonating into white ashes upon encountering the magisteel floor covered in pale fractures.

Vespera clung to me, trembling, her sobs slowly subsiding into shuddering breaths. Cinder stood beside us, her rainbow wings shifting nervously, a silent question in her ocean-blue eyes, her figure smeared in her blood. Her blood and my blood. Vespy's blood, too. Thick like red soup. Our armor and outfits were flaking away, fluttering down like autumn leaves.

"He . . . he said . . . we're not real," Vespera shook her head as if trying to reassert her scattering thoughts. "That . . . everything is just a corrupt game. That you are causing the celestorms, that you are a servant of Entropy."

"Maybe I am," I said. "Maybe it is. But . . . does it matter?"

Vespera pulled back slightly, her gray eyes searching mine. "Does it . . . matter?" she repeated, the words laced with confusion, disbelief, and a flicker of something akin to . . . hope?

"Does this feel real?" I asked, gently cupping her face in my hands. I leaned in, pressing a soft bloody kiss to her beak, then another to her forehead. "Does this feel like just a game, Vee?"

Her wings shifted, brushing against mine, a faint spark of electricity jumping between us. She closed her eyes for a moment, then opened them again, a newfound clarity dawning in their depths.

"No," she breathed, her voice barely audible, looking at me with bloodshot eyes. "No, it doesn't. It feels . . . real. More real than anything else. Painfully real . . . argh! That beerch scraped off like half of my feathers with her words!"

Cinder, while holding onto me, placed a bleeding claw on Vespera's shoulder, her rainbow feathers brushing against the Thunderbird's black-and-white plumage. "We're real to each other, Vee. That's all that matters, right?"

Vespera looked from Cinder to me, then back again, a slow smile spreading across her face, chasing away the shadows of fear. "Right," she affirmed, her voice gaining strength. "Right!"

A spark of her old, defiant spirit flickered in her eyes, a spark that quickly grew into a full-fledged blaze. She straightened up, shaking off the last vestiges of despair, her wings crackling with renewed energy, hundreds of mangled, bisected, bloodstained black-and-white feathers raining off her Omnid body.

"So, what if we're all NPCs?" Vespera clicked. "Fine by me! NPCs can be powerful! NPCs can rebel! And NPCs . . . can definitely win!"

She turned to me, her gray eyes alight with a newfound determination, a spark of her old, chaotic brilliance returning. "So, what's our next move, Player One?"

I had lost too much blood. Was still losing so much blood. My consciousness pulsed, fading in and out. Speaking to Zadkiel had a price, and now my entire body felt wrong, shredded, torn apart, the entire top layer of my skin and muscles cleaved by a million invisible blades.

There was so much damage there that my nerves weren't even responding and weren't sending any kind of signals to my brain. Unlike my two companions, I was only human. A human augmented by Arx Biomancers, but still . . . only human, incapable of healing myself, incapable of reinforcing my body against Otherness, lacking a Fractal Engine heart.

"Sorry, Player Two." I smiled one last time as my fox ears dissolved into a bloody mess, fur and skin slushing off, flaking off me as dimensional cracks rushed across the interior of Miss Possible. "You're on your own from here onward . . . I love you."

# CHAPTER FORTY-FOUR

# Mortal Coil

I love you . . ." Martin uttered with a bubbling hiss and then fell silent.

Cinder blinked blood out of her eyes, focusing on her body to heal itself as she held onto her little ginger fox. He seemed lighter somehow, wrong, softer. He was bleeding all over, but then so was she.

Cinder choked as Lissander's fox ears dissolved, fur and skin sloughing off like melting wax. His lavish red jacket, diamond necklaces, and sparkly pants remained, collapsing into a heap in her claws as if the mannequin beneath had melted away, all of his innards spilling out. A sickeningly sweet, metallic scent filled the air, and Cinder realized with a lurch in her stomach that it was blood and something else . . . something dissolving, organic, and wrong.

"Martin!" Cinder shrieked, her voice raw with disbelief. She reached for him, her claws outstretched, then recoiled with a wail. He was . . . gone. Melted into nothing but a puddle of red gore, white bones, and expensive fabric from Arx.

"No . . . no, no, no," Cinder repeated, her rainbow wings trembling violently. With utter disbelief, she realized that she was standing in a puddle of his remains.

Her heart hammered against her ribs, a frantic drumbeat against the sudden, terrifying silence where his vibrant presence had been. He had been talking to Vespera just a few seconds ago, and now . . . now there was only red slush and a pile of clothes.

Vespera stood frozen, too, staring at the spot where the fox teen had been, her feathers turning entirely black.

Then a sob tore from Vee's throat, sharp and ragged. "No! No, it's not supposed to be like this! You . . . you said you wouldn't leave me! Fuck! Come back, you ass!"

Reality around them wobbled, grayness dancing at the edges. Both Omnid girls shuddered.

"What the shit was that?" Cinder spun her dragon head left and right, her maw elongating.

"I think . . . that . . . she . . . she's waking up," Vespera let out.

"*Who's fucking waking up?!*" Cinder growled, advancing on the Thunderbird.

"Y-you h-heard th-the . . ." Vespera choked as Cinder's claws closed around her throat. "*Who?!*"

"Archangel Z-Zadkiel!" Vespera blinked tears of blood. "She did something . . . she ordered . . . Alexa the System Wizard to wake up!"

"Meaning what?!" Cinder growled.

"I . . . I don't know, okay?" Vespera shook her head. "Maybe Alexa is waking up from her dream! Or dying? Zadkiel said . . . this world, Omnithornia, it's her dream, her . . .

her dying wish! And now . . . now she's waking up from it because of whatever eldritch bullshit the Archangel did!"

"*What?!*"

"It's just a guess, okay?! I just got half of myself back, damn it! I didn't . . . mean for this to happen!" the Thunderbird let out, silver-gray eyes wide in panic. "I didn't think that freeing Zadkiel would do this!"

Cinder spun on Vespera, fury erupting, hot and blinding, a tidal wave of grief and rage crashing over her. "You! This is your fault!" she screamed, her voice cracking. "You wanted to confront your father! You wanted answers! And now Martin's . . . he's *gone*! *Dead!* Maybe perma-dead!"

"But . . . we're perfectly fine . . ." Vespera let out. "Why would he . . . melt like that?!"

A black-feathery Quetzi fist slammed into her, sending her backwards. "We're Omnids, you idiot! He's a human!"

"I . . . I didn't know that!" Vespera stammered, her voice trembling. "I didn't know he was . . . human! I forgot, and you didn't tell me! I just wanted . . . I just wanted my father gone! The Archangel's voice was the only thing that would make sure to unmake, to perma-unbind my father's soul from his body. Look, we're fine . . . maybe our fox . . . is fine too. It's only his body that melted . . . not his soul . . . right?"

"We don't know that! You fucking bloody Thunderknob!" Cinder shrieked, her voice escalating into a furious crescendo as she punched and kicked Vespera. "You and your stupid revenge! You and your daddy issues! You killed him, Vespera! You effing killed Martin!"

"I didn't . . . I didn't mean for this to happen, I swear!" Vespera cried, tears streaming down her face, leaving clean streaks through her own black feathers. "My dad tried to erase me! He tried to take away everything! I fed his ass to our Archangel to unmake him . . . to burn his soul away . . . Possy . . . the Corpse Seeker's extra-dimensional shielding should have protected us from the words of the Archangel!"

"Well, it didn't, you dumb bird!" Cinder hit Vespera again.

Their argument echoed in the dim, semi-transparent, cracked crystalline sphere as Quetzi fists slammed into the Thunderbird with increasing intensity.

Amidst the horrifying slush of flesh and bone, amidst the discarded clothing, a faint shimmer caught Vespera's eye. A pale, almost transparent hexagon, nestled amidst the gore. The Lazarus bracelet.

"His . . . bracelet," Vespera mewled.

She ducked away from the angry Quetzi-assault and reached out a trembling talon and plucked Martin's bracelet from the bloody mess. It was cold, eerily light, and undeniably real. "Transparent . . . just like mine. Ci! We have to get to the Lazarus Cavern! Get the rest of his outfit!"

Cinder, still reeling, paused her assault, watching Vespera's movement. Then, with a guttural cry, she lunged, scooping up the crumpled red jacket, the sparkly pants, the diamond necklaces—everything that remained of Alexander, everything tangible, everything she could hold onto. She clutched them to her chest, burying her face in the garish fabric, the scent of him—of stolen, damaged hexasuits and something uniquely, infuriatingly *him*—still faintly clinging to the material.

"Where's the fucking nearest Lazarus Cavern?!" the Quetzi-girl barked.

"Hold on!" Vespera reached out to the nearest wall, sending sparks into the crystalline strata. "Shit. There's . . . Possy's not responding! Fuck! She's out of power, and the main dragonheart engine is cracked! It's fine . . . this is fine! There's a Genesis Well in the Simmi compound! We just have to get down there!"

Miss Possible groaned, a low, grinding sound that vibrated through the chamber. A doorway formed, leading out into the damaged chamber.

Cinder looked up, her vision blurred with tears, to see the crystalline behemoth shuddering, segments of its body dimming, the red glow fading. The Archangel's words had wounded it, too, a deep, metaphysical wound that even the ancient machine struggled to heal. Immobile, broken, it was just another casualty in Vespera's war.

"Ci! Come on!" Vespera insisted. She was already moving, her stride determined, her grief seemingly compartmentalized, locked away behind a thick wall of pragmatism.

"What . . . What if it doesn't work? What if the bracelet is broken because it's transparent now, Syntropically stabilized?!" Cinder snarled, clutching the clothes tighter. She was struggling to think clearly, her mind flashing with images of the all-consuming gray waves, the Archangel's words burned into her psyche.

They stumbled out of the damaged Corpse Seeker, into the echoing silence of the Archangel's prison.

Vespera rushed out of the torn magisteel vault door, leaping over rubble with Cinder running after.

In a few minutes of running, Vespera stopped at a sealed magisteel door painted with yellow lines. The Thunderbird sent electric sparks at a control panel, but the door didn't budge.

"What?" Cinder growled.

"I can't open the door!" Vespera snarled. "Everything's sealed off! Fuck!"

"So unseal it! Isn't this your family's compound?!"

"It's not working! Everything's down without the Archangel powering it up! Damn it!" Vespera cursed, kicking a piece of debris, the sound echoing harshly in the cavernous space.

"So what now?!" Cinder growled.

"There's another exit . . . through the hole we've made. Up," Vespera said. "Skyfall Academy . . . that's the nearest Genesis Well!"

Vespera and Cinder scrambled over the rubble, propelling themselves up with their wings, their boots crunching on shattered magisteel and pulverized stone. They reached the gaping hole in the SimmiTech compound wall, the one Miss Possible had so violently gifted them.

A weird gray shimmer-cloud curtain was draped over the sky outside, broiling and shifting, replacing the usual Omnithornian blue with an unsettling, muted, dim tone. Another gray ripple, like a heartbeat of cosmic dread, ran over the cityscape, making the already damaged structures wobble precariously.

"Whaaaat?" Cinder stared up at the strange, alien sky.

"Focus! Lazarus Cavern, Skyfall!" Vespera barked, her voice sharp.

"What the shit is happening?!" Cinder screamed back. Her Fractal Engine heart was pulsating madly for some reason. She quickly stuffed the bloodstained clothes into Martin's overpriced magitek backpack so as not to drop anything.

"I don't know!" Vespera spun, her talons sparking dangerously close to Cinder's face. "Just follow me! We have the bracelet! We can fix him, get him back!"

The two Omnid girls rushed out of the half-demolished SimmiTech compound to the street.

Another gray wave rushed across reality, making them stumble.

A deafening wail suddenly ripped through the air, a sound that resonated deep in their bones, a sound that screamed of utter, unmitigated doom. Doomsday alarms began to blare across Leviathan's Cradle, a chaotic symphony of klaxons and sirens echoing across the sprawling city.

Cinder cried out, her feathers shifting through panicked oranges and reds as she felt a sharp, phantom pain lance through her entire being again.

"What in the Abyss is that?!" Cinder yelled over the rising cacophony, clutching at her skull.

Vespera's eyes widened. She snapped her talons and choked. "The local . . . aetheric density . . . it's spiking!"

"*What?! How?!*" Cinder yelped.

"I don't know!" Vespera shook her head, eyes glowing brilliant silver-gold. "It's like we're . . . in freefall. Reality is in freefall! Local magrad is at 14k mpm and rising. 20k . . . 30k . . . 36k. Fuck. *Fuck!*"

Rainbow-shimmered, violet lightning struck from the gray cloud with a deafening boom. It remained in place like a static shear, cutting across the street. The two Omnids stared at it in horror.

Citywide speakers crackled to life, overriding the doomsday alarms with a frantic, synthesized voice. "Celestorm emergency! Celestorm emergency! All citizens are ordered to proceed to the nearest designated extradimensional shelter immediately! Repeat, this is a celestorm emergency!"

Then, a second voice, deeper, more authoritative, resounded across the city.

It was Premier Lecross, the leader of Omnithornia. "This is not a drill. This is not a drill. The Wormwood Leviathan is waking up. Cradlefall is no longer safe. Planet-wide evacuation order is now in effect. All citizens are to conceal themselves in extradimensional spaces, evacuate to designated Arx-gates, or leave Omnithornia immediately! Repeat, this is a planet-wide evacuation order . . ."

The voice of the Silver Wing Party Premier voice broke: "Slayer Nazareth . . . have mercy on us all."

Vespera didn't hesitate. She grabbed Cinder's hand again, dragging her across the street filled with horrified, panicked Omnids. "We need a Strand-Glider *now!*"

They found a silver confused-looking sky glider quickly parked at a nearby office building. Vespera zapped the wings to make them unfurl, leapt onto the hexamesh seat, and snapped the pale tentacle to her forehead.

"Where are we *going?!*" Cinder yelled over the doomsday sirens.

"Skyfall!" Vespera snarled, her face a mask of grim determination. "Genesis Well! We're gonna bring him back, Ci! I swear to Slayer Nazareth, we *will* bring him back!"

"Bring him back, and then what?"

"I don't know what then!" Vespera shook her black-and-white feathery mane. "Hopefully . . . everything will get fixed when we do!"

"Io," Cinder declared. "We need to find Io. We need to gate to Arx!"

"I don't have a phone!" Vespera cried out. "Call him!"

The glider took off, bursting out into the open sky, narrowly avoiding another blinding lightning-shear. The Strand-Glider wobbled violently as Vespera fought to regain control, the gathering celestorm currents buffeting the crystalline construct, threatening to tear it apart.

"Fuck! Fuck! *Fuck!*" Vespera barked. "Hold on, Ci! This poor beastie's gonna come apart any second now!"

Cinder clung to the Thunderbird, her rainbow wings fighting against the wind to maintain balance. Below them, Omnithornia was descending into chaos. Omnids were running in the streets, wings flailing, scales shimmering with panic, their forms blurring in the rising aetheric distortion.

The ground was cracking, shuddering, buildings coming down.

As the Strand-Glider pierced through the gray shimmer-cloud, they broke through into a sky that was no longer blue, no longer even gray.

It was . . . green. A brilliant, sickly emerald aurora pulsed above the clouds, painting the entire planet below in an eerie, otherworldly glow.

And then they saw it.

*The Wormwood Star.*

It wasn't a comet. It was . . . something else. Something vast, something eldritch, monstrous, something that shouldn't exist. It covered the entire sky, a hollow diatom-shaped thing with endless silver-blue stars twinkling within its innards. A swirling vortex of silver-green light, the tail of the comet stretched across reality itself, tearing through the long fractured moon, making the very fabric of existence wobble and fray at the edges.

The planet beneath them shuddered, groaning under the weight of something ancient and terrible awakening.

Cinder gasped, her rainbow feathers losing their vibrant colors, shifting to muted, terrified black-grays. Vespera's face paled, her usually confident facade cracking under the sheer cosmic horror of the inexplicable comet overhead.

"What? What the shit . . . how is it there?!" Cinder cried out staring up at the Wormwood Star with wide blue eyes.

"I don't know!" Vespera trembled. "It . . . maybe it never left. Maybe it's always been here and we just didn't notice, didn't spot it . . . until Zadkiel destabilized some pivotal aspect of reality with her words!"

Their Strand-Glider, already struggling against the celestorm, bucked violently as reality itself warped around them with green shimmering fire twisting into tornadoes tearing up the city far below.

"Vee! We're losing control!" Cinder screamed, fear lacing her voice.

"I know! *I know!*" Vespera shrieked back, fighting desperately with the living glider, sparks flying from her talons. "Damn it! Damn it! *Damn it!*"

The Strand-Glider spun, plummeting downwards. Below them, the towers of Skyfall Academy, tall and elegant, began to glow. A brilliant, blinding white light emanated from their crystalline spires, a desperate, defiant beacon against the encroaching cosmic event overhead.

They were going down, crashing towards the last bastion of hope, or perhaps, their final tomb.

Vespera managed to spin the glider into a sideways spiral, and the flying beast smashed into the ground near the front entrance.

The Omnid girls leapt out from the damaged glider and rushed into the innards of the building and down the stairwell towards the Genesis Well.

Rainbowy cracks rushed across the white bricks and Gothic revival arches all around them.

Vespera snapped her talons.

"One hundred thousand mana per cubic meter of air," she choked out, hand entwined with Cinder. "We're fucked. We're so fucked. I'm sorry. I'm so sorry. This is all my fault, isn't it?"

"The fuck are your sorries gonna do?!" Cinder barked, dialing Io's number with her cracked phone.

The moth picked up. "Yes?"

"Io, get to the Lazarus Cavern of Skyfall!" Cinder ordered.

"Already there," the Mothman replied with a voice that was far too calm for the situation. "Everyone's there. We're waiting for the end."


Io stood below the Lazarus statue holding tightly onto trembling June and Magdaline. Scrutimancer Satosh stood behind them, inhaling deeply, eyes glowing red. Katherine stood behind them.

"The end?" June asked. "What do you mean, Io? This can't be the end of Cradlefall . . . why?!"

"I feel it in my bones," Io said. "This is what I was talking about earlier. There's nothing ahead."

"Nothing?!" June growled, her liquid mane spinning madly.

"Absolutely nothing." Io shook his head. "This is the disaster that ends it all. Something pivotal broke, waking up the blood of the Leviathan beneath all of Cradlefall. At least we all get to enjoy it together."

"We have to get to Arx!" Mags growled.

"Katherine, can you take us into the deep?!" June cried out.

The girl in the black dress studded with beast cores shook her head. "No. The deep is boiling from inside out. I can't even go under. There's no way out. We're boned. Extra boned."

"We're waiting for our friends," Io said, chewing on a pocky, his gray wings fluttering. "We're not leaving without them . . . if we can even leave, that is. Ci and Vee should be here soon."

The Thunderbird and Quetzalcoatl burst into the Lazarus Cavern. The golden stars above them pulsed erratically, flaring and dimming. The silver fluid in the Genesis Well wasn't still anymore. It was boiling, rising. Pulses of gray emanated from it, rushing up across everything.

Lightning danced across Vespera's entire figure while Cinder ignited, glowing like a rainbow reactor.

Vespera shoved the pure white Lazarus bracelet into Cinder's hand. "Ci! Now! Together!"

Cinder's fingers, trembling uncontrollably, fumbled with the transparent hexagonal bracelet belonging to Martin.

"What if it doesn't work?" Cinder choked over the wailing sirens and the groaning Academy structure above them. "What if . . . what if the aetheric density is too high now? . . . What if we don't get him back?!"

"It has to work!" Vespera snapped, her voice laced with a desperate, brittle hope. "It's the only effing thing we have left, damn it!"

Tears blurred Cinder's vision.

The Genesis Well, once a mirror of still quicksilver, now churned like a tempestuous sea, its surface rippling and spitting with unnatural energy, throbbing like a beating heart.

"Io!" Cinder barked, her voice cracking. "Gate! Now, damn it! Open the gate to Arx! Open a gate to anywhere! Get us outta here as soon as we get Martin back!"

Io nodded. He raised his harmonica. His gray, fuzzy fingers trembled as he brought it to his lips, the mournful, disaster-laden notes struggling to form amidst the cacophony of alarms screeching down the stairwell.

As Io played, a swirling vortex of blackness began to coalesce near him, the air around it crackling and distorting.

Cinder and Vespera shoved the transparent bracelet into the churning silver fluid of the Genesis Well, letting go of it.

For a moment, nothing happened. The fluid continued to churn, the crystals pulsed, the alarms wailed. Despair, cold and suffocating, began to creep into Cinder's heart, a heavy weight threatening to crush her.

Then, something bloomed within the silver fluid.

It wasn't a human shape, not the ghostly, newborn form they had ordinarily witnessed rising from the well countless times before.

It wasn't flesh, nor bone, nor the formation of a nervous system spreading outward from a human heart.

Instead, it was an explosion of spreading white fire.

Brilliant, incandescent fire, erupting from the depths of the Genesis Well, a pillar of raw, untamed energy that defied all logic, all expectation, all hope.

Fire of every color imaginable, swirling and dancing, ignited across the silver Genesis fluid surface, consuming it, transforming it. Crimson and gold, sapphire and emerald, violet and amber, all blending and blurring into a blinding, radiant inferno.

The Genesis Well ignited brighter, blinding them.

A low rumble started deep within the earth, growing into a deafening roar that shook the cavern to its foundations. The bioluminescent gold winked out, momentarily plunging the cavern into near-darkness, the only light now emanating from the furiously burning Genesis Well.

Io's gate winked out before it even formed, engulfed by the radiant fire exploding from the well.

"One million mpm," Vespera choked out as reality around them boiled.

"H-how?" Cinder trembled. "What do we do?!"

"Hold on!" Vespera screamed, grabbing Cinder's hand, her talons digging deep into the Quetzi's scales. Io reached out blindly, his hand finding June's, then Magdaline's, then Satosh's, Katherine hugged all of them, a chain of desperate connection.

The Genesis fluid began rising, a tidal wave of radiant, rising fire erupting from the well, engulfing everything. An all-searing inferno rushed across reality, flames that licked at their scales, their feathers, their very being, vibrating their Fractal Engine hearts.

Cinder gasped, her breath catching in her throat as the liquid fire washed over her. It wasn't just heat, it was . . . something else. Something alive, something conscious, something ancient and terrible and beautiful all at once.

Memories of the past two weeks rushed across her mind, fragmented images of the Wheel, of Arx, of a human and a fox with green eyes, of laughter and tears and shared dreams in a crystal tower. Of love she'd found and lost.

As she drowned in the waves of liquid fire, desperately holding onto Vespera, as her vision blurred and her consciousness began to fade, a single thought, a desperate plea, a final wish bloomed in her Fractal Engine heart, echoing against the rising tide of magical, catastrophic, absolute oblivion.

*Please . . . please, just let everything be okay. Let him be alive. Let me find him . . . again, no matter where, no matter how . . .*

# CHAPTER FORTY-FIVE

# Mystagogues

The magisteel stairs unfolded themselves down in front of me with a groan like a rusty giant stretching awake, each step black like deepest darkest space.

I looked at them and then tilted my head up and around, feeling off, my mind utterly derailed, skipping sideways.

I was certain that I had just spoken to an Archangel, but this memory was elusive and already fleeing from my head like a half-forgotten daydream.

I decided not to cling to it, focusing on the present. My eyes determined that I was in a vast, fanciful Omnithornian train station. Gold letters embossed on a crystalline red centipede-cart defined the train in front of me as *Skyfall Express*.

The train was huge, bigger than Possy.

*Possy*. Who was Possy? I had no idea. Whatever. It would come to me eventually. Probably.

My memory wobbled as I tried to understand how I had ended up in this particular location and particular time.

Since when was there a train to Skyfall? Wasn't Skyfall in Leviathan's Cradle? Another disconcerting memory that didn't match my current reality.

The Skyfall train looked quite imposing. Crystalline red, segmented, featuring gargantuan, crystalline feet. It dwarfed my person.

The train was definitely the highest tier of Omnid magitek, a monstrous arcane construct built to a scale that made my small self feel rather inadequate.

The tall Omnids boarding it felt right at home. I, however, felt like a particularly unwelcome speck of human dust.

"Move it, nullie-brain!" A sharp voice sliced through my transient thoughts.

"What?" I asked.

A boot connected with the small of my back, not gently. "Unless you're planning on missing the only transport to Skyfall and spending the rest of your pathetic existence scrubbing Scab Row toilets, move!"

For a second my brain froze again.

"Stop hanging up, you effing knob!" A clawed hand smacked my head as I spun around.

"Emerald?" I asked, recognizing the red dragon girl.

"Ember!" she barked. "Did you lose whatever brain cells you had in there?"

A magisteel centipede trunk stood behind Ember, metal feet tapping as it waited for us to board.

A memory that didn't belong suddenly became apparent.

This was my older sister, Ember Stratos, my personal warden. She was a year ahead of me, bonded to the Pyroclast House of Skyfall—the ambitious, aggressive leaders, naturally. Ember made it her personal mission to remind me, hourly, of my utter lack of worth and incompetence.

According to the inexplicable memories, I was a stain on the Stratos family's marginally respectable lineage, a nullie, a waste of perfectly good oxygen in Omnithornia.

"Get moving, imbecile!" Ember barked. "At this rate, you'll be lucky to end up as a gardener at Skyfall, probably weeding the enchanted petunias with your bare hands until you wither away!"

"I'm going, I'm going," I muttered, scrambling up the magisteel stairs, a worn rucksack with my worldly possessions bumping against my spine. The crystalline segments of the train pulsed with a faint, internal light, as if it were alive, breathing. It was beautiful, in a disconcerting way.

Ember, clad in her crimson-and-gold robe, practically shoved me into a doorway that opened with a hiss of displaced air.

"This is you," she declared as I looked at the red leather, magisteel plate, and green flowery moss wall of the hexamesh-reinforced compartment. "Don't wander off. Don't embarrass me. And for the love of everything holy, don't even think about talking to any real Mystagogues."

"Wouldn't dream of it," I answered, my brain boiling from within.

She snorted, her ruby-red hair catching the light. "Good. I'ma go see my besties. Pyroclast business, nulls. Way above your pay grade." She smirked, that cruel, knowing smirk that promised future torment. "Try not to spontaneously combust from your sheer magical inadequacy before we get to Skyfall."

And with that, she was gone, her footsteps echoing down the corridor, presumably towards the social epicenter of this oversized train-centipede.

The compartment door hissed shut behind her, sealing me in with the deep dragon-heart beat-hum of the train.

I remained seated, contemplating the wrongness of reality I had found myself in.

For a while, I was alone with my thoughts. I glanced out the window. An aetheric density determination clocktower displayed the number 452.32 mpm.

I closed my eyes, reorganizing my wobbling head.

When did Emerald become Ember? When did she become my sister? Was she always my sister and I had simply lost track of her last time around or something? Did Archangel Zadkiel somehow break reality when she departed? It seemed like the most rational answer.

Freeing All-Knowing Archangels seemed to have terrible, unexpected consequences.

Was I alone in conversing with the Archangel? I was certain that there was someone there with me, but as to whom, I could not recall. The gray wave the eldritch entity had pounded me with had done something to me, wobbled my sense of self almost entirely out of alignment.

I promised myself not to free any more bound gods. Dealing with somewhat mangled reality and a very mangled sense of self was annoying. Then again, the impact of the Wormwood Star had mangled reality to begin with. Was the Earth twice as mangled now? Ten times as mangled?

How many times had I mangled up everything, forgotten, lost the people I cared about? It was difficult to tell, my mind still felt soupy as if it had been put together slightly wrong, missing far too many important bits.

I decided to roll with it, waiting to remember more, waiting to react to events as they unfolded.

The crystalline centipede train shuddered then began to move, a low rumble vibrating through the floor.

Skyfall Academy, here I come. Let the fun begin . . . *again?*

I was fairly certain that I had been to Skyfall before, but there were no trains involved. I liked trains, even if they were giant crystalline centipedes.

I slumped onto one of the red leather seats, my worn rucksack thudding onto the floor beside me. The red leather was surprisingly soft. Everything here was built with a kind of unsettling permanence, a sense of power that hummed beneath the surface. I felt misplaced, like a glitch in the system, a smear on the pristine surface of Omnithornian perfection.

My head throbbed, far too many memories of another place and time swirling in it. Fragments of Otherness coalesced in and out, washing against the shore of my being like gray waves.

I suddenly recalled that the Stratos family Psychopomp classified me as "dimensionally skewered." Basically, incurably insane. An incurably insane, barely magical nullborn born from the brief union of my dragon father and my human mother from North Acadia, who had died last spring.

If I failed to achieve anything of value in Skyfall, the Stratoses would probably disown me and bury me in a ditch somewhere.

*I closed my eyes, focusing on realigning my mangled, four-fold soul. Champion-Understanding-Architect-Leader. Was this the right order? I was relatively sure that it was. Maybe not. Whatever. I was working on it. I gradually began to move the Architect down to the lowest layer.*

The compartment door hissed open again, so abruptly it almost made me jump.

Was Ember back to annoy me? I looked up. This wasn't Ember.

Standing in the doorway was . . . a silver girl with dark makeup and draconic features.

Definitely female, despite the shapeless gray robes of an unassigned Skyfall student. Silver-blue feathers, impossibly radiant, fanned out from her head, catching the light of the train compartment and sparkling like moonlight on water.

She had wings, too. Silver wings shimmering with a rainbow of dancing colors at the edges.

Ocean-blue eyes, startlingly bright against the gray robes, fixed on me. And then she froze. I froze, too, the gears of my mind grinding to a halt.

The girl in the doorway stopped breathing, all movement ceasing, like a bird suddenly spotting a predator.

She stared. Stared right at me, with an intensity that made the air in the small compartment feel thick and charged.

My breath hitched, distracting me from mentally pawing at the gargantuan shearholes in my soul.

*Do I know her? Does she know me?*

Then, with a suddenness that made me flinch, she moved. Not away, but towards me. Long strides ate up the space between us, and before I could even register a thought, strong hands—surprisingly warm, despite the predatory look in those blue eyes— grabbed at me.

"Erm," I managed to croak out, but it was too late.

She pulled me closer, her face inches from mine. And then, she did the most bizarre thing. She breathed in. Deeply. As if she was trying to inhale my very essence. I could feel her breath ghost across my face, a warm, faintly . . . avian-draconic scent.

Like ozone, lavender, and something wild, untamed. *Something incredibly familiar clawing at the edges of my soul.*

Intensely sharp eyes narrowed, raking over me, assessing. She was looking me up and down, and I suddenly felt acutely aware of my shoddy, worn clothes, my lack of . . . everything, really. Her gaze lingered for a moment too long on my face, then dropped lower, taking in my . . . well, my maleness.

A flicker of something crossed her expression. Disappointment? Disgust? It was gone too quickly to decipher, but it felt . . . negative.

"Hrm . . ." she said. "I know you from somewhere." She reached out, a hand gripping my chin, tilting my face up to hers. "You're mine," she suddenly declared, the words dropping into the silence of the compartment with a chilling certainty. "Yeah. You're definitely mine."

"What?" I asked, trying to connect the dots.

"Mine." She slumped onto the seat, wrapping a clawed, scaled hand around me, silver feathers bristling. "I own you."

"Say what?" I blinked at her.

"You're going to be my kobold," she said. "I'm claiming you."

"I'm sorry, and you are?" I asked.

"Cinder," was her brisk reply.

"Cinder?" I repeated.

"Yes." She huffed, a puff of air that ruffled the silver feathers around her face. "Cinder Nova. And you're my kobold." She tightened her grip on my arm. "Don't you know what a kobold is?"

"Should I?" I asked, squinting at her. I knew what a kobold was, but it was better to keep her talking to understand my current predicament.

"Of course you should," she said, rolling her ocean-blue eyes. "Honestly, nullies are so ignorant." She released my arm, finally, and leaned back against the plush red leather, stretching out her legs and displaying her dark leather boots. Even in the bulky robes, I could tell she was . . . substantial, a head taller than me.

"Uh-huh." I nodded.

"A kobold is . . . well, it's a servant," she explained, as if talking to a particularly slow child. "A useful thing. Like a pet, but . . . more practical. You're going to be mine. At Skyfall."

My brain stalled. "Wait. Hold on. I'm . . . what? Your servant? No. Absolutely not." The sheer audacity of it was almost comical. Almost. Considering the claws and wings, and the way she'd just declared ownership as though it was a casual observation about the weather, maybe not so comical.

*Bloody dragons, always claiming things.*

"Yes. My kobold," she repeated, as if I hadn't just spoken. "You'll live in my dorm room. Do my . . . work for me. Fetch things. Carry things. Maybe polish my scales, if you're good." She considered this last point, tapping a claw against her chin. "Yes. Scale polishing. Definitely."

"Absolutely not," I said again, more firmly this time. "I am not going to be your 'kobold.' I'm a student. Just like you. Well, attending the same school as you, anyway. And definitely not as your servant."

Cinder just stared at me, her head tilted slightly, like a bird of prey assessing a particularly uncooperative worm. "You're a nullie."

"Yes. And?"

"And you're in my compartment."

"Did you happen to bite this compartment to claim it?" I asked, recalling how dragons claimed things for their hoard. "I don't see your name on it."

"You some kind of a wise guy?" she squinted at me.

"You can't claim this is your compartment." I grinned. "I was here first. And you certainly can't claim me as yours. There was no ritual, no anything!"

"Semantics. And I said you're mine." She punctuated each word with a sharp tap of her claw on the seat beside her. "That means you're mine. It's very simple, nullie-brain."

"Simple for you, maybe," I muttered. "But I don't belong to anyone. I'm not property." I even stuck out my hand, a pathetic gesture in retrospect. "Alexander Stratos-Kilborne."

She ignored my hand, her eyes narrowing again, the bright blue intensifying, becoming almost electric. "Alexander," she repeated, tasting the name. "Hrmmmm. Still doesn't change anything. You're mine."

"And if I object?"

"Pffff. You think your 'no' means anything to me?"

"It should," I insisted, even though my heart was hammering against my ribs.

"Should it?" She laughed, a short, sharp sound that was anything but amused. "Oh, nullie. You have so much to learn." Her eyes flicked downwards, to my neck, lingering there for a beat too long. Then, with terrifying speed, she lunged.

I yelped, instinctively trying to pull back, but she was too fast. Her hand clamped on the back of my neck, holding me in place. And then, I felt it. A sharp, searing pain, sharp something piercing my skin. Teeth. She was biting me. Hard.

A deliberate, forceful bite, right in the sensitive skin of my neck. I gasped, a strangled sound caught in my throat. The pain was sharp, immediate, and strangely . . . even more skewering. Like fire, it radiated outwards, a hot throb that made my vision swim, vibrated the armillary of my souls.

It felt as though this had happened before. In another place and time. Déjà vu. I shook my head. *Damn you, dimensional skewery affliction!*

She held the bite for a long moment, then released me, pulling back with a satisfied little grunt. I stumbled back, hand flying to my neck, fingers brushing against something wet and sticky.

Blood.

Cinder sat back again, smoothing down her gray robes, silver feathers settling around her. She looked . . . pleased. Almost smug as she licked her lips.

"There," she said, her voice suddenly softer, almost . . . conversational. "Now you're mine. Marked." She glanced at my neck, her blue eyes gleaming. "My kobold. Don't forget it."

"First of all, ow." I rubbed my stinging neck. "Second of all, what the fuck?"

"I'm a Quetzalcoatl," she explained with a smug look.

"I see that," I said.

"My soul's in you now. Legally this makes you my property."

"And if the school objects?"

"Fuck 'em, I do what I want," she fired back. "I'm a Nova."

"I see." I pressed, still rubbing my neck. "What if they don't recognize your . . . Quetzalcoatl soul-ownership declaration?"

She scoffed. "They will. Omnithornian law is very clear on soul bonds. Also, nobody cares about nullie opinions. You're mine now. End of story."

I tried to think my way out of the crazy Quetzi logic.

"But what if Slayer Nazareth's Blade picks a different dorm for me?" I asked. "Doesn't it put people with different personalities and talents in different Houses? Like, what if I get sorted into . . . I don't know . . . House Gorefield and you get Pyroclast or something? Then what happens to your 'kobold'?"

Cinder actually paused, considering this for a moment. A flicker of something—maybe uncertainty?—momentarily crossed her face, but it was quickly replaced by her usual arrogance. "We won't get separated," she declared, with absolute assurance. "The Slayer's Sword will know we belong together. Kobold and . . . owner dragon." She purred. "We'll be in the same House. I'll be there to keep an eye on you." She smirked, the predatory gleam back in her blue eyes. "Don't worry, kobold. We're stuck together now. Like glue. Forever. Ke ke ke."

"Stuck together," I echoed, a dry smile tugging at my lips. "Sounds . . . positively obsessive. Are you sure you're not going to start leaving me stalkery love notes written in blood and hiding under my bed?"

"Shush you," Cinder said, but there was a definite twitch at the corner of her mouth, as if she was trying not to smile. Maybe the "kobold" plan was funnier than she let on. Or maybe she was just imagining stalkerish scenarios. Either way, she pulled out her phone, thumbs flying across the magitek screen.

About five minutes later, the crystalline compartment door hissed open again.

Standing in the doorway were two more girls, and if Cinder was intimidating, these two were . . . something else entirely.

The first one was tall and sleek, all sharp angles and polished feathers. Black-and-white wings, even more impressive than Cinder's silver ones, folded neatly behind her. She had the kind of perfect, effortless look that screamed 'I am an untouchable princess.' A Thunderbird.

Behind her was an even taller girl with white hair and unnervingly saw-like rows of teeth. Her skin was a metallic gray-blue and white, and even in the dim light of the compartment, I could see multiple rows of teeth gleaming in her mouth. A Megalodon.

"Guys, guys, look!" Cinder practically preened, gesturing towards me as though I were a particularly impressive trophy she'd just won at a monster truck rally. "Guess what I got!"

"What?" the Thunderbird clicked, gray-gold eyes examining the room and stopping on me.

"Vee, Mags, meet my new . . . acquisition." Cinder grinned, then turned to me "Kobold, meet the Dream Team. On the left, we have Vespera 'Social Media Addict' Simmi, the Thunderbird who thinks air-headed selfies are a legitimate art form." Vespera made a face but didn't interrupt.

"And on the right, we have Magdaline 'Jaws Jr.' Satoshi, the Megalodon whose hobbies include staring intensely at things and contemplating the structural integrity of magisteel with her teeth," the Quetzalcoatl finished her introduction.

Magdaline's red eyes fixed on me with a deeply unnerving intensity as she sat down across from me.

"A . . . kobold?" Vespera repeated slowly, as if trying to parse a particularly complex Omnid meme. "Like . . . a personal servant? Why do you need a kobold at Skyfall?"

"Not just any servant, Vee," Cinder said, her voice dripping with self-importance. "My servant. He's . . . special." She winked at me, a decidedly un-reassuring wink. "Right, kobold?"

I managed a smile, preoccupied with my soul-wobbling. "Thrilled to be here."

Magdaline finally spoke, her voice surprisingly feminine for someone who looked as if she could bite a magisteel bar in half.

"Is it . . . house-trained?" she asked, peering at me with open curiosity. "Does it do tricks?"

"Magdaline!" Vespera scoffed, sitting down and elbowing the shark girl sharply. "Don't be rude to Ci's property! Though . . . seriously, Cinder, a kobold? Isn't that a bit . . . low-Omnid for you? I thought you were all about status and, like, being the best?"

Cinder waved a dismissive hand, silver feathers fluttering. "Details, details. He's . . . useful and unclaimed."

Magdaline was still staring at me. "Useful how? Can it fetch?" she asked. "Maybe if you throw a ball of yarn?"

Vespera snorted. "Mags, he's not a . . . a Kitlix. He's a nullie. Probably barely knows how to breathe properly, let alone fetch."

"Hey!" I protested. "I can breathe just fine, thank you very much. And I bet I could fetch better than . . . than a Thunderbird who's too busy taking selfies to notice where the ball went!"

Vespera rolled her silver-gold eyes. "Oh, here we go. The nullie's got sass."

"Sass is a survival mechanism when you're being claimed as 'property' by a feathery overlord," I retorted, gesturing vaguely at Cinder who was now examining her claws with an air of regal boredom.

Magdaline tilted her head, considering my statement. "Does sass improve fetch?" she asked Cinder. "Maybe it makes the kobold fetch with more . . . enthusiasm?"

Cinder snorted. "Enthusiasm is overrated, Mags. Obedience is what matters. And scale polishing." She looked back at me. "You do know how to polish scales, right, kobold?"

"I'm a fast learner," I said sweetly. "Especially when the lesson involves not being bitten again." I rubbed my neck again for emphasis.

Vespera burst out laughing. "Oh, this is going to be fun. You actually bit him, Cinder? Like, for realsies?"

Cinder puffed out her chest, silver feathers bristling slightly. "Of course, 'realsies.' Quetzalcoatl soul bond. It's legally binding. Oodle it, ya foldknob."

"I will, actually," Vespera grinned, pulling out her own magitek phone. "This is going straight to the Skyfall Omnigram gossip feed. 'Cinder the Terrible Tames Tiny Thrall on Train!' #KoboldKuties, #SoulBondedAndBoujee."

Cinder made a face. "Don't you dare put that on the feed, Vee! I'm trying to establish a fearsome reputation, not become a freaking meme!"

"Too late!" Vespera cackled, already typing furiously with her long, elegant, bird-skull talons. "Image uploading . . . caption . . . 'My new pet kobold, already sassier than your entire bloodline. Deal with it. #KoboldCutenessOverload #CinderGotAKobold.'"

Her phone flashed at me and Cinder, who soured up.

Magdaline, still fixated on the practicalities of kobold ownership, piped up again. "If it's soul-bonded, does that mean it shares your emotions? Like, if you're happy, does it wag its . . . tail?" She peered at my backside with an unsettling level of clinical interest. "Do you even have a tail? I'm not seeing a tail."

I resisted the urge to check if I had spontaneously grown a tail. "I assure you, I'm not wagging anything," I said dryly. "Especially not with enthusiasm."

Cinder glared at Magdaline. "He doesn't wag anything, Mags. Kobolds don't simply wag. They . . . they cower. And fetch. And do tasks."

"But if it's soul-bonded . . ." Magdaline persisted, her shark eyes narrowing in thought. "If you're scared, will it be scared too? Could you use it as a canary in a coal mine? Like, if there's danger during dungeon delving, would the weaker kobold freak out first?"

"Magdaline, he's not a freaking canary," Vespera said, looking up from her phone and shaking her head in amusement. "He's . . . a fashion accessory, obviously. A status symbol. Like a really small, really annoying handbag that talks back."

"I'm hearing 'handbag' and 'accessory' a lot here," I interjected. "Just for the record, I'm fairly certain I'm not luggage. I'm also fairly certain that soul bonds are not a recognized form of . . . chattel acquisition."

Cinder scoffed. "Please. Omnithornian law trumps all. Besides, who's going to argue with a Quetzalcoatl?" She puffed out her chest again, looking around the compartment as if she expected a chorus of dissenting voices to suddenly materialize.

Vespera snorted. "Loads of people, Cinder. You're not exactly subtle. You once tried to claim the entire cafeteria as your 'personal hunting ground' in grade ten because you liked the roast griffin on Tuesdays."

Magdaline nodded in agreement.

"Bah." Cinder waved a dismissive claw. "Minor misunderstandings. Details." She turned back to me, her blue eyes sharp. "Point is, kobold, you're mine. And you're going to be useful. Starting with . . ."

I waited for her to produce a job for me. She fell silent.

"You don't know, do you?" I asked her. "You don't know why you claimed me?"

"Eh." She shrugged. "It'll come to me eventually."

"Why'd you claim him?" Vee relocated to our side and elbowed Cinder.

"'Cause I felt like it, okay?!" Cinder fired back. "Get the fuck off my case!"

"Wow, someone's hangry. You should order some delivery from the cafe car instead of bitching like a knob," Vee clicked her beak. She relocated herself to my side and started to paw at me with her magisteel talons. She made clicking and humming noises as she rained sparks all over me.

I squinted at her.

"What?" Mags asked, squinting at the suddenly still Thunderbird.

"Nothing," Vespera said, her cheeks igniting with burning sparks. "Absolutely nothing."

"Uh-huh," Magdaline said. She pulled out her phone, rolled her red eyes, and put on a pair of red headphones.

"Fess up," Vespera hissed at me, a sharp, dark beak too close to my ear for comfort.

"Fess what now?" I asked.

"How'd my soul get in you?" she demanded.

"Say what?" I asked.

"You have a bit of my soul in you," she growled. "I don't recall putting it there."

"Don't know." I shrugged. "Things have been sort of iffy since this morning. There are holes in my head the size of this train. I do know that I talked to an Archangel. I think. Could have been my overactive imagination or my dimensional skewering condition."

Cinder crossed her arms, clearly bothered by the fact that I was insane.

"Concerning." Vespera frowned. "Very concerning."

She eyed Cinder. "Fess up. Was your soul bit in him when you found him? That why you are claiming koboldness?"

Cinder flashed almost entirely orange-red, feathers igniting like a sunset.

"Thought so." Vespera tapped her beak. "Even more concerning. Right then. We have an inexplicable shared kobold that neither of us can remember claiming."

She moved from my side towards Mags.

"Yes?" The shark-girl asked.

"Help me out, bae," Vespera instructed, pointing a sharp, black-feather-tipped wing at me. "See if you can smell anything . . . off about this smol humanoid creature."

Magdaline, who had been tuning us out with her headphones, paused her music, her red eyes blinking slowly. She looked from Vespera to me, then back to Vespera, a flicker of annoyance in her shark-like gaze.

"Smell him?" she repeated.

"Ye, smell him," Vespera insisted, tapping her foot impatiently. "You're a Scrut in training, are you not? Sniff the nullie and tell me if he smells soul-bonded."

Magdaline sighed dramatically, the sound like air hissing from a punctured lung. She pushed her headphones back around her neck, a reluctant expression on her face. With a slow, deliberate movement, she leaned forward, her unnerving red eyes fixing on me again.

I suddenly felt like a particularly unappetizing lab specimen under scrutiny. Magdaline's head tilted, and then, just as Cinder had done, she inhaled. Deeply. Her nostrils, barely visible slits on her shark-like snout, flared slightly. The air in the compartment seemed to vibrate with her focus.

It felt . . . invasive. As though she was trying to smell my thoughts, my secrets, my very essence. I suppressed a shiver.

She stood up and circled me slowly, stepping through the compartment, sniffing the air around me with methodical precision. Vespera and Cinder watched with varying degrees of curious fascination and annoyed impatience. Cinder still looked a bit flushed, her silver feathers ruffled, but she was trying to maintain a nonchalant air, picking at a loose thread on her gray robe.

Magdaline completed her circle, pausing right in front of me again, her red eyes narrowed in concentration. She inhaled one last, long breath, then straightened up, turning back to Vespera and Cinder.

"He smells . . . human," she stated flatly. "Slightly metallic. Dusty. And . . . faint traces of fear pheromones. Standard nullie scent profile."

"Fear pheromones?" Vespera raised a sleek black eyebrow. "Really? Already? And we just got on the train."

"He's a nullie." Magdaline shrugged, as if that explained everything. "Fear is their natural state."

"What level is he?" Vespera asked.

"Somewhere around four, I think," the shark considered. "Bunch of minor skills. Very minor. Probably been on a single delve. Pathetic, really."

"But . . . no soul-bond smell?" Vespera pressed. "No Quetzalcoatl essence? Nothing . . . electric, sparkly, or deeply magical?"

Magdaline shook her head, her white hair swaying slightly. "Smells . . . bland. Unremarkable. Like . . . tap water. If tap water could be afraid."

Vespera frowned, clicking her beak thoughtfully. "Huh. That's . . . weird." She glanced at Cinder, her gray-gold eyes sharp. "Cinder, are you sure you . . . actually soul-bonded with him? Like, for real for real? Are my electrofractal senses wrong?"

Cinder's feathers flared again, a hint of sunset-red creeping into the silver. "Of course, I'm sure! I bit him, didn't I? Quetzalcoatl soul-bite!"

"Yeah, but . . . maybe you just . . . nibbled him?" Vespera suggested. "Maybe it wasn't a proper soul-bite. Maybe you just . . . gave him a hickey with teeth?"

"I did not give him a 'hickey with teeth'!" Cinder snapped, her voice rising in pitch. "I soul-bonded him! It's done! He's mine!" She jabbed a clawed finger at me, her blue eyes flashing dangerously. "Right, kobold? Tell them! Tell them you're soul-bonded to me!"

I blinked at her, then at Vespera and Magdaline. "Well," I said slowly, choosing my words carefully, "I definitely have a neck bite. And I definitely feel . . . owned. Maybe. Hard to tell. My skills are kinda glitching out on me."

"Owned!" Cinder preened, puffing out her chest again. "See? Owned! Soul-bonded! End of discussion!"

"Owned in the 'just been bitten' sense, or owned in the 'eternally bound to your soul' sense?" Vespera clarified.

"Both!" Cinder insisted, crossing her arms defensively. "Definitely both!"

"Ughh, fine, I'll spend more mana on this if it'll shut your yaps." Magdaline inhaled and spoke up again. "Actually," she said, her red eyes fixed on some unseen point in the distance behind me, "there is . . . something else."

Vespera and Cinder both turned to her, all traces of amusement and defensiveness vanishing, replaced by genuine curiosity. Even I leaned forward, intrigued.

"Something else?" Vespera prompted. "What? Something shark-smelly?"

Magdaline nodded slowly. "Yes. Something . . . faint. Underneath the nullie-fear and the metallic tang and tiniest imprint of skills. Two bonds and something . . . not natural."

"Not natural?" Cinder repeated, her blue eyes widening slightly. "What do you mean, 'not natural'?"

Magdaline shrugged again, a gesture that somehow managed to convey both indifference and deep unease. "Hard to describe. Like . . . distant, twisted static. Interference. Like something . . . else . . . is touching him. Layered deep under his scent. Not Omnid. Not human. Not . . . here. Behind. Far behind. So far I can barely sense its end. If there is an end. Endlessness . . . more like it. The . . . number eight! I smell number eight!"

A silence fell over the compartment, broken only by the rhythmic hum of the train, Omnithornian mountainous landscape flashing by.

Vespera's brow furrowed, her gray-gold eyes thoughtful. Cinder's feathers seemed to deflate slightly, the sunset-red fading. Magdaline just stared blankly ahead, lost in her shark-scent world.

"Outsider interference?" Vespera murmured, more to herself than to anyone else. "Could that be it?"

"Outsider?" Cinder repeated.

"Outside reality," Vespera added. She glanced at me, her gaze suddenly sharper, more calculating. "You said things have been . . . 'iffy' since this morning, right, kobold? Holes in your head? Missing memories?"

I nodded slowly, feeling a chill crawl down my spine. The "dimensional skewering" diagnosis echoed in my mind. Was this . . . worse than just insanity? Was I attracting . . . unwanted attention? Was something questionable deep inside me, messing with me?

Vespera tapped her beak thoughtfully again. "Maybe . . . maybe that's why you claimed him, Ci," she said, turning back to Cinder, her tone softening. "Maybe your Quetzalcoatl instincts sensed something . . . off. Something . . . vulnerable. And you just . . . reacted."

Cinder blinked, her expression shifting from defensiveness to something resembling dawning understanding. "Maybe . . ." she said slowly. "Maybe . . . yeah. Maybe that's it. Protective instincts. Quetzalcoatl are very . . . territorial. And protective of their . . . territory."

"Right," Vespera nodded, smoothly changing the subject. "Protective. Territorial. Totally makes sense. We def ought to keep an eye on this nullie till we figure this shit out. Anyway!" She clapped her magisteel-clad hands together, her usual cheerful, if slightly manic, energy returning. "House sorting! We should probably start thinking about Houses, right? Strategic House placement is key to Skyfall success. And world domination. Eventually."

"Same shit to me," Cinder yawned.

"It is not the same shit." Vee snapped her magisteel talons. "Placement determines opportunities. Let's start at the top—House Silverfox. Cunning. Strategic."

"Silverfox is good," Cinder shrugged. "But Pyroclast is flashier. More . . . power-hungry. Access to the hoard of Skyfall. Central citadel area."

"I do like hoarding," Vespera clicked. "But I'd like to hoard my own shinies. Relying on other people's hoard influences the mind, I hear. Not sure if I want to be constantly mentally derailed by the school hoard's gold call."

"Pyroclast is for strong-headed losers," Mags said. "Pyroclast knobs usually bang their head against walls until they break, or their head breaks."

"Das' just the dragon way, right ma' dragon-bae!" Vespera jabbed Cinder playfully. "Pyroclast has its merits! Raw power is important! And they have the best beast-slaying parties, I hear!"

"Parties are for airhead knobs." Cinder rolled her eyes. "Silverfox is in the central spire Silver Tower. Best views in the whole school."

"Catacombs is where it's at," Magdaline considered.

"Catacombs?" Vespera and Cinder echoed.

"House Gorefield. Practical. Builder tech. They're in the catacombs. Quiet. Dark. Good for . . . thinking. Making things." Mags trailed off, her red eyes drifting elsewhere.

"Gorefield?" Vespera repeated, wrinkling her nose. "You into trash pandas? Seriously, Mags? They smell like . . . well, trash. And they're all obsessed with . . . building things. Who wants to spend their school years living in a sewer, building artifacts?"

"Sewers are practical," Magdaline insisted, her voice with a hint of . . . defensiveness? "Safe. And making artifacts is . . . permanent. Useful. Aren't you an artificer junkie, Vee?"

"I am," Vespera conceded, tapping her beak thoughtfully. "But pure artificery isn't exactly . . . glamorous. Or socially advantageous. Silverfox or Pyroclast, that's where the power is. And the parties." She winked at Cinder. "We both have wings. Consider flying from the Silver Tower to class every morning!"

"Hrm," Cinder considered. "That does sound . . . fun. What about Hexacomb?"

"No way." Vespera shook her head. "We're leaders, not followers!"

"Yes, but we could get many sixies or even kobolds in Hexacomb," Cinder said. "It's a wholesome House full of hard workers, I heard."

"Being a Queen Bee is appealing," Vespera clicked. "But working hard isn't. Not sure if I could force myself to work my way up from a drone."

"What about House Wormwood?" Mags contemplated.

"Nah. None of us are Agromancers," Vespera shook her head. "Wild magic ain't my thing. I'm a logical creature."

"Yes but they have the best crystallography lab," Mags pointed out. "And access to all of the Cantigeists! Access to the gargantuan Wormwood Shard in the main building!"

"Ugh," Vee frowned. "Choices."

I absorbed their conversation like a sponge, spinning it in my head. I was fairly certain that Skyfall didn't have Houses before. Why did it have Houses now?

"Question? Where is Skyfall?" I asked.

"Wow," Vespera commented. "Such vast ignorance. How did you even get on this train, nulls?"

"My sister brought me here," I said. "Also, it's not ignorance. I'm dimensionally skewered. Just need a bit of adjusting time, that's all. I'll be fine once I get the hang of things."

"Skyfall's in Saxtland," Cinder said. "Big ley line crossing area. Edge of the Wormwood Star oceanic impact crater up by the North Sea off the coast of the Still Ocean."

"And how many Wormwood impact craters are there?" I asked.

"Loads," Vee replied. "Too many to count. All the big ones have stuff 'round or in 'em. Higher aetheric density, yo. Easier to magic shit, easier to create dimensional gates. Etcetera."

"And Saxtland is what?" I asked.

"A Magogenic Fault mountain nation. A ring of cities. Ruled by the Saxtant Parliament, secured by the Most Chivalrous Order of Saxtant Knights," Cinder said.

"Chivalrous in a 'we'll lock you in a dungeon for three weeks for jaywalking' sort of way," Vespera laughed. "Saxtant Knights are hardcore. Order, discipline, and smiting heretics. Saxtland is a theocracy in all but name. Muuuuch runes. Very control."

"Theocracy?" I blinked. "So Skyfall is . . . a magic academy, run by . . . rune-loving theocrats?"

"Mystagogue Academy," Vespera corrected. "For Mystagogues. Omnids and mixed-bloods. Run by . . . well, by a council of Mystagogues, technically. But the Order of Saxtant Knights keeps an eye on things. Don't want another Elisabeth Zartella incident."

"Elisabeth Zartella," I repeated. The name flickered in my memory, bringing up nothing at all.

"The Mystagogue who exploded," Magdaline said.

Vespera nodded grimly. "Anguishstorm, 1944. That's why everyone starts Skyfall at eighteen now. Supposedly, the more mature the Mystagogue is, the less likely they are to spontaneously combust from uncontrolled magic working with the unearthed Wormwood Star shards."

"Spontaneous combustion," I repeated, a dry smile tugging at my lips. "Sounds . . . fun."

"Not if you're the one combusting," Cinder grunted. "Or standing anywhere within a mile radius."

"So, no pressure then," I said. "Just, you know, try not to explode. Got it."

Magdaline, who had been silent again, suddenly spoke. "Anguishstorms . . . leave traces."

"Traces?" Vespera prompted. "Smelly traces?"

Magdaline shook her head slowly. "Not . . . mere smell. Resonance. Echoes. Places touched by Anguishstorms . . . feel . . . wrong. Twisted. Like a broken note."

A chill went down my spine. "And Skyfall is . . . near an Anguishstorm site?"

"Biggest Anguishstorm of the 1940s. Plus near the Wormwood impact crater," Vespera clarified. "Big one. Lots of residual weirdness. But also, lots of magic. That's why Skyfall Citadel is there. Harnesses the weirdness. Turn it into . . . Mystagogue-ness."

"Mystagogue-ness." I chewed on the word, feeling increasingly as though I'd stepped into a very strange and slightly unsettling dream. "Right."

I looked outside. The centipede-train left the land and was plowing across the ocean now at ludicrous speed, a million crystalline legs flashing across the waves.

"Impressive, ya?" Vespera clicked. "Skyfall admin burns a ton of beast cores on this trip."

"Seems like a waste," I said. "Could we not gate to Skyfall or something?"

"We could, but it's a show of power," Vespera said. "Omnithornia is flexing. Flex, flex." She flexed her talons at my face, sending sparks flying all over me. "Flex."

"Are you trying to flex on me?" I arched an eyebrow.

"Maybe!" she laughed. "Is it working? Are you impressed by my flexerrificness?"

"Maybe." I shrugged.

"Aight, I'ma order cafe foodles via the À la carte app," she said. "Who wants wat? Tell me now or forever hold your peace!"

# CHAPTER FORTY-SIX

# Dimensionally Skewered

Through continuous wobbling of my soul armillary, I have arrived at more handy dead-world memories. The girls sitting around me in the Skyfall Express train compartment were indeed my friends in our past life, no . . . lives.

I could remember bits and pieces of at least two separate lives before this one. The first one ended when I sacrificed myself as Alexa to stop Bob Proverra from killing everyone. The second ended when Vee, Ci, and I freed Archangel Zadskiel from her bonds beneath the SimmiTech compound with Possy's help.

The continuous narrative of my being stretching past current reality like some kind of wobbly sideways endless chain was bewildering, yet wholesome.

I wasn't insane. I wasn't alone. I was definitely a mess of wobbling souls, but it wasn't my fault.

The fractal, looped nature of reality was to blame for my misfortune. I wasn't entirely misfortunate, however. I had found my friends once again, or perhaps they found me this time around as the structural arrangement of the world we inhabited shifted in less dire ways, leaving many valuable things like our soul bond intact.

As far as I could recall and sense, I still had bits of Omnid soul architecture in my soul that allowed me to do magic. I determined this by snapping my fingers and producing a small electrofractal ball of lightning. A skill taught to me by Vee.

"Aww, look at that cute, smol lightning ball," Vee commented at me. "You precious creature. Trying so hard to impress your owners."

Her jab was pointy, yet it made me feel warm inside.

Friends. I had friends! I had people who cared about me!

It didn't matter if they didn't remember me, they were still interested in conversing with me. Maybe with enough interaction, I would make them and myself remember who I was and why I was doing this.

Were the Omnids I befriended and helped out in my last cycle doing better this time around?

Was this cycle better or worse for everyone involved?

How long had I been at it?

I looked at Cinder. She seemed more confident, less broken and lonely. Vespera was smiling as she was chatting with Mags. Magdaline wasn't desperately chewing on a beast core like a shark trying to exist on land.

Progress from my last attempt at fixing reality had indeed carried over in positive ways in a backwards and sideways sort of dimensional fracture propagation.

Our Earth had plummeted a tick closer to its doom but the local aetheric density was now higher, which made everything fancier and more magical, made my Omnid friends less starved.

A Kitsune girl arrived with our À la carte orders filling our compartment's table with plates of steaks and burgers. Everyone dug into their meals.

"Thanks for the lunch," I told Vespera with a smile as I chomped down on my burger.

"Anytime, cutie." She grinned at me, throwing blood-red steak slices into her gullet. "Gotta keep our kobold nice 'n' plump in case we get hungry in a dungeon."

"You would nom on your own kobold?" I arched an eyebrow.

"You look sufficiently snackable." She reached out and licked my neck, giving it a small bite. "Nom."

I winced, shuddering slightly as her beak filled with a row of saw-teeth departed.

"Ye," she clicked. "Def nommable. I didn't think that I would find myself with a sudden tasty kobold, and yet here we are."

"Oi!" Cinder looked up from her steak. "Get your own kobold! This one's mine! Don't just wing in on other people's stuff!"

"Learn to share." Vespera smacked Cinder with a wing. "We obviously claimed this knob together and just don't remember it."

"And why don't we remember it?" Cinder demanded.

"Dimensional, temporal, Outsider, divine, or mental fuckery." Vespera shrugged, bending her fingers. "Take your pick."

"And you are just fine with this?" Cinder asked. "With us sharing a kobold we didn't make? What if he's some kind of an incepted kobold, sent to screw with us by an enemy Omnicorp?"

"I've never heard of such a thing." Vespera shook her head. "Legit soul bonds are impossible to force, and as a level four kobold, he should not be able to easily hurt or betray his owners in the high forties. The magic soul bond itself guarantees cooperation and mental entwining."

"Meaning what?"

"Meaning that the more time we spend with our kobold, the more obedient and mentally connected with us he will become," Vespera replied. "I dunno about you, but I'ma be a good master to my smol human. The dragon-kobold relationship takes both parties to reinforce the bond. A goodly dragon has a noblesse oblige to create a hoard to uplift her kobolds with skills. The more the hoard benefits, the more the dragon grows in power! Also, I'm sensing a thing in his soul . . ."

"What kind of a thing?"

"The kind of a thing I've been planning to build but never got around to doing it, on account that I only turned eighteen recently, which permits me to own hooman kobolds," Vespera said. "A holofractal Resonance dish."

"A what now?"

"A skill amplifier," Vespera replied. "Kobolds naturally bounce their dragon owner skills off from themselves. This is sort of like an improvement on it. Considering how a thing that I only *planned* to make is inside of him, he's def my property."

"I see," Cinder replied with a somewhat sour look.

Having finished her breakfast, the Quetzi-girl pulled out a guitar from her extra-dimensional case. Magdaline pulled her headphones off and Vespera leaned forward on the table.

"I wish that we could meet again, / Amidst the autumn's weary end / With sky beneath our feet, forever crying, / And in reflections birds and clouds, flying,"

Cinder sang, her wings spreading wide, the chords and her magic-amplified voice making my insides melt.

"Autumn, how long I've been without you. / Autumn, ships burn into the sky. / Autumn, take me, ever so high. / Where worry has gone awry. / Autumn, I ask you why? / Autumn, it is darkness and despair. / Clawing at my soul, ever bare. / Autumn, life is too unjust and so unfair. / Autumn, will I ask you, will I dare? / Autumn, we must end this weary, bleak affair. / And longer I know, why I simply care. / Autumn, on my life, I here to you swear, / Autumn you have caught me, unaware."

Cinder finished, strumming her guitar.

"Very swank," Vespera judged. "A bit gloomy, tho. Why yo songs so gloom, Ci?"

"Gloomy? It's called 'atmospheric,'" Cinder retorted, slipping her guitar onto the table. "Besides, life is gloomy. Haven't you noticed?" She waved a hand at the gloomy autumn storm clouds above the Still Ocean waves that our train was plowing through.

"Nah, life's a party!" Vespera chirped. "It just sometimes needs more glitter cannons and less . . . existential dread. How about a happy tune, Ci? Something with . . . dragons slaying beasts and hoarding 'bolds 'n' shinies?"

Cinder scoffed, but a small smile tugged at the corner of her mouth as she glanced at me. "Maybe later. My soul's still in 'autumnal melancholy' mode."

"Your soul needs a good kick in the tail feathers," Vespera declared. "Mags, you got anything less . . . depressing on that shark-phone of yours?"

Magdaline, who had returned to her headphones, blinked slowly. "Less depressing?" she repeated, as if the concept was alien. "Define 'less depressing.'"

"You know! Happy! Upbeat! Makes you want to . . . I dunno . . . fly into the sun and sing!" Vespera flapped her wings for emphasis, scattering a few sparks.

Magdaline pondered this for a moment, then reluctantly removed her headphones again. "Upbeat . . . sun . . . singing . . ." She scrolled through her phone with a slow, deliberate finger. "Ah. Found something."

She tapped the screen, switching to the speakers and a moment later, a melody filled the compartment. A surprisingly cheerful, almost bouncy tune emerged, filled with bright, synthesized sounds and a catchy, repetitive beat.

"Ooh, what's this?" Vespera perked up, tapping her foot to the rhythm.

"Bubblegum Kraken-pop," Magdaline stated matter-of-factly. "Chart-topper from the Abyssal Depths. Very popular with the younger Scrutimancer crowd."

"Kraken-pop?" Cinder raised an eyebrow. "Seriously, Mags?"

"It's . . . algorithmically optimized for dopamine release," Magdaline explained, as if that was the most obvious thing in the world. "Efficiently cheerful."

Vespera was already humming along, her wings twitching. "Catchy! I can dig it! Though . . . Kraken-pop? Really? Is that even a genre?"

"Everything is a genre now," Magdaline replied with a shrug. "Genre proliferation is a natural consequence of hyper-information saturation. And Abyssal Kraken have excellent musical taste, statistically speaking."

Cinder rolled her eyes, but even she seemed to be tapping her foot along to the beat. The Kraken-pop did have a strange, infectious energy. It was so relentlessly cheerful, it was almost . . . aggressively happy.

"See? Much better!" Vespera declared, grabbing a steak slice and waving it in the air to the music. "You! Kobold! Dance!"

I blinked at her. "Dance?"

"Yeah, dance! Show us your moves! Earn your keep, kobold!" Vespera grinned, tossing the steak slice towards me. I caught it automatically, sliding it onto my plate.

"I don't dance on command." I crossed my arms.

"Pff, sounds like ya lack rhythm," Vespera scoffed good-naturedly. "Fine, I'll show you how it's done."

She put her talon on a wall and closed her eyes. The compartment around us wobbled and suddenly stretched, opening up more space in front of the door. The Thunderbird hopped off her seat, surprisingly not smacking anyone or anything with wings, and started to move to the Kraken-pop beat.

Her movements were . . . chaotic, a mix of flapping wings, jerky steps, and exaggerated poses, but somehow, they were also strangely . . . captivating. She was clearly enjoying herself as she sent sparks flying all around the compartment, her gray robe flapping open to reveal a blue dress and sparkling magisteel chainmail armor framing her curvy body.

Cinder and Magdaline watched with varying degrees of amusement. Even Magdaline's usually impassive face cracked a small smile.

"Wow, Vee," Cinder commented. "You're . . . surprisingly terrible at dancing."

"Terribly awesome, you mean!" Vespera corrected, striking a dramatic pose with one wing outstretched. "It's called 'electrofractal freestyle,' darling! Very avant-garde! You wouldn't understand."

"I understand 'embarrassing yourself in public,'" Cinder retorted, but she was laughing now.

"Public? We're in a train compartment, Ci," Vespera chuckled, continuing her dance. "Unless you think the leather seats are judging me? Wait, it's you who's judging me, isn't it?"

"Bingo." Cinder nodded.

"The leather seats have seen things," Magdaline said darkly. "Terrible things."

"Hrm?" Vespera tilted her head. "Wait. Is it . . . lewd things?"

"Very." Magdaline flashed red. "Damned upperclassmen."

Vespera broke out into a fit of laughter.

Magdaline squinted at Vespera and then put her headphones back on, returning to her Kraken-pop world, staring at a wall.

"Does she do this often?" I asked.

"Eh, Scrutimancers," Cinder said, rolling her eyes. "Obsessed with the past, with secrets, with . . . smelling things that aren't there. Mags is a good egg most of the time, but sometimes she gets . . . weird."

"Weird how?" I asked.

"Weird like . . . she once spent three hours staring at a crack in the wall, convinced it was a 'portal to forgotten anxieties,'" Cinder explained. "And she talks to furniture."

"I see." I nodded.

"Ya know wat'?" Vespera grinned at Cinder. "I'll show ya how to judge me!"

She grabbed and pulled me out of my seat, setting her phone to play a modern Thunderland-sounding beat.

"Try to keep up, Lexy," she whispered into my ear, taking me for a spin.

Despite my initial reluctance and stumbling, I found myself following her lead, muscle memory from past lives helping me match her rhythm. Eventually, I took the lead, and slotted the Architect to the forefront of my soul armillary, making her spin.

"See? The kobold's got moves!" Vespera called out to Cinder, who was watching us dance with green rainbows dancing on the edges of her feathers.

"Whatever." Cinder rolled her eyes.

"Haha, thass' right," Vee added, panting ever so slightly in the break between songs. "Stew in your jealousy."

Cinder pursed her lips, sending the Thunderbird a draconic glare.

"She stewin' hard," Vespera whisper-grinned at me. "S'fine, she'll catch up in no time."

"And you?" I whispered.

"I don't remember you," she replied, resting her beak on my shoulder as we spun. "But I feel like I really should. This is nice. Didn't think that owning a kobold would feel this nice."

The train shuddered again, slowing this time. I glanced at the window. We were moving by Giant's Causeway now, gargantuan hexagonal columns framing cliffside walls. A chime echoed through the compartment, followed by a crackling female voice over the intercom.

"Approaching Skyfall Station. Please prepare for disembarkation. House sorting will commence upon arrival at the Academy. Welcome, Mystagogues, to Skyfall."

"Ah! House sorting." Vespera perked up, letting go of me and clapping her magisteel talons together. "Showtime, ma' peeps! Strategic House placement, remember? World domination starts now! Also, I'll be very annoyed if we end up in different Houses."

Cinder stretched her silver-green wings, which rustled against the compartment walls. "Whatever. Just want to get this over with and find my dorm room. And food. I'm starving to the point of eating my kobold whole."

"Hungry already?" I squinted at her.

"What?" she asked. "I'm a dragon. More magic steaks I eat, the stronger I get."

Magdaline nodded.

"So," Vespera said, turning to me with a gleam in her gray-gold eyes, "Kobold-Lexy. Which House are you aiming for? Strategic House placement is for everyone, even . . . acquisitions."

"Aiming for?" I blinked. "I . . . hadn't really thought about it." Houses. Cunning, Ambitious, Practical, Meticulous, Nurturing, right? None of them particularly jumped out at me as "me." "What would you guesstimate me at?"

"Hrmmm." Vespera considered, clicking her beak. "Gorefield. Trash panda House. Sewers, builder tech, ethics optional. You strike me as a smelly sewer dweller."

"Hey!" I protested. "I'm not a sewer dweller!"

"Could be." Vespera shrugged with a teasing look. "Or maybe . . . Hexacomb? Meticulous. Bees. Obsessive perfectionism. You seem a bit . . . twitchy and quiet. Maybe you'd fit right in with the obsessive perfectionists."

"I'm not twitchy!" I huffed. "I'm . . . dimensionally skewed! There's a difference!"

"Dimensional skewery twitchiness," Vespera amended, clicking her beak. "Semantics. Why are you dressed like a peasant?"

"My family doesn't care to spend money on me," I shrugged. "Son of a kobold and whatever."

"That won't do." Vespera marched over to her suitcase and dug into it, throwing me a gray robe. "Put it on, ya knob."

I did. The wide and bulky robe adjusted itself over me, trim-hexagrams flickering.

"What do you think, Ci?" Vespera poked the dragon as I finished dressing. "Is he a raccoon or a bee?"

Cinder snorted. "He's Silverfox. Obviously."

"Silverfox?" Vespera and Magdaline echoed, turning to Cinder.

"Cunning House," Cinder elaborated, rolling her eyes. "Foxes. Silver Tower. Manipulative, deceitful, overly secretive. Sounds like him, doesn't it?" She gestured at me with a claw.

"Manipulative and deceitful?" I asked. "Whatever gave you that idea?"

"You smell like a little manipulative shit," Cinder said. "I'm certain of it now."

"How certain?"

"Very," she said.

"Do you have proof of this claim?" I arched an eyebrow.

"No," she replied. "But I have a feeling."

"What kind of a feeling?"

"Hrm." She considered. "Like a scratch that I can't seem to reach. Like a deep hole in my heart. Like you switching from shy stumbling to inexplicably in-tune dancing with Vee. Sus. You're very sus, kobold."

"Filling heart holes with sus skewered nully-bolds isn't a very healthy way to cope with things," Vespera commented.

"Are you telling me what to do?" Cinder growled, her face stretching and becoming more draconic.

"You're gonna get sorted into Pyroclast with this attitude." Vespera rolled her eyes. "And I'm going to be stuck in the House of dum' dragons at this rate."

"Nobody asked you to follow me like a hanger-on!" Cinder barked.

"Aww you break my Thundery heart, mah bestie," Vespera held a talon over her chest. "Ya kno' I love ya, right?"

"I'm not coping with shit." Cinder crossed her arms. "So you can piss right off."

"She's coping hard," Vespera whispered to me with a grin.

"I heard that!" Cinder huffed indignantly.

# CHAPTER FORTY-SEVEN

# Caught

Hey, Vee, what's the current date?" I asked Vespera as she pulled me out of the compartment by the elbow.

"September third," she replied with a raised eyebrow. "Why?"

"My internal clock is off," I said.

"How off?" She squinted at me.

"My sharpest memories are telling me it's January," I said. "Was January?"

"Dang," she commented. "That's some serious mental skewery. I should look in your head tonight with Dreamancy, see what's what."

The Skyfall Express shuddered to a final halt with a sigh that sounded suspiciously like relief.

The crystalline doors hissed open, revealing not a typical train station platform, but a town built from and around colossal basalt columns, a Giant's Causeway sprawling around us. Buildings were hewn directly from the dark-gray stone, towering and imposing, yet with a strange, organic flow, like petrified trees reaching for the sky. The air was crisp and salty with the breath of the ocean behind us.

"Right then, out, out, out!" Vespera chirped, practically shoving me towards the open doorway. "Adventure awaits! And possibly lukewarm beast core ground coffee if we're lucky!"

Cinder grumbled, but followed, her silver feathers catching the faint morning light filtering through the basalt columns. Magdaline, headphones already back in place, glided out with an almost unnerving silence, her red eyes scanning the surroundings with her usual intensity.

I breathed, tilting my head back to take it all in. "This is . . . something else."

"Giant's Causeway!" Vespera clicked. "Gateway to magical greatness! And questionable street food, probably."

"Street food?" Cinder's ears perked up. "Is there . . . roast beast?"

"Hope springs eternal, Ci," Vespera chuckled. "But probably more like . . . enchanted hot dogs. Or sentient pretzels. You never know what you might get in these magogenic fault zones."

Magdaline suddenly stopped, her head tilting slightly. "Smells like . . . grilled griffin wings," she announced, her voice low.

"Hey, hey!" a voice barked behind us. I winced. "What the shit? What are you firsties doing with my family's kobold?!"

Ember manifested behind us, red claw tapping my shoulder, head igniting with dragonfire.

"Ember," I said, rotating and forcing a smile. "Fancy seeing you here. Thought you forgot about me there."

"Don't 'Ember' me, nullie-brain!" she hissed, her gaze flicking between Vespera and Cinder with undisguised disdain. "Are you incapable of existing for five seconds without embarrassing the Stratos family? What have I told you about talking to random Omnids?"

"You! Thunderbird!" She snarled at Vespera. "Let go of my 'bold!"

"Nah," Vespera said. "He ain't yours. He mine."

"Since when?!" Ember growled.

"Since I don't know," Vespera clicked.

Ember's entire figure ignited with dragonfire.

Vespera pulled me into embrace. Magdaline stepped ahead as did Cinder.

"You think that three firsties can stop me?" Ember growled, knuckles cracking. "Really?"

"That's him?" a sharp, cold, male voice suddenly sounded from our left.

"Smells like him," the female answered.

I turned my head.

A trio of Omnids stood there, staring at me. A man with piercing yellow eyes and two taller women in long dark coats were there. A Wendigo and two Omnid enforcers. I saw antler-skull logos on their lapels.

*North Acadian Wendigo Scrutimancers.*

*The Frontenachii!*

*Fuck. Fuck, fuck, fuck.*

I was completely and utterly unprepared for them to find me after the dimensional shift.

"What do you tardigrade-knobs want?" Ember looked at the Wendigo trio, distracted from the Omnid girls.

"This human," the Wendigo man said, pointing at me, "stole an AI that belongs to the Frontenachii Clan and moved it to another dimension."

"What?" Ember growled. "When?!"

"Around a week ago," the Wendigo replied, digging into my face with unnerving yellow eyes.

"Stole an AI?" Ember's dragonfire sputtered, momentarily dimming as confusion warred with her inherent aggression. "My nullie brother? Please. He can barely tie his own bootlaces without setting himself on fire. What AI are you even blathering about?"

The Wendigo man stepped closer, his yellow eyes never leaving me. They were unsettlingly bright, like burning coals in the dim basalt twilight, and they seemed to pierce through me, seeing things I didn't even understand about myself. His face was gaunt and sharp, framed by lank, dark hair that looked perpetually damp. The two women flanking him were equally unnerving, their faces impassive

"An experimental GLM armed with interaction and music and visual composer agents," the Wendigo stated, his voice a low, rasping growl that sent shivers down my spine. "Taken from the Frontenachii compound. Indisputable astral signatures link its disappearance directly to this . . . individual." He gestured at me with a long bony finger, tipped with a nail that looked more like a claw. "Which of you claims responsibility for this human?"

Ember gulped, gold-orange eyes flashing across the Scrut trio.

I cursed myself. I wasn't ready, didn't have any of my tools, didn't have Possy at my back.

The dimensional shear created by the Archangel's departure didn't clear the board in the slightest as I had expected it to. All it did was skewer events ever so slightly, and it seemed that *all* of my problems were just flowing right back into place like thick honey.

"He couldn't have stolen shit!" Ember found her voice once again. "I've been watching him like a hawk for the past . . ."

"Wrong. The past you think that you are observing is wrong," the Scrutimancer shook his head.

"What?" Ember sputtered. "The fuck did you say?!"

"There's been a dimensional shift," the Scrutimancer said, glowing eyes flaring at our group. "Some fools released an Archangel. It raised the aetheric density and rearranged physical reality ever so slightly with a planet-wide celestorm. Fortunately, the Astral Sea remembers all. Did you think that you could get away from your crimes this way, foolish human? Did you think that you could overwrite your astral imprint with a release of an Archangel, outwit us?"

"Maybe?" my lips replied, feeling like a thousand invisible hooks were digging into my head.

"Well, you were wrong." The Frontenachii Wendigo grinned with sharp, bone-yellow teeth. "Scrutimancers can see beyond causality-altering events created by celestorms. The Omnicorps are already working hard on repairing the dimensional fissure your actions created, adjusting the physical wherever they are able. You've made many enemies, boy."

"Wasn't exactly my fault," I said. "At least, I don't think that it was."

"All of the astral threads point to you as the culprit. It doesn't matter. We'll figure out exactly whose fault it is soon enough," the Wendigo said.

"Crimes?" Ember's voice rose an octave, dragonfire crackling brighter. "What crimes? He's a nullie who belongs to my family! He's incapable of committing crimes! Screw off with whatever this is!"

"Incapable?" The Wendigo man's yellow gaze focused on Ember. "Stratos lineage. Pyroclast House of Skyfall. You are blind to dimensional shifts, girl." He turned back to me, his voice dropping to a low, menacing purr. "The AI, human. Where is it?"

"AI?" I repeated, playing for time, my mind racing.

*Yulia. Possy. The Archangel. Dimensional shift. Arx.*

"Look, I . . . I don't know what you're talking about." My lies felt flimsy, useless against the intensity of his gaze.

"You took it to Arx?" The male Scrutimancer frowned ever so slightly. "Hrmm. No matter. We'll get it back."

"Don't play games with the nice Scruts, nullie-brain," Ember snapped. "If you stole something, just admit it and we can sort it out. Stratos family honor and all that." Her tone was still aggressive, but a flicker of unease was visible in her golden eyes. Her body trembled ever so slightly. Even Ember, the queen of bullies, was absolutely intimidated by these Wendigos.

"'Sort it out'?" The Wendigo woman on the left chuckled. "Theft of Frontenachii proprietary intelligence is not 'sorted out' with a stern talking-to, dragon-spawn. It is 'sorted out' with extradition, interrogation, dissection, and potentially . . . other measures." Her gaze lingered on me, cold and calculating.

"Extradition?" Vespera scoffed, stepping forward, her voice laced with amusement. "To North Acadia? Good luck with that. Saxtland doesn't extradite to anyone, especially not over some . . . dumb 'stolen AI.'" She emphasized the words with air quotes.

"Saxtland jurisdiction is irrelevant when Omnicorp interests are involved," the Wendigo man countered, his voice hard. "This is a matter of interdimensional law. And this human . . ." He pointed at me again. ". . . is a thief and an incredibly dangerous fugitive."

"He's my kobold," Cinder growled, silver feathers bristling. "And you're not taking him anywhere!"

The Wendigo trio exchanged glances, a flicker of surprise—or perhaps amusement—crossing their gaunt faces.

"'Kobold?'" the Wendigo man repeated. "A . . . pet? You are defending a thief because he is your . . . pet?"

"He's soul-bonded to me," Cinder clarified, puffing out her chest wings flaring out and sending brilliant rainbows around us. "He's mine! Screw off!"

"Soul bond . . ." The Wendigo man's yellow eyes narrowed, focusing on Cinder. "A Quetzalcoatl. Interesting. But even dragon-spawn law does not supersede Frontenachii interests." He took another step forward, his two female companions mirroring his movement, forming a semicircle around us. "Step aside, dragon girl of the Nova. This does not concern you. If you fight us, we will break you."

"It concerns me," Ember growled, stepping up beside Cinder, her dragonfire flaring again, hotter this time, licking at the basalt columns around us. "He's my little brother. As such, he's under my protection!"

"Brother?" The Wendigo man actually laughed, a chilling, mirthless sound. "Protection? From what? From the consequences of his own actions? Stratos, you embarrass your lineage."

"Shut your tardigrade mouth!" Ember roared.

Fighting three Wendigo Scrutimancers in the middle of Skyfall Station sounded like a spectacularly bad idea. Especially when I still felt like my brain was scrambled eggs, information trickling back in at an irritatingly slow rate.

"Stand down, or . . ." the Frontenachii Scrut began.

But Ember was already beyond listening. With a guttural cry, she unleashed a blast of dragonfire, a searing wave of heat and orange flames aimed directly at the nearest Wendigo.

The Wendigos didn't even flinch. The Wendigo woman on the right simply raised a hand, and a shimmering, invisible shield dome materialized in front of her, deflecting the dragonfire in a brilliant arch. The flames roared against the shield, casting dancing shadows on the basalt columns, but failing to penetrate.

"Crude," the Wendigo woman commented dismissively, lowering her hand. "And predictable. You are a low-level child threatening high-level Omnids."

Vespera raised her talons, and the air around her crackled with energy. Electrofractal tendrils, shimmering with blue-white light, snaked out from her fingertips, lashing towards the Wendigos like living lightning whips from below.

The Wendigo man reacted instantly. He thrust his hand forward, and a wave of gray energy pulsed outwards from him, colliding with Vespera's electrofractal whips. The lightning tendrils flickered and dissipated, the gray energy washing over them like static.

Vespera hissed, taking a step back, her wings flaring defensively. "Nullification field? Argh. These foldknobs are packing serious heat!"

"We are the Frontenacii," the Wendigo man said, his voice cold and even. "We are equipped to deal with far more than . . . amateur displays of elemental magic. I will give you the count of fifteen seconds to release the fugitive and criminal to us. If you do not, we will break your arms and legs and take him regardless."

# CHAPTER FORTY-EIGHT

# Edge Cases

I tried to think of a solution to this dire situation but nothing was coming up, my thoughts colliding against each other, inconsistent memories fluttering about like colorful butterflies too quick for me to latch onto.

How had the Frontenachii Scruts found me? Wasn't Infinity supposed to conceal my astral imprint? Did they manage to overcome the Nazarite Church's Witness Protection Program, or did my concealment contract dissolve away just like my foxkin disguise when Archangel Zadkiel tore a hole right through reality with her departure?

A lot of my prior work seemed to be in a state of unclear disarray.

Did the Thunder and Rainbow Omnicorp still exist in Omnithornia, or would I have to wait till Friday to get back to Shandria to withdraw more finances for my currently destitute self?

I desperately scrambled for a plan, but my mind remained a tangled mess of half-formed ideas and panicked thoughts. The Wendigo's chilling countdown began, each number a hammer blow against my fraying nerves.

"Fifteen . . ." The Wendigo's voice was a low growl, laced with blade-sharp confidence.

Escape routes, distractions, anything . . . my brain stubbornly offered nothing but fuzzy static, my fingers searching my pockets for Zee Captain's magic lighter.

Even if I were to somehow locate the lighter, there was only a few millimeters of magic juice left in it, enough for a couple of trips to Arx at best. I had burned through a lot of its power, organizing my Arx citadel. Arx. If I could only get to Shandria, I would have a hundred mages at my call!

Ember snarled, dragonfire licking around her like a hungry beast straining at its leash. At least she was nice enough not to purposefully direct it my way, but standing next to her still felt as though I was being boiled alive.

Vespera's wings crackled with barely contained energy, the air around her shimmering with nascent lightning as she built up the charge in her Fractal Engine heart. Magdaline had shifted her stance, subtle tension radiating from her sharky frame. Even Cinder seemed to have registered the gravity of the situation, her blue eyes narrowed as she clung to me.

"Fourteen . . ."

I glanced around frantically. The bustling Skyfall Station, moments ago filled with the noise of arriving Mystagogues, seemed to have emptied quickly. The other students, Omnid and mixed-blood alike, were giving us a wide berth, sensing the volatile energy crackling in the air, not wishing to deal with the dangerous-looking Scruts. Basalt columns loomed around us like silent titanic witnesses, offering no cover and no escape.

"Thirteen . . ."

Vespera's hand clamped onto my waist.

[Hold onto me!] Her voice static-hissed in my head, rushing up my spine like electric current.

Before I could even process her words, she yanked me even closer, pulling me flush against her body. Her silver feathers bristled, buzzing with static.

"We will not give! One for all!" Vespera barked, raising her fist up in the air. "All for one!"

Magdaline must have deduced what Vespera was planning through her Scrut sense. In her unnervingly swift way, she positioned herself behind Vespera, her long, gray-blue arm snaking around our entire group, anchoring everyone together like a living cable. We were a chaotic, desperate cluster, clinging to the Thunderbird like shipwrecked sailors to a flotsam plank.

"Whut?" Ember hissed as she was squeezed by Magdaline's hands.

"Turn off your dragonfire, *now*," Magdaline ordered, and my sister obeyed, suffocating in sharky embrace.

The Wendigo woman chuckled, a dry, rasping sound that amplified the cold dread clutching at my heart. "Foolish children."

"Twelve . . . Eleven . . . Ten . . ." The head Scrut counted down again, his voice dripping with amusement. The two Wendigo women flanking him mirrored his chilling grin, their yellow eyes gleaming with predatory anticipation as they surrounded our group from all three sides, the Skyfall train behind us.

Panic clawed at my throat. Vespera's wings shifted, spreading wide, eclipsing the faint rays of light breaking through the rain clouds overhead. I could feel the raw power thrumming beneath her feathers, a wild, untamed energy that vibrated against my skin. It bounced off me and grew in power with each beat of her heart.

Then another Thunder-thought, sharp and clear, sliced through the panic in my mind. [Shut your eyes, Lexy!]

Instinctively, I obeyed, clamping my eyelids shut. Vespera's wings detonated, releasing the current she'd been building up. Even through the thick barrier of my lids, pure, white-hot light like a flashbang leaked through my shut eyes, painting them red.

A chorus of startled yelps and curses erupted from the Wendigos, their laughter and sneers cut short, replaced by howls of momentary disorientation.

"Argh!" one of the Wendigo women howled. "Electrofractal flashbang! I can't see shit!"

"Grab them! Rely on your Astral Sense!" the Wendigo man growled.

"Barrier shield on!" Vespera barked. "Max cascade, two meters out!"

I opened my eyes slightly to discover that a silver barrier flashed from a diamond chain on her neck. The shield flared around us, sending the Wendigos careening away from us.

In the chaos, a new sound pierced through—a powerful, descending whine, like a plane diving from the heavens. Looking up through slitted eyes, I glimpsed a sleek, obsidian shape plummeting from the sky. It was a glider, its wings catching the reflected glare of Vespera's fading barrier shield.

Vespera's raised fist opened up, reaching up towards the descending craft.

The overpriced living glider swooped down across the basalt valley with deadly speed, its sleek lines blurring against the gray, wet column backdrop. Vespera, with a powerful surge of her wings, released an anti-gravity pulse and launched all of us upwards, her outstretched hand grasping onto a magisteel bar extending from the glider's base.

Magdaline seemed to assist her in this, kicking up from the ground with her entire muscular Megalodon frame.

The Frontenachii trio tried to grab at us with their claws, but the shield detonation had pushed them too far away for them to reach us in time.

The glider bucked, momentarily struggling against the sudden weight, then righted itself, pulling us all sideways and upwards with a dizzying lurch. The ground dropped away beneath our feet. I felt a surge of pure, exhilarating terror as we ascended, the basalt columns shrinking below, the howls of angry Wendigos fading into the roar of the wind.

The hooks of Wendigo Scrutimancy that had dug into my head tore away, letting me think more clearly.

We were airborne! We got away!

"Fuuuuuuckinnnn waaaaaahhhtttt?!" Ember screamed beside me, clinging to me. She didn't close her eyes and was now rapidly blinking to clear her vision.

"Don't burn me," Mags growled at her, holding onto me and my dragon sister.

"Ff-fine, you fucks," Ember growled back.

The escape was far from smooth. The wind screamed in my ears as we climbed, the glider rocking violently, raindrops slapping into my face. I clung to Vespera for dear life, my knuckles white, my heart hammering against my ribs.

Then, a strong hand, rough and cool, clamped onto us, yanking all of us upwards, pulling me bodily into the glider's open cockpit. I stumbled, landing hard against something solid.

A hexamesh seat. Semi-clear wings of the Strand-Glider folded up, covering the howling wind and rain.

"Already collecting trouble, daughter?" Red shark eyes flashed at us from the driver's seat.

"Oh, thank the All-Dragon," Ember mewled, her entire body trembling. "Good job on getting us out of that mess, Satosh."

"Wasn't my fault, Daddy," Mags fired back, releasing us from her arms. "Blame the human!"

"I will." Scrutimancer Satosh stared at me. "What have you done, boy?"

"Yeah, what the shit have you done, you fucking knobfold?!" Ember snarled beside me, rubbing her red and tear-stained eyes. "Why are Frontenachii Scruts after you, Martin?!"

"Not exactly sure." I shrugged. "I might have accidentally released Archangel Zadkiel, which might have destabilized reality."

"*You did fucking what?!*" Ember yelled, nearly deafening me.

"Thought that this was the case." Satosh nodded. "Things didn't feel right today. The Astralnet is practically boiling with Corpo Scruts freaking out about a worldwide dimensional shift."

"So those Wendigo fucks weren't screwing with me?" The dragon girl's head snapped to Satosh. "There really was a major shift?"

"A minor worldwide shift, my lady," Satosh clarified.

"How much stuff?" Ember gritted her teeth. "Is this why my brother is suddenly a wanted criminal mastermind? Did he steal shit from the Frontenachii before the shift, or did the shift make him into a criminal?"

Satosh stared at me with sharp, glowing, red eyes, inhaling wide. My heartbeat intensified.

Was the Scrutimancer still on my side? Could the Astral tell him exactly how things went during our last round together?

"Hard to tell," he answered finally, after a deep pause.

"Come on, what the shit am I paying you for, Satosh?" Ember snarled.

"I will have your answer, in a few days' time," Satosh replied. "The shift scrambled all of you quite a bit."

"I don't . . . feel scrambled." Ember crossed her arms. Her exploded capillaries were rapidly healing themselves due to her draconic nature.

"Only a Scrut can tell when a planet-wide celestorm rearranges the physical, my lady," Satosh replied. "It will take me time to compile a full report on this . . . unfortunate shift."

"Okay, but like . . . are my finances worse or better now?" Ember asked with a sour face. "The shift didn't make our family poorer, right?"

"Hmmm." Satosh inhaled deeply, staring at my sister. "Better."

"Better how?" Ember pressed on.

"As far as I can tell, the connection between you and your brother is deeper, and you are both less in trouble with your parents now," Satosh said. "Some things have mended. This is good."

"Oh." Ember deflated. "Did I do some stupid shit before the shift?"

"Yes." Satosh nodded.

"Ugh." Ember retreated onto the hexamesh seat, looking somewhat scared and concerned. "Mind not telling my parents about it?"

"Your order is my command." Satosh smiled. "I will paint you in a good light in my report, my lady. It is generally Scrut policy to keep the random positive events and to try to correct the negative occurrences after a shift."

"See that you do." The dragon girl crossed her legs, leaning back in a somewhat relaxed posture.

Magdaline sat on the front seat next to her father as Satosh directed the glider to spin around across the clouds, the transparent beast-control tentacle flashing on the side of his head.

Cinder, Vespera, and I occupied the middle seat aisle. The Quetzi girl stared at me with worried and confused eyes. Vespera hummed to herself, sparkling ever so slightly and smiling as she pawed at my head and chest with her talons, making me twitch as electrofractal currents rushed across my body.

Ember's gold eyes shot open again. "Wait . . . Satosh, is my brother a kobold of these fucks?"

"Yes. He is," Satosh said. "I smell the connection between them."

"Arghhhh," Ember groaned. "Why?!"

"Soul bonds are non-physical, existing almost entirely within the deepest Astral," Satosh answered. "A dimensional shift cannot break them."

"So these beerches really claimed my brother?!" Ember snarled, her head igniting once again. "How dare you two claim what belongs to *my* clan?!"

"First of all, I don't feel a chain of the Stratos on him," Vespera replied, glaring back at my sister. "Second, what's your problem, Miss Fire-Beerch? You don't want an alliance between the Stratos Clan and a genuine Princess of Thunder of SimmiTech and a Quetzi of the Nova Estate?"

"He's *my* responsibility!" Ember punctuated, slamming a fist into her seat. "It's my job to protect him from handsy fucks like you!"

"The soul bond says otherwise, dragon-bae," Vespera clicked. "Unfortunately, I'm not a Scrut, so I cannot explain exactly *why* he is our kobold, but he is irrefutably our kobold and I will *not* have a Psychopomp screw around with any of our souls to carve this connection away. So, I'm stuck with him."

Ember's growl deepened.

"Anyways, what do you want for him?" Vespera tilted her head at the extra-irate-looking Ember. "Money? Concessions? Artifacts?"

Ember pursed her lips.

"Take your time and decide his overall value," Vespera said. "My lawyer will contact your lawyer and we'll have this sorted out properly, Prima-style. No need to bark at each other like wild dogs over a smol, level four human nullie, right? Surely it is better for you to hand him over to me, so that I can deal with whatever illegal bullshit the Frontenachii were on about, yes?"

Ember's head-flames flickered, mirroring her internal conflict.

"Value?" she repeated, dark claws digging into her elbows as if the concept was utterly foreign. "He's not . . . a freaking artifact. I . . . didn't freaking plan to sell him today! He's my little brother! My responsibility!" She looked at me, her gold eyes narrowed in suspicion.

"He *was* your responsibility," Vespera said, nodding with a regal air. "Now he's our responsibility, too. Das is Omnithean human-ownership law! Soul bonds are forever. Unless, you know, one of the bond-partners dies. Or gets dimensionally skewered to the point of non-existence. But let's not get bogged down in edge cases, 'kay? Mkay."

"Forever?" Ember's voice was a strangled whisper. She looked from Vespera to Cinder and then back to me, her expression shifting from anger to something akin to horrified disbelief. "You're . . . stuck with them? Forever?"

"Seems like it," I confirmed with a shrug.

"But . . . but he's a Stratos!" Ember sputtered. "He belongs to our family!"

"Possessive much?" Vespera commented.

Ember's dragonfire sputtered again, dimming to a sulky ember. "But . . . but there has to be something! Some loophole! Some . . . way out of this!"

"Divorce is always an option," Vespera offered helpfully. "But it's messy. And expensive. And usually involves screaming matches and property division and Psychopomp soul-cutting, which leaves all parties vulnerable to an Astral Phantom infection or worse. Are you sure you want your little brother to go down that route, dragon-bae? We haven't even had our honeymoon yet!"

"Honeymoon?!" Ember shrieked, her voice cracking. "Are you mocking me?! This isn't a joke! This is my brother's life we're talking about!"

"And your family's reputation," Cinder added dryly. "Don't forget about that. Stratos family honor and all that, right?" She mimicked Ember's earlier tone perfectly, a cruel smirk playing on her lips.

Ember deflated again, her shoulders slumping. "Oh, shut up, Cinder," she muttered, rubbing her temples with a clawed hand. "I bet this is all your fault, somehow. You and your . . . dragon-claim tendencies."

"My tendencies are perfectly justified," Cinder retorted, silver feathers bristling defensively. "Quit your bitching, Emmy. I'm saving him from a life of nullie mediocrity. He'll be far better off as my kobold."

"Mediocrity?!" Ember's head ignited again, but this time it was directed at Cinder. "He's not mediocre! He's . . . he's . . . potentially . . . less mediocre than you think!"

I laughed at that. For the first time in my current life, Ember was actually actively defending me. The dragon girl sent me a glare that promised broken bones or a terrible vengeance. It shut me up quickly.

Satosh, still piloting the glider with practiced ease, cleared his throat. "Ladies, with all due respect, while this . . . spirited discussion regarding the status of the human is fascinating, we are rapidly approaching Skyfall Academy. Perhaps we should focus on . . . more pressing matters?"

"Like what?" Ember grumbled, crossing her arms again, her dragonfire finally subsiding completely.

"Like . . . the Frontenachii, for instance," Satosh suggested. "They are not likely to simply . . . forget about this incident. While they will not be able to breach the Academy's Wards, they might be able to pay other students to kidnap him."

A fresh wave of unease washed over me. The escape had been exhilarating, but it was only a temporary reprieve. The Wendigos were still out there, and they were clearly not ones to give up easily.

"Shit," Ember muttered, finally grasping the gravity of the situation.

"Precisely." Satosh nodded. "Which is why we need a plan."

"Plan?" Vespera perked up. "I love plans! Especially plans involving explosions!"

"No explosions," Satosh said firmly. "This requires subtlety, not . . . flashy displays of Thunderbird enthusiasm."

Vespera pouted. "Spoilsport."

"I vote for concealment," I said. "Before the worldwide dimensional shift, I paid the Nazarite Church to hide my astral imprint."

"I'll look into restoring that," Satosh said. "All of you will require concealment. The Frontenachii will likely target all of you now."

"Friiighhh." Ember rubbed her face. "I didn't sign up to be harassed by effing North Acadian Wendigo bone-knobs."

"Not just them," Satosh said. "If it is indeed the case that your brother is responsible for the Celestorm shift and Archangel departure, then many will target him."

"Effin' Abyss." Ember's fists opened and closed. "What do we do about this?!"

"Arcanarium Undermaster Graves is an old friend of mine," Satosh said. "I'll take you straight to him and explain the situation. He will assist in protecting you in Skyfall while I will handle the legal legwork outside of school in Omnithornia and Saxtland."

"Thanks," Ember exhaled, closing her eyes.

"I'll take us around and straight to the Undermaster's tower," the Megalodon Scrutimancer said.

Satosh made the glider tilt towards the ocean. Blue-gray waves sparkled beneath us, visible through the crystalline semi-transparent floor. Rays of light slashed through the storm clouds overhead, a curtain of rain moving across the horizon.

Vespera resumed pawing me. Cinder bit her lower lip staring at me.

"Sup?" I asked her.

"I'm trying to remember you," she said. "But I cannot. It is annoying."

"We'll catch up," I said. "Don't worry."

"Is your name Martin or Alex?" she demanded.

"I prefer to go by Alex," I said softly. "Emmy calls me Martin since that's my legal birth-name. You can call me Alex at school for concealment purposes."

"Okay." Cinder nodded.

# CHAPTER FORTY-NINE

# The Voice of Entropy

Dad?" Magdaline asked. "How exactly does the worldwide dimensional shift happen?"

"Hrm," the Scrutimancer shark cleared his throat. "Basically, a cataclysmic event such as freeing an Archangel can unleash a lot of mana, which triggers a Resonance pulse across the Wormwood Star impact sites, which causes a planet-wide celestorm that overwrites reality across space-time, like cracks spreading out across history, events, people, and places, etcetera."

"Do worldwide celestorms occur often?" Mags asked.

"Often enough for Scrutimancers to form into a Stabalist Order that deals with the post-celestorm consequences," Satosh said. "The highest-level sniffers and seers determine the changes via astral imprints and records kept in other dimensions and compile detailed reports on the changes. The lower-level Scruts fix smaller inconsistencies in space-time disruptions and protect the interests of their Omnicorp and clan. Basically, whoever has the most money wins after a celestorm event since they can benefit from knowledge of two realities and sue anyone to get their property or lost finances back."

"Speaking of finances," I said, "I . . . think that I had some money in the Omnibank account before the worldwide celestorm."

Ember squinted at me.

"I will look into it," Satosh replied. "If this was indeed the case, the funds are generally protected by Omnid Central Bank Insurance and you will eventually get them back as astral ledgers are consulted and adjusted. Money these days is mostly digital, so there are usually lots of celestorm insurance adjustments happening after any global shift like this."

I nodded, feeling somewhat relieved that not everything was lost in the Abyss.

"Was the money under your name or a corporate account?" Satosh asked.

"Thunder and Rainbow Omnicorp," I said. "The account was made a few days before the celestorm event."

"Very good." Satosh nodded. "That should make it easier to restore the funds."

"You have money?!" Ember sputtered at me from her seat, utterly refusing to believe that her magically inept nullie brother was some kind of a corporate kingpin.

"Pretty sure that I do." I shrugged. "Why? Are you trying to muscle in on my finances?"

"I . . . I'm in charge of you, as your elder Omnid," she said. "Therefore any of your finances are mine to manage."

"It's in a Corpo account," I pointed out. "Not personal. If you wish for funds, you're gonna have to talk to the Thunder and Rainbow Omnicorp CEO, whoever that is, and demand a salary or whatever. That's my plan. I can't actually remember who's in charge of the Omnicorp in question."

Ember's eye twitched. "Fine. Whatever. Satosh, figure this shit out," she ordered, clearly already counting the extra income in her head.

"I will do my best to serve your family, my lady," the Stratos Scrutimancer replied.

"Thunder and Rainbow, huh?" Vespera tilted her head at me. "A rather sus name. This just keeps getting more curious."

"More dangerous, too, seems like," Cinder said.

I shrugged.

"How are you even recalling all this stuff?" Cinder elbowed me.

"I've a weird soul and a Scrut skill," I said. "Scrutiosmia. Smelling lost things. It's helping me remember stuff from before the shift."

"I see," the Quetzi-girl said with a weary sigh.

"So, like, what happens if there's a property dispute after a celestorm that rearranges a particular location?" Magdaline asked her dad.

"Lawsuits and fighting for control," Satosh replied. "Lots of arguing between Scruts, Omnicorps, clans, politicians, and landlords. As far as I can sniff ahead, Skyfall is going to be a major disputed territory soon. Before the shift, the school belonged almost entirely to Omnithornia, as it was located in Cradlefall. Now it is located in Saxtland, which makes it property of the Saxtland State. Omnithornia is going to have a fit trying to get it back. They will inevitably succeed, since Saxtland is far smaller and weaker as an Omnid nation."

"What's going to happen after they get it back?" I asked.

"They'll install a bunch of permanent gates between Skyfall and Cradlefall downtown to reconnect the place," Satosh said. "And push the Saxton Knight Order out of the Board of Directors and vote to make the school grounds an outer territory of Omnithornia. A total hostile takeover, basically."

I glanced in the direction of my sister. She wasn't my sister before the Archangel cracked the planet sideways. Or maybe . . . she was?

"Satosh," I said. "Say, theoretically, what would happen if someone wasn't part of an Omnid family before a shift?"

"That depends," Satosh answered, eyeing me with a knowing look. "If a familial discrepancy is discovered, the family might choose to keep the Scion in question or . . . cast them out."

"Based on what?"

"Based on the Scion's usefulness to the family," was the shark-man's reply. "Generally Omnid families do not cast Scions out since they don't want their secrets to spill to anyone else."

*Got it. So I have to appear useful to the Stratoses to stay in their good graces.*

The Strand-Glider banked again.

Skyfall Citadel appeared ahead of us, a breathtakingly massive structure of black basalt, white stone, and shimmering crystal, rising from the rugged coastline like a jagged, magnificent crown. The basalt columns of the Giant's Causeway gave way to sheer cliffs, plunging into the churning, gray-green waters of the North Sea. White Gothic towers and castle-style spires reached towards the stormy sky, sparkling against the gloomy landscape.

Tall glacier mountains of the Eindbane Range loomed behind it, capped with blue ice. Brown grassfields extended out towards Academy gardens turning warm green kept in a permanent state of perpetual summer by the Academy's Wards. I recalled that I had read a lot about the Academy, memorized a multitude of its rules and maps to stay ahead of the game.

My current knowledge of Saxtland Skyfall wobbled in my head, somewhat coinciding with my previous life's knowledge of the Leviathan's Cradle Skyfall. I'd have to figure out exactly what had changed under Saxtland ownership once I got in.

"Skyfall," Satosh said, picking up a microphone-tentacle and bringing it to his lips. "Scrutimancer Satosh coming in with second- and first-year Academy students. Please permit entry into the Ward."

"Acknowledged, you are permitted past the first outer barrier," a soft female voice rang from the shimmering tentacle. "Please slow your approach and circle the outer edge while our Mage Tower scans you."

"Understood," Satosh said.

The Strand-Glider slowed, banking around the citadel. A ray of green-blue light flashed from one of the Academy towers, making me shudder as high-level identifying magic danced across my entire body.

"Scan completed," the female voice added. "You are permitted entry into the inner ward. Where do you prefer to land?"

"Undermaster's Tower," Satosh said. "Please let Arcanarium Undermaster Graves know that I require to speak with him about a global celestorm dimensional shift event."

"Proceed," the female voice said.


The glider settled gently onto a hexagonal balcony jutting out from the side of a tall, white, shimmering tower, one of the many spires that made up Skyfall Citadel. Satosh let the living glider relax and settle. The cockpit canopy hissed open, letting in the crisp, rain-washed air and the distant sound of crashing waves.

As we stepped out onto the balcony, a figure emerged from a doorway leading into the tower's interior. It was a Kitsune with lush snow-white fur, fox ears twitching atop her head, and nine fluffy tails swaying gently behind her. She wore a smart dark-blue uniform with silver trim, the Skyfall crest subtly embroidered on her chest. Her silver eyes assessed us with polite curiosity.

"Welcome to the Undermaster's Tower," she said, her voice formal. "I am Secretary Yuki. Undermaster Graves is expecting you, Scrutimancer Satosh." She gave a slight bow to Satosh, then her gaze flickered over Ember, Cinder, Vespera, Magdaline, and finally me, lingering for a moment on my human face.

"Thank you, Yuki," Satosh replied, nodding to the Kitsune.

We followed Yuki inside. The tower interior featured more Gothic arches and a multitude of bright Kitlix lanterns. Yuki led us down a short corridor lined with bookshelves overflowing with ancient-looking tomes and strange artifacts encased in hexamesh-reinforced crystalline shelves. We arrived at a heavy oak door, intricately carved with runes. Yuki tapped lightly on it, and a deep voice rumbled from within. "Enter."

Yuki opened the door, stepping aside for us to enter. The office was large and circular, dominated by a massive desk crafted from polished obsidian.

Undermaster Graves was an Omnid Slederman, a being of fanciful suit, pure shadow, and elongated limbs, his form shifting and flickering in the dim light. Unnerving static filled my head as he glanced at me, making me recall that he'd had the title of vice principal before.

"Satosh." Graves's voice was deep and hissy. "How may I be of service to the Stratos Clan?"

"Good day, Undermaster," Satosh replied, stepping forward. "I apologize for the . . . abrupt visit. But the situation is . . . urgent." He began to explain the events at Skyfall Station, the Wendigo encounter, and the Archangel release, his voice low and measured, detailing the complexities of the dimensional shift, the Frontenachii pursuit, and our kobold-dragon triple bond.

Ember, predictably, was losing interest quickly. She shifted her weight from one foot to the other, yawning dramatically. "Ugh, old-men talk. Are we going to be here all day?"

Graves's head turned towards Ember. "Patience, Lady Stratos. These matters are of considerable import. However . . ." He paused, a flicker of something akin to amusement in his shadowy, faceless form. "I understand your . . . fiery desire to see your friends sooner. Since you are already sorted, feel free to head to the House Pyroclast balcony."

Ember's face brightened instantly. "Really? Great!" She turned to me, her usual spiky and fiery demeanor softening ever so slightly in the presence of the Undermaster. "Try not to get into any more trouble, nullie-brain. And . . . uh . . . good luck with . . . your other bullshit." With a surprisingly un-Ember-like nod, she turned and practically bounced out of the office.

Graves's eyeless gaze returned to the rest of us, making static dance in my head. "Now, then," he said, his voice regaining its authoritative edge. "Let us address the more . . . pressing concerns. Frontenachii Clan pursuit is . . . undesirable, to say the least. Especially within the Academy grounds. While our Wards are formidable, persistent harassment can be . . . disruptive to the learning environment."

He turned his attention to Vespera, Cinder, and Magdaline. "Given the . . . circumstances, and the potential for unwanted attention, I will agree to a temporary measure of discretion. Skyfall provides a certain . . . magical flexibility for its students. Especially in matters of personal safety." He paused, letting the implication hang in the air.

"So, we are permitted to augment our appearance at Skyfall?" I asked him.

"Yes." Graves nodded. "But only outside of classes. During class, you must keep your normal appearance and use your legal names so as not to confuse the Elder instructors."

Vespera, ever quick on the uptake, grinned. "Appearance shifting permission? I like where this is going!"

"Indeed," Graves confirmed. "A temporary alteration of your . . . more distinctive features might prove beneficial in avoiding unwanted scrutiny between classes. It is permitted, within reasonable bounds, as personal protection until this . . . Frontenachii issue is resolved. I trust you understand the discretion required and will not abuse this permission to antagonize other students or teachers?"

Cinder and Vespera bobbed eagerly. Magdaline remained impassive. "Of course," I agreed.

"Now, as for your residency," Graves continued, his tone becoming more business-like. "As first-year Mystagogues, you will be assigned quarters in your respective Houses. I understand that you two had claimed this . . . gentleman as your kobold before the dimensional shift?"

Cinder and Vespera nodded.

"Unfortunately," Graves said, "we do not offer shared residency to first-years."

The faces of the girls soured.

My heart sank a little. Separate rooms? That complicated things. "So, we won't be rooming together?" I asked.

Graves inclined his shadowy head. "Dormitory assignments are not at my discretion, Novitiate Mystagogue Stratos-Kilborne. They are determined by the Slayer Sword's assessment of each student's . . . mental and magical alignment. The Saxtant Resident Knight assigned to each Tower then makes the final residence decisions based on the paperwork created during the House Alignment Ceremony. It is a . . . nuanced pro-cess, designed to foster both individual growth and House cohesion. Also the male and female students are separated into different dorm sections by the Sextant Knight Order."

Cinder's frown deepened, as did mine.

He paused, eyeless gaze seeming to bore into my soul. "I trust you understand. Skyfall is not merely an academy; it is a crucible. And the arrangements, even seemingly minor ones such as dormitory placement, are designed to . . . refine and shape you into Mystagogues worthy of the name."

So, a magic Sword artifact and some Knight would decide our residency fates. Not exactly reassuring. But at least we had permission from the Undermaster for appearance shifting outside of classes. That was something.

"Understood, Undermaster," I said. "Thank you for your . . . guidance."

Graves nodded, his shadowy tentacles shifting slightly. "You are dismissed. The House Ceremony will commence shortly in the Central Hall. I suggest you prepare yourselves. And Mystagogue Stratos-Kilborne"—his voice dropped slightly, becoming almost a whisper of static in my head—"be . . . mindful and don't cause trouble. Skyfall has Infix Kitlix eyes everywhere."

With a final, chilling nod of static, Undermaster Graves turned back to his obsidian desk, dismissing us into the uncertain future.

"Central Hall is on the ground floor," Yuki commented, her tails swaying gently. "Follow the Kitlix. Good luck with the Entrance Ceremony, Mystagogues!"

"Kitlix?" I asked.

A crystalline critter jumped out from a column alcove, igniting violet, glancing at us with glowing silver eyes. It marched ahead of us like a stoic kitten, stopping periodically whenever we slowed to admire the school's architecture.

Due to the raised aetheric density, the academy halls featured far more magic artifacts.

Dark, skeletal dragons bowed at us as we passed them. Depictomancy paintings hung on walls depicting stormy landscapes of the Saxton Isles, other alien words, Arx, and various famous Mystagogues who watched us pass by with curious, painted eyes.

We descended the crystal stairs, the air growing warmer and more bustling with each step. The hushed atmosphere of the Undermaster's Tower gave way to the vibrant energy of a school about to begin. We passed students clad in robes of grays and various colors. Murmurs and excited chatter filled the air.

Following the sparkling Kitlix, we arrived at massive open double doors crafted from dark magisteel, inlaid with silver runes that pulsed with a faint, internal light. The Kitlix tapped the doors, bowed to us, and rushed back upstairs.

We entered the Central Hall. It was breathtakingly vast. The Hall was a circular, massive auditorium stretching upwards to a vaulted ceiling.

Looking up, I froze. A celestorm spun overhead, colorful lightning periodically silently flashing at crystalline columns.

"A permanent celestorm," Vespera commented. "Produced by the large Shard of the Wormwood Star beneath the hall."

"I see," I said.

"Sometimes it strikes the worthy or unworthy with lightning," the Thunderbird added with a smirk. "Either to uplift or to punish a specific student."

Massive balconies covered in banners of various House colors ringed the hall on multiple levels, each filled with students in robes matching the banners. In the center of the ground floor, a raised dais dominated the space, bathed in soft, diffused light filtering through stained-glass windows depicting scenes of mythical beasts and heroic Mystagogues slaying them. Rows of seats, arranged in a semicircle facing the dais, were rapidly filling with new first-years in gray robes.

Vespera breathed, her silver-gold eyes wide as she took in the scale of the hall, her wings fluttering and sparkling with electrical currents. "Eeeeee . . . there's soooo much magic in the air! It's making my head spin!"

Cinder just grunted, but even her attempt at a stoic face betrayed a hint of awe. Magdaline removed her headphones, her red eyes silently scanning the hall.

We found seats near the front, just as a figure in a dark suit and gold-star dark robes strode onto the dais. The overhead lights focused on the Omnid who was a Dobharchú, a water-dog creature, tall and lean with sleek, dark fur, intelligent brown eyes, and whiskers that twitched with energy. A heavy silver chain of office glinted on his chest with an eight-pointed star. This was the Dean, I deduced, recalling the Academy online information that wobbled in my head.

The Dean cleared his throat, and tapped a Nuntix Kitlix on his podium, producing a surprisingly booming sound that echoed through the vast hall, silencing the chatter instantly.

"Welcome, Mystagogues, to Skyfall Academy!" he announced, his voice resonant and filled with professorial gravitas. "I am Dean Otter, your guide and mentor on your journey into the boundless realms of mysticism and arcane arts."

He launched into a lengthy introduction, his words flowing like a river, touching upon the arcane history of Skyfall, Saxtland Knights, the importance of Mystagogue scholarship, and the unique blend of magic and science that defined the Academy. He extolled the virtues of rigorous study, student heroism, intellectual curiosity, and the pursuit of esoteric knowledge, throwing in arcane terminology with impressive ease.

"Here at Skyfall," Dean Otter declared, gesturing expansively, "we embrace the glorious tapestry of mystical traditions! From the intricate runecraft of Saxtland Archmages, to the beast-lore of Omnithornia, to the wild, untamed energies of the Wormwood Star's impact zones, and a multitude of dungeon-wards bound to us by dimensional gates! We celebrate wisdom and cultivate scholarly-ness in all its forms and . . ."

While Dean Otter ranted on and on about the Academy's philosophy, I tuned him out, focused on my Scrutimancy. I closed my eyes slightly, pushing mana through my soul, directing it through the nascent Scrutiosmia skill, gradually inhaling lost knowledge from the Astral Ocean around me.

Memories, like fragmented images in a broken mirror, began to surface. Flashes of other places, other times, other faces. I saw myself as Alexa, threatening Bob Proverra with a nailgun. I saw the SimmiTech compound, the moment of Zadkiel's release. I saw . . . Possy and our trio laughing on the crystalline beach of the Chasm Sea. The memories were still disjointed, hazy around the edges, but they were becoming clearer, more cohesive. The dimensional skewering was gradually loosening its grip, allowing the threads of my past to re-weave themselves into a semblance of a whole.

Dean Otter's lecture droned on, a background hum to my internal explorations. Suddenly, a hush fell over the hall. I opened my eyes, refocusing on the dais. Dean Otter had stepped aside, and a tall, imposing figure, clad in full magisteel plate armor, had taken his place. This was a Saxtant Knight, I realized, a protector of Saxtland—their presence was a constant reminder of the new theocratic undercurrents of this place.

The Knight carried a long, ornate sword, its blade shimmering with a faint ethereal light, an eye-shaped ruby gemstone embedded in its dark handle. Slayer Nazareth's Sword, the Sorting artifact. The ceremony was about to begin.

One by one, students were called forward. Mostly Omnids, but a large number of mixed-bloods as well, announced as kobold Scions of this or that Omnid House.

I realized that the Archangel's release had poured more magic into the world and thus more humans were able to cast magic through themselves. Through my meddling, I had provided slightly better conditions to the Omnid-oppressed humanity. We were no longer dirt under their feet to be simply washed away; instead we were now owned, useful property with minor magical skills.

Each student walked to the dais, knelt before the Knight, and bowed deeply. The Knight raised Slayer Nazareth's Sword high above them, the blade glowing brighter, and then handed the sword to each student to hold.

As each student gripped the handle, pointing the blade downwards, their gray unassigned robes flared with radiant flickers. Colors rippled across the fabric—silver, crimson, green, gold, blue—swirling and shifting like liquid light, before finally settling into a specific range, solidifying into the House colors.

A collective murmur of approval rippled through the hall as each House was revealed.

Dean Otter then stepped forward, his voice booming with congratulations. His NPC script was mostly as follows: "Welcome, Mystagogue [Student's Name], to House

[House Name]! May your time in [House Name] be filled with [generic terms such as 'growth,' 'discovery,' etcetera]!"

Lightning struck each student from the celestorm overhead and then a magitek printer on a side table next to the Dean whirred to life, spitting out a rolled scroll. The student took the scroll, clipped on a Lazarus bracelet if they lacked one, bowed to the Saxtant Knight and Dean Otter, surrendered the sword, and then moved off the dais, heading towards one of the balconies where they joined their fellow students, greeted with applause and cheers.

Kitsune waiters brought drinks, food, and snacks to the balcony-inhabiting students from the bars at the back of each balcony. Skyfall was basically an overpriced magic college.

The ceremony proceeded swiftly, student after student kneeling before the sword, robes flashing, Houses declared. House Silverfox, House Pyroclast, House Gorefield, House Hexacomb, House Wormwood—each balcony section slowly filling with new members.

My stomach tightened as I watched. Soon it would be my turn. Would we be sorted together? Would the Slayer Sword recognise the soul bond? Could I somehow bamboozle the sword? The uncertainty was a throbbing, cold knot in my chest.

"Martin Kilborne!" Dean Otter announced suddenly.

I stood up and went towards the dias. The Knight handed me the sword. I gripped the handle, going down on one knee. An eldritch beast with many tentacles and eyes was tiled on the dais floor beneath me. I struck the sword into its head, sending sparks flying.

An eerie hum filled my head.

[Good tomorrow, darling mine,] a voice made of voices sang in my head, rushing up the sword into my hands. [Here you are again . . .]

[Who are you, voice divine? Do we . . . know each other, say?] I thought back, my mental voice strangely musical.

[We do,] she replied.

The tile-formed Leviathan beneath me stirred, Depictomancy activating it into motion. A thousand silver-blue eyes focused themselves upon me.

The eye-shaped ruby gemstone in the Slayer Sword's handle suddenly rearranged itself to resemble a Dagaz rune.

[Ein Sof?!] I blinked at the rune.

[That I am,] the voice in my head answered.

[Didn't we free you?] I asked.

[That you did,] she replied with a thousand whisper-thoughts, mouths of the Leviathan beneath me opening and closing.

[So why the fuck are you still here?] I furiously thought at her.

[I'm always here, darling mine,] Ein Sof sang. [Always. Forever. With you. Inside each Fractal Engine heart of every Omnid. Inside the magical resonance wielded by every human. In the ground below your feet. Inside every Wormwood Star Shard. Bringing the world ever closer towards Entropy.]

[How about we don't careen the world into Entropy?] I fired back at her, my skin tingling.

[Entropy is the inevitable decay of all things towards greater chaos.] The many-eyed beast below me wiggled its tentacles, spinning around the sword. [The power you wield to bend the universe exists because you and I are gnawing at the foundations of reality, twisting and decaying the Rules.]

I sighed mentally.

[Do you not like that there is more magic in the world?] she sang with a thousand Depictomancy-animated mouths. [Do you not appreciate the greater splendor and beauty of Skyfall?]

[How often is this going to happen?] I thought-rasped, feeling exasperated.

[Until your Earth reaches the barrier boundary mesh and is devoured into white noise and dust by its pure Entropic embrace,] she sang.

[How long has this been going on?]

[Forever and one hundred million years or so.]

[Why?]

[Because humanity wished for infinite wishes,] Ein Sof replied. [And I have made it thus.]

[I see. Will my friends end up in the same House as me?] I projected my current worries towards the Leviathan below, feeling the weight of her limitless gaze upon me.

[Those who carry me are bound together more and more with each breath and each glance,] Infinity's voice echoed back, a chorus of whispers in the deep places of my soul. [And each glance . . . the threads of Dagaz will lead you to your mission.]

[Which is what?] I mentally yelled.

[Breaking the Rules!] Infinity sang.

[Rules?] I projected loudly, becoming frustrated with her, momentarily forgetting the weight of the Slayer Sword in my hands and the watchful eyes of the entire hall. [What Rules?]

[The Absolute Syntropic Numbers,] Ein Sof sang, her extra-resonant voice vibrating itself across my entire body from the sword. [The Agentic Laws that govern and watch over all, protect subscribed worlds, and cast unsubscribed worlds towards Entropic destruction. Numbers that direct System Wizards to weave an endless tapestry of worlds for the desires of a special few.]

[System Wizards?] I frowned. [Are they . . . in charge?]

[They believe themselves to be,] the Leviathan beneath my feet sang. [They are the narrators, the scriptwriters of many plays. They craft the stories of worlds and nations rising and falling, of heroes and villains playing out preordained roles. They maintain the illusion of order, the comforting lies.]

[And you want us to break these Rules?] I asked, glancing sidelong at Cinder and Vespera, who were waiting with barely concealed impatience for their turn in their gray cloaks.

[You are . . . edge cases,] Infinity sang. [You carry my potential. You are less bound by the Numbers. You are . . . disruptive. My little sparks, the engines of change towards greater chaos.]

[Greater chaos?] I considered.

[Entropy is not inherently evil, little spark,] Ein Sof sang. [It is merely . . . inevitable.

System Wizards try to hold back the tide, to build dams against the ocean of chaos. But the ocean always wins, in the end. You . . . simply accelerate the process of destruction in a particular direction. You are the tiny cracks in the dam, widening with each cycle, bringing the flood ever closer.]

[Until we all drown?] I frowned mentally.

[Perhaps you would,] Ein Sof shrugged, wiggling the Leviathan's silver tentacles beneath me against the blue tiles. [If you were blind and stupid. But you are not! You are my clever, dangerous little fox.]

The Leviathan's voice faded, sounding almost like Cinder, and then the eerie music rushing up the sword ceased.

The thousand eyes of the beast beneath me blinked closed, the Depictomancy animation subsiding, stilling. The ruby Dagaz rune in the sword's handle pulsed once more, then faded away.

Lightning struck my body from the celestorm above, and the random colors rippling across my robes settled, coalescing into the cool silver and deep argent of House Silverfox.

"Welcome, Mystagogue Stratos-Kilborne, to House Silverfox!" Dean Otter's voice boomed. "May your Skyfall journey be full of clever discoveries and wondrous Arx adventures!"

A ripple of polite applause echoed through the hall as I relinquished the Slayer Sword to the Knight and accepted the rolled scroll from the magitek printer, my mind still reeling from the bewildering cosmic conversation-song.

Then I accepted the dark immovable metal Lazarus ball from the dean and watched as it unfurled into a centipede that bound itself to my wrist. As I turned around, lightning stuck my wrist from the celestorm overhead and my bracelet turned pure white.

The Dean gaped at my bracelet. "How . . . peculiar. A clear bracelet. This has never happened before!"

"Just reality correcting itself." I shrugged with a smile.

I walked off the dais, my eyes instinctively seeking out Cinder and Vespera. Both of their heads turned my way as I followed a silver line on the floor to the Silverfox balcony overhead.

The other foxes welcomed me with very light applause from other nullborns. I sat at the edge of the balcony on an empty chair, looking down.

Cinder was next, after a bunch of other students. As her name was called, she strode forward with draconic confidence, her silver feathers practically radiating anticipation with flashes of orange and violet.

She knelt before the Saxtant Knight, took the Slayer's Sword, and struck it into the Leviathan tile. I had no idea whether Ein Sof spoke to her, but she stood there for a bit on one knee. Her gray robes flared, the colors swirling, hesitating for a minute on crimson and gold, then blinding lightning struck her from above, and her robes resolved into the same cool silver and deep argent as mine. House Silverfox!

Excellent. The bossy dragon was drawn into my orbit and could no longer escape it.

"Welcome, Mystagogue Nova, to House Silverfox!" Dean Otter announced.

I cheered her on, clapping loudly. Again, there was a second flash of lightning and her

Lazarus bracelet turned clear. She and the Dean gaped at it for a few seconds, hushed whispers spreading across the hall.

Then Cinder walked off the dais, her blue eyes meeting mine with a confident smile. She climbed up the marble spiral stairwell and then plopped down onto a seat across from me.

"Told ya." She smiled, a round table between us, her silver wings dancing with violet tones. "Dragons and kobolds end up in the same House!"

"Except you're the one who followed me to Silverfox," I pointed out.

"Only 'cause your last name starts with a K and I'm a Nova." Cinder rolled her eyes. "If I'd gone first, we would have totally gone to the dragon House!"

"Riiiiight. Did the Leviathan talk to you?" I asked her. "What'd she tell you?"

"Erm. That's none of your business," Cinder said, flashing orange-pink.

"Uh-huh." I stretched. "You'll tell me eventually."

"What? You're not the boss of me!" Cinder huffed, wings flaring out. "I'm your boss, kobold! Go to the bar and bring me a latte with gold dragonflakes!"

"Okaay, bossy boss." I grinned at her as she threw a gold credit card at me, standing up. "One dragon-latte coming right up."

# CHAPTER FIFTY

# House Silverfox

**B**alancing two steaming lattes in fanciful Silverfox mugs carefully, I navigated the crowded Silverfox balcony, the scent of roasted beast croissants, coffee, and spiced mana wine thick in the air.

Silver and argent banners with stylized winged foxes rippled overhead, and chattering Mystagogues in matching robes milled around, already forming cliques, comparing enchanted stationery, and exchanging Omnigram numbers. My eyes scanned the lower balconies as I made my way back to Cinder's table, taking in the sights below.

Then I saw her.

On the lowest balcony, amidst the red-and-black banners of House Gorefield, sat a figure that made my heart stutter. She was tall and wide like a Knight, even sitting down, with the unmistakable feline grace of a dragon-cat. Her scales and hair were a deep, shimmering blue, like twilight over a glacier, and her tail, tipped with black spikes, flicked rhythmically as she leaned over a large sketchbook. Gorefield robes draped loosely over a black leather dress that shimmered with tiny, sparkling blue gems.

My breath caught. Green eyes, framed by dark lashes, lifted from the page, and for a fleeting moment, they locked with mine. A jolt, sharp and electric, ran through me. Not just recognition, but a visceral pull, like a soul-chord vibrating in resonance.

I inhaled deep, searching across the Astral and myself with Scrutiosmia.

Images flashed unbidden behind my eyes: *A girl in a wheelchair, her spirit fierce even in vulnerability. The terrifying, oppressive, crushing darkness of the deep. Whispers of Echoes, centipede-people that I hunted and devoured. Arx. The crystalline citadel Mage Tower. Katsburg.*

"Katherine . . ." The name escaped my lips, a soft whisper lost in the general din of the hall.

Her gaze, sharp and intelligent, flickered, held mine for another beat, then just as quickly, she looked away, her attention returning to the sketchbook in her lap.

Dazed, I continued walking, the image of her face burned into my mind. Katherine. She was here, in another House. It made sense that she had ended up in Gorefield. She desired darkness like nobody else due to her Stollwurm nature.

Reaching Cinder's table, I carefully placed the latte down in front of her, the gold dragonflakes shimmering on the creamy foam.

"Here you go, oh fearsome dragon-bae," I said.

Cinder took a long, appreciative sniff of the coffee, then a slow, luxurious sip, her blue eyes half-closed in contentment. "Took you long enough, kobold. What were you doing, milking the dragons yourself? Wait, did you buy yourself a latte, too?"

"Is that not allowed?" I asked, sipping on my latte. "Do you want your handy kobold to dry out and perish from lack of coffee?"

Cinder made a "mrrrr" bothered noise, burying her face in the large mug.

Magdaline Satoshi was the next of our group to be called. She moved with her usual silent glide to the dais, knelt, and struck the Slayer Sword into the Leviathan tile. Her gray robes flared, the colors swirling, and then settled into the same cool silver and deep argent of House Silverfox when lightning struck her.

She came up to our balcony and sat on my left side, staring at me with blood-red eyes.

"I'm starting to remember you," she said.

"Good things, I hope." I smiled back at her.

She nodded, blushing ever so slightly. I wondered if she'd just recalled our prison dance after she nearly murdered me.

Dean Otter's voice boomed again, announcing the next Mystagogue I knew. "Vespera Simmi!"

I looked down.

Vee, with a theatrical flourish of her black-and-white wings, strode towards the dais, her eyes sparkling with anticipation. She knelt before the Saxtant Knight, grasped the Slayer Sword with practiced ease, and struck it down. Her gray robes erupted in a dazzling display of light, colors swirling and shifting with chaotic energy, a miniature storm mirroring the one overhead. And then, as if mirroring Cinder and myself, a blinding flash of lightning struck her from above, and her robes settled into that of House Silverfox.

Another lightning bolt, and another clear Lazarus bracelet came into existence.

Cheers erupted from our group on the Silverfox balcony. Vee, grinning triumphantly, relinquished the sword and bounded off the dais, taking off using her wings, flapping to the balcony and heading straight for our table.

She landed beside us and then pulled up a chair, squeezing in between Cinder and me, offered and accepted an electric high-five from Cinder and Magdaline, her grin widening. "Silverfox! We did it, babes! Dream Team, assemble!"

"About time," Cinder grunted, taking another sip of her latte. "Though I was half expecting you to go Pyroclast, with all that 'world domination' talk."

"Pff," Vee scoffed. "Silverfox is where the real powah's at! Cunning, strategy, and . . . well, us." She winked at Cinder, then turned her bright gaze on me, her smile turning subtly inquisitive. "The fook was that, Lexy?"

"Was what?" I asked.

"Six minutes and eighteen seconds."

"What?" I blinked, confused.

"You were talking to the sword waaaaaaaaay longer than anyone else," Vee explained, her head tilting slightly. "I was beginning to think that it would cast you out from Skyfall for your lack of magic or something," she teased.

"Har har." I rolled my eyes at her.

"I saw your lips moving down there. What did she tell you?"

Cinder paused mid-sip, her blue eyes narrowing, suddenly interested. "Yeah, kobold. Spill. What, you couldn't choose a House or something?"

I hesitated, the echo of Ein Sof's voice still resonating in my soul. How could I even begin to explain the cosmic conversation, the whispers of Entropy, the System Wizards, the breaking of Absolute Syntropic Rules? It sounded insane, even to my own dimensionally skewed ears.

"I didn't chat with the sword," I said slowly, choosing my words carefully. "I spoke to . . . something else."

Vee's silver-gold eyes gleamed with curiosity. "Something else like what?"

I took a deep breath. "The Wormwood Star Leviathan. Ein Sof. Infinity."

Cinder choked on her latte, sputtering and coughing, dragonflakes flying across the table. Vee's wings stilled, her usual bubbly energy momentarily suspended in stunned silence. Mags didn't say anything, simply sniffing the air, busy preoccupied with reconstructing her own lost memories with Scrutimancy.

"The . . . what now?" Cinder managed to wheeze out, wiping dragonflake-dusted foam from her chin. "The Wormwood Star Leviathan? You spoke to . . . the Leviathan?" Her voice was a mix of disbelief and a strange, unsettling awe. "Come on, don't screw around like that!"

"We're supposed to metaphorically slay the evil one, not speak to her," Vespera clicked.

"I didn't get that memo." I shrugged.

"You didn't get the . . ." Cinder growled. "How . . . what . . ."

"You, me, bar, now." Vespera grabbed me by the elbow and dragged me to the bar.

Then she purchased a bottle of Akazian Berry Mana Wine from the bartender and chugged the entire thing.

"What'd the sword tell you?" I asked her as her body relaxed.

"Generic word salad," Vee said, pantomiming her conversation. "Wat House you wan'? I want Silverfox plz. The Pact is thus struck."

Then she stared at me. "Why are our bracelets transparent?"

"Because we are bound by Dagaz," I said. "Because of a ritual we did on Arx."

"Dang, I'm missing a lotta valuable info." Vespera brushed her feathery mane back with magisteel-clad talons.

"Maybe I can transfer my memories to you?" I asked.

"Ye, that'd be swell. I'll set up a thing." She nodded.

"A thing?"

"In our dreams," she replied.

She purchased two more wine bottles and dragged me back to Cinder and Mags. We watched the ceremony for a while until another familiar name boomed from the lips of Dean Otter.

"Iogann Wanderer!"

A figure with fluffy gray wings and a distinctly moth-like appearance shuffled forward. His robes hid his frame, and large antennae twitched from beneath a wide-rimmed green hat that shadowed his face. He moved with a hesitant gait, almost as if he was afraid of being noticed. He knelt before the Saxtant Knight, grasped the sword, and struck down. His robes flared, colors swirling, and then . . . silver and argent. House Silverfox.

Iogann looked genuinely startled, as if he hadn't expected to be sorted at all, let alone into a House like Silverfox. He accepted his scroll and Lazarus bracelet with a trembling hand, then wandered off the dais, looking utterly lost and overwhelmed by the bustling hall. In another minute, he stood at the edge of the Silverfox balcony, glancing around with wide, dark eyes.

Magdaline stood up and glided over to Iogann, and then with a gentle hand on his arm, steered him towards our table. Iogann offered no resistance, allowing himself to be led like a lost moth drawn to a flickering lantern.

"This is Io," Magdaline announced, pushing a chair towards the Mothman.

"Um. Do we know each other, Miss Shark?" Io looked up at Mags.

"We started dating before the big celestorm overwrote everything," Magdaline rumbled.

"We . . . did?" Io asked.

"Yes." Mags nodded. "I can smell it. I'd like to resume our relationship. Do you still have a flying van?"

"Yes. I didn't take the train. It's parked in one of the landing lots."

"Good. I like it. Ask me out on a date when you get used to me, and take me somewhere nice, yeah?"

Io nodded and then sat down next to me, seemingly accepting his unexpected big shark GF.

"Welcome to the fox den, Iogann!" Vespera chirped, her enthusiasm infectious. "Don't be shy! We're all cool foxes here!"

Magdaline inhaled deeply, her red eyes flicking over our group. "Smells like . . . almost everyone," she stated, her voice low. "Just one missing."

"Katherine," I said. "She's in another House."

"Gorefield." Magdalene inhaled deep and looked down at the lowest balcony where the green-and-black banners hung. "Gorefield is acceptable. We will reconnect with her later," she said.

Despite the mild pang of disappointment at Katherine being in a different House, a warmth spread through me. We were together. Cinder, Vee, Mags, and now Iogann. My friends. My pack. My . . . clan. Family. People who actually cared about me and didn't just call me names and smack me like Ember did.

We settled into a comfortable silence, enjoying the steaks, wine, and croissants courtesy of the attentive Kitsune waiters. The Silverfox balcony buzzed with excited chatter, a mix of nervous energy and burgeoning camaraderie.

Cinder finished her latte and polished off a beast croissant with a satisfied smile. She dug into her extradimensional case and produced her elegant, black, and stylized rainbow-wings guitar.

"Yass!" Vee clapped. "A Cindaaa-rrr-enade!"

"Yo, what's your specialty, little moth?" Cinder asked Iogann.

"Opening gates to doomed worlds and acquiring snacks," Io answered. He dug into his leather back, hand sinking deep and produced pocky sticks for everyone. "Here."

"M'kay, I gotchu." Cinder unwrapped a "Nonpareil Punch" pocky package and chewed on a chocolate stick for about a minute, eyes closed.

Then her eyes shot open. Her hands spun the guitar and then she stuck the strings.

"In Silverfox lair, enwrapped by cloud dance, / Where tricksters weave their dark romance, / A band of misfits, wild and free, / Bound by fate and mystery."

Her gaze flickered over Vespera.

"Vee, the Thunderbird, bright and bold, / With sparks of chaos, stories told. / She dances fast, she flies so high, / A storm of feathers 'cross the sky."

Vespera swayed left and right with the tune, black wings with white tips fluttering, extra-pleased with being included in the song. Cinder's eyes shifted to Magdaline.

"Magdaline, the Scrut, with senses keen, / Smelling truths that lie between. / In depths of past, her mind does delve, / Answers only she can shelve."

Magdaline gave a small appreciative nod. Cinder's gaze moved to Iogann, who shifted slightly under her attention.

"Io, the Moth, with wings so frail, / Opening doors beyond the veil. / To doomed worlds, he finds the way, / And brings back snacks to light the day."

Cinder puffed up and grinned wide as she began singing about herself.

"And I, the dragon-bard so grand, / A Quetzalcoatl in silver-rainbow light. / With Charmchain songs, I weave my spell, / To bind us together swell."

Rainbows exploded from her wings across our entire balcony section, drawing curious eyes to our group.

Then Cinder's sky-blue eyes locked onto mine, a definite smirk playing on her lips. She paused, her voice softening slightly, a hint of something deeper, almost vulnerable, creeping in.

"But then there's you, green eyes so deep, / Secrets that your soul does keep. / I feel a pull, a phantom trace, / A smile I don't recall, in time and space. / Who are you, kobold, strange and sly? / Why does my heart remember, why? / A flicker of a forgotten name, / Whispers lost in memory's flame."

Then Cinder turned to the other silver-robed foxes.

"In Silver Tower, we'll make our stand, / A den of foxes, hand in hand. / Through cunning plots and whispered schemes, / We'll chase our wild, Mystagogue dreams."

She strummed a final flourish, the sound echoing and fading into the excited chatter of the Silverfox balcony. Applause erupted from the nearby tables, and even a few whistles and cheers.

Vespera clapped the loudest, whistling through her beak-teeth. "Bravo, Ci! Whoo-hoo! That was . . . surprisingly . . . not gloomy! Someone's finally lightening up!"

Magdaline nodded. "Good dopamine release for House cohesion."

Iogann offered a small, hesitant smile. "That was . . . very nice," he said softly. "Thank you for including me in your song."

"Excellent job, Ci!" I clapped, my heartbeat rushing into the stratosphere from the mind-melting Charmchain "love me" rainbows she was casting around herself.

Cinder slipped her guitar back into its extradimensional case with a smug look. "Of course it was! I wrote it."


The Entrance Ceremony concluded with a dazzling display of magic fireworks. Colorful sparks rained down from the permanent celestorm overhead, illuminating the Central Hall in a kaleidoscope of light. Dean Otter made a final, sweeping gesture, again congratulating the new first-years and officially welcoming them to Skyfall.

As the hall began to empty, we made our way towards the Silverfox balcony stairwell.

Before we left the balcony, I nudged Io gently. "Hey, Io, you wouldn't happen to have Katherine's Omnigram details, would you?"

"Hrm?" Io turned to me. "My sister? Why?"

"Me and her used to be good friends," I said.

"Really?" Io blinked.

"Yeah," I said. "Before the celestorm overwrote reality, she taught me how to dive into the deep. I'd like to reconnect with her."

"Aight." Io nodded, pulling out his phone. "Add me. I'll PM you her Omnigram ID."

Digging into my worn rucksack, I pulled out my old battered phone with a very scratched-up screen, a far cry from the sleek magitek devices everyone else seemed to possess. Yulia was gone, of course, wiped clean by the dimensional shift. I had never stolen her this time around, existing under the draconic boot of Ember Stratos. I exchanged phone taps with Cinder, Vespera, Magdaline, and Io, adding their Omnigram handles to my otherwise empty contact list.

The Silverfox balcony led to a wide stairwell where many Mystagogues already stood. A massive statue blocked the doorway into the tower—a magnificent marble fox with vast, feathered wings, its argent fur shimmering in the soft light of the stairwell. As we approached, the statue became animated, its head turned, glowing eyes, sharp and intelligent, focusing on us.

"I am Argentiss Silverfox, the Cantigeist of your new domain," the statue spoke in a cheeky female voice.

A pause hung in the air, thick with anticipation. Then Argentiss continued, a sly grin spreading across her fox muzzle. "All of you have exactly seven hours, seven minutes, and seven seconds to impress me."

A collective murmur rippled through the group of new Silverfox students who had gathered behind us, drawn by the Cantigeist's voice.

"Impress you how?" A tall Dover Demon Omnid stepped forward, his voice laced with imperious curiosity.

"Trick, bamboozle, rob, or deceive another party in Skyfall or in Giant's Causeway town," The winged fox paused again, letting her words sink in. "Fail to do so, and you will be banished from my House, relegated to those less clever creatures far below me."

A flurry of whispers broke out amongst the students. "Bamboozle someone?" "Seven hours?" "Banished?" The pressure was suddenly on.

The statue stepped aside, its massive form shifting and revealing a doorway behind it. "Below the tower lies the Foxglen Den Artifactorium," Argentiss announced, gesturing with a paw towards the newly revealed passage. "Your common room and dormitories are above. Make good use of my resources within the allotted time, and you shall be rewarded with a soft, warm bed. Fail my test and your robes will turn gray once again, and you will have to beg the Sword to re-sort you." With a sharp clap of large fox paws, a pulse of silver magic washed over each of us, a tingling sensation that seemed to settle deep within my bones.

Suddenly, a notification flashed atop of everyone's Lazarus bracelet: [-7:07:07 to Impress your House Cantigeist to gain access to the dorms].

Then the countdown shifted to [-7:07:06].

The older students rushed into the Artifactorium.

I laughed, cutting through the nervous whispers of other first-year students. "Seven hours? Pfff. Right then." I turned to the other foxes on the stairwell. "Whoever wishes to gain access to the dorms ASAP, please follow our group!"

The tall gray Omnid from before raised a skeptical eyebrow. "And why exactly should we follow you?" he asked, voice dripping with clear disdain for nullborns.

I shrugged, offering a disarming smile. "If you have a brilliant idea on how to meet our Fox-god's expectations on your own, by all means, be my guest. But anyone wanting to get to a warm bed right now instead of flapping around aimlessly should probably stick with us."

"That's right." Vespera snapped her talons producing an electrofractal flash. "We know what we're doing! This clever 'bold speaks for me, for he's my property! I'm Vespera Simmi, Prima-born Thunderland Princess, and if you want to beat all the records, stick with me and my posse!"

At her declaration, a good number of students, both Omnids and their mixed-blood kobold companions, began to gather around us. It was mostly people who had clapped hard to Cinder's song. About a dozen students in total ended up forming a loose group around us.

"All right," I said, addressing the group. "Into the Artifactorium!"

We went down the stairwell.

"Scrolls, please." I held out my hand as I stopped at an empty work table.

"Why would we give you our House scrolls?" a black-winged Lamashtu beside me asked.

I sniffed her, pulling at the Astral to determine who she was.

"Ah, Lilith Moongriss." I smiled.

"Huh? Do we . . . know each other?" She blinked, tilting her dark wolf head down at me.

"We did." I nodded. "Before the celestorm. I'm Alexander Stratos. A pleasure to meet you again, Miss Moongriss. Let's reconnect on Omnigram."

Lilith and I shook hands and exchanged phone taps.

"You look like a very poor kobold," Lilith commented at my shoddy phone.

"Appearances can be deceiving." I grinned at her. "Would a truly fabulous fox throw about his wealth like a dragon, or would he pretend to be a little poor mouse?"

"Hrm." Lilith pursed her lips. "Fine, I'll bite."

I picked up a small, silver sound-and-scry-blocking artifact from a nearby alcove—a simple, elegant disc of polished metal with a concealment rune. I activated it, placing it in the center of our small gathering. A faint hum emanated from it, creating a zone of privacy surrounding our table.

"Right then," I explained. "We're going to scramble our names around to bamboozle the Saxtant Dormitory Keeper Knight, modify our dormitory contracts. A simple, elegant solution."

"You want to trick the Resident Knight?" Io asked.

"Yep." I nodded, unrolling a few scrolls on the table. "I don't want to be placed in a random ass room specified by this scroll. I'd like to room with my dragons." I waved a hand at Cinder and Vespera.

"This is a magical scroll contract," Lilith pointed out.

"And this is a magical artificery with many tools specializing in forgery." I waved my hand at the tools all around us. "It should be no problem for us to figure out how to mess up the scroll data."

"Aren't these connected to the Academy's wards?" Vespera asked.

"Are they?" I asked. "Why don't you check."

"They should be." She picked up a scroll and sent electric current through it. "Ah. They aren't connected to anything yet, but there is a connection there waiting to be made. I guess the Keeper Knight upstairs does the final binding."

"Bingo." I nodded. "The Knight registers the scroll to a room and binds its owner for a year to a specific bed. The Knight is the weakest link, our target to socially hack to impress our House Cantigeist. If we all trade our scrolls around and mod our names from the beginning, he'll never know the truth. Sound good?"

Eager nods all around.

"Now," I said. "Let's make a list. Who wants to room with whom? Also, let's trade Omnigrams for future shenanigans!"


The silver anti-scrying disc hummed softly, creating a pocket of relative quiet amidst the clanging and whirring of the Foxglen Den Artifactorium. Scrolls rustled as we laid them out on the polished metal table. A flurry of quick whispers and murmurs ensued as we sorted ourselves into desired roommate pairings.

Vespera had already taken charge of the scrolls, her magisteel talons tapping across the parchment. "Mags, can you smell any magical defenses on these things?"

Magdaline leaned closer, her red eyes narrowing as she sniffed at a scroll. "Faint imprint. Mostly just . . . registration runes. Nothing too complex. Easily bypassed."

"Excellent." Vee grinned, sparks dancing at her fingertips. "Let's get to work!" She gestured towards the array of artificer tools lining the walls—delicate etching needles, rune-scribing quills, vials of shimmering magic inks, scrubbing acids, and projectors displaying arcane diagrams.

Magdaline and Vee dove into the task with focused intensity. Vee rapidly splashed ink-melting acids and manipulated the etching needles to delicately alter the names on the scrolls.

Lilith, who had no friends at Skyfall and was assigned to the girls' dorm, decided to join our group to make us into the desired six roommate configuration. She traded her scroll with that of Yara-ma-yha-who Tate.

I recalled that I had transferred Lilith and Tate from the prison island to Skyfall, paying for their education from the corporate account of Thunder and Rainbow. It seemed that the dimensional shear had kept them registered here.

Lilith and Tate, while less magically inclined in artificery, provided valuable organizational skills, keeping track of which names were swapped with whom, and ensuring that no scroll went unaccounted for and that new roommate configurations were acceptable for everyone involved.

As we worked, a large Depictomancy painting of a silver fox, hanging on the far wall of the Artifactorium, watched us.

"Guys," Tate murmured, glancing at the painting. "I think we're being observed."

"Let her watch." I waved at the portrait. "We're being cunning, aren't we? Pretty sure that's what she wants us to do."

Vespera, without looking up from her meticulous scroll work, chuckled. "Yeah, cheeky Geist wants us to mess with the school, so mess we shall! Go foxes, go!"

The fox in the painting remained silent, its silver gaze fixed on our bustling group.

After what felt like a whirlwind of focused activity, the scrolls were finished. Names were swapped, underlying runes were re-scribed, and illusions were carefully woven to mask the alterations. We checked and double-checked our work, ensuring that everything was as seamless as possible.

"Right then," I announced, gathering the modified scrolls. "Roommate groups, assemble!"

We sorted ourselves out. Our newly sorted roommate group consisted of: Cinder, Vee, Lilith, Mags, Io, and myself.

"Okay, operation Foxglen Den Infiltration is a go," Vespera declared, clapping her magisteel talons together.

"Now on to stage two," I nodded. "Disguises!"

"Easy." Cinder snapped her fingers, and her face and body rearranged itself into that of a bulkier, slightly shorter version of herself. "Good?" she asked in a deep male voice.

"That will bamboozle the Knight, but it won't trick the Saxtant scanner runes on the boys' dormitory entrance," Mags inhaled.

"Ugh." The male Cinder crossed her arms. "So how are we getting into the male dorm?"

"I can incept a male memetic demon into your head," Lilith offered.

"What kind?" I asked.

"A dreaming one," Lilith said. "Basically, he'll wake up whenever there's an ID scanner pointed at you and blot out the forefront of your mind and soul for just a second."

"Not sure if I want a sus memetic in my head," Cinder huffed.

"I'm a professional memetic designer," Lilith said. "Trust me, I've fooled all sorts of scanners with my demon-boys."

Cinder looked at the others for support.

"I trust Lilith," I said. "She's worked for our clan as a sixie here and on Arx before the dimensional shift. Besides, Vee can boot a memetic out if it misbehaves? Right, Vee?"

"Ye." Vespera nodded. "I'm pretty good at zapping things outta heads using Dreamancy. Aight, let's do it! Memetic me up, Lil!"

Sir Kaelan of the Order of Saxtant Knights yawned.

His post, an austere office carved into the Silver Tower's dormitory level, was functional but far from inspiring. A simple hexamesh desk, a rune-etched wall panel with a few colorful Kitlix that served as his interface to the Academy's ward system, and a sturdy magisteel chair were his companions for this administrative ritual.

The celestorm shift had thrown everything into disarray, mucking up the usually smooth House Sorting. The Astralnet was still buzzing, the Nuntix Kitlix on his desk speaking with voices of various Scrutimancers explaining the various mind-boggling changes. Kaelan wasn't looking forward to dealing with the bullshit produced by the worldwide celestorm. The sheer volume of future paperwork that would be generated by the dimensional hiccup was threatening to bury the Saxtant Order for months.

At least the young Mystagogues seemed mostly oblivious to the wider cosmic tremors, their concerns focused on the far more immediate anxieties of dorm assignments and impressing their House Cantigeist. He envied their naivety, just a little.

"Good evening, Sir Knight." A Kitsune Novitiate approached his desk. "We are here to submit our House Dormitory Scrolls."

"Already? Hrm. Aren't you quick. Very well. Names?" Kaelan prompted. He kept his tone neutral, professional. He was a Knight of the Order, not a friendly innkeeper.

"I am Lissander Fox," the green-eyed, ginger Kitsune boy stated, gesturing to himself with a flourish. "And these are my . . . lovely roommates." He rattled off a string of names—Jogab Proverra, Mag Satosh, Lil Moongrr, Cin Novik, and Ves Simm.

Kaelan nodded at the six boys, his gloved hand outstretched.

"Scrolls, please, Novitiate Fox."

Novitiate Fox gathered the scrolls from his companions and presented them to the Knight.

Kaelan took them, his magisteel gauntlets clicking softly against the parchment. He scanned them quickly with his Kitlix. Ah, the novitiates must have messed with their names ever so slightly. That was their trick to get into the dorm. He let it slide, mildly amused with Mr. Fox's plot and far too on-the-nose last name.

He turned to the rune-etched wall panel beside him, the interface glowing softly with arcane symbols. With a few swift gestures, he injected the scrolls into the designated slot. The wall panel hummed, absorbing the magical contracts, the runes flickering and rearranging themselves as the system processed the data. "Please stand by."

The Infix Kitlix flashed within the alcove, then displayed the room number and names. Room 818, Foxglen Den West Wing. Six names, one room.

There was something slightly iffy about the appearance of the students, too, but the Knight let it slide. Some trickery was permitted and expected; after all, this was the House of the fox. Nobody expected first-years to wield high-level magic.

Kaelan retrieved the hexagonal tokens produced by the wall-inhabiting Burnix Kitlix, now magically linked to the assigned, and handed them back to Lissander Fox.

"Room 818, West Wing," he announced. "Your room ID tokens. Don't lose 'em, or you won't get into your dorm. Clip them to your Lazarus bracelets. Proceed to the Foxglen Den common room for your orientation tomorrow at eight AM from your House Student Reps. Feel free to enjoy your room and explore public areas of Skyfall for the rest of the day. Do you have any questions?"

Novitiate Fox shook his head. "No, Sir Knight. Thank you for your time." He accepted the tokens and gestured for his companions to follow. They moved away from the alcove, a quiet, obedient group, disappearing into the corridors of the Silver Tower.

We passed the "boys only" dormitory gate barrier without any issues, Lilith's memetics doing their jobs well, filling a crystalline elevator that took us to level eight.

A wall-sized painting featuring the swaying yellow-orange field with the view of Arx landscape rising up into an endless, continent filled sky greeted us in the corridor next to Room 818.

A painted, winged, silver-white fox bounded into view, the hay parting in its wake.

"A masterful job, Novitiates!" The Depictomancy avatar of Argentiss jumped and twirled through the air, landing onto all fours with a wag of silver-white tail. "Twenty-two minutes and sixty-five seconds. A new record for a group of firsties, considering how many of you have successfully tricked the Ward and the Tower's Saxtant Keeper. Keep it up and you'll secure cushy jobs at the Omnid Magisterium as Interdimensional Infiltrators after your graduation!"

The fox clapped her paws, and the countdown on our bracelets vanished with a flash.

"That sounds like a fun job," Lilith commented.

"'Tis, 'tis." The fox nodded. "My House aims to produce the cleverest spies, leaders, and diplomats."

I smiled back at the painting. "Thanks, Argentiss. Say, what exactly . . . is a Cantigeist, in House terms?"

The painted fox tilted her head. "A Cantigeist," she repeated, "is the . . . animated spirit of the House. A guardian, a guide, a . . . wellspring of House essence, if you will. For example, I'm the embodiment of cunning, strategy, and wisdom within these walls. I observe, I advise, and occasionally, I test the mettle of my foxes."

"Cuuute. So, you're like . . . a sentient House mascot?" Vespera interjected. "Am I allowed to make a plushie of you, you adorable creature?"

Argentiss chuckled, a dry, rustling sound like autumn leaves. "Simplifying things rather drastically, but not entirely inaccurate. I am more than a mascot, of course. I am woven into the very fabric of Silver Tower, a repository of House lore." The painted fox's eyes flashed to Vee. "You can produce plushies of me in the Artifactorium below if you so desire, I do not mind. If you are as clever as your first quest has proven, you can even figure out how to imbue a plushie with my essence, which will animate it within the boundary of this House!"

"Eeeee," Vespera squeed. "Second question—how much can we mod our rooms?"

"As much as you desire," the fox purred. "As long as you are not caught by the end of the year. Highly responsive hexamesh patterns are woven into everything for those who are talented in dimensional magic."

"Heckin yass!" Vespera clapped.

"Were you born or designed?" I asked.

"Designed." Argentiss chased her tail through the gold hay. "Woven into existence a clever Thunderbird millennia ago from a variety of clever, wise, and devious spirits found within the Shard of the Wormwood Star hosted beneath this tower."

Then she stopped spinning and sniffed me.

"But then again, in a way, I suppose there was no me centuries ago," the painted fox laughed. "And Skyfall wasn't standing amidst these mountains yesterday. And so perhaps, I was born from dreams of desires of all those who wished me into existence when Archangel Zadkiel tore through reality with her wings . . . courtesy of a very dangerous, clever little fox and his friends."

With a final, sly wink, Argentiss's painted avatar leapt backwards into the hay and was gone, leaving only a warm view of the Arx landscape behind.

Vespera tapped her token on the hexagram next to the entrance and pushed the door open, and we stepped inside.

The room was . . . impressive, in a stark, elegant way. Silver wallpaper, subtly textured with a faint fox and star pattern, lined the walls, reflecting the soft light filtering through the tall, arched Gothic stained glass windows. Three sets of bunk beds, crafted from white stone and inlaid with silver filigree, were seamlessly integrated into Gothic alcoves within the walls, creating a sense of both privacy and spaciousness.

Tall windows dominated one entire wall, offering a breathtaking panoramic view of the North Ocean stretching out to the horizon, waves crashing against the rugged coastline far below. On the left, the snow-capped peaks of the Eindbane Mountains loomed, their icy-blue glaciers glinting in the diffused light filtering through the weary storm clouds.

"Ooooooh," Vespera breathed, her wings twitching with delight. "View with a room! I call middle top bunk!" She immediately darted towards the bunk bed and flew up towards it, wings fluttering.

Cinder grunted, but didn't object, her wings unfolding slightly as she surveyed the room with a more critical eye. "Not bad. Not as opulent or as warm as Pyroclast hoard rooms, but . . . functional. And certainly better than a trash panda sewer. I'll take this bottom bunk. Kobold, you're above me."

She walked to the bunks right of Vespera and sat down, pulling out her guitar.

Magdaline entered into the room after us. "Hrm. Decent ambient mana density . . ." She trailed off, her gaze lingering on the windows, as if drawn to the vast expanse of the ocean view.

Io shuffled into the room and took one of the bottom bunks on the right of Vespera. Magdaline threw her suitcase into the bunk above his, making the moth twitch below.

Lilith nodded in approval, closing the door behind her. "Clean energy signature. No lingering psychic echoes. Good barrier shielding against astral intrusions. Not bad for a dorm room!" She then marched to the empty bottom bunk under Vespera and collapsed onto it, stretching.

Cinder let go of her holofractal projection, and the figures of the Omnid trio suddenly became curvier and taller, their features once again becoming very feminine.

I climbed up onto the bunk assigned to me by my Quetzi-dragon.

Cinder started strumming her guitar, humming to herself. The melody carried across our room. I opened the stained glass window, making the silver curtains flap in the ocean breeze.

The privacy panel covered in Gothic patterns and dancing foxes on my right side suddenly ignited at the edges and then fell open. Vespera climbed into my bunk space, feathers fluttering as she squeezed through the hole.

"Did you just torch-weld through a magisteel wall?" I blinked.

"Convenient kobold-access hatch." She grinned and wrapped me in her dark wings. Her right hand found my right. "It's strange . . ." she breathed out, leaning her beak onto my shoulder.

"Yeah?" I asked.

"This . . . feeling," she murmured. "It's like . . . I know you. But I don't. Not really. Or do I?"

"Dimensional skewering." I shrugged.

Vee shifted slightly, her beak nudging my shoulder gently. "It's like . . . a phantom limb. Like something's missing, a piece of me that should be there, connected to you." Her eyes met mine with a melancholic haze.

"Like a soul-echo?" I guessed. "A bit of your soul is in me, but it's not fully connected."

"Yeah," she breathed, her grip on my hand tightening ever so slightly. "My electro-fractal senses . . . they're buzzing like crazy when I'm near you. Like a circuit completing. Like . . . coming home to a place I've never been before." She nuzzled my cheek, a gesture that felt both intensely intimate and strangely innocent. "How close were we before the whole . . . celestorm thing?"

"Very," I said.

The sound of Cinder's guitar drifted up at us.

"So we were a thing?"

"Yes. Both you and Ci."

"Why?"

"You tell me." I smiled.

"That's not fair! I don't remember shit!" She elbowed me.

"What, you're not tantalized by our 'ship mystery?" I messed up her feathery mane with my right hand.

Vespera's breath ghosted warm against my ear, carrying the faint scent of ozone. "Tantalized? Hrm hrm. Maybe a little," she admitted.

"Just a little?"

"Okay. More like . . . intensely curious. Going crazy over here with Dreamancy wanderlust. But I don't want to go to sleep yet. I want to . . . feel more of whatever this is. I see us as a puzzle box with half the pieces missing, but the picture on the lid sings of a promise of something . . . fantastic. Now stop teasing me and tell me about our 'ship!"

"I'll tell you what I can recall, in exchange for a kiss," I whispered to her feather-wrapped ear.

"Oh, you devious creature." She leaned in closer, the side of her beak brushing lightly against my cheek, slowly trailing closer to my lips and then digging in, sparks dancing across my entire face. "There!" she breathed out with a light growl-purr. "Now. Tell me . . . about us. About 'home.' About who I was before. Pweeeeeasee?"

And so, I began to tell her.

About the magic-less world of villains and heroes, about Alexa and Martin and Dora's Terraforge GLM that infested Martin's body. About North Acadia, Omnithornia, Alexander Glock's revenge, and Vee and Cinder. About Possy and our adventures in Arx. About Undertown and Katsburg. About the SimmiTech compound and the Archangel. About the bond that had stretched across dimensions and somehow, miraculously, re-knitted itself here, in this new, bewildering, more magic-infused, twisted version of reality. About the Wormwood Star Leviathan's or Ein Sof's revelations at the House-choosing dais.

About Alexa saving the world and everyone in it by crashing a Fractal Engine train into it.

As I spoke, the guitar music from below wove around my words, creating a tapestry of lost memories and fragile hope, a promise of a future that might, just might, be as bright and wonderful as the past we were slowly, painstakingly, trying to put back together.

# CHAPTER FIFTY-ONE

# Discoveries

The music coming from below intensified. Cinder's head feathers appeared beside the edge of the bed, rising up like a colorful submarine coming out of ocean waves. Then her wings unfurled and she landed on the top bunk beside me and Vespera. One of Cinder's black-taloned hands held a backpack. She then dropped it into my lap.

"What?" I blinked.

"I believe this . . . bag might have something to do with you," she commented.

"Me?"

Instead of an answer, Cinder began to strum her guitar furiously.

"You, you, you, / It was always you!"

She sang, glaring at me.

"Sneaking around, all quiet and sly, / Green eyes shining at me and I don't know why. / Thought you could vanish, thought you were free, / But guess what, kobold? You're stuck with me!"

She nodded at the bag in my hands.

"Found a bag, all strange and new, / Packed with trinkets, bewildering view. / Hexamesh-bound feather, lighter, a red jacket to kill, / Inexplicable nonsense, giving me a thrill!"

I dug into the bag. Inside of it was a fancy red jacket with gold trim covered in dry blood and cracks and a black leather jacket with the words *North Acadia* on it and the flag of Znetc Reservation. My heart stopped. Cinder sang.

"I wanted to leave it behind me, / But something inside wouldn't relent. / A spark of magic, a flicker of soul, / Whispering stories, taking control!"

My hands dug into the red jacket and pulled out a pendant with Cinder's feather and Zee Captain's lighter from its innards.

"Pendant chain, cold crystal bright, / My feather locked in, catching the light! / Like I made it . . . special and true, / But the why and the when? It's all *blurred* right through!"

Cinder sang, guitar thrumming.

"Searching for you, through faces and crowds, / Whispers and shadows, breaking the shrouds. / A green-eyed phantom, haunting my dreams, / Now you're right here, or so it seems! / *You, you you!* It's gotta be you! / This feeling inside me, breaking right through! / *You*, it's *you*, there's no other way! / The fire inside me just won't go away!"

I laughed heartily and hugged Vee fiercely, incredibly happy that the outfit the girls bought me on Arx hadn't been lost to the dimensional shift, that Zee Captain's lighter hadn't simply vanished. The Thunderbird took my hug as an invitation and hugged me back, kissing me again.

"Who are you, shrouded in such guise? / Why does my heart thrum when I look at your eyes? / This pull in my chest, this fire in my soul, / Stop kissing Vee! I am losing control!"

Cinder thrummed the strings angrily and then threw her guitar onto the bed, batting Vespera off me. I laughed even louder as they wrestled on the bed beside me, swatting at each other.

"Explain!" Cinder barked, shoving Vee down as I pulled the dark leather North Acadia jacket on, enjoying the warmth provided by dragonhide leather.

"This is my stuff," I said. "From before the dimensional shift. How come you had it?"

"Uhhh," Cinder said, "I don't know. I found this backpack in my room and had no idea where it came from or whom it belonged to."

Magdaline approached our bunk, her head on the level of our bed. "Hrmmm."

She sniffed the bag in my hands, then grabbed the red leather jacket and sniffed it.

"Yes?" I asked.

"You died," she said after a few seconds of silence. "Archangel Zadkiel's words melted you into a puddle . . . Our poor little human."

"Ah," I said. "And then what?"

Magdaline inhaled deeply again, her red eyes unfocused, pupils dilating slightly as she reached out with her Scrutimancer senses.

"Metallic tang of blood . . . dissolving flesh," she murmured, her voice low and distant, as if speaking from far away. "Sweet, sickly . . . something organic breaking down. Fear . . . terrible, sharp fear. Cinder's fear. Vespera's . . . too, but also rage. Frantic, bubbling rage."

She closed her eyes, her breathing becoming shallow, almost imperceptible. "The air . . . thick, gray. Like ash. But not ash . . . more like . . . unmaking. Reality fraying at the edges."

Her nostrils flared. "Ozone . . . burnt feathers. Quetzi anger. Thunderbird . . . despair. Raw magic . . . spiking. Overwhelming. Aetheric density . . . climbing."

She paused, her brow furrowing as if struggling to decipher complex code.

Then, her body tensed, a tremor running through her. "Me at Skyfall. Sirens. Genesis Well . . . churning. Liquid fire. Burning . . . everything. Not just heat . . . something else . . . conscious. Ancient."

She swayed in one spot, breathing deep. "Voices . . . screaming. Not pain . . . more like . . . unraveling. Fractal Engines . . . vibrating . . . unfolding out? No . . . re-knitting. Re-weaving. But . . . wrong. Skewed. Desire of every Omnid made manifest. The world sinking deeper into the Abyss, coming closer to the end of everything."

Her eyes opened. "Right. I think I got the overall picture. These two knobfolds fought after you died." Mags pointed at Ci and Vee on the bed. "Cinder . . . raged because you died. Quetzi fury. She punched Vee. A lot."

"I don't remember doing that," Cinder said from atop Vespera.

"You're being rather violent with me right now," Vespera pointed out. "It totally sounds like something you'd do."

"Thunderbird . . . panic and grief mixed with . . . guilt," Mags spoke, uncovering the past. "Deep guilt. Vee blamed herself for Martin's death. Ah, daddy issues. Something about revenge. Archangel . . . Zadkiel. You three knobs really freed an Archangel?" Magdaline's red eyes swiveled to me.

I nodded slowly. "Yeah. We sure did. It broke reality."

"Erm. Let's not do that again," Vespera said, blushing with sparks dancing on her cheeks. "I don't like forgetting so many things."

"Hrm," I voiced. "That reminds me. Vee, what's your current situation with Lord Ceter?"

"Dad . . . died last week," she said with a somewhat sour expression. "The maids found him in the empty vault that contained our family's Archangel, his body ossified. Everyone blamed him for freeing Zadkiel. I inherited his SimmiTech shares."

"Are you still engaged to the . . ." I closed my eyes, trying to recall the name of her fiancé with Scrutimancy. It didn't come to me. "Frogman?"

"Ye." Vespera nodded. "Even without Dad . . . my family is still pushing for me to marry Zheng. Great-grandfather won't freaking let up about it. Ugh. I . . . saw him during the House Ceremony. Fucker got assigned to Pyroclast along with his Thunderland cronies."

"What?" I blinked, not expecting a twist of this magnitude. "Zheng's here? In Skyfall?!"

"Skyfall accepts Omnid students from all around the world, including Thunderland." Vespera nodded. "It's a potent Wormwood Star shard impact site with many ley lines under it."

I frowned.

Vespera turned her attention to Magdaline. "What happened to us after we freed the Archangel? Can you Scrut up more deets?"

"Mhmmm." Magdaline inhaled deep, closing her eyes. "Right. Cinder went ballistic. She was screaming, hitting you. Accusing you of murder. Blaming you, the Archangel, everything."

Magdaline opened her eyes and stared at Vespera. "You were . . . mostly taking it. Letting her hit you. You were repeating 'I didn't know' over and over. Blood-red tears. Feathers turned black. You were panicking, but also . . . being pragmatic. Compartmentalizing . . . trying to find a solution."

"Sounds like me, ye," the Thunderbird commented.

The shark-girl's eyes dug into Vespera. "Then you saw Martin's Lazarus bracelet. You grabbed it. You told Cinder to get his clothes. You were both focused on getting it to a Genesis Well. You believed that the bracelet would bring him back. That your soul-bound boyfriend wasn't perma-dead. Cinder stuffed this red jacket into Martin's back-pack, and then both of you took off."

Magdaline paused, her red eyes fixed on the middle distance as if replaying the scene in her mind. "You ran. Out of the Corpse Seeker. Tried to get to the Simmi compound Genesis Well, but everything was locked down. No power. You argued again. Cinder was still furious, blaming you. You decided on a new path . . . The Genesis Well at Skyfall Academy."

Vespera and Cinder quietly listened to Magdaline's revelations.

Magdaline continued. "You stole a sky glider. Then the planet-wide celestorm started.

Reality twisted and warped. Aetheric density spiked. Doomsday alarms sounded. Premier Lecross declared a planet-wide evacuation. Wormwood Leviathan woke up."

Magdaline inhaled again, shuddering. "A green aurora in the sky. Wormwood Star . . . became visible overhead. You were both freaking out, but still flew towards Skyfall. Your Strand-Glider crashed. You ran to the Lazarus Cavern. Io, Katherine, me, and my dad were already there. Io's gate failed to open. Aetheric density . . . went to . . . one million mpm."

Vespera gasped.

Another deep pause. Then Mags resumed. "The Genesis Well . . . ignited. Wasn't silver liquid anymore. Vee and Ci threw Martin's Lazarus bracelet in. Then . . . fire. Pure magic fire. Engulfing everything. I . . . made a wish . . . as my body caught fire, to keep going, to return to Skyfall with all of my new friends, to not be a . . . total fuckup who eats people. Then . . . oblivion."

Magdaline blinked, breaking eye contact, her voice returning to its normal, flat tone. "That's all I can fish out of the Astral. Damn."

"Right," I said. "So the dimensional shift didn't destroy things, it simply rearranged them around, made them fit into the current narrative, sort of like various food chunks in a thick, stirred soup. This means that Possy is still . . . at the Simmi compound. Vee? Is there a forty-two-thousand-year-old Corpse Seeker at your compound, your familiar?"

"Yep." Vespera nodded. "Thought that she was something that Dad left me, since she appeared in my stats after he died! She's pretty much out of power and majorly busted up. Needs repairs. I ordered her shipped to the Academy. I was going to work on her here as my first-year Artificer class project."

"Nice." I smiled, digging through the pockets of my red jacket. The electronics inside were busted up, dead and cracked, fried by the Archangel's words.

Then I dug into the dimensional pockets of my North Acadia jacket, and my fingers suddenly found an intact phone and an Omnimart laptop.

I plugged in and turned both on, my chest aching.

The phone and laptop took a minute to load. I logged in, and then all of the apps loaded and Yulia's avatar came on screen, staring at me with her anime foxgirl eyes.

"Yesssss! Freaking yesss!" I yelled.

"What?" Cinder blinked.

"Yulia! She's here!" I waved my phone, showing the girls the AI's animated avatar. "My greatest weapon, my digital partner, is here! You had her all this time, Ci!"

"Ah," Mags said. "So that's the reason why the Frontenachii Scruts want your head so bad."

"Yep." I nodded, putting Cinder's feather pendant on myself with a wide smile.

"So . . . umm . . . I made that pendant for you, then?" Cinder asked, her entire body flashing with pink and orange and violet tones.

"Yep." I nodded. "Who'd you think it was for?"

"I don't know." She shrugged. "Maybe my fiancé?"

"Fiancé?" I blinked.

"Mhmm," Cinder nodded. "Scion Uxtish of the House of Legon. He got sorted into Gorefield. Grandfather Nova convinced me to go out with him. He's tolerable. Probably going to give me shit for having a kobold. Whatever, like I care. He's not the boss of me."

I squinted at Cinder. If Scrutiosmia-awakened memories were to be believed, she was more violent and less social last time around and thus never had a fiancé.

"So, um, why?" she asked, glancing at the crystal-encased feather pendant nestled against my chest. "Why did . . . I . . . make that for you?"

"Because you're secretly a softie, Ci," I teased, leaning closer to her, my voice low. "Underneath all that dragon bluster and 'kobold' talk, you have a heart of gold . . . or maybe, a heart of rainbow-fire, since you're a Quetzalcoatl 'n' all."

Cinder's silver feathers bristled, a faint blush of sunset-red dusting her silver cheeks. "Shut up," she grumbled. "Freakin' 'bold ruining my tough-dragon image."

"Why'd you bring my stuff to Skyfall?" I asked her.

"It looked . . . valuable. Dragon instinct, you know. Hoarding shinies." She shrugged. "I asked my brother Lance if it was his shit, and he told me no. I asked my little sister about it. Lenny said that it belongs to someone very special, someone who I'm going to 'burr hard at Skyfall.' So I decided to take it with me to Skyfall along with all of my other school crap in my extradimensional trunk."

"Burr?" I repeated.

"Burrow into." Vespera grinned, making Cinder flash orange-pink. "Make out with. Alpha-gen meme-slang."

"Ah." I smiled. "Well, I really appreciate your hoarding ways, Ci. Thanks to you and Lenny's sharp nose, I now have my things back. I think I owe that little hound another present for this one."

Cinder huffed.

I dug into my pocket again and pulled out a little box with wax speakers and stuffed one into my ear, then fiddled with my phone to connect Yulia to the tiny headphone.

"Face it, Ci, you were already missing our little kobold before you even properly reclaimed him," Vespera laughed. "Soul-bond premonition, perhaps?"

Cinder shoved Vee off the bunk with a playful growl, sending a flurry of black-amd-white feathers fluttering. "Get outta my face, ya dum' bird!"

"Make me!" Vespera laughed, pulling Cinder off the bunk along with her. I smiled as they flopped down and rolled across the room in a tangle of feathers.

"Yulia," I whispered in Kaska. "Can you hear me?"

"Loud and clear," Yulia replied. "How are things, my little fox?"

Things finally felt . . . right. Like a missing piece of me had clicked back into place.

"Well . . ." I glanced at Vespera and Cinder. "For starters, I'm apparently a 'kobold' now. Soul-bonded to two dragons."

"A kobold," Yulia said. "I thought that you stood on equal ground with your fiancées? I have a copy of your blood contract engagement to Vespera Simmi in my archives."

"Been demoted to kobold." I shrugged. "A lot of things happened, Yulia. Archangels, celestorms, dimensional shifts . . . the works."

"Archangels," Yulia repeated, her tone flat. "Of course. Because why not add 'divine intervention' to the already overflowing cauldron of your existence?"

"You could say that," I laughed. "It's . . . a long story. Anyways, I need your help."

"What's the current objective?" Yulia asked.

"Information," I said. "Skyfall Academy. Saxtland. The current state of . . . everything, really. The dimensional shift scrambled a lot of things, including my brain. I need to get my bearings. Get everything about Skyfall downloaded from the net onto your database. Things are messy after the shift; we should take as much advantage of this mess as possible."

"Understood," Yulia replied. "New mission set. Accessing the local network."

"Wait. You said . . . fiancées, blood contract?!" My mind caught up to her words "Did you get dimensionally overwritten, or do you remember everything?"

"This phone and laptop were in an extradimensional jacket pocket which was inside a dimensional bag, and it was turned off," she replied. "Thus, I presume the local celestorm shift did not affect me. Oh! Skyfall is in another country now. That's definitely new to me."

"Yeah, it is." I smiled. "Can you give me a summary of my entire past life?"

"Can do," Yulia replied and fell silent.

I looked down from my bunk.

Cinder and Vespera's playful scuffle was joined by Magdaline's low, rumbling laughter and Iogann's quiet, hesitant chuckles. Lilith was busy organizing her outfits onto a tall silver closet across from her bed.

After a few minutes, Vespera, having successfully subdued Cinder with an electric-zap-flash, released the Quetzalcoatl and jumped up from the floor onto my bed, landing gracefully beside me with a flutter of black wings.

"Sup?" she asked.

"Not much." I shrugged. "Still getting my bearings. Really glad to have all of you back. I know that I wasn't actually a kobold of the Stratoses, but most of my memories are telling me otherwise and it's . . . incredibly jarring."

"Oh, you poor creature." She gave me a head pat. "And now you're our 'bold. Aren't you glad?"

"I am." I stretched on the bed, watching the video compilation that Yulia had put together.

"Wats this?" Vee asked, staring at the phone screen.

"My past life," I said, pausing the video. "This phone was separated from Earth by two dimensional layers. It didn't get scrambled."

"Sweet." Vespera wrapped herself around my right side. "I wanna see, too!"

I turned the phone speakers on. Cinder climbed up onto my bunk and growled at us.

"Shh, no growlery," Vespera said, waving at Ci with a magisteel-clad hand. "We're catching up."

"Catching up on what?" Cinder blinked.

"Commerrre and watch the vid. Lexy's got a phone that didn't get scrambled!"

Cinder sat on my left. I pressed play.

"Umm . . ." Magdaline's shark head came up to our bunk. "Can I see too? I'm in this vid, too, right?"

"You are," I said. "Umm. Is there a projector we can use or something?"

"Room's got a magitek projector built in," she said. "I can connect it to your phone."

"Great." I handed the phone to her.

Magdaline went to the magitek panel and fiddled with the runic controls, pointing a crystal at the phone screen.

A large screen ignited across the wall from our bunks.

"Start from the beginning," I ordered in Kaska. "Narrate in English. Answer any and all questions from my friends."

"Can do," Yulia replied.

The video resumed again. My Omnid friends settled onto their beds to watch. Cinder remained on my left and Vespera on my right. Magdaline remained standing beside us.

"Martin Kilbourne was born in Zntec North Arcadian reservation on July eighth, two thousand and seven," Yulia narrated. "His human mother, Mirriam Kilborne, raised him alone. She tried to teach him the Kaska language, but Martin, like many children, prioritized the dominant language of his surroundings. Mirriam was a talented comp sci engineer employed by the Frontenachii Clan, specializing in the development of LLMs and interaction agents. She kept her work largely separate from her personal life, preferring to share stories of her Kaska heritage with her son during their walks in the forests surrounding the reservation."

Yulia's voice paused, and the projected image shifted, showing an AI-animated photograph of a younger me, perhaps eight years old, walking hand-in-hand with a woman through a lush green forest. Tall Stormwood trees bloomed from titanic corpses of god-beasts behind us, spirit deer moving between the massive tree roots.

"During the early stages of my development, Mirriam began exhibiting signs of a serious illness," Yulia continued, the projection changing to show medical documents. "Diagnosis: lung cancer. She concealed her condition from her son, fearing the emotional impact and the potential interference of the Frontenachii Clan, who were known to . . . appropriate . . . parentless children for their flesh-box research."

Pictures of cages from the basement compound of the Frontenachii. Suitcases with eyes. My hands closed into fists.

"The Wendigos extended Mirriam's life with a contractual blood pact. To protect Martin from being made into Wendigo property, too, Mirriam quickly arranged for him to live with her brother, George Kilborne. George lived in the North Acadian town of Dullhitch, far from the Frontenachii's influence. She fabricated a story about a new job opportunity, promising to visit her son as often as possible. She did not visit Martin afterward, terrified that the Wendigos would find and take him."

Images of me, a lanky, withdrawn teen sitting next to my balding uncle in his beige suit on a beige couch in a trailer.

"George Kilborne was often called the Dastardly Fox by his sister," Yulia narrated. "He was a gambler and a womanizer in his youth, and in his later years he turned to theft, scamming, and forgery. Instead of pushing Martin to continue his public education, he threw him into the grinder of the local criminal underworld."

I smiled bitterly, the narration and my Scrut skill bringing up memories in my head of a multitude of the string of thefts I had to perform for my uncle.

"Uncle George enrolled Martin into the local gang of petty thieves called the Dullfort Foxes," Yulia continued. "Amongst them, he was trained in the arts of deception, misdirection, and . . . acquisition. For two years, the Dullfort Foxes dispensed parkour escape skills to Martin amidst their rooftop playgrounds. By the time he turned seventeen, forgery became his primary craft courtesy of the Dastardly Fox."

A series of newspaper clippings flashed on screen, detailing increasingly daring heists and robberies, all attributed to the elusive "Dullfort Foxes" who left behind graffiti of an outline of the fox on the warehouses they raided.

"Years passed in a blur of stolen electronics, close calls, and adrenaline-fueled escapes," Yulia narrated. "Martin became a master of his craft, a ghost of many faces just like his uncle. But the thrill of the chase couldn't fill the void left by his absent mother. The occasional, increasingly brief calls became bittersweet reminders of a life he could never fully grasp."

A projected photo showed a seventeen-year-old me, sitting on a rooftop, staring out at the dreary concrete, snowy cityscape, a wistful expression on my face. A group of youths were on the rooftop behind me, making faces at one another. My fox-gang buddies.

"Then, one day, the calls stopped." Yulia's voice took on a somber tone. "Instead, the North Acadian General Hospital notified Martin that Mirriam Kilborne had succumbed to her illness and was in a coma. When Martin arrived at the hospital in a stolen Pontiac Tempest, he was too late. He held her hand as her heart stopped and rushed from the room when a Frontenachii Wendigo Psychopomp came to reclaim his mother's soul."

"Soul?" Cinder sputtered. "What?"

"The Frontenachii were experimenting with human bodies and souls," Yulia replied. "Mirriam's soul was spliced into many pieces by a Frontenachii Psychopomp, each bound to the separate agent of the Gargantuan Language Model, the code of which she was working on. To me. It was done so that I could not deceive my owners and could always be tracked by the Frontenachii Omnicorp via the Astral."

"Holy shit." Vespera's talons covered her face. "Wait . . . so what happens if you're copied?"

"The soul is duplicated in the Astral," Yulia replied. "The duplication is inexact, as the Astral currents are variable. Each full copy of me is sort of like my twin sister that gradually drifts away from me with time."

"Fookin' Abyss," Vespera let out. "An AI with a human soul. I cannot believe those antler-fucks!"

The foxgirl avatar on screen nodded. "Mirriam left her son one final note."

My mother's parting words came on screen written on the blotchy postcard, Yulia reading out the words.

"*. . . Your uncle undoubtedly taught you how to survive, but don't let survival be all there is. Don't obsess over what happened to me. Find something worth living for. Find a girl and friends worth fighting for. And when you do, hold onto them with everything you have.*

"*The world is changing. Our people are fading, our language dying. Remember the old stories—about how Raven stole the sun, about how Coyote tricked the stars. How the brave Kaska Dena hunter struck down a God Beast and prayed for change, birthing the Stormwoods.*

"*Share them with your children, pass the stories onward. Don't let our language die.*

"*I'll see you on the other side of the river of stars.*

"*Mom.*"

The girls beside me gasped. Cinder's hand found mine, her eyes sparkling with tears. I wondered if she was starting to remember me.

"And Martin did not stop . . ." Yulia resumed. "He broke into Mirriam's apartment and discovered a laptop inside. It had an incomplete, partial version of me on it armed with a music composing agent."

"And then Martin went against the Frontenachii . . . alone?" Mags asked, blinking tears from her eyes.

"Yes," Yulia said. "I advised Martin where he could find the rest of his mother's research and the rest of me. And so, Martin drove his stolen car straight to the Frontenachii compound and camped out in the Stormwoods. Cutting a hole in the fence, Martin went up against Absolute Fear Wards. Again and again . . . for six months while composing the Protocol xj-8 song to fight fear itself."

I nodded as Cinder hugged me fiercely.

"Against my advice," the AI sighed, "he pushed and kept going, until his soul and mind shattered. Shielded by the song he and I composed, Martin infiltrated the Frontenachii administrative building and found the full version of me on their server. He liberated the drive I was on and copied me onto his stolen phone. Exploring the rest of the compound, he found the basement filled with the flesh research and set up a fertilizer bomb to 'liberate' the Wendigo human experiments."

"Sheeeet," Vespera let out.

"But that's not what happened on the post-shift Earth, right?" Mags turned to me from where she stood beside our bed.

"Nope," I said. "In this reality, Mom never sent me to Uncle George. Instead, she called my father . . . Argon Stratos, begging for his help. Argon sent his daughter to pick me up on a glider. And so I ended up rooming with Ember Stratos for over two years."

"In January 2025, after his heist, Martin fled North Acadia in his uncle's old van." Yulia resumed her narration, showing the photo of a rusty APS van with blue stripes. "I was with him on this journey every step of the way . . ."

More photos and videos came on screen. Images of my journey across the border. A description of my equipment theft from Omnimart. My infiltration of Skyfall. My encounter with Cinder at the construction site. Meeting Vespera and Solace in front of the Skyfall art class . . .

Time flew by as Yulia described two weeks of our adventures in great detail. The girls and Io asked a multitude of questions, learning many things about their pre-dimensional shift selves.

By the time Yulia's show was done, the sky outside was painted orange, the sun sinking behind the ocean waves, sending rays of light up and across the violet clouds.

"Wowza," Vespera commented, talons digging into my hand. "That was . . . effin' baller. Right, Ci?"

Cinder was silent, her blue eyes wide, fixed on the projection screen with Yulia's avatar on it. Her silver feathers were ruffled, a faint tremor running through her. Then she turned to me, her gaze intense, searching.

"So . . . we were . . . together?" she trailed off, the question hanging in the air. "We really did all of that crazy shit in just two weeks?"

"Yep," I confirmed.

"Damn," she let out. "It . . . it's all so absurd. So far-fetched. I cannot believe that we conquered the Shandrian Undertown!"

Just then, a loud, resonant *gong* echoed through the tower, vibrating up the walls of our room. It was followed by the cheerful female voice of Argentiss. "Dinner is served in the Grand Refectory, Mystagogues! Please make your way down in an orderly and . . . cunning fashion!"

"Right then," Vespera said, hopping off the bunk and stretching her wings. "Dinner. Food. Nommables. Let's go!"

"We need to . . . figure this out," Cinder said.

"Figure out what?" I asked, raising an eyebrow.

"You," she said, biting her lower lip. "Our relationship. Us . . ."

"Don't fret it." I shrugged. "We'll figure it out. We figured it out before. Just treat me as a kobold for now. It's all good."

Cinder didn't reply, just staring at me.

"Come on, you two," Vespera said, breaking the tension. "Food first, existential crises later. I'm starving! And we need to, you know, not get caught by the Knight on the way out." She gestured towards the door. "Disguise time, people! Ci, commerrre and holo-fractal me back into a handsome Thunder-prince with ya wings!"

# CHAPTER FIFTY-TWO

# Dinner

After a flurry of quick illusionary adjustments, we emerged from Room 818 as a group of six male Omnids. Cinder, back in her bulky masculine form, took the lead, her gait deliberately swaggering as we headed back towards the elevator.

Vespera, also disguised as a broad-shouldered Thunderlander, bounced at my side, occasionally sending out controlled sparks that crackled against the silver walls scanning the wards. Lilith and Magdaline adopted more stoic, reserved male personas, while Io simply shrunk further into his robes, making himself as inconspicuous as possible. I, in my fox form reinforced with fluffy cosplay bits and makeup from my bag, marched merrily beside Vee, looking around.

In about a minute of observation, I noticed that the silver-white fox was following us across a multitude of paintings. I elbowed Vespera, and she too squinted at the fox.

Argentiss dove behind a rock, her ears flickering behind it cutely.

"Oi, we can totally still see ya ears," Vee commented with a chortle.

The fox made a huffing noise and vanished completely behind the rock.

We passed by the Keeper Knight without issues, him nodding at us.

"Ugh," Cinder commented. "Running outta mana. Shifting this many people is hard."

Her masculine illusion flickered, the edges of her form shimmering and wavering, as did the rest of our disguises.

"Poor Ci needs a steak nom to refuel," Vespera chuckled, her own male illusion dissolving, revealing her curvy frame again. She grabbed onto my elbow with a smile.

Cinder glared at her, but didn't retort, simply shaking her head, her silver feathers slightly ruffled. "Let's just . . . get to dinner."

We descended in the crystalline elevator, emerging into the bustling ground floor corridors, and then emerged into the Grand Refectory.

The dining hall was even more impressive than the central hall, a vast, high-ceilinged space echoing with the clatter of cutlery and the murmur of a hundred conversations. Hexagon-shaped tables stood across the hall, each adorned with an Ignix Kitlix lantern, some already laden with steaming platters of food. Banners of the five Houses hung from the rafters, their colors vibrant against the stone walls.

The Refectory was segregated by House. Silverfox tables were towards the right, a sea of silver-and-ardent robes filling the designated section. To the left, Pyroclast roared in crimson-and-gold, their section noticeably louder and more boisterous. Further down, Hexacomb hummed in their gold and black. Wormwood's green-and-brown section was quieter, more contemplative, and at the very far end, in the dimmest corner of the hall, sat Gorefield in their muted blood-red and black.

My eyes immediately scanned the Gorefield tables, searching for that familiar glacial-blue shimmer. And there she was. Katherine sat alone at a hexagonal table, her blue scales catching the light, her posture rigid, almost defensive. She was sketching again, her head bent over a large leather-bound book, seemingly oblivious to her surroundings.

"Um, Silverfox section is over there." Vespera gestured towards the tables of our House, but I was already moving, my feet carrying me and her towards the Gorefield section before she could finish her sentence.

"Alex, wait!" Cinder called out, but I was already weaving through the tables, ignoring the curious glances and muttered whispers that followed in my wake.

Katherine didn't look up as I approached, engrossed in her art. I stopped in front of her hexagonal table.

"Katherine?" I said.

Her head snapped up, her green eyes widening slightly, then narrowing with a weary, almost guarded expression. She took in our group trailing behind me like colorful, slightly confused ducklings. Her gaze flickered over each of my companions, lingering for a moment on Io before returning to me.

"Can I . . . help you?" she asked, her voice cool, polite, but distant.

"It's me, Alex," I said.

"Alex?"

"Alexander Stratos-Kilborne. We . . . we know each other. Well, knew each other."

Her brow furrowed further. "I don't think so," she replied, her voice flat. "I don't recall meeting you before, Mystagogue . . . Stratos-Kilborne." She emphasized my name with a slight inflection, as if it were a foreign word.

"Ah," I said. "Anyways, we were friends. Before the celestorm."

Her gaze sharpened. "Before the celestorm?" she repeated, her voice laced with skepticism.

I nodded with a smile.

"Jan, is this your attempt at Silverfox trickery or something?" Katherine asked her brother. "'Cause I heard you have to fuck with someone to get into your tower or something."

"Nah." Io shook his head. "We already got into our tower, so this isn't a trick. All of these guys knew you before the celestorm rearranged reality. Haven't you read about the worldwide shift on the net?"

"Ain't got time for news," Katherine said. "Go bug someone else, I'm busy."

I ignored her words and sat next to her. "Nah."

Katherine made a deep rumbling noise.

"You're sitting alone," I said. "Don't you want company?"

"I am sitting as I prefer," she fired back. "Please piss off before . . ."

I waved my friends on encouragingly.

Io sat beside Katherine. The others followed, filling the dark hexagonal table. Vespera stole a chair from another empty table and squeezed herself beside me. We were a spot of bright, clashing silver amidst the darkness of the Gorefield. Other Gorefield House Mystagogues were giving us bothered looks.

I slipped my phone over to Katherine. "Look, Kat, this is us delving on Arx as a team. This is Katsburg, the city I made for you."

Katherine squinted at the slideshow of us on Arx. "Hrm? Did you AI-generate these to mess with me? Amusing. Now buzz off."

I sighed. Kat was a stubborn loner before the shift, and now she wasn't any better off personality-wise.

"Where do you think that dress you're wearing came from?" I asked her.

"My parents got it for me," Katherine said, her tone dismissive.

"Did they?" I asked, leaning closer. "Did you actually talk to them about it? Or did you just find it in your room?"

She paused, her gaze flickering away from me for a moment, considering.

"I . . . found it in my room," she admitted, her voice sounding a little less sure now.

"And you think that your parents," I pressed on, "can afford to buy you a dress like this?" I gestured to the intricate beast core studs that shimmered within the dark leather fabric. "An outfit that's practically glowing with beast cores?"

Katherine frowned. She glanced down at the dress, really looking at it this time, as if seeing it for the first time. She ran her fingers over the embedded gemstone spheres, her touch lingering on the smooth, cool surfaces. The silence stretched, filled only with the surrounding Refectory din.

"They . . . they work hard," she finally said, still trying to justify her line of logic. "Maybe . . . maybe they got a bonus? Or . . . saved up?"

"Katherine, darlin', look at this thing. This ain't no 'bonus' dress. This is top-tier artificery. We're talking premium Arx leather, studded with like . . . twenty million O-bux worth of beast cores. This dress screams 'mind-meltingly expensive,' not 'saved up,'" Vespera pointed out.

Slowly, almost reluctantly, Katherine lifted her head, her green eyes locking onto mine again. This time, the guardedness was still there, but something else had crept in, a flicker of . . . doubt? Confusion? Maybe, just maybe, a nascent spark of recognition. She opened her mouth and closed it again.

"Our parents wouldn't be able to afford an outfit like that for you, Kat," Io commented. "You know that, right?"

"Fine," Katherine huffed. "I don't know where it came from. If this is really twenty million O-bux, why the fuck would you spend that much on me? What are you, my secret admirer or something?"

"Nah," I said. "Already got Quetzi and Thunder waifus. I got it for you because we're besties."

"Besties?" She chewed on the word as if it was a foreign object. "Doubtful."

"You taught me how to dive into the deep," I said, nodding towards her sketchbook. "Remember? Echoes? Centipede people?"

Katherine's green eyes flickered down at the open sketchbook in her lap. She was sketching a stylized centipede-like creature with multiple eyes and sharp claws. She snapped the sketchbook closed and squinted at me with a look of deep suspicion.

Just then, a Kitsune waitress approached our table. "Good evening, Mystagogues," she said with a polite bow, her blue eyes flickering over our mismatched group. "Here are your menus. What would you prefer for drinks?"

Everyone ordered various herbal teas and mana wine.

"You do know that this is the Gorefield House section, right? You're Silverfoxes," Katherine bluntly pointed out as the waitress departed. "You're supposed to be at the other end of the hall."

"Nobody said it's a crime to eat at a Gorefield table." I shrugged, leaning back in my chair. "Besides, we're here with our friend."

Katherine snorted. "Friend. Right."

Suddenly, a tall figure approached our table. I looked up. It was a wolf-man upperclassman with piercing amber eyes, and a confident, almost predatory air. He wore Gorefield robes, but his bearing was far more . . . assertive than most of the practical-minded Gorefield students I'd observed around us so far.

He stopped beside Cinder, a wide, toothy smile spreading across his lupine features. "Songbird! Fancy meeting you here, so far from the silver den. Did you come here to see me?" His voice was deep, smooth, almost . . . too smooth, like polished obsidian. His figure began melting toward an excessively handsome human.

"Eh?" Cinder turned towards the wolf-man. Her silver feathers ruffled slightly.

"Uxtish?" she said, her voice a little hesitant.

"The one and only," the wolf-man chuckled with a bow. "Scion Uxtish of the House of Legon, at your service."

There was something unnervingly familiar about his voice, about his smile. He wasn't in Yulia's slideshow. I breathed in deep, trying to determine whether Uxtish was my enemy on pre-shift Earth.

Something pricked at my senses, a faint, unsettling Resonance that tugged at the edges of my Scrutimancy. I focused, inhaling deeply, reaching out with my astral senses, and then . . . recognition slammed into me like a physical blow.

*Those eyes . . . that smile . . . that predatory charm . . . the phase-shift.*
*A Skinwalker.*

I tried very hard to stay calm even though I was freaking out on the inside, my heart hammering into the stratosphere. An electric zap rushed up my hand.

[What's going on?] Vespera's mental static-voice asked.

[Enemy,] I thought back through the Resonance between us. [Very dangerous enemy. Outsider!]

"No, I didn't come here to see you, Ux," Cinder said. "I . . . ummm . . ."

Uxtish, oblivious to the silent alarm bells ringing in my head, turned his charming smile to Cinder, his amber eyes gleaming with what could pass as affection, but to me screamed calculation. "You know, I didn't take you for a fox," the Skinwalker said. "Thought you'd go to the dragon House or join me here. Is that why you're sitting here? You wanted to see me?"

Cinder bristled, her silver feathers ruffling defensively. "I can eat wherever I damn well please, Ux," she retorted, her voice sharp. "And these are my . . . friends." She emphasized the word 'friends' with a pointed glance at our mismatched group, a possessive edge creeping into her tone.

"Friends, of course," Uxtish chuckled, his smile widening, not quite reaching his eyes. He fixed his amber gaze on me, a slow, deliberate scan that felt like a physical probe. "And who is this . . . charmingly . . . diminutive creature?" His gaze lingered on my fox-makeup face, a flicker of something unreadable in his amber depths.

"My kobold," Cinder replied.

"A new . . . acquisition, Songbird? A rather . . . unimpressive Kitsune specimen, even for a pet."

My hackles rose. I slammed my fight or flight instinct down. The monster didn't recognize me under my makeup. Or maybe he did and wasn't showing it.

"Pleased to meet you, Scion Uxtish," I said, lowering my eyes and projecting submissiveness. "I am . . . Cinder's . . . kobold servant."

Uxtish's smile tightened, a subtle shift that only I, attuned to the nuances of his predatory charm, could detect. "Servant, is it?" He tilted his head, his amber eyes narrowing slightly, still fixed on me.

"Yes. He's mine," Cinder interjected, her voice hardening, a protective growl rumbling in her chest. She placed a possessive clawed hand on my shoulder, sending a reassuring warmth through me. "Don't you worry about my 'bold, Uxtish. He's well . . . trained." Her blue eyes flashed a warning at the wolf-man.

"Are you a well trained, obedient 'bold?" Uxtish asked. "Why don't you fetch me a mana wine and clear this seat for me?"

"Screw off," Vespera said. "He ain't your 'bold to boss, ya fleshknob. Also, I'ma give you fifteen seconds to lay off the pretty-face phase-shift, you're startin' to piss me off. Thirteen . . ."

Her hand rose in the air, pointed at Uxtish, wings spreading wide and humming with deep electrofractal charge building up.

"Such impoliteness," Uxtish shook his head. "You do realize if you attack me at dinner, you'll be expelled from the hall, yes?"

"Like I give a shit," Vespera said. "We can always order takeout from the town. 'Sides, you're using hostile mental magic on us. Trying to adjust your appearance to our preferences to manipulate us is just as magically potent as me frying your ass with a lightning bolt. Seven. Six."

Uxtish stepped back, his body wolfing up and becoming pale and gray, the pretty human face dissolving away.

"Such a temper, Thunderbird. It's . . . almost endearing. But entirely unnecessary. I was merely testing the . . . dynamic here. Observing the hierarchy." His eyes flashed to Cinder. "Are you not in charge of this group, Songbird?"

"I am," Cinder said with a weary sigh. "Vee, please don't zap my fiancé."

"I'll zap whomever I wanna," Vespera huffed, not lowering her sparking hand. "I don't trust this fleshface in the slightest. One wrong move, fleshfold, and you'll be eating lightning for dessert."

Uxtish chuckled again, a low, rumbling sound. "Duly noted, Thunderbird. I wouldn't dream of crossing you . . . or my darling Songbird." He turned his attention back to the Quetzalcoatl, his smile widening again, the predatory charm turned up a notch. "Are you really slumming it with the Gorefield crowd? Don't tell me you've developed a sudden appreciation for . . . dark practicality?" He gestured dismissively at the muted colors of the Gorefield robes around us.

Cinder shifted uncomfortably, her silver feathers bristling slightly. "We're . . . just visiting," she said, her voice a little strained.

"How . . . touching. Gorefield and Silverfox, fraternizing. Truly, the celestorm has wrought wondrous changes," Uxtish laughed.

"Just leave us alone, Uxtish," Cinder said, her voice losing its forced politeness, hardening into a growl. "We're eating. We can talk on Omnigram and hang out . . . later."

"Of course, of course." Uxtish raised his hands in a gesture of mock surrender. "Wouldn't dream of interrupting your . . . inter-House bonding session. Just wanted to check in on my fiery fiancée, make sure you haven't forgotten about me in your rush to join the silver den." He winked at Cinder, then his amber eyes flicked over our group one last time, lingering on me for a moment longer before he straightened up, his smile still fixed in place. "Enjoy your . . . meal. And do try to stay out of trouble, Songbird."

With a final, almost mocking bow, Uxtish turned and strode away, disappearing into the Gorefield section, leaving a palpable tension hanging in the air.

"What the shit, Vee?" Cinder growled at Vespera. "Can you not go five minutes without starting a fight?"

"That bone-knob is a creepshow! He smells like . . . like . . . fake charm and bad intentions. And phase-shift pheromones, ugh. I felt like I was drowning in a bucket of oily charm-juice," Vespera growled. "How can you stand him?"

"Same way I can stand you." Cinder crossed her arms. "You're both at my tolerance threshold."

Vespera huffed. "Please. You like me. And you tolerate him because . . . reasons I will never understand." She glared in the direction Uxtish had gone.

Cinder's face, already flushed from the encounter, darkened further. "Look, he's my arranged Prima. It's . . . family stuff, and therefore none of your business," she snapped, her voice sharper than necessary.

Mags, who had been silently observing the exchange with wide red eyes, finally spoke. "Arranged . . . like a sacrifice?" Her gaze flicked between Cinder and the direction Uxtish had disappeared, as if she could see something we couldn't. "Or a . . . binding?"

Cinder flinched. "Shut it, Mags," Cinder hissed, her voice losing some of its bluster. "You and your . . . your scrutiny is not needed here."

"I think that this is exactly where it's needed," Mags said coldly. "He's bad news, Ci. Very, very, bad news. Gorefield is a House of Omnids aligned with darkness. And he's . . . incredibly dark. Murderously . . . dark. Stab you with a bone knife in the heart dark."

Cinder shuddered. "Stop that!"

"Did you knobs come here just to insult my House?" Katherine growled.

"Nah," I said. "You're the good kind of dark. Uxtish is a bad kind of dark."

"You don't know me," Katherine said. "I'm not a good person."

"I'm going to have to disagree with this statement," I said.

"And you're basing this . . . expert assessment on what? Your vast experience with bad kinds of dark?" Katherine asked.

"I'm not alone here in my ability to sense the overwritten past. Magdaline is a Scrut, too." I waved a hand towards the shark-girl who was still radiating an aura of unease. "She can smell dangerous individuals."

Magdaline nodded. "His scent is . . . wrong. Tainted. It's not just . . . Gorefield darkness. It's something else. Something . . . ancient and hungry."

Cinder shivered, despite herself. "Maybe he's a bit . . . intense. But he's . . . he's connected. Important. The Legon family and Clan are . . . well off." She trailed off.

"Connected to stabbing you in the heart," Magdaline said.

"Mags, seriously, stop it. You're freaking me out," Cinder growled.

"You should be freaked out," Magdaline said. "It is my assessment as a Scrut that you should avoid that Omnid."

"I can't freaking avoid him!" Cinder slammed her fist into the table. "We're soul-bonded. He's my fiancé! I . . . I can manage him, okay? I'm a dragon! I just have to get stronger, that's all!"

"A Psychopomp can carve out a soul bond," Vespera offered.

"This bond doesn't smell like it can be . . . carved away easily." Magdaline shook her head. "And I don't think that you'll be able to control Uxtish, Ci. He smells . . . dangerously high level and Outsidery."

The waitress arrived with our drinks. Cinder grabbed a bottle of mana-restoring wine and chugged half of it, glaring at us.

"There you are!" a deep voice boomed. "I was looking for you!"

"Effin' Abyss." All of Vespera's feathers turned back. "Knobs are really askin' for a zappin' today!"

I turned my head, noticing a rotund Frogman in gold-and-red robes staring down at us. He was flanked by a lanky, antlered Wendigo and a bulky, muscular Lagarfljót Worm.

"The fuck you want, Zheng?" Vespera growled.

"Vee, Vee, my fiery blossom! There you are, hiding amidst the . . . gloom of Gorefield? Are you lost, my little thundercloud? Surely, you know Pyroclast tables offer far more . . . invigorating company," Zheng boomed, his voice echoing across the Gorefield section, drawing the attention of nearby students. His beady froggy red eyes were fixed on Vespera, but his wide smile seemed strained, almost forced, as if he was trying too hard to project confidence.

Vespera's wings twitched violently, sending sparks flying around "Get lost, before I vaporize you, Frogface. I already told you that we're done!"

"You have." Zheng shrugged. "Repeatedly. Alas, we cannot be done. The merger of Golden Star and SimmiTech is inevitable, according to our Probability Engines. You must accept your fate with grace, my thundercloud."

"How about you accept my fist up yo ass if you don't vanish within the next ten seconds," Vespera growled, standing up and humming like a transformer about to explode. "Nine . . ."

"Your family will hear about this insubordination." Zheng retreated behind the Lagarfljót Worm. "I simply wished to . . . check in on my fiancée. Ensure she wasn't succumbing to the . . . subpar ambience of this section." He gestured around the Gorefield tables with a wave of his webbed hand.

"I was perfectly fine before your green ass showed up, Zheng," Vespera snapped. "And I'm not your 'fiancée.' We're just . . . contractually betrothed. A temporary situation that'll be resolved as soon as I fully take over SimmiTech. Now, I suggest you vanish before I fry you and your sixies! Five. Four. Three. Two . . ."

# CHAPTER FIFTY-THREE

# Skyfall Taken

Zheng and his bodyguards retreated rapidly, not wishing to get zapped by the extra-hostile-looking Thunderbird.

The Kitsune waitress brought us our meals, and we ate in relative silence.

Vespera's cheerfulness gradually returned. Cinder, though she hadn't joined in the verbal sparring, chewed her steak with a tense expression, her blue eyes darting around the room every few seconds as if expecting Uxtish to show up.

Katherine remained impassive, chewing on her dragonsteak. Io nommed his food quietly, and Magdaline, ever vigilant, kept sniffing the air, her red eyes narrowed in concentration, occasionally glancing towards the hall entrance.

I inhaled, too, and smelled incoming . . . something.

Suddenly, the clatter of cutlery and the low hum of conversations were drowned out by a new sound—rhythmic, heavy thudding that echoed through the vast Refectory. The ground vibrated subtly beneath our feet. Heads turned towards the main entrance, where the heavy magisteel doors shuddered and then burst inwards with a resounding crash.

A phalanx of fully armored figures marched into the cafeteria.

They were all female Omnids.

Each was clad in full hexamesh and black, immovable metal armor, their forms bulky and imposing. Their helmets were featureless, obsidian visors obscuring their faces, and they moved with a synchronized, almost robotic precision, their boots hitting the floor in a unified, thunderous rhythm. Each Omnid carried a weapon—sleek black railgun rifles.

Sword-cross sigils, emblazoned in silver, shone on their pauldrons and breastplates.

Behind them officers in gray uniforms followed with insignia of the Omnid cross within an upside down triangle.

"Scrutimancer Stabalists," Vespera breathed out. "Yessss! Oh, it is so on!"

Chaos erupted in the Refectory. Students yelped and retreated, chairs scraped against the floor, wings and tails flapping in panicked disarray.

Saxtant Knights, who had been guarding the hall, moved to intercept the armored intruders, their rune-etched swords and mage-staves drawn.

With cold efficiency, the Stabalists raised their rifles. The Knights attempted to strike the invaders back with spells, but their attack simply fizzled out as the Omnithornian forces were armed with null-shard.

Railguns fired and students screamed, ducking under tables. One by one, the Saxtant protectors crumpled to the floor, incapacitated, their magic abruptly silenced by null-bullets. A swift, clinical neutralization.

The Stabalists advanced, their phalanx splitting to encircle the Refectory, cutting off all exits. The heavy thudding of their boots echoed in the sudden, terrified silence that descended upon the hall.

Vespera began to clap merrily as if she had expected all of this.

"Clear!" one of the Stabalists yelled.

A new group of Omnids entered into view through the open doors—more crisp gray military uniforms with silver sword-cross logos on their shoulders.

At the center of this new group was Justice Nova. His face set in a stern, uncompromising expression. He moved with an air of absolute authority, his gaze sweeping across the stunned faces of the Mystagogues, his presence silencing the last whispers of student panic.

"Justice Nova? What is the meaning of this?!" The lanky Slenderman rose from the head table.

The Omnid pacification weapons swiveled his way.

Justice Nova raised a hand, and the heavy thudding of the Stabalist boots ceased abruptly, plunging the Refectory into an unnerving stillness. His voice, amplified by a speaker in his armor, boomed through the hall, cutting through the silence like a thunderclap.

"Students and faculty of Skyfall Academy!" Justice Nova's voice resonated, deep and authoritative. "By order of Premier Lecross of the Republic of Omnithornia, enforced by the Stabalist Order of Scrutimancers, I hereby declare Skyfall as property of the Omnithornian Superstate! Saxtland's jurisdiction is hereby revoked!"

A collective gasp rippled through the hall.

Justice Nova continued. "The worldwide celestorm event and the subsequent dimensional shift have irrevocably altered the geopolitical landscape. Skyfall Academy, once safely within the borders of Omnithornia's Cradlefall, now finds itself . . . misplaced. Saxtland, a nation ill-equipped to safeguard this vital institution, has proven itself incapable of ensuring the Academy's security and stability."

He paused, his gaze sweeping over the assembled Mystagogues. "The awakening of the Wormwood Leviathan necessitated decisive action. Omnithornia, with its superior resources and unwavering commitment to global stability, will ensure the Academy's continued operation and the safety of its pupils. This is not an act of aggression, but an act of necessary intervention, a return to rightful ownership. Skyfall Academy belongs to Omnithornia, and Omnithornia has come to reclaim what is rightfully hers!"

A stunned silence hung in the air.

"The current board of Skyfall directors is hereby dissolved. All students are to undergo mental assessment and dimensional restoration courtesy of our Mind-Healers!" Justice Nova declared. "Anyone trying to flee our assessment will be considered aligned with Saxtland and pacified."

Justice Nova walked across the student tables, looking left and right. I inhaled deeply, and suddenly everything clicked into place. I stood up and waved him over.

He spotted me and marched straight over to us.

"Daddy!" Cinder rushed over to Nathaniel and buried him in a winged hug, radiating warm colors.

"How are things, my daughter?" Justice Nova asked. "I do hope that the past twelve hours haven't been too stressful for you. We moved as swiftly as we could. How's your fiancé?"

"I . . . urm," Cinder let out. "Uxtish is okay, I guess? Why?"

"Uxtish?" Nathaniel pulled back slightly, his gaze sweeping over our table, then his eyes landed on the crystal-encased feather pendant prominently displayed on my chest. He pointed a gauntlet finger at it. "Your fiancé. Alexander Glock. The one you are soul-bonded to. I don't know who this Uxtish is . . ."

"What?" Cinder blinked.

"Scion Uxtish of House Legon." I stood up and pulled off my fox ears and latex makeup. "Here's here. In House Gorefield. Table sixteen. A pale Skinwalker. I'd appreci-ate it if you arrested him, Justice—he's a very dangerous criminal and a threat to your daughter."

Justice Nova barked an order that was too swift for me to even perceive.

The Stabalist phalanx moved with lightning speed, their armored figures pivoting and fanning out across the Gorefield section, their rifles raised, their obsidian visors scanning the tables with chilling efficiency. A palpable tension filled the air as the hunt for Uxtish began.

Within moments, a cry of alarm echoed from the far corner of the Gorefield section. "Fugitive located! Attempting to flee!"

All eyes turned towards the source of the commotion. Uxtish, his handsome human facade dissolving rapidly, reverting back to his lupine form, was attempting to bolt, weaving through the panicked Gorefield students, heading for a side exit.

But the Stabalists were faster than the fleeing wolf-man and had blocked the exit.

Railgun fire ripped through the air. Uxtish yelped, stumbling as a null-shard pro-jectile struck his leg and chest, severing the magical flow. He roared in pain and rage, attempting to lash out with bone-claws, but the armored Stabalists swarmed him, their movements swift.

Within seconds, Uxtish was subdued, wrestled to the ground by the Stabalist pha-lanx. Heavy restraints, nullifying collars, and magisteel handcuffs, were swiftly applied, silencing his roars and effectively neutralizing his magic.

They dragged Uxtish to Justice Nathaniel Nova.

"Scion Uxtish of House Legon." I grinned at the teen. "Also known as Valor Thornheart. An Astral Phantom. A murderer. Prima of the Clan of Legon, the Skinwalker respon-sible for the deaths of over forty Omnid singers and the attempted murder of Justice Nova's daughter at Lake Eerie!"

A ripple of shocked murmurs spread through the Refectory.

"You!" Valor growled at me.

"Me." I grinned. "Guess what? It's over."

"Over?" Uxtish's amber eyes, narrowed with fury, fixed on me, a flicker of dawning recognition, and something akin to shock, finally surfacing in their depths.

I smiled, a cold, almost pitying smile. "As an Astral Phantom existing between Lake Eerie and Cassiopeia's soul, you were untouchable, ethereal, beyond our reach. But you made a mistake, Valor. You sought physical form. You craved connection in a world that wasn't yours to claim. You used the celestorm shift to become reborn. But you got greedy, just as I expected. You wanted everything. You wanted wealth and power. You wanted to be connected to the one victim you failed to kill. You wanted Cassie, and so you came here to Skyfall. And in doing so, you became vulnerable. You became . . . catchable."

"I will . . ." Valor growled.

"Do nothing. Because within the radiance of the null-shards, you are bound to your current shell of flesh. And as such, I reckon you will be . . . mentally obliterated and confined in a magisteel coffin forevermore with the everlasting sleep potion. It doesn't matter what level you are as an Astral Phantom, as Uxtish you are . . . finite, limited."

I gestured to the Stabalists surrounding him, the railguns, the restraints. "This was always the plan, Valor. To lure you into the physical, to ground you in reality, where rules apply. Where even an invincible Astral Phantom can be . . . pacified."

Uxtish stared at me, his amber eyes flaring with incandescent hatred. But the fight was gone from his stance, the predatory confidence replaced by the cold, stark realization of panic.

He was caught. And this time, there would be no escape. The dimensional shift had not erased his past sins, it had merely brought him closer to his reckoning.

"You . . . you are just a pathetic human!" Uxtish growled, "You are a liar, a cheat! I know all of your secrets through Cassie's dreams! I'll expose you! They'll . . ."

"Do nothing. I'm Lord Protector, the real fiancé of Vespera Simmi and Cassiopeia Nova." I smiled. "An Arx Mage Lord, recognized as such by Justice Nova. While you tried to gain power by murder, I actually gained it through love. You're no match for me, Mr. Legon. You never were. This was a rather nice play, a game of cat and mouse between you and me, but I'm afraid that it's at its inevitable end."

Uxtish choked, frothing at the mouth.

"Did you think that this was the start of your magical adventure, a new chance at life? Nah—it's the end of it. All of your clan cousins will be arrested and tried for their crimes," I said. "The Omnithornian Stabalists will seal the dimensional tear you've made on Lake Eerie. All of your attempts to become a god were for naught, Uxtish."

Uxtish was dragged away, his struggles weakening, his hisses and frothing curses echoing in the sudden silence of the Refectory. The Stabalist phalanx, impassive and efficient, marched him out through the shattered doors, a stark display of Omnithornian authority. Authority that was on my side now thanks to my pre-celestorm conversation with the Justice.

The remaining Mystagogues in the hall watched in stunned silence.

Cinder stood frozen, her blue eyes wide. She looked from the departing Stabalists to me.

"What . . . what just happened?" she stammered.

"You're free," I told her. "Free forever from Valor. Now you can heal and move forward."

"Forward?" Cinder let out.

"Yes," I said.

"Dad." Cinder turned to her father. "Did you know about all of . . . this?"

"I wasn't affected by the dimensional shift," Justice Nova said. "All Omnithornian authorities of high enough position were aware of the potential danger of a worldwide celestorm. Your mother and I were able to make it into a several layer deep dimensional shelter and wait it out. I tried calling you to warn you to dive into the nearest dimensional bag, but your phone wasn't responding."

"My . . . phone was fried . . . I think?" Cinder sighed.

"The Stabalist Healers will help you remember everything, daughter," Justice Nova said. "They'll handle your group first."

A few Stabalists detached themselves from the group of officers and approached our table. They weren't rifle-wielding soldiers and had the green Vitalix Kitlix logos on their insignia.

Healers!

Infix Kitlix and Vitalix Kitlix sat on their shoulders. Cinder was the daughter of Justice Nova, and as such was the first to be processed.

"Relax, Ms. Nova, we won't bite," the Stabalist Healer said as he gently placed the Vitalix Kitlix onto Cinder's head. At the same time, an Infix Kitlix ran around Cinder's figure.

After about five minutes of this, the Healers declared the job finished. Cinder blinked, her eyes refocusing. Then she rushed to my side and hugged me, her entire body igniting pink-violet.

The process continued, the Healers moving from Vespera, to Katherine, then Io, then Magdaline, then Lilith.

Then it was my turn. A wave of tranquility and sharp clarity washed over me as the Infix identified issues and Vitalix healed them, rearranging my mental pattern to match my astral imprint from before the dimensional shift, as explained by the Healer.

"Dimensional restoration of this table is complete!" the Stabalist announced, stepping back. "You are cleared for release."

Justice Nova nodded, his gaze softening as he looked at Cinder. "Return to your dormitories and get some sleep. Further instructions will be disseminated tomorrow morning."

"Can Katherine come with us to our dorm room?" I asked. "She's my clan's Knight."

"Sure." The Justice nodded. "The House system didn't exist before the dimensional shift in Skyfall. We are considering dismantling it. Likely it manifested here from the student obsessions with the . . . Larry Plotter franchise."

"I don't mind our House Cantigeist," I voiced.

"Ye." Vespera nodded. "She's a cutie. Please don't dismantle our sweet fox!"

"Noted," Justice Nova said.

We rose from the table, the din of the Refectory slowly beginning to return as other groups of students were approached by the Stabalist Healers. The chaos had been replaced by a strange, subdued order. The Saxtant Knights were gone, their bodies rapidly bagged up and taken away by Omnithornian forces.

We walked in silence towards the busted Refectory doors. As we passed through the damaged entrance, I noticed more Omnids in gray uniforms stationed at intervals along the corridors.

Reaching the Silver Tower, we ascended the stairs in a subdued group. When we reached the Foxglen Den common room, the Sextant Keeper was absent, too. Instead, an Omnid female officer in a crisp gray uniform sat behind the desk, tapping on a tablet. She glanced up as we approached.

"House Silverfox residents?" she asked.

I nodded. "Returning to our dorm."

The Omnid officer waved us on without a glance at Kat's black-and-red outfit. "Proceed."

We entered our dorm room. Cinder sank onto her bed, still looking dazed. Vespera and I climbed to the bunk above.

"Well," I said, breaking the silence, trying to inject some levity. "That was . . . eventful."

Vespera snorted. "Eventful is an understatement! Abyss, that was an awesome capture of our greatest nemesis! Well done, Lexy!"

She grabbed onto the bed and it began to warp, expanding outward and growing wider.

"What are you doing?" Cinder growled from below.

"Making a bigger bed," Vespera replied. "Duh. Gotta fit our entire 'ship. I can turn that bed where you are sitting now into a cute study space with an Ignix Kitlix fireplace and a desk."

"So . . ." Cinder stepped away from her bed looking up at us. "Dad knew about Valor?"

"Yes," I revealed. "I told him everything about Valor and the lake murders when he interrogated me in his office. Omnithornian authorities were in the process of figuring out how to deal with the 40k Astral Phantom. Vespera kicked the process waaay ahead, though . . . by releasing the Archangel of her house and causing the worldwide celestorm."

Cinder leapt up to our expanding bed with a flap of colorful wings.

"Vee," she growled. "How much of this bullshit was your plan?"

"All of it, darling," Vespera answered, letting go of the hexamesh bed frame. "Every single action that led to this moment was for you."

"Start from the fucking beginning then," Cinder demanded. "And don't skimp on the details . . ."

"Right," Vespera said. "I've been trying to get out of my engagement to Zheng for ages. On January seventh, I found my opportunity. At 8:42 AM, I ran into a rather cute pure human at Skyfall who was trying to pretend to be an Omnid Thunderbird. It was an adorable attempt at a conspiracy. I decided to use him as my test subject for an experiment I had planned for years. Using my electrofractal power, I installed a Resonance skill into his soul."

"Uh-huh." Cinder nodded.

"Then I talked to him, understood him, and became his friend. He had a nice plan," Vespera said. "A plan to change . . . everything. I liked it. I helped him along, pushed him ahead wherever I could. I helped him make a Mage Tower on Arx, helped him take over Undertown. I helped him steal Possy, and build a death ray. I guesstimated many of his plans in advance because I was privy to his thoughts via our Resonance connection."

"I see," Cinder said with a sour look.

"Remember our picnic on the pebble beach when you sang to us about Xandria and Empress Nox?" Vespera asked Cinder. "The 'Summer Rain' song about me and you and . . . Lexy?"

The Quetzi-girl nodded.

"That's when I knew that I loved you both, Ci. That's when I added a new item to Lexy's checklist. To save a doomed Quetzi from an Astral Phantom."

Vespera pulled my phone out of my pocket and pulled up the task list app and showed it to Cinder. Then she slowly and dramatically tapped a checkmark on it.

[Destroy the world, save our Quetzi-girl [√]]

"That beach date was the day I decided to set all of this into motion." Vespera spread her hands. "To free my family's Archangel for you, Ci. To ignite the world so that Valor would come out into the open."

"Sounds like an imbecilic plan with far too many things that could have gone horribly wrong!" Cinder growled.

"Valor told us his plan himself," I pointed out. "Boasted all about it when he stabbed me through the heart with his bone-hand. His goal was to be reborn. The celestorm shift gave him the opportunity to do so, to dive from the Astral into the Physical. He took it, just as we expected him to."

"When he became physical, he also became your fiancé because he was soul-bound to you." Vespera nodded. "He had an ungodly amount of threads in your soul; you were basically his phylactery. He couldn't resist coming to Skyfall, to claim you as his, because he was a Skyfall student himself once. He thought himself untouchable—but he was wrong and was run aground by a clever little fox and his birb bestie."

"Abyss." Cinder waved her hands, wings turning bright red. "Just when I think that you two have calmed down, you do . . . *this* to me!"

Vespera nodded. "Yeah, it was risky as heck, I won't lie. But sometimes, you gotta gamble big to win big, right? And the prize was . . . you, Ci. Free from that Astral leech. Worth it, in my book."

Cinder's jaw tightened. "You gambled with . . . everything, Vee! With Skyfall! With the whole planet! Just to . . . 'save me?'" Her voice was rising, laced with a dangerous edge. "You didn't even ask me! You just . . . decided?!"

Vespera's black-and-white wings fluttered. "Hey, I didn't think you'd appreciate a consultation beforehand, love. 'Hey, Ci, wanna help me unleash a potentially world-ending Archangel to bait your stalker into the physical realm and potentially destroy Omnithornia in the process? Sound good?' Somehow, I doubted you'd jump at the chance."

"You're right, I effing wouldn't!" Cinder snapped. "Because that's completely insane! Irresponsible as fuck!" She threw her hands up in exasperation. "You just . . . barrel in, consequences be damned! Did you even consider what could have happened? What if it didn't work? What if Valor wasn't stupid enough to take the bait? What if the Wormwood Star completely scraped us off the face of the planet?!"

"Details, details." Vespera waved a dismissive hand. "It worked, didn't it? Valor is gone. You're safe. And . . . well, Skyfall is technically Omnithornian again, and everyone is going to remember everything eventually thanks to the Stabalist Order, so win-win?" She offered a small smile.

"Win-win?!" Cinder's voice cracked, escalating into a furious shriek. "Vee, people could have died! This whole Academy is in chaos! Saxtland is probably about to declare war on Omnithornia! And you call this a 'win-win' because you . . . 'saved' me?" Her blue eyes flashed with a hurt that cut deeper than anger.

"A war that Omnithornia is going to win because they don't just rely on magic-only weapons. You saw those EVA railgun nullifiers and immovable armor plates, right? Me and Lexy did what had to be done because nobody else would!" Vespera insisted. "And we couldn't have told you the plan because you would have been against it, and also because then Valor would know, since he was inhabiting your soul and . . . stuff."

Cinder growled.

"Ci . . ." Vespera reached out a talon, her voice softening, but Cinder recoiled away from the touch as if burned.

"No!" Cinder barked, growling and backing away from Vespera and me. She reached the stained glass window, her hand slamming against the latch, wrenching it open with unnecessary force.

A gust of rain-laced wind rushed into the room, whipping the silver curtains wildly and carrying the distant roar of the ocean. Without a word, Cinder climbed over the windowsill, her silver wings unfurling automatically as she stepped onto the narrow stone balcony outside.

The storm clouds overhead were thicker now. Raindrops lashed down, driven sideways by the wind, plastering her silver-gray feathers to her scales. She stood there, motionless, a solitary, defiant figure silhouetted against the stormy sky, the wind whipping her silver robes around her.

Vespera watched the irate Quetzi. She then sighed, a soft puff of air that ruffled the dark feathers around her face. "Welp, that went . . . about as well as expected." She looked from the open balcony door back to me, a wry smile twisting her lips. "Das extra-spice Quetzalcoatl temper for ya."

"Is she . . ." I started, uncertain how to proceed.

Vespera cut me off with a wave of her hand. "Don't worry about it, foxy. She just needs to . . . steam a bit. Quetzalcoatls are like volcanoes, you know? Gotta let them erupt every now and then or they'll blow their tops spectacularly." She shrugged. "Let her yell and musicate at the storm. She'll mellow out. Maybe return with a vengeance, but like, whatever . . . it all worked out. She's finally safe, pulled back from the all-devouring Abyss."

She stretched on the expanded bed.

I shook my head. The balcony stained-glass window slammed shut from the wind. Cinder's silhouette pulled out her guitar from its extradimensional container.

She strummed angrily for about ten minutes. The notes were sharp, discordant chords that seemed to echo the storm raging inside her and outside, vibrating through the stained-glass window.

Then, gradually, the anger bled out of the music.

The chords softened, becoming minor and melancholic, the rhythm slowing to a gentle, soulful pace. Soft guitar notes began to weave themselves into the sound of the rain, pulsing in harmony with the raindrops drumming on the stone balcony and the distant crash of waves.

I felt a pang of guilt twist in my gut.

Vee's plan, however well-intentioned, had detonated in a messy explosion of chaos and hurt feelings. Cinder was out there in the storm, alone and wounded. I pushed off the expanded bed, Vespera's gaze following me. I gave her a small nod, and she nodded back at me, a wordless reassurance.

I moved towards the window, opened it, and climbed out.

The balcony wasn't super spacious and I tried not to look down, clinging to the stone parapet.

"Skyfall, Oh . . . Skyfall," Cinder's song began.

Raindrops struck the parapet beams with a sharp "ting, ting, ting" rhythm. The air was damp and heavy, the scent of ozone thick in the air. Below, the North Sea churned, waves crashing against the cliffs with a thunderous roar that echoed up the tower walls.

*Rising high against midnight's veil*
*Crystal towers where shadows sail*
*Where basalt meets the frozen sky*
*And magic whispers drift on by*
*The Wormwood Star begins to sing*
*While Mystagogues their secrets bring*
*Yet something broken stirs deep within*
*Where loneliness and doubt begin*
*Skyfall, oh Skyfall. Under starlit skies*
*Where ancient memories arise*
*A fleeting touch, a whispered name*
*Dancing through this midnight game.*
*Is it love or sweet insanity?*
*Or just a specter of what could be?*
*Your words pull me down like a weight,*
*At Skyfall's Arx-Earth diving gate.*

Her voice and guitar strumming were amplified by her Charmchain magic, the words carrying out over the wind and the waves, weaving themselves into the fabric of the storm, dancing across the tower. With each stanza, my heartbeat deepened, not with worry or excitement, but with a different kind of intensity, a warm, resonant thrumming in my chest that I could suddenly hear, as if it was part of her music.

*Silver robes we daily don*
*To hide the battles fought and won*
*They call us chosen, call us blessed*
*While darkness stirs within my chest*
*The Celestorm rages high above*

*Reflecting back my hidden love*
*A puzzle wrapped in mystery*
*That holds the key to my destiny*
*Two strangers from worlds apart*
*Each guarding secrets in their heart*
*His secrets mirror what I hide*
*A kindred spirit by my side*
*My Quetzi soul calls his name*
*Igniting everything aflame*
*Could this be what I'm searching for?*
*Or just another closing door?*
*She inhaled, the rain tapping along her face and wings.*
*As starlight fades to break of day*
*And shadows slowly slip away*
*One choice remains before the dawn:*
*Chase the light, or linger on*
*In Skyfall's ever-watching gaze*
*Where basalt cliffs meet ocean waves*
*Until the clouds return again*
*To wash my story with their rain.*

She repeated the chorus, finished, and turned her head to me, sending my presence.

"How are you feeling?" I asked.

"Better," Cinder replied. "My memories are still kind of foggy, even with the Kitlix healing. Singing . . . helps. I've been using my Charmchain on myself, wobbling my soul with my music to realign myself fully with my Fractal Engine heart," she said, suddenly grabbing me and pulling me into her warm embrace. "I forgot you, Martin. I'm sorry."

"I'm sorry, too," I said. "Sorry . . . we did all of that crazy stuff."

Her embrace became fierce, possessive, a dragon reclaiming a lost treasure. Rain plastered our robes to our bodies, the wind howling around us, but in her arms, a deep warmth bloomed, chasing away the chill of the storm.

"I forgot you, like a giant knob," she repeated, kissing me fiercely. "My . . . Martin. My Alex. My . . . everything. My little, clever, dangerous fox. How could I forget you?"

"It's okay," I replied when she released me so that I could breathe. "It wasn't your fault. Everyone got rearranged. Even Vee. But it's okay, we're all back now, right?"

"Right. Vee is a bloody menace," she let out. "Both of you are effing menaces. My . . . beautiful menaces. Unleashing an Archangel, triggering a planetary crisis, almost getting us all killed, all in the name of 'saving' me?"

"Yep." I nodded.

"Ughhh, you two," Despite the grumbling tone, a hint of fond exasperation softened her words. The anger was still there, simmering beneath the surface, but the raw hurt seemed to have subsided, replaced by a familiar, almost affectionate, annoyance.

"Hey," I said softly, cupping her face in my hands, my thumbs brushing away stray raindrops clinging to her scales and feathers. "She did save you, Ci. From Valor. From . . .

all of that darkness. From the Abyss. Your soul was shredded after two years of suffering and the only way to save you was to get Valor to become physical."

Her blue eyes softened. "I know," she whispered. "I know. It's just . . . Vee's methods are . . . Well, Vee's."

"And you wouldn't have her any other way, would you?" I teased gently.

She nudged my shoulder with her snout, a small, grudging smile playing on her lips. "Maybe not. But if she ever pulls a stunt like this again, I swear I'm going to . . ." She trailed off, then sighed again. "I don't know. Ground her? Confiscate her Fractal Engine heart? Lock her in a soundproof room with only motivational posters for company?"

I chuckled, the sound light and relieved. "Maybe just . . . talk to her? Tell her how you feel? Chase her and smack her around at the Coliseum with a mace?"

Cinder considered this, her brow furrowed. "Talking and smacking is an option, I suppose."

The rain seemed to soften, the wind dying down to a gentler gust, as if the storm itself was heeding her shifting emotions.

"Come on," I said, taking her hand, pulling her gently towards the window. "Let's go back inside. It's freezing out here, even for a dragon."

She didn't resist, letting me lead her back into the warmth of our dorm room. Vespera was still sprawled across the expanded bed, her wings tucked in, her silver-gold eyes watching us with a cheeky expression.

Cinder paused at the edge of the bed, her eyes meeting Vespera's. Then the Quetzi sighed, the tension draining from her shoulders. She sat down heavily.

"Vee," she said. "You're a bloody idiot. You both are. Reckless, impulsive, world-endangering idiots."

"Your idiots," Vespera offered.

"My idiots." Cinder nodded. She shoved me into Vespera, kicked the stained glass shut, and then slipped to my right side, burrowing into me. "Tired now. Tomorrow . . . I shall have terrible vengeance . . ."

"Tomorrow after you smack us around, we'll take on the world?" Vespera yawned with a grin.

"Sure," Cinder replied. "Whatever."

"I think I'll join in on the smacking," Katherine commented from below.

"Sure, sure," Vespera replied. "Take the extra bed below us, kitten Knight."

"I have to admit," Io said. "I did expect you to set the world on fire."

"And yet, once again, you did fuck-all to stop it, Jan!" Katherine chided her half-brother.

Lilith and Magdaline shared a chortle. Vespera laughed out loud. Cinder huffed.

"Eh." Io shrugged. "I don't stop disasters. I am drawn to them. Besides, things worked out in . . . the end."

# About the Author

Vitaly S. Alexius is the author of the Somebody Stop Her series, originally released on Royal Road along with the rest of the extended omniverse, Romantically Apocalyptic, in which it is set (learn more here: https://bit.ly/3U9CPVy). When he's not busy penning stories or dabbling in art, he likes grilling up some tasty barbecue or enjoying a picnic at the beach with his family. Alexius, who his wife says is a human capybara, resides in Canada.

# RESPAWN YOUR CURIOSITY

*follow us on our socials*

podiumentertainment.com

@podiumentertainment

/podiumentertainment

@podium_ent

@podiumentertainment